PRAISE FOR *STONING THE DEVIL*
BY GARRY CRAIG POWELL

'STONING THE DEVIL is a mesmerizing read. You will not find another book like this one. Powell has an astonishing ability to create characters with swift and haunting power. His intricately linked stories travel to the dark side of human behavior without losing essential tenderness or desire for meaning and connection. They are unpredictable and wild. Is this book upsetting? Will it make some people mad? Possibly. But you will not be able to put it down.'

Naomi Shihab Nye

'These linked stories are utterly mesmerizing and exotic. With a keen ear for dialogue, and a sensibility of the best Conrad, Kipling, Orwell and Achebe, Powell pulls off a masterful feat.'

George Singleton

'Garry Craig Powell's *Stoning The Devil* interweaves narratives of sex, power and identity through a feminist lens, with all of the *contradictions* and myriad facets that perspective affords. This episodic novel—each chapter of which is complete unto itself—is first and foremost a work of lush and vivid prose. Various formal innovations, from the epistolary opening chapter to the syntactic feat of the chapter entitled "Sentence," demonstrate Powell's technical virtuosity. It's this skill that allows him to capture the Gulf landscape's severe beauty, alongside a wealthy city's urban sheen and excess, with clarity that feels neither detached nor heavy-handed. While the Gulf in general, and the UAE in particular, almost function as their own characters in the book, it's those souls who suffer and thrive in the foreground whom Powell trains his, and in turn the readers', attention on. The characters which inhabit Stoning 's pages are sensitively drawn and attuned readers will find themselves quickly invested in the lives of Badria, Fayruz, Alia and all the other "players" of this novel.

'Even now as I write this, weeks after reading this book, I am still haunted by the story and the traumas that befall Badria, and Fayruz—two characters who seemed to me to embody traditional Western feminist ideals of power (...)

Stoning The Devil does not shy away from controversy, nor does it provoke for provocation's sake. Barbarities and hypocrisies of both Islamic and Western cultures find their complexity—in these stories as in real life—through the individual human being. Powell's sensibility, as well as sensitivity to loaded imperialist rhetoric and post-colonial politics, offers some truly inspired and nuanced passages that work within that charged linguistic space to fret the limitations of "enlightened" thinking. Powell plays with the practice of exoticizing, in small and profound ways, but what is ultimately gratifying here is that what we're left with are not just concepts or too-easy epiphanies, but real people, written with a skeptic's compassion and a poet's clarity.'

Paula Mendoza

Garry Craig Powell

Garry Craig Powell grew up in a working-class family in Aylesbury, Buckinghamshire, when it was still a pleasant market town. He attended Aylesbury Grammar School and completed his first degree at Cambridge University. He also has an MA from Durham University and an MFA in Creative Writing from the University of Arizona. He has spent his adult life outside Albion – running his own language school in Portugal, then teaching English at an Arab university in the UAE, and finally as a professor of Creative Writing at the University of Central Arkansas. (He recommends that writers do not waste their time and money on such courses.)

His linked collection, *Stoning the Devil,* which is set in the UAE, was longlisted for the Frank O'Connor International Short Story Award in 2013, and the Edgehill Short Story Prize the same year. He believes literature has a vital role to play in the defence of Enlightenment values. Garry Craig Powell lives in northern Portugal, and writes full-time. He plays classical guitar, and loves hiking in the mountains. *Our Parent Who Art in Heaven* is his first novel.

For more information, visit his website, www.garrycraigpowell .org and follow his Facebook author page, www.facebook.com /gcraigpowell

Our Parent Who Art in Heaven

A Novel

Garry Craig Powell

Flame Books

First published in the United Kingdom by Flame Books
Isle of Skye, Scotland
www.flamebooks.net

Cover illustration by Nick Ward. Cover template design by Zack Copping. Author photograph by Dayana Galindo. Formatting and typesetting by Vivien Reis and Susan Flowers.

9 8 7 6 5 4 3 2 1

ISBN 978-1-7399164-3-5
E-book ISBN 978-1-7399164-1-1
Audible book ISBN 978-7399164-2-8

For my mother

'In times like these, it is difficult not to write satire.'
Juvenal

'Who will guard the guards themselves?'
Juvenal

'Satire is a sort of glass, wherein beholders do generally
discover everybody's face but their own.'
Jonathan Swift

'Fools are my theme, let satire be my song.'
Lord Byron

'Satire is moral outrage transformed into comic art.'
Philip Roth

ONE

As Long as You Make Me Happy

Another blissful day is beginning, Huw thought, as he made love with his wife that mild morning in March. *Yet another in a series of blissful days destined to last forever.*

Half-closed in rapture, Miranda's honey-coloured eyes gazed into his, and she gripped his arms. Huw saw her as a pre-Raphaelite nymph: lissom and pale, her face pure and plaintive. The purring sound she made was perhaps at variance with her virginal appearance, but Huw found it both fetching, and flattering. As he redoubled his efforts, a faint frown appeared on Miranda's brow, which invariably signalled the approaching cataclysm.

Birdsong and the perfume of azalea blossom poured through the open window.

It was eight o'clock, breakfast was over, and Owen was on his way to Tocqueville Junior High, so Huw and his wife were free to bellow like cows in labour. They roared—and kept roaring—and roared more.

'Do you think the neighbours heard us?' said Miranda

afterwards in her Delta belle accent. Although she was in her late twenties, her voice was still girlish, soft and high.

Huw collapsed by her side. 'Unless they're stone deaf, I should certainly think so.' She giggled; he neighed with laughter.

'I thought you Brits were buttoned-up,' she said. 'Cold. Repressed.'

'That's the English,' Huw said. 'I'm Welsh.'

'Isn't a Welshman a kind of Englishman?'

'So you will insist,' Huw said. 'But we're not alike. Look you, I grew up on a dairy farm in Cardigan Bay; my parents spoke little English and my grandparents none at all.'

'I know, honey. You've told me tons of times. You're a wild Celt.'

'An uxorious one,' he said, relishing the Latinate word. 'I love you.'

Her honey-brown eyes glistened. 'I love you too,' she said, stroking his hair.

Oh, lucky man! At the pinnacle of happiness, what more could he desire? Only the infinite extension of that happiness. And this was where, like most mortals, he made a fatal mistake. Huw was intelligent and cultivated, but not, sad to say, a wise man, although he was not far off fifty. The Fates bless the virtuous with happiness, he believed. Forever, naturally.

'I hope you will always stay with me,' he said, confident of her response.

Did she frown or sigh? Not at all. 'I'll never leave you,' she said, still smiling, but with a glassy look in her eyes, 'as long as you make me happy.'

Faintly at first, Huw heard the sinister bowing of basses and cellos, that ominous sawing that often presages a storm in the early films of Ingmar Bergman. Now he knew: his wife's love was conditional. *As long as you make me happy*. It was no different, of course, from the attitude of most people, in these enlightened times: you stay with a partner just so long as it is pleasurable or to your advantage: then you break the contract and seek another, better, companion. It is commerce: each of us has a quantifiable market value. And yet Huw had believed, with a naivety that stunned him now, that his paragon of a wife loved him as he loved her, without reservations, for as long as they lived. That was what they had vowed, on their wedding day, beside the white columns of the mansion in the Delta. *I take thee, Huw, to be my wedded husband, to have and to hold from this day forward, for better, for worse, for richer, for poorer, in sickness and in health, to love and to cherish. Until death do us part.*

'What?' she said, sitting up. 'What's that funny little smile?'

Had she meant those words? Apparently not. 'Nothing.'

'Don't lie to me. It's that twisted, bitter smile you have sometimes.'

'I can't help it, my love.' He turned away to hide the tears in his eyes.

'Did I say something wrong? I *told* you I won't leave you, silly.'

'As long as I make you happy.'

'Don't worry about that. You do make me happy. And you always will.'

She kissed his lips, briskly, with that glassy look again. *You must believe her*, he told himself. But could he still do so? For seven years he had been happy in this American Eden—and now the bearded tyrant of the Old Testament was kicking them out.

What had Eve murmured to Adam as she handed him the apple or whatever it was? *I'll always love you—as long as you make me happy. But woe betide you if you ever bore me.* Was it something like that? Was that the darker part of primordial knowledge? Not simply of our mortality, which is bearable, but of the faithlessness of those we love, which is not.

*

That afternoon, while he was speaking to his Creative Writing class about generating suspense in their stories, a beam of sunlight burst through the neo-Georgian window, which was not unusual—but then something very odd happened: gold-edged clouds invaded the classroom, and fat chuckling babies gambolled on them, and blond angels flew in, blowing trumpets, and a Michelangelo man with immense muscles and a grey beard held out his palm, arresting Time. The trumpets were baroque, Handelian, and a choir sang. *Tempus abire tibi est.* Latin. It is time to for you to leave. But time to leave what?

And was this an epiphany? Surely that was clichéd if this were a supernatural event?

His students froze like figures in a painting. Elise, the most beautiful girl in the class, or in any class, probably, was staring at something below the table—her phone, doubtless. Walt, an overweight boy with an inflated sense of his own intellect, was smiling at some secret thought. Others had the glazed eyes of kids who played too many video games. The better students, such as Jordan, the fey, frail lesbian with short-cropped bottle-blonde hair, and Charleston, the black student who led a Marxist study group, were gazing at him with an intensity which might indicate their intellectual hunger. Or maybe they were just on drugs.

Two insights struck Huw: first, that teaching Creative Writing to people who read little but Harry Potter and comics was a waste of time, so maybe the choir was telling him to leave the academy; and second, that although Time was on pause, as in *The Secret Miracle,* the Borges story they were discussing, he could still think, as the protagonist Jaromir Hladik could when he faced the Nazi firing squad. If so, were the students *compos mentis,* too? He observed them; could they observe him? If so, what did they see? A middle-aged white guy whose posture proclaimed his boredom, while a despicable glint of lechery lit up his face?

Next, assuming that he was not deranged, could he use this unique event to complete his own masterpiece, the way Hladik had used his year-long reprieve before the rifles to compose his verse drama, *The Enemies,* in his head? Huw's Modernist retelling of *The Mabinogion* had been stalled for years. Hladik had asked

God for a year, whereas Huw had not asked for Time to be halted at all. It had just happened. How long did he have? What if this tableau were frozen forever? Could the universe grind to a stop? It might get boring, even with Elise to look at in perpetuity. *Scribe, scribe, scribe,* the choir sang. Write, write, write.

Non te amat, the choir sang now. She doesn't love you. Elise? Of course not. Miranda. *Uxor tua, non te amat.* Your wife does not love you. Could he believe that? No.

And would he ever see Miranda and Owen again?

He did not have to wait long to find out. The drone of a lawn-mower drowned out the dying blasts of the angels' trumpets. The chubby babies with their tiny wings rolled out of the windows, using the clouds as slides, and God gave him one last frown, probably for ogling Elise. Then he heard a voice intoning some bloody rubbish about scenes being battles, with a winner and a loser. It was his own voice. The tableau came to life: Elise was furiously texting under the table, Walt's eyes closed in joyful surrender to his inner joke, and Charleston pointed a pencil at Huw, like a knife. It was time to leave. He had let his opportunity slip.

'Good God,' Huw said, 'did anyone else notice that?'

For once even Elise glanced up from her phone, puzzled.

'I mean, did Time stop a few moments ago? It wasn't just me, was it?'

Jordan said: 'We all get the metaphysical game Borges is playing with the reader.'

'Yes, yes, but did Time actually stop for a minute or not?'

Students giggled. 'Maybe you're overtired,' said Walt with an air of condescension.

'What's he been smoking?' Frank—or was it Hank?—said in a stage whisper. A tall, curly-haired lad with the lean physique of a rugby scrum-half, a swagger and a quick smile, he stood out among the misfits of the Creative Writing programme as oddly normal. His classmates shunned him. No one sat near him or chatted to him before class.

21

The rest of the hour passed as usual: the students 'critiqued' stories, a sci-fi by Charleston, in which an enslaved proletariat revolted against the capitalist cyborgs who controlled them, and a fantasy by Elise, whose fashionista protagonist found fame and romance thanks to the help of a squad of gay and trans elves, who had the diction of rappers. Although the sunbeam had evanesced, wisps of cumulus cloud lingered in corners of the classroom, veiling glass-fronted bookshelves and the sparkly 'Celebrate Diversity' poster. Comments on the workshop stories ranged from 'Dude, I loved this' to 'I totally identified with the main character' and 'It was awesome when you killed the boss robot, Charleston' (echoed later by 'It was so cute and hot when you kissed the Maharajah, Elise'). Huw was half-listening. He strained his ears to hear distant scraps of laughter, the beating of great wings, and plucked strings, almost out of ear-shot. Harps, lutes, lyres? Or some twit furtively playing a game on their phone? Was he going bonkers?

'You mean the protagonist, not *you*,' he said. Bloody hell, that silly prat was him!

'We identify with her,' said Truman, who last year had still been Trudy.

'It doesn't matter whether you identify with her.' That awful voice of his, badgering, bullying, professorial. He hated it but could not help himself. 'A writer's got to be able to create characters you can connect with even if you don't have a similar background.'

'Well for me it was totally awesome,' said Truman, blushing.

'But *what* was awesome about it? Be specific. General praise doesn't help.'

Again for a moment Huw saw Michelangelo's God leaning across his desk, his long hair and robes swept back by a scorching wind, his forearm muscles as prominent as ropes. His index finger extended towards Charleston's pencil, which still pointed at Huw. From the vast vaulted ceiling of the Sistine Chapel, came a booming, thunderous voice:

'Your problem is that you don't read. Your inspiration comes from television, video games, and movies. You aren't writing about people with real problems. Why not? Why do you write? Because you have something to say? Or do you just want to be J.K. Rowling and live a glamorous life?'

The students gazed back at him with baffled, hurt expressions.

'What about you?' said Jordan, with a touch of defiance. 'Why do *you* write?'

'Because you want to be famous, right?' Elise said. 'You want to be somebody.'

Huw shook his head. 'Not at all.'

'Have *you* got anything to say?' asked Broome, an ageing black-haired Goth.

That stumped him. Well, did he? Broome scowled—she disliked him, he knew, but she had a point. Was this that other cliché of the creative writing class, the *inciting incident*?

'I don't know,' Huw said, meekly for once. 'I don't know why I write half the time.'

'You just have to keep at it,' Walt piped, in adenoidal tones. His cheeks dimpled in a complacent smile. 'Follow your dream.'

Disney. What was the damned dream? To create a perfect work of art or to be seen to have created it? To be creative or admired? Echoes of the trumpets, or maybe tinnitus, bounced from the barrelled ceiling—but in the Sistine Chapel. Not here.

'Yeah, totally,' Elise said. 'That's what inspired my story.'

A pity she's not as bright as she is beautiful, he thought, *and that she's the daughter of the President of Oxbow State. What's more, she's my student, and a quarter of a century younger. Oh yes—and I'm married. Happily married. There is that, too.*

Come back to the class. Should I address the Disney dream?

No, to argue against that would be fruitless. His students, who had accepted the Disney dogma, would only think he was ranting. Already they were looking at him with anxiety, as actors regard an actor who has forgotten his lines. Jordan, in denim

23

jacket and jeans, her legs wide apart—the word *manspreading* sprang to mind—came to his rescue.

'If you're not feeling well, we could quit a few minutes early,' she said, leaving her lips open, following the fashion photographer's rules: open mouth equals sexual availability and vulnerability. Probably she knew she was cute but was unconscious of the irony of posing in attitudes dictated by the sexist patriarchy.

'I'm not exactly unwell,' he said. 'It may sound pretentious, but I've had an epiphany. Are you familiar with that term?'

'I've heard of it,' Charleston said. 'But I don't know what it means.'

'Have you read James Joyce?' Blank looks greeted the question. 'No, I suppose not. You should all read *Dubliners* at once. An epiphany is a moment of sudden clarification or understanding, usually at the end of a story, often in place of a climax, which Joyce considered rather crude.'

'Hey, I dig climaxes, personally,' said Frank or Hank.

This caused giggles, an eye-roll from Jordan, and a sigh of derision from Charleston. Elise was one of the gigglers.

'Either I have just had a hallucination—and I haven't been smoking anything,' Huw said, 'or something unprecedented outside the pages of fiction has happened.'

'Life is imitating art,' Charleston said earnestly.

'Or you were so into the story,' Jordan said, 'that it affected your notion of reality.'

'Would you say you're a suggestible person, sir?' said Elise. She was sitting very near him in a short kilt and even behind the table he could see she was scratching her thigh.

Did she mean him to see? 'I am a bit suggestible,' he said.

'The logical explanation,' said Walt with an air of triumph.

Might the students be right? Could it have been a hallucination? 'Look, if you'll forgive me, we'll take Jordan's suggestion and finish early. I apologise for my strangeness today. I'm not sure what came over me. I'm sorry if I sounded rude.'

As they stumbled out, most of the students already had their phones in their hands. Charleston and Elise approached Huw's desk.

'Hey, man,' Charleston said, 'no need to apologise. You're right, we don't read enough. Capitalists feed us on video games and superhero movies, so we can't tell the difference between fantasy and reality.' His pencil still made stabbing motions at Huw's chest. 'Our minds are so full of that shit that we can't think at all, man. All we want to do is get high and buy more of their stuff.'

'Exactly,' Huw said. 'Write about that.'

Charleston's forehead crinkled. 'I can write about *that*?'

'Absolutely. You can and you must.'

Charleston gave him a rare, disarming grin. 'Thanks, man.' He barely glanced at Elise, even though she was beside him in a minikilt and a tight turtle-neck that disclosed dangerous curves. Might he be gay? Or just shy? In any case, he was gone.

'What can I do for you, Elise?' Huw said, keeping his eyes firmly on her face.

'I just wanted to say it's all good, and I don't think you're nuts. It's cool that you're suggestible.' She paused—meaningfully, or awkwardly? 'Do you like, believe in astrology?'

'Not really, I'm afraid.'

'Pity. I can cast horoscopes and read the cards. I could tell your fortune.'

'That's very kind of you, Elise. Let me think about it.'

'Sure.' Out she flounced, doubtless aware that he was admiring her pert arse.

Outside the campus resembled a scene in some film by Joseph Losey, shot with filters to intensify the greens. Rolling lawns dotted with oaks and magnolias, Georgian style buildings with porticos and pediments, a fountain with a peristyle of white Tuscan columns—supporting nothing—and flower-beds of geraniums and wisteria. Kitschy but attractive, it aimed to resemble an Ivy League university. Huw was fortunate to have a job here. And what did it consist of? Talking about things he loved, to people who had chosen to study them. Many of his students were talented; a handful were brilliant. Aside from his teaching hours, he chose when he worked. So why did he feel so dissatisfied lately? Why had that bizarre experience befallen him? Was it a message from God—to pause, arrest the flight of Time and reflect on the meaning of his life? Or simply what the kids called a 'brain-fart'?

Before he could answer these questions, his colleagues Melvyn and Frida appeared, walking towards him—Melvyn, in jeans and trainers, with a mop of uncombed hair and a grey goatee, ambling with the loose-limbed gait of a stoned teenager, and his wife stomping alongside in a purple voodoo robe that contrasted with her pasty white face. The robe sported stars, comets, moons, palm trees, panthers, and silhouettes of feline African women. Below its fringed hem, she wore desert combat boots. Piercing her snub nose, a gold ring glinted.

Melvyn gave him a warm smile. 'Coming to the reading tonight, buddy?'

'I had forgotten all about it,' Huw admitted. 'What's her name again?'

'Savanna B. Manley,' said Frida. 'A great rider.' Huw pictured a woman with six-guns and a cowboy hat. But she meant *writer*, of course. 'You gotta be there, Huw.'

Was there a whiff of menace in her tone? As director of the Creative Writing programme, Frida had always been kind to him, even motherly, but of late Huw had sometimes caught a gleam of annoyance in her pondwater-brown eyes, and irritation in her voice. Might he have offended her in some way? Nothing came to mind. And yet she narrowed her eyes at him like Clint Eastwood in a Spaghetti Western. As she tramped away, picturesque and incongruous from the red bristles on her nearly bald head to the desert boots, her panthers prowling through the fronds of the forest, her black Amazons lurking and prancing with spears, the fringe of her dress shaking to the beat of tribal dance, an icy current tingled in the Welshman's spine. First Miranda, now Frida. But he dismissed it. Over-tired, that was all.

Don't worry, boyo, he told himself. *You are invincible.*

He was wrong about that, as he was about nearly everything that year.

TWO

So Incredibly Human

At seven-thirty Melvyn was seated in the tiered lecture hall. The whiff of marijuana smoke hung in the air, wafting from the students' clothes and unbrushed bird's nests. Predictably, Frida and Savanna B. Manley were late—whenever Melvyn was not with her to nip her heels, Frida was unpunctual—and already the students were showing signs of restlessness. Scrolling through their phones, glancing at the entrance, and even taking the extreme step of talking to each other. Vocally. In person. Without using their thumbs, without acronyms or emoticons. The two girls sitting behind and above him were talking about his wife, either unaware that he could hear them, or indifferent. The latter, he decided.

'Like, where do you think Mrs. Shamburger is?'

'It's only seven-thirty-five. She's invariably tardy.' Very odd diction for a student.

Melvyn turned. 'Not always, surely?' he said, smiling up at them.

Ashley, a young white woman 'of generous proportions',

even by Delta standards, turned the puce colour of the velveteen pyjamas she was wearing.

'Sorry, professor. I didn't know you was listening.' Her hillbilly accent and grammar distressed Melvyn's delicate New England nerves.

'I couldn't help it,' he said. The other girl—*woman*—was slim, not that he was supposed to notice their bodies, but in that dress, which clung to her athletic frame like the drapery of the Nike of Samothrace, how could he not? Her face was as blank as a phone screen. As a man, he knew he *must* not pay attention to what a woman looked like, and as a writer with a postmodern training, he knew that to describe a face, even to notice one, was bourgeois and old-fashioned: We are all faceless now. Or meant to be. But as he caught her eye, and the fixed, intense stare behind her glasses, another worry troubled him. Should he repress his urge to look? Was feminism turning him into a eunuch? Was that what women wanted? He had a moment of defiance: he *would* look if he had the urge to. Hell, yeah. But who was this girl or woman? Ashley was in one of his classes. Was her friend a Creative Writing major too? He tried a teasing tone: 'I heard you calling my wife *Mrs.* Shamburger. Hasn't she managed to expunge that term from you all's vocabulary?' *You all*: ten years in the South had turned him into a hick. He would have to curb that tendency.

'Yeah, she's like, it's sexist,' said Ashley, 'but I reckon she's just into being called *Doctor*. Or *Doctor Mrs.*'

He chuckled. Frida was indeed a pompous ass. Would he ever escape her?

The slim girl crossed her legs with the languor of a film star. Her dress was so short that he glimpsed red panties. *You are practically upskirting!* his inner Frida berated him.

'Is it true she took your name when you guys got married?' the girl asked.

You guys, not *you all*. Upper-middle class, then, if she was even from the South. Her accent gave no clues. He hoped she came from a more civilised state than this one. Might she even be a cultured New Englander, like himself? 'Yes, it is true,' he said.

'I'm lovin' it,' Ashley said, with a child's delight at her own wit.

Melvyn had endured thousands of jokes about hamburgers, and groaned.

'But why?' said Ms. Red Panties. 'I heard she's a radical feminist.'

'She sure is.' His gaze kept slipping towards her long, marble-white legs. 'I guess Shamburger sounds hysterical to you. But imagine if your maiden name was Gorgonzola.'

'Gorgonzola?' gasped Ashley, suppressing a chortle.

'Yep, like the cheese. It's a name from northern Italy. She's Italian-American.'

'Like Don de Lillo or Camille Paglia,' said the other one, whose legs were bare, in fact naked, nude, oh boy. 'But what about Frida? We heard that isn't her real name either.'

'It is now,' Melvyn said, impressed she knew the novelist and the scholar. 'Man, but that's a secret. How'd *you guys* hear about it?' *Show Ms. Smarty-Panties you're no hick.*

'She re-invented herself, then?' she said. 'Inspired by Frida Kahlo, I presume?'

'Right,' Melvyn admitted, impressed again. But how unoriginal it was of Frida.

'Cool,' said Ashley, making it two syllables. 'So what's her real first name?'

Frida had not forbidden him to reveal it, but he guessed she would be displeased if he did. And yet to make up for his shame at being married to Frida, he wanted to confide in these girls, or women. Especially the smart, stylish one with the glasses. 'Gladys,' he said.

Ashley's jaw fell open, pantomiming amazement. 'Woah, dude!'

'Gladys Gorgonzola,' Red Panties said. 'No surprise she changed her name.'

Yes, the girl or woman had breeding, class, intellect. Could he dare to hope she might like him?

'But where can Frida be?' he said, scanning the hall.

The Xenophon Fullerton Auditorium had curved banks of blackish benches and desks rising steeply from the lecturer's dais. Wainscoting and brass Victorian lamps gave the hall a warm, golden glow. Students loved the Hogwarts atmosphere. Most had draped their massive bodies in shapeless tee-shirts and jeans, though a few females—the slimmer ones—wore short skirts, and makeup. How many were here for extra credit? Half at least, probably. A wave of murmurs broke as Huw arrived with Miranda.

'Woah,' Ashley whispered. 'Get out of here! Professor Lloyd-Jones' wife is *hot*.'

'Indeed,' agreed Nike. 'Imagine making love with her.'

She was a lesbian, then. Damn! But how she spoke—almost quaintly, for a student.

'She's *way* younger than he is,' Ashley said. 'That's gross, right?'

'Not at all, he's devastatingly attractive too,' her friend purred. 'That *accent*. Those grey sideburns. He's like a sexy vampire. I'd make love with him too. Or both together.'

In fact then she was bisexual, or pansexual, or polyamorous—whatever the hell that meant. Melvyn's initial disappointment turned into relief, then jealousy, and finally resignation. Grow up, he told himself. She's a kid. Why would she find *you* hot? As for Huw being *sexy*, to Melvyn the Welshman looked typically British—just scruffy, with bad teeth. Neither tall nor athletic. *Sexy? Give me a goddamn break. I'm way sexier than he is.*

But at that moment Frida stamped into the auditorium, in a billowing black evening gown, sleeveless—revealing the dragon tattoos Melvyn had begged her not to get. The audience gasped, probably not at Frida's appalling taste, which he doubted they noticed, but at the tall, dreadlocked white woman whose cowboy boots clopped behind her.

Savanna B. Manley swaggered in like a victorious Olympian. Several girls or women—there were adults in attendance, at least people of adult age—broke into a high-pitched howling, whooping and yipping. Ululations. He had underestimated the reputation of the writer of *Bloody Blades,* the graphic novel-in-verse about a teenager's battle with cutting herself. The idol threw off her white leather jacket with a rock-star flourish, flinging it over the back of a chair, and sat with her long legs wide apart, just like a guy—a very sexist perception, he recognised and scolded himself for. Ms. Manley smiled with simmering triumph. Melvyn braced himself for the usual narcissism and stupidity, and ogled Miranda…

… Who was in a summer dress, short *and* low-cut. She reminded him of a cheerleader with her permed blonde hair and all that lipstick and mascara. Southern belle, for sure, sadly. Christ, she was hot, though. Huw turned towards him at that inopportune moment, saw Melvyn leering at his wife, and gave him a queer little smile. What exactly did it mean? *I'm on to you? I see you lusting after Miranda, but she's mine, you hypocrite, you slug?* Or maybe he was just being friendly as usual. What *did* a Welshman think? The Brits were darned hard to figure out. Enigmatic, inscrutable. Once Huw had called himself a Druid, tongue-in-cheek probably, but there was something in it. He was Oxford-educated. Smart. Mystical. Maybe just weird. Not sexy at all. Melvyn slumped lower, trying to disappear.

Frida poked the microphone, which popped, then peered over the lectern as if she were struggling to keep her head above water, clutching it hard. But by degrees, her face took on the familiar frightening smile, lips curling first, eyes crinkling next. Like a motivational speaker's, it didn't indicate joy or amusement. No, an uplifting speech was coming. Why did everyone do such sappy, cloying introductions nowadays? Virtue-signalling, of course.

Melvyn *despised* virtue-signalling—although to be fair he did it all the time himself.

'Thank you all *so* much for coming,' Frida warbled, in the unctuous voice she used to convey sisterliness and sanctity. 'I'm so happy to see all you young, creative women here.' A cue for an outbreak of whooping. 'And guys of course,' she added.

'I believe you young women will save the world,' she continued, her eyes brimming with tears. Could she be sincere? Even for Melvyn, it was hard to tell. She said stupid shit like that even at home, and yet she had never convinced him that her feminism was a true faith so much as a convenient creed that furthered her career. She had not been so fanatical when they met. All through grad school she had allowed him to support her with his trust fund money. Still, he had to admit that she was capable of working herself into a lather, as she was doing now— to masterful effect, judging by the squeals. But what about the guys in the hall? Didn't they feel a bit left out? Couldn't a few of them help save the world too?

Frida thanked the Dean and the College of Liberal Arts for supporting the Writers in Diversity series, her newly-shorn head bobbing respectfully towards the elderly Dr Jorgen Jorgenson in his bowtie and pinstripe suit, who sat beside his much younger husband, Timothy. In the spotlight her reddish bristles glinted. She reminded Melvyn of Van Gogh in his lunatic phase as her voice rose in ecstatic awe:

'And it's my great honour and pleasure to introduce to you someone *Saloon* magazine has described as 'a literary genius worthy of the Nobel Prize'.'

Melvyn smirked: Frida had written that hagiographic appraisal.

The audience was in ferment, barely reining in its desire to holler, shout and scream. Frida's voice blared like a trombone at the Pride parades they attended as allies, with traces of her childhood East Boston vowels, though she strove to speak like a Boston Brahmin: 'She has defied genre boundaries, mixing graphic novel and verse. She has fearlessly advocated for the outsider, the teenager who is transgender, anorexic, addicted, who self-harms…'

Or all of the above, Melvyn thought, having been forced to read Savanna B. Manley's 'slim volumes of prophetic power' by his wife. If they were not so woke in theme and tone, would they ever have been published? Doubtful.

'Her first novel, *Shemale*, sold 200,000 copies and *Library Magazine* hailed it as 'compulsory reading for diverse YA English classes'. The sequel, *Bloody Blades,* was an international bestseller and the movie will star Tinker Quick.' Frida paused for a collective gasp. 'Elsa has interviewed her twice, and her latest novel, *Switchbitch,* was featured on Obadiah's Book Club. She has been the recipient of a National Legacy for the Arts grant, as well as a MacAlfred 'Genius' grant, and the American Transgender Association has honoured her as a hero. *Tempo* Magazine named her one of the most influential one hundred women alive. Our last First Lady, the cool one we all love, called her 'a visionary'. In verse of breath-taking originality and power, our guest has transformed the literary landscape of the United States. I am beyond thrilled to introduce you to … Savanna B. Manley!'

Beyond thrilled? Hyperbole. But Frida had always resorted to clichés.

A tsunami of applause thundered. Amid screams of joy, the percussion of stamping feet and the snare-drum rolls of clapping, amid whistles and ecstatic howls, students brandished phones, snapped photos. Spotty cheeks and chubby cheeks shone with tears. Huw glanced around, a supercilious look on his Welsh face. He dared to smirk. Melvyn could not imagine how any professor could be so reckless.

Might Manley be the Real Thing, though? Graphic novels in verse were not really Melvyn's thing, but like all his colleagues, except Huw, he accepted that every form of art was equally valid. You couldn't cling to elitist, patriarchal notions. Pop culture was just as deep and complex as the highbrow stuff. All the cool leftist critics agreed. You only had to consider the genius raps of Mustwe East, or the inspiring auto-fictional songs of Tinker Quick. *Game of Crowns* was as universal as Shakespeare. Like obviously. Melvyn's own idol was DFW—he had slogged his way through *Infinite Jest* in a mere two years without understanding much—actually, anything—but, hell, it sounded smart. The lanky granny did not look as intellectual or as cool as DFW, but authors could not be judged by appearances. Writers were a repulsive tribe on the whole. Except the latest young women writers, of course, who were all smoking hot. Publishing houses sure knew who was marketable.

Melvyn's heart and ears were open, he told himself, suppressing a fantasy of the newest literary genius, the simpering Charlotte Silk, whose fiction was barely at his freshmen's level, though boy oh boy, she had the looks and bod of a goddamn supermodel.

Bow-legged in her cowboy boots, Savanna B. stomped to the lectern. Frida waddled to the seat beside Melvyn, gazing on Manley with operatic veneration, hand on her chest.

'Good Goddess,' Savanna said, 'thank you *so much* for that, Frida. It's totally freaking awesome to be here with you all at Oxbow State University. What a cool audience you are. You don't know how buzzed I am to see so many young women writers in front of me. Girls, you are *gorgeous*.' More yips, yowls, and squeals.

'Girls?' Melvyn whispered to his wife. 'Are you still allowed to say that?'

Frida clucked with irritation. 'Of course you can, if you're a woman.'

Huw hissed, 'Clichés,' at his wife then turned around to Melvyn and Frida and said, 'Aren't there any bloody blokes in here?'

Frida frowned. Ms. Manley—could that be a pseudonym?— began to tell her life story, in a folksy way. Sell it in fact, like an expert saleswoman.

'I gotta tell you women,' Manley said, her dreads forming

a flying halo as she shook them like a stoned reggae singer, 'you are *way* cooler than I was at your age. Trust me. I was a total nerd. All I did was read books, real serious literature,' (she pronounced it *litera-chew-er*). 'Louisa May Alcott. Alice Walker, Maya Angelou.' She let the weight of those immortal names sink in. 'I had mental health problems, too, like Prince Harry, they ran in the family, and my daddy couldn't keep his hands off me. That's right, sisters, I write what I know. So maybe it wasn't surprising that I started doing drugs, tons of damn drugs, pot, acid, cocaine, heroin, the whole nine yards, I was a real hippie. And I was cutting myself too.' She slipped that in artfully.

'She's got them eating out of her hand,' Frida murmured with admiration.

Huw shot Melvyn a *mocking* glance. Could anyone be so politically incorrect, so insensitive, so unwoke—so reckless? Melvyn pulled an inscrutable face in reply. Looking around the auditorium at all the worshipful faces, he wondered that Huw dared show his irreverence. The Maenads would tear a man limb from limb if he slighted their goddess. With a shudder, Melvyn imagined these plus-size Americans in fawn-skins, snakes coiled around their arms and thyrsi in their fists. That Manley suffered from mental illness he had already divined from her books, and her daughters had suffered from the same tragic problems, the writer was testifying now, breaking into sobs, arms and dread-locks flailing.

'That was when I found Jesus,' she proclaimed in an exalted nasal whine, 'and the mission he had gave me. He commanded me to write poetry, and promised me that he personally would inspire me, to teach noble young women like you that whatever you've been through, you will prevail, as long as you trust in Him.'

She paused, apparently seeing that these words puzzled many. *He? Him?* What was Manley thinking? Ms. Smarty-Panties said, 'Patriarchal' aloud.

Undeterred, Savanna raised her voice: 'Or Her, like obvs.'

She bit off the end of the word. 'God or Goddess, who cares, right?' She suppressed a murmur of dissent by yelling: 'I tell you this, sisters. You trust your innate beauty, whatever you look like. It don't matter if your figure is different from a model's. You own your bodies, 24/7. You're goddesses. Am I right, or what?'

Rodeo squeals, shouts, stamping, whooping, whistling and yipping.

With a jubilant grin, Huw sibilated: 'The glorification of victimhood.'

Miranda poked him with her elbow. Melvyn pictured that host of ample Maenads descending on Huw in a frenzy, ripping his flesh with their teeth and nails.

Melvyn held up an index finger. 'Don't judge her till you've heard her read.'

She opened a book—crimson as gore in a horror flick—and began to recite, in the sententious tone favoured by so many American poets. Pitched higher than her speaking voice, which was masculine, indeed manly, (hence her sobriquet?) she read mawkishly, without punctuation or pauses. Her verse was not just blank, without any rhymes, but had no meter either, or even any real content. It was indeed blank. Cliché followed cliché without rhythm or euphony; the images were obvious or stilted; nouns and verbs were tangled in webs of qualifiers; and the plot—what there was of it—was sophomoric and derivative.

In short, it was shit.

Not just common-or-garden commercial shit, either, the work of an insipid mind—Melvyn was inured to that after years teaching creative writing—but devious shit, meant to manipulate and exploit the vulnerable, the troubled, the pathetic. So he supposed. If she were sincere, the woman was as batty as a barrel of squirrels.

And yet at the end, having read in her Messianic voice, Manley bathed in applause, the women weeping and keening like Arab matrons at a funeral. They were in paroxysms; they were moved. Well, wasn't that the purpose of literature? Crying colossi stamped down the stairs, clutching their sacred books, storming the table where Manley was enthroned, ready to sign her masterworks.

Huw and Miranda were already perusing the piles of novels—that is, Miranda was reading with a solemn, sultry expression—Melvyn had to loosen his collar—while Huw was examining *Bloody Blades* as if it were spattered with snot. The guy was actually wincing.

But he sniggered as he turned the pages. Like a goddamned teenager.

'You find it funny?' Melvyn asked.

'Immensely,' the Welshman replied. 'Pretentious and portentous. I wondered if her writing might improve without that nasal, whining delivery. But no. Look at the line-breaks. Quite random. An orang-utan might have done as well.'

Miranda frowned at her husband. Oh boy, what a babe.

And then Frida appeared, her face flushed with exaltation. Was the emotion manufactured? Actors managed it through self-hypnosis. And in these hysterical times, academics had to be 'passionate', too, especially in the liberal arts. Melvyn skulked behind her, hands in his pockets, dreading what she might come out with.

'She's so incredibly human, right, Huw?' Frida said.

Melvyn cringed. Knowing Huw, he would say something withering.

Huw looked down on her with that insufferable British air of superiority and sarcasm. Lofty as George the fucking Third. 'I wouldn't go *that* far,' he said.

'Sweetie,' Miranda warned him. Melvyn repressed a smile.

Frida's gold nose ring twitched and trembled.

'Are you being enigmatic again? I can never tell when you're joking,' she said. 'You must have been impressed, though? Don't you think she's a genius?'

Huw glanced with glee at Miranda, who was immersed in

Shemale. She nodded, encouraging—no, warning. Warning, dude! Melvyn leaned in, eager to hear every word.

'Fuck me, Frida,' Huw said, 'do I think she's a genius? About as much as I think Tinker Quick is a genius, or Mustwe East. The woman's a talentless halfwit.'

Frida's nose-ring shuddered, her forehead creasing, her scalp scarlet beneath the copper brush of bristles. She wheezed, pure East Boston now: 'Unbelievable. You insult me to my face when we're surrounded by students.'

Huw rolled his kingfisher blue eyes. 'I didn't insult you, Frida, I insulted that fraudulent excuse for a writer.'

'Who *I* invited here,' said Frida, raising her fleshy arms and flexing her muscles in a weird way, so that her blue dragons convulsed.

Miranda telegraphed a reproach to Huw, who smiled back. Have I gone a bit too far? his smile meant. Not that he cared, plainly enough. She nodded at him to leave. Melvyn had a sudden inspiration: could he use Huw as a lightning rod for Frida's ire? She might spare him, then. Seldom had he had such a brilliant idea. It took possession of him at once.

He followed them out, while Frida blundered through the herd of students, scattering them, to appear at Manley's side with an apostolic smile on her face.

'That was brave of you,' Miranda said to Huw as they left the auditorium.

'Foolhardy, you mean. Unwise. Reckless. Impetuous.'

'You need that promotion, honey, and she *is* the director of your program.'

'I know. I'm sorry.'

'You don't really sound it. You sound half-contrite, half-proud.'

You go, girl, Melvyn mentally urged her. *You mean he's a patronising prick.*

'Do you always have to be so brutal?' Miranda asked.

'It's my hot Celtic blood,' he said.

'Well I guess you'll just have to write a bestseller if you lose your job.'

Huw reeled—unless it was an illusion of the mauve sunset. Neither he nor Miranda had noticed Melvyn, as far he could tell. They were passing the peristyle of the fountain, an arcade of slim columns. Students slumped on the benches, captivated by glowing screens. Some looked stoned and doubtless were. Traffic grumbled by on Connelly Street. Melvyn addressed Miranda as he caught up with them: 'Hey, so what did *you* think of the reading?'

She stopped abruptly. Underwater lights came on, illuminating the jets of water, which arched behind her, framing her dramatically. She had blue breasts.

'I found it moving,' she said, her breasts flashing like police car lights.

'Me too,' Melvyn said. 'Deeply moving. Manley is quite the genius, right?'

'Really?' To Melvyn, Huw sounded like Richard Burton or Anthony Hopkins. His voice had that sonorous Welsh cadence, but also a touch of brutality.

'But maybe I'm as half-witted as *you* think Savanna B. Manley is,' Miranda said. 'Do you think all women are sentimental? Men can be so goddamn arrogant.'

'Of course I don't think that. But tell me what you found moving in it. I couldn't see anything in it,' Huw said, not even looking at Melvyn.

'Naturally you wouldn't,' Miranda said. Melvyn's heart beat harder.

Huw watched her walking away from him—as lightly as a ballet dancer, Melvyn thought, as lightly as Frida had once walked—before hurrying after her.

'Perhaps I was wrong,' Huw said humbly.

'Won't you tell me?'

'Not now,' Melvyn heard. Miranda's tone was as final as Frida's. It would be indiscreet to tag them further, although he wished he could. Huw *was* arrogant: Miranda had nailed it. With joy, Melvyn took out his note-book and scrawled:

Oxbow State is entering an electrifying phase. Oh boy oh boy!

THREE

The Song of the Sea-Monsters

As flies to wanton boys are we to the gods, Gloucester says in
Lear. They kill us for their sport. The Bard was right about that.
They seldom even give us a warning.

The next evening, Huw was sitting on the swing-seat on
the porch, sipping tea, slipping into a trance. The garden was
lushly green, aflame with blossom; after a brief thunderstorm,
the wisteria and azalea bushes were dripping. Scraps of poetry
in English and Welsh skipped across his mind. But musical
tempests were also menacing, cellos hurrying for shelter, violins
squealing, frantic with fear, when Miranda drove up to the kerb
in her hybrid, and again he recalled the choir's command, to
leave the academy and write. He had told Miranda about the
angels with their trumpets, the cherubim on the clouds, the
patriarchal deity, the whole vision, but she had not taken it
seriously. How can you consider leaving your job when we need
the money? she had said. Was she worrying about that now?
For ages after turning the engine off she sat tight, hands on the
wheel. He had not mentioned the choir's other pronouncement,

that she did not love him. How could he? To articulate such an idea might make it happen. When she finally emerged from the carbon-grey carapace of the vehicle, looking like the actress she was often mistaken for, one famous for a role as a dancer, her face made-up, hair curled, in a chalk-stripe trouser-suit, she tripped past him, ignoring his greeting and his wave. Had she seen him? She was never rude. All Huw's doubts and fears of the past few days returned with redoubled force. Just what was the matter with her?

He followed her indoors and found her in the kitchen, at the table in an alcove festooned with potted plants. In one hand she had a glass; in the other, a bottle of port, which she clutched by the neck, upside down, like a German stick grenade.

'I need to get drunk,' she said. 'Do you mind?'

'Owen will be home soon, you know,' he said, adding in an attempt at humour, 'Please don't lob that bottle at me. It's not like you to get drunk.'

'Can't I let myself go sometimes?' Her features belied her annoyance, or strove to: her face froze in an expression of crazed beauty-queen happiness. Preternaturally bright eyes, TV presenter smile. Huw's worry that his best work was behind him, and teaching had riddled his mind with woodworm, was forgotten. A catastrophe was approaching. Just a couple of days ago Miranda had told him that she would only stay with him as long as he made her happy. Had he failed her? If he had, would she give him a chance to make amends?

He took a small glass of port to accompany her. 'It's funny,' he said, to remind her of their luck. 'People say passion doesn't last, but mine is undiminished. After six years of marriage. I know how fortunate I am to have found love so late in my life.'

She swigged the port, traces of her glassy grin remaining on her face. Huw reached across the white-painted pine planks of the table and laid his hand on Miranda's right arm, which held the glass. On any other day she would have placed her free hand over his, pressed her palm against his chest, responded somehow. But tonight she did nothing but guzzle, giving no sign that she was aware he had touched her.

'Can I get drunk, then?' she asked, looking towards but not at him.

'Be my guest,' Huw said, with a trace of sarcasm.

'Sourpuss. You're so… I don't know, so damn *American*, sometimes.'

'*American*? Me?' He wished she would look him in the eyes.

'Bible Belt Baptist. Sensible. Self-righteous. You've been here too long, Huw.'

How long had he been in the States? Seven years or so, starting with the Master's in Creative Writing at Iowa University, where he had met and married her, followed by the three-year teaching appointment in Oman, and then the return to Miranda's home state in the Deep South. Had it been too long? Was he turning into a Southern prig? The fear that he might be informed the vehemence of his denial: 'Jesus Christ, Miranda. I'm from Wales. I come from a noble line of tipplers, topers, sots, soaks, boozers, carousers, and dipsomaniacs. I'm damned if I'll let you blacken my name with an insult like 'Bible Belt Baptist.' I'm as much of a sinner as you are, so help me God.'

She smiled without mirth or tenderness. 'Let's both get drunk then.'

'What is it?' Huw asked her. 'What's going on? Tell me, love.'

'I've got to get drunk first.'

He heard the dogged resolve in her voice. 'Shall I get the dinner?' he said.

'I'm not going to eat.'

'I'll have to get something for Owen. He'll be home soon.'

'Go ahead.'

Huw cracked some eggs and beat them with a fork. 'This isn't about me resigning, is it?' No answer. 'You haven't you lost *your* job, have you, love?'

'God, no. The Department of Psychiatry couldn't function without me.'

'Car accident? Mass shooting? Not another war?'

She shook her head. Her eyes glittered like ice crystals.

'I wish you wouldn't drink so fast,' he said. 'You know it makes you ill.'

'I want to be sick. I want to puke my goddamn guts up.'

'Has someone in the family got cancer or something?'

'Nothing like that. But it is something to do with the family.'

'Won't you tell me what it is?'

'I've got to get plastered first.'

Owen sailed past the window on his bike, arms crossed, headphones on. A minute later he was in the kitchen, grunting a greeting, his eyes not meeting Huw's.

'What's for dinner?' he said, in a mid-Atlantic accent.

'Omelette, I'm afraid,' Huw said.

'Again?'

Huw nodded discreetly at Miranda.

Seldom perplexed, Owen raised his brows in interrogation.

Huw nodded back, barely perceptibly. 'I'll call you when it's ready.'

Owen left the room, all bones and long limbs. Miranda was drinking. She did not look at Huw. He observed her, though: her face was pale—or was that just the make-up?—and her eyes were remote, glazed. Her posture, usually perfect, if a little rigid, was different. She crouched over her glass, encircling it with her arms as if afraid he would snatch it away.

'Don't you want to take your jacket off?' he asked her.

'No.' The monosyllable was a body blow.

Was she working up the courage to tell him she was leaving him? Might she be having an affair? He could not imagine it. Her behaviour had not altered in the past weeks, and he had been just as loving and attentive. But he remembered her saying she had been moved by Manley's work. Perhaps he should have given that more thought. To him it was an odd confession—like admitting you enjoyed the music of Mustwe East or Tinker Quick. Was it possible to love someone who valued such twaddle? Of course it was. He put a plate over the omelette, held it in place, then turned it over and glanced at Miranda. He reproved himself for his arrogance—that was what she had accused him of. Hubris. Pride comes before a fall.

'What did you find so moving at that reading?' he said, trying again. He glanced over his shoulder as he stood at the stove. She materialised from her underworld, and visibly *collected* herself. She was in pieces, in fragments.

'I identified with her. The teenage girl.'

'But you've never cut yourself, have you?'

'Not yet.'

'*Not yet?*'

She clucked. 'I want to. It's me or my mom.'

'What?'

He gaped at her. She did not reply. He smelled burning.

'Oh Christ, the sodding omelette.' He took the pan off the burner. The omelette was seared but still edible. Or so he hoped. He started hurling together a salad. Did other people have crises while cooking for their teenage sons? In fiction a dramatic scene was never interrupted, but in reality the drama often had to wait.

'Dinner!' he called up the stairs. He hoped Owen would not notice how sloshed Miranda already was. Fortunately, he focussed at once on the food when he came down. He sat and scrutinised his plate. 'Aren't you two eating?'

'We'll eat later,' Huw said. 'Probably. How was school?'

Owen nodded rhythmically at the music in his earbuds—metal, by the sounds of the crunching guitars. 'Tastes like shit,' he muttered. 'You incinerated it.'

'Sorry,' Huw said. 'Bad day so far. And about to get worse, I fear.'

Owen glanced at his stepmother. 'Yeah, right. Chicks are all the same, dude.'

Huw expected an exasperated hiss at the sexist language, but Miranda was either not listening or did not care. She poured another glass—her fourth or fifth. Then, unsteady on her feet, she headed for the cutlery drawer, from which she took a Rambo-sized carving knife. With a dazed expression, she pondered its blade and stumbled out of the kitchen.

Huw caught up with her in the living-room, where she swayed beside the sofa. 'Drunk as a skunk,' she said, prolonging the syrupy Southern vowels. 'I just need to cut my face. Is that OK with you?'

He took the knife from her and put it down. He held her arms. She did not resist.

'Of course it's not OK with me. Why?'

'You really want to know? My mom hurt me.'

Huw knew his wife was not fond of her, but they were always courteous with one another, and he had never suspected anything sinister of his mother-in-law. 'What do you mean? Today? What's she done?'

'Nasty things,' Miranda said, in the awestruck voice of a child. She looked oddly girlish. Trusting. 'That's why I need to hurt myself. If you'll just let me slash my cheeks or stab my eyes, I'm sure I'll feel better.'

He suppressed the urge to weep. 'I won't let you harm yourself, darling. You know that.' He hoped Owen could not hear. Let him be oblivious.

'Would you cut me then? You could chop off a finger for me. This one.' She held up the little finger of the left hand. 'I'll give it to you as a present.'

'Of course I can't do that, my darling. Are you serious?'

'I've been thinking about it all week. I was sure you'd like to have one of my fingers. I was planning to cut one off and send it to you in a letter.'

Huw had never seen her drunk, let alone heard her talk about childhood abuse or such sick impulses. Horrors stampeded through his brain. It was not, could not, be happening. If she were nuts, life would be unthinkable. He would not let her be insane. If he pretended everything was all right, maybe it would be. Once again she reminded him of the Hollywood actress with the enamelled smile. He hoped to God that Owen had heard nothing. With luck, if his music were loud enough, he would not have. Right then Owen loped past them, eyeing the carving-knife in his father's hands with concern. Then, to Huw's relief, he was gone.

'When did your mother do these nasty things to you?' Huw said.

'I've had a bad day. Will you bear with me? Let's go back to the kitchen. I bet I could drink you under the table.'

He led her by the arm. She stumbled, but was not as unsteady as he had feared.

'Is it OK if I have waking nightmares tonight?' she said when she sat down.

'What do you mean? You're worrying me. What's the matter?'

'That's the question, isn't it? Everyone thinks I'm sooooo sane.'

'You are. Probably the sanest person I know.' Until tonight she had been, anyway. That was partly why he had married her, for her balance and serenity.

She gulped the port like a child gulping cola; it dribbled down her chin. 'Oh I'm fucking sane, all right. I'm the best administrator Garson has ever known, she says. Do you know why?'

He dabbed her chin with a tea-towel. 'No. Tell me why.'

'Because I can hear the monsters breathing in the sea.'

'We're hundreds of miles from the sea, you know. I wish I knew what was troubling you. I feel so powerless. I don't see any monsters.'

'I don't see them either. But I hear them.' She chugged her port. 'Gasping for air, sucking it in, sighing. Splashing, struggling to stay afloat. They get tired of swimming all the while, thrashing their tails and bellowing. They tread water.'

'I don't get it. What's that got to do with you being a great administrator?'

'Can't you see? The monsters send me messages. They're real smart.'

'What do the monsters say, Miranda? Do they speak English?'

'Don't patronise me, Huw. I know you think this is crazy. It is crazy. But what if it's true, too? Obviously they don't speak in words. They make high-pitched squeals, like whales or dolphins or submarines. What do they call that, radar?'

'Sonar.'

'Sonar, right, thank you, professor. It's a sort of language. You don't decode it with your mind, the way you do with words; you decode it with your heart. It's like music. An emotional language. I understand the monsters. I'm pretty smart too.'

'I know that. But let's get this straight. You're saying that mythical beasts in the ocean advise you how to run government mental health programmes, and a department at a Medical School. They communicate in submarine squeals, which you understand?'

'You got it.'

'Are you pulling my leg, Miranda? Tell me this is all a joke.'

'Hey, do I ever fuck with you?' Her lips tensed.

'You've got to admit, it's a stretch. Are you trying to tell me that you base multimillion-dollar decisions on what monsters squeal at you in sonar? And if so, how long has this been going on? You know what your therapist would say about these monsters, don't you?'

'That they're projections. That is what he says, you're right.'

'Well, what do you think of that?'

'I know they're projections, but they're real to me. So yeah, I do base my decisions on how I feel when I listen to their songs. It's been going on about four years now, since we lived by the Indian Ocean in Muscat. Remember those days?'

'Of course—they were among the happiest of my life.' In his mind they retained a fairy tale quality. He tried to picture what she had seen at that time as she gazed through the carved lattice-work of the window-screen at the sea. It was silver and black and effervescent. Sailing dhows rode their anchors in the bay, rocking, writhing, plunging and rearing, twisting and turning, anxious to break free from their moorings. On a cliff to the right, the floodlit Portuguese fort had overlooked Mutrah harbour. A full moon blinked like a blind eye as a cloud closed over it and uncovered it again. From behind their two-hundred-year-old house, from the entrails of the city, came the lovestruck cry of the muezzin, atop his minaret. Huw smelled fish, seaweed, spices, baked mud bricks, salt. He did not hear the monsters.

'All right,' he said. 'Let's say the sea-monsters are real. You still haven't told me what happened to you today. Can you? How did your mother hurt you?'

'Oh, that wasn't today. It was a long time ago, in days of yore.' She smiled at the quaint phrase. 'I just remembered today.'

Slowly, painfully, as she drained the bottle, it came out. Her mother had hit her very hard when she was a child; once she had choked her. She had entered the shower when Miranda was bathing, and pulled her pudenda, telling her that one day it would all be loose and ugly. Huw asked if she was sure; Miranda said she was. He wondered why she had never mentioned any of this, how it was possible she had only just remembered. She answered that the memories had been there, but confused, like half-remembered dreams. She had not wanted to think about them. In that case, he asked her, how could she be certain that she was recalling them accurately? She just could, she said. It was up to him whether he believed her.

He did, he told himself, of course he did. He allowed her to finish the bottle, thinking it might soothe her, help her sleep. He escorted her into the bedroom and undressed her. He decided to stay awake and watch over her. To his surprise she fell asleep almost at once, and slept as peacefully as an infant. For hours he gazed at her. But at some point he must have dropped off; he was startled awake by her shuffling back into the bedroom. 'I've just taken a bottle of sleeping pills,' she slurred. 'I'm fine, though. Please let me die.'

And yet she submitted passively to him wrapping her in a dressing-gown and driving her to the hospital. The doctor on duty in Emergencies reminded Huw of a figure in a Persian miniature. Miranda answered her questions like a child. Lunesta, whole bottle. Benzodiazepines. Ten, twenty? Some port wine. Half a bottle.

'Why did you do this?' the doctor asked her gently.

'I'm tired of being sensible,' Miranda said. 'I want to be bonkers now.'

'In love with lunacy, I'm sick of wisdom and reason,' the doctor murmured, in English, with a slight accent—but that was Rumi, Huw remembered. They would have to pump Miranda's stomach, she told Huw. Go home and sleep. The doctor's eyes were grave, black, beautiful, and it was shameful of him to notice them, but he could not help it.

'How can I?' he said. 'Can't I stay with her? Why did you do this, Miranda?'

His wife did not respond, but looked up at the doctor, expecting her to answer for her, which she did, in verse again: *'Every storm the Beloved unfurls, allows the sea to scatter pearls.'* She spoke in English, half to herself, half to Miranda.

But when Huw said, 'Rumi again—are you Persian?' the doctor threw him a keen glance. Curious or contemptuous? Was she reproving him for being distracted?

'Go home,' she said with calm authority. 'You may return in the morning.'

He kissed Miranda's forehead, embarrassed, and trudged out.

As he drove home, Tocqueville, with its centuries-old oaks and ashes, its bushes in blossom, and its Craftsman houses, might have represented an American idyll. And yet there was something sinister, something of *The Truman Show* about it—and Miranda, too. He had once overheard Broome loudly describing Miranda to another student, and clearly meaning him to hear, as 'Your typical little Barbie doll.' Was it too much of a strain, keeping up the glossy Instagram image of perfection?

Was this the fatal flaw of American life?

He remembered a summer's day a couple of years ago,

when he and Miranda had climbed Cader Idris back home. She had been solemn and somber, as she often was, but also calm, collected. He pictured her on the crest of the great cliff, the highest and steepest in Wales, without makeup, her face clear and sane. Even then, though, she must have been hearing her sea-monsters. Other odd recollections came to him: that she had confided that when driving an urge to swerve into the path of an oncoming car often nearly overpowered her—he had dismissed it as a joke—and that she had persuaded him to move their bedroom from the upper storey to the lower because upstairs she always had an impulse to hurl herself from the window. Evidently he was married to a madwoman. Could he cope with that? Was that a selfish concern? It was. He would just have to learn to cope with it.

The words that came into his mind were Rumi's. *In love with lunacy, I'm sick of wisdom and reason.* What a relief that might be, to abandon yourself to madness. These days, nearly everyone had surrendered their reason. Half-blind with tears, he wept as he drove. But who was he weeping for—Miranda, or himself? His self-pity disgusted him. *Every storm the Beloved unfurls, allows the sea to scatter pearls.* That was what the doctor said. Had she spoken to console Miranda, or him? But he could not think any further.

His car had made its way back to the blue house, with its covered porch and square white columns. They had bought it because it looked like a writer's house. But now it struck Huw that terrifying things happened in picturesque old houses: witches plotted to murder the innocent, impostors took the place of true brides, stepmothers treated children cruelly, and the hero had to leave home and brave terrible trials. Huw had hoped he would die in this house. Now, as dawn broke and he got out of the car, he knew it was just a temporary refuge.

FOUR

Capital Thought Crimes

In his book-lined study, seated on a buckwheat *zafu* cushion, Melvyn was meditating. Make that trying to meditate. From the lounge came the usual torrent of television din. He was a mild man, but for once peevishness had got the better of him. He had fantasies of yelling curses, switching off the TV, or better still, taking it out with a swift kick. Stifling the negativity—*Remember, the superior man controls his emotions*—he arose from his kneeling posture, took a deep breath, and imagining himself a Zen monk treading on tatami mats, glided—*No*, he edited himself, *prowled*—towards the roaring television. The sitting-room door was open. Of *course* it was. Enthroned on her colossal black leather recliner was Frida, laptop open on her hams, while *Upton Abbey* blasted from the flat screen TV.

'Sup?' said Melvyn, proud as ever of his resonant bass-baritone.

Frida was stabbing the keys in a frenzy, a Nazi wireless operator in an old movie. Caps, exclamation marks. Outrage or feminine solidarity? Both, knowing her.

'Just grading papers. And working on my novel of course.'

She was on Facebook too. 'Of course you are. How silly of me. I wondered if you might be watching television. As the volume is so high, you know.'

She cast an irate glance over her shoulder. 'Hey, *my* gender can multi-task.'

In his gentlest voice he said, 'Psychologists disagree with you there.'

'Yeah, but what do those jerks know?'

Melvyn held his tongue: *The superior man does not speak on impulse.*

Should he politely ask her to look at him? He foresaw her answer: *Can't you just walk around the couch?* He did so, negotiating the obstacle course—a fetid paper bucket of brown sludge from Sundoes, a ziggurat of paperbacks on the pedagogy of Creative Writing, a dog-eared pile of essays or stories, and the even more dog-eared dog, Darcy, unsuitably named, considering his obvious lack of pedigree, asleep at Frida's slippered feet, and nearly as dishevelled as she was. Onscreen, English aristocrats chaffed each other in refined tones, and Melvyn looked down on his wife. Literally. *I guess I shouldn't look down on her,* he told himself, *but I can't help it, after all.*

'Still in PJs, I see,' he said, glancing at his watch. 'At half-past eleven.'

'Don't guilt-trip me, Melvyn. What's the point of being a writer if I can't work in my pyjamas? Huh?'

Striped flannel PJs, bought in London during the mythical epoch of their honeymoon. They were baggy then, and stylish, in an old-school way, on her still-slender body. Now the frayed pant legs were filled like pork sausages. At that unkind simile, bells shrilled in Melvyn's mind. To compare his wife to … that unlucky animal—he repressed its name—was not merely unacceptable, but *unthinkable.* And yet the more thoughts he hacked off, the more grew back, like Hydra heads. Now the image of Napoleon in *Animal Farm* superimposed itself on Frida's face.

People said you could get used to anything, but the disastrous deterioration of his wife's figure still amazed and distressed Melvyn. Traumatised him.

How superficial, he admonished himself, hearing Frida's voice in his head. What about her noble mind, her talent, her idealism? Wasn't that the real her? Again he heard her hectoring inner voice. Maybe he should love her for her personality, but goddamn, her personality sucked too, big time. Besides, there was just *so much* of her body—it was hard to ignore. It billowed and barged and bullied its way into all his thoughts, even the ones he kept covered up in the corners. All righty, then. Be fair. Be *kind*, as Frida might say.

Her hair was no longer a cascade of Jane Austen-inspired curls but shorn, indeed shaven like a storm-trooper's. All the same, her face did retain traces of its former charm. The same low brow and startled, slightly hysterical eyes; the upturned nose, once cute, but now, with the thick gold ring piercing the columella, undeniably, inescapably porcine. His internal editor cut in again: *porcine* was not a word a man could use to describe a woman these days. *Eve*rrr! Alternatives? Piggy? Worse. Swinish? *Much* worse. What if you moderated it with an adverb? Sweetly swinish? Prettily piggy? Forget it. He half-expected her to snort. Well, he did. Her lips were pursed. Was she concentrating or just ticked off? Ticked off, of course. He felt like grinning that he had achieved that.

'I've been wondering,' he began. She did not so much as glance up. He took a deep breath. 'Whether you—I mean *we*—shouldn't maybe, uh, start exercising regularly.'

She did snort. Loudly and hoggishly. *Oops. There you go again.*

'You already do. Karate, Tai Chi. You mean me, don't you? But I go to the gym *all the time* too. Last week I went like twice. Well, once, anyway.'

Yes, and dawdled on a treadmill at 1.6 miles an hour, while reading *The New Yorker* and watching Obadiah, he thought, but had the sense not to say aloud.

'We could stand to lose a little weight,' he ventured. 'Don't you think?'

With a great shuddering movement, she turned her pink face towards him.

'You're thin as a stick. You're fat-shaming me. That's misogynistic, Melvyn. Chauvinistic. Toxic. Just fucking say it. You mean I'm fat, right?'

Melvyn was not so dumb as to fall into that trap. No woman was *ever* fat: he knew that. Everyone knew that. 'Of course—not. I'm just talking about our health.'

'Bullshit,' Frida boomed, pitching her powerful contralto even lower. A pity she did not emulate those mellifluous feminine British voices. 'You're talking about our sex life. I'm not dense. You just see me as a sex object.'

You wish, Melvyn told her mentally—a capital thought crime. Unsayable.

'What matters,' Frida declared, 'is not a woman's body but her mind.'

'I've never fully understood that. I mean, I get it that you inherit the genes for your body, so you're not to blame if it sucks, and neither do you deserve praise if you get an athletic one.' *Like mine,* he thought, proud of his awesome, ripped physique. 'But what about your mind? Isn't that just the product of your genes and upbringing too? If you're smart, do you deserve any more admiration than if you have an athletic body? Besides, just how deep are most minds? Aren't they usually kind of superficial too?'

'Maybe *yours* is, Melvyn. So now you're saying I'm superficial?'

She was deflecting again, not answering his main question. Melvyn could not win this argument. He had done his best to admire his wife's mind, but had long ago reached the conclusion that it was unoriginal, lazy, and tribal. Like many academics, she had done her doctorate to convince herself that she was an intellectual. And she clung to the belief that she was one. Clung *fiercely,* she would have said, cliché-monger as she was. She *was* superficial.

'You know I'm not saying that,' he said. *Coward,* he hissed internally.

Frida's meaty elbows poised on the padded armrests. Melvyn feared she was about to lever herself up and lurch at him. But his words mollified her: she sank back into the soft leather with a sigh. 'Anyway, it's all a matter of perspective. I mean our idea of the beautiful. It's just fashion. Look at Rubens' nudes.'

Melvyn called to mind *The Three Graces.* They were statuesque; she was—not.

'Do you know what Rocky said to me yesterday at the reading?' she said.

'Yes, I do.' He recalled Roquette Rathhaus's obsequious Southern face, seething with insincerity, as she came up to Frida. She had hugged Frida with quasi-sexual enthusiasm. 'She said you looked fabulous in that sexy violet velvet dress. She admired the way it revealed your voluptuous curves. I believe that's how she expressed it.'

'Yeah, right. Well?'

Was she inviting him to corroborate Rocky's opinion? *Sure, your curves would appeal as voluptuous—to the guy who carved the Venus of Willendorf.* Yet another thought he had to censor. When did that start, having to police his own mind?

'I see that.' Man, he was a fake, even to himself. 'Sure, it depends on context.'

'I *own* my body,' Frida said, thrusting out her lower jaw like Mussolini.

Her grandfather was an Italian Fascist before he emigrated to Boston, Melvyn remembered. Pencil moustache, mean, thin lips: he had seen the photos. He had killed Abyssinians. She must have inherited her pugnacious expression from the black-shirt bastard.

'*I* think I'm sexy,' Frida went on. 'Besides, I'm American. I'm average here.'

More's the pity, Melvyn was unable to say. Why couldn't she model herself on those slim, fey English ladies on the screen? Why hadn't he married one of them?

'But *you* don't find me sexy anymore, do you?' she said, her voice curdling with menace. The red bristles on her scalp glistened. Her nose ring trembled.

Now he was on treacherous ground. Panic surged in his throat. How might he respond? *I try, God knows, but despite my efforts, those mounds of quivering flesh overwhelm any desire I feel.* No, there was only one acceptable answer: *Of course I find you sexy, darling.* But he couldn't bring himself to lie so shamefully. Instead he hung his head like a naughty boy, hoping she would not press him.

'You only do it in the dark these days, don't you?' Frida insisted. '*Drunk.*'

He sensed that his best course was to maintain silence. But his insurgent thoughts would not be stilled. Why was he yoked to—to this 'female of repellent aspect', as Oscar Wilde might have described her? Because of the girls? They were grown-up now. *Women.* Because of the job? He had tenure. Of course it would be awkward if he and his wife got divorced but remained in the same department. Get to the point, he chided himself. Confront her. Force her to admit her fault. Be a *man.* Be like Bruce Willis. Bruce Lee. Or Clint.

'That's not true,' he mumbled. *Liar, liar, pants on fire!* 'Anyway, I came in to ask you to lower the volume a tad. Surely you could? I am trying to meditate.'

'Meditate or daydream?'

'I do meditate, you know. When I'm allowed to.'

'Geez, why don't you just shut your goddamn door?'

'Mine was shut. Why isn't yours? Ever?' A hellhound awoke in his belly, stretched, stiffened, its hackles rising. It bared its teeth. But he still had it tethered. 'Why must the whole house revolve around you, Frida?'

The scummy brown ponds glimpsed through her granny

glasses got murkier. 'Isn't that obvious?' she said, leaning forward and swamping her laptop with her belly.

It was a pivotal moment. Things were about to be said that would change his life forever. Frida was on the verge of unleashing words she had long yearned to utter, annihilating words. She would not shout. But he knew from the crimson flush on her cheeks, and the quivering nose-ring, that she would be merciless. He remembered a department meeting when a rhetorician she pretended to be friends with had dared to suggest that Frida had undeserved release time. Frida had routed the upstart with murderous invective—in fact the woman had died months later, of a sudden and mysterious illness. Death by rhetoric!

'I have no idea what you mean,' he said.

'What do you actually *do*, Melvyn? Apart from sitting on your ass all day and daydreaming? Huh?' She wobbled, threatening to upset her chair. 'How long have you been writing that so-called novel? When did you last publish anything?'

The hellhound strained at the chain, snarling. 'I might ask you the same question. I have published a collection of poetry and a book of flash fiction, at least.'

'You asshole. You think flash fiction counts? How many articles and essays have I published? How many books? I'm an *authority* on the pedagogy of Creative Riding.'

The hell-hound slavered and lunged. It wanted to bite and rip. Still, he spoke softly. 'Some might say that's a fraudulent subject.'

Her brow burned, bright red. 'Creative Riding is fraudulent?'

'The *pedagogy* of Creative Writing. What do you have to say about it? Be honest: nothing but platitudes. Those who can, do; those who can't, teach.' This was great fun.

Her nose-ring shook. 'I guess that's why you became a professor, then,' she sneered.

'Maybe—but for damn sure it's why *you* became one.'

Her trotters swung off the table on which they had been reposing, and she swept the computer off her lap. She lumbered to her feet, knocking over the foul-smelling coffee, flanks heaving, and lowered her snout—she was about to charge, surely. She was the Empress of Blandings, Lord Emsworth's prized possession in the Wodehouse stories, the stoutest pig in Shropshire. Oh man, if she could read his mind! He would be dead meat.

'All right, you asked for it, wise guy,' she said. 'Why does the house revolve around me? Try this: because *I'm* the director of the Programme. *I'm* the one with the international reputation. *I'm* the full professor. You came into Oxbow State on my coat-tails, and you're tolerated because of me. You're my sidekick. My lackey. My puppet. Have you ever dared vote against me in a meeting, Melvyn, even once?'

He hung his head again, whipped. *Pussy*-whipped. He had not.

'*I'm* in charge,' she said, 'in the department and at home. *I wear the pants.*'

The hellhound wanted to howl, but the chain choked him. All Melvyn could do was nod ruefully. 'You really get off on the power, don't you?'

'Why the hell shouldn't I? Men enjoy it, right? Why shouldn't a woman?'

'Surely it's unseemly to enjoy it for its own sake, whatever sex you are.'

'*Gender*, puh-lease.'

'Whatever. The *I Ching* says Power should be exercised for the good of a community. The superior man does not seek to gratify himself, but benefit others.'

'The superior *man*. Like you, Melvyn? When are you going to get over your dumbass patriarchal hang-ups? What about the superior *woman*?'

'What about her?'

'You just don't get it,' she said with a nasty laugh. 'You're looking at her.'

The words stung like a slap. 'Jesus Christ.' The person

before him was not merely his middle-aged, portly wife, red and vibrating with rage, but also, as she had made him see, a potentate. A petty, narcissistic one, sure—yet a potentate all the same, who wielded real power, in the university and in the heart of his own home. And he had fed this monster.

What could the wounded dog do? Snarl, flail with fangs and claws, maim and murder? How typical of a man that would be, to behave like a beast or a savage.

Whine scathing, sarcastic words, then? They would be harmless, empty. For she had spoken the truth. She had made herself his mistress, or master—whatever—and he had submitted to his thraldom. Because he believed in equality, he had always told himself: now he understood he had deceived himself. He had just been weak. And if there was one quality no woman could stand, however much she protested otherwise, it was weakness in a man. Very well. He would change. Was that possible? According to conventional wisdom, no. The leopard's spots and all that. According to the sacred laws of literary fiction, though, characters could change—*round* characters could, proclaimed E.M. Forster. But could he, Melvyn, behave like a hero in a novel? Could he find strength in himself, redeem his life?

He dared hope so. But what did he want? That was the question he asked in every workshop, of every character. Of course he wanted to leave her. He had longed to for ages but had stayed for the girls' sake. Yes, it went without saying that he would have to go. But underneath that longing was another, darker desire. He would show her who was in charge. Exact his revenge. His wrath would be terrible.

Wagner rumbled in the dark, icy caverns of his mind. He would exult in her utter humiliation. He remembered reading about a study on the cannibals of New Guinea. None of them ever expressed remorse for killing an enemy. On the contrary, years later, they recalled their murders with pride and delight. Melvyn had that primitive streak too. Not that he would slaughter and eat her, of course, heh-heh. But what about that superior man of the *I Ching?* Which was he? Savage or sage?

Darcy stirred and gazed at him with doleful eyes—in commiseration. Darcy knew a whipped dog when he saw one. But even Darcy's pity did not last long: within moments, he was licking his genitals.

Melvyn bared his own teeth in a canine grin. 'Sure, you're the Superior Woman.'

That placated Frida. She turned back to Facebook.

She was scowling and hissing about Huw, some blog post of his. All at once an idea came to Melvyn, devious, delicious, and simple. This was how he could wreak his revenge.

'Enjoying Huw's essay?' he said, his inner cannibal coming to the fore.

Frida spoke through her teeth. 'It's about novelists of genius. All male, of course. Dead *white* fucking males. The goddamn patriarchy. That English asshole.'

'Welsh.' *Twist the blade. Needle her. Make her hate him.*

'Whatever,' she snapped. 'A Welshman is basically a kind of Englishman, right?'

'I guess you're right. Those Limeys are pretty darn smug and snobby.'

'The hoity-toity way he called Savanna a talentless halfwit.' The lurid greens and blues flickering over her face turned her into a troll. 'I could tell he meant me, too.'

Inside Melvyn a joyful fire burned. 'Yeah, maybe. You've always had great intuition, Frida.' That was a lie but the rest was not: 'I have a feeling you'd like to destroy him. You *could*, you know.'

Frida gaped up at him, taken aback: 'Oh yeah, I know.'

Melvyn gloated. 'Will you?' he whispered. Now he knew what Iago felt like.

Frida's eyes were unfocussed: presumably she was imagining future deeds. The fleshy face with its skull-cap of red bristles trembled; the gold-nose ring quivered. 'I just might,' she said, hoarse with desire.

'I bet you could have him fired by Christmas,' he hissed over her shoulder.

Her fingers stubbed her keys. *What about WOMEN?* she wrote, a ghastly operatic grin on her green and blue face. 'I could, but you know what? That's too good for Huw.'

His mouth watered. The slavering of his chops flummoxed and thrilled him in equal measure. Where was the Superior Man now? Who cared? 'Oh yeah?' he said.

'He deserves to be humiliated, humbled, brought to his knees. I can think of ways of tormenting him, of prolonging an excruciating torture.'

Horror and excitement battled in Melvyn's mind. 'I bet. You're *so* creative.'

'Yeah, I am,' Frida said, punching 'Enter'. 'This is going to be so fucking cool.'

Melvyn practically snapped his jaws. He smelled blood. He savoured the tearing of flesh. He would be in at the kill. But for now, he must bide his time.

Softly, like a Buddhist monk gliding on tatami mats, or like Garfield, on his cushioned paws, he padded back to his den. To meditate. The Superior Man knows the meaning of the time. He *would* achieve enlightenment. But not yet, he prayed, please.

FIVE

The Marvels of Modern Science

No one would have dreamed that Miranda had tried to kill herself just days earlier. Of course, she was heavily medicated. Even so, as she sat on a Gustav Stickley settee, wedged between their hosts, Dr Matthew McBane and his wife NeAmber, much too intimately to Huw's mind, Miranda might have been a *Vogue* model. With her hair in a topknot, her pearls—natural ones from her first 'starter' marriage to a dotcom millionaire—and her creamy bosom half disclosed by the décolleté of her velvet cocktail dress, with her white stockings and stilettos, she was flawless, the epitome of the *lady*—an archaic term, but right for the Grace Kelly type, who inspires awe as much as desire. Huw put her on a pedestal, she sometimes complained, which was true. He had always laughed at that, but now he wondered why it bothered her. Was he Pygmalion? Did he adore her simply as an ivory statue of his own creation? If so, he was not wholly responsible. She had once welcomed his adoration—but perhaps no longer. He tried to think of something else.

Huw buzzed about in the McBanes' Prairie style living-room,

sipping Sauvignon Blanc and surveying the oak bookshelves. The complete works of Freud and Jung in black leather, but also Adler, Reich, Rogers, Klein, Neumann and Fromm. The fiction ranged from the Western canon to contemporary North American eminences. There were lots of black women novelists. Dr Matthew was literate or wished to appear so. As was Miranda's other boss, Dr Garson Gneiss, pronounced 'Nice', as she had told him with a hearty laugh. She had come with an effervescent blonde poet named Isabella DiMarzio who unlike Huw was ferreting through the shelves, making fierce, lightning jabs at books that delighted her: verse by Audre Lorde, Sharon Olds and Carolyn Kizer. A triumphant squeal accompanied each strike. But Garson's attention was diverted from her paramour. NeAmber, a woman with the muscular figure of a tennis champion and an indelible grin, had just asked her, in a voice dripping with insincere solicitude, whether Garson's tumour had been analysed yet.

'Oh sure.' Garson sat on a low Mission ottoman. To Huw she looked like Queen Victoria in her later, jowly years. 'It was malignant, all right.'

'I'm *so* sorry.' NeAmber crossed her long mahogany legs with a coquettish glance at Huw, clearly checking that he was watching. He was. She reminded him of a femme fatale in a noir movie. 'So are you going to have surgery?' she said.

Isabella DiMarzio tossed her plaited blonde mane and neighed. McBane snickered, but did not smile. He never smiled. Flat affect? Or just a serious bloke? Miranda gazed at Garson with the veneration of a peasant adoring a statue of the Virgin. Did she always behave like that with her boss, or was it the drugs? And why didn't anyone answer the question?

'What the hell?' NeAmber said. 'You guys know something I don't?'

'Apparently,' her husband said. 'Garson has already had her surgery.'

'That was PDQ,' NeAmber said, her lips contorting almost into a snarl.

The others exchanged smug, knowing looks. Music percolated from the speakers. Classical guitar, carefully curated. Lily Afshar's *Hemispheres*.

Dr Gneiss twirled the stem of her wineglass. 'The surgery wasn't performed by a human doctor,' she said.

'Do you mean the doctors used AI?' Huw said. 'Some kind of robot?'

'No,' said Dr Gneiss. 'The surgeon was alive, but not from our world.'

NeAmber shot a look at Huw. 'What the actual holy fuck?'

'Garson had it done,' said Isabella, pirouetting in her thigh-high boots, her spun-gold hair and lipstick shimmering, and flinging out her arms like a Cossack dancer, 'by an extra-terrestrial surgeon.' A flourish of trumpets seemed to accompany her words.

'You're shitting me,' NeAmber said. 'Huw? What do you know about this?'

'Nothing.' Despite his shock over Miranda's suicide attempt, which had left him emotionally drained, he had to fight the urge to burst out laughing.

In contrast to her voluptuous girlfriend, Garson sat with her knees apart, a squat, rectangular figure, oddly asexual like a pre-Colombian stone goddess, stolid and majestic. 'I've been in touch with extra-terrestrials for years,' she explained. 'I communicate with them telepathically. They have outstanding skills. They're *way* smarter than any human doctors. We have tons to learn from them.'

NeAmber's mouth gaped, pantomiming astonishment, but retained the unnatural grin. 'I'm sorry, but you shrinks fucking slay me,' she said. 'So what did you do, Garson? Call the ET dude on your cell-phone and make an appointment? Where did he carry out the surgery? In a spaceship? A planet in another galaxy? A supernova?'

Garson spoke patiently. '*She*. No, she was able to perform it at my home. And I didn't need to use my phone. I told you already, I communicate with them telepathically.'

'What about nurses?' Huw said. 'Instruments? Anaesthetists?' So dazed was he from watching over Miranda that he doubted he had understood her. Was it an elaborate leg-pull?

'You don't understand,' Isabella said, leaping into the air with her hands above her head. She was in her late thirties, a bit old for such antics. 'She didn't need nurses or anaesthetists, let alone instruments. She could see inside Garson's skull, and she operated by probing with her fingers.' She curled and uncurled hers, a pantomime witch working magic.

'Extra-terrestrials have fingers, then?' NeAmber was clearly enjoying all this.

'Sure they do,' Isabella said, with a talent show smile. 'But she wasn't using them in a corporeal sense. She wasn't there in body.'

'No?' said NeAmber. 'Just, like, in spirit or something?'

'The doctor visited in her astral body,' Dr Gneiss said. 'She used the energy emanations of her fingers, like X-rays or microwaves. They can penetrate flesh.'

Miranda nodded as if it all made perfect sense. NeAmber shook her head. 'Sometimes I wonder if y'all...' she began. Instead of saying 'are cuckoo' or something, she did not finish, seeing her husband nodding. McBane, with his flaxen curls, puffy pink cheeks and astounded, round eyes, reminded Huw of a gigantic new-born. A cartoon caricature of a baby.

'Did you see her too, then, Isabella?' Huw said. 'The extra-terrestrial surgeon?'

She hesitated too long before replying. 'Sure I did.'

'What did she look like?' NeAmber said. 'Green, four arms and all?'

Isabella glanced at Garson, who replied for her:

'It's impossible to describe an extra-terrestrial,' she said gravely. 'What you do notice is their brilliance. It's like looking at the filament of a light bulb. You can hardly see the wire. We can't properly perceive their physical bodies, if they even have them. They're just a blaze of light to us. Humans have very poor eyesight.'

'What colour are these extra-terrestrials?' Huw said.

'It depends. Blue, mauve, green. At times crimson or orange.'

NeAmber giggled. Huw imagined a psychedelic figure, face-less, a whorl of lurid hues. 'Did it hurt?' he said. 'Having surgery without anaesthesia, I mean?'

'Not at all. You don't need anaesthesia for brain surgery. The brain feels no pain.'

'Amazing,' NeAmber said, stretching and admiring her magnificent legs, which gleamed as if they had been oiled. 'I would never have guessed.'

'Nor I,' said Huw. 'The marvels of modern science.'

Garson's glance was sharp, but finding his face blank—years of dodging fights in Welsh pubs had given him that skill—she relaxed and smiled at Isabella.

'What's really amazing,' the poet said, prowling and sashaying like a model on the catwalk, 'is that the tumour has totally vanished, according to the CT scan.'

'The ET had a CT scanner? A virtual one?' NeAmber said. 'Awesome.'

'Not the ET,' Garson said. 'I had the scan performed at the hospital. On a regular machine. It confirmed that the surgery was completely successful.'

She had either imagined her tumour, Huw supposed, in which case of course there was no trace of it now, or else had really had one but had been operated on by a human, and had convinced herself and the credulous Isabella, that the doctor had been an extra-terrestrial. Huw guessed that Garson would not tell a calculated lie, but she might work herself into a hyster-ical state. She was *suggestible*, as the lovely Elise had speculated he was himself.

NeAmber had not fallen for a word of it. To her, it was just a hoot. What about Miranda? Her face gave nothing away. *Your typical Barbie Doll*, Broome had described her. Flawless, she meant, empty of emotion or thought. Was that true? Was there a person inside? Of course there was. The poor thing was drugged to the gills. Barely conscious. But was it possible to stay sane when loonies like this surrounded you? Had they infected her?

McBane rose, announcing dinner, offering his arm to Miranda, an antiquated gesture which Huw expected her to reject—yet she stood and took his arm without demur, while NeAmber towered over her on the other side, gloating, bloody gloating—or was Huw so worn out that he was delusional? And if Miranda were just a Barbie doll, a male fantasy, what did that say about *him*? Was he that shallow? Did he love *her*, or had he just been projecting all along? He had to set aside these questions as he was waved to the head of the table, while Garson and Isabella sat side by side to his left, and McBane, Miranda and NeAmber sat in a row to his right. McBane wanted to keep Miranda sheltered, or perhaps imprisoned, between himself and his wife. That must be it: he did not trust Huw too near her. Huw considered making a joke but knew it would fall flat. Americans seldom had much sense of humour, and McBane—like Miranda—had none at all. If Huw protested, he would come across as petulant, and someone would riposte with a jibe about him being lovesick or possessive. All right, he was. Was that so terrible?

They had catered sushi for starters, with a crisp California Pinot Grigio and Paco de Lucía replacing Lily Afshar on the stereo. *Entre dos* Águas, the rumba soundtrack of *Vicky Cristina Barcelona*—chosen to evoke the painter's desires for two women? Matthew quizzed Isabella about current poetry, casting titbits on trendy contemporary fiction to Huw with equal aplomb. NeAmber simmered beside Miranda, speaking sotto voce. Huw had murky inklings. NeAmber's murmurs were conspiratorial, improper—sexual, surely? He picked at the stale sushi with distaste.

McBane asked if Huw had been to Mexico—he had

not—and supposed that he must admire the country's writers, particularly Carlos Fuentes and Juan Rulfo. He did, but it struck Huw as an insidious turn to the conversation. Only last night, Miranda had suggested they visit the country, a proposal Huw had rejected at once.

'Miranda longs to go to the Yucatán,' Matthew said, stressing the first syllable of the province, as Americans usually did. 'I guess you'll be going with her, Huw?'

Annoyed that she had broached the subject with her boss already, Huw said, 'I doubt it. With the wars between the drug cartels, it's far too dangerous.'

Matthew forked sushi into his rubbery infant mouth. 'I disagree. But what a pity. I was hoping you would come with us.'

Mines detonated in Huw's brain. He turned to Miranda. 'What? You're going without me? With *them*? When was all this decided?' She avoided his gaze and did not reply.

'Miranda invited us a couple of days ago,' Matthew said. 'It'll be good for her. Therapeutic. Mayan culture is so rich.'

A couple of days ago? Before she had spoken to him? 'I see,' Huw said. 'I didn't know the plans were so advanced. It would have been nice to have been told. May I ask exactly who's going, Miranda?'

She turned her eyes on him and opened her mouth. But words failed her. Was she unable or unwilling to speak? Or not allowed to? NeAmber spoke up for her:

'Just Matthew and I.' Her eyes sizzled with excitement. Why? Huw's mind did a back-flip. 'Of course Miranda invited Garson and Isabella too.'

'Did she?' Huw said. Miranda had to be quite insensitive—or else devious.

'Yeah, but sadly we can't go,' Isabella said.

'More extra-terrestrial surgery coming up?' Huw said.

Garson glowered. 'Actually, no. Isabella's new book is coming out.'

'*Sappho's Saffron Threads*,' Isabella said with a glittery grin.

'So she'll be going on tour,' Garson said.

'What about you, Garson?' Huw said. He hoped she might go and protect Miranda from the McBanes.

'No, I can't, either. Someone has to run the department with an iron fist. Besides, Mercury will be retrograde next month. I can't risk a trip to a foreign land.'

Now Huw remembered Miranda saying that Garson would only decide on critical issues, like launching new public health campaigns, or writing major grants, after casting a horoscope. He had supposed they did it for fun. Now he suspected that Miranda's sea-monsters and the stars were responsible for all key decisions in the Psychiatry Department.

'Hang on—you're going next *month?*' he said. 'Surely that's a bit rushed?'

'The summer holidays are coming up,' Matthew explained.

'But will Miranda be fit to travel? So soon after her... '

'I can look after her if she needs professional help,' McBane said.

That was what Huw was afraid of. Babyish as McBane looked, there was something sinister about him. The psychiatrist had designs on Miranda—but what kind of designs? NeAmber cleared their plates away, with the help of Isabella, who flitted and pranced, with dance-like gestures, like a fifth century Greek *haetera* on an Attic vase.

'Miranda has suffered a big shock,' Garson told Huw, 'and will need *everyone's* understanding and support.' From the look she gave him, it was clear she meant him.

'I realise that of course,' Huw said, hurt. 'I just wish she'd included me in her plans.'

'She did,' Garson said. 'She invited you, didn't she?'

'I suppose so.'

'I'm sure you could still go with her.'

But Huw was not sure. Nor did he want to. In any case the conversation was cut short when NeAmber and Isabella brought in the second course, kimchee, which looked like tripe and smelled like hot, wet, unwashed socks, although everyone sighed and inhaled its aroma with delight. Meanwhile Paco furiously chastised his guitar, slapping its sides, knocking the top with his knuckles and fingernails, while gypsy women stamped their heels and clicked castanets, and men clapped and shouted in harsh, primitive voices. While Huw tried to eat the revolting kimchee, tears rose to his eyes. Despite his embarrassment, he did not brush them away. To make matters worse, McBane displayed no tact on seeing his distress.

'Are you all right?' he said with professional distance.

'I'm fine.'

'Are you sure? You look like you may be upset by something.'

'I'll be fine.'

'I could give you a Valium,' McBane said.

'No, thanks.' Huw flung a glance at Miranda, hoping she would come to his aid. But she was oblivious of his misery, or indifferent to it. She was talking to NeAmber in low, intimate, happy tones. Huw thought of teenage girls, discussing their dates, or the dresses and shoes they planned to wear for a party.

She had not spoken a word to him since they arrived.

On the stereo a tenor shouted out his pain, while Paco fanned and thrummed and struck the strings and a hail of notes spat at Huw and ricocheted off him.

Those hailstones stabbed his cheeks and stung like hell. *¡Ay, ay, ay, ay!*

SIX

You're So Far Above Me

Thank God, the knock on Melvyn's office door was not the peremptory, pork-knuckled one of his wife—when she bothered to knock at all—but a timid, tentative tapping. Hesitant. Arrhythmic. *Ergo,* a student; a female student, he guessed.

'Come in,' he carolled. He kept the door unlocked but shut to discourage faculty and students who simply wanted to shoot the breeze. Nothing happened. With a sigh, he rose from the deep leather armchair he had bought to impress visitors, and opened the door. Just as he had imagined. Long, straight, mousey hair, parted in the middle, and glasses. She was taller than Melvyn, although he was above middle height. Large-framed, the Kate Winslet type, but not overweight, she shrank apologetically, touchingly, inside her gabardine raincoat, which glittered with raindrops. Familiar somehow. He raised his eyebrows in enquiry.

'Excuse me sir,' she said, not quite meeting his eyes. 'Are you busy?'

'I am,' he said, consciously professorial, 'but this is one of my office hours.' That sounded a tad priggish to him, so he added, 'So of course you may interrupt me.'

'You are so kind,' she simpered, with a flat facial expression that triggered a recent memory. Her voice was familiar too: unusually educated for an OSU student, with the ringing cadence of old money. When he was at Dartmouth as an undergrad, all the co-eds had spoken like that. Still, he could not place her.

'You're not one of my advisees, are you?' he said, barring the doorway.

'No, sir. But I would like to come in. If I'm not bothering you too much.'

He fled behind the barricade of his huge desk and sank into his seat, without holding the door open for her. She shut it after herself.

'Please open that,' he told her. He smelled a delicate, costly perfume.

'Oh, is that a rule?'

'Not exactly. But it is what we call 'best practice.' Male professors keep their doors open to protect themselves from charges of sexual harassment.' *Quite apart from the greater risk of protecting yourself from your jealous wife.*

'Oh, I'm not going to sexually harass you. Not yet, anyway.'

Oh boy, she was dangerous. Weird too: her words were flirty but her expression was not. His laughter came out high-pitched, jumpy. 'Still, I would like you to open that door.'

A vertical crease appeared between her eyes, but she did go back and crack it. Two inches or so. But for sure this chick was too shy to throw herself at him, so he let it go.

'You don't remember me at all?' she said, standing before his one oil painting.

He searched his memory again. 'No, should I?'

'I met you at that reading last week. I sensed that we connected.'

Of course! Now he remembered—not her face, frankly, but

74

her voice, her manner, and dammit, if he had to fess up, her body. She was the Nike. Those legs. The *red panties*.

'Oh yeah, sure. So um, what did you think of Manley's work?'

'*Work*?' She spoke with the scorn of a Susan Sontag, a true bluestocking—whoops, like co-ed, that was another banned word. 'I found her trite and vulgar. As you must have.'

'Naturally,' he said, flattered. Boy, she was smart. He would have recognised her if she had been showing more of her body, he realised, but as soon as that evil idea struck, Frida's face intruded in his brain, a caricature cartoon, red with rage, bristles on her scalp erect, nose-ring trembling, her nostrils belching steam. He hoped she wasn't monitoring his mind again. Even so, oh boy was he curious to see what lay beneath the student's raincoat.

'You're wet,' he said, at once wishing he had not used such a suggestive word. 'Won't you take off your coat?' Did he sound like he was hitting on her?

'Oh no, I'm fine,' she said, not taking the hint. She gazed at his pictures with the attention of a museum visitor: the reproduction of Waterhouse's 'The Lady of Shallot' above his desk, and the portrait in oils of a lady with an Edwardian chignon, in a gilt Art Nouveau frame—his wedding present for Frida, which she had detested on sight.

'I love to see pictures of women on a man's walls.' Her tone was not flirtatious—or was it? 'I adore the Pre-Raphaelites.'

An undergrad who knew the pre-Raphaelites? 'Thank you.'

'Who is she?' she asked, indicating the portrait with her longish nose.

Embarrassed, he blurted, 'My wife,' although that was stretching the truth.

'Is that so?' she said. She inspected the picture. 'I can't see the resemblance.'

'Well, I bought it because she looked like my wife. Back then. To me, anyway.'

'You must be so in love with her.' Was her tone accusatory? Ironic? Just polite?

In *love* with her? How preposterous! 'She doesn't look like that now,' he said.

'No, she looks very different. How tactless of me, I apologise. Still, as Shakespeare says, '*Love is not love which alters when it alteration finds.*'

'You like Shakespeare?'

'Who doesn't?' She spoke like Sontag again.

'Most OSU students. I can't get my daughters to read him. Or even my wife.'

'Anyone with *intelligence* appreciates Shakespeare.'

Once more, hardly tactful—but he liked her forthrightness.

'He is a Dead White Male, though,' Melvyn said.

'Only a fool would fail to read him for that reason,' she said.

'That would include half of our English Department.'

'Certainly. But I think for myself.'

'So I see. But that's so rare in a university these days. Won't you take a seat?' He waved at the pair of chairs on the other side of his desk. 'And tell me what I can do for you.'

At last she sat, not provocatively—she was wearing jeans, flat pumps, and beneath the raincoat, a cashmere sweater, like the Sloane Rangers of London he had heard about on a TV documentary. *Ladylike*, if that was still a permissible word.

'I have a copy of *Flasher*,' she said. 'I hoped you might sign it for me.'

Although the collection had been published over a year ago, she was the first student—actually the first person—who had appeared in his office with such a request.

'Sure,' he said, with the debonair, dimpling smile he often practised in the mirror, for when he eventually became famous. 'I'd be delighted.'

She carried a briefcase but did not open it. Instead she spoke:

'I think you're brilliant. The equal of the greatest writers.'

Spot-on! The girl was brilliant herself. 'You're a Creative Writing major then?'

'No, sir. A Psychology major.'

That figured: they were always eccentric. 'How did you hear about my book?'

'I have a friend in one of your classes. They told me about it.'

'They? Male or female? Or are they obsolete categories now? You mean Ashley?'

'I'd prefer not to say, sir.'

Her caginess was weird. 'You don't need to keep calling me sir.'

'I'd prefer to. I can't imagine calling you anything else, ever.'

'I do have a name. It's Melvyn.' But what did she mean by that 'ever'? Was she anticipating a lifelong relationship? Planning one?

'I know that, sir. But you are so far above me…' She blushed. 'I feel I can only address you with deference, and to be frank, with awe.'

What a discerning girl she was! 'You are a mysterious young woman,' he said. And a tad nutty? Or was it only the quaint formality that was drilled into Southerners? 'You won't tell me your friend's name, or call me by mine, and yet you want to chat with me, I still have no idea about what. It's all quite intriguing.'

'I'm thrilled I'm intriguing you. I want to talk about *Flasher*. And everything.'

He coughed noisily. 'Let's start with the book. What did you like about it?'

'I loved the sex scenes,' she said, looking him straight in the eye at last. 'They're so graphic and detailed, so insightful. You understand exactly how a woman feels in bed. What she wants. That scene where the vicar and the au pair have sex standing up, and she puts her foot on a chair. I was practically gasping at that one. I found it deeply erotic.'

'It's not meant to be.' What if Frida were to burst in on them now? 'The sex scenes are disturbing, right? There's rape, sadism, manipulation. They're far from porn.' He hated his demure tone. *I'm like Mr Collins in Pride and Prejudice. Prim: priggish. A professorial prick.* 'The sex is there to illustrate how people, especially men, abuse their power.'

'I see that, naturally, that's part of its brilliance. I love the way you are able to analyse a relationship through sex.' She paused. 'I'm going to be a sex therapist.'

The panic button in his brain shrieked. 'Are you kidding?' He gulped, hoping she would not notice his Adam's apple bobbing, out of control.

'I am deeply interested in sex. It's the fundamental human interaction. I feel certain you agree with me, sir.'

'I guess I do...' What the hell was he saying? A *sex* therapist? Could she be on the level? If so, was this an emergency—or the miracle he had been longing for?

Her mouth twitched into a smile, or a facsimile of one. He remembered Olimpia, the beautiful automaton of Hoffman's *The Sandman*. No, she was disconcerting, but maybe just forward. Of course she was gauche. It was not unusual for students to ask intimate questions. Probably her intentions were quite innocent.

'I'd like to be your friend,' she said. Or maybe not innocent at all.

He fidgeted with a pen, unable to answer.

'Could we have coffee some time?' she said.

Are you out of your mind? he thought. 'Sure, why not?' he said.

'You are still married, then,' she said, glancing at the painting, 'to her?'

Surely she knew? Everyone knew the Shamburgers. 'The woman who looked like her, you mean. Frida. Yes, we are still married. For the time being.'

She smiled without showing her teeth. 'Our lives are always in flux,' she said, adding in her haughty New England tones, 'She must have been beautiful. Back in the day.'

'Kind of.' *Cute rather than beautiful. And summer's lease hath all too short a date.*

'You deserve a beautiful woman who can make you happy.'

Absolutely! 'Heh-heh, I guess I do. You're so—'

Sensitive, shrewd and smart? Or deranged, ditzy and dicey? She was not like the usual coquettes angling for higher grades, with their languid smiles and drooping eyelids, but she was definitely suggesting… something. Or was he just being paranoid? Probably the girl was just awestruck that he had published a book. How many authors could she have met? He reminded himself that she had asked for his autograph, that was all.

'Yes?' she prompted him. 'You were saying? I'm …'

'You remind me of the Nike of Samothrace. You want me to sign that book?'

She fished it out of her briefcase. 'Thank you so much, I *adore* that statue.'

Wow, she actually knew Greek culture too. 'I wish you wouldn't call me sir.'

'Sorry, sir.' The cover photo was of a woman, shot from behind, wearing a raincoat, which she held open, flashing someone. Did that explain *her* raincoat?

He turned to the title page and crossed out *Melvyn Shamburger III*. 'Who shall I make it out to? What's your name?'

'You mean my real name?'

His pen hovered like a fly above the page. 'Don't tell me you have aliases?'

'Sure. I despise the real one. And maybe it's better for you not to know it.'

Oh boy, she was trouble, all right. 'I guess it's up to you which name you go by.'

'Call me Jezebel. Guess whether it's the real one or not.'

'I imagine it's not,' he chuckled.

To Jezebel, my mysterious, appreciative reader, he wrote. *I am glad you found these stories*—he considered 'enjoyable' or 'interesting' but rejected both and settled on '*stirring*'. With a further hint of flirtatiousness, he ended: *Good luck in your future career! Yours,* and signed with a squiggle resembling Arabic calligraphy, and many dots and flourishes.

'Will that do?' he said, handing the book to her, open at the inscription.

'Oh yes, sir, thank you, that's wonderful.' She held the book to her chest as if she treasured it. But then, unfortunately, still far away, but approaching fast, came the foghorn blasts of Frida's voice. Melvyn went into lockdown mode.

'I better get back to work,' he said. *And get the timebomb out of here.*

'Yes, sir. Can I email you about having coffee?'

Better make an excuse: it was near the end of term, he was busy, maybe not a great idea, on reflection. Anything. Avoid any compromising situations.

'Sure,' he said. The blasts of the klaxon were close—when had Frida started to shout all the damn time? He stood and flailed, off balance. Jezebel stood too and held out her hand for him to shake. Irreproachable. She was not gorgeous, but statuesque. Not that he found her hot. Not at all. Not a bit. As she left, he cringed behind his desk, awaiting the collision.

A final blare presaged the crashing of the door into the wall, and cracked plaster, and there stood the Empress of Blandings, bristling, steaming, her snout lowered to charge:

'Who the hell was *that*, Melvyn?'

Oh no—she only used that snorty tone when she was suspicious or angry. 'Just a student,' he said, hunkering behind his desktop screen.

Frida's grunted: 'I smell cheap, vulgar scent. Sheesh!'

Keep your head. Don't contradict. Distract, divert, deflect. Be a politician. Sidetrack. Stir her up. He stammered, 'Uh, seen Huw yet today?'

Frida's low brow crinkled and darkened. 'Him! You'll never guess what he's been up to! I am going to nail him so good!' Smoke smouldered around her nostrils.

Melvyn fought back a snicker. *Whew, that was a close call. Well done, guy!*

SEVEN

The Phallocentric Canon

Huw always pedalled his racer like Geraint Thomas chasing the yellow jersey in the Tour de France—but since Miranda had set terms on their relationship, had her breakdown, attempted suicide, and arranged to go to Mexico with the McBanes—since his life had begun to unravel a couple of weeks ago, he had been sprinting on his bike yet more swiftly, trying to overtake his grief and anxiety. Skimming the smooth black roads of Tocqueville, brushing the white and pink blossom that overhung them, phrases curled and leapt beside him, inside him, beneath and above him, hissing, thundering. All he had to do was hold on, keep his balance, his mind clear and empty, and ride the wave. Sentences sizzled as he surfed through another tunnel of trees. Once again the power was upon him, the sacred power of the bardic tongue and the earthier one of the invaders, intertwined. They seized his heart and spirit, turned the world into a glorious blur, and Huw knew his writer's block was broken.

Then a camouflaged pick-up flicked past, nearly clipping him, with its horn blowing and mad, male shouts. Out of the windows hung naked torsos, and tattooed arms, shaking fists and beer cans. A moment of terror turned into fury. Huw yelled a Welsh curse and tore after them. But he could not hope to catch them, and what if he did? They were four, he was one; they were in their twenties, he was nearly fifty.

Besides, the swirling waves of Welsh and English had retreated, and he was on dry land again, approaching the university. Could he remember that passage vouchsafed him, straight from the teeming tongues of his ancestors? Thank Christ, he could. He began reciting as he rode, to memorise it, in a loud, exultant chant.

But disaster struck again. As a saloon car passed, a woman leaned out of the front passenger window. 'Get a fucking car!' she roared. A *woman*! He flipped her off—the indispensable gesture in American traffic. Millennials were tolerant, supposedly, and yet it was white youths who always mobbed and menaced him on his bike. What was more, the car was an Audi, driven by the lovely Elise, he saw, as it turned into the car park. Worse still, rack his brains as he might, the miraculous passage he had been reciting had quite vanished. Not a wisp, not a word, was left. Cursing in Anglo-Saxon terms now, he dismounted by the pedestrian crossing. Even so, he had to jump aside to a swerving SUV. The driver was Frida and she was texting. No one was paying attention to anything that mattered.

When he reached the classroom after leaving his bicycle in the empty rack, he found his students not chatting as students had done in his day, but scrolling through social media or texting on their smart phones. They leaned against walls, lolled against pillars, or sprawled on the floor. Elise sat on this far from spotless surface in one of her fetching mini-kilts, fingers jabbing phone keys, knees drawn together in a concession to modesty, although her ankle-length suede boots were wide apart. Her posture offered a splendid view of her legs to anyone lounging nearby on the floor, and yet not a single guy, some of whom must have been straight—surely?—nor the lesbians, Jordan in her denims, and her girlfriend Nutmeg, in her short shorts, or the transgender student, Trudy—no, Truman, Truman, he reminded himself—was flirting with her. Or even noticed her. What the bloody hell was wrong with them?

'Good morning,' he said. As usual, no one replied. Not even Elise.

The only student who made eye contact with him was Walt, the podgy boy with the piping voice and supercilious smile. 'They're like *ants*,' he said.

His tone invited a sardonic smile or a mordant comment. Huw winced: let the lad interpret that how he would.

Nonetheless, Walt's classmates were less comatose than they appeared. Charleston glanced up from his tablet and snapped:

'As a matter of fact, boy wonder, I'm working for the downfall of your class.'

Walt shot a bittersweet, patrician smile at Huw. *You see?*

'And I'm writing a piece for *The Siren* on the LGBTQIA+ community,' murmured Jordan. 'Maybe I could interview you?'

Walt disdained to reply. He was indeed gay, Huw suspected, but not out.

'Me, I'm researching organic farms in the state for a project,' said Nutmeg.

Huw unlocked the door. Elise sprang to her feet in a single, fluid movement.

'I was checking how many likes I got for my new profile picture,' she said.

'I rest my case,' Walt said, with a jubilant glance at Huw.

'Eight hundred ninety-three,' Elise said. 'Damn, I can do way better than that.'

'Let me see,' said Truman, flushing violet. 'Gosh, Elise, you look gorgeous.'

Hear, hear, Huw mentally congratulated Truman—although she, or rather he, he, he, had not dared look the President's daughter in the eye.

Once seated, after the customary complaints about

rearranging the seats—Huw insisted on a half-circle, while they preferred rows—the students crumpled in their chairs.

'You all look so eager to discuss literature today,' Huw said.

'We don't *mind* talking about novellas,' Jordan said. 'Like, we don't hate it.'

'But we prefer to watch the movie versions,' said the tall, curly boy who had just sauntered in and whose name Huw could never recall, Frank or Hank.

'What we don't get,' Jordan said, 'is why there are no women on your syllabus.'

'Surely it's not all dudes?' said Truman. 'I'm so done with the patriarchy.'

Huw crouched behind the enormous monitor on his desk. 'I'm surprised that this question is only coming up now,' he said. 'Didn't you read the syllabus earlier?'

'Hell no,' Hank or Frank said. 'No one reads shit like that.'

'If you don't,' said Huw, 'then surely you don't have the right to object?'

'We have read it now,' said Jordan. 'Leastways, I have. Could you just answer the question, please? Why aren't there any women on the syllabus?'

'I had two criteria when I chose the texts. First, they had to be under fifteen dollars. I couldn't find any novella collections by women at that price.'

'There's nothing by African-American authors either,' Charleston said.

Huw said, 'True. But not all the authors are white. There's an Asian and a Latin-American. And García Márquez did have some African ancestry.'

'They all had penises, though,' Jordan said.

'Presumably,' Huw said. 'Though I was under the impression that one's genitalia is no longer considered a useful criterion for determining gender? Isn't it a social construct?'

Everyone glanced at Truman, who flushed purple. 'Sure, right,' he said.

'Are you trying to tell us some of those dudes identified as women, or were gender-fluid?' Jordan asked Huw.

'Of course not. Look, there are excellent novellas by African-Americans and women, and by African-American women. I could give you a reading list. I will.' He hesitated, aware that the words he planned to say were potentially explosive. 'But my second criterion was that the novellas had to reach the very highest standard—be worthy of the canon. That's why I chose collections by Tolstoy, Chekhov, Mann, García Márquez and Kawabata.'

Jordan's sigh sounded like a punctured tyre. 'That's cool beans that you considered the cost. Most profs could care less. And I dig it that these dudes are all awesome writers—except maybe that one Japanese guy, who's super creepy…'

'*Eeew,*' said Elise. 'Totally.'

'But,' Jordan went on, lying back, legs spread, with the confidence of someone who knew she was the most gifted student poet, 'the canon is phallocentric. And very white.'

'Cultural imperialism,' Charleston intoned. 'Colonialism. White oppression.'

Huw was about to object that García Márquez and Kawabata could hardly be accused of that, but Jordan forestalled him: 'The tyrannical patriarchy,' she said.

'I just wish you would have included at least one woman,' said Broome.

'And a black dude,' said Charleston.

'And like a lesbian,' said Nutmeg.

'Or a gay guy,' said Walt helpfully. 'Or someone who self-harms.'

'What about a pedo?' said Frank or Hank, smirking. 'Or a trannie?'

'We don't say that word!' Jordan said. 'And you know it.'

'I don't give a damn,' Frank or Hank said. 'Well? Would you like to see transsexual—excuse me, trans*gender*—writers represented, Trudy?'

'*Truman,*' Jordan hissed. 'Asshole.'

Truman turned a rich shade of mauve. 'I would like that, yeah.'

'Do you see my predicament?' Huw said. 'Must I include every minority? And in direct proportion to their percentage in the US population? If so, how many Chicanos must I include? How many women Chicanos? How many lesbian, bisexual, or trans Chicanos? And the same with native Americans, Jews, Islanders.'

'We don't expect perfect proportional representation,' Jordan said.

Huw stood up, suspected his flies were open, and fell back into his chair behind the desk so he could check. No, they were done up. He stood again, wished he were taller, nearly sat down once more, but instead left the shelter of his desk to strut in front of the class, in the manner of an officer giving a briefing. Except that he was under fire. Friendly fire.

'I have a question for you,' he said. 'Dr Roquette Rathaus teaches a course in which all the poets are women. Does anyone object to that?'

The students were silent and their faces blank—all except for Frank or Hank, who cackled. 'Yeah, anyone pissed at that? And what's-his-face, the prof who wears Hawaiian shirts. The dude with the ponytail and the man-boobs.'

'Luke?' Walt said. 'That's fat-shaming.'

'Yeah, Lucky Luke. All the writers in that dude's creative nonfiction workshop are fags, dykes, or trannies. No kidding, man. Not one normal dude.'

The students emitted groans, grunts, growls, snarls and hisses.

'You may not approve of the bigoted vocabulary,' Huw said, 'But I notice no one denies the substance of his claim. And yet when I draw up a single syllabus featuring only male writers, there's practically an insurrection.'

'Say what?' Elise susurrated.

'Rebellion,' Jordan explained. 'But that's different,' she went on in a tone that reminded Huw of ministers in Welsh chapels. Sanctimonious. 'Luke and Rocky are redressing centuries of repression by the patriarchy. Whereas you are just reinforcing it.'

'I don't accept that. My intention wasn't political. I just wanted you to read the best novellas available.' Surely he had won the argument now? The disgruntled faces and body language—crossed arms and legs, torsos turned away, eyes averted—suggested otherwise.

'All right,' he said. 'You win. What if we add a woman to the syllabus?'

'*One?*' Broome boomed as if she were copying Frida.

'Unless you're willing to buy several new textbooks.'

'I just don't want to do any extra work,' Elise said.

'We could drop *House of Sleeping Beauties*, if you all find Kawabata creepy?'

'Gross,' said Nutmeg. 'But who would we read instead?'

'How about Muriel Spark? *The Prime of Miss Jean Brodie*.'

'Where's she from?' said Walt.

'Scotland.'

'White, obviously?' Charleston said.

'Not all Scots are white, Charleston, but I'm afraid Muriel Spark was.'

Charleston scowled—playfully, though. The lad had a sense of humour.

'Many Scots consider themselves oppressed,' Huw said. 'Like the Welsh.'

'Give me a break, man,' Charleston said.

'Our languages were banned,' Huw said. 'The Irish were starved.'

'Yeah, but not enslaved,' Charleston said.

'Actually, many Irishmen were sent to the Carolinas as indentured servants, practically slaves,' Huw said. 'But certainly it was worse for Africans.'

'Why don't we read a novella by an African-American woman?' Jordan said.

'How about Nella Larsen's *Passing*?' Huw said. 'It's about light-skinned women who manage to pass for white during the Harlem Renaissance. What do you think?'

The entire class voted to replace Kawabata with Larsen, except for Walt, who complained about the extra cost, and Elise, who had already read Kawabata and did not want her work to go to waste, and Frank or Hank, who did not explain, but sneered eloquently.

'Good,' Huw said. 'And now I hope we can leave identity politics behind and talk about literature and writing for a change.'

The novella up for discussion was *Death in Venice*, which he had picked for its imagery and symbolism, its flawless structure, and masterly use of exposition—and also, admittedly, because its subject matter was a homoerotic obsession, which he expected would please the LGBT members of the class. But he was wrong. Although Jordan said she dug it, Walt demurred, objecting to the portrayal of Aschenbach as a 'pedo'. Nutmeg said he was a Kevin Spacey type guy, and he disgusted Broome because he was not in control of himself. Huw pointed out Mann's philosophical underpinning in Nietzsche and Schopenhauer, but the students were unable to grasp the concept of determinism. Elise said it was just an old-school story about snooty Europeans, and like, who cared? Charleston jumped in: You could read it as a critique of bourgeois decadence, not as Marxist as García Márquez's *No-one Writes to the Colonel*, but clearly influenced by Weber. Huw pressed him for more.

'Give me a break, dude,' Frank or Hank said, 'it's just a story about *faggots*.'

'Homosexuals, puh-lease,' Walt said.

'I object to that term,' Truman said. 'It's homogender. The patriarchy just perpetuates the concept of biological sex to keep women and the other genders in subjection.'

Frank or Hank bellowed. 'How many are there? I thought there were two.'

'At least a hundred,' said Truman. '*Hello?* Everyone knows that.'

'That why you decided to buy a dick at the clinic and become a dude, then?'

'Let's focus on commenting on what she said,' Huw said, but although Frank or Hank's face wore a malignant grin, silence fell like a hard frost over the class. Jordan crossed her arms and glared at him. 'What?' Huw said.

'You said *she*,' Jordan said. 'Truman wants us to use male pronouns.'

Huw flushed. 'Did I say that? I'm sorry, Truman. It wasn't deliberate. It's just that for the last two years we were all calling you *she*, and sometimes I forget.' The apology fell on deaf ears. Jordan continued glaring, and Truman had a blank, autistic stare. The class was back treading the well-worn paths of identity politics, patriarchal oppression, and victimisation. Outrage at Huw's insensitivity ran high. His attempts to steer the discussion back to language and literature proved fruitless. Still, he consoled himself as the class collapsed, he had defused the unrest over the preponderance of male authors on the syllabus. The inclusion of Nella Larsen guaranteed that, surely?

While he reminded the students of their homework, Broome, the 'mature student' and former model, rushed out like someone fleeing a crime scene, in spite of her size, knocking Jordan and Nutmeg aside as if they were bowling pins. Elise advanced with a bold air. When she reached his desk she stood there with an expectant look. He had to speak first.

'I hope you're not upset about the paucity of women writers on the syllabus.'

'I'm not sure what that means. Something about women writers in poor cities? No, it's all good. I don't really give a shit, you know? I mean, sure, if Jordan and Nutmeg and the rest make a fuss I'll join in, because of feminine solidarity and all. But it's no biggie, right?'

'What is a big deal to you, Elise?'

She gave him a long look, which might have been a come-on. 'You know, fashion, lifestyle. Making it. Becoming someone. I got my own YouTube channel, you know.'

'Good for you,' he said, but it sounded condescending.

'Thanks, I've got twelve thousand followers. I was wondering if you've reconsidered my offer to read your fortune.' Her gaze was deep, unflinching. Did she mean to tempt him?

The last of the students had trooped out. Huw wavered, flattered. And worn out from stress—the indignation over the 'phallocentric' syllabus, the thugs threatening him from the pick-up, and that woman screeching at him. She had been in Elise's car, he remembered.

'Who was that girl who screamed at me as you passed me in your car this morning, Elise? Women don't usually do that. That was you driving, wasn't it?'

'Yeah, sorry. Sorority sister. It was lame. She's a hick, you know? I'm real sorry.'

'I don't understand why it infuriates Americans so much to see me cycling.'

'I guess they think you look like a pussy.'

He laughed. 'Hardly a politically correct term, is it? All right. I don't believe in it, but you can tell my fortune. How do you do it? With cards?'

Her steady look almost *smouldered*. 'No. Give me your right hand.'

After a second's hesitation, he did so. She took his hand firmly, and with her index finger traced the lines, hollows and mounds of his palm. Huw hoped she would be brief.

'I've never seen a hand like this before. A *very* prominent Mount of Venus, criss-crossed by dozens of lines. Hundreds, oh man. You are a totally awesome lover. You have a strong tendency to promiscuity, a need for instant gratification. Right?'

'I *was* a bit of a womaniser, once, a long time ago.'

'Your heart line is very long, and curvy. You express your feelings easily and are happy with your love life.'

'I am.' Was that still true, though? And should he have admitted it?

'Your headline is deep and long; you think clearly and logically. But it's also curved. You're super creative.'

'If I weren't, I'd be in the wrong profession, wouldn't I?'

'Your lifeline is long, deep and curved too. You're full of vitality.' She looked up at him, meaningfully. 'On the other hand, your fate line isn't so strong. You've controlled your life pretty much, up to now. Maybe too much.'

'What do you mean? Surely being in control is a good thing?'

'You shouldn't plan so much. Sometimes you have to let things happen. Your hand is square, the fingers short: that shows impulsiveness, creativity. You're impatient and *very* highly-sexed.'

'My sexual appetites seem to feature rather prominently in this reading.'

Instead of making a flirty rejoinder, she said, 'Just a moment. Let me look at your lifeline again. I don't like to say this, Huw, but I see several catastrophic events.'

She had called him by his first name. Not only did her insight ring true—but if it were all a game, why would she reveal anything unpleasant? Didn't fortune tellers usually say what people wanted to hear? Unsettled, Huw began to believe her, although he was conscious of his inconsistency: only last night, at the McBanes', he had felt that the astrology and other esoteric practices of Miranda and Doctor Gneiss were absurd.

'Catastrophic events?' he said.

Elise's lips twitched. 'You know, divorce, losing your home or your job, life-threatening illness, that sort of thing. Shit, maybe all of those. Yeah. I'm sorry.'

He tried to smile, but queasiness overcame him. She stroked his palm with her index finger. 'And when will these catastrophes befall me?'

'I can't say exactly. But in mid-life. Oh, man. Right about now, actually.'

At that moment in the corridor came a ponderous, elephantine thumping. Stertorous breathing, an indrawn whistling wheeze, followed by a grumbling moan. Then a snare-drum crack, as the door smashed into the wall. They both froze.

There, filling the doorframe, and jammed in it with the biggest and fullest tote bag he had ever seen, was a crimson humanoid, scalp bristling, fleshy bare arms juddering, dragons flapping their scaly wings, her mouth open in shock and horror and the thick golden ring in the snout quivering with indignation. She smelled of steam, smoke, and stale coffee.

'Morning, Frida,' Huw said, his hand still clamped in Elise's. 'How are you?'

Frida forced herself through the doorway, snatching at the bag, snorting and panting.

'How am I?' she began, with a dangerous Diamondback rattle in her throat. 'I'm fine. What I want to know is how *you* are, and what you imagine you're doing.'

Huw prised his hand out of Elise's. 'Elise was just reading my palm,' he said.

Elise nodded. 'Right, Dr Mrs. Shamburger. I have awesome psychic abilities.'

'Is that so?' Frida said, turning to Huw: 'Don't you think it's a tad indiscreet, holding hands with a student here, when anyone might happen along?'

'It was innocent, Dr Mrs. Shamburger,' Elise offered, with the self-assurance of being the President's daughter.

'I'm sure it was, Elise. *On your side*. Thanks, you can go now.'

Elise flounced out, tossing her hair over her shoulder, offended. How dare Frida dismiss her like that?

'As for *you*…' Frida began.

'Give me a break. I was just—'

'I know exactly what you were doing. Teaching male authors.

Male, *cis*gender, *heteronormative* authors. Aren't you ashamed? Not one single woman!'

How could she have heard so quickly? Then Huw remembered Broome barging her way out of the classroom a few minutes ago.

'You have a spy in my class.'

Frida did not answer. Huw insisted: 'Do you deny it? Who is it, Broome?'

'I can't tell you who told me. She just told me what's going on. As the director of the program, I have a right to know what's taught in the classrooms. You told them there were no women who have written good novellas.'

'I did not. I told them there are excellent novellas by women. Broome is a liar.'

'Or *you* are. Anyway, there are tons of women you could be teaching.'

'*Tons*?' he said, but she failed to catch his sardonic tone.

'Yeah, tons who are as good as the white males in the canon. Better.'

'I don't only have white men on my syllabus. But OK, who do you suggest?'

'Sandra Cisneros, *The House on Mango Street*.'

'Not a bad book, but surely it's a collection of linked stories?'

'All right then. Marguerite Duras,' (she said, 'Margaret Dure-ass') '*The Lover*.'

'Hardly up to the standard of *The Death of Ivan Ilyich*, is it, or *Death in Venice*?'

Frida lurched at him. 'That's your opinion.'

'Obviously it's my opinion,' he said, stepping away from her. 'What a fatuous thing to say. Who else's would it be? Perhaps you expect me to express your opinions?'

She bent one of her legs, which were encased in leggings, and pawed at the floor. She lowered her head. Huw braced himself for a clumsy charge. Her bare, full-sleeve tattoo arms rose higher and higher. Would she wallop him with those massive hams?

Beads of sweat glistened on her brow. Her tiny pondwater-brown eyes were bloodshot.

'I expect you to teach people who represent our students,' she said with a grunt. 'It's our responsibility to teach authors they can identify with.'

'Then I should be teaching a majority of immature, poorly-educated authors who spend their time playing video games, sexting, and smoking marijuana. And since virtually all our students are white and middle-class, presumably our syllabi should reflect that too? As yours does, in fact. Doesn't it?'

She snorted and her nose-ring quivered. 'You've been looking at *my* syllabi?'

'For instruction, naturally. You teach nearly all white, middle-class American women writers, don't you? Authors of a similar background to your own, in fact.'

'I don't believe it. Are you daring to criticise me?'

'I'm pointing out a fact. But you are daring to criticise me. And spy on me.'

'How dare you say *dare*. I'm the frigging director of this programme.'

'And I'm a tenured professor. So I have complete autonomy over the content of my syllabi, provided I teach the course content. And I prioritise quality of writing over identity issues and social justice. I happen to think that's more important for creative writing students. I know that's not fashionable. But it's my prerogative.'

Frida lowered her head again, apparently on the brink of charging.

He went on: 'What's more, I respond to student complaints and suggestions. I have just added a woman writer to the syllabus. Did your spy tell you that?'

'No,' Frida said, but realised her mistake at once. 'She's not a spy. Who?'

'Nella Larsen,' Huw said. Frida looked blank. 'Do you know her?'

Frida frowned. 'Of course. I mean, not in depth. Isn't she from Minnesota?'

'She was black. Or rather of mixed ethnicity: Danish father, black mother. From Curaçao. How many African-Americans do you teach, Frida?'

Frida's neck folds juddered, but she did not answer.

'Do you teach any at all, Frida? How about Latin Americans? Asians?'

'Fuck you, Huw,' she said as she stomped towards the door.

When Huw got up to the third floor and passed Melvyn's vast corner office, a girl in a dripping wet raincoat was slipping out of it. Furtively. Huw entered his own office, fell into his chair, wishing he had not been so abrasive with Frida, ignited his desktop computer—and saw hundreds of emails awaiting him, many marked 'urgent'. But one howled for attention. Its subject line, all in caps, and terminating in a thicket of ejaculatory spears, read:

A L L S T R A I G H T M A L E S O N Y O U R S Y L L A-
BUS!!!!!WHY????!!!!!!

Frida had dashed that off before clomping down the stairs. Beneath was one from Miranda, also bellowing:

PSYCHOTIC SPELLS MAY BE HOME LATE DON'T WAIT UP.

He took a deep breath to calm himself. On his desk was a framed photograph of Miranda, her hair pulled into a topknot, her face powdered, white as chalk, her lips red as strawberries, her neck and shoulders bare, vulnerable—in the same pose, maybe consciously, as the actress in the poster for *White Swans*, and with the same deranged air. Were those blue lines on her forehead blood-vessels, or cracks in the china? *Pull yourself together*, he told himself. *For her sake and Owen's. Can't afford to lose your job now. Will she keep hers? Just read the bloody thing.* Outside a chopper's rotors churned, flattening the treetops. He had the sensation that some figure in the ether was watching him. Was he under surveillance?

Having hallucinations, sea-monsters paddling in muck in my office. Psychiatrist recommends committing myself. I'd prefer not to. Garson thinks I should. Matthew doesn't think I need to. Invited me to his house tonight for dinner. Sweet of him. Sea-monsters told me to accept. One of them has a beard and reminds me of my dad. So I guess I'm going. - Andamir

No salutation, no 'love', and the odd, misspelled name. A mistake, or some kind of joke or puzzle? It was an anagram, so maybe the latter. What did she mean? That her identity was confused, back-to-front? An internet search came up with nothing. More troubling was the news that she was hallucinating again, and that her psychiatrist and Garson, admittedly not the sanest mental health professional herself, recommended urgent in-patient treatment, which would mean heavy sedation. Equally troubling was the news that Matthew had invited Miranda to his house—just her, apparently. And she had accepted. Hadn't she considered his feelings at all? Just weeks ago he was happy. *Cachu huwch,* he said. It was all fucked now.

He wanted to roar, strap on armour, hack McBane and Frida to pieces. *Coc y gath¹*.

---

1   Lit. 'The cat's prick'. An expression of dismay similar to 'Fucking hell.'

EIGHT

It is the Young Fool Who Seeks Me

Melvyn stood on the doorstep, unable to ring the bell. Jezebel's house was a McMansion with proliferating gables and roofs, windows of all shapes and sizes, disproportionately colossal porch columns, and a round tower with a witch-hat roof—but its tackiness was not the reason for his hesitation. Although Jezebel had promised her father would be out, now that he was here, Melvyn lacked the courage. Or did he have a genuine conscience? What would the Superior Man do in this situation?

He clutched his cell phone like a talisman. He pulled up an *I Ching* app, typed in the question, Should I enter? and came up with the fourth hexagram, Immaturity, Youthful Folly. *It is not I who seek the young fool. It is the young fool who seeks me. At first, I inform him with clear answers; but if he importunes, I tell him nothing. He must persevere to succeed.* The young fool had to be Jezebel, making allowances for the misogyny of the ancient Chinese sages. Not him. Obvs. He had one moving line, the third one. *Like a foolish girl, throwing herself away, a weak, immature man...* That could not mean him either. *As a girl owes it to herself to wait until she is wooed, so also it is undignified to offer oneself. Nor does any good come of accepting such an offer.* This was a tad confusing. Was the *I Ching* counselling him to desist? He consulted the second hexagram indicated by the changing line. Number 18, Removing Corruption. The Condition read, *Guilt is implied.* The Judgement added, *Inner weakness, irresolute drifting, combined with outer inaction, inertia and rigidity, lead to spoiling.* Jeez, couldn't those mandarins have been a bit less ambiguous? On the one hand, they told him not to offer himself; on the other, they said inaction led to corruption and guilt. So what was he to do? He stood paralysed, aware that anyone in a car might recognise him and have suspicions about a man loitering outside a McMansion, on a school day.

He had an itch to relieve himself so overpowering that he considered unzipping and letting go, right there on the doorstep. *Be a man*, he told himself. He raised his hand and made a martial arts fist. He could totally punch a hole through the front door, splinter it, smash it to smithereens. Or simply knock it. He let out a high-pitched, ferocious scream. His fist did not move. The damn thing just stuck there, frozen. *I'm a cartoon character, a jerk. I'm Mr Magoo.* His arm wilted, like... like—well, it was better not to think about what it wilted like. Defeated, he turned to go.

At that very moment, the door opened.

'Yes?' asked a woman's voice—but not Jezebel's. He swung round to face her. It was a real, honest-to-God adult woman, forty or so, in totally bodacious shape, yet old enough to be Jezebel's mother. Oh, my God. *Was* she her goddamn mother?

'I'm here,' he began, but stopped abruptly. How could he explain that Jezebel had invited him? Not only was it 'inappropriate', but also, he realised now, he did not even know her real name! 'I'm here... ' he repeated, stalling again.

'Yes, I can see you're here,' the woman said, eyeing him with amusement. 'I heard the blood-curdling scream. Like Kung Fu fighters make in those old movies, you know? Are you all right? You haven't injured yourself?'

'Oh no,' Melvyn said hurriedly. 'I just uh, stubbed my toe on the uh, step.'

'That sucks. Maybe you've broken it. Want me to examine it? I'm a nurse.'

'You're a nurse?' She looked like a *Playboy* playmate.

'Sure, why shouldn't I be?'

'Are you—' *Jezebel's mother,* he wanted to say, but could not without giving the game away. He started again. 'I'll be OK. You see, I was invited here, by, by—'

'My sister,' the woman said, smiling broadly.

'Your sister? You're her *sister?*' Cool it, he told himself. Like the Fonz.

'Sure, why shouldn't I be? Oh, do I look too old to be her sister?'

'No, of course not. But she never told me she had one.' Unsurprising, really—even though Jezebel was much younger, her sister was far prettier.

'You'd better come in. You're—I've forgotten your name. Is it McDonald? Something to do with hamburgers, right?'

'Shamburger,' Melvyn said testily, as always when anyone teased him about it. 'It's actually an ancient German name. Nothing wrong with it.'

'Of course not,' she said, holding out her hand like a man, and pumping his with masculine strength. 'Shamburgers are tasty. Once in a while. I'm Delilah.'

'*Delilah?*' His voice cracked with incredulity.

'Why shouldn't it be? You sure do repeat a bunch of things, Mr Shamburger.'

'*Dr* Shamburger,' Melvyn said, his amour-propre under attack also from the mounting pressure in his bladder. He was astonished as Delilah—could that be her real name?—led him through a vast, echoing atrium, high as a church nave, and then another hall of a room, destitute of furniture, carpets or curtains. Their footsteps echoed as though they were in a cavern. If only he could pee here, on the parquet floor!

'Have you just moved in?' he said in a strangled voice.

'No, we've been here a year. Oh right, the house is practically empty. That's our dad. He's into minimalism. Like the Japanese, you know?'

'But what's the point of having a huge house if there's nothing in the rooms? I'm sorry, I don't mean to be rude.' Melvyn clenched his teeth. *Hold it in, hold it in.*

'No problem. Hell, I don't know. It's his money. He lets me live here for free so I don't complain.'

They reached an immense kitchen with granite counters, an island with stainless steel stools high enough for giants, distressed 'rustic' beams, and a stained glass window, depicting a half-naked woman with a defiant expression—a reproduction of Aubrey Beardsley's *Salomé*. On the island stood a bottle of red wine, glasses, crackers and a blue-veined, crumbly cheese: *Gorgonzola*. Deliberate? Sure, it was.

'I get the feeling there's a theme going on here,' Melvyn said. When Delilah looked at him questioningly, he went on: 'I mean Salomé there, and you, Delilah, and, uh—' he trailed off, hoping she would supply Jezebel's real name.

But she did not take the hint. 'Oh the Biblical names. Right. All names of *femmes fatales* too, right?'

He nodded, frustrated he could not winkle the name out of her. She poured two glasses of Châteauneuf-du-Pape, and cut a few crumbly slices of the cheese.

'Gorgonzola?' he said.

'In your honour,' she said. So it *was* a good-humoured if sly dig at his wife's name. 'My sister asked me to entertain you for a while. Do you mind?'

Actually, it was damn embarrassing. But it was a rhetorical question. What the heck was Jezebel, or whatever her goddamn name was, up to? Keeping him on tenterhooks, augmenting the suspense? Or just inconsiderately late? He had to admit that Delilah was attractive, built like an aerobics instructor, as tall as her sister, but more willowy. Curves in all the right places. Could he flirt with her? Should he? Was that the idea? But how could he, knowing that Jezebel might appear at any moment?

'Take a seat,' Delilah said, handing him a wine-glass. Waterford crystal.

Drinking would be excruciating. He crossed his legs. 'No thanks, Delilah.'

'You're too funny,' she said, rubbing her hands, which had some cheese stuck to them, and then sailing over to the sink. Oh no—she was going to turn the faucet on! Melvyn gritted his teeth. Could he resist wetting himself? The water gushed out of the tap, in an unstoppable flood, powerful, invincible.

'Are you all right? With your face screwed up like that you must be in agony.'

He opened his eyes and uncrossed his legs. 'I am. May I use your…?'

'Sure.' She laughed with the malice of a Disney witch. 'Right over there.'

He began to sprint for it but two realisations arrested him: first, that he looked an utter dick, running for the john like a toddler; and second, that the violence of the movement might unleash the mighty torrent. Stiffly, he slogged his way across the colossal kitchen, slamming the door behind him, unzipping with frantic haste, and then, eyes shut, blissfully letting go. Oh what joy! When he came out of his quasi-orgasmic trance, his beatific face smiled at him in the mirror. And he saw what he had barely registered as he burst into the bathroom and tore at his flies: a number of framed monochrome photographs, 'Extremely *inappropriate* photos,' said his internal Frida. Of naked or nearly naked young women, clearly pornography, but 'tasteful' compared to the porn of our age. These Victorian models did not have the pneumatic figures of modern porn models and actresses, nor did they look tall. They had rounded bellies, as in old paintings. And full bushes of pubic hair. Who decided that porn models should have shaven pudenda? When? Sometime in the nineties? And why? Someone found it sexier. Because they wanted women to look like little girls? Wasn't that a tad pervy? Melvyn found the women sexy, in spite of their homeliness. They leered at him knowingly. *We know what you want, Melvyn. Sure we do. Come here. Would you like to touch me? Would you like me to touch you? Here? Or maybe here?* As he zipped up, he wondered why antique porn adorned the walls of a family bathroom. *Must be an unusual family.* But what was normal? Who decided? (Frida, in their family.) Whose values were right? Whose were more feminist? Maybe those Biedermeier pictures, with the women's black stockings and long, elaborate hair, turned on the members of the household. Aroused them. Or they just were not hung up about sex. *Imagine that.*

'Feeling better?' Delilah said as Melvyn came out beaming.

She had a hell of a nerve to tease to him like that, but he did not take offence. 'Goddamn right,' he said.

'What's your name?' Delilah said, proffering a glass again. This time he took it. 'I mean, your Christian name.'

'My Christian name?' No one said that anymore. When had Christian names become reactionary? 'Melvyn,' he said, gulping wine and wolfing the Gorgonzola.

Delilah drank too, leaning against the counter, which pushed her pelvis and hips towards him. Was that a provocative pose? She wore a tee-shirt dress, split to above the knee. *Hot* damn. Sure it was provocative. 'Melvyn,' she murmured. 'That's right, I remember.'

Melvyn hoisted himself onto a stool as high as a stepladder. 'I wonder how long your sister will be. And if your parents might worry, I mean, you know.'

'About her seeing an older man? Don't worry about that. Our mom was shot dead by an eight-year old at the shooting range. With an AR-15. An accident. I see that shocks you. It's fine, it was a long time ago. We're over it now.'

'I'm so very sorry,' he said with conscious gravitas. 'And your dad?'

'He's broad-minded, don't worry. I'm sure she told him she's seeing you.'

'I'm not exactly *seeing* her,' he said.

'You're wondering about my relationship with her, right? Since I'm so much older. No worries, I don't mind. She's a grownup. We're free. We're very liberal.'

'So I see,' he said, with an involuntary glance towards the bathroom.

'Did you like the pictures? Hapsburg Empire, 1890s I should think. Vintage porn. Taken in Vienna, Prague and Budapest. Pretty foxy ladies, weren't they?'

'They certainly were.' Once more he wondered if she were flirting with him, and if Jezebel might have brought him here to set him up with her sister, who was so much closer in age to him. But before he could develop those speculations, a door creaked and clicked shut. Someone was descending the stairs.

Jezebel entered the kitchen at a stately pace, unsmiling, in a full-length grey dress, cut low, with a high waist, right below the bosom. With her hair in a topknot, she had the air of a Jane Austen character. Her breasts were glowing white globes. She still wore her glasses.

'Hi, sis,' Delilah said.

'Thank you for looking after Dr Shamburger,' Jezebel said in a stilted tone. She held out her hand; Melvyn was forced to shake it.

'I'll leave you two alone, then,' Delilah said, with a flicker of a wink.

Melvyn had turned on his stool to greet Jezebel—rudely failing to rise, he realised, discomfited—and when he turned back, Delilah had already vanished.

'Bring your wine, sir,' Jezebel said. 'I'll show you my room.'

That was just what Melvyn was afraid of. 'Won't you have a glass?'

'I can't control myself after a glass of wine,' she deadpanned, taking one.

He climbed down from the precarious stool—how high was it, five foot?—and followed her. Even wearing ballet slippers, she was an inch or so taller than him. She moved noiselessly along bare, echoing corridors, up stairs, around corners, down steps, up more, through a picture gallery without pictures—there were hangers, and bright white rectangles where paintings had once hung, and empty, elaborate gilt frames—past numberless doors and dirty windows. He was in one of those impossible Escher houses.

'Delilah told me about your mother's tragic accident,' Melvyn said.

Over her shoulder, Jezebel said, 'I didn't shoot her on purpose. No one was to blame.'

She had killed her own mother! He did not know what to say. 'Not even the guy who let you use a semi-automatic weapon?'

'He was trying to teach his daughter to defend herself.'

In the Shamburger house, guns were anathema. 'I'm so very sorry,' he said.

She cast a sharp look over her shoulder at him, doubting his sincerity. She frowned. 'My bedroom, sir,' she said, opening a cheap, laminated door.

'At last,' he said. It was nothing like his daughters' rooms, with their posters of pop stars, clothes and shoes in heaps, teddy bears, Disney toys, photos, soccer boots, swimsuits, Harry Potter costumes, lacy pillows, and makeup. Jezebel's room was spartan: twin bed, dresser, and wardrobe, all white as teeth in toothpaste ads.

'You like it?' She sat on the white quilt, in a prim pose, hands on her lap.

'I wish my daughters would keep theirs as tidy.'

She stared, expecting him to do something. Her gaze was clinical, judgemental. He stood stricken, marooned on the parquet floor. The door behind him was still open. Should he shut it? Would she think he was making a pass at her? Did she want him to? Was he reading too much into her, or too little?

'Maybe this wasn't such a hot idea,' he said. 'You inviting me here.'

'Why not?'

'People could get the wrong idea. Your sister, my wife.'

'Does that matter? We're not that conventional, are we? What is the wrong idea, anyway? I'd like us to be…' she said, 'more intimate.'

'Geez, Jezebel, I still don't even know your real name.'

'Does that matter? What's in a name? As Juliet says.'

'It was awkward not to know what to call you when I met Delilah. If that's *her* real name. Is it?'

'She has other names too. Sometimes she calls herself Petronella.'

'Jesus, why? What was the idea of getting her to entertain me, anyways?'

'I thought you'd like to meet her, sir. And she you. We're close, although she's twenty years older. Would you like to sleep with her? Do you like her?'

'Sure I like her. But hell,' he lied, 'of *course* I don't want to sleep with her.'

'Why not? Don't you think she's hot? Most guys do.'

'Heh-heh, boy oh boy, you don't mince words. Sure, she's pretty…'

'So go for it. I bet you could sleep with her. I'll ask her if you like.'

'Oh man, what an unusual girl—woman—you are. No, please don't do that. I'm not sure I could—oh hell. You still haven't told me if Delilah is her real name.'

'Does it matter?' she said for the third time. 'Delilah, Petronella, who cares?'

'Geez, Jezebel, I guess so. I feel I've gone through the looking-glass.'

'Like Alice. Isn't that freeing—to go through the looking-glass?'

'I guess. But also kind of unsettling. We all fear the unknown.'

'I adore the unknown. I want to embrace mystery. Sit beside me, sir.'

He obeyed—at a safe distance. The door was still open. Where was Delilah?

'You are nervous, sir.'

'Damn right I'm nervous.' Why was that? She had practically offered to pimp Delilah to him, not exactly an unpleasant prospect, and he could probably have Jezebel as an appetizer. *Is this guilt?* he asked himself. *Or fear—of Frida—or what?*

'You're stiff too,' Jezebel said, 'if you don't mind me saying so. I promise you Delilah won't disturb us. You can say what you like. *Do* what you like, sir.'

Her words were unambiguous, yet her face and tone were flat; they did not rhyme with what she was saying. And her own posture was as rigid as his was. No doubt she was shy. Inexperienced. He was glad she was a bit nervous too.

It was nuts. A twenty-one-year-old *Jezebel* had manoeuvred him into her bedroom, with the intention of seducing him— and he was as limp as wilting cabbage. He blamed the tattooed, red-bristled ogre squatting in his brain.

'I wish you wouldn't keep calling me sir,' he said. Should he touch her, kiss her? That would spell the end of his marriage. Which would be fucking fantastic—but also scary as hell, dammit. 'I should be getting back to the university, Jezebel.'

'As you wish. I'm happy you came,' she said, although her face expressed neither joy nor disappointment. 'Come again. Will you think about what I said?'

'How could I forget? But—my conscience is troubling me, Jezebel.'

'Is that so? The Superego is overrated, sir. It's nothing but an internalisation of societal and parental values. You've done nothing wicked yet. But I trust you will.' She spoke without the slightest emotion. Melvyn couldn't make her out.

He gave her a lopsided smile, to which she did not respond, and stood up. She led him back through the cavernous house in silence. Only now did he start to feel the proverbial stirring in his loins. *Lousy* goddamn timing! He hoped she might embrace him at the door, but no, she only shook his hand, formal as a saleswoman.

Outside he gulped the air as if he had been holding his breath. He raced to his potent car in fear that someone might be watching—Jezebel or Delilah, from an unwashed window, or some student with a grudge. But it was none of these who saw him. Just as he unlocked the car, a pink convertible Corvette zoomed up. Like Barbie's. It was not Frida's car, thank Christ, but it was the second worst one in the world. In Tocqueville, anyhow. Rocky was gaping at him in disbelief. He waved her down, but she drove by, shaking her head.

He had become one of those guys in Greek tragedy. Yep, he was in *deep* shit.

NINE

Brutally Honest

In the small hours of the morning Huw was in his dressing-gown, on the porch-swing, waiting for Miranda to come home from the McBanes' house. The live oaks creaked, the cicadas shrilled, the tree frogs belched in a rhythmic chorus, and a bongo drum beat inside his chest. Slapping at mosquitoes, he murmured to Miranda: Are you coming home, love? What have I done wrong? Are you angry with me? His mobile showed she had still not replied to his message asking when she would be back. He called her and heard an ersatz Latina accent:

Hola, amigos! Leave a message, and I weel call you back, eef I feel like it. Adios!

He pictured NeAmber McBane saying that, the bimbo. Perhaps while wearing a Mexican hat. He tried to speak but could not. He sent a text instead. *I miss you, love.*

The azaleas that screened and perfumed the porch had a bluish tinge in the gloaming. Was that the hum of Miranda's hybrid? At last the Prius did appear, grey and ghostly. Equally spectral was Miranda, heels and slender legs emerging from the car first, glamorous and expressionless, in a skirt suit and pink silk blouse with a pussy bow, hair permed, immaculate. Too immaculate? Her heels ticked on the flagstones of the path. Would she explode? Would he? He stood. From the corner of her eye she registered movement, turned her head, and gave him a hollow stare. A mocking-bird burst into joyful song.

Come to me, he willed her. *Take me in your arms, tell me you love me.*

She climbed the three steps to the porch and halted, staring, silent, sullen.

If she came to him, she was still not lost. *Come to me, my darling.*

'What are you doing out here at six in the morning?' she said.

He could not answer. *Hold it in, boyo, hold it in. Bollocks to self-pity.*

Her straight-backed posture proclaimed confidence and power. Untouchably beautiful, the epitome of the American professional woman. He could not move towards her.

Her speech was staccato, each word a bullet: 'You guilt-tripping me, Huw?'

He shook his head and the unshed tears flew out. 'Not at all. Just happy you're home.'

'I'm going to bed,' she said, frowning. She walked in, not waiting for him, and he followed her sheepishly. He ascended the stairs behind her. In the electric light her legs in their nude tights gleamed like antique marble statuary. A few short weeks ago he would have slipped his hand up her skirt, laughing. Now he was at a loss.

Until they reached the library upstairs it did not occur to him that she was heading for their old bedroom, which they had moved out of because the height, and her urge to leap from the windows, terrified her. She paused and glanced at the filament of light under Owen's door. Was he already up? Or still up? Huw heard the clicking of a keyboard. *Still* up, dammit. But Miranda was already in their old room. A hopeful sign? In the dawn light the room was exactly as they had left it: cinnamon walls, wainscoting, the Victorian bed with the immense headboard, carved like the stern of a sailing ship. She undressed, dropping her clothes on the floor, not so much as glancing at him. The bed was made. She got in, and after a moment's hesitation, he discarded his dressing-gown and joined her.

The house held its breath. 'Are you going to work today?' he asked.

'Of course not.' She shut her eyes and opened them again. 'I guess we need to talk. About what's going on. Right now, what I need is space. You understand?'

Even *more* space? Huw knew they needed to talk, but right now he could not face the prospect of any changes. He stroked her hair and kissed her cheek.

He expected her to be unresponsive, but she turned towards him.

'I guess I have to let you have me first. Or I'll never be able to get a sensible word out of you, right?'

Was she teasing, flirting, or criticising, turning irony on him? Either way he did not halt his caresses, and she rolled towards him, less stiffly now.

'You only want me for my body.'

'Of course not, love,' he said, shocked.

'Sure you do. I'm just tits and ass to you.'

'Let's face it, they are superb,' he tried to joke.

She slapped his face, rather hard for playfulness, and then submitted to his advances. At first she did not respond, but then she did, and soon they fell into the Bossa Nova groove, in perfect time, and her accusation receded. Miranda came with her usual energy but less abandon, less tenderness. She did not gaze into his eyes. He kissed her; she did not respond.

'Feel better now?' Her tone was that of a nurse who had just given him medicine.

'Much better,' he said, hoping the sex had re-established their intimacy.

'Maybe we can discuss things, then. Now I've serviced you.'

Huw had been trying to get her to talk for weeks. 'For God's sake, don't put it like that. I'm not your client, am I? But we can talk. Aren't you sleepy, though?'

'I'm exhausted. But Matthew gave me some pills to keep me awake.'

'Whatever for? And pills, plural? He's not your therapist, is he?'

'No, but he is a psychiatrist. He can prescribe medication.'

'I know, but you're already taking medication, aren't you? Does he know that? Does your regular therapist know that McBane is medicating you as well?'

'Hey, don't freak out on me. Relax, dude. I can give you a pill if you like.'

'Jesus, Miranda, you want to medicate me now? How big is your supply?'

'Look, drop it, or I'm done. You want to talk or not?'

'Of course.'

'Good.' She sat up, ramrod-straight against the headboard. In the thin green light her torso was as white as ivory. With her breasts sticking out, taut, defiant, sculptural—and yes, wooden—she reminded him of a figurehead on the bows of a sailing ship. 'As I was saying,' she said, noticing the direction of his gaze, 'you just love my boobs.'

'You know that's not true.'

'Sure it is. If I were ugly, you wouldn't be with me.'

'I've never thought about it.' He did now. Would he? If he was frank, maybe not. The realisation shocked him: he had always believed he was in love with her soul.

'When my looks fade you'll leave me for a younger model.'

'No, I won't,' he said, meaning it, yet he heard the edge of doubt in his voice.

'Guys are all the same.'

'How sexist is that? Imagine if I said women are all the same.'

The figurehead gazed out to sea. 'You're too needy. You got

to give me more space. Right now I need to spend more time with Matthew and NeAmber. *They* understand me.'

'Are you saying I don't? Is that why you want to go to Mexico without me?'

'I never said that. I asked you to come. You still could.'

'The McBanes give me the creeps.'

'You think I belong to you. Get over that, Huw.'

'I'm not possessive,' he said, though as he spoke he knew it was untrue. But was belonging to someone a bad thing? 'I love you, that's all. Do you still love me?'

'Of course,' she said curtly. 'But our relationship has to change.'

The timbers of the old house creaked. The crickets chirped. 'How do you mean?'

'I told you, I need more space. Let me go out on my own. Have my own friends. Go on vacations without you. Do you love me enough to let me do that?'

Owen bumped about in his bedroom. Huw had no desire to have a holiday without *her*. 'I don't get it. Aren't you happy with me?'

She pulled on a pink velveteen pyjama top, a grandmother top. As he glanced down on her, she appeared to have a double-chin, and he imagined what she would look like when she was older. Not ugly but not alluring either. 'I never believed in the institution of marriage, the legality of it, the conformity, the restrictions. I agreed to marry you because it was the only way we could be together in Oman. Remember?'

He remembered, but had long believed she was as happy as he was. 'Are you saying you don't want to be married to me anymore?'

She took her time answering. 'I don't know yet. Does it matter?'

'Does it matter?' He heard a crash. A door slammed.

'I mean, what matters is love, right? Do we have to be married? Who cares? I'm not saying we can't be. I just need space, to breathe, to think. Let me have it, if you love me. Will you do that for me, for us?'

'Why do you want to go to Mexico so badly?'

'You know why. I want to see the Mayan ruins, and Frida's house.'

Frida Kahlo was the wrong model, with her self-absorption, her victim complex, her glorification of suffering, and her open marriage, but Huw knew Miranda would not like him saying that. Besides, he could not bear to lose her. 'All right,' he said grimly.

'Let me be free,' Miranda said. 'I need to put myself first. My diagnosis is serious. PTSD, bipolar disorder with schizoid tendencies, depression and anxiety.'

'Jesus Christ, when was this? So many conditions? Why didn't you tell me?'

'I didn't want to worry you. It's OK. I'm managing. I'm well-medicated.'

'I'll do whatever I can to support you. I promise. I love you.'

She nodded her thanks—but did not assure him of her love in return. 'Great. This weekend I want to go on a women's retreat. Is that OK with you?'

'What kind of retreat? Where?'

'In the country, up in the hills. The woman running it is a confidence guru. Her name's Petronella Pikestaff. NeAmber says she's the real deal. She kicks ass.'

'I'm not sure I want my arse kicked. And surely you of all people don't need more confidence, do you, love? I've never known anyone more confident.'

'Huw, you don't know me at all.'

No, he did not know her at all. He could see that now.

*

Later, Huw was stumbling about in the supermarket, alone as usual: Miranda no longer had the patience for shopping. She had stopped cooking and cleaning too—not that she had ever done much of either. Huw had left his glasses at home, so everything was a blur. Dawnesha Ceyonne sang a ballad over syrupy strings, dragging out single syllables over dozens of notes in mushy, meaningless flourishes. Supposedly *soulful*.

Huw used his trolley as a battering ram. 'Excuse me,' he called out to the sleepwalker blocking his way. He barged past him like Charlton Heston in a chariot race.

A tall, skinny shadow in a baggy tracksuit zoomed in on him. By the redolence of repellent scent and margaritas, he guessed it was a woman. By her air of focussed fury, a professional woman. By the Ozark screech— 'Heeugh! What's bitten you?' it had to be Rocky Rathaus. 'Oh, never mind. Guess what I saw this morning? Only Melvyn, coming out of one of those magnificent mansions on the west side of town.'

'Sorry, Rocky, I can't see,' Huw said. 'Why did the mansion upset you?'

'*Dude*. It was like eleven thirty in the morning. And he was so furtive. Tried to flag me down. Sneaky look on his face. Who do you think he coulda been visiting—on the *west* side of Tokeville, Heeugh?'

'How should I know? A friend? A colleague?'

'Heeugh, you are so naïve. So ingenious.'

'I think you mean *ingenuous*.'

'Uh? Oh, sure. But don't you see? We don't have colleagues on the west side. Those mansions are too pricey for professors. Except Business professors, of course.'

'I wouldn't live in one if you paid me. Nasty, kitschy things.'

'Heeugh—it was totally awesome. Heeuge, with gables and a kind of tower with one of those super cute roofs, like a fairy-tale, you know what I'm sayin'?'

'I suspected as much. Did it have columns too? Stained-glass windows?'

'Don't be so snarky, Heeugh. As a madder of fact it did. Anyways, what was Melvyn doing out there? It's so like weird. You think he's maybe having an affair?'

Good for you, Melvyn boyo, if you are. 'I wouldn't jump to conclusions.'

'I guess I godda tell Frida. I mean, it's my dooty, right?'

'If I were you I shouldn't meddle. If it's bothering you, why not just mention to Melvyn that you saw him? I'm sure he has an innocent explanation.'

'Of course, you would be on his side. As a man, I mean.'

'Not at all.' It was not so much that Melvyn was a *man*—to Huw he was a sort of superannuated adolescent, since he looked and behaved like one. 'No, I just feel sorry for any bloke who's...' *married to such a harridan*, he left unsaid.

'Who's what? And don't tell me I'm meddling. It's just solidarity with Frida.'

Frida Shamburger, Frida Kahlo. The monster in the Creative Writing Department, the monster of egocentrism, Miranda's sea-monsters. Melvyn's marriage, and Kahlo's, and his own. Too many tangles, weeds wrapped round his legs, trapping him. 'Ah, is that what it is?'

'Don't take that tone with me—that goddamn uppity Briddish tone.'

'I can hardly help being Welsh, Rocky.'

'Why not? How many years have you been here? Can't you talk like us?'

Usually he reined in his Welsh testiness. Now he did not. 'Well, I could. Let's see: I could reduce my vocabulary by eighty per cent, stop using compound sentences, mix up the collocations of my prepositions, insert meaningless phatic fillers into each phrase, and speak in strings of clichés. Yes, I daresay I could speak like you if I put my mind to it.'

'You are so *goddamn* condescending. How does Miranda put up with you?'

'She doesn't any more. Good-bye, Rocky.' He blundered off, and found himself at the checkouts. Dawnesha was still yodelling her overblown emotions. *I ee-ay, will always, love you—ooh-ooh-ooh-oohoo-ooh. I can't live if living is without you.* Why was such rubbish popular? Because we no longer have real emotions; we borrow them from movies and weepy songs. Or we do, but suppress them, because they reveal facets of ourselves we prefer to ignore. The manufactured sentimental versions are easier to deal with. Huw yodelled as he walked out. In Wales, someone might have joined in. Here people stared as if he were nuts. *Which I may be*, he thought. Maybe Miranda's madness was catching.

*

Arriving at his office after lunch, duly bespectacled, he found awaiting him a person with long, floppy hair, a suede jacket, white chinos and loafers, worn without socks. It was Timothy, *not* Tim, the much younger husband of Dr Jorgenson, the Dean of the College of Liberal Arts. Timothy had an infant's high forehead and bush baby eyes, big, blue and bulging, with purplish rings beneath them, which gave him the air of an inveterate Onanist. With those immense, doleful eyes, Timothy smiled, wistfully, and vainly. Definitely a wanker—in the literal sense. Huw would have put money on it.

'I'm *so* glad you're here, Huw,' Timothy droned, glancing ostentatiously at his watch. 'Like, finally. I need your help with this *insufferable* thesis. It's such *agony*.'

'Sorry I'm a bit late, Timothy. Just a moment.' His office was a disaster: cardboard boxes full of student work formed a Himalayan outline above his bookshelves, and his desk bore the marks of a recent Gestapo raid: open, ransacked drawers, torn papers, piles of trash.

Timothy sank with studied elegance into the armchair before it, crossing his legs as British men did, one knee over the other—which was considered effete here. A real man was supposed to sit with his legs apart. It was permissible to prop one leg up on another, but only the ankle could rest across the knee. Timothy touched his lips with his index finger, as if in deep contemplation, which knowing him was most implausible;

or urging secrecy, which was more likely; or signalling his sexual innocence, in a fey, disingenuous kind of way, which was more probable still. Huw told himself to be careful.

'I wonder if you've had a chance to read the latest section of my thesis,' Timothy drawled—not in the Southern manner, but more like a flamboyant boy Huw had known at Oxford, who had modelled himself on Oscar Wilde.

'Actually, I have.' What on earth could he say that would not traumatise the poor fellow? 'You did a good job of evoking the lives of yuppies in a Southern city. Their manners and mannerisms, their patterns of speech—even what they download to their smart phones to listen to in the gym, and what kind of latte they drink at Sundoes.'

Timothy's finger was back on his mouth. No, actually *in* his mouth. Would he suck it? He raised his eyebrows petulantly. *Is that all?* the expression meant.

'Mmm,' Huw hummed, praying for inspiration. 'Another thing you pull off well is…' (*Come on, think of something! Not Miranda and the McBanes or Frida and the prospect of losing wife and job and home.*) '… the gay scene in the state capital. The leather bars, the strip clubs, the parties. Very detailed, lots of specifics, very true-to-life. I can tell you're writing from personal knowledge.'

Timothy's bush baby eyes bulged wider. '*You* know that scene, Huw?'

'Well, no. I can't say I do.'

'You sure about that? You wouldn't be bi, Huw, but maybe chary of coming out?'

'Good Lord, no. Whatever gave you such an idea?'

'There *is* a rumour that you're gay, or bi. You must have heard it.'

'Not a whisper. How extraordinary.'

Timothy enunciated the syllables *ha, ha, ha*—less a laugh than a parody of one. 'No need to get defensive, Huw. It's not a trial. I'm not accusing you of a crime.'

'I just wonder why *anyone* would suppose I might be gay.'

Timothy tittered. 'Want to know my theory? They think you're so hot and handsome that you *must* be. They can't face the idea that you're not. They want to believe they have a chance with you, you see. My buddies have told me so.'

'Please tell them I'm straight. A hundred percent.'

'Everyone's a bit gay,' Timothy said.

'No, they're not. Never say that in a pub in Wales, boyo.'

'Oh, what a pity. My little friends will be *so* disappointed. What a heartbreaker you are, Huw.' Timothy grinned, delighted by Huw's discomfiture. 'But we're getting off track, aren't we? So what did you think of the plot developments in the novel? Terribly complex, aren't they? *Byzantine.*'

'Well, to be honest...' Huw began.

'Oh, no!' Timothy wailed, laying the back of his hand against the chalk cliff of his forehead in mock horror. 'Spare me your British honesty! Whenever you say that, I know you're going to say something just *brutal.*' He spoke with masochistic relish.

'My intention is never to wound. But if I'm not going to be sincere, why speak at all? Criticism is valueless unless it's truthful.'

'Sure, Huw, but you could be *kind*, no? That's what we all wish. Like— '

'Like who?'

'Well, like the Shamburgers, for instance. They're so *sweet*. Especially Frida. She *adores* our work. She says every single one of us is talented and special.'

'Do you really believe that?' Huw did not: Frida often lamented the banality and incompetence of student writing in private. 'Can everyone be talented?'

'Maybe it's a teeny bit of a white lie at times.'

'If she finds it all so wonderful, what do you learn from her?' Huw said.

'That's the problem, right? You're the only one we can trust. You're savage, but at least when you say something good about our work, you mean it. And when you tear our work to pieces, *unfortunately* you're usually right.'

Impatient with the affected talk, Huw had an urge to end it. 'So you want to know the truth about the novel? It's supposed to be a psychological thriller, but there's not enough action or suspense to make it thrilling, nor enough depth of character to make it literary. It's not even plausible. When the police interview Gavin, they believe his incoherent alibi. That makes me wonder how much you know about police procedure. And the crooks are Colombian drug-lords, from Medellín. A bit of a cliché, isn't it?'

'There *are* Colombian drug-lords. And some of them are from Medellín.'

'I daresay. But what do you know about them? Have you met any?'

'I've seen tons of them in movies.'

'Exactly. Your Colombian cocaine dealers conform to Hollywood stereotypes: they have ponytails and diamond ear-studs and they speak comical English. They have porn star girlfriends and they're savage sadists.'

'Do you suppose the real ones are kind and considerate?'

'No, but it's boring that they conform to our expectations. If you're going to describe them in depth they need to be complicated or surprising in some way.'

'Some people simply *are* stereotypes,' Timothy said. 'I am, for instance.'

'Absolutely.' Huw smiled to soften the barb, but Timothy looked hurt anyway. 'I know some people are stereotypes. But why put them in your novel? Who cares about stock figures? And talking of those, why does Gavin betray his husband in the first place?'

'He's so *old* and *fussy*. Gavin wants *adventure*.'

'And yet he has an affair with another old, fussy man. I wonder why.'

'I guess he's looking for a father-figure. Or he's just into older guys.' Timothy scrutinised Huw's face. Was he flirting? Christ, Huw hoped not.

Huw went on without mercy: 'Then Gavin agrees to meet Don Carlos in an empty meat warehouse—another cinematic cliché—and, incredibly enough for a young gay graphic artist, Gavin takes an automatic pistol with him.'

'You don't think gay men can use pistols? That's a tad homophobic, no?'

'I'm sure some of them can. But Gavin is such a soft and ineffectual person. He's often in tears. He can't even make up his mind about what to wear or how to comb his hair. Does he really think he's going to win a shootout with a drug-lord?'

'Sure he does, and he succeeds too,' Timothy said, pouting.

'Who's going to believe that? What are the odds?'

'It could happen. He could get lucky. Guns do jam.'

'They do in movies. But it's awfully lucky for Gavin.'

'Oh my God, you just *hate* my novel, don't you? Admit it. You think it stinks. You're telling me I'll never be a writer and I should give up, like this minute.'

How the bloody hell did Timothy guess that? 'I never said that. The novel does need work, though. Quite a bit, to be honest.'

'*To be honest*,' Timothy drawled. 'You're quite the piece of work, aren't you? So *judgemental*, so *English*.' He hissed the last word. '*Jorgen* says my work is brilliant.'

'He is your husband, Timothy. He might be a bit biased.'

'Melvyn says I'm gifted. Frida thinks I could be the next Brett Easton Ellis.'

And yet neither of them had wanted to admit Timothy to the program, Huw remembered. It was he and Luke who had argued for his admittance. Huw had discerned potential—which had not been fulfilled, since Timothy had been spoilt by his professors, all sycophants to Jorgenson. Apart from Huw, not one had dared to point out his work's faults. So naturally Timothy had assumed it was perfect.

'I'm not saying you're not gifted,' Huw said, ashamed of his hedging.

'You're not saying I *am*.' Timothy's voice wobbled on the verge of tears.

Huw sighed. How much praise did the boy need? 'You have potential. An ear for language, realistic dialogue.' Timothy still sulked. 'But a thriller must be plausible, and a literary thriller can't be full of clichés and stereotypes. You need more discipline.'

Timothy's face was flour-white. 'Thanks for your *honesty*,' he said, standing and flouncing out with the same insouciance as Elise did. Timothy flounced even more campily, swinging his hips and tossing his head like a male model on a runway. *You asshole*, that strut proclaimed. *I don't need* you *for anything!*

Huw sighed. In the past few days he had demonstrated his talent for antagonising people again and again. First Frida, then Rocky, and now Timothy. Would they all become enemies? On his desk, Miranda fixed him from her photograph frame with a glassy, incredulous, hurt look. Had he antagonised his wife too? *You asshole*, her expression proclaimed—didn't it? *I don't need* you *for anything either!*

Was he too honest? In Wales people expected honesty. At Oxford too. You mocked, ridiculed, took the piss. Blokes especially, and you gave as good as you got. It was fine to insult people to their face. Insults were not rude. You called your mates tossers, wankers, twats, prats, fairies, dickheads. Your *best* mates. In Britain blokes took it as a compliment if you insulted them or ragged them—it showed you regarded them as equals. You never did it to anyone less bright, or from a lower social class. That was bullying. And maybe the reason the Yanks were so touchy was that they had an inferiority complex. They believed Brits were brighter. And they were right. Unless the Brits were really snooty, arrogant bastards, that is.

Which some of them were. But Huw was not a snooty, arrogant bastard. Was he? *Was he?*

TEN

Is God a Guy?

A disembodied voice spoke over Melvyn. A blessing from heaven?

Thank you, Jesus, he murmured. Jezebel leaned back against the endless long pink hood of a Corvette, her eyes fixed on his, and with tantalising slowness lifted the hem of her dress to above her knees, to her thighs, to—OMFG!—to her—oh boy oh boy oh boy—right up to her goddamn *belly*button. But Melvyn directed his gaze lower.

No panties, not even those ephemeral V-string things from Vickie's Secret.

And by God, he was hard as a hammer. *Nothing* could stop him now.

He walked towards her, unzipping himself. She held out her arms to him.

Her voice croaked at him, loud and harsh. 'MELVYN! Get up already!'

He was on the brink of entering her when it cawed again:

'Melvyn, I won't tell you again. It's Sunday. Get up. Get ready for church.'

God or the Archangel Gabriel? Thunderheads filled the sky. Fork lightning flickered and crackled. Could God have that grating voice? Was He full of wrath? Melvyn lunged his lance at Jezebel, determined—but goddammit, she had vanished. Instead, *he* sprawled on the hood, arms waving, flies open, his proud Johnson exposed, vulnerable. And some stinky, slimy creature loomed over him, hissing, its scales scraping the concrete drive as it dragged itself towards him, foul smoke belching from its nostrils, jaws open, about to snap over his wilting member. He kicked at the vile monster with all his might.

'No!' he screamed, grabbing his privates with both hands. 'Leave me alone!'

'Melvyn, what the hell's wrong with you? Are you nuts? Wake up already!'

He opened his eyes and struggled to make sense of what he saw: a billowing purple pavilion, with wings sticking out of its sides, possibly vestigial, flabby, flappy, defaced by hideous pictures, yet furnished with claws, and a humanoid head sticking out of the top, a triple-chinned, blotchy head, with pink, pinpoint eyes, rust-red bristles on the scalp, a gold ring in its snout. It was no relief to find himself at Frida's mercy instead of the monster's.

'Hey, it's Sunday, right?' he groaned. 'Can't I lay in for once?' Or was it *lie in*?

'No you cannot lay in,' Frida tromboned. 'God, men are so slothful.'

You're calling *me* lazy? he nearly asked. You, who live on social media?

'On Sunday I go to church. Every goddamn Sunday,' Frida blared. 'And you accompany me. It's for our spiritual benefit, Melvyn. For the good of our souls.'

Have you even got a soul? Have I? Who cares? He just yearned to return to his dream and roger Jezebel on the hood of the

Corvette. Was that asking too much? He had been so darn close—on the point of entry. And Frida had kicked his ass out of the gates of paradise.

His loins throbbed painfully. If he couldn't bang Jezebel, surely he could at least go have a huge breakfast at Denny's, eggs and bacon and sausages and hash-browns, followed by pancakes with syrup and half a gallon of coffee? Then lounge about at home, maybe watch some football. The Patriots were playing. Pour himself a Brewski. Check out porn videos. That was his idea of a Sunday morning.

'I don't know why I have to go,' he said. 'Can't you go on your own for once?'

'Hey, I'm the goddamn subdeacon. What would the new vicar think?'

'Who cares? No one gives a flying fuck if I'm there. Actually no one gives a flying fuck about any of it. They're all just pretending to be Christians anyway.'

'Melvyn, how can you say that?' Frida tore the bedclothes off his body. Melvyn's Johnson poked out of his PJ flies. More like a garden worm than a king cobra, sadly. He covered himself, mortified.

'True, you rarely even pretend,' he said. 'Only when you put that dumbass purple surplice on. Then you think you're the Archbishop of fucking Canterbury.'

'Go fuck yourself,' Frida said quietly as she fumbled for something in her purse.

He stuck his lower lip out. He would not let her bully him. For once he would have his own way. Frida could not make him do anything. She was not his mother. Well hell, she kind of was. Anyhow, she was not his boss. Well damn, yes, in fact she was. She had no power over him. Shit, yes, she did have. Or very soon would have.

Frida had turned her purse nearly inside out. Melvyn glimpsed a black metal barrel.

'Was that a gun I saw just now?' he said.

'Oh yeah, I didn't tell you I bought one. A woman's got to be able to protect herself, right? This is the MeToo era. Broome showed me her Beretta and I thought it was cute.'

'Holy shit! You're packing heat now?' *This was bad news. Very bad news indeed.*

'Everyone has one now. Even Rocky does. We're already taking lessons.'

With a start he remembered Rocky seeing him scurrying out of Jezebel's McMansion. That was on Friday. Had she shopped him yet? He pictured her in a detective raincoat, like Jezebel's, spilling the beans, and Frida tapping a pencil as she listened. Rocky couldn't have betrayed him yet—if she had, Frida's fury would have fallen on him by now. But why not? Maybe she just had not had a chance. Or could her conscience be troubling her? He was sure Rocky did not have one. Her ethical development was at the level of an alligator's. Maybe a bit lower. Like Frida, all she wanted was power, position, and fame. And pleasing Frida was her strategy for getting it. So it was only a matter of time. When would she betray him? Of course, at church! Rocky was always there, fawning over Frida, having confidential little chats with her over coffee and cookies after the service. Could he forestall her? She wouldn't rat on him if he were standing beside her, would she? Stopping her was his only chance.

He leapt out of bed. 'I'll be ready in fifteen,' he said, heading for the shower.

Frida ballooned her cheeks, shook her head. Her tongue wagged like a bell clapper. Her jowls deflated. 'What a weirdo,' she muttered as he padded past her.

*

As far as Melvyn was concerned, the best thing about St. Michael and All Angels was that the hicks who filled the town's Southern Baptist churches and the Churches of Christ were absent. As Melvyn climbed down from the vast purple Shamburger armoured car in the parking lot, in his seersucker suit and loafers, he saw professors from Oxbow State or the liberal arts college, Prince, all dressed like civilised people from the North—which most of them were. Blazers, chinos, tweed jackets, linen suits. The women wore formless tents and jeans. No makeup. The downside, it struck him, as he opened the passenger door for Frida—she was a stickler for sexist, archaic courtesies—and cushioned her fall as she plummeted earthwards, was that no yuppie studs attended this church, which was known as an old liberal hangout. So Toqueville's babes, tanned, dressed to slay in spike heels and miniskirts and, and made-up like porn stars, were naturally absent too, and there was no eye-candy.

The second her Doc Martens hit the tarmac, Frida's face underwent its usual Sabbath transformation. Gone in an instant were the peevishness, the tight lips, narrowed eyes, flared nostrils, and wrinkled scalp. She smiled with the otherworldly expression of an apostle walking beside Jesus. She exuded serenity and saintliness. World-class acting.

'How do you do it?' he asked. 'I mean, walk that way. Like Princess Di.'

'Well done, Melvyn. Actually I do imagine I'm Princess Di. I *become* her.'

For Frida, that was an unusually frank admission. Even with Melvyn she liked to maintain her aura of sincerity and authenticity. Sometimes he wondered if her subterfuges and deceptions were so deeply ingrained that she came to believe them herself. But if you caught her off guard you might find a chink in the armour.

Melvyn was about to crow when he glimpsed Rocky and remembered he had to get to her before Frida did. Would Rocky rat on him? Had she already ratted? She would do anything to please Frida. Incredibly, several days after Rocky had caught him outside Jezebel's McMansion, Frida had still not mentioned the matter. Was she pointedly ignoring him? Or 'blissfully unaware'? Then he also glimpsed Jezebel, lurking like a detective. Oh no!

Please, God, he prayed, with more fervour than he had ever prayed in his life, *Please don't let that crazy girl make a scene. And please let me prevent Rocky talking to Frida in private. I'll give up beer and porn. I'll be good from now on, I swear. Thank you. Amen.*

'What are you smirking about, Melvyn Shamburger?' The voice was cultured, New England, reminiscent of Gore Vidal. Cooper, a Lit. professor with the etiolated, wincing smile of an elderly Somerset Maugham, a tall figure in a corduroy jacket, thin and bent as a pipe-cleaner. One of the few intellectuals on the faculty at Oxbow, he enjoyed teasing the creative writers.

'Hi Cooper, hi Burd,' Melvyn said, addressing Cooper's wife, a tiny woman with dyed blonde hair and intense, sparrow-like eyes. 'Just wondering why an inveterate atheist like you is always to be found here, Cooper.'

Cooper laughed silently but hard, his eyes closing. 'In a Southern city if you don't belong to a church, you have no social circle, so my lovely wife tells me.'

'What about you?' Burd's chuckle was razor-edged. 'Don't I recall seeing you two in the audience when Richard Dawkins came? And Christopher Hitchens?'

'We are believers,' Frida said, in bell-like Boston Brahmin tones, her face radiating beatitude. 'The concept of an after-life is comforting. Humans need it.'

'Even if it's untrue?' Burd said.

'Like fiction,' Melvyn mumbled. 'The kind of fiction Frida likes, anyway.' What the hell had gotten into him? For years he had been meek and submissive, and now all of a sudden, his impulses to rebel were breaking out, willy-nilly. It was scary, but exhilarating too. He saw from Frida's face that he had touched a sore spot.

'What's that supposed to mean? What kind of fiction do I like?' she said.

Cooper raised his eyebrows. He dyed his hair, but his eyebrows were grey.

'Let's face it, chick-lit. That *Scarf, Praise, Adore* woman. The one who wrote *The Private Life of Wasps*. Oh yeah—that other one too, the *Gaga Sorority*.'

Frida's brow darkened and furrowed. 'Chick-lit my ass,' she said, her accent reverting to East Boston. 'That's literature, but you're too prejudiced to see it.'

With that she stomped towards the imposing figure of the new vicar, who was welcoming the congregation at the door of the Victorian Gothic church.

'She likes that shit? Tonight you'll be sleeping on the couch,' Burd said.

'No sex in the foreseeable future,' Cooper added.

'I wish,' Melvyn muttered. Should he run after her? What if Rocky reached her before he did? Or, God forbid, Jezebel? To his relief, Frida was standing beside the new vicar, a woman of formidable height and build, in a purple chasuble, emblazoned with a lucent gold cross. She held her arms wide and beamed as she welcomed her lambs into the fold—with authority. Frida had resumed her gentle, beatific expression, but she was clutching a colossal silver-topped mace, which he feared she would brain him with. How had she gotten hold of that? Not only were her tats covered by the surplice, but also, as usual, she had removed the punky nose-ring. Why? Did the Episcopal God disapprove of tats and piercings? Melvyn bet he did too.

'You're smirking again,' Cooper said as the three of them edged past the vicar and Frida. 'What repression is going on in that devious mind of yours?'

'You must be the last Freudian critic alive,' Melvyn said, grateful that Frida had not cracked his skull open with that mace as they went by her.

'We're both Freudians,' Cooper said. 'Your fiction is strewn with phallic symbols. Just what are our deepest hidden urges? What are *yours*, Melvyn?'

'I hardly want to kill my father. He's already dead. And what other paternal authority figures would we like to murder?' Melvyn glanced at the mostly elderly crowd in the vestibule.

Their uniformly white faces were splashed with lozenges of bright colours from the stained windows. Jezebel, in her raincoat, stood alone beneath a panel depicting Mary Magdalene—a coincidence or conscious symbolism? The latter, knowing her. She peered at him from behind her glasses, staring in a creepy way. How did she know he attended St. Michael's? Or was she a member of the congregation that he had never noticed before? No, she was stalking him, for sure. What did she want? Hadn't he blown his chances with her? Then he noticed Timothy, a young fiction writer of negligible talent in the MFA programme, standing beside the dyed black hair and San Francisco moustache of Professor Jorgen Jorgenson, the Dean, who gazed at his husband with pride.

'I guess I wouldn't mind topping old Jorgenson,' Melvyn said.

Cooper laughed on the intake of his breath, like a Swede. 'That sounded very vehement, Melvyn. He's not that bad, is he? As Deans go, I mean.'

'He's an old bore. *The Faerie Queene.*'

'Homophobia, Melvyn? Surely not.' Cooper pulled an astringent face.

'I'm talking about Edmund Spenser. His research interest. You'd think there was nothing else of value in English Literature, to listen to him.'

'Oh that. I guess he is the best candidate for symbolic parricide. As for marrying our mothers…' he glanced around the vestibule, and located Burd, who had wandered off and was talking in assertive tones, 'We already have, no?' He laughed: wistfully, wheezing.

But Frida and the vicar were bearing down upon them, and Jezebel was still gawking at Melvyn, which he hoped his mother—or rather, his wife—had not noticed. Frida did have a condescending, suspicious smile on her face, and so did the vicar. But that was normal, of course. As a man in the Humanities, he expected women to treat him as though he had a mild mental retardation, plus sociopathic tendencies. So he wiped the

impish smirk off his face. He had been a choirboy at his prep
school and could look innocent at will.

'Hi, hi,' said the vicar, seizing each man's hand in turn and
wringing it like an orange she wanted to drain of its juice. Melvyn
nursed his crushed fingers afterwards, behind his back. 'I am
the *Reverend* Crystal Nutt?' She emphasised the honorific in the
same way that Frida emphasised 'Doctor' when she introduced
herself. He had a hunch and misgiving that the pair would get
on well.

'And what are we discussing here,' the Revd. Crystal Nutt
asked with a falling intonation, as if it were not a question.

The patronising 'we' of the authority figure.

Cooper chuckled, with discomfiture. 'Just the usual Freudian
stuff.'

Frida rolled her eyes. 'What else would *you two* be discussing?'

'Naughty boys,' the Revd. Crystal Nutt said, wagging the
nightstick of her forefinger playfully at them. 'Well, we must run
along, Frida. The Lord Awaiteth?'

As Cooper followed them into the nave, Melvyn gazed ahead
like a blinkered horse, catching Jezebel out of the corner of his
eye. Somehow she appeared at his side, in perilous proximity.
'Good morning, sir,' she said, unsmiling.

Melvyn affected surprise. 'Jezebel, I didn't see you. Are you
Episcopalian?'

'Not exactly. My family belongs to a weird cult. But you are?'

'Not exactly, but my wife bullies me into coming here.'

Jezebel stood way too close and spoke into his ear. 'Oh no,
how sad. Why?'

'She thinks it's good for her career. And it makes her feel
important.'

'How inauthentic,' Jezebel said. 'Can't you rebel?'

Could he? Instead of replying, Melvyn asked: 'So what are
you doing here?'

'I need to see you,' she said in an urgent whisper. Sweating,

Melvyn rubbernecked. Rocky was out of earshot. 'Could we talk after the service, sir?'

They had shuffled into the dimly-lit nave now. 'Can't it wait till tomorrow?'

'Tomorrow may be too late,' she said. 'It's now or never.'

Was she an Elvis fan? He pulled an ambiguous grimace of a face and fled, joining Cooper and Burd in a polished cherry pew. Nevertheless, moments later, Jezebel took a pew in front. She kept turning around to stare at him. Burd poked Melvyn's ribs:

'Who is that cute girl I saw talking to you? Does she have a crush on you?'

Luckily Melvyn did not have to gabble an emphatic denial because right then chanting began, and Frida came in, waving a censer from which frankincense poured, followed by the vicar in her purple, gold-edged robes, and a pair of acolytes. The congregation rose.

'Good morning,' said the vicar from the pulpit, with a crazed televangelist smile. 'And welcome to St. Michael's and *All* Angels? I'm the *Reverend* Crystal Nutt? It's my privilege to be your new vicar?' Her smug tone implied that the privilege was the congregation's. She spoke with the ultra-annoying upward lilt of the Valley Girl too.

'And now,' she said with the breathless excitement of a talk-show host, 'I'm going to ask *Doctor* Frida Shamburger to read the lesson for us?' Melvyn almost expected applause.

Frida stamped up to the lectern, a pure, apostolic expression on her face—who was she now, Melvyn wondered?—Joan of Arc in Ingres' portrait? Saint Theresa in Rubens'? She opened the Bible, and began to read the lesson, from Genesis, in flawless Boston Brahmin. A pity they could not have retained the noble English of the King James version, in an Episcopalian church. Instead he had to endure the flat phrases of some dopey modern translation. In a despairing moan, Frida rushed over Eve being created from Adam's rib, clearly to elide the episode, but her face glowed when she read with special emphasis that *both* man and woman had been made in God's own image. Melvyn had forgotten that bit. Her insinuation that God was transgender, or gender-fluid, made half the congregation sigh with delight. Now Melvyn pondered the matter, many of the faithful looked nonbinary themselves.

Still, he speculated, if dudes and chicks were both made in God's image, didn't that indicate that they looked pretty fit? He tried to imagine God as a squat, dumpy woman with sagging breasts. No way! On the other hand, as a supermodel, maybe without the usual sullen pout—hmm, that was *way* better. If God were female, surely she would be slender, like the naked Eves of the Renaissance, or Gisele Bundchen? He pictured a cross between a Brazilian underwear model and Botticelli's Venus. Face of the latter, body of the former. Oh boy oh boy oh boy. He could venerate *that*. Then he realised he was imagining her as white. *Racist!* hissed his inner Frida. Blushing, he remembered Jezebel, who met his gaze as he glanced at her. Hell, her body was spectacular too.

Unfortunately Frida's braying mangled his dreams. Still, his fantasies continued as she spoke. He pictured Eve strolling about in Paradise with a fig-leaf, and coming to the Tree of Knowledge, and the serpent. It reared up, like—let's face it, like an aroused prick, and no wonder, seeing that Eve, who had the figure and face of Jezebel, was on a shoot for the *Sports Illustrated Swimwear* issue. And she was in the raw, butt-naked, oh boy oh boy.

The erect reptile was hissing at her, Just taste this luscious fruit, Miss, just try it, and you shall be like God Himself. (Frida fudged the reflexive pronoun, making it indeterminate.) *Yeah, why not?* Melvyn could see Frida thinking. He read the emotions as they flickered over the screen of her face: anger that it was the woman who fell, sympathetic rebelliousness when she took the fruit, cunning when she offered it to her hapless mate, and indignation and outrage when Adam blamed her for it. But also a kind of perverse pride. After all, Eve *was* the agent of the Fall.

Woman had been far from submissive then! On the other hand, as God booted the couple out of Eden, he cursed Eve. 'To the woman He said, I will greatly multiply your pain in childbirth; in pain you will bring forth children; yet your desire will be for your husband, and he will rule over you.' Frida's knuckles whitened as she grasped the lectern and wailed those words. But her face was as purple as her robe, suffused with blood and resentment, and she ended with: 'And I will put enmity between you and the woman, and between your seed and her seed.' That was a notion Frida could get behind. She was all about enmity between man and woman.

The Revd. Crystal Nutt nodded with the approval of a teacher for a favourite pupil.

'Thank you so much, Dr Shamburger, for that impassioned reading? It was awesome, beyond beautiful? Sisters, and uh, brothers? And other genders, right? You just heard the Holy Writ on the Creation of humankind and the Fall? A neat story, right? But what I have in mind, if you'll indulge me for a while, is something I've been working on for my Doctor of Divinity degree: a feminist interpretation of the Creation story? Yes, you heard me right? The tyrannical patriarchy has misunderstood Genesis, *wilfully* misunderstood it? They emphasise the wrong parts: that God made man first, like that was a huge deal, and that woman was made from his rib, like she was just an afterthought? But think about it, guys?' the Revd. Nutt said, her amplified voice booming, and grinning with the mania of a motivational speaker: 'Adam was napping when God slipped his rib out? What does that mean. Why, the little guy was unconscious, of course, until a woman came along? And if you read without prejudice, Genesis proceeds along those lines? Adam is a dumb, obedient, dim-witted schmuck, you might say, while Eve is the inquisitive one, the intellectually curious one, the courageous one? The snake offers her the fruit of the Tree of Knowledge— and naturally she accepts it? What smart woman wouldn't. Only a man, always willing to submit to a dictator, would be content with his subordinate lot? Just notice: it's Eve who takes the fruit, of her own free will, and Eve who gets Adam to try it too? She's the pro-active one, the leader? What does Adam do. He denies responsibility? *She made me do it*, he says? *And you made her, God?* He's right there?' the Revd. Crystal Nutt said. 'God not only made Eve, but knew she would accept the fruit, and so—if God is omnipotent and wholly good—he or she wanted her to taste it? The prohibition was a trick, to whet her appetite even more? It's clear to me, sisters? Right from the start, God was trying to show us that women are smarter and braver than men? So we should be running things?'

Was the sermon satire? Stand-up? Melvyn glanced around at the congregation: most faces reflected astonishment, although many women, including Frida, were nodding in grave, passionate agreement. Melvyn remembered all the *I'm With Her* stickers during the last presidential election. Shit, even he had had one on his Hummer. What would Jezebel think of all this? She was rubber-necking again—*Ouch, horrible cliché that.* He looked away.

'But the ending's kind of a bummer, right,' said the vicar. 'God curses Eve, sentences her to the eternal tyranny of men? Sheesh. What do we make of that.'

She gloated over her flock. 'I tell you what, sisters? It was a palliative for the guys? Give them the illusion they're in charge, and they'll knuckle under? I gotta tell you, most of them are not so smart? Oh, sure, he or she might have planned a short spell, relatively speaking, of patriarchy? But make no mistake, sisters, she was already planning the matriarchy that would supplant it?'

Melvyn noticed the pronouns metamorphosising, and disquiet on the faces of Cooper and Burd, and derision on Jezebel's, unless that were wishful thinking. Yet also the unmistakable glow of triumph and vindication on Frida's.

'Now let us pray,' the Revd. Crystal Nutt said. 'I invite you to participate in a new, less toxic, less patriarchal version of the Lord's Prayer?. *Our Father* is so sexist, right. So unacceptable? How could we begin our petition instead. Hit me, sisters!'

'Our *Mother*!' yelled Rocky, squirming with excitement in her pew.

'You go, girl!' Frida stage whispered, wriggling too.

The Revd. Crystal Nutt beamed at Rocky. 'Thank you for that suggestion, Dr Rathaus? That's better than 'Father', for sure, but maybe it's like a tad exclusionary. What about our transgender friends. What about our friends who are questioning their gender, or determined to be indeterminate. We don't want to hurt their feelings, do we. I know you all agree with me?' Her face was stern. 'All righty. So I propose that we address our God as… '

'*Our Parent*,' Melvyn murmured audibly. Cooper smirked.

'Our Parent,' the vicar intoned, glaring at Melvyn, 'who art in heaven… '

'Our Parent who art in heaven,' the congregation echoed.

Melvyn wondered if Revd. Nutt would end the prayer with 'Amen'—or would it be 'Awomen', or 'Aparent'? But she stuck with Amen.

Even so, heathen though he was, he stumbled out of the church, as stunned as he would have been had he attended a torchlight Nuremberg Rally in 1936.

Burd cackled: 'Is your head reeling, Melvyn? Are you woke yet?'

He shook his head, nodded, then shook it again. 'I'm speechless.'

'A paradigm shift,' Cooper said. 'Our vicar is reinventing Christianity as a matriarchal cult.'

They had reached the vestibule, where the ritual of devouring chocolate chip cookies and swallowing brown water disguised as coffee took place. Rocky was already bounding like an overfed mastiff at Frida, who strode in with the self-assurance of a bishop, wielding the mace again. Melvyn rushed towards them, determined to reach Frida first.

He failed: Rocky assaulted Frida—that was hardly putting

135

it too strongly—and flung her furry arms around Frida's neck, tears streaming down her muzzle.

'Totally fuckin' *awesome* reading, Frida. Loved it!' Rocky said, swooning. Was she nonbinary? Melvyn wondered. She looked a bit nonbinary. Not butch exactly, but not feminine either. Maybe the new dogmas about gender were catching on because few educated men were masculine these days, and few of the women were feminine. The Revd. Crystal Nutt, who also looked nonbinary to Melvyn, was lolloping towards the two women, or gender-neutral people, and the maelstrom of their hug sucked her in too.

'Oh my gosh I'm sorry,' Rocky said, 'I shouldn't freaking curse like that.'

'That's totally fine?' the Revd. Crystal Nutt said. 'It's just enthusiasm? That means you have God inside you? Yes, she's inside you—inside all of us?'

Rocky wept. Excellent. Melvyn hoped she would forget about splitting on him.

'Your sermon was awesome,' said the poet, 'Beyond awesome. I have no words.'

Thank God for that. And how like her to have no words.

The Revd. Crystal Nutt and Frida wept too, but if Melvyn was not mistaken, at the same time they were squinting at him with condescension, or contempt. No one pulled *him* into the group hug. Why not? What did Genesis say? *Then the* LORD *saw that the wickedness of man was great on the earth, and that every intent of the thoughts of his heart was only evil continually.* Melvyn was pretty sure that meant him.

The three women loosened their grip on each other, but continued to move in a close, hypnotic circle, in a kind of dance. A pavane, perhaps. It was a sculptural composition, something like Rubens' *Three Graces,* indeed—harmonious in emotion, but chunkier than the Flemish painter's nudes. Thank God these modern American graces were draped, at least.

Cooper's eyebrows rose at acute angles; the two men

exchanged a glance of hilarity. Melvyn also intercepted a flirtatious glance from Timothy, which he ignored, and a questioning look—a summons, a call, an offer, an enticement, an invitation? —from Jezebel.

'The Holy Trinity,' said Burd. 'The Mother, the Daughter, the Holy Ghost.'

'Dr Roquette Rathaus is hardly ethereal, if she's the spirit,' Cooper said. 'As for the mother, if that's Frida—the Oedipal mother, Melvyn—beware her teeth.'

Melvyn could not grin back. The joke cut too close to the bone, and besides, Jezebel was within springing distance, her limbs tensed, her tail twitching.

He slipped away and joined her.

'Wow,' she said as he came up to her. 'And I thought the Tocqueville Church of Christ was unhinged. But these Episcopalians are insane. Truly batshit crazy.'

'I couldn't agree more,' Melvyn said.

'Aren't most of these people professors? They look like it.'

He nodded. 'I'm afraid the majority of them abandoned reason long ago.'

'I'm going to have to save you. Let's meet. Very soon.'

Oh boy oh boy. His head jerked in alarm. She took the gesture for assent.

'Great. Where? You weren't at ease at my place. Shall I visit you at yours?'

Are you out of your mind? he was about to say. Then he remembered—Frida would not be at home next weekend. She planned to attend some kind of radical feminist retreat in the mountains. And what's more, Thalia, who was still in high school, was flying to Boston as a birthday present, to stay with her sister, Clio, who was doing a BS in Journalism at Emerson with a Minor in Women's, Gender and Sexuality Studies. Having the house to himself would either be a miracle or the biggest mishap in his life, at least since his wedding.

'Shall I?' Jezebel insisted when he did not reply. 'Would you like me to, sir?'

Frida was approaching, with her deeply spiritual smile. Channelling Joan of Arc or St. Theresa. No immediate danger. Even so, he had to get rid of Jezebel fast.

'Let me think about that,' he said, fleeing.

Whew—not a moment too soon. The purple surplice flapped as it flew towards him. Hot air buffeted the fabric, which billowed about Frida's massive body. The bronze filings on her scalp glittered like a warrior's skull cap. She merely looked annoyed, not enraged.

Ergo, Rocky had kept quiet. He fell to his knees. Frida yanked him up by his elbow.

Thank you God, he mouthed. Good old Rocky had not ratted on him. Maybe she was not a servile shit after all. What was he thinking? Of course she was a servile shit.

'Melvyn, people are staring. Who the hell was that? Haven't I seen her before?'

'Oh her? Just a student,' he said, unaware that his *hamartia* was undoing him.

*

Why did therapists always have abstract prints on the walls? Did they think they calmed their clients? Or was the idea that like Rorschach tests, they would stimulate the imagination, liberate the subconscious? Nah, those tests were garbage anyway. Gauguin was Melvyn's idea of an artist, despite his penchant for young girls. Or because of his penchant for young girls? *If Frida could eavesdrop on my internal monologue, I'd be toast,* he said to himself.

'What do you really want, Melvyn?' Dr Pound was saying. 'That's what I'd like you to articulate. So far all I've heard is a litany of complaint about your wife. That's fine, but if you want to improve your life you have to set some goals. Why don't we work on that now?'

Melvyn regarded Dr Pound with respect, condescension, and consternation. Respect, because she was smart and literate, as she had proven in their counselling sessions; condescension because of her 'motherly' figure, since he could not eradicate his prejudice against overweight people; and consternation, because she had put him on the spot. He knew she was right, but that put the onus on him, and he had been hoping she would tell him what to do. Should he have a fling with Jezebel? That was what he wanted to know. He would never have a better opportunity. Should he leave Frida? He would never have a better opportunity.

'Gosh,' he said, with the smirk he had developed to signal his superior intellect, 'I guess we should start by defining what we mean by goals.'

'No need for that,' Dr Pound said sharply. 'You're smart enough to know what I mean. I'm asking you to state what you want out of life, what you'd like to achieve, what you'd like to do. Just be honest. Are you capable of that?'

'It's not so easy,' he said, eyeing her ginger hair with aversion. 'I mean, emotions are complex. I'm not a fourteen-year-old girl.'

'I see,' said Dr Pound, the blue lasers of her eyes boring into his. 'Yours are far more profound, more mature, and wiser, I imagine?'

Melvyn squirmed in his squeaky leather chair. She reminded him of Frida, that was the trouble, with that flabby figure and ginger hair. Not to mention her bullying tone.

'Well? Let me have it, Melvyn. Just talk. Let it fly.'

'I'd like to delete her. My wife, that is. Like an old, useless file.'

'What a curious way of putting it. Is that just a momentary wish or have you actually contemplated it as an action—by considering ways and means, for example?'

'At times I do feel like throttling her. To stop the ceaseless flow of inanities.'

'How interesting.' Dr Pound appeared to be enjoying herself.

'Anything else? Anything more gratuitous? Any forethought going into these murderous impulses?'

'A couple of times in the kitchen, when I was holding the carving knife, my fingers started tingling. With the impulse to stab her. Just to make a point, haha.'

She did not laugh. 'Was that unprovoked or did she say something to enrage you?'

His admission was unwilling. 'She said something to enrage me.'

'Can you tell me what it was?'

He laughed—*bitterly*, he thought, deploring the cliché. 'Always something belittling. Once she said I was *all right* in bed.'

Dr Pound made short, Frida-like snorting noises. 'Is that so devastating?'

'It was the way she said it. You know, like giving a student a C. Theoretically it means 'average' but everyone knows it's below par. 'All right' sucks, basically.'

Dr Pound sighed. 'So you feel she's not satisfied with you as a lover?'

Melvyn writhed in his chair again. 'How do I know? I guess she might not be.'

'You would like her to say you're fan-fucking-tastic in bed, then?' She was merciless. 'Have you told her *she's* fantastic in bed, Melvyn?'

'*God*, no,' he blurted, laughing. 'Are you crazy?'

'Let's hope not. Why haven't you told her she's great in bed, Melvyn?'

'Because she isn't,' he said, and then it all burst out. 'She's lousy. Just lays there, I mean *lies* there, like a beached whale. All that blubber, and those staring, pond-scum eyes. That red, raspy stubble on her scalp.' He shuddered.

Dr Pound glared at him. 'That's pachyphobia,' she hissed.

'No, Frida's not a Paki. Just an East Boston eyetie.'

'Pachyphobia means fear of overweight people. The last

acceptable prejudice. You despise fat people, don't you, Melvyn? They revolt you. Disgust you. Admit it.'

'No,' he said with all the indignation he could muster. 'That's not true. Like no.'

Dr Pound glanced at an onyx paperweight as if she had an urge to hurl it at him.

'Though I have to admit,' Melvyn went on, 'her fat turns me off. I can't help it.'

Dr Pound turned crimson, which made her hair look orange. 'You don't think your lousy sex life might be partly your fault?'

'Hell no. I never had complaints from anyone before. Jesus, I do what I can. Even with her. Last time we did it she wanted me to use a… a goddamn vibrator while we…'

'While you what, Melvyn? Go on. Are you afraid to say the word?'

Could he say *while we fucked*? No he could not. 'While we um, made love.'

Dr Pound's lips curled. 'I see. And you didn't like that, I take it. Using a vibrator?'

'It grossed me out. I had to use it while we were actually… you know.'

'Screwing? Why did that disgust you? Was it a blow to your amour-propre?'

'Well, I guess it was. I mean, can't she get off without a goddamn gadget?'

Dr Pound's face was as red as Frida's when she was furious. Redder, maybe. 'Tell me, have you ever used Viagra, Melvyn?'

'That's none of your business. Anyway, what's that got to do with anything?'

'You're getting angry. Great, that's the transference. You know what that is?'

He *was* angry. 'Don't patronise me, Dr Pound. I'm not some goddamn redneck.'

'So you know all about the Oedipus Complex? Sure you do.

141

I've read your flash fiction. Did you want to marry your mother, Melvyn? Did you marry her?'

She had him in a corner. 'I guess so. My mom was bossy too. Wish I hadn't.'

'*Have* you ever used Viagra, Melvyn?' She was a relentless interrogator.

Speak calmly. 'Of course I have. How else could I get it up with a goddamn inert whale like that? A skinhead whale with a goddamn ring through her nose like a prize pig.'

'You do hate her, don't you? And you're mixing your metaphors. But my point is this: if you need Viagra to get aroused, why shouldn't she need a vibrator?'

'You got me stumped there. But it's different, somehow.'

'It pisses me off when men are hypocrites like that,' said Dr Pound, glaring at him.

'Surely therapists aren't meant to get angry with clients?'

'We are human, too.'

'That never occurred to me. But it sounds like you're on her side. Are you?'

'No,' she said—lying, he was certain. 'I'm just pointing out inconsistencies. Trying to get you to think clearly and honestly. Let's go on. You'd like to kill her.'

'Only sometimes. Quite seldom, really. I mean, hardly ever. Haha.'

'Well, that's fine and dandy. You only have occasional murderous impulses. I think you'll agree you'd better not give way to them. So what's the alternative?'

'Divorce would be ideal. But I can't. Thalia would go to pieces.'

'Your younger daughter, right. How do you know that?'

'I asked her. She said she'd have a nervous breakdown, her grades would bomb and she'd start cutting herself again or doing heroin. Worse still, she threatened to start praying. To Jesus. God, I just couldn't handle that.'

Dr Pound smiled. 'She's already skilled at manipulating you, isn't she?'

'I resent that. She's a good kid. She adores me.'

'Another Oedipal complex? Or Electra complex?'

Fuck you, Melvyn wanted to say. 'Anyway, think what a nightmare it would be if we got divorced. I'd see Frida in meetings every day. And if I left Oxbow State, what chance would I have of getting another teaching job near here?'

Dr Pound tapped a pencil like a policewoman. 'So what else can you do?'

'I can't think of a goddamn thing.'

'What would you like to do? What do you dream of doing?'

'Getting my own back. Make her pay for all the humiliation I've had to endure.'

'Any ideas? Short of killing or maiming her, I mean.'

A sheepish grin crept across his face. 'Well, there's this girl.'

'Yes?'

'She's after me. I swear. She's the one that's making the moves. Not me.'

'One of your students, Melvyn? You could lose your job.'

'She's not a Creative Writing major. But she is a student at Oxbow State.'

'Really? What's her major?'

'Psychology, actually. Hot damn, I wonder if you know her?'

'She could've interned with me. I better not ask her name. How old is she?'

'Twenty-one, I believe. She's a senior.'

'So what's the problem?'

'What's the problem? You're kidding. She's Clio's age.'

'Is it that you'd feel guilty about betraying Frida? Is that the issue here?'

'Hell no. I'd feel *great* about that. It'd be like winning a Pulitzer. But surely you understand? Wouldn't it be vile to take advantage of such a young girl?'

'Woman,' Dr Pound said.

'Woman. Sorry.'

'We can't have it both ways. Either she's a woman once she's eighteen, as we keep insisting, in which case she's an autonomous adult with a right to her own sex life, or she's a child. At twenty-one. What do you think? Is she a virgin?'

'I doubt it. She says she wants to be a sex therapist.'

Dr Pound gave him a gleeful smile. 'You hit the jackpot, Melvyn. And she is twenty-one. *Way* past the age of consent. Even here in the States.'

'I can't believe my ears. You're telling me to go ahead?'

'I'm just asking you to think clearly. This is a grown woman, who can make decisions about her own sex life. If she wants to have sex with you, and you want to have sex with her, I don't see any impediment, unless you love your wife.'

'I'll be damned. I never expected to hear that from a woman. I told a couple of guys in the dojo,' he said, recalling locker-room talk. 'Of course they just told to bone her.'

'That's not exactly how I would put it,' Dr Pound said with a sly smile.

And yet that was *exactly* what she meant. His therapist was giving him permission to have an affair. In fact she was instructing him to. Practically ordering him to. No doubt about it. Women were a mystery, and no mistake. He found himself laughing, unable to stop. It would be one in the eye for Frida. His joy was so intense, he nearly wet himself. But a doubt struck him: What would the Superior Man do? He would ask the *I Ching*. Then just go with the freaking flow.

ELEVEN

How to be a Badass Woman

For the past half an hour, whenever Huw tiptoed into the bedroom, he had found Miranda standing in front of the tilted cheval mirror, dabbing cosmetics on her face with the passion and perfectionism of Rembrandt working on a self-portrait. Not since a Stones concert they had been to, when she dressed for a fantasy date with Mick, had she taken so much trouble over her appearance. Knowing she would be late for her retreat, Huw tried one more time.

'Nearly ready?' he said.

'No,' she said. 'Go away and don't interrupt.'

Upstairs Owen was playing his drums, or destroying them, so Huw could not write either. Instead, he flipped through the glossy brochure on the table in the kitchen. On the front page, in Gothic lettering was the legend: *The Guild of Goddesses*. There was a coat of arms in comic book style: an escutcheon with the device of a helmeted goddess carrying a spear—Athene, presumably, in a garish coppery colour—supported by a leopard rampant and a lioness rampant. Beneath was a photo of a slim blonde in a pencil skirt with a slit and thigh-high boots with spike heels. Petronella Pikestaff, the caption read. Former model, burlesque artist and nurse. Founder of The Guild of Goddesses. Beside this was a quote from Obadiah: 'Petronella Pikestaff is a badass Southern woman who will transform your life and turn you into the goddess you've always been, deep down inside!'

Inside the brochure were photographs of Petronella being carried onto a stage by muscular black and brown men; of Petronella prancing, the men ranged behind her, dancing; of Petronella with her legs apart, a microphone held suggestively between them, an expression of orgasmic ecstasy on her face.

Huw chuckled. But the picture unsettled him too. What on earth was the purpose of this 'symposium'? Who was it for? A series of bullet points gave him the answers:

For women and woman-identifying persons
Learn the ancient lore of the priestesses of the forests
Become the sassy, badass woman you know you are
Unleash the goddess within
Find the power to demand what you want
Own yourself and the courage of your desire
Free yourself from pain and guilt
Discover your secret strength
Find your Inner Dominator
Learn to love your own unique Beauty

So far, so predictable. The usual self-help recipe of positive reinforcement, unrealistic promises, and compliments. Did anyone buy it?

Apparently so. There were numerous testimonials from Guild Members:

'Petronella is the real deal. She changed my life. I love you, Petronella!'

'A weekend with Petronella left me so pumped I'm ready for anything!'

'I learned to love myself and ask for more—and hell, I got it! Thanks forever, Petronella, Mother Goddess of the Guild! Women's lives will never be the same!'

If Miranda's breakdown had shaken her and left her needing a boost for her self-confidence, the symposium was probably harmless, at least. Or was it? Did he want his wife to become a sassy badass? And what about finding her Inner Dominator? The prospect of a sassy badass Inner Dominator in his life was not enticing. Just then, Miranda came in at last.

She strode into the kitchen as if she were Tinker Quick entering the stage at a stadium and taking possession of the crowd, her face grave, imperious, fully aware how superhuman she looked, her inner goddess unleashed. She was already badass; she had found her Inner Dominator. She fumbled at her side, perhaps for Tinker's riding crop. She looked as though she would like nothing better than to give him a couple of savage lashes across his face.

'You're not pissed off with me, are you, love?' he said, standing.

'For Chrissake, Huw. I'm late. You've got to get me there in half an hour.'

As they had to drive over seventy miles, that was impossible. But he neither told her so, nor pointed out that he had been waiting for two hours. She did look spectacular, he had to admit, even by her standards: the flawless face, as blank as the face of classical statuary; the voluptuous body, sheathed in tight black silk, her legs swishing in black stockings; the black nail-polish, the glittering blood-red lips. Old habits die hard: he reached for her.

'Don't touch me!' she said in chilling tones. 'Never touch me unless I tell you to!'

She's unwell, he told himself, hurt. *Fragile. Give her time. Let her get well again.*

As they walked outside he said, 'I was wondering what this seminar costs?'

'*Symposium*. What does it matter? I'm paying for it.'

'Still,' he said, as they reached the car, 'our finances are in common, aren't they? You often ask what I've paid for things. And sometimes you aren't happy. You've been known to persuade me not to buy something *I* wanted.'

'A thousand dollars. Hurry up and unlock the car, will you?'

He fumbled with the remote key. 'A thousand dollars? For a weekend?'

She seized the door herself, preventing him from opening it for her. 'Yeah, do you have a problem with that? You know how much money I make, right?'

'Quite a bit more than I do,' he said, getting in. 'As you often remind me.'

'Sheesh. Maybe we need to have separate finances. It's my life, Huw.'

And mine, he wanted to say, as he started the engine and drove away. But maybe it was not any longer—maybe he was wrong about that.

'Can't you go faster?' she said. 'We're late. Man, you're like driving at fifty.'

'That *is* the speed limit.'

'So what? Everyone speeds. You're so sensible sometimes, Huw, so goddamn British. So *boring*. No one drives under the limit, except really old people. Old ladies.'

'I do have a son, you know. And I love you. I'd rather not kill you.'

Miranda could not fume: her internal thermostat was set to freezing. Her face was impassive, white as frost.

'Anyways,' she said. 'It's not one weekend. It's two.'

'You mean you won't be home next weekend either?'

'You got it in one, Huw. And next weekend costs another grand.'

He put the Brandenburg Concertos in the stereo. Bach always consoled him.

'I can't stand violins,' she said, ejecting it. 'They're so miserable.'

She put another CD in the slot. Electric guitars, a country beat, a woman with a harsh voice and a Southern accent. It was a putdown song about a guy who didn't have a clue, didn't know where to put his hand, and couldn't even make the singer come. At least that wasn't Huw: he nearly always made Miranda come. All the same, the misandry depressed him. Near the end, the singer told her beau to fuck off.

'Jesus,' said Huw. 'Must we listen to this? You prefer this to Bach?'

'I do, yeah. I think she's great. She's taking control. Empowering herself.'

'Oh, is that what she's doing?' He suspected the singer was a lonely, bitter woman. The photograph on the CD case, of a middle-aged, angry person, confirmed his intuition.

'Just imagine if a man wrote a song about a woman failing to satisfy him sexually,' he said. 'What would women say about that? What would you say?'

'Men write sexist songs all the time. About how hot women look, how great they are in bed.'

'That may be superficial—but it's not exactly negative, is it? In this kind of song, the woman is taking no responsibility for the failure of the relationship. It's entirely the bloke's fault, and purely because he's a dud in bed. Is that fair?'

If Miranda was thinking of an answer, none came. The car climbed into the hills beyond the city. Trailer homes, gas stations, fast food franchises, and clapboard churches with witty homilies in metal letters on their white marquee boards: IF YOUR LIFE STINKS WE HAVE A PEW FOR YOU. BE THANKFUL YOUR (sic) STILL ABOVE GROUND. HOW TO HAVE A BETTER MARRIAGE EVERY THURS EVENING. *Maybe we should go to that one*, Huw thought, musing whether it was only possible to have a good marriage on Thursday evenings. Leaving the outskirts behind, they drove through an ancient forest, along curving roads, climbing then dipping, sheltered by the Roman-esque arches of oaks and elms. Through the trees, he caught glimpses of mountains, round-backed, slumbering dragons. Reminded of the monsters again, he risked another question:

'You've been calmer recently. More stable.'

The country singer still snarled on the stereo. 'Maybe.'

'You haven't mentioned the sea-monsters for a while now.'

'Because I don't want to worry you. They still follow me.'

'Are they following us now?'

She nodded. 'Can't you hear them?'

'I'm afraid not. What are they saying?'

'It's hard to decipher. A lot of it's just noises: hissing and sighing and a kind of scraping sound, like they're scratching at their scales. A sort of swishing too. I think they must be rustling their tails and wings. You must hear that rustling noise.'

'That's the wind in the trees, Miranda. It's blowing hard.'

'No, it's the sea-monsters. They're skittering right along beside us.'

'And why do you think that is, Miranda?'

'It's obvious, isn't it? They have messages for me.'

'Can you understand what they're telling you?'

'Sure I can.'

'Will you tell me?'

'You won't like it.'

'Tell me anyway. I can take it.'

'I doubt it. They say I need to be on my own more. Maybe find my own apartment.'

He bit his trembling lip. 'Are you sure of that, Miranda?'

'It's a little indistinct, with the hissing and swishing, and the sound of the waves. And their voices are low. They croon, you know? Kind of like Frank Sinatra.'

'The sea-monsters sing like Frank Sinatra?'

'Something like that. Sorry. I know it must upset you.'

'Are you leaving me, Miranda? Are you telling me we're finished?'

'Oh no. I want us to stay together. I just need to be on my own for a while.'

'So you aren't divorcing me?'

She shook her head without looking at him.

'It does upset me,' he said. 'I'll be sad if we aren't living together anymore. I think Owen will find it a shock too. But what about you? Won't you be upset at all?'

'I might be, a bit. But it's what I need. And you can always visit me.'

'Great. Is this going to be temporary or permanent?'

'I don't know. Don't pressure me. You're always pressuring me.'

'I'm sorry. I try not to. So when might this happen?'

'See? Pressure, pressure. The sea-monsters advise the end of this month.'

'That's only ten days from now. Could you find a place that quickly?'

The angry, weary voice still sang. 'I already found one.'

'A done deal, then? Ten days. If you're spending next weekend at the retreat too, we won't even have a last weekend together. You do move fast.'

'Don't be snarky with me, Huw. That's why I got to move out, see?'

'Where is it then? The apartment?'

'A condominium. Just off Buzz Aldrin.'

'A long way. I can't walk there.'

'It's five minutes in the car. And no one walks anyhow.'

They drove on in silence, apart from the rising wail of the wind. For Miranda, doubtless, the hullaballoo persisted: the crooning voices, telling her things she wished to hear, and those hissing, swishing, scratching, flapping noises—what were they, the whisperings of her conscience? Or subconscious? Thank God she could not see her sea-monsters. But Huw fancied he saw swift shadows flitting beside them and above them, like immense clouds.

The mansion was a neo-Gothic extravaganza with towers and battlements and uplifting signs as they approached—BADASS WOMEN THIS WAY—YOUR TEMPLE, YOUR LIFE—PETRONELLA PIKESTAFF WELCOMES GORGEOUS GODDESSES TO THE PANTHEON—WOMEN WITH BALLS—DO WHAT YOU WILL—JUST ASK—YOU ARE HOLY! Huw sat in the car park, watching her legs snipping together like black scissors as she walked into the building, carrying a weekend bag. He could not face driving home yet.

He ejected the CD, got out of the car, and dropped the country singer into a trash bin. Then he walked towards the house, drawn by its weird architecture, and curiosity. He hoped Ms. Pikestaff would not implant men-hating ideas in Miranda's impressionable mind. As he approached the entrance, a woman came out to meet him. She was tall and statuesque, wearing a close-fitting grey dress, and glasses. She looked familiar. Had he seen her at the Savanna B. Manley reading, talking to Melvyn? In fact, hadn't he seen her coming out of Melvyn's office more than once lately? She was imposing, self-possessed for someone her age. Unsmiling, though—almost intimidating.

'Professor Lloyd-Jones,' she said, extending her hand as an older woman might. 'We haven't met but I know you from Oxbow State. I'm a student. My name is Jezebel. I've just welcomed your wife to the symposium. Are you a participant too? Do you identify as a woman? That was a joke,' she said, deadpan. 'I don't imagine you're one of Deli—I mean Petronella's dancers? You look fit and handsome enough to be one. But she prefers African-Americans or Latinos. My sister might be a little racially prejudiced, between ourselves.'

'Petronella is your sister, then, I take it?'

'Yes, my older sister. I'm here to facilitate the sessions and make a little pocket money. May I ask what you're doing—if you're not taking part?'

'Just dropping off my wife. I wonder what she will experience, what she hopes to find here. I don't know much about feminist retreats and life coaching. Is it terribly exciting?'

'It is for most of the women. Of course they aren't very smart. Oh, sorry. There may be exceptions. I find it all a bit silly, to be frank. I've seen it so many times now. But it makes them happy, and my sister's getting rich.'

'I like your directness. May I make a rather cheeky request? Could I watch the seminar for a while?'

'Not in the audience. It they discovered a male intruder, I dread to think what they might do. We have a security team, as well.'

'But the security team must be men, I suppose?'

'Yes and no. That is, it depends what you mean by 'men.' They *used to be* guys, but now they're transgender women. From Texas. Trans Bikers for Christ, they call themselves.'

'The mind boggles. Trans Bikers for Christ? From *Texas*?'

'Austin, obviously.' She gave him a wintry smile. 'Anyway—how could we pull this off? It might be fun. Do you mind taking a bit of a risk?'

'I'll take my chances with the transgender Christian bikers.'

'You wait till you see them—many of them are weightlifters. Real muscle men. I mean women, of course.' She flashed a brief Goneril-like smile.

He smiled back. 'Let's do it.'

'In case we meet any security women, do you mind wearing a disguise?'

'What kind? Would I have to dress up in drag?'

'No, just as a waiter. Petronella likes to have the ladies served by men. A reversal of the usual hierarchy, you see. Come along, this way. You can change here.'

She led him into a cloakroom, and instead of leaving, turned her back while he donned black trousers, a bowtie, and a white jacket.

'How do I look?' he said when he was ready. 'Do I pass muster?'

'You look Italian. Like Marcello Mastroianni in *La Dolce Vita*. Suave but also vulnerable. Perfect. Quick, this way. Your wife was late—they're already starting.'

He followed her down wainscoted corridors, through a room with hammer-beam vaulting and stuffed elk heads. Thickets of antlers. Loud thumping music was playing, with singing and rapping in Spanish.

'What on earth is that?' Huw asked.

'Reggaeton, to warm up the goddesses. Do you like it? Of course not.'

Jezebel opened a door and Huw found himself on a kind of gallery with her, overlooking what must once have been a ballroom, with a stage erected at one end, and rows of seats facing it. The seats were full, but he located Miranda, who was gazing expectantly at the stage. Not far from her were a number of Oxbow State students and faculty: Broome, Jordan and Nutmeg, as well as a transgender professor of Queer Studies called Marge, Rocky Rathaus, and Frida Shamburger, who was dressed like Toni Morrison, which is to say like the Queen at a State occasion, but with less taste, in a full-length ballgown, with a fur stole (could it be real?), a string of pearls, and a tiara. Had she concealed her full-sleeve tattoos, her buzzcut and nose-ring, she might have looked elegant. Well, maybe not, given her Hogarthian dimensions. She was talking to, or shouting at—the brazen blare was audible even above the nightclub beat—a massive woman with a butch haircut and clerical collar.

'Where exactly are we?' he asked. 'With these curtains we're nearly invisible.'

'I believe this was the musicians' gallery. This place was built for Xenophon Fullerton, the magnate who owned the mines. Convenient, sir, isn't it?'

Before he could answer, the music rose in volume. The bass and kick drum thwacked his chest, in a monotonous rhythm. The lights dimmed. A skirling of bagpipes began, and all the women leapt to their feet, shrieking, screaming, and howling.

Six dusky men came cavorting onto the stage, in skin-tight black singlets and leggings. The audience clapped. Miranda looked excited. The dancers darted offstage and returned, carrying a prostrate woman above their heads. They set her down on her feet and knelt before her, and the ovation reached a crescendo. 'Your Mother Goddess, Petronella Pikestaff!' boomed a deep DJ voice offstage. A single spot-light fell on her.

She wore a bolero jacket, a blouse with a pirate's ruff, over-the-knee boots, and a skirt so short that a broad band of stockinged thigh was visible. Her hair was a mass of gold curls. She was at least six feet tall.

'Impressed?' Jezebel shouted in Huw's ear.

He nodded. She stood unmoving in the centre of the stage, her legs wide apart, arms akimbo, smiling as the men made their obeisance, bending their powerful torsos before her, raising their arms. She surveyed the audience with the gaze of an empress. Then she flexed and cracked and struck, this way, that way, quick as a whip, sharp as a snake. The dancers leapt to their feet and capered behind her. The upturned female faces of the audience showed rapture—like Jordan, Nutmeg, and Rocky—or the transport of holy awe, like Frida, the female priest, and Miranda. They all swayed in rhythm. Shyly, joyfully they glanced at one another. Nutmeg grinned at Miranda, who smiled back.

The song, if it could be called that, must have gone on for ten minutes, though to Huw it felt far longer. The beat and the bass never faltered and nor did the dancing. Petronella had the poise and skill of a professional dancer—no, more, she led her troupe, and yet outshone them. She was better than a Bollywood star, slinkier than Tinker Quick. When the music halted, an acolyte handed her a cordless microphone, she made a Valkyrie screech, and the women whooped back.

'You're goddesses!' she yelled, her voice harsh. 'I love you all!'

Surely some of the women must storm out in disgust? Huw hoped Miranda would. But none did. Their gaze was reverent. Didn't they hear the insincerity in Petronella's voice?

'That was amazing, huh?' she bawled. 'Was it fun for you?'

The squeals and barks of the crowd were those of sea-lions showered with fish in an aquarium. Jezebel shot a sardonic glance at Huw. Beneath the epidermis of her dress, her body was taut, and yet her corporeality was the least essential part of her. Her mind informed her whole life—her clear, cold eyes showed him that. But what kind of mind was it?

Onstage, Petronella pranced and grinned. 'See, dancing releases nitric oxide in your blood. And pheromones. So you feel awesome—and *sexy*. Right? Who's feeling *hot?* Don't be shy, ladies. Come on, who's feeling *foxy?* I sure am.'

Arms went up: Rocky's, and Nutmeg's. The vicar's. Not Miranda's, thank goodness.

'Only about a third of you. That'll change, I promise ya. Trouble is, sisters, we're taught to *not* feel sexy, right? Didn't your momma teach you to be a *good* girl?'

Miranda nodded. 'And where'd that get ya? They praised you for ignoring your body, right? They praised you for being quiet, for accepting, doing what you're told. We gotta change that. We're not going to do what they tell us anymore. We're gonna do what *we* wanna do. We're gonna ask for what we want. *Demand* what we want. How about that?'

The barks and squeals of the sea-lion colony resounded.

'Beautiful, beautiful,' Petronella warbled. 'You can be sassy, see? You're all badass women, I can tell.' More squeals, yips and shouts. 'You're all goddesses. You're mistresses of your fate. Yeah, you are.' Was Miranda a goddess? Bodily, absolutely. Intellectually—she was bright, if a bit cracked, a bit potty. But was she in command of her emotions? Was there a spirit inside that perfect sculpture of flesh? She lacked the self-possession and serenity of Praxiteles' Aphrodite—but so did all these women. The essence had been left out. It was not so much that they were broken, as the old Emo song wailed, but incomplete. Despite her charisma, Huw thought, that went for Petronella too. Jezebel had a stillness and a spark—but she was an Artemis, a huntress, pitiless and cold. Welsh women often had that spark and fullness, and warmth too. So did South Americans. Unbidden, he recalled the Persian doctor in the hospital. She had that divine spirit also. But he forbade himself to think about her. Miranda was slipping away. If he wanted to keep her, he had to understand her. And change.

Petronella was summoning women to the stage, to declare something they wanted for themselves. The first was a mousey woman with poorly-cut hair and shapeless clothes who might have been a librarian.

'I wanna be a writer,' she said softly. 'I wanna be a legend.'

'Beautiful,' Petronella said. 'Put your hands together for her. What's your name, sister?'

'Delia.'

'Delia, fantastic, awesome. And what kind of writer do you wanna be?'

'A fantasy novelist. I've just been accepted on the MFA Program at Oxbow State.'

Frida and Rocky whooped frantically; Jordan, Nutmeg, and others joined in.

'That is so coo-ul. Wicked, awesome. I'm proud of you, sister Delia.'

Delia got an ovation as she strode off the stage—standing straighter than she had, and beaming like an actress on the red carpet.

Next Petronella pointed at Miranda, summoning her with a wave. Miranda shook her head. Petronella's hands flew to her hips, with a teasing smile. Nutmeg and Jordan pulled Miranda out of her seat. Everyone clapped.

When Miranda reached the stage, Petronella towered over her. 'My, you are *gor*geous,' Petronella said. Her voice had a hawkish, predatory edge to it.

'What's your name, darling?'

Her voice was tiny: 'Miranda.'

'Great, like Carmen Miranda, right? And what do you want, honey?'

A little louder now: 'I want to go to Mexico.'

'Tell us why, will ya?'

'I'm inspired by Frida Kahlo.'

'Woohoo!' shouted Frida.

'Sure, why is that, sugar?' Petronella said.

'Because she was strong. Fierce. She lived the way she wanted. She didn't even live with her husband—she just visited when *she* had the urge, when she wanted sex. And she didn't let her suffering define her. She transformed it into something beautiful, mythical.'

Petronella turned to the audience with the expression of theatrical wonderment that talk-show hosts like Obadiah and Elsa used to engage the crowd.

'Hey, this chick is the business, right? Strong, fierce—you hear that, sister goddesses? I see that strength, that fierceness in you, Miranda. Right, ladies?'

There was a howl and a roar. Huw noticed that like Delia's, Miranda's posture was already more confident—shoulders back, head held high.

'So tell me, babe, you gonna do it? You gonna make your dream come true?'

Miranda nodded with pride. 'I've bought the ticket already.' This was news to Huw.

'Woohoo!' yelled Frida. 'You go, girl!'

'You going alone?' Petronella asked Miranda.

'No, with friends. My husband didn't want to come.'

'Terrific, terrific. What do we need men for, sisters?'

'Nothing!' the gigantic vicar bellowed. A lot of women laughed.

'That's right,' Petronella said. 'I know some of you are into men. And that's okay. But you don't *need* 'em. Right? They need *us*, right? And we gotta teach 'em that—all of us goddesses. Show 'em who's boss. Right, ladies?'

Frida Shamburger roared. So did many others. From the podium Petronella produced a bullwhip, and handed it to Miranda.

'Take it, it won't bite you, honey.'

Don't take it, Huw pleaded. Miranda accepted it shyly.

'Crack it, sugar. Show him. Show us.'

'Sick,' Huw said.

'Oh, are you're into that?' Jezebel said. 'The kinky stuff?'

'Actually I meant the word in the archaic sense. Perverted. Depraved. Warped.'

Miranda's arm rose, hesitantly: then flashed out. The whip cracked.

Everyone screamed. Miranda walked offstage, clutching the whip, to another ovation, beaming as Delia had. Childish and absurd though it was, apparently the course worked. Huw wondered if he had never noticed a part of Miranda. He had considered himself a model husband. But what if he had not responded to all her needs? What if he had not nurtured her deepest desires? What if he had failed to draw her out, to listen to her when she spoke?

He spent another couple of hours in the gallery, in fascinated horror. More women came onto the stage and gave their testimonials. Then there was a period of 'quaking': women testified to their pain, howling and wailing while Petronella cradled them. Then more reggaeton, Daddy Yankee and Maluma, with wild dancing. When Petronella asked the audience who felt foxy again, almost all the hands shot up. Including Miranda's. She had been dancing with Jordan and Nutmeg, and exchanging smouldering glares with them. In the last session before lunch, a pompous-looking white man came on stage and sat behind a desk. He was middle-aged and bald, a portly figure in a business suit and tie.

One by one, women mounted the stage and asked him for things they wanted. To begin with all were hesitant. Petronella had to goad some into asking. Their initial demands were modest:

a kitten, a box of chocolates, a bunch of flowers. He shook his head irritably at each one. The women started laughing. Since he refused all their requests, it freed them to ask for more. One wanted a Porsche, another a black man with a huge dick. Many cheers. One shouted that she wanted multiple orgasms every single night. More cheers and whoops. The aspiring fantasy novelist wanted to be loved. The vicar asked to be an archbishop. Broome requested celebrity. Jordan asked if she could have a baby with Nutmeg. Nutmeg asked if she could be polyamorous. Rocky asked if she could be a full professor. Frida demanded the Pulitzer Prize—no, the Booker—no, the goddamn Nobel Prize. Miranda begged to see her sea-monsters. Then she asked if she could make another request. Petronella nodded. *I want my husband to see me as I am. Let me live my way. Can you do that for me?*

The man in the suit shook his head, without feeling. Was that how Miranda saw him, Huw, as a pompous old guy, denying her nature, scotching her desires and aspirations?

All at once he found the event unbearable. 'Thank you very much,' he said.

'Are you OK?' Jezebel said. 'You look shaken.'

'I am, but I'll be fine. I appreciate your kindness.'

They walked in silence through the halls with the elk trophies, until they reached the main doors, where Jezebel said:

'I'm delighted to have met you. I wonder if you'd be willing to help me with some research I'm doing for the Honours College? I'm going to be a therapist, you see.'

He nodded, too upset by it all to ask her what kind of therapist she wanted to be.

TWELVE

The Opportunity Must Be Seized

When Melvyn consulted the *I Ching*, he got the third trigram, Resolving Chaos, with a moving fourth line. The oracle proclaimed: *The opportunity must be seized. Don't allow false pride or false inhibition to hold you back.* Did those oriental sages nail it or what?

So he invited Jezebel to the campus Sundoes, bought her a cup of sludge, and mentioned in passing that the following weekend, his wife and daughter would both be away. Jezebel did not take the hint. How could he nudge her, subtly?

'I may get a tad lonely, all by myself. All weekend. Alone.'

Tinker Quick was squeaking about her useless boyfriends on the sound system. Students eyed Melvyn and Jezebel with the curiosity of paparazzi.

'Unless you'd maybe like to keep me company,' he murmured. 'Would you?'

Her answer was startlingly loud. 'I want to make sure I understand. Are you suggesting that I come over to your place and copulate with you, sir?'

Heads turned. Someone took a photo with a phone, he was pretty sure. 'Of course not! Please speak quietly.' In a nearly inaudible whisper, he added: 'I was thinking along more romantic lines, but now you mention it, haha, sure, sex is good too.'

She gave him a clinical look. 'I'll see what I can do, sir.'

'So you'll pass by—Saturday? For um... lunch?'

'I'm busy Saturday. Maybe Sunday? If I can.'

Slack-jawed students gaped after her as she strutted out.

*

Melvyn was on tenterhooks that Sunday morning. He had bathed in Thalia's bubble bath—soaking in the tub, which he had not done for years—shaved with a real razor, and drenched his chin and cheeks with cologne. The house was clean by Shamburger standards, which were far from exiguous, but little could be done about Frida's pagodas of papers and books, rising from tables, desks, floors, and any other vacant surfaces. Melvyn had bought and lit aromatic candles. Norah Jones sang seductively on the stereo. His most daring move had been to defer dressing: instead of his usual professor clothes, he wore only a white towelling robe, and a pair of Aladdin-like red leather slippers. Dr Pound had licensed him to be wicked. But would Jezebel appear? Had her reticence been a deliberate strategy, to keep him in suspense? A bit of sexy teasing? Or might she simply have lost interest in him?

Melvyn prowled around the house, watched curiously by Darcy and indifferently, or scornfully, by Garfield, the corpulent marmalade cat. For once Melvyn did not open his email. Nor did he enter Facebook, where he would see constant updates from Frida, gushing about the powerful, beautiful young women at the symposium, with photos of her glowing like a red traffic light beside other women, all wearing triumphant smiles. Perhaps one of a margarita or a plate of sushi. He turned off his cell phone. It would infuriate Frida if she texted him and he failed to answer, but fuck her. He had withheld the number from Jezebel too, like obvs. So the question was, what could he do until she arrived—if she did?

He was way too excited to write, or even read. What would the Superior Man do? A spot of Tai Chi? He did a sequence, but could not concentrate, and kept forgetting the next pose. He sat on his zafu cushion to meditate. All he could think of were his bare legs, which were muscular and manly, embroidered with a dense, curly mat of dark hair. At their apex was the tabernacle, the holy of holies, the secret, venerable organ, dangling in a state of readiness—a dangerous, mysterious demi-urge. Would it behave? He had his anxieties on that score. He hoped it would spring into action at the first whiff of hand-to-hand combat. As it reposed on the pillow of his balls, he felt its weight: yes, it was satisfyingly, inordinately, unwontedly large. He flipped back the dressing gown to have a peep. Yep, no question, it was a solid-looking member, a veritable African python, thick, long, sinewy, magnificent. It had been such a stalwart, faithful friend. *Where would I be without you, old buddy?* He flicked the sacred serpent back and forth, a contented smile on his face.

And yet his worries interrupted his musings. What time was it? Would the neighbours see her arriving, if she came? They were a nosey bunch, seldom far from the folds of their curtains. And if they observed Jezebel's arrival, would they report to Frida? They ought to have arranged to meet in a motel. No, that would have been beyond sordid. He was not *positive* that Jezebel intended to have sex with him. Bullshit, of course he was. But what if there were some emergency? What if Thalia had one of her panic attacks, and needed to fly home? If she called in desperation and he did not answer? Above all, should he pop a Viagra? No, relax, the python said. It was eleven o'clock, then twelve, twelve-thirty, one. The candles burned low. Norah Jones kept singing. He was getting hungry. Damn her, she wasn't coming.

But just when he was about to give up, there was a timid

knock on the door, not preceded by the whoosh of an automobile engine, or the slamming of a car door.

Melvyn arose from his zafu cushion and slithered over the carpet, watched sceptically by Garfield. Checking quickly that the serpent was concealed behind a flap of the bathrobe, and taking a deep yogi breath, he seized the door handle.

As he opened the door he realised he had forgotten to prepare any lunch.

But there was Jezebel, with her impassive, sculptural face, half-hidden by glasses, wearing the Grecian dress she had worn to receive him at the desolate McMansion, and bearing gifts: some sort of meal, by the look of the Styrofoam boxes, and a bottle of sixteen-year-old single malt Scotch, which she thrust at him.

'Come in,' he said, ushering her inside, and scanning the neighbours' windows for white faces or moving curtains. Nothing he could see, thank God. 'Where's your car?'

'Around the corner. I didn't want to attract attention.'

'You *are* smart.'

'Thank you, sir. I'm flattered by the bathrobe. How thoughtful and sexy.'

'You don't think it's overdone? It's not exactly subtle, is it?'

'Who wants subtlety? You're being confident and masterful. I find that thrilling.'

Melvyn had imagined their passion overtaking them. In his fantasies, he had thrown off his robe, or she tore it off his body, while she flung off her own clothes, and quickly they were fused on the floor. But they had not so much as touched one another. He had forgotten the etiquette, the ritual. *I must be patient*, he thought.

'You've brought a meal,' he said. 'I forgot to get one. Thanks so much.'

'It's Italian. *Pollo a la cacciatore*. Do you like Italian food?'

'Like it? I love it: I am Italian-American, you know. I'll open a bottle of wine.'

He swept three or four towers of Frida's books off the table on to the floor.

'No need to do that, sir,' Jezebel protested, 'you may damage them.'

'It's only my wife's creative writing pedagogy,' Melvyn said, with visceral hatred. 'Some of it written by her. Vacuous baloney. I think I'll set fire to them, actually.'

While Norah Jones warbled, he microwaved the meal, and they drank a plummy Montepulciano. The wine helped him relax. Jezebel nodded with what he took to be philosophical approval as he put the books in the fireplace, and set them alight, which was harder than he expected. The flames only burned the covers and blackened the edges. Obliterating Frida's name felt great, though. As they ate, apropos of nothing, Jezebel said:

'Do you appreciate lingerie, sir?'

'Depends what kind,' he said, recalling Frida's drawers, capacious enough for the hindquarters of a carthorse, and the massive contraption meant to check the uncontrolled swinging of her pectoral appendages. How she managed to funnel all that flesh into those 'cups'—buckets would be a more accurate word—was a puzzle. How did she strap it all together? Frida in her underwear was not a pretty sight.

'You might appreciate this kind, sir,' Jezebel said, lowering her décolleté and giving him the briefest glimpse of a boldly-cut, black lace push-up bra.

'Oh boy oh boy oh boy. God yes. May I see more?'

'Soon,' she said, a drop of red wine on her chin. He ventured to lick it off. 'We don't want to rush things. What about this?' She sat sideways, raised the hem of her long dress with tantalising slowness, until he saw stocking-tops and suspenders, then covered up.

'You are a major genius. Um, would you like to see my bedroom now?'

'Yes, I think that would be appropriate, sir. Let's have a glass of Scotch first.'

'Aren't you afraid you might lose control of yourself?'

'Oh yes, sir. That's precisely what I'm afraid of. Make it a large one, please.'

The whisky was rich, complex, and peaty, with caramel tones. Melvyn flushed as he drank with her. They ascended the stairs, Melvyn kicking piles of Frida's papers out of the way, and found themselves in the bedroom, where Jezebel's Grecian robe dissolved at his touch, magically, leaving her Nike-like body resplendent in the lingerie—black bra, stockings and suspenders, and a suggestion of a V-string. Melvyn's own bathrobe fell open. Jezebel's astonishment at the sight and touch of the python was a connoisseur's, not a virgin's.

She spoke in awe. 'How huge, how… swarthy. This is a black man's penis, sir.'

Melvyn took that as an entirely non-racist compliment. 'Gee, thanks.'

No need for Viagra with a nubile woman, it struck him. He was virile, manly, *huge*. He was a man of the jungle. They crashed down together, scaring off the curious Darcy, and *desecrating* the connubial bed—what a delightful word. Their coupling was athletic, aerobic, a middle-distance run, ending in a sprint neck and neck to the finish. Hardly spiritual, but one hell of a blast. Boy oh boy oh boy, Melvyn had not had such an awesome time in years.

'You're a fantastic lover, sir,' she said as they lay together afterwards. She still had her stockings on. 'Sensuous, but brutal. The perfect combination in my opinion.'

If only Frida could have heard that! Melvyn's pride in himself mushroomed; he grew; he glowed. *And* she believed him to be brilliant!

No one had ever spoken to him like *that* before. 'Do continue,' he said.

'Yes, precisely. Do let's continue. I see you are ready. If you would like to, that is.'

'I sure would,' he said, clambering on top of her again. 'I'm even beginning to enjoy you calling me sir.'

'I'm glad, sir.' But somewhere under her dress on the floor, her phone rang. 'I'm afraid I need to take that call, sir,' she said, pushing him off. 'Please excuse me.'

Well, I'll be darned, Melvyn thought, as she snatched up her bra and dress and left the bedroom, whispering into her phone. What the heck could be so urgent?

He fancied he heard her pronounce the fricative F—maybe Frank?

Surely not. Could anyone take precedence over him, the brilliant writer with the black man's penis, the sensuous but brutal lover? The hell they could! He would show her. He would be masterful again, snatch the phone from her, hurl it away, drag her back to the bed and ravish her. She would enjoy that. But by the time he got down the stairs, she had her ballet flats on and was slipping out of the front door.

'Sorry, sir, I must go. I can't explain now. Thank you, it was beyond my dreams.'

The girl was kind of a nut. Still, he had got his revenge on Frida. No one could take that away from him. What a chick. He hummed the Ode to Joy as he showered. He was *way* too happy to think about tidying up before Frida came home. Unfortunately for him.

THIRTEEN

A Germ of an Idea

A stained glass Tree of Life, a vintage reproduction of the Tiffany original, hung in a window in Huw's study. Behind a slender golden trunk in the centre of the panel were hills, a lake, and a river zigzagging towards the tree. Foliage and flowers filled the lower foreground. In the upper limbs of the tree hung red and orange fruits and purple blooms. Branches trifurcated from the trunk and spread in an orderly tangle, like a Celtic knot, reaching upwards, towards the fruit, the foliage, and the flowers. Gazing at this glowing panel as he wrote, Huw was inside the sap of the tree, his spirit rising, racing through leaves and twigs and petals, into the hearts of those fruits. He was surging, humming, spinning. One with life.

You may imagine he was in ecstasy, filled with mystic joy. Sometimes he was. But not today. Sadness abides in the core of life, in the heart of the oak and the orange tree, in the capillaries of the leaves, in the stamens and pistils of the blooms, in the probing roots, in the deep, dark earth where the worms toil and burrow. Joy animates every fibre, but it is fleeting. The tree carries the knowledge of its own decay and demise. Even at its zenith, in that crown of leaves burnished by the hot liquid light of the sun, it feels the creeping of the rot—so distant and slow that it could surely never reach these heights—and yet it can and it must.

Every evening for the past fortnight Miranda had come home late, often in the small hours. All day, every day, Huw dreaded her planned departure for her own flat. Still, he hoped to persuade her to change her mind. If he could just reassure her that he would give her space, respect her desire for independence, let her 'find herself,' wouldn't she stay with him?

The day before she was due to leave, she came home from work early and agreed to take a short hike with him. 'Isn't this beautiful?' he said on the overgrown trail in the mountains. Now and then he had to use a stick to part the undergrowth.

Miranda kept her eyes on the ground. 'I'm afraid of the snakes,' she said.

'You never used to be. If there are any, they're sure to feel us coming.'

'I'm not so sure. I'm so frigging scared.'

'Just tramp heavily. Like this. They can feel the vibrations.'

He demonstrated but she did not follow his example. 'There might be bears.'

'I haven't seen any signs. And if there are bears, they'll only be black ones. They're just like big dogs. You wave your arms and shout and they go away.'

'If you haven't gotten between them and their cubs.' She stopped dead.

'Come on, Miranda. We've only been walking ten minutes.'

'I can't go on, Huw.'

'You want to go back already?'

Tears glittered in her eyes. She nodded. He sighed. 'Well, come on, then.'

'I can't walk back through that undergrowth. It's infested with snakes.'

'I'm sure it's not. But what are we going to do, then? Stay here?'

'Could you carry me?'

'If you really can't do it, of course I could.' He tried to hug her, but she was stiff as a statue. He picked her up easily—she weighed a hundred and ten pounds.

When they reached the car at the trailhead, he set her down. She was panting.

'All right now?' he said.

She shook her head as children do.

'What's going on? I haven't spoken to you all this week. I don't like that.'

'Don't be so demanding, Huw. I told you I need some me time right now.'

'I understand that. But there's so much me time. I hope we still have a marriage.'

'Of course we do.'

'Even though you're moving out?' She didn't answer. 'And you're spending so much time with the McBanes, too. Is that helping?'

'I guess. Although they can be a tad weird.'

'I've noticed. But how do you mean?'

'You know Matthew's OCD, right? I think he's gotten a bit obsessed with me.'

'Go on,' Huw said grimly.

'He's asked me to tell him each month when I get my period. He insists.'

'What did you say?'

'He's afraid I might get pregnant. He doesn't want that.'

'What's it got to do with him?'

'Well, he's afraid he'll impregnate me.'

'Jesus Christ. Are you sleeping with him, then?'

'Of course not. I think I'd remember if I was.'

'Are you sure?' She was so heavily medicated, he wondered if she would.

'Sure I'm sure. He's a marshmallow man. Physically repulsive.'

'But if there's nothing between you, how could he get you pregnant?'

'He believes he has the power to impregnate me by looking at me.'

Huw had to let that sink in. 'Christ, he's off his head.'

'He's convinced that if he covets me lustfully, I could conceive his child.'

'An immaculate conception? What exactly do you do with those loonies?'

'Talk, eat. Drink.'

'You're not supposed to drink at all because of all the meds you're taking.'

'I know. But Matthew is a doctor. He won't let me do anything dangerous.'

'You're so naive. *He* is dangerous. They're both dangerous. They're scheming.'

'What do you mean, scheming?'

'My guess is that they want to have a threesome with you. I saw how NeAmber ogled you. They're taking advantage of your illness, Miranda.'

'That's a horrible thing to say. But I guess it could be true. They have been kind of creeping me out lately…'

'Really? Then surely you aren't still planning to go to Mexico with them?'

'I have to. I have to see Chichen Itza. Frida's paintings. It's important to me.'

'You don't have to go with them. I'll go with you—as long as they don't come.'

'It's too late. We have the tickets.'

He could not say he knew that already. 'You've actually bought the tickets?'

'We're going at the start of May. You couldn't go then anyways, because of the university exams.'

'Couldn't you change your ticket? I'm afraid you're falling

into their power. And drifting away from me. I feel I'm losing you. I love you, Miranda.'

'I love you too,' she said—glibly, the way children say it when pressed.

'Really?' She nodded, faraway. 'And you'll stay with me?'

'As long as you make me happy.'

'Of course. So long as I make you happy. As you told me a few weeks ago.'

Now, in spite of his anguish, as he sat beneath his Tree of Life, words poured from Huw's pen. His ancestors murmured in his ear: all he had to do was listen. More medium than poet, he wrote, and what he wrote was good. Even so, he shared the knowledge of the tree. Sorrow accompanied the incantation, like the strains of the Bach B Minor Mass. Grief informed the myths of the Mabinogion, even as they blossomed and bloomed and formed wreaths, bright and quick and playful. He was in peril of losing her—and his own life.

That was his secret knowledge, as he composed on the beautiful, bleak morning after Miranda had gone. He had to finish the book and provide for Owen's future. Last night Miranda's brother had come to fetch her. She had taken little: her clothes, her profusion of shoes, a few books and pictures. Miranda's brother was a big man with red hair who so exactly matched a second century statue of a Roman soldier in the Uffizi that he could have been the model. He had said unkind things about Huw which Miranda had reported to her husband. Huw had wondered if he would have to fight him. If the red-haired Roman insulted him, he would punch him, even if it meant a humiliating defeat. Luckily no violence was offered. Huw did not plead with Miranda to stay, so there was no ground for conflict. Brad averted his eyes from Huw's, embarrassed to be there. He hefted the heavy suitcases like playthings. Huw did not offer to help. She was dry-eyed, lifeless as the doll in *The Sandman*. Had Huw fallen in love with an automaton? If so, who was her Coppelius?

Who had created this beautiful automaton? Her mother, her father? The McBanes? Might it be Huw himself?

On the lawn a cardinal pecked at something, and a blue jay bullied the crimson bird out of the way. Huw had left his study door open. Owen paused in the doorframe on his way downstairs, either not noticing the tears on his father's face or not remarking on them out of embarrassment. Indeed, what he said was probably a tactful attempt to distract him.

'Hey, I saw that skinny dude you work with the other day. The one with the punky, chunky wife.'

Punky, chunky. Huw gave Owen a feeble smile. 'Melvyn. Was he with Frida?'

'No, some chick. Quite a hot one.'

'A chick? Melvyn? Are you certain?'

'Dude was in Sundoes with her, near my school. They looked intimate.'

'Really?' That did not sound like Melvyn, but right now Huw could not think about him. He could think of nothing but Miranda's departure.

'I expect he's banging her,' Owen said. 'I would for sure.'

Huw attempted another smile, but did not reply.

'Hey, who was that last night?' Owen asked.

'It was Brad coming for Miranda. She's gone.'

'Oh yeah, I know. We said goodbye. I didn't see Brad, though.'

'Did she say anything to you?'

'Just that we'd stay friends. Oh, yeah. She asked if I'd help her paint her apartment.'

'Did she? Will you?'

'Yeah, probably.'

'Out of friendship? Love?'

'Well, she's cool, for an adult. Also she said she'd pay me.'

'Did she?'

'Yeah, and I could definitely use the money. Well, see you later,' Owen said.

He slammed the door on his way out, and moments later

Huw was on his bicycle, sailing into the street with an abstracted expression. Huw's grief coursed through him. For hour after black hour, no image arose in his mind but Miranda's face, sorrowful, distant, and unreachably beautiful, like a mural of a medieval saint in a Spanish church. Only her face, offering benediction or malediction. But then, merciful as rain, the words began dropping around him, in Welsh and English, a murmuring, a whispering, a rumour, a scratching he saw as well as heard, for he saw the Gothic letters, the calligraphy of the quills, the flourishes, the illuminated capitals, the bold colours and gold leaf. Voices, as bell-like and clear as those of chanting monks, gave him their words. He thanked God for that blessing.

*

He was less thankful for his role as thesis committee Chair at Timothy's defence later that day. His advisee had rejected all of Huw's suggestions for revisions, so the text was littered with wrong collocations, tense switches, clichés, and redundancies. The prose was turgid. Because Timothy had turned in the novel over a month late—with Frida's approval—Huw could not demand changes, so his only choices now were to either fail or pass the blasted thing. He ought to fail it. But that would displease Frida, and might put his promotion in jeopardy, or even his job, at a time when over half the family income had vanished at a stroke. He decided to pass it, since the other committee members planned to. Looking back later, his decision to appease would seem injudicious and cowardly to him.

The atmosphere in the Conference Room was celebratory but nervous. Jorgenson was there. It was not unusual for the spouse of the person defending to attend, but usually the Dean did not. The old man made Huw uneasy. It was the Chair's job to ensure an impartial examination, and how could he, given such pressure? Jorgenson was the kind of older man you found in the *Prairie Home Companion*—big and smug, in a Truman

Capote dickie bow and seersucker suit, with dyed hair and a San Francisco moustache. Timothy pranced and preened among his pals, mostly male, white, and gay, although Charleston and Broome were among them. Timothy had a blonde floppy fringe reminiscent of David Bowie in the early eighties. Like the singer, too, he sported a suit that hung loosely on his epicene frame. Although he neighed at the jokes, his face had the pallor of a pre-Raphaelite princess. As they all took their seats, he cast a pleading look at Huw, who pretended not to have seen it.

The other committee members were Marge, the transgender Queer Studies specialist, and Melvyn, in a pumpkin-colour shirt, grinning like a rapscallion. Lucky Luke was there, in his usual Hawaiian shirt but with a tie featuring fists raising the middle finger, and Rocky sat beside her idol, mimicking Frida's earnest expression and wearing the same kind of purple pavilion of a dress—in fact, maybe the very same one—a vast garment with mysterious folds and flaps. It swamped Rocky's thin frame. Frida was dressed soberly, in a black business suit. Hippo legs descended from a swollen skirt, but her feet, in ballet flats far, far too small for her—had she cut off bits of her heels, like Cinderella's sisters?—failed to meet the floor.

Frida glared at Huw, and if he was not mistaken, at Melvyn too. The gold nose-ring gleamed with menace. Her bristles, surely freshly rasped for the occasion, glinted like rust shavings. The monstrous effort of breathing made her shudder with each exhalation.

Huw sat at the head of the table. He began the proceedings with a quote from Dylan Thomas' 'How to Begin a Story', which, judging from the blank looks of his audience, even the faculty, no one recognised or appreciated. Marge (*née* Marvin—her new name was a tribute to her 'hero' Marge Piercy), broke protocol by interrupting Huw in her baritone:

'Oh puh-lease, spare us the wisdom of your dead white males.'

Rocky's head nodded with manic emphasis. Melvyn audibly

sniggered. At the irony of her berating white males? The fatuousness of the remark? Was Melvyn on Huw's side?

Huw noticed he was slouching and flicking his swivel chair about in a frenzy. He had to pull himself together, or the pack would fly at his throat. He asked Timothy to introduce his thesis. He reminded the audience that the purpose of the Critical Introduction was to show that the writer was familiar with similar works, acknowledging influences and comparing his own text analytically with others, pointing out where it was original and unique, and its merits and weaknesses.

Timothy stood, hands in his pockets. 'I am *beyond* thrilled to see you all here. I love you all so very much. The title of my thesis is *Derridean Rent-Boys.*' No one laughed. 'It's named after French philosopher Jack Derrida,' he sighed, 'who was this awesome Algerian post-modern neo-Marxist guy. But you all know that, right? So I guess I want to tell you how I got the inspiration for this incredibly complex, profound, challenging philosophical fictional novel of mine. Yeah? I know we're meant to read the classics, but that's so old school, right? Like, who cares? All those dead white males,' he said, looking at Marge, who nodded back encouragingly, 'like *whatever.*' He glanced at Huw, who did not nod back encouragingly. Timothy had read none of the psychological thrillers that Huw had recommended to him.

'So in fact my handsome husband had the idea of getting some inspiration from more modern artists, I mean the truly profound pop singers, like Lil Bitch or Meltdown at the Motel. And diverse geniuses like Mustwe East and Benno Venus. That's where I get the hip-hop rhythms from, and the street-cred. OK, cool, but what about the plot and the themes? Well, Jorgen helped me out there too. I must admit I'm a fanatical gamer, I play eight, ten hours a day, and I'm a devotee of the LGBT games especially, like the Assassin's Creed and Borderlands series. Street Fighter, too, which has a transgender hero,' he said, with an ingratiating smile for Marge.

Charleston rolled his eyes. Most of the others nodded gravely.

'And I was inspired by the masterpieces of modern television too, obviously, like Cracking Meth or Game of Crowns. I think you can see that in the really deep philosophy my hero Dominic gets into. I could compare it with The Matrix, but it's on the next level, haha. Sure, *Derridean Rent Boys* is a nail-biting, sexy thriller, but it questions the meaning of existence too. It's kind of metaphysical. Jorgen compares it to Sartre and Camus.'

Although this drivel lacked even the most fatuous post-modern critical content, Huw noted, the earnest faces of Timothy's audience indicated fascination. 'I must admit,' Timothy went on, flicking his hair out of his eyes, 'that at times I gave in to despair, especially when the draft I had poured my heart and soul into was ripped to shreds by *someone*,' he said, casting a baleful look at Huw. 'I knew deep down in my heart that this novel was a masterpiece, as Jorgen said, but at times I lost the track, like that old school Italian dude, you know, the one with the comedy. I was *literally* in hell. Sometimes I wanted to give up, and just drink margaritas on a beach, you know? So I'm so humbly grateful to God, and my dear husband, and the incred-ible, amazing, brilliant Frida and Rocky and Marge, who were so supportive.' His voice trembled and tears fell. He clutched the leather-bound copy of his manuscript to his chest. Broome, Rocky, Jordan and the youths began to yip and squeal.

'Thank you, Timothy,' Huw said, 'if you've finished. However, I failed to see any analytical elements in your introduction, or even a cursory attempt at a bibliography.'

'Brutal,' someone hissed in a stage whisper. Huw could not tell who had spoken. The frosty silence indicated that most of the audience agreed.

Huw asked Timothy to read from his work. The slender boy smiled self-consciously, flicked his floppy fringe out of his eyes again, and began to declaim in a melodramatic tone, his voice rising at the end of each sentence like a Valley Girl's, his free hand fluttering like a bewildered bird, his hips swinging to the rap-influenced rhythm of his prose, his shoulders shaking with insincere emotion like those of a televangelist. It was mindless entertainment, certainly, and pretentiously mindless entertainment at that, Derridean, Foucaultian entertainment, a detective story with long digressions on the stupidity and bestiality of the cisgender, heterosexual police, ponderously explaining the machinations of the patriarchy who ruled Southern cities, and using its characters as mouthpieces to deliver diatribes against the canon of Western writers. As literature it was inferior even to Savanna B. Manley's, if that were possible. It was, just about. Huw unmoored his mind, let it drift, allowed the words to coagulate, congeal, clot, into a sticky, affected mess, whose import was indiscernible, because it was meaningless, as Jacques Derrida himself might have agreed—and indeed decreed. A beam of sunlight gushed in through the windows, golden and green, filtered by the foliage of the oak trees, and Huw hung suspended in that stream, swimming upon its surface.

And then it happened again: Time stopped.

The moment caught Timothy like a choir-boy, mouth agape, eyes round; Jorgenson beamed with paternal pride, a white hand with slug-like fingers reposing on his paunch. Broome had an index finger thrust inside a warthog nostril. Rocky was staring at her phone. Charleston frowned, possibly deep in Marxist dreams or dialectic. Melvyn Shamburger smiled, yet kept a wary eye on his wife. Lucky Luke was fast asleep. Jordan's bony legs, in black silken trousers, were wide apart. She pouted like a model. No one was listening to Timothy's twaddle, as far as Huw could tell.

Except Frida, perhaps. Her legs resembled the ruined columns of a lost civilisation. The dirigible balloon of her suit floated above the granite stumps. But her squat, stony face, with its gold ring and rust-shavings on the scalp, wore an expression of fierce concentration. Had Timothy offended her? Unlikely. Because he was gay and the Dean's spouse, he had a free pass, although no one would ever admit that. Might Frida be cross with her husband, then? Melvyn had cast sheepish, guilty glances at her. What was going on there?

On this occasion, no cherubim gambolled, rolling and laughing on cushions of cloud; nor did blond angels blast away on trumpets, or massed choirs sing in Latin. This time a massive, darker presence lurked among the treetops outside in the unearthly, roiling light, a figure with a human shape, but with wings, as far as Huw could tell. An angel, or archangel? Once again there was music, a lugubrious organ fugue, with dissonances, irresolution, and ponderous silences. While the pedal notes rumbled in his entrails, the Presence in the oak tree, half-veiled by branches and leaves, raised a sword or lance. St. Michael? Huw heard him intoning verses in Latin: *Non te amat, tempus abire tibi est.* She loves you not, it is time for you to leave. Am I off my head? Huw asked himself. What could be more natural, after all this? Yet again, Huw wondered if this pause had a cosmic purpose. The previous episode had left him with nothing comparable to Jaromir Hladik's respite in *The Secret Miracle.* The novel remained incomplete and he had not given up teaching. Yet in these moments of stillness, he had the certain knowledge of the futility of his job, the triviality of the minds of most of his students, the vanity of his colleagues, the theatricality of the proceedings, and the malevolence and megalomania of Frida Shamburger, who seethed as she faced him. *Te odit.* She hates you, the archangel told him. But like Jaromir, he had no way out but to play the part of enemy. And it was possible that the pause was a mere illusion—because his mind had faltered and failed momentarily. Or was Time the illusion? Perhaps the human brain was too crude to perceive that the eternal moment was the reality. In that case, the chain of events, life itself, was nothing but a dream. *Non te amat.* Miranda loves you not, the Presence repeated.

Frida's tundra-cold eyes brimmed with murder. Huw shuddered. A white whippy thing reared over him, poised to strike. Timothy. His eyes too glared at Huw. Tiny black points—heroin eyes. Of course he was a junkie. The treetop stirred. The arch-angel wielded his sword. The skirling of the organ culminated in a flourish, a skein of terrifying treble notes.

The music held a warning and a command, but the message was muddied. He heard the ticking of a loud clock and his own voice:

'Thank you, Tim. You may sit down.'

'*Timothy,*' Timothy hissed, but Huw did not apologise.

'Dr Shamburger,' Huw said, addressing Melvyn, 'would you like to comment on Mr Jorgenson's *novelette,* I mean, uh, story?'

Melvyn blushed, stood, fiddled with his tie. 'He evokes Tocqueville well,' he said, pronouncing it Tokeville, as the locals did. 'I mean Tocqueville.' Tockville, Frenchified.

'It's not set explicitly in Tocqueville,' Timothy said.

'I know,' Melvyn said, 'but come on, dude, we all recognise it.' Jorgenson scowled. 'What I mean,' Melvyn went on, 'is that it's so very true to life. Of any Southern college town.' He cast a helpless glance at his wife, who was regarding him with blatant scorn. 'And uh, Tim, I mean Timothy, does a real good job of describing the queer sub-culture of Tokeville—a town like Tockville. The sex scenes are a tad graphic, and some might argue gratuitous... '

'Would *you* argue they're gratuitous, Dr Shamburger?' snarled Timothy.

'Hell no,' Melvyn said, chuckling with embarrassment and turning redder. 'I never said that. They're realistic for sure. You feel the raging lust of the young gay guys. And the philosophical digressions are... how shall I put it? Interesting? I subscribe to post-structuralist theories myself, and I found Timothy's extremely detailed and at times verbose explanations—how shall I put it? Informed? Maybe a tad didactic? As if they were written for Wikipedia or a Young Adult audience. Which is your intended audience, right, Timothy?'

'What*ever,*' Timothy said, disdaining to look at him. 'It's littery fiction.'

'Literary fiction, right. Of course, no one would call it original, but what is?'

'I seem to recall your own fiction was described as 'a long-winded, unimaginative re-hashing of French post-structural philosophy',' Timothy said, 'by a famous critic.'

A ghastly glint appeared in Frida's eyes. 'Sachiko. In the Noo Yorker.'

Melvyn babbled, 'Right, right, but it got awesome reviews too, for instance...'

'Would you mind sticking to Timothy's work?' Huw said.

'Oh sure. What I mean is that, in spite of a few faults, a handful of trivial defects, this is, as my wife Frida puts it, a novel of remarkable poise and ambition. How many students dare to write philosophical gay thrillers? How many are as bold in their condemnation of the canon? How many dare do away with prescriptive grammar, and even conventional English usage and spelling? I can safely say I've never read a novel like this. Well, I guess I have seen a few,' he laughed, 'but not *exactly* like this.'

Basilisk stares met him. Charleston choked with laughter.

'In other words, what I mean is that it was quite good,' Melvyn said. 'In fact, like totally excellent. If you're into that kind of thing. Of course, I wasn't reading for pleasure, but if I had been, make no mistake, I might have enjoyed it. Maybe. Well done, Timothy. Yeah.'

Timothy lurched to his feet, flailed as if throwing a punch, flicked his fringe out of his eyes, loosened his tie as if it were throttling him, and collapsed back into his chair, grunting.

'Thank you, Dr Shamburger,' Huw said, 'for that deft, articulate analysis. Dr Piercing, would you like to add your comments?'

Marge, whose short hair was dyed in the full spectrum of LGBTQ colours, frowned, deep in cogitation. 'It was an awesome read. I mean a real page-turner. Perfect for the beach. I just got back from a long weekend in Cancún with my honey,' she said—she had transitioned from straight male to gay female, 'and boy were those sex scenes hot! Very courageous, I thought, yeah. Props to you, Timothy, for describing the delights of using dildoes. As some of you might know from my prize-nominated, trend-setting blog, *Trans-aggressions,* I've tried my hand at that. To considerable critical acclaim.'

Huw sighed, recalling the sickening detail about her sex life in Marge's blog.

'Very interesting, Dr Piercing, but we're discussing Mr Jorgenson's thesis.'

'Right, sure, of course. What I like most about this marvel of a fictional novel is the ideology. I mean, the whole plot is a clear metaphor for the stranglehold the white patriarchy has over the rest of us. Right? I mean, all the bad guys are white.'

'Apart from the Colombian drug dealers,' Huw said. 'In fact most of the bad guys are brown. The good guys are all white. Didn't you notice that?'

'Oh, sure, I may have been on the beach with my honey, and maybe drinking a few margaritas too many, but I read it real carefully,' Marge said, unflummoxed. 'But the good guys are all gay, you notice that? Very cool. It's the evil capitalists and criminals who are cisgender, heterosexual—I mean hetero*gender,* sorry. Gender is a social construct, as I teach in my classes. Nothing to do with biology. *Everyone* and his dog knows that. You choose your gender and your sexuality. As long as the patriarchy doesn't impose one on you.'

'And yet,' Huw interposed, 'Dominic says he feels like a girl trapped in a boy's body more than once. Doesn't that suggest *he* believes there's a biological element to it?'

Marge snorted; Frida snorted; Rocky snorted; Timothy snorted. Soon everyone was snorting or squealing like the Gadarene swine plunging off the cliff.

'*Hel-lo?*' said Marge. 'This is the twenty-first century, right, Dr Lloyd-Jones? We don't need old-school reactionary theories like that here. We're *Americans.*'

'I don't follow you,' Huw said. 'What do you mean?'

'Like duh. We believe in *equality.*'

'So do I. I just don't think that assigning the status of heroes and villains to entire groups of people aids equality. But we're getting off topic. I take it, Dr Piercing, that your final verdict on the...' unable to utter the word *novel*, he said, 'this mystery, this gay philosophical detective *epic*, was positive?'

'I already said it was awesome. I mean sure, like Dr Shamburger said, bits of it are maybe not so well-written, but who cares? What matters is the message, right? And let's face it, it helps that Timothy is gay. I mean, he's white—which is bad, obviously—but he's diverse. He's a minority. And he's not exactly cis-gender, either. He has transgender leanings. That is *so* cool.'

'You mean Dominic, my protagonist. Not me, surely?'

'Yeah, right,' Marge laughed. 'But we all know Dominic is your alter ego, Timothy. No need to blush, dude. I don't mind what you do with your dildo.'

A ripple of laughter turned into a wave, then a tidal wave. Timothy smiled. Huw did not. Frida was orchestrating the swings of emotion, a potentate on her overburdened swivel chair.

But now the moment Huw was dreading had come: he had to deliver his opinion on the thesis. Everyone looked expectant. Frida's scummy brown eyes burrowed into his. Timothy shivered. Jorgenson glared. Only Melvyn smiled at him, as if egging him on.

'*Derridean Rent-Boys* is a rotten title,' Huw said, 'although it does indicate the themes of the story. As I've said to Timothy, the thesis has its virtues. There's a certain facility with language, self-assured, realistic dialogue, and also, as Melvyn noticed, the setting is evocatively described. On the other hand, as a thriller, the story is slow and clogged with philosophical musing. As philosophical fiction, it's not only puerile and derivative, but difficult to understand—'

'That's because it's so incredibly, amazingly complex,' Timothy said.

'I disagree. Thought should be clearly expressed, as

Schopenhauer held. Muddy expression is infallibly the result of muddy thinking.'

'Why don't you tell us what you *really* think?' Timothy said.

'Sarcasm—that is the prevailing tone of the so-called novel, isn't it?'

'*So-called?*' Timothy's eyes filled with tears. 'Don't you love it at all?'

'It isn't a novel yet. It could be. You have a germ of an idea but you haven't developed it. And it's too disordered. And there are too many egregious language errors. I'm passing it because it's no worse than the usual thesis standard, which is frankly abysmal. But you'll have to do a great deal of revision and editing to stand any chance of publishing this.'

Timothy bit his lip and wept. A shocked hush prevailed. Old Jorgenson visibly trembled with rage. Marge and Rocky gaped at Huw. Frida sneered at him. Lucky Luke snored. Jordan knitted her brow, and Charleston looked as though he were planning the revolution. Broome lumbered to her feet and charged from the room like an enraged rhino. Only Melvyn smiled in weird way. Again Huw wondered if Shamburger was on his side.

There was a groan of stressed steel, followed by a sharp snap: Frida's chair had collapsed. She sprawled on the floor, her skirt torn, revealing frilly bloomers of a quaint, possibly Victorian design. Her short thick limbs flailed helplessly. Rocky, gasping with the effort, managed to flop her idol on to her side, and a group hoisted her up.

Once she was on her feet, Frida directed a venomous look at Huw, uttered what sounded like a curse in a rare tongue, perhaps Uto-Aztecan, and aided by Rocky, staggered towards the door. Although Melvyn had not got up to assist his wife as she lay helpless on the floor, he jumped up now, but Timothy laid a hand on one of his bright orange sleeves, with the grin of drunken peasant in a Breughel. 'Hey, Melvyn, buddy, join us for a drink.'

Melvyn gave him a guilty grin, and made a rush for the door, as if eager to escape. He got there just before Rocky and Frida, practically pushing them over in his haste to get out.

'I need to talk to you,' Frida said. 'Rocky told me she saw you the other day. On the *west side* of the city.'

Instead of replying, Melvyn fled—at least that was the way it seemed to Huw. What was all that about? Frida got stuck in the doorway again and Rocky forced her though it with the loud pop of a cork being pulled, and more curses.

At last Lucky Luke stretched, raised the bill of his cap, and said, 'Is it over already?'

Charleston approached Huw. 'I dig your honesty, prof. You want my opinion, Timothy got what he was asking for, the pompous little prick.'

But Huw wondered if he had overstepped the mark. He feared repercussions, even reprisals, but was not sure he cared. With Miranda gone, his job mattered only for Owen's sake. Huw had failed to rise to the challenge of Whoever was freeze-framing time for him. Twice now. Would such an ellipsis ever occur again? And if it did, would he be ready?

FOURTEEN

Low Animal Cunning

When Melvyn got back from drinking margaritas with Timothy and his buddies, photographs of him grinning like a stoned bonobo were already on Instagram—he had smoked a little Maryjane too—he sneaked inside the house, slipping off his deck shoes at the door and tiptoeing in his socks towards the stairs. He glimpsed Frida, marooned on the settee, her Pearbook perched on the crests of her breasts and belly, a bag of ice draped over her brow. A terrifying noise issued from her throat—*a death-rattle*, he told himself, with a wild surge of hope, but no, that was too great a miracle to ask for. *Please God, if I can just reach my study without waking her, that's all I ask. I managed to evade the inevitable cross-examination by fleeing to Timothy's thesis celebration. She may forget if I can avoid her now. Dude, be a ninja. Move like Garfield.*

He inched his way up with the patience of a cat burglar, and had almost attained the safety of the upper storey when he trod on the step that creaked. He cursed and halted.

'Melvyn, is that you?' The voice was lupine, savage, thick and phlegmy.

Go back to sleep, he prayed. He did not answer.

'I said is that you, Melvyn?' Her voice was louder, and proto-human now.

'No,' he said. *Jesus, did I say that? That was dumb-as-dogshit.*

'Who the fuck is it, then?' That voice might have made a hardened criminal quail. Bumps, thumps, crashes and metallic clicks followed. Moments later Melvyn turned to face Frida, who was at the foot of the stairs, still in the skirt she had torn falling off her chair at Timothy's thesis defence, her forehead bruised and bumped like a boxer's. She swayed drunkenly, and clutched a nasty-looking Colt Cobra snub-nose .38, which, he saw with mounting panic, was pointed at his genitals. She did not look happy to see him, either.

'Haha, joke,' he said quickly. 'Of course it's me. Darling.'

'Don't *darling* me,' Frida said, without lowering the weapon. 'Scumbag.'

'Gladys, I mean Frida, put the gun down. I only had a drink with Timothy.'

Frida lolloped up the stairs, the Colt still aimed at his privates. 'I'm not pissed at that, you slimy snail. I want to know what you were doing on the west side two weeks back. Outside a *gorgeous* mansion. Looking as guilty as *sin*, Rocky said.'

Melvyn feigned incomprehension. 'Uh, Rocky? Why, whatever do you mean?'

'Just move, *buster*,' she said with relish. Boy, had she been bingeing on Turner Classic movies, or what? He turned; she jabbed his back with the barrel.

'You want me to put my hands up?' he said. No answer. 'I have no idea what this is about, Frida,' he stammered, preceding her into the bedroom. 'Oh, maybe you mean that day I visited um, uh, an English professor on the west side?'

'Oh yeah? Which one? What were you up to while I was at the retreat, huh?'

Melvyn assumed his Anthony Perkins expression of

half-witted innocence that, he realised too late, confirmed his guilt. 'The usual. Writing. Tai Chi. Karate.'

'What were you doing right here?' Frida said. 'In our bed?'

'Um, sleeping?' He gave her a weak smile. How could she possibly know?

'Where are the stains, Melvyn?' The effort of holding the pistol up to the level of his chest had tired her, so once again it was pointed at his penis, which shrank and shrivelled, as it did in icy water.

'Stains? What do you mean, Gladys, uh, Frida? I washed the sheets.'

'Yeah, you washed them all right. You think you're real smart, don't you, Melvyn? That's tantamount to admitting you cheated. You think you got rid of the evidence, don't you? Which English professor did you visit?'

'Uh, Cooper.' Damn, he would have to beg Cooper to cover for him now.

She snorted through the thick white rubbery snout. The nose-ring shook.

'So this is the gun I saw in your purse on Sunday before church?' he said.

'Shut up, Melvyn. Don't change the subject. Why did you wash the sheets?'

'Well, haha, I washed the sheets because they uh, looked dirty. Obviously.'

'I bet they were dirty, all right. Real dirty. Like you.'

'I can't see why you're suspicious.' She couldn't prove a thing, he was sure.

'Let's say it's a woman's intuition. Let's have a look in the bedside tables.'

'Go ahead,' he said, relieved. Thank God, she had not a shred of evidence.

She dug through his drawer: smelly socks, gum, expired rubbers, Viagra, ancient after-shave. Nothing incriminating. He was grinning now. 'See, dear?'

Then she stamped around the bed and rummaged through her own drawer.

'Oh, wonderful. Oh, Jesus, yes. Look what I found in this one, Melvyn.'

With her left hand she fished out a tiny scrap of red lace which she held between her thumb and forefinger as if it were toxic. Oh no oh shit oh fuck oh Jesus—it was Jezebel's absurdly miniscule V-string panties. How could she be so damn dumb? Or had she planted them deliberately? Could she be so devious?

'That,' he fumbled, with a nervous giggle, 'must be... uh, Thalia's? Clio's?'

Frida jerked the gun up to head height. She was going to pistol-whip him.

'Don't tell me you're fucking your own daughters, Melvyn.'

'For Chrissakes, no!' he yelped. 'What do you take me for?'

'A dirty slug. You better come clean, Melvyn, or I'll blow you away, I swear.'

'All right, you want the truth? OK, I admit it, I did entertain a—how can I put it? A girl. A woman. While you were at that wacky retreat. I'm so sorry, Frida.'

'A *girl*, Melvyn? What kind of a girl? A stoodent?' Totally East Boston now.

'Yes, a real smart one. And it only happened once.'

'I don't *give* a damn how many times you boned her, you amoeba, or what her IQ is. How old is she?'

'Like twenty-one. Honest. She's an adult, Frida.'

'You call that an adult, Melvyn? Jesus Christ, that's only four years older than Thalia. The *same* age as Clio. It turns my stomach. You are such a filthy pervert.'

'I'm not sure that's fair. It wasn't my fault, exactly. She was hounding me. I kept turning her down. She just wouldn't take no for an answer.'

'You mean you're so spineless she forced you to fuck her?'

'Exactly—I mean, hell no,' he said, as Frida pointed the pistol at his privates again. 'My new therapist said I should, Frida, I swear.'

Frida's features slid into Picassoesque disarray: snout on the side of head, one pink eye migrating to her forehead, the other one next to a pointed ear. 'Say *what?*'

'She said we were both adults,' he stuttered. 'She couldn't see the harm.'

'*She?* A woman said that? Who the *fuck* is this so-called fucking *therapist?*'

'I can't say that,' Melvyn pleaded. 'Confidentiality? You understand, right?'

Frida aimed at the floor and pulled the trigger. A crash and smell of cordite. An elliptical hole appeared in the floorboards, right between his stockinged feet.

'Jesus, Frida, control yourself. Please. Don't shoot me in our bedroom.'

'Next bullet, it's your foot. I'll nail you like Jesus. Who's the therapist?'

'Dr Pound,' Melvyn whimpered. 'Dr Eliza Pound.'

She grunted again. 'What about the *smart girl?* She one of our stoodents?'

'Yes and no. I mean, she is a student at Oxbow State. But not a Creative Writing major. Truth. Believe me. I would never stoop that low.'

'Sure you would. You got the morals of a marmoset.'

'Hey, very witty.' Melvyn tried to laugh. 'Maybe lower than a marmoset.'

'You got that right,' Frida said. 'You know what, Melvyn? You make me puke, spew, barf, heave, gag. You make me chuck my fucking guts up.'

'Boy, Frida, you're a walking thesaurus. What a terrific bunch of synonyms.'

'Don't be a smartass, Melvyn. You're dumber than dogshit.'

'Yeah, right.'

'I mean it. You're *chicken*shit, you know?' She waved the Cobra at his cock.

He hung his head. *Yeah, yellow. Where is the Superior Man?*

'I oughta plug you. Right through your little wiener.'

'Not there, please. Anywhere but my little wiener. That would be a terrible idea.'

'Give me one good reason why I shouldn't shoot you,' Frida said.

She was having a hell of a time playing the tough broad with the gun—he guessed she had been watching Lauren Bacall or Bette Davis movies—but it might not be wise to point that out. 'For a start,' he said, 'you could go to prison.'

'Are you kidding? I'd say it went off on accident. Who would they believe?'

Damn, that was true. 'And I'm repentant. Like a Republican politician caught rogering an intern, or a Catholic priest poking one of the choir-boys.'

'You mean you're a liar and hypocrite, just pretending to be repentant?'

'No, I mean I'm really, really, truly, sincerely, deeply sorry, and willing to debase myself. Demean myself. I'll do anything to prove how sorry I am.'

'Anything?'

'Scout's honour. Cross my heart and hope to die if I tell a lie.'

One of the few benefits of being married to Frida was that her mind worked so sluggishly that it was easy to follow her thoughts as they plodded after each other. She considered his offer. To use one of her clichés, her face took on an expression of 'low, animal cunning'. Actually, she did look remarkably like an animal, and a very low, cunning one, at that. A fox? No, that was way too hackneyed. A sneaky dog? Better. A sly stoat? Hmm. A crafty, wily… hog? *Yeah*, she was probably saying to herself. *It could be kinda fun to debase him, like really demean him, humble him, show him who's the boss. And useful too. He'll be my slave. I can use him for…*

'Okeydokey, then,' she said.

'Okeydokey? I'm in the clear?'

'Melvyn, you're in very deep shit. Let me make this plain. You are not in the clear. I'm gonna make you suffer for the desecration of our marriage bed. In more ways than you can imagine. You're about to experience suffering without end.'

'Oh thank you, dear. Certainly, I understand. It's so generous of you.'

'You're gonna grovel, Melvyn. Big time.'

'More than I'm grovelling already?'

'Way, way more, Melvyn. Mark my words. You just wait, buddy.'

At least she isn't going to blow my pecker off. Nothing could be as bad as that.

Slowly, the barrel drooped to her side. Without the gun pointed at him she was just a battered porker stuffed into torn clothes. Hideous, sure, but nothing to be afraid of. Not for the time being, anyway.

'Dang, Melvyn, what the heck is that smell? Did you just soil yourself?'

Uh-oh—the turd was heavy in his boxers. He smelled it himself now.

'Gee, I'm sorry. I didn't know I had. But you understand…'

She broke into swinish merriment, snorting and squealing with joy. 'That is so disgusting. So perfect. You've made my day, Melvyn. You *filthy* little child.'

He waddled past her to the bathroom. Boy, would she pay for this!

*

Later, long after he had dumped his boxers in a jiffy bag, had a painstaking shower, and endured a period of sober penitence on his zafu cushion in the study, meditating on the Way of the Superior Man, with only occasional fantasies of Samurai

vengeance, the deafening roar of the television led him downstairs to the lounge. He found Frida 'reclining'—how refined
that made her slumping sound—on her colossal dentist's chair,
Upton Abbey on the flat-screen as usual, her Pearbook perched
on the St. Michael's Mount of flesh around her middle. She
was scrolling through her newsfeed, perusing pictures of the
Loathsome Leader, and Meghan, Margaret Atwood and other
mavens, Syrian kids, and cute kittens. She was jabbing likes,
emoticons with tears and gaping or grinning mouths, in response
to each. But he could see she was also 'working', from the pile
of coffee-spattered papers beside her, and a book pillowed on
one of her knees, whose cover showed a beautiful black woman
wearing a tall African headdress and scarf, glaring with penetrating elegance at the camera. Its title was: *Becoming the Brilliant
Writer You Are – Effortlessly.*

'Sup?' he said. Had she forgiven him? Would she remind him
of his shame?

'Just working on my novel.' Yes and no, then, thank God.
'Such a struggle. The agony of creation. Self-doubt, ecstasy,
misery, transcendence. You know?'

'Of course. You might like these, darling.' With the deference
of a butler from *Upton Abbey,* he stooped and extended a box of
Belgian chocolates towards her.

'Oh Melvyn, how sweet, haha. Did you make sure they're
Fair Trade?'

He had not; he had no idea if they were; nor did he give a
damn. 'Absolutely.'

'That's lucky. I could never eat all these delicious chocolates
if I suspected they were the product of child slavery in West
Africa.'

Sure you could. 'Naturally not. Would you like some coffee with
them?'

Her cheeks dimpled. 'Are you trying to butter me up?'

By the time he had made it and brought it back into the
lounge, where strings screamed over a 'tragedy' on *Upton Abbey,*

he saw the chocolate box was empty—she had not left him one. Melvyn set the large bucket of sticky, sweet goo in a cup-holder on her armrest, and turned to dart away on 'velvet paws'. But before he could exit, he heard, above the roar of the television, a sucking, slurping, repulsive noise. By now he should have gotten used to Frida drinking like a thirst-crazed simian. A burp followed the gurgling of the drain, and a sergeant-major shout stopped him in his tracks: 'Hey, was it really a girl you boned, Melvyn? Or like, maybe a dude?'

'Say what?' He turned. She had half-rolled over like a beached whale.

'You're chummy with Timothy. Are you into dudes?'

'Hell no. I'm straight. Heteronormative. You know that.'

'That's so old school, don't you think? Kind of right-wing? Such a drag.'

Was she joking? 'I guess it is. But I can't help it, can I?'

She took another slurp. 'Don't you think you could make more of an effort?'

'Gladys, shit, I mean Frida, what are you *saying*? What *are* you saying?'

'I'm just sayin' you're a cisgender, straight, white, middle-aged *male*…'

'I admit it. But I'm not sure I follow. You're suggesting I should be ashamed of my gender, my skin pigmentation, and sexual orientation?'

'Let's get real, bud. You epitomise the white patriarchy. Not cool, dude.'

'I guess,' he said, hanging his head. 'I'm sorry, I guess.'

'You should be. You are responsible for all the evil in the world, Melvyn.'

'I am?'

'Not just you, dumbass. But your kind. White men. Think of all the people you've enslaved and exploited—all the ethnicities. All the poor *women*.'

'Sure, I get that. I'm a liberal. But it wasn't just me. And white men have done a few good things, right? Think of the glories of Western civilisation. All the art.'

'Dude, give me a break. It was all propaganda. Designed to victimise women and other genders and people of colour. All the so-called art—all that highbrow stuff—it was nothing but marketing. To keep you cisgender white guys in power.'

'Hang on a minute: what about Michelangelo and Leonardo? Bach, Mozart? Homer, Dante and Shakespeare? Kafka and Dostoyevsky? That was all just marketing?'

'Sure, those guys were just ad men. Sidekicks of popes and kings. Lackeys. But it's all over now. It's time for you guys to change. Get with the programme.'

'I see your point—but I spend nearly my entire life apologising as it is.'

'I appreciate that, but it's not enough, Melvyn. That's *so* last century.'

'Well, what should we do? How can *I* make amends?'

'For a start, I think you could do a dude, maybe Timothy or one of his buddies. Or a transgender person. Go gay, Melvyn. Take a walk on the wild side.'

What would the Superior Man say? Nothing, probably. Melvyn wrinkled his nose. 'Just imagining it makes me want to barf.'

'That's a prejudice, though, right? You've been assigned a gender and a sexuality, and you've accepted it like a goddamn moron. But it's your choice. You could change all that, Melvyn. Reinvent yourself. Assert your freedom for once.'

'I totally want to, but hell, not like a pillow-biter!'

'How bigoted. How disappointing. I expected more of you, to be honest.'

It hit him like a karate kick to the temple. 'Frida, are you trying to tell me that you might be bisexual yourself?'

She smiled in a surprisingly natural way, for her. 'Well, I might not use that terminology. But I am totally like polyamorous, Melvyn. And proud of it.'

'Doesn't that basically mean you're a promiscuous slut?'

'Melvyn, you are *so* unhip. No, it means I reject monogamy and exclusivity.'

'You do? So you don't mind that I banged Jezebel? Is that cool now?'

'That was her name, was it? No, Melvyn. You can bang *Jezebel* all you like. Hell, bang anyone you like.'

'Gee, thanks, Frida. I really appreciate your generosity. I might just do that.'

The smile of low, animal cunning reinstated itself. 'Provided you don't mind *me* banging someone, naturally. Tit for tat. Quid pro quo.'

'Mind?' he said quickly. 'I'd love that! I'd adore it!'

'You would, Melvyn? Maybe you'd like to join in, too?'

'You gotta be shitting me.'

'Have I ever shitted you, Melvyn?'

'All the time,' he said. 'So you're seriously saying you want me to join you in bed while you fuck some other guy? I never knew you were such a slag, Frida.'

'Hey, I didn't say it'd be a guy, did I? So here's another big reveal: I'm pansexual, Melvyn. I discovered that at the retreat. Can you handle that?'

'I'm not sure what it means, to be honest.'

'It means I'm into everyone—not just dudes and chicks but *all* genders. According to the Canadian government, there are like sixty of them.'

'Wow. I would never have guessed *they* had so many. Those Canadians.'

'You need a minute to let it all sink in. Yeah? But I sense that you're down with the idea. And you did promise you'd do anything to prove you're sorry.'

'I sure did. Though I'm not certain I need to be so apologetic now.'

'That's the spirit, Melvyn.'

'So let's get this straight: you're inviting me to some kind of threesome?'

'Wouldn't that be awesome? Imagine being in bed with two hot women.'

He did. The trouble was, one of them would be Frida. 'I can't do it.'

'Way disappointing, Melvyn. You're so uptight. But okay, as a first step, how about being a spectator? Like from outside, through a window or something.'

'You mean like a voyeur? I guess I could be a voyeur.' A 'stirring in his loins' surprised him. Oh boy oh boy oh boy. 'Yeah, sure.'

Frida beamed like a hag in a Bosch painting. 'Coo-ul.'

'But wait—who will it be? Oh no, not Rocky?'

'Melvyn, I can't exactly do a colleague, can I? Especially not a colleague lower in the hierarchy. That wouldn't be right, would it? I mean ethical, and all. Huh?'

'I bet Rocky wouldn't mind. I think she'd jump your bones in an instant.'

'Right, she'd be down with it. But *I* might feel badly about it.'

Give me a break. 'You got so many... scruples, right?'

'Calms?'

'Qualms, right. You're so amazingly sensitive, Frida. And articulate.'

'I guess I am, thanks. You know what? It's gonna be wicked *hot*, Melvyn.'

'Sure. But won't you tell me who it is? It's driving me wild imagining it.'

'That's the idea. Keep going wild. No, you'll find out soon enough.'

'I can hardly wait, Frida.'

'Attaboy. Thanks for understanding me, Melvyn.'

Melvyn gulped. 'Did you just thank me—for real?'

Enjoy it while you can, Melvyn. Summer's lease hath all too

short a date, as the bald white dude with the goatee said. You know, one of the old school lackeys.

Like you, Melvyn. Like you.

FIFTEEN

Women and Girls Rule His World

A woman, Huw guessed from the softness and tentativeness of the knock on his office door, if that was not a sexist inference. Theoretically prepping classes, in fact he was gazing with nostalgia at a picture of Miranda in her wedding dress, her brow garlanded with flowers.

'Come in,' he said. 'Door's open.'

In came Jezebel, the girl he had met at the feminist retreat. He wondered what she wanted, not that he much cared. Her face provided no clues. For a student, her clothes were too formal: a black pinstripe skirt suit, with black tights and heels. She carried a briefcase. She wore her hair swept into a ballet topknot, as Miranda often did, which in Jezebel's case emphasised the sharp angles of her face, unsoftened by makeup. She could have been a lawyer. In other circumstances, he might have been intrigued, but since Miranda's departure, having to talk with anyone was a trial. He hoped he could get rid of her quickly.

She shut the door behind her. 'May I talk to you in private, sir?'

As a rule he insisted on keeping the door open, but exhausted and grieving as he was, he simply sighed. 'All right, then. Take a seat.'

She pulled back the armchair opposite his desk, away from him. He understood why when she sat down: she was now far enough away for him to see her long, shapely legs. She crossed and re-crossed them. Her skirt was only slightly above the knee. Even so, it was an impressive display. But perhaps he was imagining things. Her air was professional.

'How are you, sir?' she said crisply.

Because she was a stranger, and looked older than she probably was, he almost confided in her. But if he blabbed about Miranda leaving him, he might end up blubbering. And he could not divulge to a student his anxieties about his job, or frustrations with his colleagues. No, better keep it buttoned-up, the British way.

'Fine,' he said, hands thrust in his blazer pockets. 'What can I do for you, Jezebel?'

'You remember my name. How flattering. Thank you, sir. I believe that's your wife?' She nodded at another photograph of Miranda, on the wall.

'Yes?'

'She looks like that actress. The one in *White Swans*.'

He smiled wanly. 'She does. Although I find my wife more beautiful.'

'You must love her very much.'

'Yes.' And yet she did not love him, the angel had said. *Non te amat.*

'Did she enjoy the retreat with my sister?'

'She said it changed her life.' *And mine, and mine. Tempus abire tibi est.* Had the archangel meant that it was time for him to leave, or her? Would she have left him so abruptly if it had not been for Petronella and her goddamn goddesses? He doubted it.

'That's what most of the women at the symposia say,' Jezebel said. 'Personally, I have my doubts. They feel empowered afterwards, sure, which I guess is a good thing. They often take drastic actions right afterwards. But I'm not sure the transformation is deep. It's not based on self-knowledge so much as obedience. It's a kind of cult. Petronella tells them what to believe, what to do. They exchange one kind of subjection, one kind of conformity, for another. The patriarchy for the matriarchy. Most people can't face freedom. They'll do anything to avoid thinking for themselves or figuring out who they really are.'

Huw listened aghast. Was she as mature as she sounded? Without question she was bright and articulate. He remembered she wanted to be some kind of therapist.

'Have you divulged these thoughts to your sister?' he asked.

'Oh yes. She doesn't disagree. We often laugh about it.'

'I see—so basically, to be blunt, the retreats are just a scam for relieving privileged white women of their money? For milking the insecure and the foolish?'

Jezebel offered him a brief, brittle smile. 'Petronella wouldn't put it like that. They get value for their money. And the symposia are not just for white women. All ethnicities are welcome.'

'I don't remember seeing any other ethnicities in the hall.' She made no reply to that. 'But you still haven't told me why you're here.'

She crossed her legs again, slowly. Her eyes never left his face. She did not smile or flirt and yet he had a gut feeling that she desired him. But if that were so, why would she behave with such ambivalence? Was she so sophisticated that she understood that ambiguity, mystery, and uncertainty, were ways of heightening tension, of stimulating desire?

His intuition told him that she was. Fate was offering him yet another nubile young woman, and unlike Elise, this one was not even his student. If he wished to, he could.

'A number of reasons,' she said. 'For a start I've been reading your first novel, *Ceredigion*. You're a brilliant man. You belong on the shelf with the greatest British writers.'

'That's kind of you.' In his opinion it was not true, but all the same it was touching to hear. 'What did you most like about it?' The psychological acuity, he expected her to say.

'The sex scenes,' she said without a moment's hesitation. 'They're so sensual, and yet rather brutal too. Isn't that the perfect combination? When Blodwyn finds Llewellyn on the beach after his boat's sunk, believing he's drowned, and they make love on the wet sand, while the freezing rain lashes her back—I was practically gasping as I read that one. You understand exactly how a woman feels when she makes love.'

'Do I?' He curbed his amusement. Perhaps she was more ingenuous than she looked.

'Absolutely. Would you mind signing my copy of the novel, sir?'

'I'd be happy to. Do you have it with you?'

'Yes,' she said, but made no move to open her briefcase. What would her next move be? Clearly she had a strategy. He did not. He was only responding to her moves.

After a thoughtful pause, she crossed her legs with a swish of her stockings again. 'Do you remember me asking if you'd be willing to help with my research?'

He did, and nodded. 'No need to keep calling me sir.'

'I'd prefer to. I intend to train as a sex therapist after I graduate with my Psychology degree. My Honours thesis is based on some original research. On relationships between young women and older men. My hypothesis, which of course I'm testing experimentally, is that such relationships may be very valuable for both parties.'

'I see,' Huw said with alarm. 'For the women, for material reasons, presumably?'

'Not at all. I postulate that young women use these relationships to grow intellectually. They learn so much from intellectual, wiser men. Like *Pygmalion*.'

She knew Bernard Shaw; impressive. 'And the standard view is that the men do it simply for the sex—but I imagine you'll tell me that they have nobler motivations too?'

'Not necessarily nobler. Of course they enjoy the sex with the younger woman. But the emotional and spiritual effect on them is far greater than the physical one. They get a renewed sense of confidence, they feel infused with life, they rediscover the selves of their youth—the true selves, the ones with heroic ambitions—that they had to abandon as they compromised with life.'

'That's a remarkable analysis.' And an accurate one: that was exactly how it had been for him when he met Miranda. But however flattering it was that Jezebel was offering herself to him now, as she clearly was, and however tempting it might be to allay his misery with some meaningless sex, he knew he would regret it. 'How did you develop this theory?'

'Partly from reading—not just psychology, but literature, including your own deeply penetrating novels, sir—and partly from observation and experience. But I need to confirm my conjectures, with a careful collection of data. That's where you come in.'

'I'm not sure I follow you. Would you like to interview me? Because I have a younger wife?'

She hesitated. 'To start with, yes.'

'To start with? What else do you have in mind?' Would she proposition him?

'Dr Shamburger is one of my subjects. He has helped me considerably.'

'Has he indeed?' She was skilful at deflecting questions she did not want to answer. But it was odd that she had asked Melvyn, since Frida was not younger. Was he actually having an affair with this girl? Huw recalled Melvyn's blissful reveries, the gloating grins, the guilty glances at Frida, and his apparent flight after Timothy defended his thesis. Huw had seen Jezebel leaving Melvyn's office too, more than once. It all added up. Could Melvyn be having an affair with such a cool, distant girl? It beggared belief but Huw really hoped so.

'Oh yes. I've learned a great deal from Dr Shamburger.

Although he has that somewhat affected New England manner, deep down he's more primitive. I mean that in the DH Lawrence sense. As a compliment.' She crossed her legs again.

'You astonish me.' *And scare me a bit,* Huw did not add.

'And so if you'd be so kind as to answer some questions… to start with. Nothing more. It will be *completely* confidential, of course. No names.'

'I should hope not.' Her request was not precisely improper, since she was not his student or even in his college, but it was questionable in taste, and might be risky. Bright as she was, and professional as she presented herself, he had the sense, in spite of her strictly controlled manner—or because of it—that she was a bit unhinged. Her stare had the intensity of the fanatic's. But what might she be fanatical about? She was unusual—intriguing. Still, his impulse was to refuse. Miranda would strongly disapprove if he told her. Then what made him waver? he asked himself. The very fact that Miranda would disapprove, he realised. It was a way to assert his independence. He remembered the Persian doctor, and a line she had quoted from Hafiz: *How did the rose ever open its heart and give the world its beauty?*

He longed to open his heart, whether he had any beauty left to give or not. 'I could answer a few questions. But I reserve the right not to reply to any that I find indiscreet.'

Jezebel fixed him with a clinical gaze. 'Thank you,' she said, bending to reach into her briefcase, and giving him a glimpse of her bra as her ivory blouse opened. She handed him a first edition hardback of *Ceredigion*, and a fountain pen. He took them and wrote:

To Jezebel, with admiration for your perceptiveness. Just remember that, as Blodwyn finds out in this novel, passion can lead us astray: life should not be reduced to a single obsession. Was that too moralising? Too late to change now, anyway.

'Will that do?' he said, signing it and passing it back to her.

'Wonderful, sir. Wise, as I expected. I'd like us to be very close friends.'

'That's flattering, but probably not appropriate, as people say here.'

'I feel that you have so much to teach me,' Jezebel said, crossing her legs.

'Everything of value that I know is in my novels.'

'Oh no, sir,' she said, standing. 'I know that's not true at all. Goodbye for now.'

She held out her hand; he shook it. Intriguing though the girl was, he hoped he would not see much of her in the future.

*

Miranda's condo was in a complex on the west side of the city, where only white people lived. Although no law forbade African-Americans to reside there, any black male engaged in suspicious activities in the newer subdivisions, such as walking from his car to a shop in a sinister manner, or exercising a dog in a park, or jogging on a public path, was likely to be reported, arrested, pistol-whipped, or shot once or twice, if he were lucky just in his legs, to discourage returning. Huw hated the area and marvelled that Miranda would choose to live there. She had wanted to live in the historic district for its 'diversity', after all.

She opened the door to him with her now customary glazed smile. The product of all the opiates, he supposed. Pink velveteen pyjamas, which did not flatter her flour-white complexion. No make-up. Disappointing, because she had known he was coming.

'It's sweet of you to visit with me.'

Odd though it was to be visiting his own wife, Miranda's formality struck him as odder still. He did not reply. As so often in the States, he felt he had stepped into a TV show. In her lounge, the awful *White's Physiology* was on the screen. Miranda settled on her sofa, so he had no choice but to join her. 'What do you think of my apartment?' she said.

He had been too shocked to notice when he entered, but

now he did. The walls startled him: ochre and magenta, apricot and damson, cherry-red and Prussian blue.

'Did you paint this all yourself?' he said, evading the question.

'I sure did. With Owen's help. He's a great little worker.'

'The colour scheme is inspired by Frida Kahlo's house, I suppose?'

'Spot on. Which I'll soon be visiting in Mexico. I'm so wired about that.'

Posters of Frida's paintings hung everywhere. Above the mantel, Frida's head with antlers, and the body of a doe, stuck with arrows. Was that how Miranda saw herself? As a vulnerable, lovable animal, chased and tortured? On another wall was Frida surrounded by black spider monkeys, one of them clinging to her back, his very long thin arm fondling her breast—Frida, with her adolescent boy's fluffy moustache, in the midst of mischievous emblems of lust. Again, was that how Miranda saw herself? Besieged by little simian men, snatching at her with their phallic arms and prehensile tails? Then there was Frida and the Broken Column: naked from the waist up, nails driven into her face and all over her body, her torso split open to reveal a shattered stone column. She was weeping with tightly pursed lips. In control, triumphing over her pain, glorying in her beautiful breasts, which were similar to Miranda's in size and shape. Yes, of course she identified with her.

'Isn't she great?' she said, following his eyes. 'No, you hate her, don't you?'

'I don't hate her. She was imaginative, and quite accomplished technically—nearly as good as Diego Rivera or José Clemente Orozco. But rather solipsistic, surely?'

'What does that mean?'

'Focussed on oneself. Self-absorbed.' Did that describe himself too? he wondered.

'But you only really ever know yourself,' Miranda said, pushing her hands into the little pouches on each side of her top, which made her look pregnant.

'Yes, that's the philosophical justification. But I disagree. With empathy, you can understand others. And paint them. Rembrandt did. So did Vermeer. Augustus John, too.'

'You're lecturing me again.'

'Just giving an opinion. I don't mean to lecture you.'

'And yet you do. It makes me feel dumb. You see, you would never have allowed me to have these pictures on the walls of the blue house, would you?'

She had him there. 'Well, they wouldn't go with the style of it, would they?'

'You see? It's always *your* vision. What about me? This is me, Huw.'

He saw her point. 'Yes, I'm sorry. If you come back, you can hang your pictures.'

'Gee, thanks.' Her tone was sarcastic. 'All over the house? Or in one tiny corner?'

'How about a whole room? Would that be enough? A study just for you?'

'Who's being solipsistic now? Did I use the word right?'

'You did. Touché.' He allowed her room to submerge his senses: the hot, throbbing hues of the walls, the images of exotic suffering. Immersed in the flood of colour, in Frida's dreamworld, which was Miranda's dreamworld, where women sprouted antlers and arrows, and monkeys patted their breasts, where nails were driven into their flesh and their chests were ripped open, but they kept on their corsets and pursed their lips, he wondered if he had misjudged his wife, underestimated her. What if this bold décor indicated a passionate, creative, sensuous soul? And what if she *were* a bit self-absorbed? Did he have the right to judge her for that? Wasn't he equally self-absorbed? And had that insight come too late?

'I'm sorry,' he repeated. 'I feel like I'm only really getting to know you now.'

She looked up at him with a secretive smile—a *solipsistic* little smile.

'Is it too late?' he said. 'I could change, I swear. Or is it too late now?'

'I don't know,' she said—and settled down to watch the drivel about jealousy among glamorous doctors on the telly. Incited by Frida's monkeys and bare breasts, Huw gave in to the temptation to caress. His hands probed and wandered, from the nape of her neck to the plump swellings beneath the pyjamas—stroking the velveteen, striving to slip under it and embark on pilgrimages to the south—the Eternal City. She did not respond to his advances.

'How could anyone with a modicum of intelligence watch this rubbish?' he said.

'I guess I must be a dumbass, then, because I enjoy it.' She got up, turned off the television set with an exasperated sigh, and put a CD in the mini-stereo.

'Oh no,' he said, identifying the shrill caterwauling of Tinker Quick.

'I like her,' she said, returning to the sofa. 'God, you're like an octopus.'

'I don't use my arm to deliver semen. Not yet, anyway. You really like her—what shall I call them? Her soulless, formulaic, squeaky ditties?'

'You're so judgemental. So patronising. So *superior*.'

'Critical. Discerning. I have impeccable taste.'

'How nice for you.' She did not smile but she did allow him to undress her.

Afterwards, he nodded off. Ideas purled through his dreams. What if the Kahlo obsession were not an index of Miranda's sensitivity, but simply another pop culture trend she was following? Frida was in fashion. Women all over the world adored her. Because of her unashamed narcissism, her obsession with her suffering, which to her was more painful and more noble than all others, and her belief that she was a victim of existential injustice. Naturally women identified with her. Huw did not resent Frida, who had coped as well as she could with a life of physical and emotional pain, but he did resent the halfwits who had turned her into a secular saint, an example of suffering womanhood, persecuted by insensitive men. *That asshole Rivera fucked Frida's own sister! That asshole Trotsky jilted her! Good for Frida for flaunting her lovers, male and female—especially the female ones! You go, girl!*

Frida Shamburger had adopted her first name, Huw understood in the miasma of his dream, to signal to everyone that she was creative and unconventional, wild, uncontrollable, masterful, pitiable, but also formidable, stronger than any mere man, and *way* more exciting.

'What's the matter?' someone was saying. *What's the madder?* Or was it, *Who's the madder?* 'You're grumbling. Snarling. Making fists. Wake up, you.'

No, *Huw.* Tears stood in Miranda's eyes. 'I love you so much, baby,' she said.

So much—an infallible indication of insincerity. This time he was unable to reply.

*

When he got home he had an email from her:

> *Huw, I've been thinking about our relationship and although I love you dearly I see it isn't going to work. Better if we make the split clean. I could date you but although you say you love me you'd just be 'shagging' me, right? So I think a divorce is best. Don't try to dissuade me. As you know, I'm super stubborn. I've decided. Don't write. I'll talk to you after I get back from Mexico with NeAmber and Matthew. (I'm leaving the day after tomorrow, remember? Bet you'd forgotten.) You'll be fine, you'll find someone. Give my love to Owen.*
> *Randima.*

Unable to face the house he had shared with her, or the university, he called in to cancel his classes and drove to the trailhead at Elk Creek for a run. He could either expend energy in fight or flight, or explode. He sprinted off down the trail without a warmup. No one else was running or walking. He flew along, doing six-minute miles: he timed them. His heart pumped like a piston, smacking against his ribcage. He hardly saw where he was going. His feet barely touched the ground. Nearing the bridge at the midway point, he almost stepped on a copperhead sunning itself. Presently a female figure in a tracksuit came jogging towards him. A familiar figure, he was half aware, but he paid little attention to her until she was almost upon him. It was the doctor who had attended to Miranda after her suicide attempt. She glanced at him, but he could not tell if she recognised him. Once again Huw had the sensation that he knew her well, and they had in the past been close, long, long ago.

She stared ahead. She was not going to greet him. That upset him.

He considered calling out to her. Would she respond? Why was she so aloof?

He hurtled towards her. She did not swerve. Set on her course, she would not alter it.

He deflected his own flight somehow. She neither averted her gaze, nor saw him.

But she had to have done. And be impressed by his speed. What a vain, immature hope, he thought as he bolted past.

As he ran, faster still, nails pierced him, the pistons clanked, clattered, and hammered, the pain grew, and some colossal force, a sledgehammer weight, hit him in the chest, knocked the breath out of his lungs—and felled him.

He sprawled on the path, gasping, unable to get any air inside his lungs.

He could not even cry for help. What bad luck that the doctor had passed him.

And that his life was over. He wished he could see Owen before he died.

His lungs had collapsed—he had no lungs.

An age passed. He could not breathe. He was going to die. Then the doctor loomed over him in her olive tracksuit. Kneeling, she held his wrist and listened to his chest.

'How do you feel?' she said in a calm voice.

At last he swallowed a gulp of air. 'Not great.'

'You were running at an insane speed for a man your age.'

'I'm in tiptop condition.'

'Your pulse is too fast.' She smiled—kindly or mockingly? He must have sounded vain. 'Sure you're fit. I can see that. Even so, try taking it a little easier next time, okay?'

'Okay. Do you know who I am? You recognise me?'

'How is your wife?' she said with the same wry smile. 'Better?'

'She thinks she's better. She's going to Mexico next week. She's left me.'

The doctor gave him a sharp look. 'I'm sorry.' Was she upset? Why would she be?

'I wasn't asking for your sympathy. Sorry, I don't mean that. Can I get up?'

'No. You need to rest until your heart rate goes back to normal.'

'Have I had a heart attack?'

'The wound is where the light enters you,' she said, her hand on his heart. 'That's Rumi again, but I guess you know that. You're a professor of literature, aren't you? I don't think you've had a cardiac arrest, but you should see a cardiologist for a check-up. This is a warning. You may have a heart attack if you don't change your way of life. Here's my card.'

'Thank you.' He hoped he would see her again. But that was wrong, wasn't it?

The wound is where the light enters you. The Welsh myths proved that—without suffering there was no learning. All the rest of the day, although his chest burned, Huw felt that a taper was alight there. Inside his heart a new radiance glimmered. He hoped the small flame would not go out.

SIXTEEN

Presumed Guilty Until Proven Innocent

Frida was not just late by faculty standards, or even hers, but insultingly late. Twenty minutes and counting. Lucky Luke had already pulled the bill of his ball cap over his eyes.

'Do you think, like, maybe Frida really isn't coming this time?' Rocky said.

'She said she was on her way,' Melvyn said. 'Right before I came in.'

But he was buzzed anyway. His plot was proceeding according to plan. Not only had he boned Jezebel and got his revenge on Frida, but she had accepted it, and everyone had taken the places he had assigned them. Huw was playing his part as if he were intent on his own destruction. He had insulted Frida's friend, Savanna B. Manley, and defended a womanless syllabus; offended his female students and defied Frida, and trashed the thesis of a vulnerable gay student, in public, and actually made him cry. As an extra bonus he had affronted Rocky, who was dim, certainly, but not too dim to take offence. Could it get any better? Yes, it could: Thalia, who was in Owen's class at High

School, had told him that Miranda had left Huw. For the past few days the Welshman had been stumbling about the campus like a wino, unshaven, muttering some kind of gibberish. Welsh, maybe. The dude had lost it. Totally. His days were 'defiantly' numbered, as most of Melvyn's students spelled 'definitely'. And the purpose of this meeting—if Frida could get off of her fat ass, and Facebook, and stagger here—was to decide the guy's future. Would Huw be promoted?

Melvyn was confident of the outcome. And now that Miranda was available, and Melvyn had recovered his virility so gloriously, he thought he might just bone her too. Why not? For sure he deserved another conquest. His mind drifted off in pleasant pornographic fantasies. Oh boy oh boy oh boy. This position. No, that one. Hell, both. All of them.

Seated across from him, Roquette Rathaus thumped the keys of her laptop. The Conference Room had mahogany tables and glass-fronted bookshelves. Empty, of course. It looked and smelled like a corporate board room, with its leather armchairs, wax polish, and synthetic air freshener. Two twenty-five. Lucky Luke was wearing his standard orange Hawaiian shirt, jeans, and monumental work-boots, lavishly decorated with mud, which reposed on top of the polished table like an art installation by Tracey Emin. Lucky Luke was himself in an artistic pose: tattooed Popeye arms behind his head, baseball cap shielding his eyes, a smile on his lips. Asleep? Or, as student lore had it, permanently stoned?

Stoned, was Melvyn's guess. *And* asleep. If only Melvyn could relax like that.

'Should we maybe adjourn the meeting?' Rocky said. 'Or start without her?'

Melvyn was chairing, and Frida would not forgive him if he did either.

'I'm sure she'll be here directly,' Melvyn lied. 'She's not usually so late.'

Lucky Luke raised the bill of his cap an inch, winked like a crocodile surfacing on the Nile, murmured 'The hell she isn't,' then pulled the bill down again to settle into muddy dreams. Or else he was composing deathless poetry. Rocky glanced at Melvyn with an irritated expression, then returned to her abuse of the keyboard.

A little after two-thirty, the door cracked against the wall with a report like a rifle, and in lurched Frida, panting, red-faced, exuding the fetid fragrance of Sundoe's. Sugar and crumbs liberally dusted her pink LGBTQIA+ tee shirt.

'I am *so* sorry for the delay,' she gasped. 'Something urgent came up.'

Oh yeah? Like an irresistible urge for coffee and cakes?

'No problem,' Rocky said, as the squat figure struggled to drive herself through the doorway. 'We've only been here a couple of minutes anyways.'

'Over half an hour,' mumbled Lucky Luke beneath his visor.

'I *am* the director of the programme, you know,' Frida snapped, collapsing into an armchair beside Rocky, 'and I have a ton of responsibilities. Unlike some of you.' She glowered at Lucky Luke, who showed no sign of having heard.

No hint of anger towards himself, though, for once, Melvyn reflected. In fact she showed no sign of having noticed him at all. She opened her Pearbook, which was covered with stickers of flowers and kittens, and the legend, in blobby pink letters, *Women Rule,* with a decal of a grinning Meghan Markle next to it. With her black goggles on, Frida looked rather like Von Richtofen, the First World War fighter ace. She panted and snorted, her thick nose ring shivering in time with the machine-gun rattle of the keys as she pounded them.

'Now we're all here, the purpose of today's meeting...' Melvyn began.

'Is to discuss Dr Lloyd-Jones' application for promotion,' Frida said. Ack-ack-ack-ack. You could practically smell the cordite. 'Rocky, will you be our secretary today?'

'Sure, Frida, I'd be delighted to,' Rocky simpered. 'I just love to help.'

'Uh Frida, you know I'm the chair of the tenure and promotion committee?'

The goggles swivelled towards Melvyn, her face a murderous mask. She rattled off another burst, typing and snapping like the Red Baron. 'It's obvious from his portfolio,' Frida said, ignoring him pointedly, lifting a folder from a *Save the Whale* shopping bag and hurling it across the table, so that it crashed to the floor, 'that Dr Lloyd-Jones does not deserve promotion. Especially after his shameful humiliation of Timothy the other day. A *gay* student. It was so homophobic and uncaring of him. A display of toxic masculinity.'

Rocky, who had just put on a pair of black goggles too, looked up from her typing. 'We all totally respect your opinion. I'm sure we all agree with you.'

Melvyn crawled under the table for the portfolio, thought, *Screw it,* and left it there.

Lucky Luke raised the bill of his cap, like a yawning crocodile. Would he snap those jaws?

'Let's not jump to conclusions,' Lucky Luke said in his Southern drawl, although he had grown up in Lodi, California. 'We should examine his achievements in each field, right, Melvyn? Teaching, Service, and Scholarly or Creative Work. Surely we want to be fair?'

'Of course we want to be fair,' Frida fumed. 'I'm all about fairness. Like in the courts, I believe everyone is guilty until proven innocent.'

'Don't you mean the opposite?' said Luke. 'Innocent till proven guilty?'

'Yeah, right, except in rape cases—then you have to believe women,' said Frida.

'Right on,' Rocky said. 'Always believe women.'

'We're getting off-track,' Melvyn said. 'Let's discuss his publication record.'

'It's stellar,' Luke said. 'Three novels, all with independent presses, admittedly, but prestigious ones. Gungate, Pepper, and the last one, *Ceredigion,* came out with Blossomsbury. Sachiko gave him a great review in the *New Yorker.* He won the Wholegrain Award and was short-listed for the Brooker Prize. Not too shabby.'

'Yeah, but that was like centuries ago,' Rocky said. 'What's he done in the past five years? That's the period we're looking at. Huh? Zip. Zilch. Nada.'

'Squat,' Frida said.

Melvyn grinned: given her shape, that was funny. 'Diddly-squat,' he chimed in.

'All right, he hasn't published a novel in the past five years,' Luke said, pointing his boots at Frida, 'but who has? We know he's been working on his *Manicomium,* or whatever. And he's published extracts from it in *The New Yorker.*'

'No one cool reads *The New Yorker* anymore,' Frida said. 'Only assholes.'

'Right,' said Rocky. 'It's so elitist—so patriarchal—so *white.*' Her mouth contorted with nausea as she spoke. She poked inside it, making convincing retching sounds.

'Isn't that envy?' Luke said. 'I'd love to be in *The New Yorker.* All that dosh.'

'Luke,' Frida said, 'who cares about money? We're *artists,* not whores.'

'Yeah, what she said,' Rocky added, blazing at the keyboard. 'You go, girl.'

'Melvyn?' Luke said. 'You're a fiction writer. What's your opinion of him? Everyone said he was brilliant when we hired him. Even Frida. Has he lost his touch?'

Damn, this was awkward. Melvyn could not afford to antagonise Frida, but on the other hand he might need Luke's vote when he, Melvyn, came up for promotion himself next year. Besides, much to his surprise he discovered that he had qualms—he still had the vestige of a conscience. And Huw's publication record was way better than his own, not to mention Frida's, which was pathetic by any standards.

'His stories are not so bad,' Melvyn said. 'But he should have published a book recently. Maybe with some small but highly-regarded micro-press.'

'Like yours?' Luke said. 'Or all of ours—mine included? Huw's the only one of us with a national reputation, let's face it. We wouldn't be jealous, would we?'

'Of course not,' Frida said. 'Okay, as a writer I admit he's not so bad. For a straight white male. An *older* straight white cis male. But what about his service record?'

'Stellar again,' Luke said. 'Faculty Senate, University, College and Department committees, many of which he chaired, Editor of the *Starving Artist Review*, judge of national and state literary contests, arts advisor for the Tocqueville City planning committee. He's advised a bunch of graduate theses and organised our Writers-in-Diversity series. He's been on state television and NPR. He's been giving creative writing classes in prisons and mental institutions too. *Pro bono.*'

Rocky wrinkled her pug-like nose. 'Yeah, but he could have done like way more.'

'Have you done more, Rocky?' Luke demanded. Was he defending Huw so hotly out of sheer decency? Melvyn wondered. Could any human be that nice?

'Not in like quantity, I admit. But it's the *quality* that counts,' Rocky said.

'What do you mean?' Luke said.

'Like, what's he done for the LGBTQIA+ community? Or for African-Americans or other oppressed minorities? What's he ever done for *women?*'

'Yeah, what's he ever done for *women?*' Frida grunted behind her goggles.

'He doesn't have the safe space decal on his office door,' Melvyn said.

Luke frowned. 'So what are you saying? He's racist or

misogynist or homophobic? I'm queer and I've never found him homophobic.'

'Luke—we saw him make poor Timothy weep. How heart-less of him. Anyway, even if he's not homophobic,' Frida said, 'he is racist and misogynist. Just look at his syllabi.'

'We're discussing his service right now. Can we agree that it's acceptable?'

'Like barely,' Rocky said. 'He might could volunteer at a women's shelter.'

'We're agreed on that,' Frida said, rubbing her stubby pink trotters together.

'No, we aren't,' Luke said. 'At least I'm not. Are you, Melvyn?'

'On to his teaching,' Frida cut in. 'Where there are obvious deficiencies.'

'Not to me,' said Luke. 'Be fair. His evaluations are way above average.'

'But there are lousy ones too,' Frida said. 'I noticed a disturbing tendency for his students to complain of his arrogance and their inability to understand him. Someone rated his competence in English as below average.'

'Does that reflect his competence in English or theirs?' Luke said. 'His English is flawless, you know that. We've all had students who hate us and give us zeros on everything.'

'In any case, we shouldn't pay too much attention to evalua-tions,' Frida said. 'They're notoriously unreliable.'

'That's the opposite of what you usually say, Frida.' She did not deny it. Luke went on: 'The word is, Huw's an excellent instructor. Tons of students have told me he's the best they've ever had.'

'I don't believe you!' Frida said. 'Students always say *I'm* the best.'

Because you give so many As and tell them they're all special, Melvyn thought.

'And what about this recent scandal over his syllabus?' Frida said.

Rocky nodded *sagely*. Luke indicated puzzlement by raising an eyebrow and bending his knees slightly, retracting the gun barrels of his legs. 'What scandal is that?' he said.

'A student complained to Frida that Huw's novella syllabus only had like *white males* on it,' Rocky explained. 'And he actually said women couldn't write to save their lives. Or ethnic minorities. Or gay or transgender people. He said they all sucked, big time.'

'Nonsense,' Luke said. 'Huw never uses American slang.'

'It's totally true,' Rocky said. 'Trust me.'

'How do you know that?' Luke said.

'Dude, Frida *told* me—*duh*.'

'Holy fuck, Frida, those are serious charges. Are you saying you have solid evidence that Huw made bigoted statements about women and minority writers?'

Frida's nose-ring shook and her scalp flushed crimson. 'I'm not saying I heard it with my own actual ears,' she admitted. 'But I know it's true.'

'So whose testimony are you relying on?' Luke said.

'Can't say. FERPA. Student confidentiality,' Frida said.

'Jeez, Frida, I have to know if you have evidence for those accusations.'

'All right, it was Broome,' Frida said. 'A mature student.'

'In age, yes,' Luke agreed. 'But mentally and emotionally— sweet Jesus. For a start she had the hots for Huw. We all know that. And when he rejected her advances, she turned sour. Second, she's mentally unstable. She carries a loaded pistol in her purse. She actually showed it to me.'

'Hey, so do I,' Rocky said. 'Like *hello?* Women have to protect themselves.'

'Me too,' Frida said. 'All men are rapists—except for gay men, of course.'

Melvyn snapped out of his reverie. Miranda, dressed as a Japanese schoolgirl, in black knee socks, had just laid down, or rather lain down, her eyes drooping seductively.

But Luke accepted the reproach. 'Maybe that's commoner than I realised,' he said. 'But third—well, you must have noticed that Broome is desperate to curry favour with you, Frida. She's looking for fellowships, prizes, recommendations.'

'She has a genuine admiration for me,' Frida said. 'A reverence, you might say. For my scholarly work and my example. I find that deeply touching.'

'Exactly. She's sycophantic, and makes no secret of it. So don't you think she might just be willing to besmirch Huw's name to gratify you?'

'Luke, are you suggesting that I'm biased against Huw?'

'Well, the idea had occurred to me.'

'I'm shocked that you'd consider me capable of bias,' Frida said. 'I believe in humanistic values. I'm a progressive. I fight for social justice. I read the PuffPost.'

'Maybe so. But ever since Savanna B. Manley's reading, when Huw said she was a shit writer, you got to admit you've held a grudge against him.'

'I don't know what you mean!' Frida said.

'Yeah, what do you mean?' Rocky said.

'You took it personally,' Luke said. 'I heard the conversation. I think you've been out to get him since. You want revenge.'

'I never heard anything so insulting, so false—so preposterous!' Frida said.

'Yeah, *preponderous*,' Rocky said. 'Props for the cool word, Frida.'

Melvyn decided to cut short the confrontation. 'I think we've had a very thorough discussion of Dr Lloyd-Jones' portfolio,' he said, toe-punting it further beneath the table. 'And now, maybe we should put it to the vote?'

'Yeah, let's put it to the vote,' Rocky said. 'I'm so like *done* with this baloney.'

For Melvyn, though, it was a tricky decision. He knew his wife would vote against Huw, and Rocky would support her, and Luke would vote for Huw. That made Melvyn's the decisive vote.

If he voted against, the Department Committee disapproved of the proposal, and it was unlikely that Dean Jorgenson, who had been incandescent at Timothy's thesis defence, would gainsay that vote. But if Melvyn voted with Luke, for Huw, the votes would be evenly split, and the Provost and President might give Huw the benefit of the doubt.

The Neolithic hunter in Melvyn wanted to see Huw defeated, thrashed with sticks, pelted with rocks, driven from the warm cave and the comfort and safety of the tribe. And the beta male in him, who feared the matriarch, cowered beside her heaving flanks, grateful for protection, willing to obey. Yet another part knew that Huw deserved to be a full professor—far more than Frida did, or Rocky. So maybe he should vote for him? Against the women? To stake out his independence? Defy the bloated Red Baron crouching with her black goggles on. That was what Dr Pound would urge him to do. But did he have the guts? Did he?

'Clearly we should vote by secret ballot,' he said. Luke nodded.

'Should we like vote by secret ballot, Frida?' Rocky said. 'You're the boss.'

'I'm not ashamed of my opinion,' Frida said. 'Are you ashamed of yours?'

'A secret ballot is the correct procedure,' Luke said. 'As you well know.'

'Votes for Huw's promotion…?' Frida snapped. Ack-ack-ack-ack.

'I do this under protest. Please put that in the minutes,' Luke told Rocky.

'And against…?' Frida said, with a *grim smile of satisfaction*.

Rocky's arm *shot up* like an infant's; Frida's followed at once.

Melvyn was paralysed.

'Are you abstaining, Melvyn?' Frida asked.

Damn, he could abstain—he had forgotten that. Should he? He would avoid having voted against anyone. But no one would be pleased if he sat on the fence. Who was more powerful? That was obvious. *I am a good person,* he told himself. What would the Superior Man do? He had not consulted the *I Ching* that morning, but it would counsel him to follow his conscience. Vote for Huw's promotion. He *would* vote for Huw. He would show Frida.

Feebly, uncertainly, his arm began to rise, then drooped.

'Three votes to one against,' Frida said.

'Are you sure?' Luke said. 'That wasn't clear to me. Melvyn, were you voting for Huw or against him? Could you verify that?'

'*Ich habe durchfall,*' Melvyn mumbled, remembering a phrase from German 101. I have diarrhoea. It was true. If he didn't get to a toilet real soon, he was in trouble.

'What the hell does that mean, Melvyn?' Luke said.

'Is there a motion to adjourn the meeting?' Frida said.

'I vote to adjourn it,' Rocky said.

'Seconded,' Melvyn said. 'I declare the meeting adjourned.'

'No, *I* declare it adjourned,' Frida said, snapping her Pear-book shut.

Lucky Luke mumbled something that sounded like 'hypocrit-ical bastards'. Oddly enough, Melvyn agreed with him, although he had got the outcome he planned. With luck he would soon be the alpha male of the department—but right now he had to reach that toilet.

SEVENTEEN

Heartline and Lifeline

How much worse can my life get, Huw asked himself, now Miranda wants to divorce me?

As it happens, Huw, far worse than you can imagine.

The day had passed quietly. In the morning he was able to write, to his astonishment, and in a final exhilarating spurt had completed his novel. Before lunch he lifted weights in the university gym with ferocious determination. His heart raced, his muscles tearing apart, but he ignored the pain. He ate in the cafeteria, which was unusual for a professor, and afterwards took a stroll in the university nature reserve, an area of prairie grasses and woodland frequented mainly by the amorous: condoms hung on shrubs and strewed the trails.

Sans glasses, he failed to recognise the person he was approaching, but he could tell she was female, and even from behind had a hunch she would be attractive. Her light, balletic gait was familiar: she pranced along, slowly, her feet hardly touching the ground. She wore headphones. The stateliness of her step suggested music. Twice her bare, slender arms rose, unhurriedly, gently, gracefully, as if choreographed. She wore a filmy blouse, a longish skirt of peasant inspiration, but of a more diaphanous fabric than peasants wore, and espadrilles that laced up her brown calves. She had her hair in a ballerina's shiny, tight topknot.

As he caught up with her she twirled, in fact pirouetted, rising on her tiptoes and trembling—smiling with joy and self-confidence, as if she expected applause.

'Elise, how graceful you look, floating along this woodland path like a nymph. You must be a dancer.'

'I am,' she said with pride.

'What are you listening to?'

'Chopin. The *Preludes*, played by Maria João Pires.'

Although his heart was in bits, he smiled. 'How fitting.'

She descended from her trembling points pose and stood squarely before him, far closer than usual for an American. 'Thank you, Huw. How are you?'

Should he confide in her? It might be unseemly to discuss his private life with a student, and impolitic, even though he had no intention of seducing her. But he needed to tell someone, and her use of his first name invited intimacy.

'Rotten, to tell the truth. You may have heard my wife left me.'

She nodded rhythmically, probably still listening to the music.

'She wants a divorce,' he added.

'How *splendid*,' she said, beaming. Huw guessed she had picked up the phrase from Masterpiece Theatre, maybe *Upton Abbey*. 'I mean what a splendid opportunity for you and her, to grow, to find yourselves, to explore new ways of being. It could be awesome, Huw.'

'I daresay that's how she looks at it. I confess I don't.'

'It's natural that you don't right now. But Time will heal you. I foresaw imminent catastrophe in your life, do you remember?'

'Yes, you did, Elise. What do you foresee now?'

'Give me your palm again.'

'Is there any point? You read it so recently.'

'The lines can change. In a remarkably short time.'

He surrendered his hand to her. When she took it in hers, the pleasure was instant—not exactly sexual, but certainly sensual. To be touched by such a pretty sprite was a joy. Women could be kind to men. Some of them still liked men. She stood so close that their bodies nearly touched.

'Yep, it has changed all right,' she said, peering at his palm. 'I saw the rupture in your heart line a few weeks ago, when it was kind of a crack. See? Now it's broken. Sorry.'

'Yes, it's broken. No hope at all, then?' he said, half amused, half wistful.

'You must *embrace* change,' she said. With a hint of suggestiveness? Or was that his imagination? 'Decay and dissolution bring new growth. Go with the flow.'

She said the last words with the glibness of Andie McDowell in *Groundhog Day,* and Huw had to resist retorting with the cynicism of Bill Murray.

'Philosophically, I agree. But my feelings are stuck in the Stone Age.'

She laughed. She smelled of apples and lavender. 'Now look at this, though. See this fork, right here in the lifeline. I don't remember seeing that last time. Maybe it was there already, but not so pronounced. It's crystal-clear now.'

'What does it mean?'

'I think a choice, maybe work-related. To stay here or work somewhere else.'

Tempus abire tibi est. 'Anything else?' He found himself believing her.

'Look here on the heartline: a clear break, but then there's this new line—I think it's new—connecting to the heartline. That could be a fabulous new love.'

She looked up at him and he nearly fell into the clear pools of her eyes. He had to change the subject. 'All I can think about is my old love.'

'Of course you feel hurt now. But you'll rise again—like the phoenix. Hey, I got a new tattoo. Of a phoenix, as it happens.'

Huw despised tattoos but asked politely, 'Where?'

She flushed. 'Close to my lady parts.'

'What a quaint phrase. In that case I don't suppose you can show me?' He was surprised that his tone had come out flirtatious, although he had not meant it to.

'Hell, I don't care,' she said, at once peeling back the brown film of her skirt—down over the flat abdomen, to the tops of her panties, a mere membrane of white cotton. Still no sign of the tattoo. With the titillating skill of a striptease artist—and yet too shy to look him in the eye—she pushed down the top of this garment too, revealing the mythical bird, beak open, wings wide and beating, rising from a pyre of curling flames and an equally thick fire of curling reddish hair. At last Elise dared to look at him. Across her face flittered embarrassment, but also pride, pleasure, and a challenge. It was not the saucy glance of the temptress, but the graver one of the princess offering herself to the prince.

'How extraordinary,' Huw said, embarrassed, because his voice shook.

'You like it then?' she said, still holding her skirt and panties down.

'Oh yes,' he said, far too quickly. 'It's wonderful.'

'I was afraid you might not dig it. A guy your age.'

'Usually I dislike tattoos. As most old fogeys do. But this one was done by an artist. The phoenix is alive—about to take flight.'

'Isn't it, though? It's so cool that you're into it, Huw. You want to touch it?'

A swarm of impulses assailed him, stung him. Of course he wanted to touch it! But no, of course he didn't! What was he thinking? What about Miranda? And Elise was not just a student, but his student! And what if anyone came along? They were standing in a glade of oaks and hornbeam, through which sunlight poured in melodramatic shafts. Luckily, there was no sign or sound of anyone. Just the humming of insects, and traffic not too far away.

'I probably shouldn't,' he said.

'Why not give in to temptation? You may.' Another quaint turn of phrase.

His hot blood often got him into trouble. But he pictured Miranda's face.

He shut his eyes. 'Better not. For both of us.'

'What a shame,' she said, covering up without rancour. Again there was distance between them. What terrible timing. If it had been a year hence, when she had graduated and he had got over his grief—*if* he ever got over it. 'Maybe some other time?' she added.

'I'd better turn back,' he said. It made him feel old, passionless.

'Sure. But before you go, there's something I got to tell you.'

He expected a gauche declaration, or more pressure to succumb to her advances. But she looked ashamed, or indignant.

'It's very hard to say. Maybe I shouldn't. I mean, this is in confidence, right?'

He nodded, fearing the worst. 'Of course. Go on.'

'You can't say I told you, or I'll get in trouble with my dad. Big time. You know the Shamburgers have it in for you, yeah?'

'I know Frida has. But both of them?'

'Yeah, I think so. They're lodging some kind of complaint against you. Because of how you conducted Timothy's thesis defence. Frida was furious.'

'I gathered that. But how do you know all this, Elise?'

'My dad told me—because I'm in your class and I have a major crush on you.'

'Jesus, your dad knows you have a crush on me?'

'No worries, I told him you're irreproachable—which is true, though I believe you could be tempted, frankly. If I work on you a bit more. See, you're blushing. That's so cute, Huw. Anyway, dad told me that Jorgenson and Timothy are making the complaint and the Shamburgers are backing them up. Or vice-versa. I'm not exactly certain. The little bitches.'

'Thanks for warning me.'

'Sure, no problem. Let me know when you change your mind about the phoenix.'

When, not *if*. 'Thanks again, Elise. May your phoenix fly.'

'Oh, it's about to take off, trust me.'

The encounter had unsettled him. On the one hand he was flattered that Elise was courting him, but also aware that his emotions were a bewildering mess of grief, anger, regret, pity, self-pity, confusion, denial and despair, all bubbling and boiling together. And on the other hand, there was Elise's worrying revelation about the plot against him.

But all that was forgotten when he got back to his office and saw the email from Miranda, blaring in caps: RAPE!

The message was incoherent, so he called her. To his surprise, she picked up.

'What happened, love? How are you? Can I come over?'

Her voice was tiny. 'Yes, I'm at home. Thank you, Huw.'

EIGHTEEN

Masterful Melvyn

Feeling as tough as Tom Cruise in *Mission Impossible*, Melvyn put on his burglar gear: black jeans, socks and shoes, a black polo shirt with the NaNoWriMo logo, and its fatuous slogan, *The World Needs Your Novel*, and a black bomber jacket. What about a ski mask? Nope, if anyone saw him, they'd call the cops. *How about blacking my face, then, like Justin Trudeau? People would never forgive me: you have to be the wet dream of liberal women to get away with shit like that.* Still, he had not shaved for a week and the face of a caveman stared back at him from the mirror. No doubt about it: he looked totally awesome.

Should he drive or walk? Each option had drawbacks. Even the smaller of the Shamburger SUVs was identifiable by the array of stickers: *I'm with Her, LGBTQIA+ Alliance, Teach Tolerance, Hillary for President, Black Lives Matter, Thank a Teacher,* and many more. On the other hand, the citizens of Tocqueville regarded pedestrians as tramps, malefactors, and madmen, and some hick with a BB gun or even a shotgun might well snipe at him from a dormer window as he walked past. Jezebel's strategy was best, he decided: he would drive to within a block of the address Frida had given him in the Historic District, then slink under the shadows of the oaks and maples on foot.

On the way out, with his heart thudding as though John Bonham were using it as a kick-drum, he picked up a pair of binoculars, and a natty device which he strapped to his temples. Garfield watched from the upstairs landing, peering through the banisters with an expression of undisguised scorn. Melvyn dismissed the fancy that the cat knew what he was up to and would confabulate with Frida later. Darcy wagged his tail hopefully.

Melvyn patted his head. 'Tough luck, pal. This one's for the dawgs, dude, not the dogs.'

Then he sprinted to the tank-like purple jeep, and vaulted up into the driver's seat. He set off, gripping the wheel, imagining machine-gun fire raking the road at any moment, and listening to *The Eye of the Tiger*. He sang along about the will to survive and the thrill of the fight. Tocqueville slashed by his windows, a Southern Gothic city, old wooden houses with porches and turrets lurking between trees, hounds howling at the moon. He left the car in the unlit parking lot of The Seventh Day Adventist church, in a deep pond of shadow.

As he flitted between the trees, crossing his fingers, he considered Huw's fate. Timothy had lodged a formal complaint, first with Frida, which she had supported with enthusiasm, then with the Dean, Jorgenson, who had naturally endorsed it, and thus it had reached the President, who had sent it on to the Board with reluctance and anger, so he had heard. The university lawyers were meant to be in discussion with him and the Board of Directors, right now, in an emergency session, as Melvyn stole towards his destination. Huw would be fired for sure, tenure or no tenure. If he were lucky, they might just castrate him, meta-phorically speaking—force him to make a grovelling apology, which would leave him impotent in all departmental matters, a minion of Frida's. Melvyn preferred that possibility. *Because of my innate kindness and humanity*, he told himself. *I'm not such a bad guy. Not like Frida, who's evil.* After tonight, if his dreams were realised, he would turn the tables on the lot of them. *He* would for sure soon be the alpha male in the department. Oh yeah.

He crept up to the house like a panther, not on all fours, but with the stealth of one. It was a white nineteen twenties Arts and Crafts home, with a porch on which stood a rocking chair, a derelict sofa, a coffee table, ashtrays, beer bottles and cans. Screwed into the siding was a metal plate emblazoned with an axe-wielding warrior and the legend, *Go Goths!* The football team of an adjacent state, he remembered. Melvyn edged around the side of the house. Who *did* it belong to? Some slovenly student. Or an equally messy professor. Lucky Luke? No, he was gay; an unlikely lover for Frida. Still, anything was possible these days. The crickets and katydids chirruped, covering his almost soundless approach. A bat skittered above his head, making him duck and nearly cry out. An owl screeched as he took up his position at the back, behind a bush close to the French windows. The scene was just what a third-rate writer like Frida would come up with. The bedroom on the other side of those windows was brightly lit, as she had promised. Melvyn had no need of the binoculars. A huge sleigh-bed, with a poster of dubious taste—atrocious taste—hanging above it. A sexy squaw, built like a glamour model, with a fierce expression, carrying a bow and arrows, surrounded by friendly wolves and bears, in moonlight, with dramatic snowy mountains in the background. Dream-catchers hung over the bed, which was empty.

For now.

No books on the bedside tables—so the resident was not a literary person. Next to a vast flat screen television hung a poster of a sultry Tinker Quick, her long legs wide apart, in thigh-high boots, her arms akimbo, her black hair flying in the wind, an expression of triumph on her heavily made-up face.

Evidently the tenant was a student, or an immature adult.

More evidence for this hypothesis was the profusion of Goth

garments scattered on the floor and hanging from the furniture: black leather pants, spike heels, fishnet stockings, suspenders, a brassiere fit for a Valkyrie, a corset—man, did women still wear those?—and a spiked collar and a riding whip. Real kinky. The wait was unbearable. It was seven-thirty, the time Frida had said. So where was she?

From deep inside came a cacophony, some kind of music— not Tinker, but Metal. A guttural, growling voice, the clanking of heavy machinery, the pounding of jackhammers, drums, guitars, shrill, hysterical solos. Melvyn smiled: Frida hated this kind of music. Despite the volume, he heard a feminine shriek, of laughter or pain, it was impossible to tell. Who could the mystery paramour be? Marge, maybe, the trans professor? Melvyn's mind boggled, ran riot, imagining all possible anatomical permutations. Oh boy oh boy—or oh girl oh girl.

However, when the bedroom door opened, with a tsunami of metallic din, it was not the Queer Studies professor who entered: this woman's hair was long and black. Otherwise, since his wife's bulk nearly hid the other figure, entangled as they were, all he could see was that she was also 'large', and taller than Frida. The women crashed about in the throes of passion, but Frida's paramour somehow kept her back turned towards him. She was wearing a black leather sleeveless jerkin with a skull in studs on the back; a black leather skirt, wider than it was long; fishnet stockings and suspenders, which slightly attenuated the chubbiness of her legs, and the black jackboots of an SS officer. A spiked collar. From behind she looked familiar. She had Frida in a combination of a bear hug and head lock. Was the woman a professional wrestler? Frida's copper scalp barely came up to her shoulder blades.

Nonetheless, Frida was impelling the pair towards the window, in her hideously short purple minidress, staggering as if her ankles were cuffed together with chains. Damn, they *were* cuffed together with chains. Only when the couple stumbled to within a foot of the pane did they pause, still kissing, or was it biting? Frida knew she had an audience of course. What about Alaric the Goth? Melvyn guessed Frida had discussed her fantasy with her 'mistress'—and had her consent. Maybe she was an exhibitionist too? Only now did Melvyn remember the action camera strapped to his forehead, and turn it on. Would they realise they were being filmed? And if they did, would they cease their lovemaking? He would just have to risk it.

Neither of them gave any sign that they were aware of his bearded head poking out of the bush, beyond the extraordinary violence of their kisses. It was a relief, but also a slight—was he too insignificant to notice? Besides, what did he feel, watching Frida? Horror, sure, but arousal too. Melvyn had rejected her invitation to watch lesbian porn with her, but Sapphic love turned him on, he knew now, even in the guise of bull hippo-potami in combat.

But the tableau was changing with breath-taking speed. The living sculpture writhed and wrenched itself around, so that the women, who were not ten feet away, presented their profiles to him. The woman gripping Frida in strong, if flabby, arms, was none other than their 'mature' student, Broome. His first thought was that he had been right that the tenant was not a literary person: though a creative writing major, Broome preferred trash television and video games to books. His second thought was: a *student*. His third: *Frida's* student. As that sank in, Broome broke free—maybe he had been wrong about who was clasping who or whom—and ripped off Frida's dress, thrust her face down on the bed, snatched up the riding crop, and lay into the vast Gorgonzola backside as if she were giving a public flogging in Saudi Arabia. Whack! Thwack! Swish! God, it was good! He was invisible, invulnerable. Had he orchestrated it himself, it could not have been more perfect. Doubtless Frida had wished to demean him by making him watch her with a lover, but with each of Broome's brutal blows he became more aroused, more potent. The whip whistled above the death metal—he could not hear it of course, but he *saw* and *felt* it whistling—and Frida squealed, or was that Dimebag Darrell? Nope, he would know that sow-like panicked squeal anywhere.

In the interest of decorum, what happened next should be elided from the record. It should be, since this is not pornography, but a work of serious literary fiction, as any discerning reader will agree. But we must remember that Melvyn's camera was recording every nanosecond. So, however offensive it may be, there is a record extant, and thus we are with regret *forced* to dwell upon the squalid incident a little longer, as judges and juries must when trying unspeakable crimes, regardless of their inclinations. *We could at least speed up the video, though, surely*? we seem to hear the more delicate readers among you pleading. Very well: clothes flew off and fell in a flurry of leather and lace. Broome and Frida engaged in acts of—ahem— 'oral love'. Broome spanked Frida with her blacksmith hands, then again with the whip. Frida threshed and wobbled. Heads shook and nodded. Mouths gaped in terror, and delight, to shout, to imprecate, to implore, to slobber, gnaw, suck, and bite. Melvyn stifled the urge to rush in and join them. Broome seized a fearsome mauve cudgel—in fact a dildo, a *circumcised* one—Jesus, were there special Jewish dildoes?—and looking as cruel and triumphant as Tinker Quick, committed an unspeakable act on Frida, who screamed above the cataclysmic noise.

You go, girl, Melvyn urged the savage Goth. An eardrum-perforating screech accompanied each jab of Broome's brawny arm. What could diminish Melvyn's joy? Only the realisation that never again could he possibly be so happy. He gave thanks, to God or the Goddess, Whofucking*ever*. His life was complete. This was nirvana, the purest ecstasy.

It ended abruptly. Broome snatched up scraps of leather and fled. Frida floundered on the bed in a state of shock, her back bruised, cut, covered in welts, Melvyn was delighted to see. When she rolled over, wobbling, quivering, and shaking, mascara and tears streaked her face. Superb, very gratifying. And then it happened: she broke the fourth wall. As she levered her squat body into a crouch on the bed, she looked out of the window—directly at him.

Could she see him? It was bright inside, dark outside, and on an instinctive reflex he ducked back into the foliage of the hibiscus bush. Still, her face, with the gold ring dangling from her snout, stared straight at him, and her expression dumbfounded him. She tried to smile, but the effort was too much: her lips contorted into a sneer, then a snarl. If it was not love her face showed, it was *something* erotic or pseudo-romantic. Or plain perverted.

Unable to contain himself any longer, he burst from the bush, heedless of whether his wife would be angry that he had not waited, and heedless of his swollen member. Would she notice that, concealed within his pants? He sure hoped so.

Melvyn tapped his watch, and beckoned to her to follow him. For once he knew she would do his bidding. He sprinted round the block to his car, hardly caring now whether the neighbours might see him and phone the police, or blast away at him with their semi-automatic weapons. He raced home like Vin Diesel in *The Fast and the Furious*, yelling.

He was right: he did not have to wait long. He had just checked that Thalia was still out, bribed Garfield with a saucer of milk, and swallowed a stiff Scotch, when Frida's SUV screeched into the drive. The car door thunked as if an Olympic weightlifter had slammed it.

Battered, bloody, her dress in shreds, a ghastly grin on her face, Frida looked more fearsome than a Russian weightlifter when she came in. It was a decisive moment. He jumped on her, pushed her roughly up the stairs into the bedroom, swept the mewling Garfield off the bed, and deposited Frida on it. He tore at her garments as Broome had done. Her dress disintegrated.

And then—well, dear reader, you can guess what he did, and how. He proved himself a *man*. Or rather, a Silverback gorilla, an alpha male, just as he had hoped earlier. For once Frida was not on top in any sense. And for the first time in many, many years, he enjoyed it.

'Wowee,' Frida said afterward. 'I never knew you could be so… *masterful*, Melvyn.'

'Neither did I. To be honest.'

'But what's that weird flashing gadget on your forehead?'

'Oh, this? I forgot to take it off. Just a light. For seeing in the dark.'

'Right. Genius. You are smart.' For once, Frida was happy, relaxed. *Nice.*

'I feel fulfilled,' he said truthfully. 'I never dreamed I could want you so much.'

'Oh Melvyn,' she moaned. 'It was all for you, sweetie. I *love* you.'

He had not heard that for a decade or two. Did she mean those gooey words? In her Disney-distorted mind, maybe. He did not repeat the formula. *No need. I have all the power I could ever desire, right here, digitally saved. My Third Eye. From now on she can never bully, browbeat, humiliate, or degrade me. She can never scorn me or scoff at my words. All these years she's been the boss. Now it's my turn.* As he lay on his back, with Frida's bruised flesh flopping over his chest like a burned omelette, Melvyn considered revealing what he had done. Not yet, he decided. Even so, he could not resist teasing her about Broome:

'I have to admit the identity of your lover surprised me.'

Frida's gaze was adoring. 'Because she was a woman, you mean?'

'No, because she's a student. One of *our* students. That's risky, surely?'

She chuckled. 'Don't worry. I'm pretty powerful at Oxbow State, Melvyn.'

'All the same, you'd be fired in a heartbeat if anyone found out.'

'But Broome will never tell. And I know I can trust you.'

He smiled *duplicitously*, as Gardner and Chandler might have put it.

'Sure you can trust me, honey,' he said, smirking with his secret knowledge of the footage. *Blackmail*—what a cool word. He had turned into a *film noir* tough guy, like Humphrey Bogart. And Lauren Bacall was awaiting him in the wings.

NINETEEN

The Voice of God

Oh dear, the poor old Welshman. Even by the standards of his *annus horribilis*, Huw is having a rotten day. Let us divulge, lest the reader despair, that despite the slings and arrows of outrageous fortune, and his own *hamartia* and *hubris*, our handsome dark-haired Celtic hero will receive another chance to save himself. Already Time has twice churned to a halt for him and yet Huw has gone back to his stale old life. Will he have the wisdom to seize his last chance?

Here he is, at Miranda's front door, frantic after the email titled 'RAPE', his heart racing, having sped in his car and sprinted up the stairs. He is sweating, panting for breath.

Miranda has accused him of arrogance and self-centredness, of superficiality and insensitivity. We have seen him struggling with that knowledge—recognising the truth in her words, yet, so far, failing to change much. And from folk tales, including the Welsh ones, we know that the man who cannot change is doomed to an inferior existence, or punishment. We know too that the hero only has three chances. Huw is no boy—his hair is greying at his temples. And yet he is not yet fully grown up. The dominant myth of his time is that one need not mature, ever, that it is more fun to be a boy, to play, to evade responsibility, live a life of fantasy. Huw has accepted this creed, like most men. Only now is he starting to question it.

He knocks. No response. He tries again. He's heard something inside—a monotone nasal squeak, some announcer on a television, or an irritable seal—and a shuffling noise. He imagines Miranda in her fluffy pink slippers and pyjamas. Is she hurt? Is she still in danger?

He does not suspect that his own life is in danger.

From our Olympian halls, we observe as he confronts his fate. Will he understand in time that fate is not the same as destiny—that destiny is what one makes of one's fate? He has not avoided the catastrophes, cannot avoid them, but he could find self-knowledge, wisdom—and face his troubles with dignity, like the heroes of ancient Greece and Wales.

'Miranda?' he calls. No response. 'Are you there? It's me.'

He sat down on the top step to wait. His ears whistled, his left arm ached, his jaw and the left side of his face ached, and the pressure in his chest mounted. *I should go to the hospital,* he thought. *But I've got to see Miranda first. If I can just hold out until then.* He wanted to lie down but forced himself to sit up.

At last the door opened, very slowly, silently. 'Huw?' a tinny voice said.

He jumped up to fling his arms around her—but seeing her in her pink fluffy slippers with the pom-poms, as he had guessed, and the pink pyjamas with a design of teddy bears, her hair uncombed, lank and greasy, her face bare of makeup, and yet as white and blank as a geisha's, he restrained the impulse. If he touched her, she would crumple like cardboard.

'What are you doing here?' she said. Her face was not anguished, but blank, numb.

'You know what I'm doing here. You told me to come. You

said you've been raped. Oh my God, Miranda, I'm so sorry. How are you?'

'All right, I guess. I know I look like shit. What do you want?'

'For God's sake, you invited me. Just now. I'm worried. Can I do anything?'

'No. I don't think so.' She did not move aside for him to enter.

'I love you, Miranda.'

'I love you too,' she said mechanically. *Non te amat,* the choirs had sung.

'Will you let me in?'

'My apartment is a trash-heap. You'll have to wait while I have a bath.'

'I don't care what you look like.'

'Wait in the living room. I can't talk to you till I'm clean.'

On the television, a woman with blonde hair and the manic smile of a patient in an advert for dentists was talking in sotto voce squeaks with a rodent-faced politician. Huw sat on the sofa, clearing a space among the medical books, health magazines, medicine bottles, and a menagerie comprised of a stuffed toy poodle, a panda, a duck, and the Pink Panther. They looked brand new. More disturbingly, amid the detritus was a carving-knife. From the bathroom he heard the hissing of water. Miranda's shower lasted half an hour. Then she padded to the lace-and-satin bedroom, where she cloistered herself for another half an hour.

She emerged in full regalia—dressed rather like the TV announcer, in a royal blue skirt-suit, her hair curled and blow-dried, her lips scarlet. Only the celebrity smile was missing. She sat in a pine-framed armchair, crossing her slender, stockinged legs, obsessively rather than seductively, despite the stiletto heels. Behind her, Frida Kahlo with antlers and arrows in her body frowned down on him.

'Why have you gone to such trouble dressing up?' he asked her.

She shrugged. 'You expect me to look nice.'

'I expect nothing of the kind. Don't you believe me? I love you.'

'Me or my body? Would you love me if I were fat and ugly?'

'Oh no, not again. Won't you tell me what happened? From the beginning?'

'I told you, he raped me.'

'Who did?'

'Matthew, of course. McBane. My fucking boss.'

I knew it, he almost said. 'Go on. Where? When?'

She spoke with the detachment of a perfect witness. 'Last night. Their house. I drank a ton of wine at dinner—he kept refilling my glass, although I told him not to—and they led me to a bed, so I could rest, they said. They put out the light and I fell asleep. When I awoke I found them on each side of me, stroking my body. Both of them. I told them to cut it out, but I was still plastered. I stumbled out, half-dressed, intending to drive home. But Matthew caught up with me, and pushed me into a dark room.'

She stopped as though someone had punched her in the gut.

'Was NeAmber with him too?' Huw asked.

'No, he was alone. He said he needed me. He said I had to help him. Only I could save him. He said I couldn't tell anyone. He tore at my tights. Then he did it.'

'He raped you.'

She gulped. 'Yes. Digitally.'

The computer meaning struck him first. Had McBane hacked her laptop? No, she meant with his fingers. She was speaking clinically, as the traumatised often did.

'I'm going to kill him,' Huw said.

'Please don't. I've lodged a complaint with the police. I did a DNA test. I can nail him, Huw.'

'Good. But I still want to kill him. Or at least beat him to a pulp.'

'I beg you not to. He needs to be shamed. To lose his job.'

241

'Yes, you're right. So what do you want me to do?'

'Just be here for me. And try to be more understanding.'

'I am trying. I'll try harder, I swear.'

'The sea-monsters say I need to affirm my independence from men. Do you realise, I got married when I was nineteen, and apart from the two years after my divorce, I've been married ever since? To *men*. I don't know who I am. I've spent my life pleasing men. Being what they want me to be. I need to find out if there's anything inside of me.'

She glanced at Frida Kahlo split open. Then at two seated Fridas, holding hands. Each had her internal organs revealed, her chest dissected. The Fridas all gazed coldly back at her.

He did not know how to answer. Was there anything inside her? What did he love? Had he fallen in love with his own image of the perfect woman? A picture?

'If I don't exist, I figure I may as well kill myself,' she said. 'Right?'

'You do exist. Please don't hurt yourself.'

'I'm not sure, Huw. Most women don't exist.'

'You mean they simply perform functions and roles, don't you? Like that woman with the glazed smile on the screen, talking to the squeaking rodent.' She nodded. 'If you need to divorce me to find yourself,' he went on, 'I will accept that. I have thought about it. I just want to be in your life, somehow. Help you if I can. And see justice done. Retribution.'

'It's coming. The sea-monsters told me. He'll be swallowed up. Believe me. Leave me now. If you don't hear from me again, remember that I will always love you.'

As he drove home, his chest still hurting, in fact hurting more, the song with those lyrics, which he had always hated, bellowed hysterically, swooped like a sick swallow in his brain. I-ee-ay, will always love you—oo—oo—oo-oo—oo. Hold tight, Huw, boyo. Be brave.

*

Instead of going straight to the hospital, as he knew he should, why did he decide to ride his bicycle to work, when a heavyweight boxer was punching his chest, he had pins and needles in his left arm, and his jaw ached and throbbed, right up to his left eye? He knew it was daft. But there he was, flying under a canopy of oaks and maples like Geraint Thomas again, head down over the drop handlebars, quads and calves taut, sweat streaking his face, mind empty as a Zen monk's. As he neared the final intersection before the campus, a series of mishaps befell him. Three dogs tore out from a porch and chased him, barking and snarling at his heels; next, a pick-up truck brushed his elbow, with drunken boys hanging out of the windows, screaming and making him swerve; then a pink Corvette barrelled by, piloted by Rocky, who was staring at her mobile phone. At the red light, she kicked the brakes, and Huw, already off balance and too far from the kerb, hit her back bumper.

He performed a gymnast's stunt—clinging to his handlebars, upside down—then the tarmac rose to crack his head and knee and elbow, and he lay tangled beneath his bike. A car door thunked shut. *Rocky will help me up,* he told himself. But no—she only inspected the back of her car for damage, muttered about fucking jerks, and got back inside, without so much as a glance at him. Possibly she had not recognised him. As she drove off he read her bumper stickers: *A Woman's Place is in the White House. Practice Compassion. Be Kind.*

Someone lifted his bike off him. The sky pulsed around the white-hot heart of the sun. Long legs, disembodied, rose out of suede ankle-length boots and ascended like temple columns towards the empyrean. Gentle hands touched his face, held him under his armpits.

'Don't lift him, Elise. He could be injured.' The voice was Charleston's.

'Sir? Huw?' Haloed by a corona of sunlight, her face floated among cirrus clouds. 'Are you OK?'

'I think I'm having a heart attack. I'm pretty sure I am.'

'Oh man, this sucks,' said Elise.

'It's probably a mild one,' Huw said. 'Don't worry.'

'Shit,' Charleston said. Huw still could not see him. Where was he?

Huw closed his eyes and flew off among the clouds. The pain would soon be over. People shouted, cars passed. Charleston gave directions to the emergency services. Elise unfastened his helmet. The strap had been tight around his windpipe. Someone wet his lips with water. He was dying, he suspected. He did not mind, although he wished he were not in an untidy heap like this, bleeding, one leg buckled under him, among people who did not love him. If only he could see Owen one last time, and Miranda. Would he last long enough to say goodbye to them? That was all he asked. The novel would have to fend for itself. The hardback drifted into the sky, trailing clouds of glory, as medics lifted him on to a stretcher, shovelled him into the ambulance and strapped him in.

A blue light pulsed, a siren wailed, and Whitney Houston kept bawling that she would always love him. Was he imagining that? He could *not* die listening to Whitney Houston. Someone held his hand. Miranda? No, Elise.

'Thank you,' he said.

'Hey, no worries.'

Charleston chuckled.

He passed out, or was sedated. When he came to, he was in bed in a blinding white room. God's voice blared above him, loud, authoritative, deep and confident. What was he saying? Or was it a She? Had he made it into heaven? Or was this place purgatory? As Huw's eyes focussed, he saw that God was black. A black woman. She spoke in orotund tones, to polite applause. She wore her hair in a shoulder-length bob. Her face was smooth, and a marvellous coppery colour. She was promulgating laws, commandments, something about *freedom, dignity, humanity, sisterhood*. He could not follow what she was saying. His eyes hurt so he shut them. When he opened them again, God's face was on the TV screen, and she was Obadiah. Her guest, she said, was a great musical genius: Mustwe East.

Huw wished he could lower the volume of the voices, and dim the dazzling light. His weariness overpowered him. If only he could sleep for centuries and wake up in Carreg Cennen, with Owen Glendower beside him, and his own son Owen. A harpist would play Welsh airs and a bard would recite the Mabinogion in Middle Welsh. *He* was the bard. It was his voice. He recited to his dear son and the last native Prince of Wales. He was fulfilled. Joyful. *That* was how he should live.

*

'What's that you're saying? We can't understand a word.'

'I'm not surprised,' he murmured, opening his eyes. 'I was speaking Welsh.'

An olive-skinned woman leaned over him. She had noble, intelligent features, which expressed a gravity Huw was unused to seeing.

'Welsh? Don't the Welsh speak English, Dr Lloyd-Jones?'

'Most of us can if we want to. Am I alive? What happened to me?'

'You had a cardiac arrest,' she said. 'Two of your arteries were blocked. You've undergone surgery. I've given you a couple of stents. Yes, you're alive, luckily. You didn't take my advice to consult a cardiologist, I suppose? You certainly didn't come to see me.'

'I'm afraid I didn't. I should have. Are you the surgeon?'

'Yes, I am.'

'Thank you for saving my life. We keep meeting, don't we? Is that fate?'

She murmured something. 'That means, Who knows God's purposes?'

'What language is that? May I ask where you're from?'

'I'm a US citizen. But I was born in Isfahan, in Iran. I spoke in Farsi.'

'Persia: the land of Hafez and Firdaus, Rumi, Omar Khayyam.'

She susurrated a few more words in Farsi, presumably. 'Is that Rumi again?'

'Omar Khayyam. You look tired. Sleep if you can.'

'Could you do something for me first? Turn off that bloody racket, please.'

'You don't like the television? All Americans love it.'

'But I'm not American, see you. I'm a Welshman. And I loathe it.'

'So do I,' she said, silencing it and dimming the lights. 'I'll drop in on you soon.'

'I shall look forward to that. May I ask your name?'

'Nasreen Shirazi.' She did not hold out her hand but she did smile at him.

He closed his eyes and was soon paddling a hide coracle along the River Teifi. Whenever he paused it turned in the current, like a leaf. It was soothing. The little leather boat drifted downstream. Life could be like that. No need for worry or strife. He cut and peeled a hazel wand, like the wandering Aengus, and hooked a berry on a thread, and dropped it into the water. He caught a silver trout, which turned into a glimmering girl with apple blossom in her hair. She called his name and ran and faded through the brightening air.

He woke up, old and weary from wandering through hollow lands and hilly lands. Owen was sitting beside him, not in his usual hoodie, but a smart blazer and chinos.

'Owen, lad,' Huw said. 'I'm happy to see you. I will find out where she has gone,'

'Miranda, you mean?' Owen said. He had grown up overnight.

Huw smiled and went on reciting. 'And kiss her lips and take her hands.'

'You're a bit delirious. I told her that you'd had a heart attack.'

Stuck in the poem, he could not stop. 'And walk among long dappled grass…'

'I told her to come and see you. She said she would if she could.'

He shook his head, laughing. 'And pluck till time and times are done…'

'But don't count on it. She's been so weird lately,' Owen said. 'Dad?'

'The silver apples of the moon, the golden apples of the sun,' he finished.

'A gorgeous girl was here a minute ago,' Owen said. 'Elise something.'

'What about Miranda? Is Miranda coming? I love you, Owen.'

'I love you too,' he said, sounding embarrassed.

'I must live differently,' Huw said. 'No more bloody silly games. I need to listen to more classical music. Write more. Go home to Wales. Drink more single malt Scotch.'

'Dad?' Owen said. 'You got a call from a woman in New York. Your agent, I think. Sherry Glass? Is that right? It sounded like a joke. I started laughing.'

'That's her real name, believe it or not. What did she say?'

'Something about an auction. An advance? Does six figures sound right?'

Huw whistled. 'I'm going to have another heart attack.'

Nasreen Shirazi entered as he spoke. 'Please don't make so much noise.'

'Sorry,' Huw said. 'But we've got something to celebrate: a publishing deal.'

'Congratulations, Huw. But the main thing to celebrate is that you're alive. Don't forget that. Worldly success is unimportant. You are *alive*. Be aware of that.'

'You're right.' The way she had pronounced his name, with a slightly guttural consonant, was enchanting, and he was touched that she had called him by his first name. All the same, he ached to see Miranda. Would she come? Alive, the doctor said—and he knew she was speaking not of his body alone, but his spirit.

Everyone visited: Lucky Luke and his partner, an ex-Marine, who talked only of catching alligator gar; Cooper and Burd, who brought books by Dylan Thomas and Richard Hughes; and many students, Elise and Charleston, and Jordan and Nutmeg, who held hands and announced that they were engaged, and Truman, who had once been Trudy, and needed a shave; and Walt, who gave him a box of chocolates and, incredibly, the selected verse of Rumi; and even Frank, or Hank, who with a grin left a *Playboy* on his bedside table. Huw longed to see Miranda, but she did not appear, even when Owen returned, as he did every day. On the other hand Nasreen often looked in on him. Apart from using his first name, she avoided familiarity, indeed was formal, but always recited a verse for him, and gave him her deep, melancholy Leonardo smile. He looked forward to her visits and Owen's most of all.

Less welcome was the visit Frida and Rocky paid him. Long before they entered his room, where he was reading John Cowper Powys, he heard the brassy blare, the trombone of Frida's voice, and the trumpet of Rocky's. Even though he was clutching a copy of *Owen Glendower*, dread gripped Huw. He simply could not face them yet. He shut his book and his eyes, and pretended to sleep. The horns gusted in, their boots beating a dirge-like rhythm.

'But what about riding, Frida?' Rocky said. 'I don't know how to teach creative riding.'

'Haven't you read all my books yet, Rock? There's nothing to it. You just tell the students they're all talented and special. Positive reinforcement. Give them As, as long as they condemn right-wing values. Our job is to mould the next generation. That's all.'

'Gee, Frida, you're so inspiring. I always feel so like uplifted after we speak.'

'Thanks, Rock, because I value loyalty above everything. I'm a leader, but I don't lead by fear like some goddamn fascist. I'm kinda like Michelle, or Meghan, or Obadiah. I want my followers to think for themselves. And you do that, Rocky. I know I can trust you. In fact we should think about promoting you. Women should be in charge, right?'

'Are you shitting me?' the trumpet sighed. 'Gee thanks, Frida. I love ya to bits.'

Snuffles and sighs indicated a tearful embrace. The women hurled their chairs at the wall with a crash. 'We better end our visitation,' Rocky said. 'Dude's asleep, anyways.'

Frida dropped her voice to a whisper. 'So I heard it was your car he ran into, right?'

'Uh, yeah. Thing is, I was tweeting with Sheena Grayham, you know her?'

'No way! Sure I know her, she's a genius. The creator of *Bitches*. Very cool.'

'Right, so like I never saw him. Then when I slammed on the brakes and I felt him crash into the Corvette, I never realised it was Huw laying in the road. Like honestly. I just thought it was some fucking jerk.'

Frida laughed. 'You got that right.'

'Haha. John Cow-per Powys,' said Rocky. 'Who's that, some dickhead phallocrat?'

'The hell I know,' Frida said. 'Some dead white male no one gives a shit about.'

'You got that right.' Their boots beat a tattoo on the floor, a rattle and a snare drum snap, and the horns receded, the trombone sliding, the trumpet blasting brief treble bursts.

Not only were they gone, thank God, but Nasreen was coming in.

'Who were those, er, ladies?' she said. 'Relatives? Friends of yours?'

'More like enemies, I'm afraid. Colleagues from the university.'

'I'm sorry. Is your work environment stressful?'

'You could put it that way.'

'You must change that. I noticed they didn't even speak to you. Not once.'

Had she been listening? Did she care enough to do that?

'They never speak to me if they can help it. And when they do, they don't listen to what I have to say. If you don't agree with them, you aren't merely misguided, you're scum, beneath notice. That's what's wrong with academia—with our society as a whole. No one is listening to anyone else. They talk about freedom, but they don't understand it.'

Nasreen shook her head. 'I know what you mean. When people find out I'm a Muslim, they nearly always ask how I can accept the domination of men. It's no good trying to explain that I don't. They've already made up their minds. Those poor women.' She spoke not with scorn but pity. She was a different kind of woman altogether—one who not only spoke of compassion, but practised it.

He knew he would miss her when he left the hospital. However, he was convinced that she would play some part in his future life. But he tried not to think about that. Hurt though he was that Miranda had not visited, he had to see her and ask for another chance.

TWENTY

No Laffing Madder

Melvyn was in an annexe of one of the classrooms in the Harriet Tubman Building, a kitchen intended for grad students, although he had never seen them, or anyone else, use it. The room had become his private domain. He would sneak in to scoff chocolate chip cookies, his secret vice, and watch porn on his tablet—his *top* secret vice. The 'actress' in the video reminded him of Jezebel, which gave him an idea: what if he lured her here for a quickie? The risk would be an aphrodisiac. She would be up for it, he was sure. Oh boy oh boy oh boy.

To enquire what he was doing while engaged in his viewing would be indiscreet, and indeed vulgar; in any case, female voices in the adjoining classroom interrupted him. As there was a door, fortunately locked, into that room, he could hear every word, and since the voices were as harsh and loud as foghorns, he knew he was eavesdropping on Rocky and Frida.

'I gotta tell ya, Rocky, I'm real worried. The Board still hasn't decided if they're going to fire Huw. What if he gets off scot-free, after bullying Timothy so shamefully?'

'We can't let that happen. But like, what more can we do?'

'Remember what we discussed the other day?' Frida said in an affable voice.

'Accusing him of sexual harassment? That'd be awesome. Then he wouldn't stand a chance. Trouble is, he hasn't like actually sexually harassed anyone, right?'

Melvyn's mind did a backflip. Was Frida so malicious and devious? So evil?

'Oh, Rocky, you're so innocent. You can fabricate evidence. In fact, guess what? I caught him holding hands with Elise, you know, the President's daughter.'

Oh boy, Frida was *evil*. Huw and Elise, though? Really? Melvyn was envious.

'You did?' said Rocky. 'That's not like fake news? Gosh, sorry. You did?'

'You bet. They said she was reading his palm, telling his fortune—a likely story! But here's the snag: Elise won't back me up on it. She says he never touched her.'

Melvyn closed his tablet with a sigh and adjusted his dress. He was glad Huw had not banged Elise. That would have been unbearable. Oddly, he was relieved for Huw's sake, too.

'That girl's no feminist, Frida. Too pretty. No solidarity. Got any other ideas?'

'As a matter of fact, yeah, I do. Broome.'

'Are you shitting me? Huw boned Broome? For real?'

No way! Melvyn nearly yelled.

'Between you and I, Rock, no he hasn't. He hasn't laid a finger on her.'

'Right. But isn't that kind of like a problem?'

'Not really, Rocky, because Broome is willing to testify that he harassed her.'

'You mean she'd lie through her ass just to fuck Huw over?'

'Let's not put it like that. I wouldn't call it lying. It's more like metaphorical language. Because she feels he would like to sexually harass her. At least *she* would like him to. Get it? It may not be strictly true, in the literal sense, but it's figuratively true. In her mind. She fantasises about it. And reality's subjective, like Derrida says. See what I mean?'

'You mean if she lies it's like a poem, right? Basically flowery bullshit?'

'Exactly. You over-exaggerate a tad, but it's the lie that tells the truth. In a way.'

Silence followed. Melvyn imagined Rocky's perplexed expression: the knitted brow, the pursed lips, the murky eyes. 'Yeah. Coo-ul, I guess.'

It sounded fool-proof. Huw would lose his job, Frida would invite Holly Tuwuwanda to apply for it, and Melvyn would be appointed Director of the Undergraduate Programme of Creative Writing. Since his recent gold medal performance in the bedroom, Frida had mostly been pleasant. He might not even need to leave her. After all, she had assured him he could bone whoever he liked. He could openly continue his affair with Jezebel. And maybe start one with Miranda too, now she was available? The only trouble was that Melvyn felt sorry for Huw now, just when the finish line was in sight. *Damn my conscience!* he thought.

Melvyn heard muffled words, and pressed his ear to the door. Frida spoke slyly:

'Don't forget you're going to be Director of the Undergraduate Programme, Rocky.'

What the fuck? She'd shaft me like that? Frida had assured Melvyn that the post, with release time and more money, would be his, if they could get rid of Huw, the natural choice.

'But like, what about Melvyn?' Rocky said. 'Won't he expect to get the job?'

'Oh screw Melvyn,' Frida said, with a peal of laughter. 'I mean, he may be a tad disappointed, but he's obedient. Spineless. Kind of a chump, to tell the truth. I got him wound round my little finger. Once Thalia's gone off to college, I'm gonna move a lover into the house. Then we can have a ménage à trois. Melvyn hasn't got the guts to object.'

Are you crazy? Melvyn's mind screamed. *With that freak?*

'Melvyn's in my good books at the moment. He's even been kind of a good lover for the first time in like forever. Still, you gotta remind them who's boss, right? He's just a *guy*. Like I said, I got the jerk wound round my little finger.'

That's what you think, bitch. Melvyn had been obedient—and what had he got out of it? Nothing. Well, the worm was turning.

'Just wait and see,' Frida said. 'It'll all turn out the way I plan. It always does.'

Over my dead body, Melvyn swore.

*

Later, at home in his study, where Melvyn was pecking at his keyboard and wishing he could write like Huw, a sudden corvid screech of alarm sent chills down his spine.

'Mel—vyn! Get your caagh-caagh ass down here! Like this caagh minute.'

Fuck you, I'm not your flunkey anymore, Melvyn mouthed.

He went on typing and slurping toxic Sundoes slush. He heard a crash, a curse, and the thump of feet on the stairs, then stertorous breathing, coming in thick pants, with a wheeze and a whistle and a cracking sound. Frida was wedged in the doorway.

'Melvyn, brace yourself. I've got bad news and worse news. The worst.'

'Oh God—not Clio? An overdose? *Another* drunken fuck with a linebacker?'

Frida struggled to squeeze herself through the frame. 'Caagh—no—caaagh.'

'Don't tell me Thalia self-harmed again and bled all over the Turkish carpet.'

'Worse than that.' Finally she squeezed in with a plop. '*Way* worse.'

He was in a sweat. 'What could possibly be worse than Thalia cutting herself?'

'Try this: those goddamn attorneys say we don't have a case against Huw. Can you believe it?'

Melvyn sighed. 'Well, that sucks. I am glad Thalia's fine, though.'

'One goddamned lawyer said the charge of bullying and homophobia was sheer bullshit, and he had the gall to tell me not to get on his ass about stuff like that again.'

Melvyn wished he had been there. 'Were those his exact words?' he grinned.

'Of course not. He said it was a frivolous accusation. Completely unfounded, the hick said. Just because he's a man. He had the nerve to suggest Timothy and I were delusional.'

'Hmm, he has a point,' Melvyn said. *Rub it in, dude. Look at her face now!*

'What the hell do you mean by that? You hate Huw as much as I do. More.'

Melvyn got out of his chair and stood very close to her, so she had to crane her neck to look into his face. He was a foot taller and she disliked him towering above her. But it was time to show her she was no longer the boss. 'We should re-evaluate our strategy,' he said.

Frida was speechless—which was unprecedented for her. He went on:

'I admit I was jealous of Huw. Still am, to be honest. But don't you feel sorry for him at all? I mean, the guy's just had a heart attack and Miranda wants a divorce. He has to be worried about money, big time. If you get him fired, how's he going to support that kid?'

'He has plenty of money, and unfortunately he's about to get much more.'

Melvyn pressed his point, without asking her to explain. 'We've gone too far.'

'Too far? We haven't gone far enough. That bastard deserves

to lose his job. You're way too tender-hearted, Melvyn.' Frida snorted, her flanks shuddering. 'Tomorrow I'm going to tell the President that Huw has been hitting on Broome.'

'Are you crazy? It's not even true,' he said, forgetting to put it as a question.

'Well, not in the literal sense, no. I bet he'd like to, though.'

'God, I doubt it. Huw can do way better. Anyway, it won't work. Broome is one of Elise's sorority sisters. I'm sure Elise would tell her father that the allegation is nonsense.'

Frida stepped back. 'Give me a bit more space, I can't breathe. Damn, I don't know what to do. We *have* to fire his ass. The Provost won't give us a new tenure line, so we can only hire if we fire. We need more diverse faculty. We could do with an African-American. Preferably a woman. Maybe gay. Trans would be cool, too.'

Melvyn advanced on her again. Frida flattened herself against a bookcase. The appeal to her better nature had not worked, predictably, because she did not have a better nature. She was fond of cute pets, it was true, but then so was Hitler. No, he would have to appeal to her self-interest.

'Do we really want to fire him now, right after his heart attack? It wouldn't look so good for us. For you. You'd look heartless, Machiavellian.'

'I don't *give* a damn what anyone thinks.'

Melvyn echoed what Luke had said. 'Are you sure? Besides, he's kind of a brilliant writer. Original, bold. Incredible gift for language. James Steele said in the New Yorker that he's the most exciting stylist alive. He makes the programme look good. And us, Frida.'

She shut her eyes. 'Yeah, maybe, but he is a white male. Hetero too.'

'At least he's not a dead white male,' Melvyn said, pleased by his own wit.

'Not yet. Oh my God, that's it! That's the solution.'

Melvyn shivered. 'Surely you aren't saying you'd rejoice if he croaked?'

'Well, let's be honest, it would be convenient. Painful, maybe, but hey, you can't have everything. If only that heart attack had killed him. It would have been perfect.'

Would Huw's death have made *him* happy? Maybe. But a smidgeon of pity surprised him again. Like Chandler's hard-boiled detectives, he actually did have a conscience. Weird.

'Anyways, you said you have bad news and worse news,' he prompted her.

'Yup, there's more. Wait for it. According to Lucky Luke, Huw's been offered a contract for his novel by Sloane Square, after an auction. Apparently all the major houses wanted it. It's even in *Publishers Weekly*. I've never heard such shitty news.'

'Geez, isn't Sloane Square the most prestigious house in London?'

'You bet. Holly Tuwuwanda publishes with them. All the best black and gay writers do. And what's more, it's going to come out simultaneously over here with Brooklyn Books. Obadiah is bound to have him on her show. What can we do?'

Melvyn was envious, and filled with schadenfreude. '*You* must be devastated.'

'He's going to overshadow us all. Especially *you,* sweetie.'

What a bitch. 'You sound jealous yourself, *sweetie.*'

'You know me better than that. There's not a jealous bone in my body. I'm totally delighted to see a colleague's success... But it wouldn't be right if the programme became famous just for his work, would it? With him being a man and all. What kind of example does that set? What if all our MFA candidates are white dudes from now on? What would that do to our diversity ranking and funding?'

'Our candidates are more likely to be straight chicks, you know. Our female students find Huw pretty hot—he's got a Chili pepper on *Rateyourprofessor.com.*'

'That is so gross. I mean, what about *me*? Broome says I'm super-hot.'

Melvyn coughed hard. 'Sure, honey, you are sexy as all get-out. Anyway, the question is, what can we do about it? Nothing. I guess he's getting a big advance?'

Frida wept. 'Six figures, Luke said. Or was it seven? I told you he has money.'

'Holy shit. Well, we can forget getting Huw fired. He'll be outta here, pronto.'

Frida fell into the recliner. Springs bent, boinged, and broke. 'I'm so bummed.'

'Look on the bright side: if he resigns, you can hire Holly Tuwuwanda at last. I remember seeing her on Obadiah recently. She's quite the celebrity now.'

'Sure she is. She's African, queer, and HIV positive.'

'Ticks all the right boxes, then. What more could anyone want?'

'She's also drop-dead gorgeous. *And* wears those super-cool ethnic clothes.'

'On the other hand, she can't actually write, can she? I know she's published a couple of derivative novels. But she's not much of a writer. In fact she sucks. Big time.'

'That's subjective, Melvyn. And a tad racist, homophobic, and misogynistic. I think she's a significant voice. In fact I'm writing a piece about her for *Saloon* called 'Black. Queer. Pos. And Highly Significant.' '

More of the usual, then. 'Significant? What does she signify?'

'Well, you know—oppression by the white patriarchy, and all that.'

'Yadda, yadda, yadda. Same old, same old.'

'Melvyn. Get a life. Dude, you are so out of touch.'

'I don't think I am. I'm all for equal opportunities. Sure we should be inclusive. But must we exclude all white men now? How inclusive is that?'

As she shifted, Frida's belly made a weird noise, like a new tyre inflating and popping on to a wheel. 'Melvyn, you're clueless. *You*'ve excluded *us* for centuries.'

'OK, men have. Granted. Not me. And that was wrong. Men had prejudice against women. And gays. And different races. And now we recognise that all forms of prejudice are wrong—except for the prejudice against white men. That's fine, right? No one questions it.'

'But Melvyn, that's not a prejudice. It's just common sense. I mean it's only fair we get our own back, right? And besides, the science backs us up.'

'What science?' It irked him that he was being reasonable again.

…Since she was not. 'Social scientists agree on this. They all say men are evil.'

'I know they do—but do they have any evidence at all to support their claims?'

Frida attempted to lever herself out of the recliner. She propped her heavily-cushioned elbows on the armrests, leaned forward, screwed up her face, and strained like a toddler evacuating her bowels, then crashed back into the chair.

Melvyn laughed. Loudly, openly. At last he let the hellhound off the chain.

She spoke pure East Boston now. 'What are you laffing at? This is no laffing madder. You goddamn misogynist homophobe racist—you're such a goddamn big *man*, aren't you?'

'I can see we're going to have to buy one of those recliners with a motor that tips the chair forward when you want to get up. You know, for geriatrics and *obese* people.'

'That is so mean. What's come over you? I hate you. Help me up.'

This was fun. 'What if I don't want to?'

'Are you losing your mind, Melvyn? Remember, I *own* you. I made you.'

'You need to ponder *your* position. In fact you depend on me, fatty.'

'If you don't get me out of this chair, I'll—I'll tell Thalia. I'll tell *Clio*. She'll be pissed, Melvyn. And she's got a new knife. A real big one. Practically a machete.'

'Clio thinks you're a goddamn pain in the ass. She can't stand you.'

'What? My dear daughter? Melvyn, you get me out of this chair this minute. Or I'll tell Rocky you were fucking that student. The smart one. So help me God. And Rocky will tell *everyone*. As you know.' She grinned as if she were holding a straight flush in poker.

'What if I tell Rocky you've been fucking Broome? How'd you like that?'

Her astonishment was as exaggerated as a ham actor's. 'You'd never dare.'

'Wouldn't I, though? I know you're planning to promote Rocky. Over me.'

'How the fuck do you know that? Did that dumbass redneck tell you herself? Anyways, Rocky will never believe anything bad about me. She's loyal. My minion.'

'She might believe this,' Melvyn said, with grim satisfaction. He sat down at his desktop, clicked on a file, and played the video of Frida and Broome. From the recliner came the kind of moans large female mammals make when they give birth.

'You wouldn't. You couldn't. You wouldn't, Melvyn, would you?'

'Oh wouldn't I? Think how you've treated me all these years, Frida.'

'What do you mean? I've always treated you with love and affection.'

'You've treated me like a piece of shit. Consistently. Like an inferior.'

Frida chuckled. 'I gotta be honest, Melvyn: you *are* inferior.'

'Oh yeah? In that case I'll send this to Rocky right now.'

'Melvyn! Please! I beg you. I'll do anything. Anything! What do you want?'

What did he want? Freedom, peace, respect. Someone who actually *liked* him. Good sex would not hurt, either. But of course he was not going to get any of that from her.

'Independence,' he said, moving to the door. 'The end of your tyranny.'

'Melvyn! Don't you dare leave me in this recliner. I'll—hey, it's not tyranny, it's benevolent despotism. I love you, sweetie. I do. But if you don't help me, I'll, I'll … '

'I will do such things—what they are, yet I know not,' Melvyn said, recalling the lines from *King Lear*. 'But they shall be the terrors of the earth. Yeah, yeah, yeah.'

Frida gasped and pushed, fell back and fumed. 'That's what I'm talking about,' she said, sweating. 'Huw needs to die, all right. And you do, too, Melvyn.'

'You're losing it, *sweetie*,' Melvyn said, shocked by her words but not taking them too seriously. Empty threats. Hysteria. 'You're getting deranged.'

'Deranged or inspired? You remember *The Maenads*, right? You don't realise what a group of strong women can do.' She made one last heroic effort to lever herself up out of the chair. She leaned forward, pressed her hams into the chair's arms. She screwed up her face, panting and grunting. She kicked her tiny feet. Her flesh wobbled, shook, shivered. She fell back and broke wind.

Melvyn laughed again. 'I'll leave you to consider your options, then,' he said. She sobbed as he left the room. Darcy came towards him on the landing, wagging his tail.

Melvyn patted him gently, picked up his cell phone, and called Jezebel.

'How about now, babe?' he said, his voice rising like a lark's. 'Your place?'

'I'll kill you!' Frida shrieked. 'I'll kill the pair of you!'

TWENTY-ONE

Taking the Plunge

It was perfect weather for a picnic: sunny but not sticky. No Mitsubishi Zero mosquitoes whined in the air. Even so, Huw's uneasiness about taking part in the picnic was growing. When he had received the 'invite,' as even faculty called it these days, on a card decorated with Pooh bears and red hearts, Huw's impulse had been to bin it, even though the picnic was ostensibly in his honour, to celebrate his book deal and recovery. That was hypocrisy, of course. Since his return to work, Rocky had told him she was delighted he was back, and tried to deny that it was *her* pink Barbie Corvette that Huw had run into on his bike. But she had missed him so much, really. Everyone adored him. And everyone said he was a genius.

Rubbish—but in the end Huw decided to go for Owen's sake. It would be a while before he saw the advance for the novel, so he could still not resign. Besides, he owed his presence to his students, who apart from Elise, knew nothing of the plots against him.

As Huw arrived at the trailhead with Miranda, who had

agreed to come reluctantly, Melvyn jumped down from the colossal Shamburger Hummer, which was painted a nauseous purple. Melvyn was wearing his pink *I'm With Her* polo shirt and the khaki shorts of a Raj policeman, circa 1923. Frida did not descend from the armoured car and Huw guessed why. Melvyn smiled when he saw Huw—not that Huw trusted him much more than he did Rocky.

From the rear of the car, Melvyn took out a step-ladder, a pulley, and a coil of rope, which he rigged up by Frida's door. He busied himself with the rope.

'Gee, Melvyn, your shorts are so *short*!' screeched Rocky, in a camo dress and combat boots. Was she packing her Beretta too? 'You'll creep out all the women.'

Melvyn glanced at his chicken thighs with a fond smile, and grinned at Miranda, who had just got out of the car. Was his recent friendliness genuine? Huw wondered. Or did he have an ulterior motive? Frida abseiled to the ground, half-falling, half-bouncing off the steps of the ladder, banging it against the bodywork. Somehow Melvyn managed to catch her.

No sooner had she alighted—outfitted in a canvas cape, a skirt the size of a spinnaker, rainbow tights, what looked like deep-sea dive boots, and a broad-brimmed hat, trimmed with ostrich feathers—than she uttered a pterodactyl scream: 'Miranda! I'm *beyond* thrilled to see you!'

So she did not have the courage to address him yet. Since getting back to work Huw had managed to avoid talking to her, or even being in the same room.

The programme writers, students and faculty, and a number of guests—the enormous female vicar Huw had seen at the retreat, who was talking to Rocky, and also, he was surprised to see, Petronella herself—were milling around a minibus and cars, with coolers, picnic hampers, rugs, folding chairs and tables, gas stoves, and enough provisions for a safari. Frida stormed across the piles of food and furniture, paying no attention to anything that her dive boots smashed or squelched. Each footfall was a leaden clump. Chairs splintered or snapped as she stamped on them. Cakes and quiches splattered into mush. She looked as intrepid as Allan Quatermain in *King Solomon's Mines*—a short, inflated, nose-ringed Allan Quatermain. In drag.

Miranda awaited Frida's approach with the passivity of a pawn. Melvyn came up too.

'You like my new hat, Miranda?' Frida gasped, planting a kiss on her cheek.

'It hides the sunburnt skinhead scalp nicely, right?' said Melvyn, smirking.

Taking the piss out of Frida was not like Melvyn, it struck Huw. Had he become more assertive? Or had their relationship changed? Frida glowered—but there was something pitiful and imploring in her expression too. However, she addressed Miranda, not Melvyn.

'It's a *statemen*t, you know what I'm saying?' Frida said. 'A political one.'

'Oh no,' Melvyn said. 'Spare us your sophomore pretensions, please.'

'Meghan Markle wore one like it,' she panted. 'I bought it in solidarity.'

Miranda frowned. '*Solidarity?* You mean, with the British royal family?'

Frida chuckled. 'Meghan's a minority, right? She's black, right, Miranda?'

'Yeah, sure,' Miranda said, with glazed eyes. 'Biracial, anyway.'

'You're not actually black, Frida,' Melvyn said. 'Have you noticed that yet?'

He grinned at Miranda in a new way, even as he spoke to Frida. It was a matinee idol smile—suave, debonair, confident. Something must have changed him.

'Not in the lideral sense,' Frida admitted, in hurt tones. 'Not in like actual pigmentation. But I do have the soul of a black woman. Big time. I'm a soul sister.'

'Cultural appropriation,' Melvyn said. 'Very tacky, Frida.'

'You hear me singing Aretha Franklin in the shower, right? I should have been born black. I wish I was an African-American rider. Or an Asian rider. Why couldn't I have been a cooler colour? White is so goddamn *meh*, right, Miranda?'

'I guess,' Miranda said. 'I just feel guilty for being white, you know?'

But Melvyn would not let Frida off the hook. 'Let's get this straight, honey. You're telling us you identify with Markle because you have a black woman's soul?'

'No, dumbass, I identify with her because I'm an oppressed minority too.'

Melvyn sniggered. Miranda, who without a trace of makeup seemed transparent, stood by, inert and expressionless as a China doll, her mind elsewhere or switched off.

'You got me confused, Frida,' said Melvyn. 'I mean, Meghan was a celebrity before she married Prince Harry, and now she's a member of the British royal family. That's oppressed? And how the hell are *you* oppressed? Your crime boss dad was loaded, you have a doctorate, you live the American dream. You live a life of white privilege, Frida. We all do.'

Frida's lower lip quivered. 'Right, but I'm a woman too. A *pansexual* woman.'

'I'm not sure you need to boast about that,' he muttered. She glowered at him.

Meanwhile Rocky was stamping across the debris left by Frida, leaving very little of the picnic, and enfolded her in a python's embrace. Broome, in a somewhat fey Goth outfit of black lace, leather, and chiffon, joined them. So did the vast vicar. It was a living sculpture, similar to the Laocoon, the four figures showing signs of intense emotion, ecstasy or perhaps agony, all writhing together, caught in the coils of the serpent. None of them had the athletic physiques of the classical originals, but in sheer mass they outdid the Trojan priest and his sons. They must have looked heroic or maybe just 'bizarro' to the students, who surrounded them, snapping pictures with their phones. They

were all there: Charleston and Elise, Walt, Truman, Jordan, and
Nutmeg. Even Frank or Hank, who had no interest in writing.
His presence was explained by Elise's: he never left her side.
Timothy was absent, thank God. Only Lucky Luke failed to
join the melee. He sat on a rock smoking a herbal roll-up with
a suspicious odour. In a mini-skirt and above the knee socks,
Petronella swaggered over and drew Miranda aside too. They
whispered together as if they were intimate, Huw noticed.

'Let's get going,' Frida said. 'But I warn you, I can't do a huge
hike.'

'It's half a mile,' Melvyn said.

'That's what I said: how do you expect me to hike a long-dis-
tance trail?'

The party made off, entering a sandy trail among pine trees.
Everyone but Frida carried a backpack. She huffed and puffed
in short, agonised wheezes.

When they reached the bluff where they planned to have the
picnic, Frida sat down on a rock overlooking a lake and miles of
mountain and forest. The women spread out the remnants of
the picnic on tablecloths, and, while the men busied themselves
with drinks and the stove. Frida lost her balance and sprawled,
limbs flailing, like an overturned insect.

Rocky tried to get her arms around her but could not,
and failed to wrench her up by lifting under her armpits. She
seized her hands, and bending her knees and leaning back,
with a weightlifter's groan, managed to lever Frida into a sitting
position.

'Congratulations, Rocky,' Melvyn said. 'That was quite the
feat of strength.'

'What the hell are you grinning at?' Frida asked Melvyn.

'*Du bist scheisse,*' he said. You are shit. Frida huffed, nonplussed
by his German.

Broome grabbed Frida's left armpit with both hands. Rocky
seized the other side. The vicar thrust her hands under her
backside. 'One, two, three, *lift!*' Rocky said. Somehow, they got

her up. She wobbled, but with their help, she waddled over to the picnic site.

She kept away from Melvyn, and did not sit down—there was no picnic chair large enough for her to fit in—but propped herself on a rock, beside Broome and Rocky.

The vicar talked to Jordan and Nutmeg, about their upcoming wedding.

Huw found himself beside Melvyn and Elise, on the edge of the cliff.

'Oowee!' said Elise, laying a hand on Huw's arm. 'Just look at that view.'

'We must be four hundred feet above the lake,' he said.

'Celtic hyperbole,' Melvyn said. Whatever had come over him? It wasn't like him to take the piss.

All three stood on the edge and gazed down: far below, the lake swirled and foamed beneath a cataract. Beside the water was a massive slab of rock.

Over his shoulder, Huw saw Miranda frowning at him, as she talked to Petronella. What was that about? Had she arranged to meet Petronella here? Or were the sea-monsters bothering her again? More hallucinations or delusions? Huw was about to go over and comfort her when he caught Melvyn winking at her. Abruptly leaving Huw's side, Melvyn strutted towards her, stiffly as cockerel. Curious, Huw decided to wait a few moments. Hank or Frank was opening brown bottles, and pouring their contents into paper cups, which Elise was receiving. Further back, Lucky Luke was smoking, probably wacky baccy, with Walt, Truman, and Charleston. Jordan and Nutmeg giggled with the vicar to Huw's right. Frida, Rocky and Broome were sneaking hits on a silver hip-flask and making gecko-like screeches. Huw saw the curling lips and imagined a conspiracy. Nah, he told himself, don't be paranoid.

Elise handed him a cup. 'Beer?' he asked. 'Is that allowed?'

'A malted beverage,' Hank or Frank said. 'Don't tell anyone, prof.'

Huw sipped it, looking uneasily over his shoulder again. Melvyn was grinning at Miranda, and touched her bare shoulder. She shrank from his touch. Petronella spoke, saying something cutting, probably. A flotilla of clouds sailed across the sky, hiding the sun.

Then it happened again: Huw heard eerie music, violins like crying children. A deep sawing sound, double basses, sinister. Timpani, French horns, a choir. A baroque requiem. He looked over at his wife again. He could not hear their words, but he lip-read Melvyn's.

I like you, Miranda. Or was it *I love you?* Petronella snapped a phrase at him.

Huw told Elise about the music. 'I hear it too,' she said, close by his side.

'Really? Be careful. You're too close to the edge.'

She smiled at him. 'Live dangerously, right, Huw?'

'We are. Look over there: Melvyn's flirting with my wife, but for some reason I just feel sorry for him, maybe because I can see he's no match for that woman, the feminist guru. And over there, the three witches. What's happening? Tell me. You're our Cassandra.'

Elise shut her eyes and pursed her lips. 'A tragedy is imminent.'

Melvyn stumbled back towards them, with a downcast expression.

'What kind of tragedy?' Huw asked Elise.

'Is there more than one kind?' Elise said.

'For the Greeks, the tragic hero is a victim of the gods. He or she might be anyone. But in Shakespeare it's the hero's character that impels the catastrophe.'

'Boy, you really live in your head, don't you, Huw? You need to listen to your body more. Your feelings and intuitions. Your life might depend on it.'

'You're way too close to the edge, guys,' Melvyn said as he came up to them.

Frank or Hank put his arm around Elise, drawing her gently but firmly away.

And yet Huw remained where he was, on the very edge of the precipice, and Melvyn stood right beside him, with the air of a kid who has been dared to show his courage. Kettle drums beat below the mixed choir. Shadows skipped over the rocks. Huw felt no rancour towards Melvyn. He spun round. 'Who is that?' he said, glimpsing a shape that melted into the shadows. 'See him by the trees? Tall bloke, dark, Van Dyck beard. Do we know him?'

Melvyn followed his gaze. 'I think I saw him earlier. Must be a hiker.'

Frida got to her feet with the help of her friends, lowering her head, as if she were about to charge. A hand signal of some kind passed between her and Broome and Rocky. They all stood. They stared at Melvyn, who began whistling—embarrassed or ashamed.

'I believe Frida is planning to kill me,' Melvyn said. 'And you too, I'm sorry to say.'

'What are you talking about?' Huw said. The women formed a circle, holding hands, and turned, with odd chirping noises, keeping their eyes fixed on the men.

'Look at them,' Melvyn said. 'See how they're staring at us? The question is, what would the Superior Man do? Know what I mean? I just wish I had consulted the *I Ching*.'

'You can't be serious, mate. In broad daylight? It would be insane.'

'You might not have noticed, but they are batshit crazy. And look at Miranda: she knows.' She had clapped her hands over her ears. Her mouth opened in a silent shriek. 'Strange woman, your wife,' Melvyn said. 'She looks like that Munch picture.'

This is it, Huw knew, *my last chance. The critical moment of my life.*

Now the women formed a line, Rocky and Broome on each side of Frida, hands joined, trotting towards them. Broome and Rocky were squealing like teenage girls.

'Should we move? Could it be a joke?' Huw said.

'That's what they'll say,' Melvyn said. 'If they succeed in pushing us off.'

The women lumbered towards them in a sort of slow stampede. Jordan and Nutmeg laughed, obviously thinking it a prank. The vicar looked aghast, and Elise signalled frantically to Huw to move, but for some reason he could not. He had to face them, even though Elise yelled at him to get back—which Miranda did not do. It was clear now that Frida *was* charging, her face ferocious, tattooed arms thrust out, to push him—or Melvyn?

'Yes, they mean to kill us,' he said. Thunderheads rose in mauve-black columns.

It all happened very fast. Frida lurched to her right, barging into Broome, who plunged towards Melvyn and Huw. Rocky made a grab for Frida, who was off balance, but only caught her cloak. Frida was about to crash into Melvyn, but at the last moment he twisted away from her on the lip of the cliff on one leg, in the Crane pose.

Soprano voices shrilled in Huw's ears. French horns brayed. Trumpets blared. The charging women reminded him of the rugby field, when, once again, as he knew it would, Time juddered to a halt. *Tempus abire tibi est,* the choir sang. It is time for you to depart.

Miranda's hands no longer covered her ears, but her eyes. Petronella had her arm around her. *Non te amat,* chanted the voices. Seeing him shattered on the rocks or drowned might shock Miranda, but mostly, Huw knew, she would just feel sorry for herself.

She had seen, but not warned him. She loves you not. Knowing it was a relief—it ended the uncertainty. Why hadn't he believed the warnings? Time to leave. *Non te amat.*

What if he used this pause to take evasive action, like a lucid dreamer? He tried to move but he was paralysed. When he looked at Melvyn, he saw he was exultant.

The music thundered around the mountain, male voices

predominating now, basses and baritones, in a kind of dread-filled requiem, and a mighty drummer thrashed the timpani. A shape was so close that Huw smelled the acrid odour of their sweat. The colossal figure was no longer holding hands with Broome and Rocky, but reaching out to push him over. The brass and woodwind whirled in a spiral of hectic sound. Instinctively, Huw side-stepped.

He grabbed the strong, satanic arms, twisted around, and flung the figure behind him.

Time was flowing again, slowly, but accelerating. Figures seethed around him, yet Huw saw everything clearly. The satanic shape he had grappled with turned into Frida, who flurried between the two men, head flung back, scrabbling at the air. She spun and grasped Melvyn on the lip of the cliff, her back to the abyss, overbalancing, her arms attempting a sort of butterfly stroke, fury and panic on her face. Did Melvyn push her? If he had, it was too swift to register. Rocky clung to Frida's cloak, in peril of going over too.

Lightning lit up a black and crimson face, with white teeth. The devil was still there. Thunder tore open the sky. The mountaintop shook. Frida lost her toehold and overbalanced.

The violins teetered at the top of the E string, vibrato, the timpani thumped, the thunder crashed and cannonaded off the cliffs, the sopranos shrieking as they plunged into the bowels of hell. *Gloria scriptori.* Glory to the author, they sang. *Scribe, scribe, scribe.* Although it was dark as night, with another lightning flash Huw saw Frida's body dangling, her claws clutching one of her husband's arms. Melvyn stood with legs apart, wrenching backwards. Trying to heave her back over the brink, or just save himself? Rocky had let go of Frida's cloak and seized her arms, but she was kneeling, off-balance, slipping slowly over as well. It was like a modern ballet in which dancers leap then freeze in sculptural formations.

Will Rocky and Melvyn manage to pull Frida back from the brink? Huw wondered.

271

He hoped not. He wanted to see the devil fall.

Forked lightning split the purple sky, thunder shook the mountain at the same moment, and in the blink of an eye Rocky tumbled off the cliff, and was clinging to Frida's back, her arms around her boss's neck. Broome dived headfirst into the abyss. Frida slipped out of Melvyn's grasp but clutched at an outcrop of rock beside his feet. The agony on her face as she tried to hoist herself and Rocky up to safety was indescribable. Melvyn bent over as if to save her. But as the cymbals and the thunder crashed and the wind screamed, and rain lashed them in torrents, he straightened up, stumbled, and the next thing Huw saw was Melvyn's hiking boots on Frida's fingers. Was that an accident? Melvyn looked serene. But he did grind those chubby fingers with his steel-capped toes. Hard. Was it an accident?

Then he *stamped* on her fingers. But he might have slipped. Possibly.

Frida let out a heart-splitting shriek, the music stopped with a peal of thunder and a final thump of the drums, and she plummeted, her cloak fluttering around her. One after the other, Broome and Frida splashed into the lake.

Melvyn looked down. 'Man, was that intense,' he said—with relish, Huw thought.

Elise flung herself into Huw's arms. 'The tragedy I foretold. But you saved yourself!'

Hank or Frank shook his head. 'What were those ditsy chicks smoking?'

'Shut the fuck up, Hank,' said Elise.

'Frank,' said Frank. 'I'm Frank, don't you remember?'

Jordan and Nutmeg wept in one another's arms, although Jordan was also giggling hysterically. She soon had her phone out and was taking pictures. The vicar had her hands together in prayer. 'Heavenly Father, I mean Mother,' she said. 'I mean, Heavenly Parent: you have not made us for darkness and death, but for life with you forever.'

Miranda was in a foetal position, Huw saw as he prised Elise off himself. Petronella had one arm around his wife, and with the other was stroking her hair and murmuring to her.

In moments, everyone was on the edge of the cliff, gaping, gasping, shouting.

'It was a terrible accident,' Melvyn said. 'It may have been some kind of prank that went wrong. A true tragedy. The worst of it is, they weren't even taking a selfie.'

'Are they all dead?' said Elise. She too was already taking pictures.

'Broome never surfaced,' Melvyn said. 'The fall must have broken her back. Sadly, it's clear that Frida has passed too. I believe she's in a better place.' He spoke in pious tones, as he would later at the memorial service, Huw supposed. He spoke like the Superior Man.

'What happened to Rocky Rathaus?' Lucky Luke said. 'Is she dead too?'

No one knew. Peering over the edge, secured by the surprisingly strong arms of Elise around his waist, Huw scanned the foot of the cliff. Nothing. Then he surveyed the cliffside, and discovered Rocky on a ledge, fifteen feet or so below. She had wrapped her arms around the trunk of a young pine growing out of the rock and clung there with her eyes shut tight.

'You bastards,' she whimpered. 'None of you loves Frida like I do.'

Elise got spectacular footage of her weeping on the ledge, and of herself, heroically throwing a rope down to her. She shared the videos and selfies on her page, and in an hour racked up 17,453 likes and over two thousand shares. By late afternoon it had gone viral. That night she appeared on Fox News and CNN as 'the glamorous girl hero of the Westmoreland Gap tragedy.' The following day she had offers from three modelling agencies, and Hollywood scouts calling her. She was an instant celebrity.

Huw drove home later, shaken but feeling free. Miranda had

not spoken to him once since their arrival, and did not speak to him again. Petronella said she would drive her home.

Huw's destiny had been fulfilled, he sensed, except for one thing. But what was it?

He knew he had to do something, but it took him months to figure out what it was.

Envoi

'It's incredible they survived such a high fall,' Nasreen Shirazi was saying as she examined Huw in her office, six months later. On the walls were several framed Persian miniatures and a large reproduction of Leonardo's *Adoration of the Magi*. The scent of flowers pervaded the room—not cut flowers, but potted plants. Orchids, pink roses, poinsettias, and African violets. She had just taken his blood pressure, which was healthy. 'You say they fell two hundred feet?'

'A hundred and seventy. They were lucky to fall into the deepest water and not hit any rocks. Frida was very badly injured. She's still recovering, I hear.'

Nasreen told him to open his shirt, and listened to his heart with her stethoscope. 'That's fine. Vigorous—my, it's beating hard. Are you excited about something?' He was too embarrassed to answer. Smiling, she went on: 'What happened to them? The newspapers said there were charges of attempted murder.'

'I dropped them on a lawyer's advice. Impossible to prove,' she said.

'Didn't I read that your boss accused her husband of attempted murder, too?'

'Yes, initially. But she dropped that as well. In return for being allowed to keep her teaching job. There was an almighty scandal. Elise wanted her father to fire her.'

Nasreen placed her palm flat on Huw's chest—not seductively, but he sensed that she enjoyed touching him. She pressed hard, gazing steadily into his eyes. Her hand was cool and strong. 'She did lose her position as director of the programme, though, didn't she?'

'Yes. Melvyn, her husband, took over. They switched roles. Ever since her fall, Frida has been quiet, almost sweet. She behaves exactly the way her husband used to. She never contradicts him or votes against him, although she's still a bit peevish. I never thought I'd see such a transformation. And her disciple, Rocky Rathaus, changed in just the same way.'

Nasreen threw back her head and laughed. 'In Farsi we have a word to describe women like that. But I had better not say it. So Frida continues to teach with you. She must hate Melvyn as much as you. Isn't it very uncomfortable?'

'It is,' he said, buttoning up his shirt. 'May I tell you something in strict confidence?'

'Of course you can. I'm your doctor.'

'I feel a certain guilt about her. I was to blame for her fall.'

Nasreen frowned. 'What on earth do you mean?'

'Frida thought it was her husband who grappled with her and swung her and made her lose her balance. But actually it was me.'

Nasreen's face paled. 'You struck a woman?'

Huw's gaze wandered to Leonardo's painting. 'You won't believe what I have to tell you. But I believed I was face to face with a demon. I didn't exactly strike her, either.'

'Go on.'

He told her how he had heard the celestial music, with the angelic choirs, the counsel in Latin, the kettle drums, the sinister sounds, the archangels, and that day, the mysterious shape of the bearded man whom Huw had glimpsed several times, a man of immense height, who had an acrid smell; he spoke of the three occasions when Time had stopped, and of Elise's warning of an imminent tragedy, and her advice, to heed the voice of his intuition.

'When the three of them were almost upon us, I swear that that devilish figure was among them. At least I thought so. His arms reached out to push me and I felt his hands on my chest, shoving me backwards, into the abyss. I didn't think. I acted. I didn't hit him, but seized his arms and swung him around. It's a move I did once in a rugby match.'

'And what happened?' Nasreen's had changed; she no longer spoke with anger.

'It all happened in a moment, you have to understand, it was confusing, with women shouting, and losing their balance, and slaps and punches and kicks. But I think that...'

'What? Just say it.'

'The devil turned into Frida. I know it sounds like a lie, or lunacy.'

Nasreen sighed. 'Far from it. That was just what happened.'

Huw laughed nervously. 'You can't be saying you believe me, surely?'

'I believe you. It was no hallucination. You fought with a djinni.'

'You believe that? Is it possible?'

'I'm absolutely certain. You fought a djinni and you won, may God be praised. It was his will.'

Huw shook his head. 'I'll have to think about that. Thank you.'

Nasreen shook her head too. 'God bless you. And what now? What are you going to do?'

'I've given my notice at the university. Finally. Next semester will be my last. I'm going to dedicate myself to writing. Sink or swim.'

'I hope you will succeed.' On her lips, it did not sound an empty phrase.

His heart beat harder. 'I wonder if you'd have dinner with me one night?'

Her face darkened—with anger, plainly. 'Aren't you still married?'

'Not any more, no. My divorce came through a couple of months ago.'

Her mouth softened. 'That is sad. I could see that you loved your wife.'

'Yes, I did.' It embarrassed him to say so, but he had no desire to mislead her.

'You speak with sorrow. You still love her.' It was not a question.

Although his momentary impulse was to deny it, he had to be honest. 'I'm not sure you ever cease to love someone you have truly loved. I do still care about her. And I'm happy that she has found peace and happiness in San Miguel de Allende.' *Even with Petronella.*

'Is that in Mexico, the home of my poinsettias?' she said, glancing at them.

'Yes. She followed her dream, see you, a dream of Frida Kahlo.'

'Like a Disney princess,' she said, with amusement and maybe disdain.

'She went with a woman named Petronella Pikestaff. Do you know her?'

'Ah, the famous feminist. I read about her in a magazine. So many American women are confused. I know it's politically incorrect to say so. Do I offend you?'

'Very little offends me. You aren't a feminist, then, I take it?'

'I am a woman,' she said, almost fiercely. 'I believe in equality, of course. I'm not an idiot. But few American women under-stand what it means to be a woman. Or is that just my backwards Middle Eastern mentality? What do you think?'

'It intrigues me. I don't think you're backward. I hope you'll tell me what you believe in much more detail. You still haven't said if you'll have dinner with me.'

'You need another check-up in six months' time. Earlier if

the results of your blood tests don't look good. Your cholesterol remains a little high. You should eat more anti-oxidants. Eliminate the stress from your life, if you can.'

She was evading the invitation again. He would have to try once more.

'I am trying. I've resigned, and am no longer living with a disturbed wife.'

Nasreen gave him a long, hard look, gauging whether he was really relieved. 'What happened to her boss? You told me he raped her, didn't you?'

'Did I really? That was very indiscreet of me. Perhaps it was the drugs I was on after the surgery. Yes, and he lost his job over it. Dr Gneiss saw to that. But Miranda didn't press charges. She foresaw ugly cross-examinations and knew she would go to pieces in court.'

'So how is she living? In Mexico?' She tapped a pencil, impatient or nervous.

'Her partner runs self-fulfilment feminist retreats. For white Americans.'

'Of course. And Miranda helps her, I suppose? She's very pretty, isn't she?'

Was there a twinge of jealousy in her voice? Huw hoped so. 'She is.'

'And didn't you tell me that this Petronella's sister used to assist her?'

'You have a remarkable memory. I must have done. And it transpired, in the welter of accusations and counter-accusations after the incident on the clifftop, that Melvyn was having an affair with her. The sister. She called herself Jezebel, like the temptress in the Bible.'

'Oh no.' Nasreen steepled her hands. Her eyes were merry, though.

'She's doing a Master's in Psychology at Cornell now. She aims to be a sex therapist.'

'And how would *you* know that, Huw?' Nasreen's voice was sharper.

'She told me,' he said sheepishly. 'I think she may have been after me too.'

'I bet. Sex therapist, indeed. We also have a word in Farsi for women like that.'

'I can imagine.' Her intimate tone encouraged him. 'And another scandal that started to break but somehow didn't was that it turned out Frida was sleeping with her student, and mine, Broome—the other woman who tried to push us over the cliff.'

'It gets crazier and crazier.'

'I believe Frida is still seeing her. And Melvyn is still seeing Jezebel.'

Nasreen shook her head. 'I don't want to hear more about these sick people.'

'All right. So—will you have dinner with me? Do you like Indian food?'

'I love it. But you aren't ready to date me yet, Huw. I can see that.'

'I think I am,' he said at once, but unsure of himself.

'No, you aren't. Take it from me. We'll wait six months. Then ask me again.'

'You'll have dinner with me in six months? Do you promise?'

'I told you to ask me again then. *If* you are over your grief for Miranda.'

He saw she would not be swayed. He stood and held out his hand, which she took firmly. She did not shake it, but held it in hers. He wanted to take her in his arms, but knew she would not let him, even if she were feeling the same desire. 'I shall look forward to my next appointment,' he said.

'So shall I,' Nasreen said. 'Behave yourself meanwhile.'

'What do you mean?'

'Don't give in to temptation with that model. The one who's in California.'

'Elise? How in the world do you know about her?'

'How do you think? Her father is my patient too. I can be quite jealous, you should know. Like most Middle Eastern women. Dr Goldsmith told me she has a crush on you. I know she's beautiful. It would be fun for you—but not healthy.'

Huw reddened. He had considered giving Elise a call and more than once had got as far as picking up the phone. 'I won't go near her,' he promised.

She susurrated a few words of Farsi. 'Goodbye for now, then.'

It was hard to let go of her hand, which she still held, as people from the Middle East often did, without embarrassment or sentimentality. It obviously betokened something stronger than friendship. Would it be foolish to fall in love with her? If she were to return his love, would she love him forever, or would her love be in vain, as Miranda's had been? As he looked into Nasreen's grave eyes, those deep, deep pools, he saw she was a different kind of woman altogether. And he had become a different kind of man. He would not expect her to comfort or reassure him. Nor would he ever take a woman's love for granted again.

For now, he had a happy day ahead of him—and that was enough.

The End

ACKNOWLEDGEMENTS

I wish to thank the following friends who generously read drafts of this novel, critiqued it and encouraged me greatly:
David Joiner
Jacqueline Newman
Jack Gaiser
Jemima and Rupert Copping

Milton Keynes UK
Ingram Content Group UK Ltd.
UKHW011837260224
438492UK00004B/214

One Shot
in the
Storm

CHRIS OSWALD

NEWMORE PUBLISHING

First edition published in 2020 by Newmore Publishing.

ISBN 978-1-9160719-5-7

Chris Oswald has lived in America, Scotland and England and is now living in Dorset with his wife, Suzanne, and six children. For many years he was in international business but now has a little more time to follow his love of writing. His books have been described as dystopian but they are more about individual choice, human frailty and how our history influences the decisions we make, also about how quickly things can go so wrong.

Main Characters Appearing in One Shot in the Storm

Non-fictional characters marked *

Mr Amiss, father of Amy Tabard.

Anne Aspley, burgeoning business owner following a close shave with family bankruptcy.

Lieutenant Aspley, young officer serving in New England.

Mr Aspley, silk merchant in Dorchester.

Mrs Aspley, his wife, mother of Lieutenant Aspley and Anne.

Captain Gerome Barceau, Huguenot soldier in William's army.

Michael Bars, governor of the prison where Simon Taylor is held.

Corporal Bing, English corporal who takes a dislike to Henry Sherborne.

Sally Black, Penelope's maid and lover.

Lieutenant Blades-Robson, company commander to Henry Sherborne.

Tristan Browne, Irishman born in Barbados, now staying with Thomas in Dorset, cousin to Bridget.

Sergeant Bullen, English sergeant who mentors Henry Sherborne.

Lord Cartwright, previously right-hand man to Parchman, now a Minister of State.

Bridget Davenport, née Browne, married to Thomas, historian, cousin to Tristan.

Eliza Davenport, née Merriman, owner of Bagber Manor.

Matthew Davenport, oldest child of the Davenport family, recently married Lady Eliza Merriman.

Thomas Davenport, second son of Luke and Rebecca Davenport, builder.

Major Davidson, commander serving in New England, youngest brother of the Duke of Wiltshire.

Mr Fellows, very old and successful merchant in Dorchester, befriends Anne Aspley.

Michael Frampton, Bridget Davenport's publisher in London.

Private Fugini, soldier in Henry Sherborne's platoon, resourceful cook.

Grimes, henchman to Simon Taylor and Parchman, married to Amelia.

Amelia Grimes, daughter of Simon Taylor by his first marriage, known to her friends as Mealie.

Colonel James Hanson, friend of Thomas and Grace, Colonel in the Dorset militia.

Sergeant Holmes, English soldier serving in New England.

Plain Jane, friend to Thomas and Grace, married to Big Jim.

Mr Jarvis, debt collector who advises and befriends Anne Aspley.

Big Jim, friend to Thomas and Grace, owns a successful hauliers firm in Dorset, married to Plain Jane.

Mr Milligan, builder who trained Thomas before turning over the firm to him.

Milly, maid to Eliza Davenport.

Dr Mowbray, quack doctor who is more interested in selling remedies than curing patients.

Sir Neil O'Neill*, general in James' army.

Fr O'Toole, parish priest for Ballydalgagan.

Parchman, ex-government agent in hiding, owner of several inns in the South West of England, key person in the prior imprisonment of Lady Merriman, has a deep-rooted grudge against the Davenports, the Merrimans and the Roakes.

Private Parker, soldier in Henry Sherborne's platoon.

John Parsons, godfather to Milly.

Sir William Phips*, New England adventurer and leading citizen in Boston.

Lady (Alice) Roakes, previously Mrs Beatrice before she married Sir Beatrice Roakes (now deceased), owner of the Great Little Estate.

Alfred Rose, sailor who becomes assistant to Parchman.

Sarah and Kitty, sisters, maids to Eliza Davenport at Bagber Manor.

Duke of Schomberg*, second-in-command of William's Irish army.

Meinhartd Schomberg*, the Duke of Schomberg's son, a general in William's army.

Grace Sherborne, Countess of Sherborne, wife to Henry, daughter of Luke Davenport.

Henry Sherborne, Earl of Sherborne and illegitimate son of Eliza Davenport.

James Stuart*, previously King of England, Scotland and Ireland.

Amy Tabard, married to Paul, lives with Mr Amiss in Dorchester.

Paul Tabard, government contractor at Tabard and Co.

Elizabeth Taylor, née Davenport, elder daughter and second child of Luke and Rebecca Davenport, married to Simon, known by friends as Lizzie.

Tomkins, factor at the Great Little estate.

Earl of Tryconnell*, general in James' army.

William III, Prince of Orange*, King of England, Scotland and Ireland.

Penelope Wiltshire, Dowager Duchess of Wiltshire.

Duke of Wiltshire, inherited the title following the death of Penelope's husband.

One Shot in the Storm

Chapter 1

New England 1690

S imon Taylor used his knife to cut a hole in the groundsheet, imagining the width of his head as he did not want to make the slit any longer than it had to be. The first attempt was too tight so he added an inch to the length and tried again.

"What're you doing, Private Taylor?" came a voice from behind a tree.

"Improvising, Sergeant Holmes, to keep dry."

"Let me see." There was movement from behind the tree. A solid man with too much weight around his middle and a limp from the distant past, came into view, brushing against the undergrowth. He peered at Simon's creation in the light offered by the early dawn, light lost to a great extent in the mist patches that had kidnapped their feet. The head hit a low-hanging pine branch, the mouth swore when a shower of rainwater soaked his shoulders, a quantity running down his neck. "Damned rain!" he muttered, attacking the branch with his arm and thus loosening another assault upon him.

The rain was heavy but the most noticeable thing was its duration. It had started raining on Sunday and now it was Friday. Five days without a hint of stopping; five days bivouacking pointlessly, in Simon's opinion, for the French and their Indian allies would not come in such a downpour. Looking up at the sky, it seemed it would continue forever. Maybe God was cleansing his wicked world.

Or maybe He wanted something to dilute the blood that had spilled everywhere around them in the last few weeks.

"Good work, soldier," came the waterlogged voice of the sergeant. Then a thought crossed his weary mind. "It's alright for you now, isn't it? But what about the rest of us? There are no more bleedin' groundsheets?"

"I know where to get some, Sergeant."

"Don't tell me to apply to the bleedin' quarter-master, for that won't bleedin' well work." It was understandable that blood and bleeding was on the sergeant's mind; there had been much sight of it recently with the war in America mimicking the one in Europe. And now his platoon was in the thick of it, thrust deep into enemy territory, protected only by the rain and the mist which had become both friend and enemy to the twenty soldiers under the sergeant's command.

And it was his command for the officer-in-charge, Lieutenant Aspley, was useless. His parents had purchased a commission in 1689 and sent him on his military way in the vain hope that it would make something of the young man. But over the last three months, the soldiers in his platoon had barely seen him as one illness followed another. Hence, the sergeant felt the burden on his rain-soaked shoulders.

"No, Sergeant, I would not dream of discussing it with the quarter-master. I know exactly where to get twenty-plus groundsheets plus a host of supplies including some cooked meat, even steal some time at a warm fire."

"You're kidding me, sonny-boy." Simon had ten years on his sergeant, making the appellation comical.

"Not at all, Sergeant. Listen to me a moment. It means splitting our little force but I think it can be done."

They stood in the persistent rain, for there was no joy to be had in squatting in puddles of water. They stood with their boots lost to the greedy mist, like clouds fallen from the sky. They stood as Private Taylor outlined his plan.

Sergeant Holmes would never describe himself as a coward, more that he had developed a finely-tuned sense of self-preservation over the years. A career soldier, now in his early-forties, he was starting to feel the pressure of an ageing body combined with a demanding lifestyle.

But he was also thinking as the years rolled by that he might actually live through his army career and have a comfortable retirement. He looked forward to the possibilities, aware that his life could be snatched in any one of a hundred different ways.

Maybe there was an inn he could buy near an army base where his long, sometimes amusing, stories would be appreciated. Maybe, even, there was a woman somewhere who would take the heavy-set body and slightly grumpy demeanour and see something of worth in it. He had saved enough to make him an attractive prize. And then there was the booty he had secreted, a little here and a little there. Most now was converted to cash and held on account at various jewellers and antiquarian establishments across London.

Suddenly, there was hope. But that hope demanded he stayed alive. What could hope offer without blood pulsing it around his portly body?

"I can't leave my post," he said flatly when Simon's plan was aired. "The officers are depending on our intelligence." He hoped that sounded convincing enough.

"Give me ten men," Simon replied. "I'll do it with ten men."

They settled on six, plus Simon to lead.

"I'll make you a corporal to give you some bleedin' authority." Everything was bleeding before the rain washed it away.

Corporal Taylor responded with a request that he be allowed to choose his six men.

"Take who you like but only one musket for each soldier. Do you need rations?" Simon did not; he knew there would be food at his destination. He just hoped six soldiers would be enough.

Galley Gorge was so called because a great rock formed one side of the gorge and it was crudely in the shape of a Spanish galley-ship. It projected above the cliff as a long thin vessel, even having a rising prow like galleys do. The finishing touch was a series of different darker veins of rock or ore that ran at right angles to the line of the ship down both exposed sides. They looked exactly like oar-ports set at intervals into the body of the ship.

The first time Simon saw Galley Gorge, it was during the middle of a gale. The stone-boat seemed to be moving with the wild waves, bending up with them and then crashing down.

It was an illusion, of course, but it did not stop Private Tucker from asking how they were going to board.

"In the dark, with the rope you brought, Tucker. Get some rest now, men, we've a busy night ahead." He took off his makeshift cloak and tied it between two trees for some minimal shelter. "I'll take first watch as I want to observe their camp for a while."

"Yes sir," said several of the six, even though Simon was no more than an acting-corporal.

The soldiers under his command, Corporal Taylor thought, wanted to be told what to do and when. And that is what he did, with clarity and sufficient precision to ensure everyone knew exactly where their duty lay.

"It's critical that we catch at least seven horses from the enemy camp on top of the Galley and let the rest run wild. They will be for our getaway so it is vital unless you want a Mohawk spear through your guts. Johnson, I know you're an experienced horseman so you're in charge of the horse section. I'll lead the camp section. Now, let's move out quietly. Who knows what we will find up there on the rock but at least they won't expect us to be so foolish as to attack in this weather." Simon grinned as he spoke and received six good grins in return. There is not much to this leadership business, he thought, except exercising the mind, clarity of purpose and half an ounce of humour.

"Acting-Corporal Taylor to the Major's tent."

They were back at the main camp after three days of action that Simon could barely believe. Their tiny mission to seek rainwear and food had grown out of all proportion.

There is another aspect of leadership, Simon reflected; opportunism or carpe diem, as his Latin teacher had trotted out all those years ago.

Simon hurriedly stepped out into the dark but dry evening. The rain had ceased the moment he had decided there was more to this raid than groundsheets and beef; as his orders had flowed from their position at the top of the rock they had scaled, the sky had cleared, as if God was just waiting for someone to take charge down there on the waterlogged earth.

He followed the sergeant to the major's tent, not knowing what to expect but surprised by the warmth from this otherwise aloof officer who bore the whole responsibility of the hastily put together regiment that Simon had volunteered for.

"Sit down, Taylor. A glass of something?"

"Ah, brandy perhaps, sir?"

"I can't abide brandy. You've got a choice between whisky and whisky. What will it be?"

"Tricky choice, sir, but I think I'll opt for the whisky."

"Good man, never trust a brandy drinker, I say." Simon had always enjoyed brandy but nodded his head in agreement as the major snapped his fingers for the orderly.

"Now, Taylor, I want to hear what went on, straight from the horse's mouth!" His baying laugher sounded more like a donkey than a horse but seemed to suit the occasion.

"Well, sir, it was like this." He settled back on the folding camp chair, whisky with a splash of water in his right hand, dangling from that hand as if the muscles employed in holding glasses upright had suddenly spasmed and were now rendered useless. "I admit when I first thought of Galley Gorge, I was thinking of my platoon's comfort. If we could get groundsheets for protection against the rain plus some half-decent rations, it would improve morale no end."

"Good thinking, Taylor. A man who thinks about the comfort of the men under his charge is going to go far."

"But then I thought about it a little more deeply, sir. It was held to be impregnable and was the base of operations throughout this area. The French and Indian raiding parties could retreat there knowing they would be safe. The Galley Rock could hold several hundred men and horses with sufficient supplies to last months, if not years. To all intents and purposes, sir, it's a natural fort."

"I know its strategic value, Taylor. I understand the brilliant element of surprise you brought to the scene by climbing up the face of the cliff at night and in intense rain, very commendable action indeed. What I want to know is when did you decide to capture and hold it?"

5

"Ah, that, sir, is the crux of my story. Bear with me a moment longer, if you would be so good, sir, all will be clear soon enough." The decision to turn a raid for supplies into a key strategic matter had come to him just as his tiny force spread out on the cliff top, having scaled a treacherous overhanging projection with just two ropes to prevent falling to their deaths two hundred feet below.

They had surprised and captured a small picket-line easily, no shots fired, "That was the element of surprise, sir. Seven of us took 35 prisoners because they could not see how few we were in the dark. They must have thought it a major assault."

"What happened next?"

"I realised that the night was both friend and foe, sir. It hid our weakness of numbers but also posed obstacles for we did not know the terrain in the slightest. Then we had the most enormous piece of luck when…"

"You make your own luck in this army, Taylor, in life too, I suspect, although I am just a simple landowner in peace time."

"Thank you, sir." It seemed the most appropriate reply. "Actually, it was two or more strokes of luck we made for ourselves." Simon noticed, as he paused, the major sitting up straight in his camp chair. He had his commanding officer's attention. "First, we found a real babbler amongst the captives. A big man, he was, that you might expect to have more courage. I speak French, sir, so was able to converse with him easily. He told me that the camp was set back a quarter-mile at the foot of the Galley Rock and he would be happy to take us there; all he wanted in return was his freedom and to go home to his miserable farm carved into the woods in some awful backwater." Simon stopped, thinking perhaps he had gone too far. The major was a farmer. Would he take exception to condescension?

"What did you do with him?" No, there was no damage done. But he would be more careful in future.

"I let him think it was a bargain done, sir. But I consider such cowardly actions no better than desertion. I determined to use him and then hand him over as a captive which is exactly what

I did. It's not my fault that he tried to run a few days later and was shot as a consequence."

It was at this point in the narrative that Major Davidson, a fairly large landowner in the wilderness of New York state, realised he had someone unique sitting in his tent. Taylor looked over fifty years old; too old and too clever to have remained a private soldier until a few days ago, especially with the initiative he had recently displayed. And he spoke French and expressed himself exceedingly well. He was clearly educated.

The militia major was out of his depth; being one of those intensely practical men, he looked at himself and knew exactly what he could and could not do. He was never a soldier so why had he accepted the commission to defend upstate New York from the mixed bands of Mohawk, Algonquin and Frenchies that terrorised their homes? He thought back to that grim day, three months ago, when the few survivors from Schenectady had arrived at his home, struggling in the snow and ice; the warriors who had murdered their families were swooping down on them, anticipating the joy of the final kill. Only a few had survived the massacre at Schenectady; most were slaughtered or taken away to a life of slavery. In response, Davidson had turned his home into a fortress and beaten back the triumphant force of French and Indians. Shortly afterwards, he had let it be known that he would be willing to serve in any capacity against the cruel raiders. But he had never expected command, especially of such a critical force when he had so little experience.

Other than of being a gentleman.

But there was something about this acting-corporal sitting before him. The major held up his hand for silence, called to his aide who was busy writing down the details and whispered something to him. The aide went back to his packing case desk and took a fresh sheet of paper from the satchel that lay propped by its side.

"Continue, Taylor," the major said, noticing the shrewd eyes trying to work out what had just been set in train.

"Of course, sir." Simon leaned forward and placed his empty glass on a similar packing case to his right. Immediately the

7

aide retrieved it and poured a generous second glass. Simon's eyes met the aide's and there was a flicker of a smile before the aide looked away. But the look had been equal to equal; that was significant.

"Sir, the second bit of luck was that the picket we captured did not consist of thirty-five of the enemy but just fifteen. The numbers were made up by twenty captives from our side. They had been brought there to dig graves for six French soldiers recently killed in action against our forces. But for us it meant a sudden and dramatic increase in our numbers, trained soldiers I mean, sir. Furthermore, at the camp ahead, there were no more than 100 of the enemy and a further 200 English fighters held captive. And we had our guide, who was prepared to lead us right into the camp."

The major asked many more questions. How could Taylor rely on the guide? Simon had determined the exact whereabouts of the guide's family and promised an unpleasant visit should there be any treachery. Did they free the captives first? Yes, it was a two-pronged exercise, actually three-pronged, as Tucker and six others were detailed to lead the horses out of the camp, the thinking being that with daybreak coming, mounted soldiers would be far harder to deal with than those on foot.

"The two main prongs, sir, were a body of men that released the first tent of captives, overpowering the guards. They had instructions to move on and release further tents of prisoners in some order. Then, using some of the freed soldiers, I led a silent attack on the enemy, tent by tent. Of course, sir, it did not stay silent long but the element of surprise and the arising confusion meant an easy victory for us, sir."

At this point, the questioning turned a different course. The major asked about Simon's past and why he was here. Simon noticed that the aide stopped scribbling the answers down in his notebook and took up the other piece of paper to work on.

"I volunteered, sir. You see, it was either seven years indenture or seven years in the army. Despite being quite old for a soldier, I decided to take my chances with the military rather than

8

working my old bones to an early death in some swamp or bleak mountain-side farm in Virginia. There were six of us convicts on board but I was the only one to sign up."

"Quite and we are pleased that you made such a decision." The major was verging on pomposity, almost regal in his recent pronouncements. Perhaps he felt it appropriate for the decision he had come to over the last half an hour. He glanced at the aide who nodded in reply, then spoke.

"I just need one thing, sir, if I might?"

"Go ahead, Charles." The aide turned to Simon and asked for his first name.

"Simon, sir."

"Any middle name?"

"Edward, sir, and Browning after my maternal side."

"Have another whisky, Taylor," the major said, topping up the glasses while the aide wrote carefully on his paper.

It was only after the fourth whisky that Captain Simon Edward Browning Taylor left the colonel's tent, clutching a hastily drawn-up field commission and following an orderly who had been instructed to find him space in an officer's tent. "And make sure it is a damned decent one for the hero of Galley Gorge."

"Yes, sir, of course, sir," the orderly had replied.

Major Davidson and his aide had a fifth whisky once Simon had gone.

"It's strange, sir," the aide said in contemplation of what they had just done.

"What's strange, Charles?"

"We only have two soldiers directly from England in our militia, other than Sergeant Holmes, who has been with us a long time. Both the newcomers are now officers. Lieutenant Aspley is useless while this bod seems to hold much promise."

"Yes, Charles. I think he will be the saving of us, for one thing is certain; I do not know what to do next. But something tells me Captain Taylor will know exactly, thus filling the gap nicely. To that end, have him come around at eight sharp tomorrow morning and we'll put him through his paces!"

"Yes, sir. Goodnight, sir." The aide stood up and saluted but Major Davidson waved him away with the comment that they were old friends and hang military procedure.

Chapter 2

Every second Friday, Henry and Grace Sherborne rode towards Sturminster Newton. Usually Henry rode on Champion, so called because he was sturdy enough to take part in a joust. Sometimes, Henry would charge ahead after using his knife to chop at a hazel stick, then turn in an exaggerated circle to run back at his wife. He always missed her by a good distance for he did not want to risk pinning her to the trunk of a tree on the side of the road. But he would always lean down from his high horse and take her captive, swinging her up so that she perched on the horn of his saddle.

Grace rode several different horses, her choice on any one day depending on her mood. Once or twice she had selected a horse almost as tall as Champion and then they had raced down the two verges of the road or in the field that ran along the side. But often she chose a very good-looking mare by the name of Straw, for she was the colour of straw just at the point of harvest. Straw was her favourite horse of all time.

They did not go all the way to Sturminster Newton for their destination was Bagber Manor, the home of Eliza Davenport, once Lady Merriman before her marriage to Grace's brother, Matthew, the unshakeably serious one of the family.

Bagber Manor was also home to Elizabeth Taylor, the wife of Simon and the sister of Grace, Matthew and Thomas. It had been the home of all the Taylor family up until last year.

But not now, thought Grace every time she rode up to the house. It was a sad story that led to the break-up of the Taylor family. Simon had been transported to the American colonies for the enormous fraud he and others had committed against both the Bagber and the Great Little estates. This fraud had hit the two landowners badly, particularly Great Little where much of the venom was directed.

Simon was the only person convicted for these crimes. Parchman had disappeared completely, presumably with much of the money obtained from the fraud. Candles, or Ferguson to use his real name, had been dismissed from his government post for incompetence but the evidence against him was too sparse and no prosecution had resulted. He had returned, grumbling mightily, to his waiting enemies in Scotland. Even Grimes, accused of murdering the sad and lonely messenger, had been freed on a technicality and remained a tenant of Bagber with his wife, Amelia Taylor, the daughter of Simon and his first wife. Hence, only Simon received punishment and only Elizabeth and her three young children remained at the manor house.

It was a family split into many parts and no part could be described as fully happy.

Grace, in her response to this, alternated between sadness at the outcome for the Taylors, and intense joy for her own situation being married to Henry, the Earl of Sherborne. But today, it was a different mixture of emotions. On the positive side, it was early May of 1690 and a good time to be young and alive.

And wealthy and married into the aristocracy.

Except this particular aristocratic family was Catholic. And that meant no public life. The Test Act of 1673 had barred Catholics from office. But it was the extension to cover nobility in 1678 that particularly jarred, for now Henry could not even take up his position in the House of Lords, still less take a commission in the army, his preference. James II, still seen by some ardent Catholics as the real king, had granted dispensations against these two acts when he had become king in 1685.

James II's dispensations had provided only a temporary relief for they had not survived the Glorious Rebellion when the Calvinist Prince of Orange and his wife, Mary Stuart, had swept to power in an almost bloodless coup to take the throne. The fact that Mary was James II's daughter and William of Orange was also his nephew meant little when thrones and kingdoms were at stake.

That last statement would be pulled apart by countless historians, examined carefully and then stitched back together again. Was it really an individual snatching the throne from his uncle and father-in-law, acting out of personal ambition? Or were William and Mary just the vehicle for the establishment to regain control after the brutal battering from the brief reign of James II? The main island of Britain was Protestant but not, perhaps, so Protestant that the masses could not be persuaded to change religion once more. But a change of national religion meant a wholesale sweeping out of the ruling class, as began to happen under James II.

And wherever privilege and power sit in society, they are jealously guarded. James Stuart was the right and lawful king yet the establishment decided on another, one who was more appealing to their particular needs for security.

But Grace was not thinking of the broad perspective of history as she pulled on the reins having just won a canter across the lawns surrounding Bagber Manor. Her thoughts were on the frustrations of her husband.

He wanted to join the army, felt it was his destiny, yet was not permitted as a Catholic to hold a commission.

"Grace, how nice to see you, Henry too." Eliza met them at the door as she always did. "The others are in the library. Matthew is newly back this afternoon from London."

Grace hurried through to the library to see the eldest of her two brothers, but bumped into Thomas, the younger brother, as he came out.

"Careful, Grace," he said irreverently.

"You be careful, Thomas," she replied, bouncing the same tone back to him. "Where's Matthew?"

"Sitting on his throne, of course!" Thomas was alluding to the large carved wooden chair with its high back and scarlet seat and back pads fastened with broad-headed nails evenly spaced around the edges. Matthew always made a bee-line for this chair whenever he managed to come home.

"I was working to draft a new bill that just went through Parliament," he told everyone after warm hugs of greeting. Eliza had come in and taken a seat on a stool beside them. She looked not just like his wife but also his most loyal subject. "It's been named after you, sister." Matthew looked at his youngest sister, resplendent in an ivory silk dress with a tulip-red underskirt, matched by a tall riding hat pinned to her hair so that it leaned over like a quirky folly she might easily have had built in her grounds at Sherborne Hall. She had raised the veil on entering the house and now reached up and drew out three long pins. She was with family and did not need to stand on ceremony.

Kitty, one of Eliza's maids, was there to take the hat and the pins.

"Whatever do you mean, Matty?" As their eldest brother had become their friend rather than the disciplinarian of their childhoods, they had warmed to him. As they had warmed to him, they had shortened his name; it was something Eliza had noted with delight, although Matthew seemed entirely unaware of the progression from Matthew to Matt and then on to Matty.

"Why, the King's new law is given your name. He signed the Act of Grace the day I left Westminster for only on his signing did I know my work was done."

Matthew had everyone's attention as he went on to explain that the Act of Grace was a generous and warm-hearted forgiveness of almost everyone involved with James Stuart's stand against the new king.

"Do you agree with this, Matty?" Henry asked hopefully. If the king could be this generous with those who could have been held up as traitors, might there not be hope that he would bring Catholics back into public life?

"I do, Henry, for the older I get, the more I see the virtues of toleration." This was getting more and more positive for Henry. Then reality hit like a dip in the cold Divelish river on a hot day. "But you have to think of the setting of this new law, the perspective if you like. Westminster is rife with plans for King William to go to Ireland. He has been rightfully afraid of going for the risk of upset at home in his absence. This new law is a clever move to settle England so that he might leave for Ireland safely."

"It should also undermine James' support in Ireland a touch," Thomas said, thinking of his time in Ireland the previous year.

Then thinking of Father O'Toole and the beautiful, lulling Latin mass he had been forced to attend. He often replayed the chanted responses in his head as he went about his building business. He had tried to banish them from his mind but they would not leave, would not quit the proud church that was his body and from which they seeped steadily into his soul.

But now was not the time for reflection. Matthew was back home and Kitty and Sara were bringing out wine on trays. He should do a toast to family or to returned members. He raised his glass. He would do both toasts, one after the other.

Mrs Amelia Grimes and her husband were always invited to these weekends but never came. Amelia knew better than to plead, for the more she wanted something, the more he took pleasure it its denial. But the invitations kept coming. Every second Tuesday, a lad brought a note to Grimes Cottage and handed it to Grimes. Every second Tuesday evening, the lad reported to Eliza and Elizabeth as to what he found.

"There are empty bottles everywhere."

"Mrs Grimes had a bruise on her cheek."

"There was such a smell coming from somewhere, it remained in my nostrils all the way home, my lady and miss." His terms of address were interesting in respect of both of them. Eliza Davenport had been Lady Merriman before her marriage the previous year to Matthew. No-one was quite sure whether she was entitled to the honorific as the heir to Lord Merriman or whether the title had lapsed on his death; moreover, did her marriage to Matthew make her plain Mrs Davenport? To answer these questions, they need only look at the world around them. All the staff and tenants of Bagber Manor still referred to her as Lady M. Everyone except her personal maid addressed her as 'my lady'. Milly, her sapling of a maid, got muddled every time and Eliza never knew whether she would be addressed as 'my lady', 'miss', 'ma'am' or a host of less frequent terms. But she did not care what Milly called her for she was a breath of fresh air and she loved the girl dearly.

With Elizabeth, it had been a sudden change when her husband, Simon Taylor, was convicted and sent to the colonies as an indentured servant. Most people automatically reverted to 'miss', as if Elizabeth had never been married, three young children notwithstanding. It was a sub-conscious and collective attempt to cope with the disgrace, removing Elizabeth from any connection with her wicked husband.

"She's not coping well," Elizabeth reflected on hearing the latest reports from the messenger lad, who had pocketed his two pennies and left, calculating all the way home how many more fortnightly visits it would take to buy his own horse. He had his eye on a beauty and somehow in his imaginings the horse stayed at the prefect age as he slowly accumulated the pounds and shillings he needed for the purchase. He had defeated the aging process, if only in his mind.

"But what can we do? Grimes won't let us near her. And with, well with Simon not employing him anymore, he is around the house much more."

"What does he do for a living?"

"He works occasional days on the neighbouring farm I hear, sometimes he substitutes for a driver who is sick for Big Jim at the haulage business. He scrapes together enough to buy his beer and brandy but little by way of food. I spoke to the steward about him. He is behind with the rent. Smith wants to throw him out but I can't do that for Mealy's sake."

"We must find a way to get food and essential supplies to her."

"I wonder whether that will just prolong her misery by extending the period Grimes can continue with his drinking. If things are coming to a head, that is surely a good thing?"

"No, definitely not, Eliza. What if 'coming to a head' means some terrible injury to Mealy?"

It was a problem they had no answer to. But Thomas did, when they consulted with everyone later that day.

"Easy," he said, "we kidnap her and bring her to some place of absolute safety."

Every second Friday, the Davenport brothers and sisters and their wives and husbands congregated at Bagber Manor. They caught up with each other's lives, taking walks and sometimes dipping in the river. They ate well and did not rush when they woke the next morning. Except Thomas, busy at his building business, and Eliza, who went about on estate matters in the morning. At lunch time they all got together again and Matthew practised his sermon for the upcoming Sunday morning service. They often took it slightly less seriously than Matthew would have liked but he had mellowed considerably since marrying Eliza.

This particular meeting stayed with them long afterwards, not because of the barmy May weather or a particular point to tease Matthew about, but because it was dominated by the sober matter of Amelia Grimes. They kept coming back to Thomas' idea. At first, it had been dismissed out of hand.

"It's crazy, Thomas," Grace said on hearing it.

"I agree," Bridget Davenport, Thomas' new wife, added in her captivating Ulster accent, shaking her head so that a large strand of hair fell onto the collar of her dress. "He'll go straight to the law and the law is quite clear that a wife's place is with her husband."

Surprisingly, the only person in favour from the start was Matthew.

"Desperate measures for desperate times," he said from his dark wooden throne.

Gradually, however, the others came around, at least closer to acceptance. Eliza was the first; no doubt thinking of her own captivity; five long years in Bristol.

"It would be a merciful thing to get her away to safety."

"I've an idea," replied Thomas, sensing the tide turning. "Let's meet again on Wednesday and all of us think on it between now and then. If we can come up with a workable plan then we can decide on Wednesday after church whether we will do it."

Lots of nods, then Grace stood up to say they must go. It would take several hours to get back to Sherborne.

"It will be a pleasant ride today in the evening sun, don't you think, husband? Henry?"

"What, oh sorry dear. Yes, quite acceptable to me." It was a neutral statement that could fit any number of questions.

Grace did not pick him up on it, not wanting to embarrass him if she could help it. Instead, she would talk to him on the ride home.

But Henry spoke first as they wound their way across the North Dorset countryside.

"Did you hear what Matty said about the King?"

"You mean the new law named after me?"

"No, dearest, not that. Rather him going to Ireland to…"

"fight!" Grace wheeled her horse, nudged it from trot to canter and called something back over her shoulder as she moved off perpendicular to their line of travel. Henry did not catch it all but heard 'men' and 'always fighting' floating back on the wispy wind.

Afterwards, close to the gates to Sherborne Hall, he spoke to her again.

"I mean to go to Ireland, Grace. I have to do something in these extraordinary times we are in."

"But how, dearest?" She leaned over in her side-saddle, almost falling off in order to kiss him on the lips. "You can't be an officer."

"Then I will enlist. My mind is made up, my love."

Grace did not reply with words. Words were insufficient. Instead she leaned over again. Henry, naturally understanding her intentions, lifted her with ease and put her on his horse, directly in front of him. He held her tightly, her legs stretched across the horse's back and playing havoc with her skirts.

She laughed, they both laughed. She understood his need and would not stand in his way.

No words were necessary but she said a silent prayer, pressing God to keep her husband safe.

And asking for a speedy return.

Chapter 3

Penelope slammed the library door so that it bounced against its frame and flew open again, flecks of the new green paint launching into the air.

"Have you seen Sally?"

"She's with Tomkins, I believe."

"She's always there these days. I know, I know, Alice, you don't need to remind me every time I ask after her. I did agree to my maid helping the steward but I did not think it would be all day and every day." Penelope Wiltshire had laid particular stress on the word 'my' and now looked sharply at her only friend, Lady Alice Roakes. She did not count Sally as a friend; Sally was a necessity, like lungs or a heart or a head. Without Sally, Penelope was nothing, could not exist. With her, she was complete.

'My' implied absolute property rights, only nobody knew this except Penelope. Most of the time, she did not want legal ownership of her maid but occasionally some devil put it back in the front of her mind.

"She loves the work, my dear Penelope," Alice replied, while also watching young Sir Beatrice crawl across the floor towards her. Penelope observed her friend a moment longer before concluding that she suspected nothing.

"I beg pardon, I was not listening. Please start again."

"I was just saying, Penelope, that you need something to occupy your time."

"I have my horse." This was said with slight indignance, as if Alice was rapidly going through her nine lives in making such observations. But Penelope was sufficiently fond of her to grant a few more.

"I knew you would not take it well," Alice replied. "Sit down a moment. I'm worried you will trip over Sir Beatrice." The baby boy, as if understanding his mother's words, chose that moment for a move that entangled himself in Penelope's skirts.

She was turning in her rapid walk up and down the length of the library, a flaring of skirts. To avoid Sir Beatrice, she tried to side step, stumbled and fell onto a low table.

"Ouch!" she cried, rubbing her shin. Turning around she sat heavily on a table which broke with a loud crack, sending Penelope to the floor.

"I'm so sorry, my dear." Alice checked her son and then came over to look at Penelope's bruised shin.

"It wasn't Sir Beatrice."

"What was it then?"

"The hem of this skirt has come loose. I asked Sally to sew it back up." She waved the skirt in the air and Alice saw it was torn badly.

"Did you ask her nicely?" Alice knew her friend well, having lived with her over a year now, sharing the solitude of a single friendship.

"I might have been a bit cross, Alice, but she is never around." She did not mention that Sally spent every night with her. She did not need to mention it for Alice knew well enough; it was unspoken between them as if speaking would bring a hundred practical and moral questions to the fore that were best avoided.

The door opened and Sally came in, already talking as she came through the door.

"Lady Roakes, do you have a moment to go over a few ideas?" she blurted out. "Oh, Pen, I didn't know you were here. Have you hurt yourself?" She broke into a run down the length of the library and slid to a stop by Penelope on the floor, broken wood from the table scattered around.

"It's your fault, Sally."

"My fault?"

"I trod on the hem I asked you to sew up for me."

"Oh, my dearest, I am so sorry. I'll do it right now." Her small black face shone with concern.

"It's a bit late now, talk about shutting the stable door after the horse has bolted!" But her anger was spent, dissipated into the warm air around them, chased out by Sally's sweet frown and anxious look. "The mending job is much bigger now, see

I've torn the skirt. I don't want the other servants to see me like this."

"That is easily fixed, Pen," Sally replied. "I'll pop upstairs for another dress and for my sewing box. Then we can do it here together by the…"

"Oh, I'd like that, Sal. You could show me how to do it. I'm a good learner, don't you think?"

"A fine student, I would say!" They refrained from kissing due to the presence of Lady Roakes, who had watched keenly and now felt a need to look away but kept snatching glances back. She saw Sally help Penelope up from the floor and into a comfortable chair. She saw her pat her cheeks and feel her forehead, but they could have been actions of elementary nursing. She saw Sally pour a glass of wine for Penelope, then accepted one herself and went to sit next to her friend by the fire, facing away from Sally so she saw no more. But she heard the swish of skirts as Sally curtsied to her back and then the door opening and closing.

My goodness, she thought, this is a complicated relationship. And complicated relationships have a habit of causing trouble. She could never feel that way for another woman but longed for a man. Yet they met nobody. They lived virtually in exclusion on their Great Little Estate, not affording a social life and not knowing how to go about one. The recovery from the disasters of 1689, when bankruptcy had stared right at them, was underway but their finances were still precarious and work on the half-complete house was halted. It would be years before they could afford to give a ball or have a summer gathering of all the notables of the area. And even then, would they come? She inevitably thought of Eliza Davenport, from the other great estate in the area. Their lands abutted in two places on this side of Okeford Hill. Eliza, who used to be Lady Merriman, known more commonly as the Witch of Bagber, had been polite about it but was firm that she wanted nothing to do with Alice Roakes.

And who could blame her? Alice had pleaded for forgiveness yet known all along that forgiveness was impossible after what she had done. She might as well be a murderer for she had stolen five long years of Eliza's life, imprisoning her and treating her like a skivvy. It had suited her purpose and her income at the time but she shuddered to think of it now.

"Are you cold, Alice?"

"No…I was just thinking on the past."

"Don't do that, my dear." For a shit-shoveller's daughter, Penelope, the Dowager-Duchess of Wiltshire, could be incredibly patrician, commanding, proud. Yet she was putty in Sally's hands, more like a young girl anxious to please her betters.

Such a complicated relationship.

The messenger was shown in to the library an hour later. He saw a domestic scene with two great ladies sitting by the fire, a maid with her back to him on a low stool working on some needlework. It was a scene he expected so nothing alerted him. He did not notice that there were three wine glasses, rather than two. Nor did he notice the laughter on Sally's face as she was relating some silly, early morning antics of the Dowager-Duchess of Wiltshire, the lady for whom he had the message.

"Your Grace, I bring you sad news." He handed over the note. Sally stood, the half-mended skirt dropping to the floor.

"Would you care for some refreshments, sir? Sir?" He was staring, having never seen a black girl before.

"Ah yes, thank you, miss." But the servant girl did not leave to fetch beer and something to eat. Instead, she rang the bell and another maid answered.

"Ellie, please take this young man to the kitchen and see that he is fed. We may have a message for him to go back with."

The door closed behind the messenger and Ellie.

"It's from my mother." No more need be said.

Sir John Withers, Penelope's father, had been ill for some time. Now he was dead. He took nothing with him, of course, other than the fondness of his dogs and a slight feeling from his wife that something was now missing. He had been a hard, manipulative, sometimes cruel, man. At the height of the Great Little problems the previous year, Penelope had gone to see her father and begged for a loan. It had been refused and she had pawned all her jewellery instead. That jewellery was still pawned, although thankfully to a considerate merchant who would not dispose of it without giving Penelope every chance to repay the loan.

But now that he was dead, Penelope was one of the richest ladies in the country. Her mother, who had been much kinder towards her, had ample provision to live a quiet but comfortable life, all she wanted. The rest of the vast fortune was Penelope's.

Or so she thought.

The reading of the will took place at Withers Court four days later. Penelope's father had been buried that morning. He had commissioned a large monument to stand on his grave but that would be some months in the making.

"Besides, the ground has to settle a while, Your Grace," the priest had said. "It's a pity we did not see more of your father in church," he added but Penelope had already turned away. She was not interested in the past.

The attorney cleared his throat to dampen the light flutter of voices in the horribly uncomfortable study. There were six chairs posted around Sir John's desk where the attorney now sat. But only three of them were occupied.

Sir John had accumulated enormous wealth but would be forgotten within days of his departure, remembered only by his widow in a vague, slightly unsettling way. Certainly, his only child, Penelope, did not care for him.

"There are a few minor bequests which I shall read first." These were to be expected. Between £5 and £50 went to each of the 28 servants, following some formula that seemed to recognise their seniority within the household and their length of service. Penelope started adding the amounts to come from the residue, her residue, but soon lost count. Maybe they came in total to a round thousand. There was her mother, of course, who had the house and an income of £2,000 a year for life. But none of this made a dent in the vast fortune Sir John had acquired.

Now would come that residue.

But there was one more gift to make, one that made Penelope sit bolt upright.

"I give the sum of £10,000 to my only child, Penelope Wiltshire, nee Withers. And that concludes the specific bequests."

"What of the residue of Father's estate?" Penelope called out.

"Ah, yes, the residue," the attorney spoke as if will-reading was something entirely new to him. He turned the page slowly. Was he following Sir John's instructions to turn up the suspense to the maximum? Or, perhaps he just enjoyed a little fun in his otherwise dry world. "Let me see, now. Yes, the residue of approximately £100,000 in investments plus the absolute interest in Withers Court and its 3,000 acres of arable land, subject to the life interest held by Lady Withers, will be held in trust."

"Trust? For whose benefit?" Penelope stood, felt her legs give way and then saw Sally coming to assist her, holding on and guiding her back to the chair. How had Sally managed to enter the study for a private family meeting? Sally whispered that she had thought to check on Penelope.

"It's common knowledge downstairs that Sir John left an upsetting will. They were talking about it in the servants' hall and I thought I had better come upstairs to be with you. Something about a trust, I believe."

The attorney was fumbling for a new document.

"I'm sure I had the trust deed with me somewhere. No doubt you will want to know who benefits from the trust?" He was an expert fumbler, eventually managing to find the trust document on the study desk, right in front of where he was sitting. He cleared his throat again. The room silenced in expectation.

"The trustees of the trust are myself and the Withers Court steward, Mr Johnson, who I see here today." Mr Johnson nodded. He had clearly known about this new arrangement and had therefore occupied the third chair alongside Penelope and her mother. "The beneficiary is Sir John's daughter, Penelope Wiltshire…"

"Thank God!"

"I had not quite finished, Your Grace. I was going to read the condition."

"What condition?"

"On condition that my daughter produces a male heir to be named after me. The father of the heir will be someone approved by Lady Withers. Should no heir be forthcoming by my daughter's thirtieth birthday, the entire estate will revert to a suitable cause to be determined by the trustees, provided my daughter does not benefit from such distribution."

The attorney stopped reading, looked over his spectacles at the four of them, for Sally had taken the seat next to Penelope and had her hand raised, ready to support her mistress should it be necessary.

"He finishes with a declaration that the Withers family will continue come what may. And that, ladies and gentleman, concludes the reading of the will of Sir John Withers, lately departed and sadly missed."

Later that day, Sally knocked on the door of Penelope's suite of rooms, the same ones Penelope had once slept in with her prospective husband, the Duke of Wiltshire, "to try the goods before purchase" as it had been described. She knocked for she knew that Penelope's mother was in there, trying to lessen Penelope's anger. It would never do for the mother to know what the daughter did with her maid.

Sally opened the door, slid inside and curtsied. Then she remained still a moment as she caught the tail end of the discussion between Lady Withers and Penelope.

"Penelope, my dearest, what is wrong with your father wanting an heir from you to take over the estate? It is quite natural to want his name to live on. After all, he made something of the name from a very unpromising start."

"Do you know what Wiltshire was like to me?"

"No but I can imagine, my little one." She leaned over and stroked Penelope's hair. "I never liked Wiltshire but your father would have you married to him for the sake of the name." She paused, continuing to tangle her fingers in Penelope's hair in a way only a mother can do. "Your father was not good to me, Penelope, so I have some inkling of what it was like for you." She refrained from pointing out that Penelope had been married to Wiltshire for a matter of months, whereas it had been close to twenty-five years with her husband. "We will find a nice and gentle man for you this time around. It is my choice, as you know, and I shall not be unkind. Surely you know that?"

"Yes, Mama, but I just do not want to do it. Oh, hello, Sally." Sally had moved into the room, not feeling good about eavesdropping.

"Good evening, Your Grace, Your Ladyship." She curtsied again. "I've come to get Her Grace ready to dine."

"Ah, I must go and get ready too," Lady Withers exclaimed, standing up and freeing her hand from a knot she had made in her daughter's hair with her ever-twisting fingers. "Sally, my dear, you will need to make a good job of Her Grace's hair as I have jumbled it up quite terribly."

"Yes, of course, my lady."

The door closed. Sally waited a minute then turned the lock in the door. She came back to Penelope and kissed her on the lips, hanging her arms round her neck and standing on tiptoes to reach up to the taller girl.

"I love you, Pen."

"I love you too, Sal." Penelope pulled the ribbons and loosened Sally's cap so that her wiry hair sprung into life. "We've just got enough time to examine what the bed is like."

Penelope was late into the dining room, keeping her mother waiting quite some considerable time.

Chapter 4

Thomas closed the ledger, sighed and went to find his angular, strangely-pretty wife. They had been married only eight weeks and, looking back, it had been the oddest of weddings. Take the weather first; winter had refused to move on, lasting to the beginning of May, white frost remaining when the snow had eventually cleared. Then from the middle of the month, summer had set in with its lazy, trickling ways and gentle heat building day on day. It had been dry throughout May, making spring growth possible only because of the melted snow now rushing through the streams and rivers of Dorset, as if given wings to fly to the sea.

The weather had been odd but it was not the strangest factor; more that the compression of spring into a fortnight seemed a reflection of deeply pinched emotions. Amelia Taylor, now Amelia Grimes, was ever-present in their relationship like the third leg of a stool. Not that she was present for she was not; it was her absence that was a presence in their marriage, like a ship with all sails set but an anchor still firmly dug into the harbour bottom.

But even stranger things were to come in the next few days for Bridget begged Thomas to take a few hours off work on the Tuesday after they had all discussed Amelia's plight when together at Bagber Manor. They were due to meet again on Wednesday and Bridget wanted to see something for herself.

"We're going to Mealy's house," Thomas said. "Is that wise?"

"Wait and see exactly where we are going, my darling." The twang with which she said 'darling' filled Thomas with desire; his wife was beautiful, wise, so full of life inside that angular body. He supposed that her soul, like most souls, was round, while her body was all sharper, leaving the soul sometimes perilously close to breaking through the surface of her skin. He knew this for at times Thomas could see the very essence of her shining through.

But their talk as they walked was not so deep. They discussed Thomas' building projects, wondering if the work at Great Little would ever start again.

"They were hit so badly by Parchman's fraud." Bridget tactfully referred to it as 'Parchman's fraud' in order not to mention the Taylor name. Parchman had been the organiser in the shadows but Simon Taylor had been the man on the ground; it had been a partnership, a joint-stock company as was becoming so popular for ventures across the world.

And they had heard that Simon Taylor, one half of that joint-stock firm, was sent to a far part of the world, to Virginia where he would be working day-in and day-out for some desperate settler hoping to scrape a living and build a life for his growing family.

They talked, although it was not raised by Bridget, of her new book, commissioned by Mr Frampton, her publisher in London. It was a survey of modern England from a woman's perspective.

"You know I'll have to travel across the country for my research."

"I'll come with you, my Bridge." She was unlike any bridge Thomas could have built, fine though his bridges were. She did not offer a way across rivers or streams. She was a bridge from Dorset to Ireland, a bridge to education and intellectual thought, spurned by Thomas when sent to Dorchester to attend school at the age of thirteen. He had spent his childhood yearning for the woods and streams and fields he knew so well and only now realised what he had been missing.

His wife was a bridge to so much more, to love, to adventure, to new things that were exciting because they were new.

And right now, she was a bridge to Amelia, who he loved dearly, had always done so. But the bridge did not go directly to Grimes Cottage. Bridget was too sensible for that. She led them instead to the copse on the hill behind the cottage from where they had watched Grimes' movements last year in the hope of getting a chance to talk to Amelia.

It was also where Bridget and Thomas had first been intimate when on watch-duty together one very still morning when their emotions had danced and mixed together and their eyes had been for each other rather than set on movement around Grimes Cottage in the hollow below.

It had also been the day when they had finally seen Amelia and she had blessed their union, urging them on, stating baldly but painfully that she was lost, given to another.

And Amelia had appealed to Thomas to live twice the life, once for himself and once for her.

Bridget made a decision as they made a wide circle around Grimes Cottage and approached the copse from the rear. She was in charge of this walk and she would not take her husband to the particular point where they had first held hands; it may have been a tacit acknowledgement that Amelia was the third leg of their stool, it may have been something simpler. Instead, she led Thomas straight through the wood on the left-hand side where a tall hedge, stacked with old oaks like grandparents watching the grandchildren play, ran down the hill towards the back of the cottage.

"The hedge has grown since last year and no-one has cut it back."

"Exactly, my darling." Again, Thomas heard the twang that made the endearment so special. "Now it's the perfect way to sneak up on the cottage without being seen."

And that is exactly what they did. And they waited there, not holding hands because they needed to be two independent witnesses when they saw Amelia. Thomas actually put out his hand for hers but Bridget was focused on their view of the cottage eighty yards ahead.

But sight was denied them at first. Instead, it was another sense that operated.

"Listen to that," said Thomas. "Are they having a fight?"

"I hear Grimes shouting but it is one-sided. Mealy is not responding."

"I'm going in."

"No, Thomas!"

He moved forward and up from his crouched position but then shrank back for the door opened and Amelia came out. It was the first time Thomas had seen her since Grimes had been released without charge six weeks earlier.

Thomas saw on her face what the messenger lad had been reporting back. He saw the bruises, the dark rings around her eyes, the hair straggling around her neck, lifeless as if a predictor of things to come.

He stared a moment, a moment too long, unable to take in the deterioration that had occurred. It was a moment of hesitation that made all the difference, both then and into the future.

For Bridget Davenport, his wife, was moving her tall, thin body across the open space between the hedge and the outhouses. She was bent double so it looked like she might topple over at any minute, her legs propelling rapidly to try and keep up with the change in balance from bending herself forwards and running, stopping, running down the slope. Her efforts did not work as planned for she fell over the short stone wall that marked the end of the field and the beginning of the backyard. Amelia, despite her exhaustion, moved after a moment of hesitation. She dropped her chamber pot and made her body into a buffer to block Bridget's fall.

Much later, on the way back to Sturminster Newton, Bridget explained the physics.

"Thomas, my dear, you must expand your outlook. Am I married to a boorish builder or someone with a brain that seeks new knowledge?" By which light-heartedness one will gather that the meeting with Amelia went either exceedingly well or exceedingly badly; humour as relief or reinforcer.

"You are married to an ignoramus but you will take me, no doubt, to another place altogether." It was the bridge metaphor again; even those who never travel should not stay still and bridges take one over difficulties a plenty. They are built by the few to benefit the many.

"Have you not heard of '*Principia Mathematica Philosophiae Naturalis*'? It is a remarkable work by a man called Isaac Newton, a supremely intelligent man. My tutor in Londonderry had a copy of this treasured work and spent some time going over it with me. The essence is that every action in nature has an equal and opposite reaction."

Bridget explained how things such as the energy behind momentum just do not go away. "Instead they transfer into other things. And they react exactly and precisely to the force applied. Thus, I had a force from the energy of running and my weight contributed too."

"Like a combination of the two?"

"Exactly so, sir." The formality of her address added to the sense of learning. "When Mealy stood to block my fall from the wall, what happened?"

"The two of you fell back against the outhouse wall."

"With considerable force, would you say?"

"Yes, you cracked your head on the stone and for a moment I thought…"

"I'm fine, my love, but the point is Mealy's body was so light, it could not withstand my momentum. I'll hazard a guess that she has not eaten this week."

"No more than a nibble, if the messenger-lad speaks true. I've heard dreadful things directly from him these last few visits."

They walked in silence, across fields of young wheat and oats, every so often seeing cows and sheep grazing in adjacent fields. Bagber Manor, less hard hit by Parchman's fraud than Great Little, was recovering quickly. Perhaps, Thomas thought, that was something to do with equal and opposite forces as well. While Bridget was reflecting on something else entirely; that silence can mask a hundred raging emotions or even the blankness we feel when we don't know what to feel. And the same silence can mask different things for different people.

Everything within Bridget screamed to take her husband away; this was not their fight as Amelia had been keen to point out in pressing their wedding on them.

*You must lead twice the life, Thomas, one for you and one for me
for I am not available to you.*

Had Amelia not given her blessing to their union? Why
had Bridget even taken Thomas there this morning when she
had known exactly what they would see?

And where it would lead them to, these newlyweds?

"I'm behind you, sir."

"Behind me in what, Bridge?"

"We have to get Mealy out of there and soon." It was the
ultimate sacrifice, risking all she had recently gained.

They all met again on Wednesday evening at Bagber Manor
as arranged. Bridget stood as soon as everyone was gathered
and spoke of what she had found. She did not go into forces
and reactions but spoke plainly about the bruises she had seen,
the torn dress that hung upon Amelia's skimpy frame and the
hollowed-out eyes that said it all.

After she finished speaking, standing like a willow in the
wind, she asked each person who agreed with her to stand.

Thomas was the first to stand. Then Eliza, visions of her own
captivity haunting her; something she had promised herself
never to dwell on.

Eliza was followed by Elizabeth, then Big Jim and Plain Jane,
asked to come along due to the importance of their discussion
and in the hope that they could add something practical to
the solution. Ever since meeting Thomas and Grace in Bristol
five years earlier, they had become firm friends. Big Jim was
so called for his diminutive size, Plain Jane for her incredible
beauty. They had settled just outside Sturminster Newton where
they ran a successful haulage business, often supplying Thomas'
building materials.

Matthew then stood from his self-chosen throne, grim face
hiding the outrage he felt as he worked his thoughts into a new
sermon. He played with a title in his head and came upon 'The
Sacred Chalice of the Human Body; a diatribe against physical
harm by the strong against the weak'. It would have fitted well

with his father's Man Against Man series published in 1685 to universal acclaim, and mostly written, or at least put into order, by Matthew himself.

That left Grace and the sudden recognition by everyone that Henry was not by her side. She rose hurriedly, aware of the eyes upon her.

"I agree with Bridge," she said but with a veil over her emotion.

"Where's Henry?" Thomas asked.

"He's gone to be a soldier." It was said with such a small voice that the words split upon the air and filtered along to the others in the room as ricochets, splinters of meaning.

"How, why, where?" they cried. Amelia was put to one side for a moment.

"He has enlisted as a private soldier and is going soon with King William to fight in Ireland."

"Let us bow our heads and pray for his safe and speedy return," Matthew said, bowing his own head low to set an example. "O Lord, the master of all that is good…" Thomas bowed his head like the others but he knew his sister well and had moved to stand beside her, taking her hand in his as Matthew led the group in prayer.

It was a long prayer, quite proper from a Presbyterian minister, son of the great sermoniser himself. It wound on, imploring God the Father to look after his child, Henry, to care for him and to bring him safely back to the fold.

It was vintage Davenport, yet Thomas was barely listening. He kept hearing the lulling Latin chants of the Catholic mass he had attended in Ballydalgagan, led by Father O'Toole who had helped in their escape both on their way to Londonderry and on their way home again.

After praying, they ate a simple meal that Sara had prepared. Cold roast beef with bread and pickles, followed by a warm apple pie.

"That's the end of last year's apples," Eliza said as Sara cut pie for everyone. "Now, what shall we do about Mealy?"

"We have a plan," said Thomas and Bridget in unison, both talking with a mouthful of apple pie.

Chapter 5

B y the start of summer proper, Lieutenant Aspley was no more.
No more a drag on the regiment's proficiency for the simple reason that he was no more.

Major Davidson, his commanding officer, had written a letter to his parents with glowing comments and sad reflections on a life lost at such a young and promising age. Mrs Aspley, the mother, kept the letter in a slim silver box under her pillow for the rest of her life, together with a lock of his hair from his first ever haircut and two of his baby teeth. She read the letter just the once and then put it away. She knew inside her that the message was a fabrication so would not read it again lest its mischief spill out and infuse the memories she had carefully selected of her only son. They were not wealthy people. Mr Aspley was the junior partner in a firm of silk importers based in their home town of Dorchester. He liked the ring of the firm's name but was saddened that it did not include his name alongside the other two. Perhaps if he worked harder still, as he faced little other prospect because of the loan to buy his son's commission and the considerable expenses to equip him for the army, they would eventually add 'Aspley' to the current title of Goodman and Ellis.

He was not a particularly good silk merchant with one success to his credit towards the end of an otherwise unremarkable 25-year career. He had stumbled upon a young man from London called Paul Tabard and offered him employment as a salesman. The Londoner had done extremely well in the few short months he had been with Goodman and Ellis. But it was inevitable that he would leave to set up his own firm. Roger Aspley had heard that the backing came from the fierce but beautiful Dowager-Duchess of Wiltshire who was also on the verge of bankruptcy. He hoped the rumours were untrue for his own precarious affairs were wound up a little more with

Paul Tabard. He had borrowed further in order to invest for a 3% share in Tabard's new venture, believing in the young man. The interest on this new loan was crippling and his wife was completely unaware of the transaction.

It was his little private investment for he believed young Tabard would do very well.

But now, there seemed little point in planning for the future. His son was deceased, lying in some godforsaken overseas territory. He was secretly pleased that the army refused to ship the body back to Dorset; bodies were always expensive to move around the world. He had a daughter but she had always been so difficult with him, as if she had never been explained the rules of whatever game they were playing. Perhaps that omission should be added to his long list of faults.

What should he do now? He could approach Tabard to sell back the 3% investment and thereby repay some of his loans but he knew Tabard had no cash. He felt listless, tired of trying to please everyone around him. He would sit a while by the window and enjoy the sunshine, let it wash over him.

It was his daughter, Anne, who found him. She raised the alarm and the doctor came from just around the corner but only to shake his head.

"Mr Aspley has had a heart attack," he said, feeling he was stating the obvious. "I expect the grief at his son's death did not help."

"My poor man, my darling husband. Gone, gone…" Mrs Aspley was distraught.

It was on the day of the funeral that practical matters came to the fore. It was sparked by a visit from a debt collector. Mr Jarvis was unaware of the death of Mr Aspley but was well known to the family as a frequent and polite caller. He graciously offered to withdraw when he was put in the picture.

"Sir, please wait a minute," Anne called across the room. She beckoned for him to follow her into the study. "Mr Jarvis, could you please let me know how much we owe your client?"

"£554, 12 shillings and threepence ha'penny," he replied, looking at his sheet.

"That is a lot, sir, a powerful lot."

"It is, I understand, the price of a commission these days. Well the lieutenancy was the original loan of £400 with interest and fees taking it to the current total, including some extra fees for missing instalments. But, miss, there will be other loans too, I dare say."

"How do you know?"

"I've never known it otherwise. When first a man goes down the road of debt, it multiplies many times over. That's the main reason I stick to the old motto, neither a borrower nor…"

"A lender be!"

"Exactly, miss. You understand that I am not the lender, merely his representative? Now, I don't want to intrude in this time of grief so I will come another day to talk about payment." But Anne had always liked Mr Jarvis and decided to press him a little further.

"Sir, would you be kind enough to take a little time and help me sort this out?" She pointed to the piles of paper on the desk, chairs and bookshelves. "My father shared his business matters with no-one and it will be a sore trouble for Mama and me to make some sense of it on our own."

"Well…," he hesitated, wanting to help, sensing something in this 20-year old girl that her father clearly had not seen but also aware of his own enormous workload. He received no salary, just commission from the successful payments he obtained from debtors in default. "I tell you what I'll do, miss, I'll come by after work each day for a few minutes and see what I can sort through." He waited to see the reaction, noting a brave attempt to hide her disappointment. "And, Miss Aspley, I'll make a start right now, if you would like me to, that is."

"Yes, thank you, sir. I'll just explain what is here for I have done a little initial sorting since…"

"No miss, if it's the all the same, let me sniff around on my own. Your mother is distraught in the next room and I think you should go to her. I'll come and find you before I leave."

Three days later, having spent much longer at the Aspley house than he had ever intended, he summarised for Anne.

"I still have some papers to sort through, Miss Aspley, but I believe I am correct in stating that your father died intestate which means…"

"That my mother inherits everything. Good, at least that is clear."

"But here's the rub, miss, for the assets are considerably less than the amount owed. Your father's main asset was his share in the business of Goodman and Ellis. A clause in the partnership agreement says if a minority stakeholder wishes to sell, it has to be offered first to the other partners. This puts you, frankly, in a position of difficulty with regard to the valuation of the stake. The other two partners can offer you almost anything. I took the liberty of having a quiet word with Mr Goodman and Mr Ellis this morning. They have indicated that your father's share is worth about £500."

"It's worth four times that at least," Anne replied, feeling her face flush hot. Would Mr Jarvis challenge her on how she got to that valuation?

"But I fear they have the upper hand in this situation, Miss Aspley." No challenge to the valuation for the reality was plain.

"And the investment in Tabard & Co?"

"Three percent is very much a minority holding, I'm afraid to say. Especially as the business has only just started trading. I don't know this Tabard but I strongly suggest that you keep ownership rather than try and sell it. You will get little hard cash for it right now but it just could make a nice surprise one day in the future."

"No other assets?"

"Just over £300 in cash, miss."

"And the house?"

"Yes, but the house is mortgaged. I am upset that your father saw clear to grant security over his house to other creditors but not to me. It puts me in a difficult position. I believe he was taking advantage of my good nature." Mr Jarvis expected to be argued with hotly on this point but felt he was justified in making it; secured creditors would always stand above unsecured, yet he represented the largest creditor of all.

Instead, Anne Aspley nodded her head in agreement.

"All creditors will be paid. I just need time." There was a firmness in her words that made Mr Jarvis take special note.

The debts, including unpaid trade bills and accumulated interest, came to more than the declared value of the assets, leaving the Aspley family technically bankrupt. It all depended on what could be arranged.

"Have you any relatives you could stay with?"

"My parents had no surviving siblings and my grandparents are all long gone so the answer is no, sir." She looked hopelessly young, a child thrust by chance into a cruel adult world. But she needed the whole truth.

"The debts now fall due with the…"

"Death of my father. Yes, I appreciate that, Mr Jarvis." She seemed in a trance. He had seen this once or twice before when tragedy had struck a middling family who, for whatever reason, had extended themselves to the point of self-destruction. There was nothing to be done; the harsh reality had to be faced.

"Will you do something for me, Mr Jarvis?" Here was the plea for debt forgiveness which he could not grant. His role was not to deal in hope or mercy but in real-world facts.

"If I can but I am restrained by my duties as an agent of your largest creditor."

"Will you please co-ordinate with the other creditors to grant me a week in order to sort out our affairs and make payment to you?"

He looked at her long and hard, saw both hope and hopelessness in her. Which would rise to the surface? He sighed.

"I wish I could, miss," he said as gently as he could. "Unfortunately, the creditors have already met." He had argued, as the representative for the largest debt, for a grace period of a fortnight but he had not succeeded. "The most they will give you is three days."

"Then I must move fast, Mr Jarvis. Thank you for all your kind assistance." She stood and offered her hand. He stood, kissed it and bowed to do so.

"You know where to find me if you need me, Miss Aspley."

"I do, sir, thank you."

Three days and fifteen minutes later, the late Mr Aspley's study was full of a dozen creditors or their representatives. Mr Jarvis rose from his seat.

"As the representative of the largest creditor, I shall take the chair unless anybody has an objection?" Nobody had but before he could continue, Anne spoke from her chair behind the door.

"Thank you, Mr Jarvis," she said shakily. "You have been very kind to my mother and me."

"It's quite a shock losing a loved one so suddenly and…"

"We've come to hear about payments, foreclosures and such like," came a sharp voice across the room. "I've not come to listen to the sorrows and tribulations of those that borrow recklessly and then look for sympathy from every quarter."

"As you know, Mr Shapely, I had asked for a fortnight to allow Mrs and Miss Aspley to get to grips with their altered circumstances and…"

"Do a runner, no doubt." That was Shapely again, judging others by his own standards.

"The vote was almost unanimous against my request. Only Mr Fellows voted with me. So now you have your way and we are meeting three days later to discuss how to manage the outstanding debts."

"Declare bankruptcy, is what I say."

"That will only be necessary if the harshest response to the Aspley's plight is adhered to. I would exhort you again to think differently on this matter."

Mr Jarvis was about to delve into his argument for leniency once more, having honed it and improved it over the last few days. Yet he did not for one simple reason. No-one was listening to him.

Instead, they were watching Anne Aspley rise from her chair behind the door, step around the other chairs to the desk pushed to the back of the room. There was no chair at the desk for it had been pulled out to accommodate one of the creditors. But she was not looking for an alternative seat. Instead, she took a slender key tied around her wrist and opened the central drawer of the desk. Mr Jarvis stood again, moved quickly to her side of the desk, quicker than his old bones would normally allow. He had been reminded of one of his early debt collection exercises from years ago. A young gentleman had been in the middle of discussions about repayments, seemed reconciled to his situation. He too had opened the central desk drawer, had pulled out a pistol, thrust the barrel in his mouth and shot himself. Mr Jarvis would never forget the pool of blood, like spilled ink, on the desk top. Then, looking up from the crumpled body, he had seen the man's brains spread across the ornate wallpaper.

The expensive decoration of the gentleman's home was one reason why he was in such debt.

Mr Jarvis had been taking as hard a line as any of the creditors that day. He had vowed then and there never to push anyone beyond their limit again. And it was this vow that had defined him as a person over a forty-year career in the unsavoury world of debt collection.

Mr Jarvis arrived at the desk in time, whereas before he had been too late. He might be forty years older but his senses were sharper, all six of them. He placed a large hand on Anne's thin wrist.

"No," he mouthed. She looked at him, understood his concern and whispered for him to trust her.

He did, releasing his grip, but staying close. She pulled out a pewter money box, took a second key from her wrist and opened it.

"I have here fourteen shillings on the pound for everyone. I beg not for forgiveness of the remaining debt but for time to pay the six shillings I cannot pay today."

"No, little miss, everything or nothing." Shapely was determined for blood. Had he not learned any compassion during his career chasing debts? Or was he just made of different material to Jarvis? Whatever, he was going to walk away with a pound for every pound owing in principal, interest and fees, or take possessions to the full value of it. "If you can't pay me right now, it will be bankruptcy for you, little miss."

"That won't be necessary." Mr Jarvis heard his own voice talking. "I will pledge as much of my share as is necessary to cover the shortfalls of all those not prepared to wait."

"No, sir. You cannot do that." Mr Fellows spoke from his chair. He was ancient. Some said he had spent his early years in the reign of the Virgin Queen. Others that he had voyaged across the world in his long-ago youth with great names such as Raleigh. "You will be dismissed from your position and sued for the difference. I know who you represent well enough."

"There we have it, then. We are back at the beginning!" Shapely's voice rose as he became excited. "Full payment or bankruptcy, which one is it to be?"

"Neither, for I will back Mr Jarvis' position with my own money. I will forego whatever of my funds are required and shall work out a separate payment plan with Miss Aspley." Mr Fellows' voice wavered, age affecting the vocal chords, giving a tremor that remained after the words had finished their journey. But no-one, not even Shapely, argued the point any further.

Within a half-hour, Anne's pewter box was almost empty but the room's occupants had dwindled to three. Anne took an empty chair next to Mr Fellows. Jarvis came to sit with them. There were only two creditors now and Mr Fellows was the bigger of the two.

"How did you raise so much money, Miss Aspley?" Mr Jarvis asked, still stunned from the day's proceedings.

"Oh, that was relatively simple," she lied. "All I had to do was make my case. I persuaded Mr Goodman and Mr Ellis that their debt to my father was worth an additional £1,000!"

"Do you have any money left? For essential requirements, I mean."

"Just this," she said, pulling a handful of small silver from a pocket sewn into her dress. "Just enough to start again!"

"What will you do now?"

"Why, I think we will take a smaller house, something less draughty for mother. Then, I will go into business."

"Bravo," said Mr Jarvis and he meant it.

Chapter 6

They took up station in the copse above Grimes Cottage. "Just like the old days," Big Jim said. But, unlike the year before when they had sought just a meeting with Amelia, today's objectives were much more ambitious.

They had decided to act when meeting at Bagber Manor the previous Wednesday. They planned their moves meticulously, going over the details until they had covered everything a hundred times; challenging and checking understanding so that everyone knew the plan perfectly. It was a plan that could not go wrong.

Yet it did. And in almost every respect.

The weather was against them first and foremost. May had been as dry as old bones baking in the sun. June seemed set to follow suit. Yet the day they chose was an aberration, one day in the first week of June when the heavens opened. Within minutes, the hard-baked ground of yesterday was a slippery mud bath. It was hard to move without sliding along and landing in a heap. Rain poured constantly, briefly holding over on three occasions for great claps of thunder before taking up its relentless beat again. It made movement and sight hard, and the noise of the rain and wind made communication difficult too. Each of these aspects was vital to the overall plan.

Grimes' hangover was also against them. He had drunk even more heavily than usual the night before. The ache that split his head open was only partially assuaged by beating Amelia twice before ordering her to give her meagre crust of bread to the starving hens.

"If you looked after them in the first place, woman, we might have eggs to eat." There had been no eggs for two weeks now. No food in, no food out.

"I'm sorry, sir. I will try harder in future, sir." She had learned that appeasement was the only way. He had five times her strength in normal times but she was weakened now. At first, she had stood proudly, using her intellect to argue points and principles. But now she just did as she was told.

Grimes went out most days, scavenging for food or work but never bringing much home to her. At least he was out during the daytime.

She had secreted half a sack of potatoes several weeks ago but it was now all gone. The only other edible things on the property were the chickens from the dilapidated hen-hut in the back but she dared not cook one without his permission and Grimes never gave it when she hinted. As long as he had his beer and brandy, he was content.

His hangover on the chosen day was the worst Amelia had witnessed. After the second beating, he sat in the parlour, head in hands, groaning. He had overseen her donation to the chickens so she no longer had a crust to chew. She stood there in front of him and knew hate for the first time.

But Amelia was a good soul, one of the best. And, despite never experiencing hate before, even when teased mercilessly at school, she recognised the symptoms and applied a remedy immediately.

"Oh Lord, grant me obedience to my husband. Banish all vile thoughts from my mind and replace them with consideration of my duty and the honour it is to be a wife in this world." She was vaguely aware of the poetry in her prayer but only vaguely. Hunger ate into her like a ravenous beast. It chewed at her flesh, it worked its tendrils through her body, it made her sick.

No, the sickness was something else, she realised with growing horror. It was to be expected.

She was pregnant.

It was bound to happen. But it filled her with horror.

"What's wrong, woman?" She did not have a name any longer, was just a sub-classification of the species. "You look like death." He stood, wavering a bit as he did so. She knew the signs; a third beating would follow shortly. Grimes saw her backing away from him and it enraged him. "Come here, woman. I like my woman to look good not like death warmed up. I'll teach you once and for all how to look for your man." He reached out to grab her, caught her by the wrist and pulled her towards him. But this action on unsteady feet caused him to stumble. She landed on top of him, smelt again the vile, sweet smell of sweat, alcohol and his revolting tobacco; the combination of odours marked him out like the scent of a wild animal.

He beat at her from below. It was not like the normal beatings where the weight of his body added force to the blows. Grimes, in this position, was more like a feeble child than a strong, grown man. The blows did not hurt except they pummelled at her resolve.

He wriggled out from underneath her, kicked her in the side. That did hurt. Then he picked himself up and left the house, forgetting his hat and coat and going out into the heavy rain, leaving the front door swinging on its hinges and banging against an ill-fitting door frame.

Thomas was in the front parlour first, the others, particularly Bridget, holding back to give Thomas a few moments with his first love, ripped away from him by the consequences of a simple mistake.

He had barely knelt beside the prostrate, whimpering body when the door opened. He looked up to ask for more time alone with Amelia.

But it was Grimes come back again. The rain and wind had swept the hangover from him and given new sharpness to his senses.

"You didn't bloody well hand me my coat and…" He stopped when he saw Thomas kneeling on the floor next to Amelia. "What the hell…"

But Thomas was upon him, knocking Grimes to the floor with his body-weight, raising his head by pulling on his hair and thumping fist after fist into his face. When Grimes recovered enough to protect his face by lying on the ground with his arms covering his head, Thomas took to kicking him in the side, the legs, the neck, any part of Grimes that was within reach.

Thomas had long legs giving him a wide swing with plenty of force and range.

It took Tristan and Big Jim and Elizabeth to pull him away. "You bastard!" he cried repeatedly. 'You bastard! You bastard!"

There are lots of words written about stillness. Mostly they evoke a sense of calm, of peace or of solitude. It can be the lonely side of solitude or it can be born of contentment, when people, maybe approaching their final days, like to sit absolutely still and experience the world as if it was new again.

But there is another type of stillness that cannot possibly lean towards any form of happiness. Picture a totally still body, lying on the floor without even the tiny in-out movement of the shallowest breathing. This is the body you have just been striking out at with both fists and feet.

At first, your adrenalin is still pumping. Your heart is racing, your blood pulses around the body. You feel righteousness on your side. So what if Grimes is lying motionless by the paltry hearth, the only movement a seeping of blood from his skull across the floorboards and spilling slowly down the gaps between? He had it coming to him.

But then the enormity of what you have done spreads, just like the blood, but across your consciousness. The adrenalin slows right down so that the pump falters for lack of anything to push around. It is replaced, even the blood in your veins, with ice.

The ice of fear. For you have broken the law and killed a man in anger.

You can justify it all you like but the jury is the one who has to believe you and the facts are clear. The judge will point out that the character of the slain is not relevant, will probably rule inadmissible the defence attorney's claim that he was a bad one.

And the penalty for taking a life is to have your life taken. No matter that you are a newly-wed, a successful businessman employing forty or even fifty men. No matter that you loved the woman this dead-still body abused. No matter that you adored her and happily struck at the abuser with knuckles and shins now torn and bruised.

You broke the law and the law knows no mercy. The law is outside mercy, that much is clear. The law stands alone, not as

Solomon with capacity to vary, but long written down by clerk after clerk, whiling away their lives in dry, dusty pursuits. And the danger of words is that, once written down, they are there for ever and cannot be changed.

"You've been stock still, staring at Grimes, for over two minutes now," Tristan said. They had arrived, crowding into the small parlour, Elizabeth immediately attending to Amelia, her step-daughter and friend.

"What's the matter, Thomas?" Bridget asked, coming over to his side, taking his hand, looking earnestly at him.

"I killed Grimes."

"Nonsense, Thomas," Grace replied, lifting Grimes' head by pulling back on his hair with her lace-gloved hand. Grimes sagged a moment then pulled himself out of his stupor, spluttering, blood and spit stretching from his open mouth to reach the floor.

The relief flooded like the rivers of rainwater outside, coursing and chuckling as they made their way to lower ground, always on the move.

"He's not dead?"

"He is most certainly not dead." To mark this statement from Grace, Grimes made the effort to raise his eyes to hers then spat at her. It landed on the embroidered overskirt of her beautiful orange silk dress. Tristan pulled the cloth from the table and wiped Grace's skirt then threw the cloth at Grimes.

"Clean yourself up, man."

Was Grimes still defiant in the face of overwhelming strength? He did not say anything in reply, no actions either apart from remaining on all fours and drooling on the floorboards.

Thomas stood, a part of him not wanting to be on the same plane as Grimes. He walked over to Grimes, ready to kick again if required. Grimes stared at him blankly. Grace bent down and twisted his head into a more normal position. It swung back to somewhere near where it had been before, staring at the space where Grace had once been.

It was almost three hours before they judged it safe to leave Grimes.

"I'll stay," Amelia said shakily. "I am his wife, after all. I'm not sure it is safe to leave him on his own."

But in the end, it was others who stayed. Big Jim and Plain Jane volunteered after Elizabeth convinced Amelia she should leave in order to recover elsewhere.

"You need a great deal of care, Mealy. After a hot bath, some good food and a few nights of untroubled sleep, you'll feel like a different person." What Elizabeth did not say was that most of the improvement would come from the lack of terror at what her husband might do.

And what Elizabeth could not know was exactly how weak and ill Amelia was. She put on a brave face but stumbled and dragged her feet with weariness until Thomas stepped forward and held her on one side, Bridget rushing to do the same on the other. Three legs of the same stool.

There was no more talk of kidnap. Thomas, who had been the main instigator and planner, was just relieved to see Grimes alive. The others felt it wrong to mention the permanence of their intentions when Amelia, despite the horrors of life with Grimes, clearly was driven by duty.

A duty that persisted despite her evident weakness.

There could never be love between this husband and this wife. But sometimes, and in some people, duty is a far stronger emotion than love. It sends soldiers out across the battlefield when they are wracked by fear. It sends them marching in bright red lines to their death and away from the ones they love.

Duty makes them march away from love.

But duty, Amelia reflected much later from the comfort of Bagber Manor, also destroyed when its intention was to care. She thought of her father. She and Elizabeth had tended him through his stroke, not from love, for love was difficult with someone so hard and calculating, but from a sense of duty. It was understandable that they had not conducted their care with love. But had the lack of love in their ministrations made her father boil over with hatred and commit the terrible crimes he did?

Or was that evil always inside him? Was she feeling the guilt of the victim and there is, in actual fact, no obligation to love?

She held herself short a moment, actually stopped breathing. How silly she was being. How could she speak, albeit it in thoughts and not words, of an obligation to love? Love was natural; it happens not at our choosing. Perhaps God in Heaven makes the individual pairings of lovers across the world for we humans do not have a say in who we love.

We love where we are led to love. And where love is not, we follow duty, compassion and obligation and try, if we have the mindset, to avoid hatred and other dark emotions of the soul.

"I know," she said to herself, "I will talk to Bridge about it; she will understand what I mean."

And when she eventually did, much later on, it gave rise to new consideration and became the basis of a whole chapter in Bridget's book.

But that was very much later for all Bridget saw now was the way her husband looked at Amelia. The uncertainty it engendered in her broke the surface of her angular body and let her soul out. And that soul saw the bleakness of the world and knew despair again.

Chapter 7

"£10,000?" Alice said in a state of shock. There had been a time, quite recently, when such a figure would not have impressed her greatly. But perspective marches in step with circumstances; reduce one and you reduce the other. "What will you do with it?" For a moment, she thought Penelope would leave Great Little. She had heard the other side of the tale already, from one of the servants, the £100,000 waiting on her marriage and the subsequent production of an heir. Would she leave Alice and Sally and find a husband?

"I'm not going to buy back my jewellery," she said, as if what she was going to do could be defined by what she would not do.

"Why not?" Alice's hopes were a little raised. If she did not desire her jewellery, Penelope was surely not serious about finding a husband. Then she thought how despicable she was being; if her friend had a chance at complete financial security, why should she not take it up?

"And I will not leave here, Alice, not unless you throw me out! I would prefer to forego the larger sum, make do with the smaller, than take up with another man." Again, she was defining her future by what she would not do.

"Are you sure about that, Penelope? You are in a position to guarantee lifelong security."

"I am sure, Alice. Here's what I am going to do with my ten thousand."

Her plan was revolutionary, such that Alice Roakes had to sit down, call the nursery maid to look after Sir Beatrice, ring the bell again for two, no three glasses corrected Penelope, and a decanter of brandy.

"Sally will no doubt be here in a minute," Penelope explained when the maid had left the room.

Sally did enter a few minutes later, curtsied to them both and accepted the offer to sit down from Alice. It was a delicate line between formality and familiarity. Whereas Penelope had no such concerns. She jumped up on Sally's entrance, poured a large brandy and took it to her.

"I've been telling Alice about our plans," she said after Sally had taken her first sip. "Do you like the brandy? I can send for something else if you prefer."

"It's fine, Pen. It's strong but I'll just sip it from time to time."

The plan was as much Sally's work as Penelope's. Or rather, the ideas were Penelope's and the detail had been worked out by Sally.

"We want to buy a stake in Great Little, Lady Roakes," Sally said when Alice asked her to explain it all again. "But not to put cash in your purse, rather to invest in the estate, really get it up to strength again. It would be a real partnership. I know that Pen, I mean the Dowager-Duchess, has lent you several thousand to pay for builders and to pay estate wages last year when everything looked so dire. That would become part of the investment and we would add a further six thousand."

"For a half share?" Alice asked, thinking it an excellent deal.

"No," said Penelope. "Please explain further, Sal, you're better at the detail than me."

"Great Little is your home, Lady Roakes, and it should stay that way. We will start a joint-stock corporation in which we will be equal shareholders. We hear they are all the rage in London amongst the merchants, financiers and courtiers, even the King and Queen invest in them. This is how it will work in our instance." Sally stopped to draw breath, noted Penelope looking adoringly at her and launched into the next stage. "The corporation will pay rent to you as the owner of Great Little. The corporation will farm the land and sell the produce and collect the rents. The profits arising will be shared equally between us as joint stockholders."

"Our only condition," Penelope added, "is that you let us live here for as long as we want. This is your home and it always will be. The corporation is shared between the three of us but the house and the land belong to you totally."

"So you mean one third of the business each?" Alice asked, not really knowing what else to say. But there was a further pleasant surprise to come.

"Not at all," Penelope cried. "Sal and I are one person in this arrangement. The corporation's shares will be held half by you and half by me. Is this a satisfactory arrangement, Alice? Shall we instruct the lawyers tomorrow? Why are you crying, Alice? I thought you would be happy."

It was just like Penelope to mistake tears of joy for tears of sadness. She lived most of her life on the surface and only once in a while dug down into the depths.

But when she did, it was deep indeed.

The Great Little Agricultural Produce and Trading Corporation was born a week later. Tomkins shook his head when he heard, not from disapproval but from incomprehension.

"Perhaps Tomkins is too old to take on new ideas," Alice said.

"Meaning we have to find someone else?"

"Sally is the obvious choice, Penelope. She has excelled at helping to manage the estate. Tomkins tells me she is a natural."

"No."

"But, Penelope dear, she is perfect for the position."

"She is my maid and that is the way it will stay. I don't mind her helping out a little bit here and there but you must remember that she is mine, Alice."

"What on earth do you mean?" Alice's eyebrows raised, suddenly aware of some form of hidden meaning, some allusion to something significant. But it passed as quickly as it came, leaving Alice with just the faintest idea she could not quite grasp.

"I mean she is in my employ. I do not... I will not give her up." Penelope blushed and turned away from her friend. Alice thought about persisting but realised that Penelope would hear no more of it. Instead, they reached a compromise, as good friends do. Tomkins would stay on as steward but Sally would help him in the office each morning when Penelope rode across the estate. Sally would officially be the assistant to Tomkins.

"There is something else we need to discuss, Alice," Penelope said as the first corporation decision was made, albeit Alice wondering how Sally would take it. "We need to consider the building work."

"As soon as the dividends start to come in," Alice replied.

"No, before that." This next stage was pure Penelope, both the original idea and the detail. But she had anxiously sought Sally's approval before airing it with Alice. "There is an advance to be made on the dividends to the tune of £1,000, sufficient I believe to get the building works going again.

It was the precise sum that Alice had set herself as a target to recommence the works. She had put aside £260 so far, now she had in excess of twelve hundred. She clapped her hands like a little girl, then placed them firmly under her skirts.

"That's very kind, Penelope. It brings me great joy." She had learned that when Penelope, her dear friend, brought joy into any situation, it was advisable to acknowledge it in plain, simple and respectful language.

Thomas came two days later, bringing John Milligan with him. Mr Milligan had fully retired now but loved to take an occasional day to visit some of the larger projects his old firm was working on.

And Great Little had been the largest of all, could be so again.

Thomas also brought Bridget.

"I hope you do not mind the liberty of my tagging along with the men," she said to Alice and Penelope after the introductions. "I have been desirous of seeing Great Little since I first came to Dorset last year."

"Mrs Davenport, you are most welcome." That was Alice, always open to appreciation of her home, the home she had found and taken to immediately. Nothing, however, from Penelope except the usual haughty expression with a long proud nose to send it down.

The two builders, young and old, were excited and spoke expansively about the project.

However, they were due to be disappointed, at least initially. It was Sally behind it, although they were not to know this for everything came through Penelope with Sally, the mute maid, standing in the corner, awaiting requests for refreshments.

"We have decided to leave the house as is for the time being."

"Then why call us out, Your Grace?"

"Because we have other work. We would like every estate cottage brought up to standard. We will have several new barns built, some to replace dilapidated ones which should be pulled down, but we also want completely new ones on Home Farm and on Stretcher's Wood Farm. We also desire brand new stables as our tinkering with horse breeding has convinced us that we can do well in this endeavour and we will shortly be buying new breeding stock of the highest quality. We aim to look after them, Mr Davenport!"

"Nothing to the house, then?" Mr Milligan asked, wondering if he would ever see its completion. Recently, he had become stiffer and found he tired more easily. Penelope seemed not to hear him as she turned to face her maid.

"Sally, please go and tell the kitchen that Mr Milligan and Mr and Mrs Davenport will be joining us for lunch."

"Of course, Your Grace." All the correct protocol with a curtsy and instant obedience to her mistress, but Bridget sensed Sally's annoyance across the span of the library.

"And then we have no more need of you here as we are going to take a ride across the estate to see the work to be done. Have the groom saddle Hector and Paris. Bring Grey Lady for Mrs Davenport and two suitable horses for the gentlemen. You may then attend to the alterations on that new gown, as we spoke earlier."

No response this time, just a stony silence as Sally curtsied again and left the room, turning away so that only Bridget, sitting slightly to one side, could see the flash of anger on her face.

"We would like some modest work to the house," Penelope said as soon as the door had closed behind Sally. "Principally to the staircase." She went on to explain her plans for the elaborate new decorations, all centred on the depiction of the Little family at feast that wound up the main staircase as if telling a story to all who lived there of the abundance long ago that was Great Little. "But, gentlemen, as you plan for this, please do not tell anyone of it. I want it to be our secret, just Lady Roakes and myself. Is that clear?"

It was clear to Bridget, who nodded her head along with the others, that the person she did not want to know was Sally, the maid. She had heard rumours about a relationship but why then hide things from one half to the other? And why treat her with such disdain, dismissing her so abruptly?

"I don't know if I like the Dowager-Duchess," she whispered to her husband as they were mounting up in the courtyard that made the grand entrance to Great Little. It was half derelict, not yet recovered from the fire of '88 and presumably was now low down on the list of priorities. Yet it had a grandeur in its dereliction that struck visitors, warning of great things to come. It was an impressive house, even in its half-built state.

"She takes some getting used to, I'll grant you that. But she behaved magnificently when Eliza discovered who Lady Roakes really was. She went out of her way in a really generous fashion to bridge the gap, really beating against the tide. It did not work but she tried when many would have turned away. I have a lot of time for the Dowager-Duchess because of that."

"Really? I much prefer Lady Roakes. But maybe the impression she gave was superficial, maybe there was more than immediately meets the eye."

"She was the one responsible for the imprisonment of Eliza but she seems a different person altogether now." Thomas thought of the woman he had met on the doorstep in Bristol. Lies had come so easily to that woman. There had been no gentleness as now, just hardness. Could people change so much?

"It's a strange world for sure," Bridget replied, thinking of her book and how she could make a chapter from her observations of Great Little and all that went on there.

The ride around the estate was focused; Penelope clearly knew it intimately. She took them to each of the sites where Sally had decided to build, explaining crisply in her authoritarian style what was required. She never once dismounted and her side-saddle seemed like a distortion of a throne; a tall lady on a tall horse, both animal and human erect and proud.

"All this can be done easily enough," Thomas concluded as they toured the last site and turned their horses for the house.

"When can you start, Mr Davenport?"

"I think a week on Monday. I have a lot of the materials at the yard and can easily get the rest. With your permission, Mr Milligan and I will go back over the various sites after lunch and will make a plan."

"And Mrs Davenport? Will she take an interest in the building works?"

"I fear only a casual interest, Your Grace. Might she stay with you this afternoon? I am sure she would like to see your library. She has a much finer education than I can lay claim to. I believe the library contents were largely untouched by the fire."

"It will be my pleasure. Don't look so glum, Mrs Davenport, I promise to behave myself." With that, she spurred Hector on to a canter and never looked back until she reached the house some three minutes ahead of the others.

Bridget was quite intimated by the thought of an afternoon with the Dowager-Duchess. But she had nothing to fear.

"This is Sally Black," Penelope said, shyness and pride competing on her face, all disdain chased out momentarily. "She will better show you the books. I was never much of a one for looking into books." She proffered her maid forwards, as if lending Bridget a precious piece of jewellery. "I prefer riding to reading."

"I take pleasure in both. I greatly enjoyed my ride this morning, Your Grace. The estate is beautiful. Now I am looking forward to a pleasant time in your library."

"Well, Sally will be happy to show you what is here," she said. "Won't you, Sally?"

"Yes, Your Grace. It will give me great pleasure." She bobbed, the perfect maid who knew her place.

A little later, when taking a break from Herodotus, the father of history, Sally and Bridget fell into casual conversation.

"Tell me, Sally, are you…?"

"No, I am not a free woman. I am the property of my mistress. But…"

"But what, Sally?" Bridget had never met a slave before. Her cousin, Tristan, had told her of them but actually meeting one was fascinating.

"But nobody knows this. Even the Dowager-Duchess, does not know that I know. She thinks it her secret. I would not have it any other way."

"The knowledge is safe with me." It meant including only generalities and broad observations in her book but so be it. Trust was a delicate thing and not to be treated carelessly. "You are so bright, Sally, you could do lots of different things, even as a woman."

"I think the Dowager-Duchess would miss me sorely if I left, as her maid of course, and I would never leave Pen." The damage was done, as so often happens when people speak frankly. No normal maid would refer to her mistress by the shortened version of her first name.

Not unless there was a lot more to the relationship.

"Tell me more about the Dowager-Duchess."

"Well, I was with her from an early age. I used to hate and fear her." The natural emphasis in this last sentence was on 'used' not 'hate', utilising the past tense but also implying that a whole different set of emotions were in play now. "I sensed something about her that scared me but I realise now that she was trying to be friendly."

Bridget knew what their relationship was by now. She had worked it out. Sally knew that Bridget knew. Yet neither would bring it out in the open.

"When did you change your opinion of her?" Bridget felt like adding that she was still in the fear stage, or perhaps it was merely uncertainty around her.

"I suppose it was when I realised that she was even more tangled up than I was. She was trying to be kind in her own way. She is incredibly kind to me." Sally fell silent and Bridget felt there was enough disclosure for the present. They returned to Herodotus, yet the words from the pages passed through Bridget's mind without registering. Once or twice she told herself off for missing a great opportunity.

"This is a splendid library," she said, trying to shake off her contemplative state.

"Thank you, Mrs Davenport. I like to come here and read from time to time. You know, it was Pen that taught me to read?"

"Really"

"She can't abide books herself, yet went to great lengths, straining her patience incredibly to teach me. It was then that I first, I mean when she was teaching me, I felt…" Sally trailed off, not finding the sanitised words, not knowing how else to say that she and Penelope were lovers.

"I understand, Sally. And I think we will be friends, you and I, so please call me Bridge as all my friends do."

"Thank you, Miss Bridge. Now, what do you know of Virgil?"

Chapter 8

Henry had never found it difficult to rise early. But to rise to the interminable routine of the drill square, at the mercy of a corporal who obviously enjoyed inflicting misery on his charges, was not what he had imagined when he had signed on three weeks earlier.

"Why do you want to volunteer?" the recruiting sergeant had asked in Salisbury.

"Because I want to fight for my country."

"No doubt you do but that doesn't wash as a reason with me." The sergeant had a modicum more sensitivity than Henry had expected and it threw him. In the end, he found himself admitting what he had not known.

"I am a Catholic and I want to prove my allegiance to the Crown."

"You are clearly an educated man but will never be an officer unless you can take the oath." The reference was to the oath of allegiance which involved a declaration against the concept of transubstantiation, the principle doctrinal difference between the Catholic and Protestant faiths.

The question of whether God the Son was present in the bread and wine of Holy Communion or whether they remained bread and wine and symbolised His body and blood.

It seemed like a simple difference of opinion; the two views could have sat together down the decades, like whether it was best to drink beer or cider for breakfast.

Only they did not and many thousands, many millions even, suffered horrible, painful deaths because two different ideas would not sit at the same table, eat from the same plate and drink from the same glass.

At a national level, it decided which countries were your friends and which your enemies. It split countries like Ireland and France, putting hatred and division amongst their best producing crops. It fermented that teeming tribal hatred that made up Europe, adding a further divisive split; rather than heal wounds, it opened them up repeatedly, fouling them with vile poison. And then it spread to the New World, replicating the misery of the old.

It drove Henry Sherborne to a mean pub in the backstreets of Salisbury, borrowed for the day to be a recruiting station for the English army. It promised to send him to another civil war that should never have been fought.

"You know you will be nothing but cannon fodder," the sergeant said before Henry signed. "There is no glory in lying deserted in a ditch to die, your blood pooling with the filthy water and the pain wracking your body, making you pray in screams for the release of death."

"I thought you would want people," Henry replied.

"I do, we are desperate. I'll take you happily enough but my conscience demands that you know what you are entering into."

"I know well enough." But how could he? How can anyone know the actual experience of war before they have entered into it? They can imagine some facets, such as the filth, the wet, the hunger, the cold, the heat, the boredom. But can you imagine all these together and then add the gut-wrenching elements of fear, hatred and pain?

Henry faced another week of the corporal ruling the drill square with his petty rules and punishments. Then they would be shipped to Ireland. The news had come through a few days previously. The king had gone ahead and this new regiment was to follow in support of the main army.

"You're a sorry bunch of no-hopers yet we are sending you to Ireland to stand by the King." The officer's contradictory statement was not lost on Henry. If they were no-hopers, why send them at all? They would surely fail anyway. This led Henry to deduce two things. They were not as hopeless as those in charge repeatedly said. And a battle was coming very soon. Why else beef up your ranks by cutting training to the bone and sending all available soldiery to Ireland?

"Sherborne to the Adjutant's office."

"Got yourself in trouble then, my lad?" The speaker was one of the few regular privates incorporated to provide some backbone into the new regiment. By and large they were condescending and this one was no exception. Except that the 'my lad' tag was understandable for he was in his mid-forties against Henry's twenty-four years. "Adjutant means big trouble." That was added because Henry did not show sufficient fear at the prospect. "I remember when…"

"Sherborne, are you going to come or shall I tell the Adjutant that you're too busy chatting to your new friends?"

"No, Corporal, I'm coming."

"Ah, Sherborne, is it? I hear you've done well in training this last month."

"Thank you, sir."

"You also come with a recommendation from Sergeant Bullen."

"Sir?"

"The recruiting sergeant who got your scrawl on a scrap of paper and sent you to us."

"Ah, yes Sergeant Bullen, sir."

"I'm making you corporal. It will mean considerable extra duties and also an increase in pay. But I don't somehow imagine you are here for the pay."

"Thank you, sir." Henry was learning the correct way to address an officer. There were two rules; words to be kept to the minimum and put 'sir' in every sentence.

"You can take this chit for your corporal stripes. You'll be in 2nd platoon. There's no point in moving to the NCO block for tonight as we are going early in the morning. That's all.

"Sir!" Henry saluted and turned to leave.

"Oh, one more thing, Corporal, do you know who the sergeant for 2nd platoon is?"

"Is it Sergeant Bullen, sir?"

"Correct, how did you know?"

"I thought, sir, that you would not ask me otherwise, sir." He saluted again and left the room. The adjutant was left thinking what a bright spark Private, no Corporal Sherborne was. Solid material for the future.

It took ten days to get to Ireland, half the time in boats, half waiting on land. Of the time in the boats, they were only actually sailing a day and a half.

And waiting the rest.

"Welcome to army life," said Sergeant Bullen. "It's a case of hurry up and wait!"

"I see that, Sergeant." Henry accepted the cup of brandy Bullen poured from his flask.

"Still, it gives me time to teach you a thing or two. Corporal Sherborne, this is where your training really starts."

Corporal Sherborne led his troop of ten men down the gangplank to dry land.

"Hurrah for solid land beneath our feet!" cried one of the more vocal new recruits.

"Quiet, Parker." It was the order he had issued most often since becoming a corporal. It seemed silence was a military strategy all of its own. Words flowed down the chain but rarely went back up.

He liked Parker, thought he was a good man, just prone to letting his tongue wag. He liked all of his ten men, although was only just getting to know the quieter ones. He had done his training in 3rd platoon, not 2nd. The men of his new section had been just shapes ten days ago but he had made the effort to get to know each one, a practice Sergeant Bullen had endorsed enthusiastically.

"Someday your life may depend on the man in the rank beside you. Get to know them like your own family, man."

"Where're we headed next?" Parker asked, unable to keep his mouth shut for long.

"To have a bloody picnic with the enemy, now shut up soldier." Henry span round and saw the old drill corporal of 3rd platoon leering at him in a conspiratorial way. "So bloody green these new recruits, they don't even know the meaning of the word discipline. Ain't that the case, Sherborne?"

"Not at all, Corporal Bing, I find you get much more out of treating people well and fairly."

"Tosh, what is the army coming to these days? Promoting new recruits five minutes into their service, what do you expect?" Henry chose to ignore this comment and turned his back on Bing, suddenly losing himself in the details of his ten-man section, preparing them for the route march ahead.

"All officers and sergeants to HQ."

"Get the men something to eat while I'm away," Bullen told Henry and the other two corporals of 2nd platoon.

"Where do we get food?" one of the other corporals asked.

"I sent Parker and Fugini out to scout for food and water," Henry replied, knowing these were the best two to send. "There's a cookhouse tent over that dune, out of sight from here. They've got beef stew and bread, even some old apples, I hear."

"Good work, Sherborne. Get the men over there before everyone knows about it and make sure to stock up on water, I expect we have a long march ahead of us."

"We've only just got here." This was the same corporal that had asked about the food. Henry looked at him again, really seeing him for the first time. He was tiny and wiry, middle-aged, with eyes that kept darting around – fear or something else? His uniform, despite twenty plus years in the army, seemed new and ill-fitting, as if one size was made to fit all.

"Haggerty, my friend, now why did you think we came to these lovely shores? For the rest and change of air? Think man, there is a hoard of Catholic bastards waiting for us out there somewhere – my apologies, Sherborne, no insult intended."

"None taken, Sergeant. Will you give me your mess tin?"

"Why?"

"To get you some stew, Sergeant."

The intention had been to move out an hour later; those were the orders given. In fact, it took a day and a half before all the stores were found and the preparations complete. Several sets of scouts were sent out and Henry volunteered for one expedition which rode out in the late morning of the first day and did not return until early morning of the next.

They had fanned out to cover as much ground as possible. The scouting party was led by a young lieutenant called Blades-Robson who seemed intelligent but hard.

"Corporal, take five men and circle those hills. If you see nothing in your circuit, get up into them and use the standard signals back to me to say what you find there. Got it?"

"Yes sir." Henry turned the army horse away after just remembering to salute. He called for Parker, Fugini and three others.

"We're going to circle those hills and then go into them if it all seems quiet. We'll go north first and circle around anti-clockwise."

"Why's that?" Parker asked. "Why not clockwise?" It was said with cheeky abandon and Henry was just about to issue a standard army rebuke when he stopped and thought. An idea came to him.

"You've given me an idea, Parker. We'll split up. You take two men clockwise and I'll take two anti-clockwise. That way we will complete the circle in half the time and meet on the far side. Now, any questions? Good, let's get going."

"What are they doing, sir?" a young ensign asked. "They seem to be splitting up."

"Good," replied Blades-Robson. "I wondered whether he would think of that. Don't you see, man, it saves valuable time before dark sets in. It seems Corporal Sherborne has quite a head on his shoulders. No doubt we will have need of that head before the week is out."

Chapter 9

Poor Lieutenant Aspley was no more. Simon heard Sergeant Holmes comment that it was no great loss, "for the man, if you can call him a man, was useless." He made no rebuke to the sergeant, for the truth was the truth. Besides, Simon Taylor was in contemplative mood.

He had earned his commission, leapfrogging corporals, sergeants and lieutenants, through a daring initiative. But the reality was, it had been no more than a plan to get protection from the weather and some food in their bellies. It had been nine parts necessity and just one of initiative and that had come right at the end, almost by accident.

The problem now was that it had gained him a reputation as the hero of Galley Gorge and reputations needed maintaining. He had achieved the one significant strategic breakthrough of the war so far. In contrast, his current role was undemanding, amounting to occasional scouting trips through the woods of New England, with barely ever anything to report.

"The war is just tit-for-tat raids across the frontier," Major Davidson said when Simon had reported seeing signs of a raiding party north and west of them, some thirty miles away. A party had been sent out to intercept them while Simon's men got some rest and food and cared for their horses. The mounting of scouts had been his initiative; Simon had argued that moving fast was essential, particularly when there was information to communicate back to headquarters. Major Davidson invested his own money in dozens more horses and they had been used extensively.

"We need to act more effectively," Simon heard himself say, surprised by his words. What gave him the authority to speak on military strategy? What did he even mean by these words?

"I agree, Taylor. Phips had a significant victory in Acadia last month, just before you joined us. Did you hear about it?" The major referred to William Phips. He was a wealthy, highly intelligent but virtually illiterate adventurer from Massachusetts, more famous for finding lost treasure ships than anything to do with government or the military. He had made King William a pot of cash with a particularly good treasure find and been appointed Major-General as a result.

"Yes sir, at least some of it. He took several ships to Port Royal and the French governor surrendered after a couple of days."

"Yes, but did you hear what happened next?"

"No, sir."

"There was some disagreement and Phips decided that the French had broken the terms of the surrender. He let his troops plunder the town."

"Not a clever move, sir. These people will be our neighbours when this war ends." Simon thought he had got the tenor of Davidson's thinking just right, matching his own response accordingly.

"I agree but he got a knighthood out of it. Yet I dare say it will move the war effort not a jot further forward. Sir William, as he now is, has left Port Royal and gone back to Boston. The whole campaign amounts to no more than another petty raid upon the enemy, an expensive folly." Simon wondered, on seeing the anger on Davidson's weathered face, whether there was not some political rivalry or personal jealousy behind his anger at Phips. What did he know of Davidson? He farmed, the major had spoken of his land. He was educated, solid, a minor aristocratic figure gone to the New World to make something of his life. On a sudden whim, chasing the fragment of an idea, Simon launched his boat into uncertain waters.

"What we need is influence in the right quarters, sir. I'm a self-made man. I have few contacts, I lack your pedigree, sir." An ounce of flattery would grease the way; Simon felt like a tiny cog trying to make one big move. It was all to do with… what was the term? Gearing, that was it. A small wheel moving very fast could force a large wheel to move at moderate speed.

"Too true, Taylor, too true." He was clearly racking his brains for the right contacts. Simon, acting purely on instinct, decided to help him on his way.

"Your brother, sir," he ventured, thinking Davidson was definitely a younger brother.

"My brother is a fool."

"But I hazard a rich fool and one with some influence." Simon had no idea who Davidson's brother was but his first guess had been correct, the major at least had an older brother.

"The Duke is a bore of a man, quite dedicated to his comforts," said with some finality; it would seem that the venture was over almost before it had begun. It would not make it into the history books; there was simply no substance to hang the tale on. "But, Taylor, I believe you are right. It might be worth an approach. Besides, he only recently inherited and may not have spent all his money yet. With the right person to approach him, we may be able to tap him for influence in Whitehall and even for some of that cash. Of course, I've not seen him for years but it's worth a try."

It had not been planned by Simon, more one of those accidents that make all the difference. But an hour and several whiskies later, Simon was back in his own tent packing his scant goods. He was, after all, the obvious choice to go and see the Duke of Wiltshire, Major Davidson's older brother by some fifteen years.

"Sir?" The voice came from outside the tent.

"Who is it?"

"The Quartermaster, sir." The senior NCO saluted sharply when invited into the tent Simon had shared until recently with the unfortunate and sickly Lieutenant Aspley.

"Sir, the major said you were going to England."

"That is correct, quartermaster. May I be of some assistance to you there?" A short while ago, when Simon was a private soldier, he would not have dared approach the quartermaster.

"There is one thing, sir. Would you be so kind as to take the Lieutenant's personal belongings with you and deliver them to his parents in Dorchester? The Major said to ask you, sir. He prefers someone he can trust to take care of them, rather than relying on the army."

"I'd be happy to do so. Have them packed up quickly for I am leaving within the hour."

"Thank you, sir." Another crisp salute and the tent flap fell back into place, leaving Simon to wonder at such coincidences that sent him back to Dorset, the very place he had come from.

It was that same coincidence, he reflected, that might raise his hopes to ridiculous heights and then strike back with a deathly blow, perhaps stumbling under a heavy cart wheel or lying in the gutters of Boston, knifed by a common thief within eyesight of the ship to take him back to England. Life was all important, to be nursed and treasured. Life and liberty. He would remember that.

But there was something else tugging at Simon as he arranged a spacious cabin, paid for by Major Davidson, on a fast and sleek ship bound for Bristol. He tried every way to dispel the feeling; it was a nuisance to be wrapped in it when he should be enjoying his new freedom, guaranteed by the fact that no-one would arrest a commissioned officer sent on a mission by his commanding officer.

He hoped the strong winds that bowled them across the Atlantic would drive this strange feeling out. He hoped the colder temperatures as they sailed through the icebergs would freeze out the obligation and leave it perched on the ice to wither and die. He wanted no part of it. He hoped the storm that hit them off the coast of Ireland would blow it from him.

"The weather is not on my side," he said as he walked the deck, trying to wear the sense of duty out through the soles of his boots and into the planks that made the deck. At least it would be in the ship then and he could skip ashore and leave it behind. The ship would take it back to America and he would be free of it. No need to come back himself; he would send the duty back in his place.

But that was the crux of it; Major Davidson was relying on him coming back.

"Don't take long, Taylor. We need action quickly. Besides, I will miss our chats." These had become frequent. Simon had noticed a tendency with the major to rely on Simon for advice on almost everything.

Major Davidson looked the part. He was tall, well-built, handsome in his uniform. He seemed decisive but Simon had come to realise that he barked his commands with false confidence, trying hard to disguise the fact that, as the senior commander in the area, he did not know what to do.

Simon had tried out his newly-determined theory once or twice.

"Sir, I think the men need a rest. Can I suggest a revised rota to allow longer periods on duty followed by forty-eight hours of local leave?" It had been dismissed at the time but three days later a similar scheme had been announced by the adjutant.

Simon's instincts were not to go back, not to risk his life in a pointless war where death lay around every bush and across every stream and meadow. But there was something gnawing at his insides, settling into his soul.

"I will see what sign you send, God," he concluded as the ship tacked up the Bristol Channel, swinging from bank to bank. Then he realised, it was the first time in decades he had talked to God. He did not refer to 'Our Lord', that would be too presupposing of a normal relationship. The word 'God' seemed to him like a strange form of nickname from one bod to another, equal status in all likelihood.

That fitted exactly the terms under which he prayed; equal to equal, more an interesting discussion than any type of supplication.

Once landed in Bristol, Simon went straight to Davidson's agent and cashed a promissory note for £50. It was his expense account for the next two weeks. After those two weeks, he would board the ship again for the return journey.

"By all means take Aspley's belongings to his parents, see your own family if they will see you, but make it your priority to see my brother early on. I think he might need a lot of persuasion to make him move."

He had thought he could just disappear into England. But what would he do when the money ran out? Starve, beg, steal? His life had always been clear before; he did what he wanted to do. Now this strange thing called duty poked its ugly nose into the scenes containing Simon and upset the delicate balance he had innately known all his life.

That was why he had made a bargain with God. If God sent a sign, he would do his duty. Otherwise, he would find a way to hide.

Somehow.

No sign came that day or the next, or even the one after that. He hired a fast and swanky carriage which the owner claimed to have the latest in modern suspension and was certainly more comfortable. He had hesitated before deciding in favour of a carriage. It was not a consideration of expense, rather that he thought maybe a military man should be mounted on a strong and elegant horse rather than closeted within luxury. But, despite promoting hoof over foot in the wilds of New England, he actually disliked riding ever since he was forced to ride home on a donkey five years earlier during the height of the Monmouth Rebellion. It was Sergeant Roakes, later resurrected as Sir Beatrice Roakes and now the deceased husband of Lady Roakes of Great Little, who had chosen to humiliate him in this way. He had not forgotten it yet somehow it seemed less important now, as if part of the last play his troupe of actors had performed, now moved on to a different story altogether.

Out of habit, he negotiated hard for the carriage hire.

"I'll take it but this new-fangled suspension is far from proven. I am happy to try it out for you but will need a discount if I am to do it."

"Of course, sir, would you say a reduction of a penny in each shilling of charge?"

"I was thinking of sixpence."

"But sir, that would not cover my costs!"

"Nor will having it sit idle while potential passengers choose more moderately priced contraptions. Besides," he lied,

"I am a man of considerable connections and, provided the ride is comfortable, will be happy to tell all and sundry of my experience. I go now, for instance, to see the Duke of Wiltshire on important business."

They settled much closer to sixpence than a penny and Simon reflected that six months in jail and the military had not diminished his capacity for business.

But no sign came to him as the carriage rushed over the rough roads towards Wiltshire. His driver was in a quandary; charged by the owner with demonstrating how smooth the ride was but by Simon with getting to Wiltshire House as soon as possible. The two aims were incompatible and Simon was ever present to enforce his will.

"Go to the stables and find a groom for the horses, then to the kitchen and get yourselves something to eat," he told the driver and footman when they pulled up outside the broad expanse of the Duke of Wiltshire's family seat. He saw, with approval, that the duke had come to the front door himself, curious to see who this glamorous traveller might be. He had stopped at an inn two miles away to straighten his appearance and brush the dust from his uniform. He had no doubt that he made a striking impression.

"Your Grace, I bring the warmest greetings from your distinguished brother, Major Jack Davidson, who thrives in the colonies and directed me to come to you."

"That wastrel? What does he want?" That was not a good start. Simon recognised the mean, narrow eyes and suspicious countenance; he had seen it often enough in business before.

"Grave matters of state, Your Grace, grave matters which I am charged to bring to you in total privacy."

"You'd better come in then," he grunted, moving his fat body to one side as if he had found employment as the doorkeeper to a private kingdom. "You'd better come in but don't expect any hospitality from me. I'm a poor man with not two pennies to rub together."

Miserable words but Simon was one step ahead of his host.

"No need, Your Grace. For I have something for you as a gift from your brother and myself." Strictly, the brother had paid for it; Simon's purse was empty except that which had been provided by Major Davidson.

"What would that be then?" He perked up at the thought of something coming his way. Had he not been complaining to the pastor this very morning, when he came looking for a contribution for the church roof, that everyone expected him to pay out all the time?

"It's all one way, that's the trouble with this world," he had grumbled to the pastor.

"Why, I have a hamper of choice food and drink." Simon turned to the footman he had arrived with. "My man, bring in the hamper and set it wherever His Grace desires it to be."

The top part of the hamper was given over to a vast selection of sweetmeats. The duke took one look into it and decided this Taylor was a splendid fellow. Below the sweetmeats were several bottles of cognac, six bottles of fine Bordeaux and delicacies from various places, all purchased the previous day in Bristol.

Simon reflected how grand modern commerce was that one city on one day could supply so many luxury goods from so many countries across the world.

It was the modern world, exciting and unpredictable; where anything could happen.

Chapter 10

Big Jim had a rule he followed in the haulage trade; whenever he won a large contract, he always did the first delivery.

"It's to scout out the project," he always said. "I need to see where the materials are going, what restrictions there are on site and what the access is like."

"But you've done that at Great Little already," Plain Jane pointed out, anxious that her husband not strain himself too much. "You've been working so hard, my Jimmy."

Jim would not bend; his rule was not to be broken. He explained that Great Little was an established project but that this was a new contract within it. "We're doing the farm buildings now. I won't rest until I've seen the lay of the land."

"Jim, the estate must be 3,000 acres! Are you going to traipse over every bit of it from Okeford Hill to where the Kingston Hall estate starts?"

"No," he laughed, "just the bits with buildings on! But, Janey, the Great Little estate does not extend east of the Dorchester Road, unless I am very mistaken. There must be quite a stretch of land before one gets to Kingston and Wimborne Minster."

"Yes, I exaggerated but I don't doubt that they will adjoin within our lifetimes. As soon as Lady Roakes and the Dowager-Duchess recover from the fraud last year, they will be expanding in every direction they can."

"And they can't go too far west for they'll soon come to Bagber land and Eliza will also be buying again soon enough."

"That still leaves east, north and south!" laughed Jane.

It was the longest day of the year. He had selected the largest wagon he had, four strong horses pulling a heavy load of timber. It was mainly oak for the beams of the new barns but also elm and pine for various uses. All was loaded and waiting to go. He looked at the large clock in his yard, wound every day by the youngest apprentice, a slip of a lad called Nick. It was five minutes to five on a beautiful bright morning. Would Thomas be late? No, here he was.

"Morning, Jim."

"Morning, my friend. Do you want some breakfast before we go?"

"No, I've brought some refreshments for our journey."

"Let's get going then." It would take three hours to cover the eight miles to their first stop. They would unload a portion of their haul then move on to the next site. They planned four more stops, making it a long day ahead.

"Just as well we chose the longest day of the year," Thomas laughed as the horses took on the slope of Okeford Hill.

But when they reached the top, Big Jim drew the heavy horses to a halt and the two of them turned to look at the view to the west. Thomas always swore he could see his house across the river in Sturminster Newton, some four miles away.

"I never can see it," Jim said.

"See the white building quite close to the church? That's it."

Privately, Big Jim thought it was not Thomas' house at all but he decided to say nothing about it. He was thinking of another time, two years earlier, when he had used his dear friend to obtain information about early plans to remove James II from the throne. Matthew Davenport had been sent as a Williamite spy and Big Jim refused to accept that Thomas, as his brother, knew nothing about it. He had placed religion over friendship and would never do that again; not that religion was less important, just that there were lines you should not cross.

And it worked both ways. Friendship and religion should stand as two pillars bearing the same load; holding a man's head high as he walked through this world.

"I was so blind then." But the wind was rising and Thomas only heard the word 'blind'.

"You are blind, my friend, if you cannot see my house from this great vantage point. Now, I can pick out yours in Fiddleford with ease." Thomas pointed towards the long line of thatch with smoke rising from the kitchen-end as the new day got underway.

Big Jim clicked to his four horses and the great heavy wagon moved off down the other side of Okeford Hill. He had a lot to be grateful for but what, at that moment, he gave thanks to the Lord for, was the simple friendship he and his wife had found in these northern fringes of Dorset.

Penelope snapped at the groom and at the new maid that served breakfast. She was barely civil with her friend, Alice, communicating her intentions through a series of grunts. She reserved what gentleness remained in her for Hector, her horse, who she would never treat poorly. She rubbed her long fingers through his mane, made an acerbic comment about the standard of grooming, climbed the mounting block and sheered away, glad to leave human company well behind.

Or rather most human company for she ached to rerun last night again but without the row with Sally. But no-one gets two chances where time is concerned. There is no machine that even halts time, let alone one to wind it back in and make it start all over again. If there were, Penelope would gladly have spent her remaining inheritance on it.

She usually found riding to be soothing, mainly because she put everything into it. To be a good rider, one has to live in the present, not in a past world or any sort of fantasised rehash that gives a superficial sheen to reality. It was sheer concentration on the now that did it for her.

Or so Sally had told her in her considered and self-educated way. What she told herself, as she cantered across the parkland, heading first for Home Farm, was that by the time she reached the woods, she would be soothed.

When she reached the woods without any calming of temperament, the soothing point became when she would reach the stream. But the stream was too shallow and barely made a splash as Hector's hooves ploughed through.

"It doesn't count with so slow a motion of water," she cried into the trees around her. "But I shall feel better by the time I leave the woods. Yet when the trees thinned and she passed into the sweet meadow that marked the approach to Home

Farm, she felt none of the usual uplift. She broke Hector into a gallop, hoping to leave her moodiness behind but it rode out ahead of her, turned and was waiting when the meadow ended and the wheat fields started.

Why had Sally been so obstinate? Penelope had done everything for her that morning; had brought her tea, brewed on a little stove she had had installed in her dressing room. She had woken Sally with a thousand tiny, speckled kisses upon her face, her shoulders, her tiny pert bosom. She had knelt beside the bed and played with her maid's hair, untangling the knots. She had straightened the bedcovers around Sally, then stood at the end of the bed hoping to be granted an invitation to join her lover.

"I've got your clothes all ready for you, Sal," she had said, hope emanating from each of her words.

"I'm not wearing my uniform today, Pen." And with that sentence, the row of the night before had swept out any hope of reconciliation.

Penelope prided herself on giving to an argument far more than she received. But not with Sally. She could not say things to hurt Sally until she finally lost control and then she said everything.

Well, almost everything, for she had not done what she had promised herself she would do that short but so long night; the shortest of the year yet the longest for Penelope as she lay awake on a sofa in the dressing room, hearing the beautiful rhythm of her beautiful Sally breathing next door in the bedroom. She had not revealed that Sally was her property, given to her as a wedding present from her father. Sally, presumably, thought she was in Penelope's employ by choice, something she could end at her own choosing. But the single piece of paper, hidden amongst her private things, said otherwise. She had the title deeds on Sally Black, a negro girl imported from the West Indies.

The delivery wagon was already there by the time Penelope arrived at Home Farm, two men unloading large beams of wood and stacking them beside the roped-off area where the new barn was going.

"That's no good," she called, making both men turn so that the beam they hoisted was flanking her. Hector shied at the sudden movement of a large object. She fought to control him as he moved away from the danger.

"What's no good, Your Grace?"

"Oh, Mr Davenport, why are you here? And Mr Bigg, do you now do your own deliveries?"

"First one always, Your Grace. You see I like to get the lay of the land, as it were."

"And you, Mr Davenport, have no more pressing business?"

"I do, Your Grace, but Jim is short of good hands and I volunteered to assist him. It gives me a chance to see the various sites again before building work starts next week. I have an idea or two about the design of the barns and it is fortunate that you are here. If you have the time, that is, Your Grace."

"I shall make time, Mr Davenport, for you did excellent work at Great Little last year and I would like to see more of your expertise."

Thomas and Jim bowed at this praise, then Thomas offered his hand so that Penelope could slide off the now quietened horse.

The next move surprised Penelope as much as the two men. She watched them for twenty minutes as they laboured under the developing sun. They had unloaded all the heavy beams but there was a lot of lighter stuff to get down. She was hardly dressed for physical labour with a luscious red and brown riding dress gathered in a great knot in the small of her back. The collar was high and stiff, adding to her distant, patrician appearance that made both Thomas and Jim feel uneasy as she watched them work and swished at her surroundings with her whip.

"You'll be here all day," she said, her voice remote, as if watching their work through a telescope. She walked to the back of the wagon. "Help me up." Big Jim was there first, made a stirrup of his hands and loaded her carefully onto the wagon bed. "I'll drag the items to the edge and then you can lift them down. Be sure to put them in order of what you will need first."

Fifteen minutes later they were finished. Thomas looked at the Dowager-Duchess. She could still pass for an aristocrat but one who had been dragged through a bush. Her hair was a little misplaced, her high hat at a slant despite the quantity of pins holding it in place. It gave her a cheeky, rakish air, reminding Thomas of the chestnut leaf that had fallen on Bridget's head last year and had marked the steps to intimacy which had led to their wedding three months ago. That made him think again of Amelia, the one he had not married. She was at Bagber Manor, her old home, but not recovering since her dramatic rescue the previous week, remaining in a trance. Why had they not heard from Grimes in that time? Big Jim and Plain Jane had reported back that they had left him when he seemed recovered but he would not talk, would barely recognise their presence.

He had volunteered to come today and had suggested to Jim that they could handle the unloading themselves, partly to see the building sites again but mostly to quiz him about Grimes. Was he scared that his crazed-assault had caused major damage or was his concern for Amelia? Whatever the reason, he had learned that Big Jim had been back just once and been chased off the premises with the lead of Grimes' old blunderbuss.

"Have you thought to water the horses?" Penelope asked from her towering platform. "No, I thought you had forgotten. Look after your horses if you want them to look after you." She was now on the box in front, picked up the long whip and clicked to the horses, leaving Thomas and Jim to walk behind, down to the trough in the farmyard, Thomas thinking at the last minute to lead Hector. By the time they caught up, she had unhitched the first two horses and led them to the trough. Jim, ashamed at his oversight, unhitched the second pair and brought them alongside.

They made four further stops before the wagon was empty.

"I'll send another driver with the next load tomorrow," Jim said as he put up the backboard of the wagon.

"Good, all will be ready for our Monday start, Your Grace, I will be here on Monday morning and will spend the day travelling between the different sites. We've got four barns to build and a new milking shed. When these are up, we'll start on the cottage refurbishments. Everything should be complete by the end of September."

"Excellent, Mr Davenport, all ready for the winter. In fact, all complete before the harvest festival at the start of October. Now, come back to the house for something to eat and drink before you make your way back. The journey will be quicker on the return for there is no load to carry."

Great Little had a lovely approach; Thomas appreciated it every time he came down to the house. The drive followed a curving ridge, first to the north then bending east, making a protective buffer. The house and immediate grounds were on a series of terraces carved into that ridge at the eastern end, just as the ridge sloped down and opened out to the kitchen gardens and the orchards. But the drive turned sharply back on itself at the last minute and went around to the front of the house which faced south and a little west; somewhere around 195 degrees on the compass, Thomas estimated.

They were met at the door by Sally, resplendent in a magnificent and pristine uniform. She curtsied deeply, held the door for them, took their hats and showed them, on Penelope's instructions, into the library where Lady Roakes sat with Sir Beatrice, or rather she sat while he crawled across the floor, picking at loose strands in the rug.

Penelope did not enter immediately. She was delayed a moment in the hall. Sally left the library and closed the door behind them, ostensibly to organise some refreshments.

"I thought you were not going to be a maid today, Sal?" Penelope could not help the rapidity of her breathing. "I thought you were to spend the day with Tomkins instead."

"I decided, Pen dearest, that I was being unfair on you. I am sorry for fighting with you and making you miserable. I just want…"

"To be more than a maid. But, Sal, I am a selfish thing and want you for myself. I'm sorry too. I'm worried about losing you, is all."

"You will never lose me unless you give me away!" Sally's answer made Penelope look at her sharply. Was she aware of her legal status? Had she found the title document? But she saw only love in the shining black face circled by her large white cap and ribbons and frills to match; love and an ounce or two of cheeky mischievousness. That was a big part of what she loved in the girl, the juxtaposition between reverence and tomfoolery. As she stood before Penelope at that moment, Sally was suddenly like she had been in the first days of their relationship; slightly uncertain, anxious to please, aware she was the junior partner. It sent a thrill of desire into Penelope, yet it was more complicated than lust. She loved Sally so that it hurt, a physical presence in her side. She wanted nothing to change yet everything to change; Sally to stay her maid forever yet to achieve great things in her own right.

They kissed, then Sally mentioned something about refreshments. She turned away to the kitchens, turned back after two steps and did another deep curtsey.

"Mistress," she said but her eyes looked up into Penelope's from her lower position and sparkled with love only. And Penelope did not know what to say back for happiness made her mute, more so for it was tinged with awkwardness. She did not move until Sally had long gone. Then, with a big sigh, she walked towards the library and opened the door.

Inside, Thomas was deep in discussion with Alice, while Big Jim studied the paintings with a deliberate air of not-listening. Penelope noted that they had not seen her enter; she had no scruples like Big Jim, moving immediately to the centre of the room where she had a chance of overhearing what they discussed.

"She is a lovely person, Lady Roakes. I suggest that you keep trying and she will come around in time. She is not vengeful, just needs time, is all."

"What are you two talking about?" Penelope could not go longer without being accused of eavesdropping, a claim that would mortify her despite the truth of it.

"Oh, just a common acquaintance, Your Grace, nothing of significance."

But Penelope knew exactly what it was and how significant too. Alice, her friend, had suffered enough for her past and, if it was the last thing she ever did, she would bring a reconciliation between her friend and the Witch of Bagber.

Who, by all accounts, was no witch at all.

That evening, Penelope claimed a headache and retired early. Sally came in as soon as she heard that Penelope had gone upstairs. Penelope stood as soon as Sally entered the bedroom.

"Sal, you came to me and offered me everything you thought I wanted. You did it with humility because you love me."

"I do love you to pieces, Pen." Sally moved across the room but, surprisingly, Penelope moved around the bed; she had to keep some distance while she presented her compromise.

"I know, my dearest Sal. But you failed in your endeavour, my dear, because I've changed my mind." There, it was said now, come out in a rush. "I want you to be the new steward. I mean, I want you to be happy. You have to stay my maid for appearances' sake. How otherwise can you have free access to my rooms? But I see no reason why in the privacy of our own home here at Great Little, you should not be both steward and notional maid, but steward first."

"Do you really mean it, Pen?"

"I do, Sal, I really and truthfully want you to be happy. You see, when you are happy, I am happy too." It was vintage Penelope to put a shine of the self-centred on an act of generosity.

They spent that evening sitting together on the bed and working on their new arrangement. Sally would serve her mistress first thing and again at night but during the main of the day she would be the new assistant-steward of Great Little.

They both knew that there was as much serving as being served in their relationship, evidenced in Penelope's next statement.

"I've laid out your yellow dress for tomorrow, Sal."

"But that is for special occasions."

"Exactly!" replied Penelope, twisting off Sally's cap with her right hand and placing it carefully at the foot of the bed. "Exactly."

Chapter 11

Anne had no idea what to do. During the week following the settlement of the debts her father had left behind, she was occupied with putting the house up for sale and finding new lodgings. It kept her mind focused on something for a while, but then the problem of their future returned.

"We have no income, Mama." She tried to talk to her mother about it but the replies were vague and lacked logic. "We must cut our cloth accordingly."

"I must have a drawing room."

"You shall have one, Mama."

"And a dressing room. And a breakfast room that looks east while the dining room faces the opposite way."

"We shall have ten rooms, Mama, no more. That includes the kitchen, scullery and washroom in the basement. I have seen such a house and mean to take it. The ground floor has a dining room and a study. The first floor has your bedroom and a room that can be a dressing room as well as the drawing room. The top floor has two attic rooms, one for me and one for the cook and the maid to share.

"What about the other servants?"

"Two is all we shall be able to afford, Mama."

"But the money from the house?"

"That is our capital, Mama, to be invested and not spent. Now, put on your hat and come and see the house I have found us."

It was four crooked stories. Mrs Aspley declared it totally unsuitable and was still complaining about the rooms being too small and ill-appointed when they moved in four days later.

Anne had stabilised their finances successfully but did not know how to turn their modest capital into an income. The maid and cook were paid for the next quarter, the larder was quite well-stocked and there were a few coins in her cash box, but nothing after that.

"We've got three months, Mama."

"You only took a three-month lease? Where will we move after that?" Her mother had visions of being told that ten rooms were too many and they had to move to six, then three. Where would it end?

"I mean we are paid up for three months. By the end of that period, I must have found a way to earn a living."

She sought the advice of Mr Jarvis and he brought Mr Fellows with him. They sat on the only two chairs in the study so Anne perched on the windowsill like a robin looking in at crumbs on the table.

"Let's start with the obvious." She noticed that Mr Jarvis had a waggle to his grey-flecked beard as he spoke. She wondered if it got more pronounced under certain circumstances; perhaps when he was seeking payment from some recalcitrant debtor it worked itself up into a fine display, wagging like the tail feathers of some exotic bird. "You cannot borrow money without the means to repay it. Well, there are those that will lend it to you at a considerable cost but that way lies ruin."

"And," she replied, nodding her head and wondering what strange quirky action she was demonstrating in answer to Mr Jarvis' beard-waggle, "we have just over £184 with our attorney. This is from the sale of the house and some furniture we did not need here, less his fees, of course."

"I started with less," Mr Fellows said. Anne turned and looked at the old man properly for the first time. He seemed ancient; she could imagine him being a young man when Queen Bess was on the throne a hundred years ago. But there was a twinkle in his eye, in both eyes in fact.

"How much income do you need?" The grey-flecked beard waggled again.

In answer, Anne pulled a piece of paper from the sleeve of her dress. "I've worked that out to be £30 a quarter. The biggest part is domestic wages, then there is food, rent, fuel for the stove and clothes, plus a little allowance for the unforeseen."

"You need an investment where you can contribute your time and talents…"

"I don't have any talents to offer."

"Oh, you have considerable talents, my dear, believe me you do."

Amy Tabard was in tears again. She had cried often since her boy had been born. The tears came when she did not expect them, certainly could not explain them and castigated herself for being unhappy when she had everything in the world.

"I will not show this unhappiness to my husband," she told Mr Amiss. "It is so illogical and I do not want to upset him when Paul has so much on his plate right now. I should be so happy with baby Martin. I just cannot understand it."

"There, there, my beloved daughter." Mr Amiss used this term now for every day he was more convinced he was her father. He saw so much of him in her, including this tendency for melancholy. He did not resort to tears for he held them in check but every so often a great sadness overwhelmed him.

Instead, he allowed it for a short while, wallowing for an hour. Then he would summon every resource in his elderly and now stooped frame to fight it. He would pull out paper and pencil and write down his blessings, always placing the family he had suddenly gained at the top of the list.

Another tactic was vigorous exercise. He would walk the full circumference of the town at speed, sometimes lengthening the walk by criss-crossing it in a pattern that added a second hour. On these walks, he would recite his blessings as if ticking off the items on a recipe or shopping list, bending the fingers of his left hand with the fingers of his right to count each point in favour of happiness.

It worked for Mr Amiss but it did not work for Amy.

"Perhaps the root of my sadness is different to yours, Father."

"I think you should tell Paul."

"Never, Father! He has so much to worry about. He is working so hard that I never see him." And the tears bubbled up again like an underground spring breaking through the surface with liberating force.

Sometimes, tears are the only answer.

"How did you start in business, Mr Fellows?"

"First I saved £50. I was working as an apprentice carpenter and then a master carpenter. It took me six years to save the money and during that entire time, I lived in one small room. It was the cheapest rent I could find. I ate scrag ends of meat and vegetables the shops were going to sell to the pig farmers. I paid a farthing less but took them off their hands rather than have the shopkeepers deliver them in bulk to the pig farms. I saved three-quarters of my income every week without fail."

"I can't do that with Mama to care for."

"No, but you already have your seed capital so while there is a need to be very careful, there is no need for the extremes that I went to."

"And then what did you do, sir?"

"All that time of scrimping and saving I was looking for opportunity on every corner but nothing came to me. I started to feel a growing despair, wondering if I would ever find a way to make my fortune. I was convinced I just needed one good idea but everything seemed closed to me."

"What happened then, my friend?" Mr Jarvis asked, interested in what had happened in Dorchester thirty years before his birth.

"I couldn't find opportunity but opportunity found me. That is to say, I was trying too hard. I was examining everything I came across to see whether it would be a viable enterprise. One day, someone said an old adage to me 'All work and no play makes Jack a dull boy', you see my first name is Jack. I thought on this for two days. Then I spent some of the money on new clothes. I realised I had no friends; my childhood friends had fallen away because I only did the work bit and not the playing. I volunteered at my church for a big restoration project. We built a new church hall with a room off it so those that were desperate could stay there. I built the bunk beds. They are still there today."

"You mean at St. Peter's? I know those bunks well indeed!" Anne cried. "I have helped there also although my parents would have me not. They said it demeaned me."

"Well it made me! Within a month, acting on a recommendation, I got a contract to restore the furniture in another church. A year later, I had a thriving building business. But I faced a shortage of building materials so I became part-owner of a ship. The idea was to bring the timber in from other places by sea."

"And now you have a whole fleet of ships," Mr Jarvis said.

"Yes and several manufactories making things to fill up those ships. But the point is, it all started from giving rather than taking. And the giving was genuine although prompted by an observation that, to this day, I do not know if the lady who said it meant to be cruel or kind."

"Bad actions can have good consequences and likewise the other way around."

"Exactly, Miss Aspley, exactly. Now there is a very pleasant new coffee house in Dorchester and I have an appointment there at noon so I must be on my way. Will you accompany me, Mr Jarvis?"

"Certainly, if Miss Aspley does not mind."

"Not at all. You have been very kind, both of you. I would not want to stand accused of keeping the boys from their pleasure!"

Anne sat alone in the study a long time after her two new friends had left. She had risen to see them out but went straight back to her perch on the windowsill rather than taking one of the two comfortable chairs. By leaving them empty, it was almost as if her friends were still there, smiling up at her higher position.

Despite the beauty of Mr Fellows' story, it was the few words of advice from Mr Jarvis that constantly went through her mind.

You need an investment where you can contribute your time and talents...

But she was unaware of any talents. Certainly, she was a moderate seamstress, could paint reasonably well and knew how to make bread and clean a hearth if she ever had to; when younger, she had watched one of the maids kneel in front of the hearth. She had asked incessant questions as to why and how it was done.

While the sun reached its high point and slipped down the other side of her new crooked house, she remained still, frowning slightly in her concentration. The study faced east so darkened a little as the sun went to the west. Her mother had questioned the need for a study, saying the room would make a passable breakfast room.

"At least it looks out the right way, my dear."

Anne would not have it.

"I need a study, Mama."

"Can you not use the desk in the dining room?"

"No, Mama, I must insist on having a study, somewhere to have meetings, to do paperwork in privacy and to think."

"Well, dear, don't go thinking your little head off! How on earth could I marry off a headless girl?"

These words came back to Anne as the unseen sun did its usual trick of sliding down the western sky, dragging afternoon, evening and night on long cords behind it. Then she realised one asset she had and that her mother was referring to in mentioning marriage.

She was a beauty. Her long, curly blonde hair, pretty grey eyes that shone with straightforward honesty, pert nose and milky white skin, all contributed to her beauty, as did her smile which was ready to jump in at any moment.

Yet she did not want to marry to get out of their predicament. Her frown deepened as she considered these options, revealing how she might look in future years when care lines had worked into her face. She did not consider it, had no way of knowing it, but she would be termed a beauty at whatever age, for real beauty shines from within. Her beauty in later years would reflect what she had achieved, against the odds. But right now it was all promise and no plan.

Except she planned never to marry, certainly not to hang on some rich gentleman's arm as a common adornment.

This all lay in the future; for now she was just like Mr Fellows and his six long years searching for opportunity.

…it all started from giving rather than taking…

She sighed, stood and left the study. She would check on her mother, check on the work of the young maid and then go over the two-weekly household budget she had set up.

She looked back from the door at her study, pausing to plan the changes that would be made. She was all plans, this girl; plans that made the road to the future, although the destination remained a mystery. Best, she reflected, to steer clear of the philosophical and keep to the practical.

Now, where was Betty, their only maid? Anne would help her for there was much to be done.

The sun did its job on the other side of the world while the new Aspley household slept. It kicked morning in across Dorset at an early hour, it being still close to midsummer. Anne rose early then went to her mother's room on the floor below and helped her dress. It was too much work for one maid and Betty had already crumpled under the strain.

"No matter, Betty, if you help prepare breakfast and tend to the fires, I will dress my mother."

"But miss, that is my job."

"You will be doing me a favour, Betty, in allowing me to spend some time with Mrs Aspley. Run along now, there is still a lot to do!" This order was accompanied with a smile that seemed to penetrate into Betty's being; certainly she forgot to curtsey on leaving.

Anne did not call her to account for this omission. Betty was young, only fifteen. There was plenty of time for her to learn.

Anne got her mother downstairs for eight o'clock.

"Where are we going, Anne?" she asked. "Surely not work before breakfast?" Anne answered but first she sprang ahead and opened the study door.

"No Mama, I am simply starving and would die if I do not eat within the minute."

"Oh my dearest, you should not have done this." Inside the room, Betty remembered to curtsey and then turned to the sideboard, opening the silver domes to show what cook had prepared for their breakfast.

"Good morning, Mrs Aspley, welcome to breakfast served in your new breakfast room!"

Chapter 12

"She won't talk. I don't know if it is because she cannot speak or she chooses not to." Thomas was beside himself. Bridget placed her long, thin arms around his neck and kissed him full on the lips. It was not an easy time for her either. Her husband had a first love and that first love was seemingly damaged beyond repair. How could she hope to smooth his way when the road was rutted and pitted beyond belief? She felt such anger at those who had laid this road with malice or carelessness.

But anger is the most negative of all emotions. She searched her soul, her very self, for some little part of hope to lay before her beloved husband.

"I would not have you suffer so," she tried, realising the futility of her approach soon after the idea left her brain but not before they had been formed into words and sent out into the room. She was lost in misery in case he took those words badly but her worry was needless as his response demonstrated.

"The poor girl. What can be done for her? What doctor can help with such a terrible malady?" He simply had not heard Bridget speak and she rushed to catch her words, gobble them back up before they might register in delayed fashion in his mind.

"I will go to London and find the best doctor to bring here." This was surely an altogether better idea. Rather than try and take the words back, she would drown them in a different plan.

"Bridge, we can't go to London. I can't leave Mealy as she is now."

"I will go, Thomas, you stay here and tend to Mealy." She hated the thought of her husband tending the woman he had first loved and still loved, yet it had to be done. She had to put him and, by default, Amelia before herself.

She had to put her husband and his needs first. It was a matter of duty, but not duty over love, rather duty through love. This thought was something to hang onto.

"But, on your own?" He had shifted from denial to entertainment of the proposition.

"I'll take Tristan. My cousin will want to go. He will want to help, my dearest."

They left that morning, riding to Shaftesbury from where they caught the London coach.

"You will go and see your publisher?" Tristan asked as they settled onto the thinly-cushioned seats.

"Of course, we shall see Mr Frampton but only after we have found a doctor."

"That is foolish, cousin. You should see him first."

"But our priority is…"

"Bridge, our priority is to find a special kind of doctor in what is probably the busiest city in the world. We must use whatever resource we have if we hope to succeed."

"You mean?"

"Yes, we must ask Mr Frampton who he might know."

"I knew there was a reason I brought you along, cousin!"

They stopped that night near Andover in a large inn called the Homeless Pig on account, so their driver said, that the landlord had a very low opinion of pig farmers.

"The new landlord changed the name which is always bad luck, I hold. Not that you ever see the landlord, madam and sir. He's a rare one for hiding himself away. Most landlords are the life and soul of their establishments but not this one. I've been driving this route for a year and not seen him but once in the distance. You don't get to see him, sir, at his other place on my route."

"Where is that?"

"Down near Wincanton, sir. It was called the Dancing Thief, on account of dancing at the end of a rope, sir! But he changed it on purchase to The Crooked Way."

"Very interesting, my fellow." Tristan slipped him a coin and thought no more of it.

But another gentleman, in fact an officer of the Massachusetts militia, was far more noticeable.

And it was Tristan who saw him first.

"My Good Lord!" he said, pulling on Bridget's arm so she spun away from a near encounter with Simon at the foot of the stairs. "Bridge, that is Simon Taylor, I swear."

"It can't be, Trist. He was sent to the colonies in chains. He cannot be back here and in uniform too!" She could see the man walking away down the corridor from her position in the shadows beside the staircase. "I grant you, Tristan, he certainly looks similar to Taylor from behind."

"I saw him from front-on also. It is definitely Taylor."

They decided to ask the landlord but was told by Holly, who seemed to be a much put-upon deputy, that he was away on business. He owned four or five inns and needed to journey from one to the other. That would explain the coach driver never seeing him.

"Can you tell us, Holly, who is that gentleman in an officer's uniform, but not a uniform I've ever seen before?"

"Why that is Captain Taylor, lately come over from the Americas, I believe him to be. Would you like to be introduced?"

"No," said Bridget.

"Yes," said Tristan.

Thomas got up from his bedside chair and walked to the window. He could see nothing outside for it was the middle of the short summer night; even the stars were covered from earthly sight by a thick cloud covering. No doubt they shone still and made a million tiny lights for the pleasure of God in Heaven. Thomas wondered whether they really could be vast burning balls of matter so far from earth yet looking like tiny specks of lantern to be plucked from the sky on any clear night but not that night. Looks were so deceiving. He suspected that the heavy clouds were much closer to earth than the stars yet what force, he wondered, could keep stars and clouds pinned up at various altitudes below the heavens but above the reach of man? Was there a hierarchy of bodies in the sky? Did king stars or queen clouds give patronage to lesser kinds?

Why was he even dwelling on this? Anything but face the truth that Amelia was lost to them. Anything to divert the mind, to fill it with pointless speculation. Grief is crooked and works upon the mind in many subtle twists and turns, as well as the obvious blatant rage.

He returned to his chair by Amelia's bed and felt her head. It was burning hot yet earlier had been ice-like. He rinsed the cloth in the basin set recently by Becky on the bedside table; the faithful maid had checked on Amelia's condition before retiring long after dark. She had stayed the last few nights here rather than in her estate cottage in order to be on hand when needed. Little Milly had been an enormous help too, despite barely knowing Amelia, who was married off shortly after Milly had arrived last year. It was Milly, in fact, knocking on the door right now.

"I couldn't sleep, Master Tom," she said. She had her own nomenclature for members of the household and Thomas found he liked being 'Master Tom'. Again, grief could employ humour and divert the griever with odd and grim appreciations.

"Come in if you want to, Milly. Mrs Grimes is sleeping." The name seemed so wrong so he corrected it. "I mean, Miss Amelia is sleeping." Milly was sixteen years old yet, as Eliza had often mentioned, she sometimes seemed to have the wisdom of an ancient.

While, at other times, she deserved her nickname of Silly Milly, given to her by Sara and Becky on her arrival a year earlier.

"Has she stirred, Master Tom?"

"No, please take the chair, Milly."

"I couldn't, sir!"

"I will fetch another from the dressing room. Please sit down, you look exhausted, Milly."

"I am tired, Master Tom." And in explanation to his question as to why, she told him she had been unable to sleep since Miss

Amelia had come home. "It's terrible to see what a wicked person can do to a good and kind one, Master Tom."

"You take too much on yourself, Milly dear."

"This is my family, sir. Your people took me in and gave me a home. I would think very ill of myself if I did not feel your woes keenly in return."

They chatted intermittently for an hour, a significant chunk in relation to the short night. Amelia sweated then froze before sweating again; it seemed the life within her escaped and headed towards oblivion, was gathered in again at the last moment through their careful ministrations, only to find a new way out. Thomas let Milly do the immediate care for she seemed to want to and was naturally good at it.

"You look in another world altogether, sir," Milly said after a long period of silence between them.

"Oh, well, yes I was, after a fashion." He was in a black and white world where Grimes was held to account for every single offence. "Grimes should be made to pay for what he has done."

"My opinion is as yours, sir, but I also pray that something positive might develop from all this worry and upset."

"Milly the Wise!" Thomas joked to force himself back into the real world.

"Hardly, Master Tom, my nickname's Silly Milly."

Simon Taylor stood before Bridget and Tristan, placing his weight alternatively from one foot to the other. He had been offered a chair but had declined.

"Sir, your daughter, Amelia, is gravely ill."

"It grieves me mightily to hear it." Why sometimes did every utterance sound wrong, insincere? He shifted the weight from left to right. Would that shift the balance of humours within him? Could a little foot-adjustment give his words a sheen of sincerity?

"I know not what circumstance brings you back to England but you seem not to be a fugitive from justice."

"I was given the choice between servitude in Virginia or the army."

"You were given a commission?"

"No, madam, I earned the commission." Again it sounded wrong, as if he were profiting from his misdeeds. He tried shifting the weight back again. "I was promoted for initiative, you see."

They did not see but smiled out of politeness and returned to the plight of Amelia.

"Can you go to Bagber Manor and see her?"

"I…fear…I fear not, at least at present." That, at least, was honest, although veiled in unintended mystery.

"Sir, she might well die!"

"I cannot, I dare not right now." He hung his head. With his height above the cousins who were seated, he had to look at his shiny boots in order to avoid eye contact. He was not behaving at all like an officer, a king's man.

"Should Colonel Hanson know of your presence in the country, perhaps?" Tristan asked; everything about Taylor's attitude seemed odd, incongruous with the status of an officer.

"I have to go, madam and sir." He bowed low, as if shutting the curtain on the conversation and took his leave, almost hitting the door frame in his haste to be gone.

"I think we should inform Colonel Hanson," Tristan said into the gap caused by Taylor's sudden departure. "His behaviour in response to the serious illness of his daughter is quite incredible, as if the most important consideration is not her wellbeing but to keep out of sight during whatever sick purpose he has in coming back here. Surely there is some law against his quick return?"

"I agree as to the strange behaviour but we cannot divert ourselves most of the way to Sherborne," Bridget replied. "Cousin, you are forgetting the main purpose of our trip."

They settled that they would send a letter to Colonel Hanson and hire a messenger to take it direct to his house. The wording was quickly done and Holly summoned to arrange a carrier to take the letter.

The fact that Captain Taylor quietly took her aside and offered his services to Holly for no fee satisfied her enormously.

She could pocket the five shillings and boost her nest egg. A little more and she and her husband could leave their employment at the inn and buy the smallholding they yearned after.

Tristan and Bridget left with the coach in the morning very much focused on their main task of seeking out the best doctor for Amelia. They travelled all day and stopped one more night in Camberley before arriving in London late in the afternoon on the third day of their journey.

Simon Taylor was a little behind in his schedule for he had to set out for the south west, in the direction of Sherborne. He also wanted to avoid the Browne cousins and so waited until a safe distance from the Homeless Pig before wheeling around and heading north at speed. He reached Marlborough, stopped briefly for a change of horses, then turned east along the road to London but approaching the city from a more northerly route to the one taken by the coach service. He stopped for the night in Reading and moved on early in the morning, arriving several hours earlier than the Brownes.

He went straight to Whitehall where the letter he carried from the Duke of Wiltshire secured his immediate entry and quick access to the minister he needed to see.

Bridget and Tristan also acted with haste, calling on Mr Frampton at his office within minutes of arriving in the capital. He did not know of any doctors specialising in trauma and the nerves but would make urgent enquiries. Then he turned to his duty as host.

"I won't have you staying at the inn when you could both stay with us."

"We would not dream of imposing, sir." Tristan trotted out the polite response but was stopped from going further by Bridget.

"Just think, cousin, if we are here at the centre of things we shall locate the doctor that much faster. It might make all the difference. Time is not on our side with this illness. Poor Mealy deteriorates with every moment."

A junior employee was sent to arrange collection of their bags and delivery to the Frampton home in Tulip Street. Two other employees, more experienced ones, were sent to make enquiries; one was despatched to the Company of Barber-Surgeons, the other to the offices of the Royal College of Physicians near St Paul's.

"Between them, we should have a recommendation," Mr Frampton said. "Now, I know Mrs Frampton will be delighted to see you so we must hurry away home and not risk displeasing her."

Chapter 13

Paul Tabard checked the ship's manifest for the tenth, eleventh, maybe twelfth, time. It had to be right. He had checked each line with a pencil mark the first time, then the mark had become a cross on second checking. Now the single sheet of paper was marked time and again on both sides. It did not matter because Paul knew the cargo list by heart.

He knew he was taking a big risk. There was every chance that a French privateer would attack the ship he had rented and take the cargo. He could lose everything. Mr Fellows could lose his ship.

He wondered again why old Mr Fellows had agreed to rent the ship to him rather than fill it with the various things he made and sold throughout Europe and beyond. Why take the risk when he had no need to involve his ship in supplying armaments to King William's army in Ireland? Moreover, why did Mr Fellows want to see him later in Dorchester? It would mean a long ride from Poole when the ship had sailed, which it was scheduled to do in a few hours with so much still to do. It would also mean, however, a rare night with Amy and Martin and Mr Amiss. The thought cheered him up enormously; it had been nine days since he had seen his family, nine days of relentless toil to get the cargo ready. He had overseen all the work himself, overhearing his new nickname of 'Hands-on Tabard', or 'Mr Hot' for short, whispered and later called openly by the loaders and the crew.

He ran through the cargo list again. It was not what old Mr Sanderson would term an initial shipment of heavy equipment such as wagons, horses and cannon. That had all gone with the main army. This was termed 're-supply' in the trade: muskets, shot, powder, boots and tents.

The expendable items of war. Which led him to think of the men. The ship carried fifty new recruits, their red uniforms indistinguishable from their red faces as they settled into the scorching life below decks in the heat of summer. How many would return? More to the point, what could he do to ensure they made it? He had undercut the Bristol firm that expected to get this series of replenishment orders by offering to take the men for no charge. The government had jumped on the idea and piled as many soldiers as they could onto each vessel. It was Paul's responsibility to ensure each man arrived in Ireland fit and ready to fight. He had spoken to the master about it, would do so again.

"Captain Jones, I want an exercise routine with every man getting time on deck."

"It will be awkward with the working of the ship, sir, but I see the sense of it and would not put these lads in more discomfort than is absolutely necessary."

"I know that to be the case and I thank you for being prepared to meet my concerns with action." Jones was a good master. Paul had seen many worse in his time at Sanderson and Sanderson where they had little choice over who would captain the ships they hired. But still he worried. This was the first shipment of twelve. If they all went well, he would be firmly established as a trader with a specialisation in government contracts. He thought of Mr Sanderson who had taught him everything before being hacked to death in his own home in London last year. Paul had fled to save his own life and lucky chance had taken the destitute young man to the inn Mr Amiss was selling.

More good fortune, for his single penny had bought endless bounty from the serving maid, Amy Barratt, now Amy Tabard, his wife and the mother of his child.

But if this shipment went badly, the clever government officials had put a clause in the contract allowing them to terminate without compensation. Paul would be ruined on his first assignment.

"Good afternoon, Mr Fellows." It was strictly two minutes to midday but their appointment had been for noon so a 'good morning' would have only lasted a short while whereas the afternoon stretched out before them.

"Good day to you, young Mr Tabard. Has the Sea Voyager departed then?"

"It has, sir."

"Forgive me, I did not introduce you to my good friend, Mr Jarvis." They had known each other a long time as acquaintances, occasionally Mr Fellows had hired Mr Jarvis to get repayment of a particular loan. But he had been so impressed by the way Jarvis had stood by Anne Aspley that he had sought out his company and they had become friends recently.

Hands were shaken while an attendant found a table in a booth with high sides for privacy of discussion. Baldock and Oates was like any other coffee shop. It had been converted from a milliner's emporium and the deep bay window that had once displayed hats now contained a large table full of broadsheets and lists of many things to do with commerce: ships' schedules, tides, port fees for various places and prices of commodities from near and far. The central part of the shop was filled with light tables and chairs that could be easily pushed together or pulled apart to accommodate a varying number of businessmen. Along the two sides were the booths, designed for more private business matters.

A coffee shop was a place of business. And the business Mr Fellows had summoned Paul to was the matter of insurance.

"The cargo is worth £4,000, am I correct?"

"That is the contractual selling price, sir."

"And my ship would cost about half that to replace. Plus any sailor who dies at sea, I give his family a pension. I think that should be extended to include the soldiers. How many are there, Mr Tabard?"

"Fifty, sir." Paul went pale with the thought of the mounting liability. It came as the tail-end of enterprise, the cost of failure. Some would cut the tail off, walk away from any consequential liability if they could, but not these fellows.

"So, sirs," Mr Jarvis interjected, enjoying the mathematics, "we are probably talking about £20,000 if the ship should be captured or else sunk. I calculate the cost today of a continuing pension to be £200 a head and there are fifty soldiers and twenty crew so £14,000 alone for the pensions." It was an enormous sum of money, enough to buy a large estate.

"Before arrival that is. I doubt the returning cargo will be worth much more than £1,000. And there will only be twenty sailors returning."

"The risk therefore is £20,000 on the way out and £7,000 on the way back."

"The question now is," Mr Fellows took over, knowing where he wanted this conversation to go, "could you take that loss, Mr Tabard?"

"I could not, sir. Almost everything I have is tied up in this venture, including buying the second and third cargoes of the twelve-ship contract."

"If you lost the ship on its outward journey, therefore, you would find it extremely difficult to continue in business. But if you were to share the risk of loss you would be reimbursed."

"But who would willingly take such a risk?"

"Nothing in life is free, Mr Tabard, but for a fee it could be arranged. I am interested in trying out an insurance operation for shipments from and to these parts. I myself have lost upwards of a dozen ships over the years. It has been an area of interest for quite some time."

They discussed fees. Paul declared early on how much money he had and Mr Fellows agreed to do it for that amount.

"It's a lot to lose," Paul commented as they concluded their negotiations.

"I will spread the risk by selling on a portion to other investors," Mr Fellows replied, sitting back and sipping at his hot chocolate.

"Count me in for a tenth," Mr Jarvis said.

"Are you sure?"

"Yes, I will also spread my risk." And he knew exactly who to start with for the first portion.

The Sea Voyager made excellent progress to Ireland and disembarked both goods and humans in good order. The local commander wrote a glowing report to Whitehall concerning the operations of Tabard and Co. who he described as a 'first class operator and a firm to be remembered for future contracts.' Captain Jones picked up wool and sheep to pack out the now empty holds but also added several thousand yards of an Irish tweed that appealed to him. The ship had a completely uneventful voyage back to Poole Harbour laden down with £3,790 worth of goods, almost as much as the outward journey. It made for a very healthy profit.

There was no call on the insurance money. Anne Aspley could pocket her share of the fee without having to pay anything. She had been in for one fifth of Mr Jarvis' £2,000 and would have had to sell all the remaining furniture had a total loss occurred.

"Next time I will go for a little more," she said to Mr Jarvis and Mr Fellows. "And I would dearly love to learn the mechanics of this trade in risk."

It was the start of Aspley and Associates, Insurers to the Marine Trade.

And Anne Aspley had found her way forward; trading risk for risk in a game of never-ending daring.

Chapter 14

"Ah, Blades-Robson, isn't it?"

"Sir."

"Don't stand on ceremony, man. Father says he knew your grandfather back before the world was begun! He was a young man then, my father I mean, and your grandfather was an experienced officer, taught him a few things, I dare say. Join us for a drink." There was a group of about twenty officers squashed around a camp table that obviously doubled for a dining table. They were sitting on trunks and camp chairs. One shuffled up to make space on an ancient studded-leather trunk that looked as if it had been made for the father all those years ago, before the world was begun.

"Gerome Barceau." The captain held out a hand. Blades-Robson shook it while sitting on the trunk.

"Peter Blades-Robson,' he said in reply. "Are you French?"

"I certainly am, Peter. But you have not stumbled upon the wrong army, mon ami, I am a Huguenot, hence unwelcome at home." Gerome referred to the 1685 Revocation of the Edict of Nantes. For close to a century, the Edict of Nantes, issued by Henry IV of France had guaranteed freedom of worship for French Protestants, known as Huguenots. The revocation by Louis XIV, the Sun King, had set France on an altogether different path. It had forced the Schombergs, recently settled in France, to leave, aligning them and thousands of others with William and, ultimately, Great Britain.

In effect, it sent a whole section of the French population into exile, forced to choose between their religion or their country. Most chose their religion. Henry Sherborne, suffering under the Test Act that made it impossible to be a Catholic in England and hold public office, could only be thankful that the restrictions imposed on those following another religion were so much milder his side of the English Channel. He shuddered to think of what he would have to give up if the French level of intolerance existed in his beloved England.

Brief introductions were made all around. Peter was both the youngest and the most junior present. Meinhardt Schomberg sought to make this the vehicle to explain their objective.

"You might wonder, Blades-Robson, why a spring chicken like yourself is to be included in the menu which is otherwise old mutton."

There was no sensible answer to this opener, or none that Peter could think of. He fell back on the standard army issue instead.

"Yes, sir."

"All of you might also wonder why this meeting is held so late at night." There were nods and grunts in reply but no-one said anything.

"To answer your unspoken question, the meeting is being held now because I have only just got my orders. These are orders, gentlemen, for tomorrow morning. All of you will be up in a few short hours from now and some will be moving out with first light." Now he had everyone's attention. Peter thought Meinhardt, their commander, placed his eyes squarely on him and Barceau when he mentioned moving out at first light.

"We are to be a diversionary force to disguise the main attack. Within that diversionary force, we want to create our own diversions."

"To give the illusion, sir, that we are the main force?"

"Excellent, Blades-Robson, you come recommended and I am starting to see why. You and young Barceau share more than a trunk to sit upon. You are each to lead a minor diversion within the larger diversion, precisely in order to give us the semblance of being a main force, thereby gaining as much deception as possible."

There was to be another part to the plan. Meinhardt, the son of the Duke of Schomberg, explained their dual purpose. After the diversionary manoeuvres had accomplished their task, they were to form the right wing of the attack across the river. "We hope that James Stuart will panic when he sees so many men marching west and will send a good body of his troops to meet us. This will weaken the centre and allow our main army to ford the river and attack the enemy with devastating effect. Meanwhile, deceit complete, we will form the right wing and ford the river and sweep around the back of the Jacobite rabble."

It seemed a neat plan but most plans need time to settle, questions arising slowly after the details have been spelt out.

"Sir, have we sent out scouts to gauge the lay of the land?" an old Dutch colonel asked. "I remember when on campaign in…"

"Keep your sorry memories to yourself, Colonel." The shocking response made Peter sit up. Was Meinhardt's earlier pleasant banter nothing but veneer?

"Sorry, sir, it's just that I've seen promising strategies come to disaster through a lack of preparation."

"You think it advisable to scout, you go and scout. In fact, keep on riding, Colonel, because I don't want doubters in my command structure. Be off with you, man!" The colonel sat a moment longer, blushing deep red against his thick white hair. Then he rose, saluted and left the tent.

"Well, gentlemen, where were we before that rude interruption?" But no man can switch jolliness off and on like sliding the shutters of a lantern. The mood had changed; most of the officers had put down their glasses half-finished. They would not raise them again. This meant a pleasant surprise for the orderly when he cleaned up later. He knew better than to drink it all so he sipped a few times from one glass then looked for a bottle and used a jug as a siphon to refill the bottle and then another one. He called it Old Schomberg and sold the bottles for four shillings each.

The purchasers assumed it was brandy straight from the old duke himself. In fact, it was the son, also a general but there was nothing old about him. He had recently turned forty-nine but looked well for the approaching half-century; average height, fit and slender, yet muscular from long days in the saddle, he had a semi-regal air about him. He was the type one treats with a dose of reverence just in case he is connected to royalty in some minor way.

But everyone who knew him knew to keep away when a black mood descended.

"I did not know the man before these three weeks," Gerome told Peter as they made their way back to their tents to brief their non-commissioned officers and get things ready for early morning. "But I suffered at the end of his tongue pretty quickly. You might be the favourite right now, Peter, but just wait until he turns on you."

Henry got no sleep the night of the 30th June. He had been trying to resolve a dispute between Corporal Bing of 3rd platoon and Private Fugini of his own section within 2nd platoon. Bing had been relentless in deriding 'Private Spaghetti', as he termed the quiet Italian who always seemed to have a thought for satisfying his section's hunger with ingenuity. Fugini had several pouches of spices and herbs hidden about his kit and seemed to be able to turn the blandest stew into something fit for a king. The basis of the complaint was that Fugini had fed Bing's section with some of that 'foreign muck the man calls food'. The fact that they all kept coming back for more had little to do with it in Bing's eyes.

"All NCOs to Company HQ," was whispered around the tents, as if the army opposite on the southern bank of the Boyne might be alerted and then listen into their plans with ears pressed to big brass horns to aid their hearing.

"Most of the regiment is staying with the centre but you boys in A Company are going to have a little more excitement!" Blades-Robson explained to the ten corporals, five sergeants and company sergeant-major crowded into his tent. The regimental adjutant was in attendance but was letting the lieutenant do the talking, laying out the plan he and Gerome had finalised during their walk back to camp after the briefing with Meinhardt.

"Our job, boys, is to create a diversion. We want the Jacobites to think we're going all the way to the bridge at Slane. We want them to move troops from Duleek to Slane, hence weakening the force at Duleek. Our company has got to look like a scouting party going ahead of the main force. That way we give real credibility to our diversion. We've got to be visible which is why we're only going at first light; no night manoeuvres this time, my lads!" The NCOs made their dutiful titters.

"What do we do when we get to Slane, sir?" Henry asked as the laughter died away.

"We're not going all the way, Sherborne. At the last moment we shall wheel away and join the extreme right of our right wing. Company Sergeant-Major?"

"Sir!"

"I need a suitable signal for turning around."

"Whistle, sir.'

"I doubt very much my feeble whistling will be heard across two-hundred yards of terrain." He put two fingers in his mouth to give evidence to his claim.

"No sir, of course not, sir. I meant, sir, for you to utilise a whistle, like one I have here, sir." He pulled a whistle from his tunic pocket and passed it to Blades-Robson.

"Excellent, CSM, excellent." He gave a low blast on the whistle. "That's a significant improvement on my efforts, CSM!"

They spent twenty minutes on a system of signals. Three short blasts was the main one, representing the order to wheel about and march east not west, returning to the banks opposite Duleek. Two long and two short represented an order to advance at speed while three long blasts meant retreat back to the camp, presumably to abandon the planned diversion within a diversion.

"General Meinhardt is the right-wing commander," Blades-Robson said, as if announcing the winner of a raffle outside the village church. "The man is most particular with regard to the following of instructions so I do not want anyone to veer from orders unless absolutely necessary. Is that understood, lads?"

"Yes, sir." It was the politest way the company commander could indicate that General Count Meinhardt Schomberg had a ferocious temper. Henry noted the way the lieutenant laboured his words and took the warning to heart.

Their departure was timed to perfection. There was no attempt to hide their progress; indeed, the opposite was their objective.

Trumpets and commands were bawled across the camp from long before dawn. Soldiers were formed, marched and reformed as the light rose on a calm, sunny day. A seasoned observer might have suspected something, seeing a greater flurry of activity than the underlying movement warranted.

But that was the gamble that King William had blessed in his final planning meeting.

It was a morning that promised to show Ireland in all its peaceful glory, decrying the fact that two large bodies of men intended raining slaughter and misery down on the other. Both claimed right, both claimed God to be on their side, not pausing to consider the incongruity of a situation where two opposing parties claimed the exact same. Each soldier looked forward to victory and prayed to avoid injury or death, promising all sorts of extravagant things in return for safety, the chance to live another day. Two armies broadly similar although, as is often the way of men at war, one side had much more fear than hope.

In the case of this meeting by the banks of the Boyne river on the first day of July, 1690, 35 or so miles from the prize of Dublin, there was a considerable imbalance between one army and the other. And this was not down to numbers, which favoured the Williamite faction by a margin of over 10,000. Good commanders have routed much larger forces countless times across the ages. Even the fact that the Jacobite army was less well equipped, pikes instead of muskets for the Irish infantry, would mean little to an able commander-in-chief.

Which James Stuart most definitely was not.

He went with the wind, this one-time and would-be-again monarch. But the wind was almost non-existent that bright summer day. Instead, he went with the last person who had spoken; his plans changing and changing yet again.

He called a Council of War, attended by all his generals and regimental commanders. It had seemed the right thing to do. But the prevailing opinion, that they should retire behind the Shannon, stuck in his gullet; retiring was a polite word for retreat and he felt this to be an affront to everything he was.

"But there is another aspect, Your Majesty, that we need to consider. Orange is hopelessly dependent on his ships for resupply, yet we have command of the Irish Sea. It would be a simple enough task to take Carrickfergus harbour and cut him off, make him live off the land." The Earl of Tryconnell spoke for most advisers to James Stuart.

Sir Neil O'Neill took up the argument at this point, a fatal mistake for it made James think it a conspiracy against him.

"Our spies tell us Orange is keen to get back to England to supress the subversion we've engendered there. If he is faced with a protracted campaign in Ireland, he will do something rash to try and end it quickly. That is when we need to strike and annihilate him."

"I won't do it, gentlemen. I won't retreat." He could not appreciate that sometimes retreat in war is the wisest move; indeed, it can win the fight when managed well, turning the opponent's brazenness into stumbling death in the ditches of the battlefield. The surprise contained in retreat followed by sudden new assault can make all the difference.

But when a man turns and turns again, turning before the first turn is complete, he ends up revolving on the spot and going nowhere.

When that man is also a king, or else claims the throne, other men's lives are thrown into that spin too. And suddenly fear pervades the air, the heavy sweet smell of doubt that soldiers pick up instantly.

And, as James was about to learn, that doubt was a bigger opponent than the whole of William's army.

Chapter 15

Simon sat and waited. Tired and hungry, he just wanted the job complete. He never would have thought it but he missed the simple days in New England, following orders and using his boundless initiative in tiny ways to improve his comfort and that of those around him.

It was a simple life without deceit. It was a life where his cunning was directed at the common enemy of hunger and discomfort instead of aiming at his so-called friends and family around him.

As it had been before.

He would go back, he knew that now, at least until his term of exile was over. He was not the labouring type and the thought of indentured service had filled him with horror, making him jump at the opportunity to join the army instead. Afterwards, who knew what the future held for him? He was over fifty, approaching old age with nothing to show for a life of calculation and deception. Perhaps it was not too late to try some other way?

"Captain Taylor? Come this way, sir." The voice belonged to a tiny man, bent over at the waist to further diminish the profile he presented. He evidently knew his way around Whitehall for his posture put his eyes to the ground yet he managed to avoid crashing against the elaborate furniture that adorned these rooms. Simon looked from the doubled-up old man to the large window he was standing next to. It overlooked a tranquil courtyard and, as Simon stood, he gained an angle of sight down to the ground below. The beautiful day seemed to beckon, to be pulling him outside, bidding him go far away from intrigue. He wondered what it would be like to be a gardener all his life like the two in the courtyard below, young and old, student and teacher no doubt. Yet his sudden urge for this simple life involved the very greatest complexities he had ever been engaged in. He had to bring a result back to Davidson and that meant persuading these people that he had a plan to beat the French in North America.

Where, in actual fact, he had none. Events had moved far too quickly for him; he had always preferred to consider at length and then move in deliberate and carefully planned steps. Yet the greedy-eyed, balding and pot-bellied Duke of Westminster had reacted immediately when Simon had arrived at Wiltshire House a few days earlier. It was almost as if he had been wishing on a star for someone just like Simon to turn up and there he was, on his very doorstep.

And, just to add further to the mix, he had bumped into the Browne cousins at the inn two days ago and had learned from them of the terrible illness Amelia suffered from.

Amelia was not his only child. He had three more with his second wife, Elizabeth. But Amelia was his oldest and the only child of his first and greatest love. The news that she was critically ill made him feel powerless, confused, desperately unhappy.

Especially as he had been the architect of the rain that had flooded into her life; he had pulled the drawstrings and unleashed the drenching that now left her, dumb and motionless, lying in her old bed at Bagber Manor. Yet he could not go to her for the only reason he was back in England was to perform the same old intrigues he had done all his life long.

Yet this time, at least, the intrigues were of noble origin.

"Lord Cartwright will see you now, sir." The aide bent backwards precariously in order to raise his eyes to see why this military gentleman in the strange uniform was not following him. Could he not understand English? Or maybe he was a half-wit? But then why would his master waste time on a half-wit? He sighed; his responsibility was to get this strange man in to his appointment with Lord Cartwright. He had no need to fret over the particular quirks of the visitors, however peculiar they might seem.

Dr Haliburton was running late for the appointment but that pleased him considerably. He felt it his prerogative to live according to his own version of time and would sometimes spend precious minutes in idle chat to ensure he was not prompt for his next meeting. Sometimes, he declined to turn up at all, pretending he had much more important things to attend to.

He had discovered as a young man that medicine was a business and the best way to create demand, as with most businesses, was to act as if you did not want it at all. The more arrogant he became, the more people just had to see him. In his thirties, he had lived a dance between feigning indifference and raking in the guineas; another lesson he had learned early on was always to charge in guineas. It just sounded better. Now, graduated to his forties, he delegated to a growing number of assistants, allowing him to spend as much time as possible with his cheery, rose-cheeked and intensely sexy mistress.

"Will he come, do you think?" Bridget asked.

"Maybe he's been called to an emergency," Michael Frampton replied.

"Mealy's case is an emergency."

"Yes, I know, Bridget. It is a distressing time for you but the doctor is not to know this. I simply told him there was a case that would require him to be away from London for some weeks. I gave briefest details, that it was a young lady much traumatised and now awake but unable or unwilling to respond, even to her family. Remember, Bridget, he is highly recommended. Ah, maybe that is him now." They all heard the front door close and male voices talking in the hall of Mr Frampton's home.

They waited for the library door to open, for Dr Haliburton to present himself as Amelia's saviour.

"Dr Haliburton? My name is Frampton, I'm pleased to…" Michael rose to introduce himself before the servant could announce the visitor.

"No, sir. My name is Mowbray, Dr Mowbray. I am assistant to Dr Haliburton who sends his…"

"Is this man so great that he cannot come himself?" Tristan rose, his annoyance like lightening stabbing at the sea. "Must he send his assistant in his place? Are we to imagine he is too important and too busy to attend this dreadful case?"

"Quiet, Trist, for nothing can be solved by blaming Dr Mowbray. Please, sit down and listen to what the doctor has to say."

"Good people," he started, sounding like an actor giving a carefully rehearsed speech, "I have studied long and hard under the great master's tutelage. I cannot hope ever to be more than a shadow of him but flatter myself that I have picked up sufficient of his great ideas to be of some assistance in the matter of your traumatised friend."

"Tell me, sir," Tristan had sat but now stood again, his anger much increased, "exactly what is it that you have spent your years in studying? Is it acting, perhaps? Or maybe verboseness?"

"Hush, Trist, you do our cause no good." Bridget urged.

"I am, in my small way, somewhat of an expert in the matter of trauma in ladies." Dr Mowbray twisted his fingers behind his back, giving an odd impression of a man who constantly flexed his shoulders. "If you would not mind telling me something of the patient."

"I won't have an assistant dealing with Mealy."

"Please, Trist, hear the man out," Bridget replied, whispering further that he could do no harm. "Dr Mowbray, do you mean you have a genuine interest in such matters or are you instructed by the elusive Dr Haliburton, to claim expertise?"

"Speak to me for twenty minutes, Mrs Davenport, give me the background to this case and I promise I will speak honestly at the end as to whether I can help or not.

Simon Taylor was convinced he had seen Lord Cartwright before but could not place him. He was not an attractive man; slick black hair combed away from his forehead, a slight stoop as if he was going the way of his bent-double aide and would get there in another twenty years. And then there were his hands that would not keep still. He was an oily man, the type who has no great ability and, most significantly, no great weakness.

The hardest types to manipulate.

"I understand that the Duke of Wiltshire has given you an urgent letter of introduction.'

"That is right, my lord. You see this delicate matter hinges…."

"Pray present the letter."

Cartwright read it three times. The first reading settled his doubts as to Taylor's genuineness. He recognised his friend's signature and knew the letter not to be a forgery. The second reading, convinced him to act along the lines of the duke's suggestion. He was halfway through the third reading when he remembered who Simon Taylor was.

"I re…" Then his mouth clamped shut as he further considered. Taylor did not recognise him and that gave him the advantage.

"My lord?"

"I was about to say that I realise the importance of what my friend, the Duke, writes about." Cartwright paused, thinking how to go on, noticing Simon's shoulders slumping an inch.

Simon was expecting the next sentence to be a denial of further action, something along the lines of appreciating the need but this was not the time and then a quick dismissal, bending to the papers on his huge desk to indicate he wanted no further disturbance.

"And I see a need to act accordingly."

"What? I mean I beg your pardon, my lord." Had Simon slipped from one play into an entirely different one? One with a happy ending? But then the weight of Amelia came back to him.

"I must say you worry me, Taylor. You travel across the vast Atlantic to impress upon me a scheme you argue will benefit the English in North America in their struggle against the French. I am receptive to it and make various suggestions as to how it might best be done. Then, you appear as glum as a little boy who has lost his prize conker!" Cartwright tried to smile, tried to indicate it was a joke, but all facial expressions came across as smirks or frowns; he could not manage a smile other than the sickly, obsequious type he had employed on his way up.

116

But now he had arrived at the top; a minister of the crown. He did not need to be obsequious again other than with a handful of the most senior.

"I'm sorry, my lord." Simon gathered himself. "I've just had some bad personal news."

"Out with it, man." In a sick parody of caring, Cartwright rose and came around his desk to where Simon was sitting on an upright chair. He sat upon the edge of the desk so he could place his hand on Simon's shoulder, as one did when one cared. But the desk and chair were too far apart and Cartwright had to stretch across the divide. He slid off the desk and only just stopped himself from falling in an undignified heap on the floor. Turning it into a rush to the window, he put his back to Simon, telling himself he was making it easier for the man to talk without embarrassment.

As a result of this floundering between desk, chair and window, Cartwright missed entirely the narration Simon gave about the condition of Amelia.

"Well, I'm sorry to hear it, Taylor. Now, on to the plan. This is what we are going to do."

Dr Mowbray had one desire in coming to see the Browne cousins at Mr Frampton's comfortable but unpretentious house in Tulip Street. Debtors were pressing on every side. If he could get away for a month or so and earn a fat fee in the process, he might be able to sort out his difficulties.

"I am your man, Mrs Davenport," he cried as soon as Bridget had finished telling him about Amelia's condition. "I have made a particular study of such conditions in recent years, much of the last decade in fact. I would relish the opportunity to treat your friend and to earn, I mean extend my knowledge a little further."

"Do you have Dr Haliburton's recommendation?" Michael asked.

"I do, sir." He pulled a letter from his tail coat.

"This is a powerful letter, Dr Mowbray."

"Indeed it is, sir. Thank you, sir." No need to mention that Haliburton had said this was the last thing he would ever do for Mowbray.

"Be gone and take your nasty debt collectors with you."

It was a type of endorsement.

"There is just one more thing, sirs and madam. It concerns the delicate matter of the fee, some of which will need to be in advance if I am to leave my beloved family for an extended period."

"You are a family man, Dr Mowbray?"

"Oh, indeed, madam." He had a bastard son somewhere so it was not a lie. The mother had come looking for help in the early years. Perhaps he would seek her out and give her a few shillings if the fee allowed it. "There is nothing quite so endearing as family. A mutual bond that ties individuals forever together through thick and thin. Yes, madam, I am a family man."

"We will need to leave today, Dr Mowbray," said Bridget a few minutes later while counting the coins into his hand.

"Yes, of course, allow me to take the money to my wife and pack a few belongings for the trip." He would buy a new coat for the journey. He deserved it. "I'll be back within two hours if that is permissible to you."

"There is a coach leaving here at noon, sir. We will purchase three tickets while we wait for you."

He bowed and left the room, thanking the Good Lord who always seemed to provide, albeit at the very last moment.

Chapter 16

"Penelope, even Hector is feeling the strain. You have taken him out for hours each day, riding early after breakfast and not returning until evening."

"I am merely doing what you suggested, Alice. I am taking an interest in something other than…well, never mind what other than. And I am also improving the estate with a multitude of suggestions."

"Orders more like, not suggestions."

"So be it, Alice, someone has to be in charge. Today, for instance, I rode to the two farms we have by Okeford Hill. I took both tenants to task for they have not repaired fences nor planted hedges along those fences to last for the long term. One has planted too much oats and not enough wheat. I called him Mr MacPearson instead of Mr Pearson and asked him what clan he belonged to for he would have porridge galore this winter but not enough bread."

"Penelope, you are impossible! Surely it is their choice what crops they grow and whether they expend their energies in repairing hedges or barns in any particular year?"

"No Alice, my dear, there you are wrong for I checked this with Tomkins and their tenancy agreement requires them to maintain the farm they lease in accordance with reasonable standards set out by the landlord. I inform each tenant that I am merely inspecting their property in this regard. The fact that I also make suggestions as to how to maximise their income is something for them to take or leave."

"You know what they call you, Penelope dear?" Why mention it now, she wondered. Her friend might take offence. But it was too late, the words were out. Sometimes, it seems, we cannot help ourselves; emotion rules us like no other creature of God's creation.

"Tell me."

"It's nothing." But that same emotion is something hard and tangible when let out of the bag, even between the closest of friends.

"I want to know, Alice."

"Well, it's more how they style you, in jest and from affection, of course." This was another example of the homo sapiens species wasting precious time and energy trying to wind back in what could not be wound; a result of striking out with words or ideas that were instantly regretted and wished never said.

"I want to know, Alice Roakes." It was going to have to be said. Alice took a deep breath and launched in.

"They say, here comes Her Grace, the Commander-in-Chief of Great Little." That was true, but not the whole truth and Penelope knew it to be only half the story.

"And?"

"That she offers her tenants great things of little consequence."

"I don't understand." Yet she sensed some of the import because she turned bright red and avoided eye contact with Alice.

"It means, Pen," Penelope swung around at the new voice to see that Sally had entered the room, "that you pronounce from your high horse, Hector, in a very proud way, things that they know already. For instance, I asked Mr Pearson to grow more oats this year because I knew that we planned to expand our horse-breeding and wanted plentiful supply of oats for the horses you are going to buy."

"Me? Buy horses?" It was a clever and loving change of direction and Alice breathed again, thankful that Sally had entered the room when she did.

"Yes, for no-one knows horses like you do, Pen. Now it is time for us both to change. Come along, my dearest. I'll tell you more as we get dressed."

Penelope jumped up, full of questions but aware that Sally had said she would explain upstairs in their rooms. This left Alice alone in the drawing room, wondering how on earth Sally Black could control this proud, arrogant woman she had become so fond of.

Alice had been given such love in recent years. True, some had been snatched away again. Sir Beatrice, her husband, had been murdered in his study next door to the drawing room where she now sat. The murder had been just a few weeks after moving in to Great Little. Then, the house and the estate she had loved from first sight, had been damaged beyond belief by others through vengeance and wild jealousy. The house had burned almost to the ground two years previously. Alice had responded by using her wealth to start building a better and grander house in its place. But then, the estate, just last year, had been brought to the brink of financial ruin by the evil machinations of Parchman, the man who had once paid her a satisfactory pension to hold and guard Lady Merriman, or Mrs Davenport as she now was styled. That was a bitter regret and one she hoped someday to remedy, if only partially, for how can one compensate for the theft of time? The stealing of valuables is one thing, they can be replaced. But to take a chunk of a lifetime for no other reason than it provided temporary security for the taker, was despicable and should never be forgiven.

Yet forgiveness was the one thing Lady Roakes yearned for. She had been given much in recent years. Her friendship with Penelope, for instance. Her son, the new Sir Beatrice, to replace the old. Even the Great Little estate, back from imminent bankruptcy and showing every sign of flourishing again under Sally Black's careful and inspired management. But she craved one more thing and this was denied her. She craved forgiveness; she wanted to like herself again and this could not happen with the great cloud of her past hanging over like a pending storm, pegging down the sky with oppression.

Upstairs, Sally said she had two surprises for Penelope as she lay back on the big bed while her mistress got their evening clothes together. She carefully laid out Sally's uniform on a chair, for this was the agreement they had reached; maid in the morning and evening, assistant-steward by day.

"Shall I change you, Sal?"

"No, dress yourself first, Pen. Don't worry, I'll help you with the buttons and hooks and pull your stays tight to bursting! But first I want to sit on the bed and tell you my plans, especially as they involve your inheritance!"

It was as Penelope had imagined when following Sally up the stairs to their rooms. Penelope was to invest in at least two-dozen mares and several fine stallions.

"I want you, Pen, to go out and find these horses and I want you to manage the whole project for the long-term."

"You mean I am to run the horse-breeding without interference?"

"Without unnecessary interference, Pen, but I will have oversight and will intervene if required, but only if required."

"So I will answer to you?"

"You will answer to me, Pen." For some reason, Penelope sought to make light of this answer, no doubt to hide her embarrassment. She had removed her overskirt and underskirt and her petticoats. She now turned to Sally and curtsied in stays and underwear.

"Yes, Great Steward of Great Little, I will accept the position of Horse-Breeder answering to you and you alone."

They collapsed in fits of giggles on the bed. Only when they heard the gong bang in the hall below did they rise and dress quickly, for they were both late for their different obligations that evening.

It was much later that night when Penelope woke with the memory that Sally had mentioned two surprises. Sally was asleep at her side, her shorter body shunted against Penelope's and her arm around her waist, causing Penelope's nightgown to ride up. Air had become caught in the nightgown like a balloon, gradually releasing as Penelope shifted her position this way and that.

It was mid-summer and early morning so there was already the start of the new day showing as light around the edges of things. They had kicked off the blanket as it had been hot that night. Now, Penelope could see the contrast between white sheet and black skin, the dividing line moving slightly as Sally stirred in her sleep. She placed her right hand on Sally's perfect face, stroking her jet-black skin and settling her back into a deep sleep. She thought back to before they had been together. Penelope then had everything but nothing, for nothing else mattered except this curious creature with a mind that could work wonders.

No, that was not quite right, as Alice, her only friend, mattered.

She fell back asleep with her hand in Sally's hair, subconsciously twisting the curls in her fingers, feeling the wiry yet soft frizz she loved so much. In the morning, she would brush it thoroughly, standing behind her at the dressing table and loving every minute of it.

But when she next opened her eyes, it was mid-morning and there was no Sally in the bed. Instead, there was a note from her propped on the pillow where her head had been so that Penelope's fingers were closed around it. She opened the note after staring blankly at it for a moment, fearing something terrible, short of breath as a result. She saw Sally's large handwriting, a neater version of her own; after all, she had been Sally's teacher.

Dearest Pen, I forgot two things last night in our desire to be together. I forgot firstly that I have to be away today. I have to go to Dorchester to see the Tabards about a shipment of meat to the army in Ireland. We have become a supplier of beef and mutton to the soldiers there! And wheat too, should the campaign extend past the harvest. I will stay at least two nights with the Tabards for they want me to meet with some business acquaintances of theirs and to discuss some propositions.

Penelope paused, overcome with sorrow that it would be two or three days until she would see Sally again.

"I'm not jealous to share her," she tried convincing the room around her. The whitewashed walls, awaiting the rich wallpaper they had selected but not yet paid for, accepted her words and stripped out the negative.

"You are jealous, Your Grace," they seemed to bounce back. "You do not want to share her with anyone."

"I'm not jealous, I'm really not." Then, to break the deadlock, she returned to the note.

I would urge you, dearest one, to travel yourself in order to occupy the time whilst I am away. I understand there is a good horse market outside Sherborne and thought you might stay with the countess, of whom you once told me you enjoyed her company. I've sent Tomkins ahead with a note to say you are coming. He will stay at Sherborne Hall for as long as he is needed. He used to be under-steward there and said he would like to return and see old friends. I have packed some clothes for you – yes, you see I have been industrious in the early hours of this morning! The dresses I have packed are numbered in the order to wear them so you do not need to worry yourself with what to select each day. And I have laid out your mauve dress with the black underskirt for today. I know you do not like this dress, finding the collar too high and the brocade netting too stiff about your body, but you are to be obedient to my wishes on this for you look truly glorious in it. I will picture you haggling for horses in all your regal splendour! Peg, one of the new maids will dress you and accompany you to Sherborne Hall, as she comes from the area and would like to see her family. She has asked that her brother, Johnnie, who is a farmhand at Home Farm, come along and I have agreed to her request. Be nice to them, Pen, and you will please me.

Another maid, an ordinary dull maid, one who would perform her tasks and leave the room with a final curtsey. But not *her* maid. Penelope looked again at the note. There were two more paragraphs.

I have one more promised surprise for you, my dearest Pen, but bear in mind some surprises might not be termed pleasant. Duty sometimes gets in the way of pleasure, as evidenced by my trip started today. I have an idea concerning your inheritance. I will tell you more when we are next together but I can say now that I will require your absolute obedience in this matter, never minding how distasteful any particular aspect of my decision and resulting instructions might be.

"Damned cheek," she said but her heart had already promised the obedience Sally required.

It only remains, my dearest Pen, to say that, as you well know, I love you hopelessly and absolutely. Write to me each evening, care of the Tabards in Dorchester, and do as I say with a heart that knows it is loved dearly. I know also that my love is returned completely. Yours in love, Sal.

"Would you prefer another dress, Your Grace?" Peg said, curtsying yet again.

"Why would I do that?"

"I...I was just thinking, Your Grace, that...that, um..."

"That this one is a little stiff for travel?"

"Yes, exactly, Your Grace." She seemed relieved to have the words dictated for her. "Of course, this dress is very elegant, it's just that..." Again, she did not know how to say it."

"Are you concerned about dressing me, Peg?"

"Well, it's just I haven't done it before, Your Grace." The poor girl, no older than sixteen, saw herself being sent away and another taking her place. She would not see her family and would be a disgrace in the lower household.

"No need to worry yourself, I know how it goes and can direct you at each stage. The buttons are numerous and fiddly, and the hooks are cumbersome but we will manage it by working together." Penelope had planned to say something much more caustic but the words that came out seemed to belong and she was pleased with them. She had made a little friendship with kindness, something new to the dowager-duchess.

And it felt rather good, particularly as it would please Sally when she heard of it.

An hour later, still just about morning, Penelope left Great Little bound for Sherborne Hall. She was dressed impeccably in her mauve dress with matching black and mauve hat and veil. She drove herself in the trap. She had two attendants, Peg and Johnnie, both delighted to have an opportunity to visit their parents and numerous siblings at home. They shared the backwards facing bench that Sally had often sat on as they had travelled across the county on trips to Bagber or Dorchester.

Chapter 17

The history of battles is more the history of failure than success. Ignore for a moment the inconclusive battles and concentrate on the clear victories. Consider the proposition that they are all about the weaknesses of certain key characters, history being a human phenomenon built up from a million-million-character traits, good and bad.

For what is history outside human involvement? Take out the people and you have history as no more than the passage of time, the constant and regular climb and descent of the sun in the sky.

Now turn to the particular battle in question, fought for control of the Boyne River on a fine 1st July in an Ireland in the midst of a hellish storm. James Stuart was clearly indecisive but there was an element of this indecision that spoke volumes about his confidence; confidence being, in military terms, the art of expecting to win and acting accordingly.

For if battles are all about weakness, winning them is all about confidence.

James had twelve cannon in his possession. These were twelve weapons that could wreak havoc on the enemy. They were a key asset and one that the Duke of Schomberg feared greatly in advising William to caution.

"Sire, the enemy cannon will do us great damage as we try and cross the river. Our infantry will be mown down as they wade across."

"We have to force our way through," William had replied, fearing other things to Schomberg, in fact a whole other layer of worry weighing upon him as monarch. His fear was that the campaign might be protracted, causing an extended stay in Ireland. Sometimes, he wondered whether this was all intentional, a grand alliance against the throne he had only just taken. James Stuart was no more than a pawn in the overall game, his job to keep William in Ireland and thus leave England, the real prize, exposed to invasion on the south coast, or from the Jacobites in Scotland. The invasion, of course, would be instigated by Louis XIV of France, the Sun King and the chief backer of James in Ireland.

The King of France's purse made trouble far beyond the borders of France. As William, Prince of Orange and fierce defender of Dutch independence, knew so well.

William felt a desperate need to get back to England but twelve cannon stuck their ugly muzzles into that determination.

And then, inexplicably, six of the cannon were moved away. Schomberg's spies said they were being transported to Dublin. Why would James make such a move? Was he hoarding his menacing weapons to use another day? Did he therefore expect to be defeated on the Boyne? Such thoughts would occupy the minds of the more intelligent personnel on both sides of the river. But the average soldier would feel it rather than think it; quite possibly more powerful, as feeling did not allow for counter-arguments.

For this was the crunch. James' army could accept an amount of vacillation, courses and plans being changed before they were even set in motion. But what would they think of anything that spoke of defeat before the battle had even begun?

Removing six of the cannon to safety was not the only move James made that had the effect of destroying his army's confidence. Rumours were rife that their leader had plans in place for his immediate return to France after the battle. Rumours may be true or false but that matters little; what really matters is their persistence and their quantity and then the efforts made to counter them. These rumours about James' flight preparations were, in fact, true. They were persistent and there was absolutely no consideration as to countering them. James was blissfully unaware of the effect certain of his actions had on the mass of troops under his command.

To most of the rank and file, James believed his own army would lose and that is the main reason why it did.

Henry's section was at the front of the company that marched west, following the course of the river. The only two soldiers in front of Henry were Blades-Robson on the left-hand river side, and Sergeant Bullen on the right.

"We have to do all the marching," Corporal Bing complained loudly. "It's the bleedin' infantry doing the donkey work, day in and day out while the cavalry…"

"Silence there," Bullen shouted against the beat of the drums and the clomping of boots. It was not noise he was objecting to, in fact they wanted noise as part of the diversion. It was just Bing himself that Bullen found unbearable.

They marched a little further, the morning sun beating on their backs as they moved west towards their deceptive objective. However, very little in battle works out as expected.

A scout rode up to Blades-Robson, pointing across the river. The lieutenant spoke with him briefly and then waved him back towards the company of soldiers he was leading. The scout saluted, turned his horse and urged it back into a trot. Passing down the line of soldiers he spoke to each NCO in turn. From there the word travelled along the ranks.

"The plan is working. There is considerable movement across the river. See the dust?"

"Infantry doesn't cause that level of dust!" Sergeant Bullen had walked across to Henry. "That must be cavalry."

"And cannon perhaps?"

"What was that, Sherborne?" Blades-Robson called from his position eight paces ahead.

"Sir, I just wondered if the level of dust meant they were moving their cannon to oppose us on our flank. It will weaken the centre considerably."

"Precisely, Corporal, good thinking. The scout is reporting this back to HQ as we speak." Henry turned and saw the lone rider now cantering towards the main army; good news always travels fast for the carrier has the heart to speed it.

The clash happened a half-hour later at a crossing of the river that Henry later learned was called Rossnaree. The wheeling back to the Duleek crossing that Blades-Robson had so carefully planned, never happened. Instead, Henry found his section, indeed the whole company under Blades-Robson, in support as Meinhardt's cavalry forced their way across the river at Rossnaree. It was Barceau, the Huguenot captain who had shared his trunk with Blades-Robson in Meinhardt's tent, that slogged on to Slane and crossed there. Henry's fight was at Rossnarce and it almost went horribly wrong.

Battles turn on a sixpence, of course, and this one almost went the other way. James had, reluctantly, done one thing right. Late the evening before, he had given way to the urgings of his subordinate commanders and sent a strong cavalry detachment under Sir Neil O'Neill to defend the Rossnaree crossing. This man fought like someone possessed, like the berserks of old, and a living, shining example to the capable mounted soldiers under his command.

Sir Neil went a long way towards countering the damage done by James. But he was just one commander of many and his main enemy was not the opposing army but the expectation of failure in the forces behind him.

Henry was first in the water, thinking if he was not prepared to plunge in, how could he expect his men to? The water was cold, despite the warm day. It was deep, rising as he waded out to the centre, musket and powder bag held above his head. But it was not the coldness nor the depth that made an enemy of the river. It was the current that caught any man not sure-footed and sent him violently downstream, thrashing for a foothold on the muddy river bottom.

And while they were in the river, they were sitting ducks to be picked off one at a time. Not only was James' infantry moving into position and firing volleys into the rushing river but Sir Neil's cavalry could plunge in and strike.

And the soldiers in the river could not even run away. They were caught, virtually stationery targets for the bullets, sabres and lances bearing down on them.

Henry had ensured each of the men in his section, several of the other sections too, had loaded their muskets before entering the river. That would give them one shot each, for they could not hope to reload mid-stream.

He and Sergeant Bullen worked as a team. Bullen stayed on the far bank to organise the men, section at a time, into ranks to wade in, reminding them to watch for the current. Two sections remained with him on the northern bank and gave covering fire. Henry, in the middle of the river, now in flowing water almost up to his armpits, shouted out orders with two purposes in mind. The first was to keep the men moving through the river in order, ten men, one section, making a line. The second purpose was to call each section in turn to lower their muskets and fire, not haphazardly but as a concentrated volley.

The far bank was steep at that spot, unlike the slow slope that had gradually introduced them to the swift running water, still full of winter snow and spring rain.

And then there was the opposition trying to force them back into the water. Henry's first attempt was repelled with a vicious stab of a pitchfork, the blades lodging either side of his arm and pushing him back into the river. Without thinking, he grabbed the pitchfork handle and pulled on it; the Irish soldier came tumbling down in to the river. A soldier in the rank behind pushed the body underwater, drowning him in a fit of violent struggles.

"Thank you," called Henry, his voice hoarse from shouting commands to his section and the others.

"They're peasants," the soldier replied breathless from his effort. "Nothing but farm tools to fight us with."

Henry took this in, thought how to take advantage. They had first to gain a foothold on the bank. He looked up and down the river.

"This way," he cried. "To the tree." Ten yards downstream was an old oak, slipping into the water from erosion of the river's edge. "Grab the roots and haul yourselves up," he shouted, although his order seemed drowned in the noise of war.

Fugini was the first to react, taking his small and wiry frame up the bank with ease.

"It's easy, right foot on this root, left hand on the branch and swing up."

Henry called to the next man, the heaviest in his section, "Don't worry about what's up there. The trunk of the tree gives you protection and Fugini's got you anyway." Henry was right; both the tree and Fugini meant none of the enemy could endanger them as they climbed out of the river. Henry went third after giving instructions to the others. Within a minute and a half, the whole section was established on the bank.

Henry called to Corporal Bing to bring his section up next, only Bing seemed not to hear and ordered his men to retreat instead. One was swept away by the current, three others stumbled into the third section and several people went down into the water.

"Hold on, face the enemy, quick march!" Bullen called through the confusion, steadying nerves. "Bing, take your men to Sherborne. Surely you can see he's got a foothold on the far bank? Make something of it, man!"

It took twenty minutes but they got over one hundred men up by 'Sherborne's Tree' and settled in several defensive semi-circles around the area.

"Advance!" called Bullen. "Keep in line, not too fast, steady goes it. Our first objective is to advance on Duleek. Let's make history, boys!" Henry was in the first line, Bing in the second row, directly behind him, not looking at all as if he wanted to be a part of any history creation.

The hurried plan Sergeant Bullen had put into place after consulting with Blades-Robson and the CSM was for the third and fourth lines of their formation to spill out either side of the first two lines in order to lengthen the attack as they moved forward from the tree. Henry, waiting for orders, noticed that the lieutenant was limping badly while the CSM, the next in command should Blades-Robson fall, had a rough bandage around his head in place of his hat.

"Damned musket ball," he mouthed when he caught Henry staring at him.

They walked at a steady advance, covering ten then another ten paces. The enemy seemed to melt away before them, as if they were little people and could make their bodies evaporate like morning mist. They seemed to roll back each time the Williamite forces advanced. Were they terrified? Yet Henry sensed some order in the rabble, as if some external force was controlling everything.

"They're luring us forward," he cried, hoping the still day would allow his words to reach more senior ears behind him. Certainly, he was not going to take his eyes off the front, other than the quickest raking glances side to side. No, the sides were not a problem; the attacking lines were spreading out nicely to prevent any flanking movement by the enemy. In a moment, the cavalry would be over on this bank, then followed by the main force of the right wing of the attack. They only had a handful of minutes to hold on while the real strength got established. They were doing their job; another ten paces were advanced.

"Fifty yards to go, lads," called the CSM. Blades-Robson was quiet throughout, limping badly, dazed by whatever had struck him. But knowing his duty and plodding on.

Another five paces, five more yards accomplished.

It was Parker who saw the trap first. The line was not quite straight and he was the furthest forward, pushed a little by Bing's constant whine behind him.

"It's getting really soft going here, Corp.," he shouted. He took one more step, sunk a foot into the bog and this step saved his life. The musket shot had been aimed at his head. It passed two inches over its sunken target and hit the man behind straight in the chest. The soldier screamed, a single unvarying pitch that seemed to last forever. Then he dropped to the ground, his bulk hitting Fugini and knocking him over into the swamp.

That was the signal for general firing from the enemy. All of a sudden it was chaos. Far worse than the river crossing, men were stuck in the bog up to their knees. When they freed their feet, they found their boots clogged with a rich, black mud that clung to everything and doubled the weight they had to move forwards. Soldiers started dropping. Henry urged on the front rank under his command, knowing that some would die before they got to settled ground.

"We've got to get over this and find firm ground," he called. "We can do it, lads. Men have achieved more with less promise before. Don't let us be remembered with shame, boys, it is only one final effort to glory!"

Thankfully, the Jacobite infantry was poorly trained and ill-equipped. Only one in three had a firearm and some of those dated back to the Civil War. The rest of James' infantry could only wave their pikes and pitchforks and wait for this advance company to come to them. True, the cannon were being pushed into place but the same spread of swamp swept around in an arc to the south making it even harder to move them into range.

It was a hundred-yard slog through the mire, at the end of which five hundred pitchforks leered down at them; not the happiest of prospects.

Afterwards, Lieutenant Blades-Robson wrote a report on his piece of the battle. It was full of extremes but the two of most note were the steady, plodding and inspiring courage of Corporal Sherborne and the wild and disconcerting panic of Corporal Bing.

Henry was one of the first to reach the stable ground where James' army waited for him. He dealt with several peasant-soldiers by pulling them into the bog by the shafts they poked wildly at him. Once down, they were hacked to pieces by his followers. When Henry heaved himself up, Parker, Fugini and Bullen were already there. They provided protection while Henry pulled up another dozen or so soldiers. The first rank of the enemy dropped their pitchforks, raised their hands in the air and fell to their knees. They looked a pathetic assembly of farmhands, not an army at all.

"Don't kill them," Henry shouted, but it was too late. Bing, newly arrived on the certain ground, lunged forwards and stabbed his bayonet at two of them. They could not run, nor could they dodge the clumsy blows, for they were on their knees. "Don't kill," Henry shrieked again. "We must question them."

Henry's plan was brilliant, especially so as it was made on the spur of the moment. He pulled Bing off the already dead man he was puncturing repeatedly and held him back while he explained his idea breathlessly to those in charge.

"Cavalry get through, must be a path, hidden path. Question the prisoners not kill."

Blades-Robson seemed to rally; Henry never knew it but his plan had buoyed the wounded officer to new effort. He called for the CSM.

"He went down in the bog, sir. I can see his body now."

"Bullen, question the Irish like Sherborne says." At that point, he toppled over, fainting from loss of blood from the vicious wound to his right leg. A lone Irish soldier saw his opportunity. He stood and charged at the fallen officer, grabbing Blades-Robson's sabre and raising it to strike.

But Parker was even quicker, not that his actions did him any good. He ran forwards, tripped on a root and took the slashing sabre on his neck. Henry bayonetted the Irish soldier then turned to see the lifeless stare of Parker looking up at heaven and two blackbirds in a branch above him.

"Brave man!" said Blades-Robson, somewhat recovered now and picking himself off the ground by rolling from underneath the dead soldier. "I owe…" But now was not the time for reflection so he shook it off and returned to the main purpose; how to get the cavalry and then the main body of infantry across the bog without suffering as the advance force had done.

They took the oldest looking and the youngest looking captives and Sergeant Bullen questioned them severely for several minutes. All the while, Henry was right behind them, holding back a furiously angry Corporal Bing; a pertinent reminder of what the prisoners could look forward to if they did not co-operate.

"Where is the path through the bog?" It was the only question they really had to have the answer to.

Henry had expected the younger man to give in first, yet it was the older soldier who told them what they needed to know.

The first cavalry unit through the bog stopped as they passed Blades-Robson's exhausted troops, still formed in defensive positions on the firm ground. Their very young lieutenant called over to them.

"You've done pretty well for damned foot-sloggers. Now, take it easy and let us clear up the mess!" He kicked his horse, then pulled on the reins when he heard Henry's voice.

"How's the rest of the battle going, sir?"

"Didn't you hear, my man? King William gave the order not half an hour ago for a general advance. The Duke's forces must be crossing the river this very minute. They're in the centre, while most of the rest of the cavalry are out on the other wing. I dare say it will be over in a couple of hours so keep your spirits up, lad."

It was not over in a couple of hours, proving that expectation, however fine and nobly meant, is just another emotion playing upon the human race.

But the Battle was won.

Or rather, James had lost.

Chapter 18

Thomas barely ever left Amelia's room, sitting night after night, often with Milly in attendance. The hours had stretched into days and Amelia's ragged breathing was the only sign of life remaining.

They frequently felt for a pulse, Milly becoming expert at seeking it out when Thomas was in despair.

"Hold, sir, I think I have it," she would cry into the still, warm air. Then she would rise and adjust the windows or straighten the bedclothes while Thomas wiped the sweat from Amelia's face.

"We should wash her, sir." And activity gave them purpose as they waited for salvation.

There were several false starts to that salvation, evidenced by horses or carriages clattering up the drive. Each time, Thomas rushed to the window. Milly noticed how his shoulders slumped when he recognised a casual visitor or someone arriving on business.

Mr Milligan arrived, drafted once more out of retirement into the building business that bore his name, seeking Thomas for some decisions on major projects.

"Not now, Sara," he said when the maid came up to Amelia's bedroom to announce Mr Milligan's arrival. "Maybe tomorrow, or the day after."

Surprisingly, it was young Milly who took Thomas to task.

"Go, sir. Miss Mealy would not want you neglecting important business matters." Thomas looked at her, wondering what stuck out from her imploring statement. It was only afterwards, on the way back up the stairs following the brief meeting with Mr Milligan, that it came to him. Milly, a junior maid, had used Amelia's nickname, albeit it with a 'Miss' posted in front of it. He could not help but chuckle, despite everything, as he crossed the upper hallway and opened the bedroom door.

"Hello, sir, sir, sir!" Milly was excited. "She just opened her eyes, sir. Miss Mealy opened her eyes, sir. She looked right at me and I swear she smiled."

Thomas rushed to her bedside, knocking Milly so that her slight body wobbled and fell against the bed, her elbow landing in Amelia's stomach.

It was a trigger, a wonderful trigger. Amelia opened her eyes again, looked at Thomas and smiled before dark shadows came over her face. She tried to rise, was too weak and sunk back into her nightmare again. It was his reward, his kernel of hope for the future.

"You opened your eyes, my Mealy, I saw you looking right at me!" Thomas was all attention to Amelia for quite some time, not noticing the dance Milly did across the bedroom floor, out of the door onto the landing.

"Miss Mealy has woken!" she cried down the stairs, her thin voice bubbling with joy.

Amelia's bedroom was soon full of people, excited chatter broke the sombre mood like the snap of relief when one wakes from a bad dream. But Amelia did not perform; her bad dream was not ending yet. She slept on, her pulse weak and her breathing ragged. No eyes were opened, no smiles for her friends and family, just the steadily sinking despair of illness gaining its grip.

There is something terrible about the brief uplift of hope in an otherwise spiral downwards. It raises the spirits to absurd heights, making the inevitable slide more pronounced than ever. And then traces of that uplift linger tauntingly, like the memorised touch of a lover long gone.

Sally jumped from the cart and thanked the farmer for the lift, pulling her bag behind her.

"How will you get back, miss?" No-one on the estate really knew how to address Sally Black. She was lady's maid, assistant-steward and special companion to the dowager-duchess, all rolled into one. The farmer fell back on politeness and respect; it was the easiest way.

"I'm staying in Dorchester a few days, Mr Hopper." She held the bag in front of her as if presenting evidence in a court of law. "You'll be going back after the market, I expect?"

"Yes, miss. My lad's coming down on Friday if that is any help? Shall I get him to call here at Mr Amiss' house to see if you are ready to return?"

"That would be very kind, Mr Hopper."

She turned to see Amy Tabard waiting at the door.

"Welcome, Sally."

"It is kind of you to invite me to stay, Mrs Tabard."

"Please call me Amy and my husband is Paul." As if summoned by mention of his name, the door to the ground floor business room opened and Paul strode out.

"Sally, it is a pleasure to see you." He hesitated, similar to old Mr Hopper, before bowing to Sally. In return, she curtsied but not quite as deeply as usual. "Will you please come this way? There are some people I would like you to meet." Paul stepped to one side of the doorway to allow passage for Sally.

The room had once been a dining room and the walls were painted a deep pink. It set off a particular hue in the wooden floor perfectly. Sally, used to cleaning and tidying, noted the heavy scratch marks on the floor where presumably the dining table had been moved back and forth to clean around. Now the room contained two large and ornate desks, remarkably similar in appearance, against two of the walls. Plus there were a half dozen upright chairs in a semi-circle in the centre of the room. Sally wondered whether they had been the original dining chairs. Then she forgot the furniture and started paying attention to those present.

Mr Fellows caught her eye first because he was ancient yet, on second glance, she picked up on something else. Was it gentleness or wisdom or kindness? Or all of them? He wobbled as he rose on introductions, thankfully leaning on his stick and quickly returning to the safety of his seat.

"The body fails but the mind goes on," he said.

"And the spirit that binds the two, sir."

"Well said, Miss Black. This is my dear friend, Mr Jarvis."

"We have met," Sally replied. "Last year, when Great Little was struggling under a burden of debt and deception, you visited regarding some loans we had that were overdue. Actually, they were not so much loans as selling forward our harvest."

"I remember the occasion, Miss Black, but sadly not meeting you."

"I served coffee in the library, sir. It was intended that I should not be noticed."

"Yet Sally was the mastermind behind the idea of selling the harvest forward," Paul said. "I helped her a little with the contracts but it was her idea entirely. For this achievement along with several others that saved the Great Little estate, she was made assistant-steward earlier this year."

"You present me in too great a light, sir, and correspondingly it dims the great contribution you made."

But the big introduction of the day was between Sally and Anne Aspley, the occupant of the last chair, set under the window. She looked shy when they gave brief curtsies and Sally took the seat next to her. But the shyness did not last.

"I asked to have the chair next to you," she whispered as the others settled in their seats. "I want very much to get to know you."

Sally nodded with a smile, not sure what else to say.

Paul called the meeting to order.

"Ladies and gentlemen," he started, smooth as ever, "the purpose of this meeting is to discuss the next stage of development of a particularly interesting business opportunity which, by virtue of your presence here today, you are cordially invited to take part in. I should add that Mr Amiss, whose house this is and is known to you all, has pledged £500 for shares in this investment. Sadly, Mr Amiss is ill and unable to be with us at present."

"But he also sends his very best wishes to everyone and to the success of the venture."

"Well said, Amy my dear." Paul looked lovingly at his wife for a moment before continuing. "The particular business opportunity we have in mind is to expand the capital of a fledgling insurance operation of some considerable promise. Fellow men and women of business, I now call upon Anne to explain further."

The proposal was simple. Aspley and Associates had underwritten several voyages over the last few weeks. "We are to be specialist marine insurers," Anne explained. "We have insured four projects with no loss and one where, sadly, one of the sailors died in a storm. Following Mr Fellows' long practice and shining example, our insurance includes a small pension for the families of those lost at sea. That same voyage also resulted in some damage to a cargo of wheat. The total loss, including the capital value of the pension, is just under £400. However, against that we have fees from the five shipments insured totalling just over £800."

"A profit of over £400! Sorry, I did not mean to shout out."

"No Sally, it is fine to do so," Mr Jarvis spoke now. "The problem is about the risk. We can easily afford to pay smaller losses but the total loss of a ship will run to many thousands, more than wiping out our capital and thereby preventing us from staying in business."

"You want to raise capital against that eventuality?" Sally asked.

"Exactly, Sally. The founding members are Anne, Mr Fellows, the Tabards and myself. This amounts to capital of £12,000, either paid or pledged. We seek to raise another £3,000 or more, of which Mr Amiss has put up £500."

"I have no money, sir," Sally said.

It was Anne who answered her. "Yes, we imagined that to be the case. However, you represent two principals who have access to wealth. You are assistant-steward to the Great Little Estate and you are…"

"Companion to the Dowager-Duchess of Wiltshire." Sally finished the sentence for Anne, helping her avoid the embarrassment of touching upon Sally's complicated relationship with Penelope.

"And," Anne continued, "Paul speaks most highly of you and of the way the Dowager-Duchess helped him set up Tabard and Co."

"It was a contract in which Paul fulfilled his side and the dowager-duchess hers." Sally said the words but they could have come from Penelope herself. Sally recognised the arrogant mask behind every act of kindness; the pretence that it was just duty or business. It was Penelope's mask lent to her to hide behind.

It made her think what would Penelope do in this situation? Would she commit her remaining capital, perhaps cutting back on the horse purchases, to make it available? She knew Lady Roakes had little money, yet Penelope had purchased a share in Tabard and Co for her benefit alongside her own. Should she make a similar commitment now to Aspley and Associates?

She looked at the associates. Mr Jarvis had been firm but kind when discussing the outstanding payments with Penelope. Sally had sold the harvest forward but then half the wheat had burned in a great fire in the Home Farm barn, making the contract impossible to fulfil. Mr Jarvis had listened to the whole story and then unpicked the contract, breaking it down into two parts. One was fulfilled by the delivery of the remaining wheat. The other was converted into a loan that Penelope had then repaid with the proceeds from pawning her jewellery; jewellery she still had not regained possession of.

She knew Amy and Paul Tabard quite well. They had often been to Great Little, first to help when the estate was under terrible threat from Parchman and his evil plans. Then, when Penelope had set Paul up in business, they had come regularly to discuss matters with his two fellow shareholders. Penelope had been insistent on Sally being present at these meetings, trying at first to uphold the appearance of Sally being a maid waiting on them, then abandoning all pretence and simply referring to Sally as her friend. The Tabards were rock solid as business partners and she did not doubt them at all. By extension, Mr Amiss, whose house the Tabards shared, must be a fine partner.

That left Mr Fellows and Anne Aspley, both unknown to her before today. The former was well over ninety, the latter around nineteen; opposite ends of life. She looked at them and made a decision.

"May I have a private word with Mr Fellows and Mr Jarvis?"

The others rose to leave, promising to return in the morning. Anne gave a warm smile, placing her hand on Sally's shoulder.

"Go easy on Mr Jarvis," she said, "he has not the strength of Mr Fellows!" It raised light laughter all around, evidencing the tension. They clearly wanted the investment. Dare Sally make such a commitment? As the room cleared, she went through the numbers again. Penelope had £4,000 left of the £10,000 she had inherited, having made a new investment of £6,000 in Great Little. She had that morning sent her lover to Sherborne to buy some excellent horses for breeding. They had agreed always to keep a reserve in order never to be in such difficult straights as they had been the previous year. But they had never discussed what would be a reasonable reserve? Maybe £1,000? Now she was being asked to invest £2,500 into Aspley Associates. That would leave just £500 for the horses. Perhaps Lady Roakes could put up a hundred but then there was the pawned jewellery to pay off.

The numbers just did not add up.

But, she reminded herself, fortune favours the brave.

She wished desperately for Penelope's presence. She realised now that she had sent her to Sherborne, even laying out the dress she knew she hated as being stiff and uncomfortable, as an exercise in control.

But how on earth does control sit comfortably between two lovers? She felt foolish on her own, more arrogant than her arrogant mistress, more presumptuous too. She ached for Penelope.

How would she decide? Should she climb down and meekly say she would report to her mistress and let her mistress make the decision? Perhaps that was for the best.

"Sally?" Sally sat up straight, as if being told off for slouching. "I believe you were miles away. Too many worries, perhaps?"

Sally had intended questioning the pair of them, praising herself in advance for her astute judgement and perception, reporting back to Penelope in a blaze of pride afterwards, saying something like, "I made the decision after careful questioning and I do believe it is for the best." And Penelope would agree because Penelope agreed with everything Sally did and wanted.

Instead, she found herself pouring her innermost thoughts out to Mr Fellows and Mr Jarvis, both of whom had built success in their lives by listening carefully to others.

When she had finished and every probe and point had been teased out and examined, she felt exhausted but as light as the trap Penelope drove at speed around the lanes. Both men left, saying, like their friends, that they would return in the morning. Sally sat back down on her upright chair, feet dangling just above the floor. By rocking her feet, she could press either her toes or her heel to the floor, but not both at the same time. It seemed to reinforce how junior she was, like a child sitting for a special occasion on a chair too big for her. For a long time she sat and examined her feet from the sitting position, not wanting to leave this limbo and face the real world again. There had been much encouragement from Mr Fellows and Mr Jarvis.

But also many warnings.

Finally, she got off the chair and went to the door. She went upstairs to the drawing room to find Paul and Amy waiting for her there.

"Mr Jarvis thought you might take a while coming to a decision. Do you need to consult with Lady Roakes and the Dowager-Duchess?"

"No, I've made my decision and this is what I would like to do."

Chapter 19

"You know Corporal Bing's complaint will have to be taken seriously?" Sergeant Bullen looked worn out. Henry, seeing his weary features, could only imagine that he looked the same. They had fought the same battle, experienced the same horrors and seen the same deaths. Even their levels of injury were comparable. Bullen had a bloody bandage around his head and a stab wound in his right leg that hurt badly when he tried to walk. Henry had his arm held with two musket straps making a sling. He also had a grubby bandage covering his right hand.

"The lieutenant will need to speak to you about it." Henry nodded, too tired to care; let the authorities do as they will. The two missing fingers on his right hand meant he would be going home regardless. The only question was whether it would be an honourable or dishonourable discharge.

"I believe I acted for the best, Sergeant."

"I know it only too well, Corporal." There was a boyish grin surrounding his words, something Henry had not seen before in this serious man.

They had followed orders but combined it with a dose of initiative. It was this initiative that Bing exclaimed so angrily against. Initiative was anathema to a certain type of career soldier such as Bing. One of his favourite stories when on the parade ground was a tale about two very different soldiers.

"What happened to Private Initiative?" he would bellow.

"He came a cropper at the first hurdle," the ranks would chime back, once they had learned the right response.

"And what happened to Corporal Obedience?"

"He got a medal for following orders, Corporal."

"And lived to a ripe old age into the bargain."

Another was, "We don't want no bleedin' heroes, instead we depend on the dependable types". There were several others, all revolving around the fact that the army was not a place to tolerate individuality.

"You left your bleedin' character at the recruitment office," he would say, as if the soldiers he was drilling were wooden toys and he had painstakingly lined them all up in neat, motionless rows until the sweep of history knocked them over.

Which, in a way, was true.

Blades-Robson had given the order to move back to the east, but this time along the southern bank of the River Boyne.

"We're going to do the same again, lads," he cried after twenty minutes' rest. The cavalry and the main body of the right wing were well established now at Rossnaree, although fighting continued sporadically as James' forces gradually moved back. "We've achieved what we set out to do here, thanks in no small part to your bravery and determination. Now we're going to create a similar bridgehead for the centre so they can get across the Boyne with minimum harm." Such was Blades-Robson's character that no-one questioned why they should do it all over again, risking their lives to enable others to cross the river in safety.

It was a good idea, in theory at least. Perhaps William's scouts should have known better. Perhaps they did but their voices were lost in the euphoria of the early successes that day. Whatever the reason, Blades-Robson led his company into a hellhole of fortifications, adapted and improved by the French engineers James had brought with him, or rather Louis XIV had insisted he take. The fortifications reminded Henry of a spider's web, luring them in and then pummelling them hard.

The Dutch contingent was first in the river from the centre, led by the Duke of Schomberg. They were brave and capable soldiers and waded out the other side, much as Henry and his colleagues had done on the right wing. Here they met the Earl of Tryconnell, filling in for James Stuart, who suddenly was nowhere to be seen. Tryconnell fought bravely, leading by example. It left people wondering how James could be commander-in-chief when absent from the field. Those same people started asking other even more serious questions about the man who would be king again.

Despite their valiant efforts, Tryconnel's troops were no match for the Dutch and fell back, just as they had earlier done by Rossnaree. It seemed the attack from the centre would be the right wing all over again; brave men wading through the river and subduing the enemy who were equally brave but lacked the equipment.

And the spirit instilled into hearts by leadership.

It was the Duke of Schomberg's turn to enter the Boyne and he did it with great bravado. He led the main body of the attack vigorously. He had motivation of a sort for his son, Count Meinhardt, was commander on the extreme right wing, leading the fight for Duleek. The count was beating his way from the right to the centre; slow progress due to the boggy terrain and fierce fighting from O'Neill's remaining troops. These heroes fought on without their leader, suffering huge casualties, for O'Neill had been cut down when the first cavalry charged through the river.

It was time for Schomberg to act; it would never do for the son to get to the centre ground and engage the enemy there before the father. This gave some urgency as he plunged into the water on his horse.

Henry could see Schomberg clearly from his position close up on the southern bank, formed into an arrowhead to fire on two sides, southeast and southwest. Henry was firing in the ranks, with Bullen taking command of the volleys on the southeast flank and another sergeant on the southwest. They fired in two ranks to allow time to load, giving Henry and the other quick loaders a few precious seconds each cycle to look around before the next order to aim was given.

That was how Henry saw that the duke was in serious trouble.

"Am I to understand that you broke ranks when you saw the duke being attacked?" Blades-Robson hung his weary head as he went through the motions.

"Yes sir." Remember, the inner voice told him, never say more than you have to and every sentence has a sir or two dotted somewhere within it.

"Tell me what you saw." That was a difficult question to answer minimally.

"The Duke was attacked in the river, sir, by infantry and cavalry. Private Fugini and I broke ranks and went to help, sir."

"What did you think you could do, Corporal?"

Henry thought back to the scene at the height of the battle the previous day. It seemed so distant now, like he had gone to see a play at the theatre.

It had been around noon, not that he had checked his watch. He went by the sun that beat down on their heads as they fired and reloaded, fired and reloaded in a never-ending but ruthlessly efficient routine; certainly there was no time to consult his pocket watch. The duke had gone into the river to defend some Huguenots who were being attacked in force. The Dutch advance party for the centre had established a bridgehead on the far bank, just as Henry had done at Rosanaree but the cavalry could ride around them and plunge into the water, causing chaos as the subsequent Williamite forces tried to cross.

Then there had been a cry from the enemy that the duke was midstream and vulnerable. Tryconnel's mounted troops had rallied. Joined by some foot soldiers, they charged and soon were hacking at the duke's small contingent.

"We just went in, sir, without thinking. Fugini lost his arm, I got a musket ball in mine and an axe took off two of my fingers, sir." Henry recounted the injuries as if a kitchen boy at home, charged with memorising a shopping list of required ingredients. "Sir, Fugini's arm came clean off above the elbow from a sabre blow. He is in the sick bay right this minute, fighting for his life."

"Thank you, Sherborne. I shall attend on him and the other wounded presently, in fact as soon as this distasteful report is done."

Blades-Robson looked hard at Henry for a long moment, thinking two divergent things. He, too, had several wounds following his active role in the battle. The CSM, Parker and four others had lost their lives. Henry was more badly wounded than most, evidencing either his bravery or his stupidity. Yet Corporal Bing, who accused him of breaking rank, endangering the whole arrowhead and charging off against orders, had not a scratch on him. He looked at the battle's end as he did every day when marching off the parade ground.

The second thought was prompted by the first but took him off at a tangent. Henry Sherborne claimed to be an unemployed labourer but his smooth hands were evidence that this was not the case, as was his cultured voice and evident education. Why, then, had be joined as a private soldier before being promoted corporal when someone had the sense to acknowledge his nascent leadership skills?

"Thank you, Sherborne, that will be all."

It was only when Henry had turned smartly around and left the tent that it came to Blades-Robson.

"Corporal, come back," he called. Henry returned and saluted once more.

"You've lost two fingers, you say?" Blades-Robson looked at the bandaged hand.

"At least two, sir. The axe-blow got my thumb as well. I pray the thumb will survive.

"I pray too, Sherborne. You know that you will be discharged? We cannot have soldiers that cannot fire a musket."

"Sir."

"I have one final question for you, Corporal."

"Sir."

"What shall I call you when you turn in your corporal's stripes and get your coronet back again?"

Henry stared a moment, wondering how the lieutenant could have worked out his identity. Then he rallied, like a soldier in battle.

"I hope you will call me Henry, sir, like my friends do."

Blades-Robson started to laugh, yet it hurt the side of his face where the sword blow had taken a chunk of his left ear and sliced into his face, causing a bloody gash on his cheek.

"And my name is Perseverance but my friends call me Percy. Share a glass of something with me, Henry."

"I'd gladly do so." Henry was in a halfway house, the 'sir' was gone but he had not quite adopted 'Percy' in its place.

Inevitably as they drank they talked about the battle, concentrating on the second half.

"It's a sad loss," Percy started.

"It is indeed," Henry agreed, knowing instinctively that Percy was referring to Schomberg's death midstream in the Boyne. "There was nothing we could have done."

"Demonstrating the army's wisdom in actual fact, whereas everyone always assumes the army to be a stupid, cumbersome and uncaring thing. There was nothing you could do to save the Duke so you were more use maintaining the square and using your musket against the enemy."

"Yes, I see that now, with the benefit of hindsight."

"You must have seen the old man being killed?"

"Yes, the shot came from nowhere but caught him in the arm. He stopped momentarily, looked confused, as if after sixty years in uniform he still did not think it could happen to him." Henry sipped his whisky; it was excellent quality. Maybe he would ask Percy where he got it from and take a few bottles home with him.

"It's not Irish," he said. "It's made on our estate. Have you heard of Invergordon?"

"No."

"Inverness, then?"

"No."

"Oh dear, we will have to correct that when you come and stay."

"Is that an invitation? Excellent and I would be remiss in not issuing one to you in return, except it is not motivated by mere politeness but a desire for friendship."

"I know, Henry, I think we will be fine friends. Now, tell me more about what happened in the river."

It was quite a simple tale, did not take long in running through it, yet caused them to sip in contemplation for a quarter-hour afterwards. Schomberg had been thrown back by the musket ball in his arm but somehow had stayed in the saddle.

"Perhaps if he had fallen into the river at that point, he would still be alive today. His contingent was not quite surrounded at that point and could have probably dragged him back to the bank and to safety."

Henry went on to describe how Schomberg had recovered and urged his frightened horse on again, transferring his sword to his left arm and holding the reins between his teeth.

"He guided the horse with his legs mostly, I could see them working the horse's side to gain advantage over the enemy. He struck out several times with his left arm. Once he downed a brute of a man who died under his own horse's hooves." But the enemy's concentration on him meant he was doomed. They struck and struck again and soon Schomberg was hit with a sword. He recovered once more and struck out again in a marvellous display of bravery before the next blade hit him viciously on the head. He had rolled off his horse and fallen into the water where the swift running river washed the blood from his body. There had been nobody left from his immediate contingent to rescue him so Schomberg's life was dragged out of him by the swift-running Boyne, the river that gave its name to the battle that was the duke's last.

"It produced a rage amongst our side and the enemy was pushed straight out of the river," Henry concluded. "In fact, it was almost as if the Duke had given up his life in a trade for victory, for the centre soon after took complete control and James Stuart's troops moved back thereafter."

"The day was won but the life was lost. That sounds rather poetic, don't you think?"

Percy wrote his report, adding in a postscript that Henry had displayed huge courage and leadership throughout the battle. He strongly recommended an honourable discharge.

The court martial, held on the 8th, was brief, many cases to handle in its sole day of sitting.

"I applaud your bravery, Corporal, but can never condone any man deserting his post and conducting himself as he sees fit. Where would the army be if it allowed everyone to do as they please?" He droned on, adding snippets of his own history in his one indulgence against the brevity of the proceedings. The old colonel looked so sombre that his gloom started to descend on Henry. "I am inclined to punish severely but the representations from your company commander are quite outstanding and I fear a custodial sentence to be too severe. Corporal Sherborne, you are fined six months of wages and hereby dishonourably discharged from His Majesty's service. Once the fine is paid, you are free to go."

Henry had not received any pay from the army to date and, in fact, never did. He happily paid the six months' fine, purchased some civilian clothes from a local doctor about his size and took temporary lodgings in Duleek with the same doctor.

"Why don't you go home, Henry?" Percy asked.

"I want to see Fugini better first," he replied, a plan developing for the now one-armed cook who held fiercely to life when many others with less serious injuries had given up on this world and moved to the next.

Chapter 20

Penelope waited on the seat of the trap drawn up at the side of the road.

"Is everything alright, Your Grace?" Peg called from behind.

"Quite so, except…attend on me a moment, Peg."

Peg jumped, first digging her brother in the side.

"Help the Duchess down, Johnnie," she whispered. They both scrabbled out of the rear-facing and backwardly-inclined seat and ran around to the front of the trap.

"Where're you going, Johnnie?" He was on the wrong side to help the dowager-duchess down. He ran around the back of the trap, boots clumping on the dry earth, while Penelope maintained some form of dignity by sitting ramrod straight and staring into the distance as if suddenly fascinated by the shapes of the oak trees that made the boundary to the next field.

"Thank you, my man." Penelope was clearly embarrassed. "Be so kind as to walk ahead a quarter mile and check for the turning to Sherborne Hall. I am concerned that we may have come along the wrong road."

"It's the right road for sure, Your Grace," Johnnie replied, thumping one heavy foot after the other as if testing the ground beneath his feet. "You see, I know this road because we grew up…"

"Go and check anyway."

"But…"

Suddenly, Peg realised what was happening.

"Your Grace, I have another idea. Could we not send Johnnie jogging on to warn the hall of your impending arrival? I am certain we do not have need of male company now we are just half a mile from our journey's end."

It was arranged in a second. Both Peg and Penelope watched Johnnie trot off until he disappeared behind the hedge.

"Can I be of assistance, Your Grace?"

"It is my dress." Free of a male presence, Penelope turned so that her back was presented to Peg. "Something has come loose."

"Ah yes, Your Grace, several hooks are apart and your overskirt needs adjustment." What Peg referred to as the overskirt was the stiff mauve netting that covered the dress completely from collar to hem. It was awry, one side sagging as most of the buttons and intricate bows that held it together had come undone.

"I fear driving the trap does not make for keeping one's attire in order."

"You were driving fast, Your Grace. Johnnie and I were fair bouncing along at the back!"

"It is the way I always drive." This Peg knew as a fact; the dowager-duchess' reputation for driving at speed was well known amongst the servants of Great Little.

"I'll have you adjusted in half a moment, Your Grace." Peg stared at the mass of dress folds, hooks, buttons and ribbons, not knowing where to start. But she made a job of it, of sorts, sometimes undoing parts she had just done up. She was reminded of a childhood game where they would tie one of them up as elaborately as possible and then count the time it took for them to struggle free.

"There, Your Grace, I think that will hold well enough." Peg had also straightened her stockings and retied the laces on the tall boots Sally had laid out for her mistress. "It is not, I think, the most comfortable dress for travelling."

"Thank you, Peg, but I do not need judgement on my lady-maid's dress sense."

"Of course not, Your Grace. I didn't mean to be rude, Your Grace." Peg blushed, looking to the ground, making Penelope wish she had not said those words. But apology was not something that came easily to her. Instead she waited for Peg to curtsey in acknowledgement of the error the young girl had made.

"We need to get going, Peg. Come and sit beside me." The tension was enormous, straining every nerve. It made Penelope feel a deep yearning for human contact, as was her way and so often unfulfilled before Sally. Peg was bony and, when Penelope shuffled up close, she poked into her side; it gave a degree of physical reassurance that at least partially satisfied that yearning. She ached, also, to tell of her concerns but could not bring herself to do so. Instead, she snapped the whip above the heads of the horses so that they moved off in a fast trot and the trap itself moved off down the road.

"How nice to see you, Penelope."

"Likewise, Your Ladyship. I hope my arrival is not inconvenient to you."

"No," laughed Grace, "it is not as if I did not have warning. First old Tomkins arrived early this morning, as grave as ever. Then, half an hour ago, Johnnie Peacock came, breathless from trotting up the drive to announce your imminent arrival."

"I did not want to arrive unannounced."

"You very thoughtfully gave me buckets of notice. In fact, enough time, should I be so inclined, to disappear out the back door and find some urgent reason to be away from here!"

"You do not want me here?"

"Of course, I am delighted to have your company. See, Penelope, I am here, waiting for you. My point was that I could have gone away but I chose to stay. I welcome the company and the chance to get to know you better." Grace sensed the awkwardness about Penelope, even more so than normal. She stood, not just on ceremony but on tiptoes. They could either play a game all visit long, dancing around, fencing words and phrases, with Penelope hiding behind her pride, or they could cut through it all and do as Grace expressed, get to know each other.

"Leave us please. I shall pour the tea, thank you." The maid curtseyed and the footman bowed, both withdrew.

"Penelope, you are most welcome here."

"Thank you, Your…"

"I attach two conditions to your welcome. First, you drop this ridiculous ladyship business. We have previously called ourselves by first names and I am determined to do so again, in order to be good friends. Do you agree to this condition?"

"I do."

"The second condition is that, as your new friend, you are honest with me at all times. I do not want my friends hiding behind a veil of insincerity or pride." To make her point, she stopped pouring tea, rose from her place and crossed to where Penelope sat. She pulled out hatpins, preventing Penelope from obstructing her efforts by standing very close to her. Then she took Penelope's hat from her head and placed it on the table with the tray of refreshments, the veil hanging over the side and making the hat wobble precariously on the edge.

"There, that is much better. I can see you so much more clearly." She looked into Penelope's eyes and saw the uncertainty, the worry. "You're not happy, are you?"

"I have some concerns, it is true." But Penelope was struggling to maintain her reserve. Then, quite suddenly, it collapsed, just as two large hooks on the back of her dress, probably dislodged by Grace's dress brushing against hers moments before, pinged open and her makeshift net overskirt peeled off like the skin of a lizard on a hot desert rock. Penelope stood up, awkwardly at first, then stepped out of the overskirt and kicked it to one side.

"I feel half-naked, Grace," she said, her mouth turning up.

"You look splendid," Grace replied, matching her mouth movement and catching her eye.

Then they were both laughing, giggling like girls. The footman and the maid, listening in turns at the keyhole, shrugged to each other and walked off, wondering at the ridiculous antics of the upper class.

The letter arrived the next morning, delivered by a special carrier who had galloped most of the way from Dorchester. Penelope broke it open without even seeing whose seal it was.

She knew it was from Sally and she knew it was important.

My dearest Pen,

I wanted you so badly yesterday. I was confronted with a decision on an investment, placing your inheritance at risk in the expectation of considerable reward. I was bound up in pride in sending you to Sherborne Hall while I took off secretly for Dorchester. Then, when faced with the facts on this investment, I just wanted to ask you, discuss with you and have you by my side to share the decision. I had a grand picture in my head about presenting you with the wonderful news of a new investment. But the reality was that I struggled so hard with the decision on my own. Loneliness was my leveller, Pen, my dear and it has brought me to my senses at long last.

Penelope placed the letter down for a moment, unable to take in what her lover was writing.

"Is everything alright?" Grace asked, seeing her pale face.

"It's Sally, my maid, I mean the assistant-steward of Great Little."

"Not more problems with the estate, I pray?"

"No, with an investment she was to make. I'll read the pertinent bits aloud."

I will relay the facts and then the decision I felt forced to make. The proposed investment is in Aspley and Associates, insurers of marine vessels and the goods they transport. Anne Aspley is young yet, with some help from Mr Jarvis, who you know, and a Mr Fellows too, has set up in insurance. The Tabards are also investors. They seek additional capital to cover risks and the returns, absent disaster, are very good indeed. They sought £2,500 from me, although as I pointed out to them, I have no money and Lady Roakes has little also. It would be your money going into this venture and I hesitated a long time because had I not just sent you to buy horses? Should I then be dashing off a curt note to you to say hold on the horses because I believe I have found a better use of your money?

"She *sent* you to buy horses?" Grace asked, the incredulity showing in her face.

"Yes, she is the business sense behind the scenes, hence she is now assistant-steward at Great Little. I know all about horses but rely on Sally for the business portion."

"But she sent you? Well, never mind. Continue, Penelope." The world seemed upside down when maids gave instructions to their mistresses. But Penelope had always been an unusual sort.

I thought long and hard and put several questions to Mr Jarvis and Mr Fellows, who were most helpful. After much consideration, I concluded that it was a solid venture indeed but that I did not have the right to ride over our decision to enter into horse breeding, especially as we had decided always to keep an amount in reserve to cope with nasty unforeseen events in the future. This investment would mean no reserve and probably not enough for all the horses we require.

"She goes on a lot about numbers next," Penelope said. "I think she is justifying her decision to me. But let the numbers be hanged!"

"What do you mean, Penelope? Let us go carefully through the figures and see what makes sense."

Penelope was reluctant to bend her head to the numbers, preferring to grant her beloved Sally whatever she wanted. But Grace was both insistent and persistent in making sense of it all.

"We should send the messenger back with a reply," she said after thirty minutes of concentration.

"What reply can we give?" Penelope asked.

"That we are coming on behind him and will be with them before nightfall. The message should be in your hand and should go to Miss Aspley, imploring her not to offer the shares to anyone else."

"You and me? We go to Dorchester together?"

"Yes."

"For what purpose?"

"To make the investment together, of course. You are not going to deny your newest friend a modicum of profit, are you?"

They made it long before nightfall, for Penelope drove her trap faster than ever before. They took a footman on the back-facing seat; he was bounced and jolted across every bump from

Sherborne to Dorchester. Grace explained more of her purpose as they trotted along the road.

"All 'those numbers', as you refer to them, showed that Sally decided against the investment for a lack of £1,000. I have that much to invest and Henry and I have been looking for something to do with it for a while. In his absence, I am sure he would be fine with me putting it into Aspley and Associates. So that is the obvious answer to the problem Sally Black has presented to you."

"The Earl is not here?" Penelope had been so tied up with her own concerns that she had not even noticed his absence.

"He is in the army, fighting in Ireland."

"But he's a Catholic, is he not?"

"He is a Catholic." Grace knew immediately what Penelope meant in asking this question; as a Catholic, he could not hold a commission. "He joined as a private soldier in May and left for Ireland two weeks ago. I pray every moment of every day for his safety and that somehow James Stuart gives up without a fight and scurries back to France."

"I thought you Catholics supported James Stuart as a Catholic king."

"Some do but many are more practical than that. This country is Protestant and no king, however devout or appealing, is going to change that fact. James was not a good king and brought much of his fate upon himself. We do not feel any loyalty towards him whatsoever. Besides, I was raised a Presbyterian."

"And you converted?"

"I converted in order to marry. Penelope, I'm one of those types that don't care for particular rules regarding the practice of religion. I think God loves a Calvinist every bit as much as a Catholic, or a Jew for that matter."

They drove on in silence for a while. Then Grace, unwilling to let the subject die completely, asked Penelope for her views on the matter.

"I don't concern myself with religion," Penelope answered. "I deal only with those things I can touch and feel." Like Sally's thin fingers tracing across her back.

The message sent on ahead had asked for everyone involved with Aspley and Associates to come to Mr Amiss' house. They arrived between six and seven in the evening, wondering why they had been summoned. The trap drew up at the front door at twenty-five to eight. Sally seemed shrunken as she curtsied to Grace and Penelope in the drawing room on the first floor. Introductions were made and seats taken, Sally reluctant to sit until urged to do so by Anne and Penelope, one either side and escorting her to a chair.

"Now, it would seem from the message I received earlier this afternoon, that there is some interest in this investment after all." Anne started the proceedings, her voice a little higher than usual then alternating in tone as she fought to control it.

"That is correct." Grace stood up as she spoke. "That is, if you would allow a further investor into your group. The proposal is that the £2,500 sought is split three ways. £750 will be held by the Dowager-Duchess of Wiltshire, £750 by her friend who is known to you." She paused at this point. She could not bring herself to mention the name, Lady Roakes, the captor and enslaver of her beloved friend, Lady Merriman, now Eliza Davenport, married to Matthew and residing at her family home of Bagber Manor. Thomas, her brother, had come closer to forgiving Lady Roakes for her cruel actions, perhaps assisted by the magnificent building contract she had given his firm, but Grace was some way behind.

Penelope shifted in her chair. The year before last, she had tried to broker some peace between the two parties but it had not worked out.

"And the remaining amount?" Mr Jarvis asked gently, knowing a little of the history between them.

"The last £1,000 would be held by my husband. I can have the funds transferred shortly, if you are in agreement with the Sherbornes being shareholders in your venture, Miss Aspley."

"I will ask the lawyers to draw up the papers tomorrow," Anne replied. "And if we are to be shareholders together, I would entreat you to become our friend as well. I am Anne."

"Grace," said Grace. "But there is one other price to pay for this solution, if I may dare mention it." Her young face had a cheeky twinkle as she tried to hide her grin. "Penelope and I are in need of beds for the night if anyone has some to spare!"

Chapter 21

D r Mowbray was adamant he should be paid the remainder
of his fee.

"And carriage back to London, sir," he demanded of Tristan,
who had to consult Bridget and Thomas for he had no money
of his own.

"It's a damned cheek!" Bridget fumed. "The man is a rogue.
He's done nothing for Mealy."

Thomas said nothing but went to the cashbox Mr Milligan
had brought him and pulled out a bunch of coins.

"How much did you agree?"

"Five guineas. And the coach to London is fifteen shillings
including lodging and meals overnight."

Thomas counted out £6, letting the coins fall one by one
onto the side table on which his cash box sat.

"Let's pay the quack and see the back of him."

"He was useless from the start, Thomas," Bridget complained.
"But if it is your decision to pay him, I will abide by my husband's
will as always." This was said stiffly so that even Thomas, awash
in his private concern for Amelia, looked at his wife closely
until the moment passed. Bridget would not look back at him,
preferring to make angles of her vision down the side of the
room and out to the gardens beyond.

Dr Mowbray had been a lot of hot air. He had arrived late
at the meeting point in London so they had missed the first
coach and had to wait for the next. He had talked the entire
first stretch about some complicated derangement of the mind
he had just solved, building their faith incredibly until he
overdid his claims and they started questioning why someone
so accomplished would be a mere assistant to another.

He was a fussy eater and one who was determined to dine in
private rather than in the common room at the inn, despite the
expense. On the first night, Bridget and Tristan had suffered

him at their table, only to agree in fits and giggles afterwards that he had no manners.

"Indeed, he has manners," Tristan corrected Bridget, "it is just that every single one of them is bad in the extreme."

The next night. Tristan had feigned illness and Mowbray was forced to dine alone, slurping and burping to the four walls of his room.

At each stop, however brief, he pulled bottles of medicine from his case and tried to sell them to fellow travellers. At one inn, the Homeless Pig again, Holly, the stand-in for the landlord who never seemed to be present, made such a fuss over the medicine-selling that Bridget and Tristan panicked, thinking Dr Mowbray would follow through on his threat to pack up now and catch the next coach back to London.

"Please, Holly, lay off the gentleman a little. We need his healing skills for our sick friend."

"I would as soon employ a village idiot as that man," she retorted. "Fancy putting your faith in him." A declaration which turned out to be all too true. But at that moment in time, all faith was not lost, although the doubts were working their way in. Besides, Bridget had another question to ask Holly.

"Did you send the message we left for Colonel Hanson?"

"Of course, Mrs Davenport. I was about to run and hire a messenger when that kind gentleman who was staying here said he would take it himself. He was going towards Sherborne."

"Which man?" Both Tristan and Bridget shared the same misgiving.

"The nice gentleman in the strange army uniform. He said he had a fast trap and could be there within the day. It was so kind of him to offer his services."

"Oh no!"

"Did I do wrong?" Holly was wondering whether her little money-saving initiative would be found out and the fee for sending the message demanded back. That morning they had paid for a smallholding on the Salisbury side of Andover. It had taken every penny they had saved. There was nothing left for refunds. "You seemed to know the man so I assumed it was a sensible thing to do."

"The note was about that man," Tristan groaned. "I think it highly unlikely that the note was delivered."

"Well, sir and madam, you should really have told me." Holly was the type who could not possibly be in the wrong; someone else would fill those shoes.

Once at Bagber Manor, Dr Mowbray was due to start work on his patient. They arrived at lunchtime and he caused some astonishment by insisting on eating several courses before seeing Amelia Grimes.

"I shall now retire a short while,' he announced, on standing up from the dining table. I pray I have a room that faces west, I so detest the early morning sun.

"Sara will show you to your room, sir. When might you attend upon Mrs Grimes?" Thomas asked.

"Who? Oh, the patient," said as if referring to a specimen in a laboratory, "I will attend to her directly after I have rested my weary bones. Travelling goes hard on me, sir."

"Well, what do you make of that?" Bridget asked, as soon as the door had closed behind him.

"It's as if he were dragging out the time until he has to see Mealy," Thomas answered his wife.

"Either he has no confidence about her affliction or…"

"Or he has to spend a certain period outside London," Thomas interrupted her.

"Why would one have to be out of the capital a certain period?" Eliza asked.

Matthew then spoke for the first time since they had sat down for lunch.

"There's no goodness in that man. He's out for what he can get from you. I sense deep selfishness. I strongly suspect he has a mountain of debts in London; that is the most common reason to flee the city."

"Quite the man of experience, brother dear!" called Thomas, for which comment he got a kick in the shins.

Dr Mowbray was leaving. He clinked the coins in his pocket as he climbed into Eliza's trap to take him to Shaftesbury and the London coach. He might dally a few days, maybe take a week's holiday in one of the inns on the way back, selling a few bottles of medicine to cover the extended stay. Once back in London with a couple more weeks come and gone, he would change lodgings and start again.

He looked out from the trap at mid-summer Dorset. The ripening wheat pushed up everywhere, fuelled by the sun which felt good on his back. This was what it was like to be in the country. The driver of the trap was a young man, full of talk about horses. He was saving up for some horse he kept referring to.

"I have just the thing to keep a noble horse in fine fettle," he said into the warm, strengthening sun. 'Fettle' had come to him as an inspired choice of word for horse-talk. It sounded equine to Dr Mowbray.

"What might that be, sir?"

Dr Mowbray did not answer, instead took a bottle of cough mixture from his bag and held it up to the light.

"I tell you what, my man, I'll let you have this for sixpence."

"But I don't have my horse yet, sir."

"Ah, but preparation is the key to success, young man. Just as the Good Lord said, 'be prepared for you know not the time or the day'. Imagine, young sir, you have just taken purchase of your fine mare…"

"I had thought to buy a stallion."

"Ah, even better then! You ride your stallion proudly home and place it in your newly-built stables. You notice it slightly off-colour and feel a rising panic at the possible immediate loss of your pride and joy; the culmination of your life's work."

"That would be terrible, sir."

"Yet, all is not lost, for you, young man, have had the foresight to be prepared for every eventuality. You go to the locked cupboard in your home, the one where your most precious articles are stored. You take down a bottle of Mowbray's Tincture for General Wellbeing. You measure out a spoonful – for that is all it takes – and add it to the oats…"

"I should not feed him oats, sir, rather a mash of bran and…"

"Well, whatever. You add the mixture and give it to the horse. The next day, he is right as rain and bursting to go. All because you had the foresight to purchase in advance and against the future need, a bottle of this fine supplement to happiness and health."

"I don't know, sir. I've never spent a penny of my savings in order to buy the horse that bit quicker, sir."

"What if I reduced the price to fourpence, just for you? You would thus be saving tuppence which would be a not inconsiderable addition to your horse-savings, would it not?"

The deal was done as the trap rattled up St John's Hill and it became warmer by the minute. Shaftesbury is a hill town, set proudly north of a great swathe of beautiful countryside. Dr Mowbray alighted at the Red Lion in the centre of the town and took a room for a few days. Why not stay a while and sell a few more bottles to brighten up the lives of a few of these simple Dorset folk?

It was almost like the final send-off, such was the level of despair amongst the gathering. Thomas was easily the worst affected, although all the friends and family felt it keenly. Eliza and Elizabeth both looked to be in mourning for their dear friend and, in the case of Elizabeth, also her step-daughter. Milly was there, standing outside the main circle as was appropriate for a servant, right behind Thomas, the man she worshipped. Gloom crowned them, sending its pervading fingers scratching and worming into every heart, rendering the spirit helpless and defeated. They had tried and they had failed. Was it now a case of watching the demise of Amelia Grimes?

Thomas stood out from the general despair with his own particular hopelessness. But another looked equally forlorn. Bridget loved Thomas completely and absolutely. She had been the driving force to go to London in an attempt to get the help they needed. The fact that no knowledgeable doctor, only a disreputable quack, would leave the lucrative city for the distant countryside was not her fault.

She had tried and she had failed. It did not escape her that her sorrow was second-hand, derived more from the misery of the man she loved than her concern for Amelia. True, what little time she had spent with Amelia had impressed her with respect for the woman but here she was trying to help her husband's first love. Had this been nature, resplendent in its naked cruelty, Bridget would have gone in for the kill by now; determined to see off her rival for all time. She contemplated how human artificiality stood outside the natural order of things. Then she prayed again to the God who had made the world and made man and woman to stand out from the other beasts by giving them a soul which He had filled with love.

Both the love from Him and the capacity to love others.

But then she wondered at His ability to seemingly give with one hand and take with the other. Why endow humans with love and then space out the resulting joy with tragedy? Why not, instead, leave us as simple beasts of nature, fighting for survival in field and hedgerow, amongst the trees and below the skies that make a dome under Heaven?

Was she losing the grasp she had always had on her simple faith?

Amelia chose that moment to stir, shaking Bridget and others back from dark thoughts to the hard reality of illness. Her eyes fluttered but did not open, fluttered again and did open. But it was so quick that some did not even take it in. Thomas saw and he squeezed Amelia's hand, laid out in a medieval posture of death on top of the sheet, as if she were a cast for the tombstone of an ancient aristocrat.

But Milly, standing directly behind her hero, saw his other hand do something completely different. It scouted out, feeling its way, to find the left hand of Bridget, standing next to him. He clasped that hand and Milly saw the grateful and loving look that this strangely pretty lady gave her husband in return. Their eyes met and made a sort of love in the midst of all that despair.

Milly did not understand what she had witnessed; she just ached for someone to give her that type of bond, that great big volume of love that her heart, beating wildly in her slight body, was more than capable of bouncing right back.

Despair is a very strong emotion; one of the strongest. Amelia did no more fluttering of the eyes, no more tiny signs of hope.

And Milly, standing behind her hero, noticed both his hands slipping away from contact. He folded Amelia's cold hand under the sheet and needed his right hand to accomplish the task, relinquishing the grip he had on Bridget's hand. When all was done, the mood had moved to new depths and he did not seek Bridget's hand again.

Although Milly was quite sure that Bridget would have taken it.

Chapter 22

The plan was ingenious, more so because there had been no plan just moments earlier. Later on, in another place altogether, Simon had time to contemplate. He considered that this plan represented a summit of all his lifelong efforts; it was a natural conclusion to his fifty-plus years on this earth.

"My lord, we clearly need an alternative to the wild recklessness of Sir William." He was referring to Sir William Phips, the new major-general in the Massachusetts colony, an adventurer of the first order of whom many legends were told, even in his own lifetime. "He may have enriched the purse of King William but he is hardly a strategist for war." His ability to find sunken treasure was second to none. The king had helped finance one venture and gained enormously from it.

"And you are a strategist, Captain Taylor?" That was a simple question to answer, one he had anticipated and rehearsed on the voyage over from New England.

"Yes, my lord. I may look an unlikely soldier but my field commission should attest to hidden talents in this direction. Six short weeks ago, I was a common private soldier. Six weeks before that, I stood a condemned man, sentenced to be transported to the Americas for my crimes. Consider, my lord, that no one could rise from such depths to such relative heights without some considerable talent previously unknown." It was an excellent argument, echoes of Cartwright's own rapid rise, but not quite enough.

"How do I know that you are not an imposter?" And this is where the first stage of the inspiration came in, the pre-inspiration as it were.

"My lord, you know me from the past." Simon still could not remember where or how he knew Cartwright but was certain that he did.

"True, sir, we both worked for Parchman, I remember you well." So that was it; Cartwright, now a lord, had been the oily part of the duo that had carried out Parchman's orders. The man was babbling on about rising much higher than Parchman ever had but Simon was not listening, rather he was thinking back to those glorious days of intrigue and scheming, underhanded in every way.

But then he thought of Amelia, lying half-dead in her bed at Bagber Manor. And the man who prided himself on his total lack of principles, knew regret for the first time.

"But, Taylor, you need to demonstrate your recent and rapid success. Taylor, do you hear me?"

"Sorry, my lord." He had to ask for the question to be repeated, which Cartwright did with impatience.

"That's easy, my lord." He passed the commission paper over, unrolling it so Cartwright could see the careful handwriting of Davidson's aide. "Major Davidson is the younger brother of the Duke of Wiltshire, my lord. His letter of introduction to the duke included some family code that I know nothing about. This was why His Grace accepted me and took me in." That and the delicacies he had purchased in Bristol, now all consumed by the duke.

"Can you get me some more when in London, my dear fellow? There is a delightful shop in the street next to St Paul's." The request came back to Simon now as a reminder of tasks still to perform.

"I am satisfied," Cartwright said. "Now to the plan. You want to have Phips dismissed and replaced with a more capable, or should we say cautious, commander?"

"Yes, my lord." He opened his mouth to explain and this is when the main body of inspiration tumbled out.

"Remarkable," Cartwright sighed, appreciating the ingenuity, working out how to present it as his own. "Leave it with me and call back this time tomorrow."

"Yes, my lord. I look forward to resuming discussions in the morning." He would visit the shop near St Paul's that afternoon. He had plenty of money still from the allowance Davidson had given him plus the money he had asked the duke for; it had been a grudging gift but a gift nevertheless. It would do no harm to return a little portion of that gift to the odious duke.

The horse market was heaven on earth, more so because Penelope and Sally went together, sharing every single moment. They had missed the first day but they discovered that very little had gone on other than looking, sounding out what was on offer. The auction ring was only open on the second day.

"We will listen to the first few sales to get an idea of how the system works," Penelope said. Sally was content to agree, glad to belong next to Penelope, to be a part of her.

"Have you been to an auction before, Your Grace?" Sally asked, using her correct title as there were so many strangers around.

"No, Sally, and you?" Likewise, there was no 'dearest' or 'darling' in her address.

"Only the one, Your Grace."

"Was it a horse sale or other livestock?"

"It was other livestock, Your Grace. We all fetched quite handsome prices."

"Oh, I'm sorry, that was thoughtless of me."

"It matters not for I am free now."

Penelope did not answer for she alone knew the truth; her dearest lover was also her legal property and there was a paper to prove it. As Penelope moved to examine the horses on offer, hiding her confusion under a veneer of strained concentration, she did not consider the obvious, that there were levels of freedom; it was a quality that came in many varieties.

Penelope proved her expertise in horses over and over again. She turned away two gorgeous palomino stallions where the reserve was £60 each.

"We need browns, nice rich chestnuts for the main breeders," she pronounced, explaining to Sally's inevitable question that she preferred this colour on horses. "And if we are to breed, we must produce not just fine horses but lovely colours as well, for it is the good-looking ones that will get the best prices!" Just as

Sally must have raised a record price at sale some years before Penelope first knew her.

A moment later, Sally pointed out a fine horse that would seem to match all requirements.

"No, he won't do at all," Penelope said in a loud voice. "See, his feet are too large while he has a clumsiness about him. I fear he will be inclined to stumble when he is running. The purchaser of this horse will not be happy to spend £30 or £40 only to have to take a gun to the poor brute's head. I predict this animal will break a leg in the first ditch he is tried on. And what would that do for you reputation, Mr...?

"Carter, Your Grace." The poor man looked miserable to have the faults of his prize horse enunciated at high volume across the crowd of visitors. He had hoped for fine things that day.

"I take it, Mr Carter, you will withdraw your poor creature from the undignified prospect of failing to meet the reserve at auction? £40 is a lot of money for damaged goods, Mr Carter."

"But...what will I do, Your Grace? I have bills to pay."

"I think we might be able to come to some private arrangement, Mr Carter." Penelope's voice was much quieter now, intended just for Mr Carter's ears, although Sally heard it clear enough. "Shall we say £50?"

"What, but that is more than the reserve!" His surprised look was remembered fondly by Sally and Penelope long after the event.

"Take it or leave it, my man." Penelope turned from the horse dealer, catching Sally's eye with a tiny wink.

"I'll take it, Your Grace, what man would not?" He scurried after her.

The deal was done in a few minutes. But Penelope had another surprise for both Mr Carter and Sally.

"If you find another of similar quality and bring it to Great Little, I'll give you £50 for that one, and the same for a third and fourth."

"I'm already looking, Your Grace."

"See to it, Mr Carter, see to it. Now, Johnnie, where are you?" Deal done, her voice rose again to its natural volume.

"I'm here, Your Grace." Johnnie came running to them.

"Take this fine animal to the temporary stables over there. Rent a stall and give it some bran. Also give him a rub down, as if he were your own. Do you hear me?"

"Yes, Your Grace." Johnnie seemed anxious to have the responsibility.

"And get your sister to help you. She cannot spend all day galivanting with the young men while you do the work!"

"Yes, Your Grace." This time he shared the joke, a wide grin evidencing the humour.

"Why did you pay more than the reserve, Pen?" Sally whispered as they walked away.

"To clinch the deal, dear Sal. I wanted to make the purchase right rather than bid on it in auction where it would likely go for much more."

"But the big feet?"

"Big feet? What big feet would they be, Sal? He's got quite the most normal size feet of any horse."

"You rotter, Pen. You've cheated the man."

"No, I've given him a certain £50 plus his profit on three more horses provided he brings them to me. He'll buy them for no more than £30, I imagine. Mr Carter will do well enough."

"What will you call this beauty, Pen?" Sally asked, looking at Johnnie leading the young stallion away.

"Why, that's easy," Penelope replied. "I think a good name would be Damaged Goods. What do you think?"

"I think that is an excellent choice, Your Grace." Her title quickly employed again as they passed near to others on their way to find the mares.

Simon left Lord Cartwright's office full of purpose and vision. This was his destiny; many things had gone wrong in his life, now they finally promised to turn for the better. He understood that, as a convicted felon, he could not take the limelight; that properly would go to Cartwright, the man who could make it happen.

"I've taken your shred of an idea and turned it into a fully-fledged plan, Taylor."

And he had, there could be no denying the incredible detail the government minister had evolved over the last twenty-four hours.

"Your task is that of messenger now," Cartwright explained. "You are to take ship back to Boston and, once there, to hand these documents to Major Davidson who, on reading them, will know exactly what to do. With your task complete, you owe your allegiance to the major. Much as I have enjoyed our two audiences, you are not to be seen in this country again. I hope I am understood?"

"Yes, my lord, just one question. Should I not know the content of the messages, in case they are lost at sea?"

"No, they are too sensitive."

"But the risk…"

"It is a risk I am prepared to take. Speed is of the essence. It is imperative that you arrive before Phips carries out his next foolhardy plan. Do you understand me, Taylor?"

"Yes, my lord. With your leave, I will depart immediately for Bristol. I assume you will fund this voyage? Chartering a ship will not be cheap." Cartwright was prepared for this eventuality. A small bag of coins was slid across the table.

"I have sent a messenger this morning to take care of your passage. The only purpose you have now is to carry these messages to Major Davidson. Is that clear?"

"Yes, my lord."

But there was something niggling at Cartwright, some detail he had left unattended. Taylor bowed and left the room.

"Taylor!" was called to the closing door.

"My lord?"

"Can you think of anything missing from these plans?"

"No, my lord. The scheme seems brilliant in its simplicity. No doubt there is real ingenuity contained in these messages which I am bound and concerned to deliver as speedily as possible. I will leave London within this half-hour, my lord."

"Godspeed, Taylor. You are a good man. We will not meet again so I bid you good luck in your new life as a soldier."

"My lord." This time the door completed its swing shut and two pairs of footsteps, Taylor and the bent-double aide, completed their dwindle down the passageway to silence.

Something was bothering Cartwright but he could not put his finger on it. He went through the plan again, using different voices to play it out in his mind.

"My lord?" The aide was back again, his footsteps not heard by Cartwright. "My lord, dare I ask how it went?"

Cartwright, in his determination to grasp what could not be grasped, broke his own rule and told his subordinate everything that had passed. The aide shuffled his feet, as if a dance to push along his thoughts.

"That's easy, my lord," he said, waiting for Cartwright to finish. "The missing element is that Captain Taylor did not ask for anything for himself."

That left a worrying niggle in Lord Cartwright's mind as he moved on to the next stage of his master plan.

Chapter 23

He kicked out at the kitten, sending it hurtling through the doorway from its supposed sanctuary. Grabbing another bottle, he cracked off the cap against the doorframe and drunk from the broken neck, long and hard.

It was the second-to-last bottle, just one more in the shed. He would worry about that later, after a drink. He would go back inside the house, find a chair to sit on and make a plan.

First of all, he had to get his wife back. He would have done it days ago except he had to make a plan first. It was her fault; had he not told her to lay more brandy in? Now, when he had need of it most, the bottles were running low. No, correct that. He did not need the brandy at all. He needed his wife back.

Another long draft from the bottle and his mind became clearer. Except his head hurt so much. It told him to close his eyes but the injustice of the situation kept them open, tying the eyelids back so the distasteful light of yet another day burst in.

He slept a moment, except it was not sleeping, eyes open and staring at the point where two walls and the floor met in a corner. He wondered why he was at the same level as the corner when he had sat on a chair. He remembered clearly sitting on a chair but maybe that was another time, another day. He needed a drink to assuage the dreadful thirst; was that glass that went down with the brandy he gulped? Something sharp amidst the welcome liquid, something painful hidden in the relief it offered.

He tried another swig. It gave the same painful mixture; rich, fiery liquid containing a thousand points of pain.

That is when he coughed up the blood. It filled his mouth with its sickly-sweet taste. He liked it at first, but not the vomiting that followed, nor the urination that trickled through his clothes. Everything seemed suddenly liquid and warm. Was his whole body turning from a solid state into a mass of uncontainable liquid? He opened his already open eyes to see the panic before him. If he was turning to liquid, he would drain away.

"Grimes will drain away," he called gently to the corner. Could a man exist in a flowing state? Logic said one could, provided the tank was kept topped up and brim full. He took another drink, just to top up the tank.

Soon, he would go and find his wife. She would know what to do. She would sort out the cottage and make a meal. He thought a moment of roast beef then vomited again and reached for his second-to-last bottle, the one with the broken neck, looking just like the other ones with their broken necks.

Simon Taylor was gone from London even before the half-hour he had allowed himself. Because he had purchased the duke's sweetmeats the day before, all he had to do was return to the inn, order the horses strapped to his trap and collect the bag containing his spare and freshly laundered uniform. He had gone early to see Cartwright and now had most of the day to make progress westwards. He had almost fulfilled the task set to him. Just recently there had been no hope and now it was flooding back like the sun flooding the new day, like the sun that stilled and warmed after the storm.

Yet it seemed a new storm was arising for the wind fairly bowled him along the road, bringing frigid temperatures from the east to mix with the humidity of the English summer. Dark clouds raced him, treating him with disdain for, despite his excellent trap, he could never hope to move as fast as they could. Simon wondered whether he would get to his planned stop that night before the coming rain drenched him.

He nevertheless made excellent progress, arriving with two tired horses late in the evening just as the downpour started. Holly met him at the bar of the Homeless Pig.

"The same room, sir?" She had the letter to the landlord in her dress pocket. She liked to feel its presence, reminding her of a new life, a new start away from this terrible place.

"No, the best rooms you have, madam, and a little company, if you please, for a weary traveller."

"I'll attend to that directly," she replied, thinking some gold from this strange soldier might allow her to make an offer on those two additional acres along the river.

"I'll show you. My body might be flowing away, but I can still stand…like a man…don't mock me or I'll tear you apart, stone by miserable stone." His voice was hoarse. He was sick. Where was his wife? That was it; he needed to collect her. "She'll be at the manor. She likes the manor. I'll fetch her home." Another long day was coming to an end and the brief dark of mid-summer was spreading throughout the cottage. It was humid. Thick clouds blocked the sky, seeming to imprison him in darkness. But that was nonsense. He knew his cottage well. He did not need light. If he could just work out which room he was in, he would know exactly how to leave and then find the way to the manor.

He rose slowly, got more confidence, then tripped on something hard and metallic on the floor. He put out both hands to break his fall, dropped the bottle which crashed against the stone floor, the sound lost to the raging of the wind outside. Again, he felt the flow of sticky sweet blood, but not for some minutes after the fall. It was pitch-black inside but outside was lit with jagged stabs of lightening as the storm flew westwards; it was a dry storm in Dorset, the worst type in Grimes' experience, no rain to wash the edges off the violence. He stretched out his arm, felt the old blunderbuss lying where he had tripped against it. He used it as a prop, congratulating himself on his ingenuity. He would soon be up. He was a strong man, could take a few cuts and bruises.

He would get the next bottle, the last bottle, then go to the manor, find out why Mrs Grimes had not brought back the new brandy he was certain he had sent her to collect.

Simon woke in the early hours to find Holly in his bed. She was not unattractive with her arching back, pretty eyes and long brown ringlets. She was mumbling in her sleep about two acres. He remembered from last time that she was obsessed with

178

buying a small farm with her husband. He toyed for a while with the idea of tracking down her husband and explaining just exactly how she earned her generous tips. Instead he rolled on top of her and entered her again while she half-slept, moaning with pleasure.

For some reason, he wondered next about how many children he may have fathered over the years from nights like this. He knew he was virile; three children in four years with his second wife, Elizabeth, gave evidence of that.

"What are you thinking of?" she asked, snuggling further into the bed.

"My children," he replied automatically. Then told her of the four he knew about.

At some point, Holly sat up, clearly wanting to say something. "What is it, Holly?"

"Your grown-up daughter. Is her married name, Grimes?"

"It is. Do you know her?"

"No sir, but I know a physician who has lately been attending on her. He is staying here at the inn. He has apparently saved her life and she is now mending well."

"This doctor, which room is he in?"

Grimes used the blunderbuss like a crutch. It enabled him to fetch the last bottle from the shed. Now it was raining, great belts of water riding on the wind, battering at Grimes as he crossed the ten yards from back door to shed. For some reason, some instinct, he took off his coat and used it to cover the blunderbuss, protecting the powder from the rain.

When the bottle was drunk, he would go and find his wife. But first, he would stay in the shed where it was still dry, although the gaps in the weatherboarding gave spreading damp patches in places, also allowing a modicum of sight from the lightening. It was just enough to spot the bottle, alone on the shelf. He cracked it open and sat on the floor, waving his gun at the world outside. It should be loaded and ready; he always kept it so. He looked down the barrel. It was hard to hold it slumped as he was. He propped his foot against the stock and held it by the trigger to steady it. The sound of one shot was lost in the crescendo of the summer storm outside.

Summer can be a time of benign weather, gentle warm breezes and strong sunshine. Yet the storm in summer can be the very worst, catching us unawares and drowning our cries of pain and despair.

Dr Mowbray, to give him credit, tried earnestly to sell Simon a bottle of his medicine when moments earlier he had been rudely shaken awake.

"It will control your temper, sir, make you sleep much better." He jumped out of bed, nightgown billowing as he scrabbled on the floor for the coins Simon had dropped.

"I'll buy your damned medicine but it is information I am after."

"What information might that be, sir?" Mowbray saw the possibility of gold replacing the silver he had collected from the floor. "I usually peddle in medicine for the body and mind but might be persuaded to trade in information."

A blow to his head from Simon persuaded him to do so. And, for once, Mowbray was truthful following that blow, telling Simon that he had been unable to help Amelia Grimes.

"I don't understand it, sir. I've had numerous successes under similar conditions." But other cases were not what Simon wanted to hear about. He rose, dropped more coins carelessly on the floor and left the room.

Ten minutes later, Simon was waking the grooms, demanding his trap be got ready immediately. They rose grudgingly, feeling the tension in both man and climate.

"I'll warrant there's a fair storm in Dorset," the oldest said. "I can feel it moving west on the wind."

"No matter, old man, I just need my horses then you can sleep through the worst God can throw at you."

"Best you sleep through it too, sir, it's not a night to be out in, I'll say again." But two gold coins pressed into his hand decided him to put his warnings away and harness the two horses.

Simon watched, wondering why the pair seemed so skittish, not thinking that the weather was felt by horses more than men.

If he drove hard all day, he could make Bagber Manor by evening. He would change horses at Bagber and ride on through the night in order not to be missed at Bristol. Hang the storm; he would drive right through it to see his first-born.

For one last time.

Frustratingly, the bottle lay now on the floor just out of reach. Grimes could see its shape in the gloom but not grasp it. He did not feel like moving yet wanted the brandy to blind the pain. There was so much noise outside it damaged his capacity to think. There had been a storm like this when he had been a child in the slums of London. He vaguely remembered losing himself in the skirts of a woman. His mother? Or just a random woman in whatever house was then his shelter? If it was his mother, it was his only memory of her. Why these thoughts now? Why live in the past when there was the present to sort out, his wife to get back, more brandy to fetch?

He would gather his strength and try again. A few more minutes of rest and he would make his move. Would the coming day prove to exert a calming influence or a continuation of the violent storm that was wearing out the short night? What did he care? He just needed one final effort to reach for his bottle, his love, his life.

Simon knew exactly where his daughter would be. Even when Simon had owned Bagber, she had refused one of the grander bedrooms on the first floor, opting for a room at the corner on the second, where east met south.

"It gives me maximum sun," she would explain. The room was plain, no lavish wallpaper, and sparsely furnished.

He bounded up the stairs, swinging through the landing, one hand on the banisters for a guide, then onto the second stairs, less wide, less sweeping than those rising from the ground to the first floor.

It was the middle of the second night of the storm and he had been driving hard all day, his progress impeded by the lashing wind and rain. The horses outside stood foaming, breathing heavily, until a groom, wakened by the noise of a household being disturbed at night, used his initiative and took them away for a rub down and feed.

Simon reached the door to Amelia's bedroom, a chain of servants and relatives behind him. He saw his other three children, born of Elizabeth, his second wife, poking their faces between the banisters of the third floor where the nursery was. But he paid them no mind. His goal was to see Amelia.

Who opened her eyes the moment his voice carried across the room.

"Amelia, what is this?" he said, not yet seeing who else was in the room. "Why do you lie in bed all day and all night?"

"She won't answer you. She no longer talks." That was Thomas's voice. As his eyes grew used to the dark, he noticed another person in the room. It was the maid Eliza had brought back from London; he did not remember her name but remembered afterwards a part of his brain telling him that it was serious if two people were staying up all night to tend to Amelia.

"How is she?"

"She sleeps as always."

"No, I am awake, Thomas." Her quiet voice somehow drowned out the storm beyond the windows, made nature stop and take breath.

"Amelia!" said Thomas. But this was Simon's moment; a moment he had driven all day and into the night to have.

"Father, is that you, sir?"

"It is. What ails you, daughter?" He would have said her name but the name was chosen by the mother, his wife who had died and taken his ability to love with her.

"Do you need to ask, sir? Do you really? It was the husband you chose for me who has put me here in this condition." She sank back on the bed, exhausted, her eyes starting to close again. Simon grabbed her hand.

"Don't sleep, daughter, stay awake a little while. Do you want me to stroke your hair like when you were a child and Mama…" He could not finish his sentence but she nodded and his other hand moved towards her hair. "Don't worry, dearest, I will sort everything out." He suddenly knew what he had to do.

"She's asleep again," he said to no-one in particular. Then he turned to Thomas and bade him continue to care for her.

"And you too, Silly Milly." The name of the maid had come to him at that moment. "I have a visit to make and then I must on to Bristol. I probably won't be back."

As Simon left, the storm opened up its fury once again, enveloping him in a tiny moving capsule on to his destination. He did not care, however. He knew the path and nothing God or nature could throw in the way could hope to stop him. And certainly not Thomas, who came towards the bedroom door as soon as he realised Simon was leaving.

"Simon, I need to…"

"Not now, Thomas, too much to do, too little time to do it in." Thomas checked himself momentarily, then thought he would question Simon anyway.

"Simon…"

But Simon was gone, out of the door, down the steps and back into the fury of the summer storm.

Simon found the dead body of Grimes in the shed. Blood was oozing from a nasty face wound, one arm stretched out towards an empty bottle of brandy with a broken neck. There was a puddle of brandy and it was mixing with a puddle of blood. The right side of his face was mangled, torn flesh pulped and raw. His one good remaining eye stared towards the bottle, as if concentration alone could somehow wind it in towards him.

There was no storm now. Nature had given in and calmed its fury as a new day began.

"The bottle was empty, Grimes you idiot." Was he reaching for an empty bottle or had there been brandy in the bottle but his efforts had tipped it out? "Whatever way, you died in frustration and pain and I can have no more anger against you."

He stood there in the shed with the early morning sun rising against the spent energy of the storm, sweeping its broom to clear the sky. By one version of the story, he spent hours there alone with the dead Grimes. Others said it was a shorter period, for how else could time have worked out? Colonel Hanson's report said he arrived at eight to find Taylor standing there, empty blunderbuss in his arm, as if it was an extension of his body, reaching out to do justice where justice had long been required.

Hanson took him by the arm, removing the gun, noting that Grimes' face was smashed on one side and that the butt of the blunderbuss was dark and dirty.

"You could have reloaded the gun and used it to stop me," Hanson said as he led Simon away. But Captain Simon Taylor said nothing in reply. There was no storm where he was now, but equally no sunshine.

Chapter 24

It took a week for Fugini to regain consciousness.

"Who will ever hire a one-handed cook?" he asked from the depths of despair.

"I will," said Henry.

"Don't jest with me, Corporal. Now is not the time for poor jokes. I know you are an educated man but not a rich one. It is never right to taunt a man by parading false hope."

"You know very little about me, Fugini. First of all, I am no longer a corporal. I have been dishonourably discharged for disobeying orders." Henry related what had happened a week earlier.

"The injustice of it!" Henry saw Fugini's rising anger, evidenced by the Italian trying to rise from his bed; being too weak for the task he fell back, sunk in a mass of sweat and pumping blood that at least brought colour back to his face.

"The army has moved to Dublin and James Stuart has left for France, panicked by our success at the Boyne. Your terrible sacrifice, Fugini, has not been in vain."

"But what now?" Fugini replied. "What hope for a one-armed cook who has no other skills?"

"Like I said, soldier. I have need of your skills. And I think you will like it on my estate in Dorset."

"You are a landowner?" It was the ultimate in wealth and status. Fugini's voice had a strain of hope to it.

"I am indeed." Henry suddenly felt a shyness about declaring the extent of his wealth.

"Are you titled?" It was the obvious next question but the supposition sat so oddly with his easy-going attitude and the fact that he had joined the army as a private.

"I am the Earl of Sherborne. And, yes, I am rather wealthy and we have a fine house outside Sherborne in Dorset, where you will be most welcome to stay and work.

To Fugini's next question, Henry replied that the girls in Dorset were exceedingly pretty, in fact prettier even than those from Tuscany.

They took ship together for Bristol two days later, berthing next to the sleek, vessel that was meant to take Simon Taylor to Boston. The master had sent urgent messages to London when Simon had not turned up. Lord Cartwright, in response, had detailed a dozen men to track him down. Two got as far as the Homeless Pig and there the trail went cold.

"I believe he stayed here but I was not in attendance," the landlord said, rubbing his shoulder constantly so that the enquirer suspected this man may be a retired soldier with a wound that nagged at him day and night; if Cartwright's man had known the true cause of the ache, and therefore the landlord's true identity, he would have smiled, his mind on the reward being offered. "I've asked my people and they remember he left in his own trap early in the morning, destination unknown." The way he said these last two words ensured the enquiries were at an end. The landlord had no desire to bring attention to who he was.

"Your name, sir?" Cartwright's henchman asked.

"My name?"

"Yes, sir, I can hardly put 'the landlord said' in the report to my superior."

"Ah yes, well it is…Parkins," lied Parchman.

They all thought, in searching for him last year, that Parchman had fled abroad. It had been a stroke of genius, he told himself, to spend some of the proceeds of his fraud on four inns in the West Country, then hiring deputies to look after the day-to-day needs of each while he remained in the background, a shadowy figure; exactly where he wanted to be.

There were two people who might have helped with the enquiries but neither was questioned. Holly had left the inn, forcing Parchman to manage everything and to receive the pair of interrogators. He was in the limelight until he could find a replacement. He had had a furious row when Holly gave notice, saying she would regret her decision to leave for some ridiculous smallholding in the middle of nowhere.

"And don't come back to me when your miserable enterprise fails," he had shouted to her departing back, making Holly even more determined to succeed. He was tempted to give Holly's address to these unsmiling agents, just to cause her some difficulty. But then he remembered that she knew something of his past and could easily return any difficulties he gave to her. Best to let sleeping dogs lie, so when Parchman was asked about the whereabouts of the person in charge of the inn at the time of Taylor's disappearance, he made up some story about her marrying a merchant from the north and going off with him to start a new life.

"It's quite romantic, don't you think?" he said, trying to force a smile.

The other person who might have helped was Mowbray; in fact, he would have been more helpful than Holly for he had an inkling as to exactly where Simon had gone. However, the questioners disregarded him as a harmless quack when he tried to sell them a bottle of 'Mowbray's Tonic, for the fulfilment of health and happiness'.

"Out of my way, quack. We have important business to attend to." As so often is the case, their arrogance denied them the vital information they sought. They charged off the next morning without paying for their board, too busy chasing shadows and rainbows and other things that cannot be caught.

The master of the ship next to theirs saw Henry and Fugini climbing over his ship to step ashore. It was an easy mistake to make; wounded officer and wounded servant, no doubt lost in their search for the shore. Both were out of uniform but that was to be expected; so often these secret people needing transportation at speed were involved in espionage and other shady matters. It gave the ship's master a thrill to be on the fringe of such activity.

"Sir, you are late indeed but better late than never. We will leave immediately and float out on the tide."

"I do not comprehend you, sir."

"Are you not Captain Simon Taylor of the Massachusetts militia?" the ship's master asked, a sudden premonition as to his error.

"No sir, I am Henry, Earl of Sherborne. And this is Private Fugini. We are returning from the Irish wars."

"A great victory, my lord," he said politely, imagining the earl to be a general or some such. He loved to mix with aristocracy. On this occasion, it did something to assuage his temper. He forgot for a moment that he had a cargo to deliver and had been cursing the day he had agreed to take Captain Taylor back to America.

"I know a Simon Taylor but this one was sent to the colonies for some despicable crimes. I suppose it is a common enough name. Why do you seek a militia officer?"

"Lord Cartwright paid me to take Captain Taylor across to Boston in a hurry and then the gentleman does not turn up, my lord. Every day in port costs me money for berthing fees and wages. This officer who disappeared was sent to the colonies for misdemeanours aplenty, so the message said. I was not to trust him at all."

"That sounds like the Simon Taylor I knew. He is married to my wife's sister."

"Will you take a drink with me, my lord?" The idea of sharing a bottle with an earl warmed him considerably.

"I would like it and thank you but I have a pressing engagement and must be away. We have just arrived back from the Irish wars, as I said." Did Henry allow the ship's master to assume they were involved in an all-important and secret mission or was it entirely innocent and just down to the man's imagination? Henry shook his hand; could there be a conspiratorial wink associated with the shake? "I suspect there is only one Simon Taylor, my man. You seek him but I have no desire to meet him again. If I find he has sloped back to Dorset, where we are headed with some urgency, I'll arrange an escort to send him back to his ship."

"It's not his ship, my lord. It belongs to a consortium. I have a sixteenth share in it."

"You have done well for yourself, Captain," Henry replied, shaking hands again, definitely a wink this time. Or was it just a nervous twitch? The earl had just recently been in battle so a nervous reaction could be expected.

"Good day to you, my lord." He bowed, knowing he would dine out on this story, gradually developing it over the months to become a great work of fiction.

Henry did see Simon Taylor two days later, but not until after a happy reunification with Grace.

"I pray you will not criticise me, sir," she said after they had kissed and strolled in the grounds and kissed again. It was high summer, hot and lazy, the oaks dotted on the lawn offering deep or dappled shade, depending on their age and stature. "But I have found a home for the £1,000 you left me in case I came across just such an opportunity." She told him about the insurance investment. "Mr Fellows thinks it will pay a handsome return, even after putting some aside to cover future disasters." She told him of the other investors and then about Anne Aspley. "I declare she is younger than me yet has such a business head on her shoulders!"

"Far from criticising you, my dear, you would appear to have made an excellent choice and placed the money to advantage when before it was sitting in that lockbox feeling sorry for itself! I would like to look at the investment in more detail and meet the other investors. Of course, I know the Dowager-Duchess but the others are not known to me."

"You will like them, I'm sure, my darling."

"Shall we go to Bagber this afternoon, Grace dear?"

"If you would like to see your mother, sir, it would please me greatly. Now, tell me again of your exploits in Ireland. I want to hear every detail."

"Well, it was hardly the longest career in the army!"

"I am pleased, my love, for I have missed you dreadfully. It has been eight weeks, four days and almost three hours since you 'marched' out of here to the recruitment station. Tell me, did you adopt a false name?"

"No, I was plain Henry Sherborne. I just did not mention any titles. I was made corporal, you know."

"How clever of you, sir!" Grace was bubbling with excitement, clearly the sudden return of her husband was a part of it but there was more. This excitement descended on Henry, like fine weather settling, only there was no weather on that perfectly still day, like time stood still. "You will have such stories to tell your children!" She could no longer refrain from mentioning children.

"We do not have any children, Grace."

"We do now, sir." She suddenly turned grave, for gravity and joy march side by side in this world, like the left and right of the soldiers' beat. She also turned to him and looked up at him. "We do now, sir," she said again. The first time the comment had passed over his head to hang in the air like a common mistruth.

"You mean?"

"Yes, husband! You are to be a father."

It was at Bagber Manor that they learned of Simon Taylor's arrest.

"James Hanson is holding him," Matthew said. "He is accused of murdering Grimes."

"Grimes is dead?"

"Certainly, and that means that Mealy is a widow." They all thought of Thomas, upstairs with Amelia. Yet he was married to Bridget, sitting downstairs with a mask upon her face.

"Is Simon guilty of this crime?"

"He was found holding the gun that shot Grimes. I don't think there can be much defence against that."

"More so because he will not talk. He has been in a daze since the arrest, as if he was in another world already. James said he found him that way and he has remained so where he is being held. He will not talk and he will not answer questions, even as to his name."

190

He would hang, of course, if a court found him guilty. By rights, he should have hanged last year but Eliza had used her little influence with the judge and had managed to secure indentured service instead, more so because he had pleaded guilty. But, if he would not talk at all, he certainly would hang now.

And then Elizabeth would be a widow too. And the three children, growing tall like Simon, would be without a father.

Forever.

Upstairs, Amelia had made little progress. After Simon's visit, she had sunk back into a deep sleep. Thomas and Milly never left her side in case she should wake again. Thomas, his hope now riddled with holes of despair, remembered a sermon his father had written, or was Matthew the real author? It mattered not, what did matter was the import of the words.

"Sorry, sir?" Milly asked so Thomas said it again, this time quite aloud, as if breaking through the mumbling to find new voice and a new tune to dance his mind to.

I have nothing to offer you, Lord, other than my weaknesses. I am naked before you, a creature of sin. I search my heart, my soul, and find nothing but despair in there. That despair is overflowing, causing a great wallowing of self-indulgence, itself, I suspect, a sin of distorted pride.

Then, I realise, I do have something to offer you, Lord. I have buckets full of hopelessness and I offer them to you in the hope that you will empty my tank of all despair and fill it instead with hope. And the very fact that hope is twice mentioned, now a third time, illustrates your love in mankind, including me.

For where there is despair, you will sow hope. I offer my despair up to you, my Lord God.

And wait for the hope that you will return.

"Gosh, sir, that seems to be overpowering with meaning and such like. I just pray that Miss Mealy becomes better, sir."

Chapter 25

The question is, does the world contain an equal amount of emotion or does the level vary according to particular factors, increasing and decreasing as the world moves on? And does the world move on, make progress? Or does it go in a perpetual cycle around a central core, essentially never changing, just varying marginally as it revolves, emotion never breaking out of its orbit around the earth? As despair lifted in Thomas, heralded by Amelia once more opening her eyes, sitting up and chatting as if nothing had happened, it settled on Major Davidson, far across the ocean in New England; as the old world rose, the new world sunk, suggesting, but not proving, that there is a finite, fixed amount of such emotion shared around everyone, rising and lowering forever like the tides.

Major Davidson had links into Boston and every report he got out of the city caused him alarm. Phips had not been replaced; moreover, he was moving ahead with an ambitious plan to attack Montreal. It was madness in a world already mad. As July moved on, he heard of Phips' plans to lead an expedition against the French.

"He is not the man to do so," Davidson proclaimed to everyone who would listen. "Find out for me where this expedition is going, Grenville, and I'd be grateful for the knowledge," he added in exasperation.

"I'll try but they're keeping it pretty close to their chests." Grenville Roberts was a solid man, a good friend to Davidson in the twenty years he had spent in America. They had met during Davidson's first week in Boston when, friendless and lost, he had wandered the streets of the city, thinking of his capital that diminished each passing day. He had dropped into a coffee house hoping to meet someone who might advise him honestly. Grenville Roberts had been alone, sitting at a table in the crowded room.

"Would you mind, sir, if I sat at your table?"

"Not at all, sir." It turned out after a few minutes that Grenville was not in a position to advise Jack Davidson or anybody else concerning the Americas.

"I was hoping," he said, "to meet someone in here to give me exactly such advice."

"Well, sir, it seems we are two peas in the same pod, both up a creek without a paddle, so to speak." If they were two peas, they were of different varieties for they looked completely different. Jack was stick thin and tall, Grenville was shorter and tubby.

"I guess our total measurements are about the same but I'm more loaded around the middle, whereas you have your head in the clouds!" Grenville joked from time to time.

But these, now, were far more serious times. They had been young then, looking out at a life full of adventure. Now they were twenty years older, each established on their own farm, each married with children. Their farms lay at either end of a short valley that billowed out into rich farmland in the middle. The water tasted divine, there were great expanses of woodland for firewood and hunting and a small, growing town lay over the mountain in a parallel valley. Other than worries over harvests, weather and the price of corn and beef, their only concern was the French, who incited the native Indians to attack at every opportunity, as the British-Americans did with their own Indian allies in return.

"We've carved a good life out here in Spring Valley,", so called because of the huge flood water that came each winter's end from the mountains around. They flooded the low ground at the bottom, leaving rich sediment which resulted in excellent yields on the crops provided the seeds were not planted too early and washed away by the water. "But the damn Frenchies threaten to ruin it."

"More like that damn Phips threatens to ruin it with his wild adventuring ways, disregarding the rights of those who he meets along the way."

"He's an intelligent man," Jack said.

"But intelligence does not predict success, far from it."

"And without Taylor back again, we have little chance of stopping Phips."

Little did they know it, but, at that moment, a subdued and silent Simon was standing before a judge in Salisbury.

"We have to assume, Mr Taylor, that your lack of response is a plea of not guilty. I'll ask you again, do you have any comment to make to the court at this time? I urge you, sir, to answer me for your own benefit." Simon did not respond, did not even acknowledge the judge's not unkind words.

"It's like he was already half way to the next place," whispered one clerk to another.

"I bet he can feel the heat of the flames," his colleague whispered back.

How do you try a man who will not talk? He had a lawyer to represent him, as Amelia, now up and about although still quite frail, had made sure to get the best one they could find. But the lawyer shook his head, saying there was little he could do if the client would not talk, would not even look him in the eye.

"I call Colonel James Hanson of the Dorset Militia." After swearing as to the truth and the whole truth, Hanson related the facts as he knew them.

"Sir, I arrived at the remote cottage occupied by Mr and Mrs Grimes at three minutes past eight o'clock on the morning of July 12th. I had my sergeant and two other militia members with me. We did not see anybody else around the houses or in the grounds."

"You say 'houses', so there was more than one?"

"Yes sir, there are two houses next to each other but I understand the other house has been empty for some years. The next nearest house is Smallwood Farm, almost a mile to the south and west. It is a remote area between the towns of Sturminster Newton to the south and Gillingham to the north."

"I see, so there were unlikely to be any people around – it is hardly a bustling metropolis, is it Colonel Hanson?"

"No sir, as I said it is remote."

"Tell the court what you found when you arrived at", he turned the page of his notebook, "at three minutes past eight that fateful morning."

"I take exception, my lord." Simon's barrister rose from his seat. "Mention of a 'fateful morning' suggests that Mr Grimes' demise occurred during the morning, with a further suggestion that it was when my client was there at the house in question. It is not proof, far from it, mere supposition." It was a good attempt and it half-worked.

"The jury will ignore all reference to 'morning' in the prosecution's question or the witness's answer."

Simon's barrister was a reasonable man, many would call him kind. He had thought long and hard about how to present a defence case when the accused insisted on maintaining silence.

"I actually think, in all likelihood, that your father is innocent of the murder of your husband, Mrs Grimes." Amelia had dressed and come down to the drawing room to receive the attorney; it was the first time she had come out of her bedroom in over six weeks.

"It hinges on the time of death," she replied.

"Precisely, because Thomas and young…eh…Milly have sworn that he was at Bagber Manor as late as half past six that morning. He drove his trap to the Grimes house, which would take thirty minutes at least"

"More like forty-five, sir. The horses had been rubbed down and fed by an enterprising stable lad, but they were exhausted from a long journey prior. I do not believe he could have arrived at Grimes Cottage a moment before a quarter past seven."

"The doctor examining Grimes' body put the time of death as probably before 4am."

"Meaning it could not be Father who was responsible for Mr Grimes' death. He is saved by analysis of the facts, sir. Now, I am somewhat weary and must rest. You say the case starts on Monday? I wish you luck, sir."

"You won't be attending, Mrs Grimes?"

"No, I won't be attending but thank you for deducing my father's innocence. Good day, sir, and thank you again for your endeavours.'

But those endeavours did not allow for the fickle nature of a jury. The word around the inns of Salisbury afterwards was that the twelve true men did not buy the old silence trick, believing anyone not willing to protest his innocence must be guilty.

The decision was unanimous, eleven grave faces stared straight ahead as their foreman pronounced 'guilty' towards the clerk who asked the question. Almost before the single word had spread around the room, the judge was placing the black cap over his wig and preparing again the words he knew so well; something about being taken from this place to a place of execution.

Everyone looked at Simon who shrugged his shoulders and turned to start his final journey.

"It's Lord Cartwright, let me in."

"It's not getting in that's a problem, mister, it's getting out again." That said to a howl of laughter from the jailer's sycophantic assistant.

"Do you know who I am?"

"You just announced yourself. Paul Cartwright you said, have you forgotten your name this last half-minute?" More dutiful laughter from the assistant.

"I said Lord Cartwright, man. I am a government minister and I must see Simon Taylor immediately.

"Oh, sorry, my lord. I thought you were some silly common man wanting a glimpse of the condemned, is all, my lord."

"Apology accepted provided you take me straight to see Taylor."

"Right away, my lord. No Jenkins, I'll do this one seeing as how he is a government minister." He led Cartwright deep into the heart of the prison and down several flights from ground level, introducing himself as he went.

"Name's Michael Bars, my lord. Was such a laugh we had when I first applied for a job here…bars, you see, my lord? Michael Bars being my name. That was half a lifetime ago and I've worked my way up to chief jailer. Not bad, I hear you say, my lord. Not bad indeed." The monologue continued until Cartwright bade him shut up if he wanted to keep the position he had spent half a lifetime arriving at.

Cartwright's ultimatum produced the strangest of results. Most would be torn to shreds by the put-down. It seemed to bounce off the chief jailer, who heeded the advice to keep quiet but did so with determined good humour. He would still be making merry, Cartwright surmised, if he were led onto the scaffold himself.

"Leave us a while, Bars, wait right outside for me." The jailer opened the door and took up a rigid, almost comical, pose in the passageway, like a sentry outside the palace. The natural cheerfulness made Cartwright stop a second, like feeling for a candle in a darkened room. Something was missing.

He remembered a song his mother had sung long ago when he was small and she had not yet taken to the bottle:

Ambition is fine, but I think you will find
Love wins over, every time.

He could hear her voice now, teasing at his soul. He stood momentarily outside himself, looking in and noting that his ferocious ambition sat awkwardly with his mother's love. But then she had turned away from him, putting drink above her young son, leaving him to rot in deception and calculation.

He had never seen it that way before. How could one man, a perfect stranger, bring painfully sweet memories flooding in like a stream in springtime, running high against its banks and eroding those banks as it rushed everything to the oblivion of the sea?

"Taylor, what on earth has happened to you?" Cartwright had evidently entered the condemned man's cell, although he did not recall crossing the threshold; before him lay a shrunken Taylor curled on the bed. It was as if the dreadful sentence in court had opened a wound in Taylor's side and the life-blood was slowly draining away. Cartwright estimated him to be half way to empty on the gauge of life.

"He won't talk, my lord," Bars called from his station in the corridor, bending around to see into the cell, yet keeping his feet placed squarely on the ground, anchoring them to the corridor floor so whatever the top half did, the bottom half would always be stable. "He hasn't said a word since he came in here, my lord."

Yet this time, Simon did reply. It was nothing, just a series of grunts and grimaces with a few words thrown in. Cartwright was an intelligent man and could piece the meaning together when most would give up in frustration.

"So, you are innocent?" Cartwright wondered as he asked this question, whether Taylor would be truthful; surely, he would temper his answers in a last-minute attempt to save his life? But ten minutes in the dark and dank cell convinced Cartwright that his accomplice was telling the truth. Moreover, there was nothing about his future that he feared, either in this world or the next.

"Have you seen a pastor?" It seemed the thing to ask. Simon shook his head. "Do you want to see one" Another shake. "Do you want to see anyone at all? Family or friends? I have enough influence, even in this deserted part of the realm, to arrange a visit." Again met with a shake of the head.

"Why did you divert here instead of going to the ship in Bristol? None of this needed to happen, Simon." There was a sudden glance at Cartwright following use of his first name but it did not last. He released the grip he had taken on Cartwright's arm and let his hand fall like an unwanted toy.

There was one more tack Cartwright could try.

"You've completely messed up the plan I put together, Taylor." First names were out now. "Remember your other life, Taylor? Do you recall you had responsibilities which you so easily turned your back on? Did you ever think of the chaos you have caused with your selfish actions? Can you not spare a word for me in explanation, bearing in mind what trouble you have caused?"

Absolutely no reaction to this. Cartwright had spoken to the defence barrister, knew about Taylor's silence, but had expected the man to open up to his seniority, failing that perhaps to the tenderness he suddenly felt towards the convicted murderer; instead he remained as tantalisingly aloof and other-worldly as ever, just a few short grunts and sparse words to punctuate his silence.

"Is there nothing I can do for you, man?"

In reply, Simon took from his pocket a scrap of paper and did, at last, speak. He asked for it to be delivered to Amelia. Cartwright left then, placing one hand on Simon's shoulder in what he imagined was an appropriate goodbye, the other hand knocking for the jailer to open the door. Once out of the cell, with the door slammed behind him, he pulled the letter out of his pocket and read it. It was not long, scratched on a single folded piece of paper with a pencil, both unasked for but given to Simon by Michael Bars, the chief jailer, on instinct.

I am sorry, Amelia, for all I have done against you. My heart was filled with bad things like envy and pride. It is pumped much cleaner now. I will miss you and will always remember how it was before ambition took hold of me. Take care, my sweet daughter. I failed you so often in life but know two things about me. I have voided all my vile emotions and only have love left in my heart. And I did not kill your husband. I arrived to find him dead already. I said nothing because it is my way of making some little amends for how I have harmed you. I know the reasoning will seem twisted but as I stared down at the dead body of Grimes, I thought that my responsibility for your suffering and the pain I have caused you and all you hold dear is worse than any murder.

There were several mentions of Thomas in the next few attempted sentences but all were scored out and crossed through. Cartwright knew exactly who he was referring to. He remembered Thomas Davenport well enough; he had twice escaped from Cartwright's grasp. He placed the scrappy letter back in his pocket.

"I shall keep this as it may prove to be evidence of the highest order. For if Taylor did not kill Grimes, who did?"

"What was that, my lord?"

"Nothing, Bars, nothing that need concern you at any rate. I Iave a boy run to enquire as to the next coach; I must get back to London." The veil of office was back over him, hiding his vulnerability from the world. His mother was put away again; it did no good to dwell on the past. There were only two tenses in Cartwright's world; present and future.

"Yes, my lord."

"And Bars, there is no need to ensure a swift death in the morning. I think our common criminal needs to dangle a little in order to make a final contemplation of his crimes." He stepped outside the prison gate, practical matters dominating once again. Taylor could not help him any longer but a quarter-part of him asked why am I willing to promote agony to someone when nothing is to be gained by it?

Then the three-quarters replied; it was the fate of the losers and that was all there was to it. If they did not matter, what did it matter if they suffered?

"Yes, my lord, of course, my lord." But in his half-lifetime in the prison, many thousands of hangings, he had never once prolonged the agony of execution and had no intention of starting now. Hanging made him sick, often rushing to the privy to vomit. Mrs Bars had always said he should have been a gardener or some such. "For you do care for your charges like young shoots, only to cut them down as they start to flower."

It was a strange world and he made his living as best as he could.

"My lord," said the boy, expanding his chest to grab more air, "the next coach leaves in forty minutes."

"For London?"

"Yes, it stops tonight near Andover and then on to Guildford, I believe," the chief jailer added, pleased to be of assistance.

"I asked after space, my lord, and there was one seat left which I took on your behalf."

"You have done well, boy." Cartwright handed over a penny. "Now, I must be off."

Chapter 26

"What was your other idea, Sal?" Penelope was busy sorting through stockings, rather enjoying the discarding motion she accomplished with a flick of the wrist. "Why do all your uniform stockings break so? Is it because you don't care for them? Or have you personified them into the wicked mistress who keeps you scrubbing floors and sewing hems all day?"

"Well, Pen, which question would you have me answer first?"

"As you will, Sal, but the only serious one concerns your other idea, the one you put in your letter to me." She tapped the pocket to her dress, through her chiffon overskirt. The note was still there, where she kept it.

"It was hardly a letter, just some thoughts."

Penelope, with half an ounce of sensibility, did not mention that the note had actually been a set of imperious instructions from maid to mistress. That was in the past now.

"The idea, Sal?" she prompted.

"It was nothing, just an idle thought."

"I still would like to hear it, Sal." She had to make several more requests before Sally took her by the arm and led her away from stocking-duty to the deep sofa under the window that looked out to the side, to the library and the terraced garden beyond.

"I just had an idea, Pen, but I am ashamed to mention it now. It was before…" They both knew what it was before.

"Sal dear, I won't rest until you tell me. In fact, you are ordered to as my maid." She looked at the clock on the sideboard across the room. "You see, it has just turned seven o'clock and you have not yet changed." Seven in the evening had become the dividing line, the time when Sally came up to the bedroom and changed from one of the dresses she wore each day for steward duties into her maid's uniform for the evening shift. Penelope made sure she was there to assist, hanging up the dress Sally had just shed, commenting on the shape of her legs or the arch of her back, smoothing her black skirt; the minor tasks of involvement were never-ending.

"You would order me?" Sally asked.

"As you order me!"

Sally rose from the sofa, pecking her on the cheek. She walked across the room, loosening her skirt as she went, pulling on the laces that held the skirt to the bodice so that it fell to her feet as she walked.

"It's like this, Your Grace," she said, labouring the last two words, liking the pout it produced on her lover's face. "I had an idea."

"We've established that," replied Penelope, mesmerised by Sally's movement across the room.

"To secure your inheritance." She stepped out of each petticoat in turn. "But, like I said in the letter, you won't like it at all."

"Try me," Penelope said, watching Sally in nothing but underwear and stays; her small body moving over to the bed where Penelope had earlier laid out both sets of evening clothes.

"It's a wicked idea, Pen." She picked up the coarse black dress and dropped it over her head. Not finding the hole for her head she looked like a great clumsy monster. Penelope was on her feet in a moment.

"Let me help you." It was often like this, Sally feigning incompetence and Penelope rushing to help.

"There is nothing subtle about you, Pen," Sally would often say, "you're just you and I love you for it."

When Sally took longer to right the dress, Penelope stalked back to the sofa, complaining that Sally was trying to make her forget about the idea.

"Which I never will so you might as well out with it."

"Will you brush my hair, sweetie?" It was the latest name she employed and Penelope could not resist it.

It usually extended to ten minutes. Penelope would start with a general brushing all over. Then she would concentrate on the delightful tight curls around her neck and ears, brushing them repeatedly and noticing how they sprang straight back again after each stroke. After that, she would tease out the wiry spirals that made the bulk of her hair; strangely some parts were almost blond or at least a dirty sandy colour.

"I thought negroes had black hair," Penelope had once said thoughtlessly.

"We differ, Pen, just like the whiteys, except we are far more attractive!"

"You said it."

This time, however, the hair-brushing stopped abruptly, just after the springy bit and before the wiry bit.

"You can never be serious!" Penelope exclaimed, dropping the brush and stepping back from the dressing table where Sally sat.

"I said to forget it, Pen, but you insisted on knowing what the idea was and so I told you."

"Me and him?" she asked, her patriarchal face shocked to a snowy white as if Sally had opened a tap below and was draining out all the blood.

"Of course, it was a silly idea. I wish I never had thought of it."

If there was one thing about Sally that Penelope found even more irresistible than her cheekiness, it was when she was quite contrite.

"How would I even approach him?" But actually she was thinking could she go ahead with it?

"What if he refused me?" Sally translated this next question by Penelope as, what if he laughed me out of his house?

"I don't think he will laugh at you, Pen. I think he needs an heir above anything else."

"But he is ugly and old; he snorts and farts."

"So do you, in your sleep at least."

"I do not!" But Penelope knew that she did. And that, surely, put her on the same level as the lewd, pot-bellied, old Duke of Wiltshire.

Who, Sally was spot on, ached for an heir to prevent his brother from succeeding him when he died.

"What's the relationship, Penelope?" Alice asked in the dining room that evening when Penelope confided in her, unable to banish Sally's idea from her mind.

"He is a second cousin to my dead husband, is all."

"That's no real relationship."

"And the real beauty, Lady Roakes," Sally spoke from her position near the side table, "is that he is unlikely to live a long time."

"That's wicked, Sally." But Alice was smiling as she said it. "But you are right. The odds must be that dear Penelope will not be away from us for long."

"I feel like one of the horses at the horse fair," Penelope complained.

"You are a lot more valuable," Sally said, then stood back to attention as the door opened and two footmen came in to help clear the plates.

The idea sat about for several days as August came. Some ideas sit and grow while others waste away. Which category would Sally's idea fall into? Grow or diminish? It seemed the latter for no more mention was made of it. And then the harvest came, two weeks earlier than the previous year due to early rain followed by the strongest sunshine. Following the tradition they had set last year, everybody went to help with the harvest. To Penelope it was like a religious service and one in which she partook gladly.

Yet Alice was called away on the first morning while they helped on Oak Grove Farm, a small tenanted property, where the family had fallen on hard times. Mr Aiden had died suddenly, leaving his widow and eight young children on a holding that could not feed them. Concentrating on Oak Grove's harvest first meant that the Aiden family would likely get the best price for their grain.

A man came riding hard across the fields.

"I believe it is Mr Tabard," called Sally, straightening up from her work tying bales of straw.

"Lady Roakes, can you come now? The time has come."
Without a word, Alice half-ran to her horse, standing under one
of the oaks that gave the farm its name. Sally saw her purpose
and ran to assist her into the saddle.

"Thank you, Sally, please tell Penelope I'll be back before
nightfall."

'Where are you going, Lady Roakes?" But there was no
answer for she was away, weaving her horse around the bales
of straw and through the gate, Paul struggling to catch up on
his gasping horse.

The rest of the harvest work, usually enjoyed by Penelope,
seemed second rate compared to the mystery of Alice rushing
off that morning.

"The yield is better than last year by a little, miss,"Tomkins
tipped his hat to Sally, the girl he had taught the rudiments of
stewardship to but who now surpassed his knowledge easily.

"Yes, indeed, Mr Tomkins. I believe it has exceeded our best
hopes. How is the price at market?"

"Also a little up on last year, miss."Tomkins returned to the
harvest work, as he had done for the last sixty years, since before
he could remember.

"Why do you treat everyone so politely but are so rude with
me?" Penelope giggled a few minutes later. To which, Sally
turned and gave an exaggerated curtsey.

"Oh, Your Grace, I pray you are not angry with your poor
maid again. What is to become of her delicate constitution with
cross words from every angle?"

"Delicate constitution, my arse!"

"You are saying, I assume, that your behind also has a delicate
constitution?"

But even with such banter and with the harvest to do, the
day dragged on.

Until Alice came back that evening, exhausted and dispirited.

"He won't sell unless everything goes to one buyer," she said,
sinking into a chair and accepting a glass of madeira.

"So buy everything!" Penelope said, knowing now where Alice had been that day.

The Bunhop estate had been for sale for some time. The owner, Sir Giles Lythorpe, had huge gambling debts but somehow seemed to hold out against his creditors.

"His latest move is a court order that forbids the estate being split up on account of an ancient land grant from King John. I had hoped to persuade Sir Giles to part with it one farm at a time."

"How much is everything?"

"It's 4,000 acres of mostly prime farmland around the three villages of Lythorpe."

"That is twice what we have here."

"Plus the house."

"The house is virtually derelict, Lady Roakes," Sally added from her perch on the window seat. "I visited there earlier this year because of the boundary dispute between the two estates." Sally had negotiated a favourable outcome with the steward of Bunhop which had added a few acres to Great Little while giving a farm on the southern edge of Bunhop access to a tributary of the Stour, thus greatly improving it. "The value is in the land, pure and simple."

"We could renovate the house and rent it out." They had no use for a second mansion.

"Except for the problem of the price he is asking."

"How much?" said Sally and Penelope at the same time, Sally adding a 'Lady Roakes' to the end of the question so that it was her voice that lingered on in Alice's conscious.

"He is asking £5 an acre and £5,000 for the house."

"How much does…" Penelope started, mental arithmetic having always alluded her.

"£25,000 all in," Sally interrupted. "More than the whole worth of Great Little," she added as an afterthought.

At breakfast the next day, Penelope announced that she was going away for a few days.

"There are some horses I wish to see near Devizes."

"You're not thinking of taking Sally with you? I do not think we can afford to let her go right in the middle of harvest."

"No, I think you have need of her here. There is also the matter of Oak Grove to sort out."

"The Oak Grove farmland would certainly be a useful addition to the horse breeding enterprise. The fields adjoin the park and some are better suited to pasture than crops. We will have to find something else for the Aiden family to do."

"They could still live in the house there."

"Except it is too small. I will talk to Sally about it this afternoon. I need to visit Sir Giles again this morning. I want to try one more time to convince him it is in his interest to sell me a section of his estate." And so the subject of Penelope's absence was put to one side during a busy day.

"Did she not tell you she was going?" Sally was making report to Lady Roakes on the terrace outside the library. It had been a long day and, even now, the sun seemed stubbornly determined to stay with them. They looked across the park to Oak Grove Farm, fresh chequered with stubble in most fields. Tomorrow they would move south to Home Farm, the biggest block of land within Great Little.

"No, Lady Roakes, and that means she is up to something."

"Well, dear, we have the matter of Oak Grove to consider. Penelope wants it for an extension to her horse farm and I agree."

"Young Joe Aiden can help with the horses," Sally said immediately. "He shows great promise. And there is a house in the village they could have. I know the rector of Whatcombe has need of a housekeeper. He is not wealthy but if we could manage a small increase in his stipend..." Sally was in the world she loved, working constantly at improvement of the estate she had come to think of as home.

Chapter 27

Parchman had time to ponder matters as the ship sailed out of sight of land. He had never enjoyed the sea but the thought of a complete pardon, all over again, was too much to resist.

"I will be able to enter government service again," he told the waves of green and white. They answered his words by chopping around the place, never keeping still and throwing the deck he was standing on in every direction at once, although others on the same deck seemed barely to notice the motion.

But, in reality, there was no government service, no service to others of any kind, as Parchman reminded himself now.

"Everything I do, I do for myself entirely," he told the seagulls as they fell astern, calling to each other across the wavetops and ignoring whatever Parchman said. "I am free!" Parchman shouted to the rigging of this sleek ship, then curtailed his voice for two sailors were looking at him strangely instead of coiling their ropes.

"I am free," he said silently, time and time again, "as free as the sea, the gulls and the fish." And this marvellous prize of freedom is what he now pondered as the ocean took control and the sailors performed their every day tasks in order to make passage across it. He contemplated his negotiations with Cartwright that had led to this sudden offer of freedom, of a glorious return to the life of intrigue he loved so much.

"Will you go in Taylor's place, sir?"

"I will not, Cartwright." There was a distinct sameness about their address. Cartwright had worked for Parchman but now he was a lord. Yet Parchman addressed him as he always had and, in return, the one-time subordinate still referred to Parchman as 'sir'.

"I can make it worth your while, sir." Cartwright surveyed the room Parchman had for his own use at the Homeless Pig. "I'll grant you this accommodation is satisfactory, even comfortable, for an inn, but there are far finer places to put down your hat."

This is where the negotiations began. Parchman aimed high.

"I want your job."

"What will become of me?"

"You made a good assistant before and you will do so again." Parchman had stared at Cartwright, cold eyes making for an uncomfortable presence. But Cartwright had not gone all out for promotion just to give it up again.

"I don't choose who succeeds me," he replied after a moment's thought.

"Who does?"

"The King."

"The King?"

"Yes, did you not know that I am a minister of state?" The stakes were being raised.

Round one was to Cartwright. Parchman licked his wounds and regrouped, summoning up the energy for the second.

"You have quite a track record in deceit, Cartwright."

"All gained under your expert direction and oversight, sir."

Was this oily man with his slicked hair and shifty eyes really to get the better of Parchman?

"Ah, but therein lies the difference." A strong punch to the midriffs was coming.

"What do you mean?"

"I mean, Cartwright, that I have been found out and disgraced. Consequently, I am low and can only go up. You, however, are at a pinnacle of achievement and, from your current position, can only go down. Look around you, Cartwright, everywhere there are ambitious people who would have your power and position in a heartbeat. You need a savvy friend and I can be that person, your guardian, if you like."

They settled it after a while. Parchman was to get a full pardon, engineered by Cartwright, and a new job of at least the same seniority as before.

"And not reporting to you, Cartwright."

"I agree, sir, not reporting to me." He did not rate the chances of long survival with the old boss in his camp. But running some other department he would be a useful ally.

But the main prize for Cartwright was to get a replacement messenger to go immediately to New England, one with enough intelligence, credibility and force of personality to carry the plan forward.

"Nothing is to be in writing, other than a single letter of authority," Cartwright said as they toasted their agreement in brandy. "All messages, passwords and secret codes are to be learned by heart."

"Nothing in writing," Parchman agreed.

Soon there was nothing to be seen of Bristol, then nothing of England either. Parchman could not stare at the waves for three thousand miles. That was for the proud figurehead. Parchman felt suited not to prominent poses but slinking in the shadows, weighing up the situation and pouncing when the time was right.

"Sir, the captain sends his compliments, sir." A small boy tugged at his bare forehead. "And he would be desirous of your company for dinner, sir."

"Tell the captain I will come at seven. To his cabin, I suppose?"

"No sir, you have his cabin, sir. He gave it up to you, as you being such an important gentleman, sir. He wants to come to you, sir, if it ain't too much trouble, that is, sir."

"Very well." He would do his duty, see the captain tonight and then keep to himself for the rest of the voyage.

"Sir, I hope it isn't too much trouble to dine here. It's just that it happens to be the only cabin of any size on board this vessel."

"No trouble at all, Captain." He assumed one called the captain of a ship by his rank. It was, in actual fact, a considerable inconvenience as his stomach was churning with the motion but he would do his duty now and be finished with it.

"I brought something for the sea-sickness, Captain. I hope you will join me in a tipple." Parchman crossed the cabin to his only bag and pulled out a bottle of a reddish-brown liquid. "I don't drink as a rule but am drawn to celebrate my passage in this remarkable boat."

"A drop or two will go down very well indeed, sir."

The trouble with a drop, as Parchman found out that night, is that it makes the next drop more desirable and then even more the one after that, but the information he gained was worth the hangover he woke with; at least it put his sea-sickness into perspective. He struggled the next morning on to the deck to find the captain in the best of health bellowing orders and mixing that bellowing with humorous observations. When Parchman's head rose through the hatchway, the banter he had heard from below ended immediately. Parchman nodded at the now serious faces and walked to the stern of the ship, once more to stare at the waves as if they did not belong in the sea at all.

There was nowhere to hide on a ship, nowhere to be alone and keep to the shadows. Everywhere you went there were people bustling about, just like London. But unlike the city, a perfect place to hide, everybody knew each other on a ship; there was no anonymity amongst a ship's complement.

"I'll keep to my cabin," he said to himself, and did so for most of the rest of the fast passage across the Atlantic.

For he had a great deal of planning to do, especially with the information he had extracted from the captain with the help of the bottle he had brought with him. He had pulled it out entirely on impulse, for Parchman seldom drank; about that he had been honest enough.

Parchman was the substitute messenger when the first choice became unavailable. It should have been Simon standing on the deck, feeling the sharp breeze and the salty spray, rather than Parchman sulking in his cabin. Instead, that same morning, when the hangover bit deep into Parchman's conscious, Simon was being led in chains to the scaffold. One of the jailers spat as he passed. It was an excellent shot, landing on Simon's upper lip.

"Have that man report to me afterwards," the chief jailer cried. 'Afterwards' stuck in Simon's mind as he dragged his manacles towards the scaffold; 'afterwards' referred to his pending death, when he would be no more. What could he expect to happen? He had spurned the visit of any religious person. Should he have asked for one? He turned now, one foot on the first step of the stairs. He would ask the chief jailer.

But his voice would not work. Too long in silence and choked-up at the thought of life ending or was his body already shutting down, inessential functions like speech deserting him? A wild panic gripped his innards; he could not communicate the most basic of needs.

He saw the chief jailer look at him, not an unkind face yet responsible for so much death.

Death meant being no more; not breathing, not looking down his nose at the world around him, no schemes to play, no tricks to pull and no warm bodies for the long nights.

Why had he surrendered to it?

He felt the piss dribbling down his leg. Why did it choose the left and not the right leg? Why waste the precious moments left considering such inane matters? There was pressure behind him to take the next step.

"It's always the second step onto the scaffold that is the hardest, it commits the whole body. With one foot on the ground, there is still the illusion of escape and prolonged life. When both feet are on the scaffold steps, the illusions evaporate like mist of a morning. I have noticed this of long experience, my friend, and mention it now only to prepare you as best I can." Those were the kind words of Michael Bars who had visited him several times and spent much of the previous night with him, after Elizabeth, Amelia, Thomas and Bridget had departed, sorrow chiselled on their drawn-out faces.

And now the chief jailer was talking again.

"Just nod your head if you want a religious." Simon nodded his head vigorously, giving the hangman a first sight of the length of the neck so he could plan how the rope would best fit. A young man, dressed soberly, stepped forwards and onto the steps beside him. The jailer had been prepared.

"Come, my son, and meet your maker." The young man's face shone with kindness; he had been selected for the position of prison chaplain when the old one had retired last year. The number of executions this young minister had attended was still under forty. He was raw but keen to do well.

"I am too old to be your son, my son." His voice was back! It had not deserted him at all. And, the moment before death extinguished life, it had come back with a joke. "And too wrapped in evil to be of interest to God."

The chaplain looked puzzled a moment, then replied, "but not too old to be His child and do the Scriptures not say that The Father loves every starling in the bush at two a penny?"

"It does."

"You have one thing left to do, my son." The last two words were emphasised by the minister, pronouncing that Simon's argument had been considered and dismissed. Simon did not pursue it.

"Being?" Simon did not want to commit.

"To be sorry for your sins, for your crimes against the nation and against those dearest to you." The chaplain had always taken his brief seriously. He read the backgrounds of all the condemned men, in fact, of all the prisoners as it was not just the condemned in need of the mercy and love he dispensed.

In his own right and on behalf of Another.

"I don't believe." But then, quite suddenly, he did believe. He had completed the steps, side by side with the chaplain. He turned and looked at the crowd; the crowd that had come to see him die. He imagined the usual bunch that enjoyed such spectacles. He was not concerned with them. He searched the sea for fishes he knew. There they were; he saw Amelia first, still pale from her ordeal. She was half way back through the crowd, supported by Elizabeth on one side and Thomas on the other. Would his voice carry that far back? Did he even want to say anything?

In the end, he said nothing until the noose was around his neck, the trapdoor under his feet; these were the two mechanisms that would bring death to him. Death and oblivion?

Or death and the fires of hell? He pissed again but jerked his body slightly to ensure it ran down the right-hand leg, giving a sweet symmetry to his last moments. His jerking caused a shudder of expectation across the front of the crowd; those that were there for the spectacle.

Then, as if someone else was talking through his mouth, moving levers and wires deep within him, he cleared his voice and waited for the crowd to become silent.

As they always did for the last half a minute.

"Repent, Simon, repent and be with Our Lord this very day," the chaplain urged. Simon looked at him in bewilderment.

"I was taught sinners go to hell…predestination, all that stuff."

"I believe otherwise, Simon Taylor. I promise you this, repent genuinely and, in a few minutes, you will be welcomed by Our Father in Heaven. Such is my absolute faith in His splendour and love."

Simon, in response, cleared his throat again but could not clear his mind. Instead, he clung to the pastor's words as if he had believed them all his life. He started talking at the top of his weakened, fear-riddled voice. And Amelia and Elizabeth and Bridget remembered the words off by heart. Thomas claimed to but got confused and ended up with several different versions.

I've been a bad man all my life. But evil can love, in fact the bad may love as fiercely, or fiercer, as the good. But our love is peppered with selfish thoughts and considerations, like an old tin bucket full of holes. And we use our love in a manipulative way, in a way that you do not, daughter dear and wife dear. Know please and remember always that, despite my evil, I loved in my particular way and, given the time again, I would resolve to love you wholly and completely, no tin bucket draining away the love. I am sorry for the suffering I have caused and the injury I have done.

"That's certainly enough, a grand mixture of repentance and regret. One could not ask for more." The words of the chaplain were the final words Simon Taylor heard in this life as the trapdoor sprang open and his body fell to the cracking sound of a broken neck.

But he did hear one more voice, whether from this world or the other. It was distant but seemed welcoming and warm; like he remembered his mother being before she had died. Perhaps it was her voice.

"Mother!" he said as the life went out of him.

Chapter 28

Penelope did not slow her horses until the very last minute. "Whoa!" she cried. She would not forgive herself if she got the timing wrong and hurt her beautiful new horses. Her ostentation might cause them to crash against the steep stone steps that led up to the ugly front portico.

But they shied away and, with Penelope pulling on the reins, veering the pair left, they came to a halt just before the steps.

"That was a foolish move." The duke's voice hit her pride dead on. It's one thing to recognise faults oneself, quite another to have them pointed out to you.

"A slight misjudgement, Your Grace."

"What brings you here? Not, I pray, a request for more money."

I'll wager you've never prayed in your life, she thought, then considered that neither had she.

"Far from it, Your Grace." They had reached a settlement two years earlier when her husband, the previous duke, had died in the fire at Great Little without producing an heir. The current duke, a second cousin, had inherited the title and the property. Penelope had negotiated hard for a portion of it.

"Then what? I doubt it is a social call."

"It is precisely that, Your Grace." Then she realised that her statement was implausible; nobody made social calls on this fat and selfish pig of a man. "And to ask your advice on something, sir."

"You'd better come in, then…" He left her name unsaid, for he could not remember it. "But don't be expecting anything by way of hospitality. You cleared me out two years ago and I've been struggling ever since."

"How old are you, sir?" Penelope asked the next morning.

"What's that to you, madam?" He still could not remember her name.

"I just was thinking, Your Grace, about priorities, is all."

"I'm sixty-six."

"You look a little younger, sir." She stressed 'a little' to gain credibility. "I am twenty-five."

"So come to crow it over me? Display your youthfulness in front of a poor old man, is that it?"

"No, Your Grace. I came to ask your advice, like I said when I arrived." She had not been able to talk to the duke all of the previous day. He had taken the sweetmeats she had brought with her and shut himself away, only surfacing this morning to ask if she had any more about her.

"I have a little, Your Grace, but first please bear with me. I'll fetch them in a moment." Somehow, she had to make it the duke's idea to join their bodies and souls forever. Her mind worked furiously on the problem. She had come with a lot of hope but no plan at all.

"Who will inherit when the sad day of your passing comes, I pray not for many a year?"

"I have two brothers, madam. The older of the two will inherit." He seemed fit to burst with anger at the thought. Penelope pressed on.

"Your Grace, thank the Lord, I was concerned that the title would fall into abeyance. Well, that is my task settled, then. I shall finish the breakfast you have so kindly offered and trouble you no further."

"Wait a minute." The duke looked every bit his age now, also frothing with anger. "Did I say it was a satisfactory situation? No, far from it!"

Penelope then did a terribly bold thing. She rose from her chair, came around the table and knelt before the odious man, placing her hands in his lap. His pot-belly protrusion was such that his chair was eighteen inches from the table, sufficient room for Penelope to come in from the side and underneath the belly. She felt like a spy in hostile territory.

"Tell me, sir, why your rage is so extreme? Unburden yourself to me, Your Grace."

He did and it was an extraordinary mix of anger and jealousy. Major Davidson, the younger brother, had emigrated to New England, done well for himself by all accounts and had been in contact recently about some urgent and secret matters of state which the duke had handled rather well, he thought.

"It's the middle brother that is the problem. He's a wastrel of the first order, never amounted to anything yet sucks off others like he was royalty." Penelope knew something of this. She had done some research, asking Henry, Earl of Sherborne, newly back from the wars in Ireland with suitable bandages and slings to show for it. Henry had been briefly engaged to Penelope when they were younger, in fact at the height of the Monmouth Rebellion of '85. It was an arranged match and they were hopelessly unsuited for each other but had developed a mutual respect. Plus, the countess, Grace, had made it a point to befriend Penelope.

It had been easy to stop at Sherborne Hall for two nights and find out more about the current Duke of Wiltshire's background.

"Why are you so interested, Penelope?" Henry had asked. "Are you planning something devious?"

"No," she had lied, "I just want to make sure there is an heir when the current duke dies. I don't want the dukedom to die out."

Henry had looked at Grace and she had smiled, her hand covering it nicely. They both knew Penelope was up to something.

Now, she was soothing a man she despised, whispering earnest and reassuring things as if she cared.

She did care, but not for the man.

"And what are his children like?" she asked.

"What children? Did I say my brother had children?" It was a serious mistake and the duke jumped on it. "How do you know he has children?" he demanded suspiciously.

"I just…assumed, sir, because you said he was married." Would that suffice? "I see, sir, that you are angered beyond belief by the situation."

"My brother who will inherit has six sons and he would love to pass on a dukedom to the oldest one!"

"I wonder if there is anything we can do about it?" Penelope asked. He saw her relief and mistook it for concern. He was, after all, the centre of his world. She decided to leave it there; better several small steps than risking everything at once.

After a breakfast of cold chops from the previous evening, Penelope moved to the next stage.

"I always thought the grounds delightful. Will you walk in them with me, Your Grace?"

"I don't walk far."

"We won't overcommit ourselves, sir. I certainly would not want to strain your heart overly. Perhaps just to that copse and back? I am thinking that maybe a little fresh air and exercise will stimulate the mind as to what to do about your predicament." Penelope knew exactly what idea she would suddenly discover when just starting back across the lawn on the return leg. She would remind him of the sweetmeats she still had in her luggage, then develop the idea with him when he was in the best frame of mind.

Only, he got there first. They had just started walking across the lawn, dropping down from the long terrace that went from the front to the back of Wiltshire House. Penelope had noticed the dilapidations the previous day when touring the grounds and planning her moves. She knew from Withers Court, her childhood home, that big houses needed a lot of care. There were numerous loose flagstones, iron railings worn to the metal and the mortar between the great yellow stones of the house had disappeared in places. She was puzzled because she knew the duke to be wealthy. Was it just that he did not care?

The duke needed help down to the lawn.

"I told the buggers to mend these steps," he said. "They're bone idle, every one of them."

"You can't get good staff these days." It sounded like the correct response, capitalising on an old man's grumpy attitude to the world.

"Talking of staff, are you still rutting that blackie you keep?"

"What?"

"Your maid, the darkie." Penelope was speechless for a moment. Did the duke really know or had he guessed?

And if he knew, then likely everybody else knew too.

"Don't worry, my dear," he still could not remember her name. She was called something to do with money or perhaps he just associated her with money because she had extracted so much from him when he had first inherited. "Don't worry, it's not universal knowledge. I just have put two and two together. But you are, aren't you?"

"Are what?" Penelope was desperate for inspiration, playing for time.

"Having your wicked way with the girl, of course!"

Then it came to her. It was a little bit of a tortured path but she played it with a sweet smile and kept the hand that had helped him down the steps in his, tickling his palm with her long fingers.

"I admit it, Your Grace, but only because I have never found a proper man." She wondered if she could be any more tart-like.

"She's good?"

"She's tolerable, I suppose." The lie trotted out easily from Penelope's lips; she was playing for high stakes.

"I wouldn't mind having a go myself."

"What?" This was going to a place she had not foreseen. For the briefest of moments she thought it would serve Sally right to be bedded by this awful man. But she loved Sally and in twenty-five years on this earth, she had not found much to love.

"But I expect I will just have to put up with her mistress instead."

"Sir!"

"That is what you came about, is it not? You want a son and that little darkie can never give you one. I want to stop my brother inheriting. It's the obvious solution to both our problems."

"Of course, Your Grace, how clever of you. I was stumbling about in the dark trying to think of a solution and you had

221

it all along!" At least he did not know about her inheritance clause, the £100,000 coming her way on suitable marriage and production of an heir.

"I knew you'd see it my way," he replied. "Besides, there is the matter of settling your inheritance as well. Help me down, my dear."

"What?"

"It is the customary posture, I believe."

"Of course, Your Grace." She helped the wobbling man to gain stability with one knee on the grass. She looked around and saw the splendid old oaks of the copse behind her. And there was an old man kneeling before her; they remained holding hands as he asked for hers in marriage.

"Dearest, will you have me to be your husband in order that we might bear a son to our mutual benefit?" There was not one jot of romance in his address.

"I will, sir," she replied, her heart as cold as a stone in winter, yet it was the height of a lazy summer.

"Just one other question, my dear."

"Yes, sir?"

"Remind me of your name."

"It is Penelope, Your Grace."

"Well, I shall call you Penny." He knew there had been some connection to money.

The arrangements were discussed in short order. The duke would talk to the vicar about the banns, by which he meant they would not be a problem.

"We will marry next week unless I am much mistaken. There is no need to waste money on a pretty dress, my dear, you will pass very fine in your regular clothes. We won't bother too much with guests. I find guests to be an unnecessary expense in any arrangement. We just need a best man to witness the nuptials."

"Can I suggest someone, sir?"

"Anyone you like, my dear. I don't have any friends, never saw the need. Friends are always after you for this and that. I expect you are similar, hiding yourself away in that place in Dorset and playing little games with your maid!" He patted her bottom as he spoke, examining the livestock he had just purchased.

"Leave it with me. I'll sort out a respectable man for you." She would take her trap and go that very day to Ashenham; better, she reasoned, to be away from her fiancée whenever she could. "I might be gone a few days but I will be back by Sunday for certain."

"Then, let us set the date for Monday!"

"As you wish, Your Grace." She pecked him on the cheek and bade him goodbye while she went in search of a best man.

Chapter 29

Anne Aspley looked at the collection of her dead brother's belongings on the floor of the breakfast room that had originally been her office. She had not shown them to her mother yet, fearing too strong a reaction.

"Thank you again, Mr Davenport, for bringing these to me but I have to ask how you came about them?"

"They were in that box with my sister's late husband's belongings. He had recently returned from America, where he was a soldier, and, sadly, died shortly afterwards." There seemed little point in telling the details of Simon's death to a stranger.

"My consolations to you and your sister, sir, but that explains it. My brother was a newly commissioned officer sent to help the colonials with the war against the French. That must be where your sister's husband met him."

"The box was addressed to your family but at another address in Dorchester. The occupants of that house directed me here."

"We have recently moved. It was very kind of you to track us down."

"I shall leave you to peruse the belongings, Miss Aspley." She looked up on hearing these words. There was something about his voice; a tone she had recently noted in another.

"Sir, by chance you would not be related to the Countess of Sherborne, would you?"

"She is my sister, Miss Aspley, my younger sister of two. Do you know her?"

"Yes," she replied, "the Countess is also one of my shareholders, Mr Davenport."

"Shareholders?" He had supposed Miss Aspley to be another, slightly down on their luck, middle class lady. Yet she had used the word 'my' in relation to the shareholders, suggesting an enterprising side to her.

"In Aspley and Associates, insurers to the marine trade." Her pride was evident. "We only started a few months ago and have made over £900 in profit!"

"I'm clearly in the wrong trade. That is considerably more than I made throughout the whole of last year." He told her about his building business, stressing the ups and downs and the difficulties that gave him in keeping a steady workforce. "It is important to me to be able to meet the wage bill each week and not to have to lay people off when times get bad."

It was several days later that the idea came to Anne. She was in her new office, set up in Mr Fellows' establishment, working on some proposals for a different type of insurance on ships; insurance that worked all year around and covered the vessel for certain limits, above which for specific trips additional cover could be purchased at special rates.

"It smooths out our business, Mr Fellows. True, it lessens the total profit a little but it means we have income week in and week out."

It was the smoothing concept that had generated a new idea in Anne's mind.

Thomas had business of his own to attend to and it involved his building work only superficially. One day in mid-August, he asked Bridget to walk with him.

"I'm going to visit that row of cottages we're building at Dewdrop Farm. The foreman is having some problems with the thatcher and I thought to try and sort it out. Will you come with me and we can take a picnic, Bridge?"

"Of course, sir." But her response was evidence of the reason for asking her to come; it was wooden, functional.

They walked across the bridge over the Stour, turned left towards Fiddleford, rather than the usual right, being the way to Bagber. The road was not paved after the bridge. It was dry and the ruts were baked into the ground, making walking difficult in the road but Thomas had a stick with him and went first, swishing the long grass by the hedgerow, making a path for Bridget to follow. They stopped in Fiddleford, close by the inn.

"I just have to pop in to see the Biggs," Thomas explained.

"I'll stay by the bridge," she replied, still functional, desultory even. "What is this stream, sir?" Thomas looked surprised a moment, then remembered that Bridget had only been in Dorset a few months and much of that had been a long, hard winter, lasting well into May. He had never taken her this way before.

"It's called Darknoll. It flows into the Stour just over there, close to the manor." Thomas pointed with his left hand, using his right to help her over a style. "Are you sure you want to stay here on the bridge, Bridge?" She laughed at his joke but it was a dutiful laugh, or rather one where the joy had flowed away to another place sometime ago.

"I don't understand it," Thomas said to Plain Jane and Big Jim a few minutes later. "We've only been married five months and she is as cold as anything."

"You silly man," laughed Plain Jane, over thirty now but looking even more beautiful with every year. "Don't you see what you've done?" Thomas did not.

"You bring her here from another country. You wed her, despite having a thing for another woman who has become no longer available while you were galivanting in Ireland…no, let me finish, Thomas. Then you spend all this summer obsessing with the other girl who, admittedly, has been through hell, and you expect Bridge to be unaffected by all this?"

"But we love each other, we vowed for better or worse, in sickness and in health."

"You are such an idiot at times, Thomas. Now, to cap it all, Amelia is suddenly available again yet you expect Bridge to react as if everything was alright."

"But she wouldn't even come in to see you. She preferred to wait outside on the bridge."

"She's here? On the bridge and you let her stay there?"

"She wouldn't come in."

Jane Bigg stood up, asked her husband to watch "Thomas, the simpleton" and left the kitchen where they had been drinking beer brewed by Big Jim. He poured more into their glasses

226

and they sat in awkward silence for fifteen minutes. It was not complete silence; more the type where each participant thinks laboriously of something to say and, as they pronounce it, they feel the irrelevance of it already. It was the silence that only two men who know themselves well can have. It was the silence employed to avoid more painful things.

They heard Plain Jane long before they saw her return. Her voice rang with deliberate laughter as it wound up the short road from Darknoll. Thomas hoped it was not the case but then knew it to be, first possible, then probable and finally certain.

"I found this young lass astray by the roadside," she called before re-entering the kitchen.

Big Jim rose, crossed the floor to hug his best friend's still-new wife. Thomas rose but would not look at her directly, preferring the floor, the dresser stacked with bottles of beer, the window above the sink with a view up the hill to Piddles Wood, leaning over the long, thatched house that Thomas had built for the Biggs just last year.

Yet he did sneak looks at his wife on every occasion when he could. He was struck again by the curious and beautiful angles that made her body and face. It seemed to him that intelligence came in corners, more so if they were of varying angles around the body. Perhaps common sense was more rounded, more worn away at the edges. He would like to build a house like her.

Bridget, his wife, was all edges and was on edge herself.

She caught him looking from time to time and then, of course, he looked away, finding more purpose in examining his boots or the buttons on his coat. But once, as Big Jim did what he did best, opening more bottles of beer, they held their gaze; long, steady and deep.

Afterwards, as they walked on to Dewdrop Farm across a field where they could walk side by side, Thomas tried apologising. Bridget let him stumble through a few words then found his hand and took it. Thomas turned, reasserted the grip but without looking down. Their eyes were fixed on each other's.

"Don't try and apologise anymore. Jane explained to me, Thomas my dear. She gave me a severe telling off on the bridge, calling me a fool and a simpleton for complaining about you caring for Amelia. She made me feel quite small indeed and then she built me back up again on the walk from the bridge to her house. I am sorry, too, Thomas. I've made your life harder than it had to be because of my jealousy for Amelia."

"Oh Bridge, I do love Amelia but in a different way now, more as a sister. It is you…" No more needed to be said.

They were late at the row of cottages but Thomas could see immediately what was wrong.

"It's not the thatch at all," he said. "it's that the roof line is too low. The cottages look like a row of soldiers without their hats! Take the roofline up eighteen inches and you have a whole different perspective. See, also, there is room now to make a proper attic in the roof space. We will amend the plans to build a dormer window in each attic and put a tiny staircase here so we have permanent access."

"I see, Mr Davenport. Thank the Good Lord you came along today."

And Bridget spent the entire picnic afterwards doing a very bad imitation of the foreman, her Ulster accent making a disaster of the Dorset dialect.

"Mr Davenport, thank the Good Lord you came along in my life," she said repeatedly, doing what Bridget Davenport did best which was to use the strange, sharp angles of her personality to build bridges from one side to the other.

Mr Amiss knew he would not see much more of this world. But the end, when it came, caught even him out, for it was not the growth in his belly that caused it but an accident. On a good day, he could still be up and about and he was running a few errands one mid-August day, looking forward to returning home to Amy and the baby. He stepped into the road to avoid walking under a ladder, chiding himself gently for being superstitious, when the cart struck him. It was not a heavy cart for it was empty, returning to the grocers' shop from where it had begun its journey early that morning. Half an hour later and it would be loaded again. A strike at that time would certainly have killed instantly.

An observer said that frail Mr Amiss seemed to bounce across the road and straight into the ladder he had sought to avoid. The ladder came down on him, bringing the window cleaner and his two pails of water tumbling after. The witness reported that the top of the ladder struck a hat shop window, smashing the various panes and sending shards of glass showering over the scene.

Certainly, Mr Amiss had multiple cuts to add to his more serious injuries.

"His leg is broken, I believe, also he seems to have fainted." The first person to kneel beside the body was no physician, just a practical bod who had attended a few similar scenes over his long life.

"It's Mr Amiss," said Mr Fellows, turning the body over as best he could. "Run and get Mr and Mrs Tabard."

Mr Fellows tried to move the body, he later told everyone, in an attempt to make him more comfortable. But he stopped when Mr Amiss screamed in agony. Instead he let his friend lie in a heap by the side of the road; a strange and twisted pile of bones and flesh, like a person half way through the process of being melted down for scrap. He crouched down low, itself a feat for a man approaching his century, to try and get on the same level as Mr Amiss.

Amy Tabard was there next, running the six hundred yards from the house without stopping. She fell down to her knees and Mr Fellows made way for her, sitting back on his aching legs, then stretching them carefully one by one.

"Father," she said, for everyone now accepted that she was his daughter. "Father, we must get you to the house and get a doctor." There is something in desperate hope, an easily snapped thread running from reality to fantasy. Amy clung to it, eyes open but shut to all reality.

"Can't move, Amy, my dear daughter, can't move." He said four more words but first he closed his eyes so that Amy panicked and sought to cling him to her.

"Hold on, Father, help is coming." Looking up, she could see Paul running up the street.

"Don't move him. I think his back must be broken. It is agony for him to be moved." Mr Fellows placed a restraining hand on Amy's arm. "He can't be moved," he reiterated, as if repetition would add to his argument.

"Then how do we help him?" She looked up desperately again. Paul was only fifty yards away now, chugging valiantly to get there.

"He can't be helped, my little one. He is dying, Amy, he is dying." Again the repetition, for what else does one say?

But Mr Amiss had four more words to say in his time in this world. He said these in perfect lucidity and with his eyes wide open. He said them to Amy, just as Paul skidded to a stop and came down beside his wife on the ground.

"I love you, daughter."

The funeral was well attended, for Mr Amiss had been a popular man. There were no relatives other than Amy and Paul. They sat in the front row, constantly making way for others to pass and take seats further along. Amy cried every moment, fresh tears to mark the passing of a lovely man.

"We ought to signify his passing in some way," Mr Jarvis said at the party afterwards. They were in Mr Amiss' house, now passed into his daughter's ownership.

"You mean a monument or a park bench?"

"No, I had something else entirely in mind. Think, Paul and Amy, how he helped you start in business."

"He gave us somewhere to live and an income while we developed the business. He also backed us in a small way."

"I think we should set up a fund in his name to help other young people aspiring to enter into business."

Mr Fellows gave the most money, followed by Amy, from her inheritance, and then Mr Jarvis. They decided to keep the subscription open until the end of the month and a surprising number of his old friends and customers at the Red Lion gave pennies and shillings and even the odd larger amount. Combined with the founding donations they had sufficient in the trust to provide a small income to several young people headed into the business world as well as a modest amount to back them.

"It's the model my father followed in helping us getting started," she said, anxious as trustee to get it right from the beginning.

They debated a name for two weeks before settling on the simplest: The Amiss Trust for Young Business Folk.

"And I hope, Mr Fellows and Mr Jarvis, you will join me as the first trustees," Amy said when the lawyers were ready to finalise the trust documentation.

Chapter 30

"What do you mean, he is not here?"

"Sir William Phips has left the city on campaign, sir."

"I wish him well in it," Parchman lied, "but I come from Whitehall with important despatches for him. I must reach him urgently."

"You should catch him if you take your fast ship, sir. You came in the White Lady, I believe. Sir William has nothing so fast as it, I'll wager. May I see the letter of introduction again, sir?" It was the only letter Parchman had from Lord Cartwright, addressed to whomever it may concern and placing a burden on the recipient to assist his trusted emissary, Parchman, in any way in which he required. The original had said 'trusted servant' but Parchman had insisted it be changed to 'emissary'.

"First, you will give me a complete run down of the strategy. Then you will find me suitable accommodation for one night. I depart in the morning, not by sea but by land."

"Yes sir."

Parchman insisted on a large escort, courtesy of the local militia. He had slept well that night, the first night on land for three weeks. It had not been an easy crossing; well over a month in which they lay becalmed for four days. There had been no motion to throw his stomach but the absolute stillness and the attendant heat had, in many ways, been worse. It had driven him from his cabin to the deck again.

"When do you think the wind will return?" he had asked the captain.

"Three more days, I believe, sir." And it had been exactly that, a wind had threaded its way through the lank sails on the evening of the fourth day. It had increased steadily to the point where Parchman thought there was nothing but extremes from the sea.

"When will this gale end?" he had asked, thinking he must sound like a small child repeatedly asking when…when…when.

"Sir, this is hardly a gale, more a brisk breeze. We will have two or three days of this if we are lucky, sufficient, I pray, to take us to Boston."

As if the captain were directly connected to God, the stiff breeze blew them for three days almost to the minute from Parchman's question and brought them to Boston harbour on a bright, sunny afternoon in late August.

And now Parchman was back in his element, playing the daring-game with both feet on dry land.

"What, sir? You want an escort to go by land?"

"Is that not what I have just said?" It was convention to attach 'sir' in addresses, even to someone quite junior. But Parchman would not do it, would not demean himself by recognising anything of worth in the bureaucrat before him.

Besides, he rather liked the discomfort his arrogance and disdain provided.

"Might I ask where you intend to go? It is not possible to travel overland to Quebec, sir."

"You may not ask. Just provide the escort as is my right."

"Yes, sir. Might I ask, sir, whether your ship…"

"It is not my ship. I merely berthed in it."

"I see, sir. Might I enquire whether it brought the requested munitions for Sir William's expedition? He was loathe to leave without them but the summer was pressing on."

"I neither know nor care what the ship's cargo is." He did know, for the captain had listed in detail the munitions he had separately contracted to carry to the New World, for the planned invasion of Quebec.

Parchman had fumed on hearing this from the captain. Was nothing secret from the common man? But then he had realised that an attack on Quebec was the obvious next step after Phips' success at Port Royal earlier that year. The captain would have easily guessed the purpose of his cargo.

He had asked the captain for maps of the New World early in the voyage and had poured over them for countless hours.

It was during one such hour, alone in his cabin, that the idea of his own plan began to form.

"Hang Phips and hang Cartwright, "he muttered to himself, "my plan shall serve my needs much more closely." Then he recoiled.

But it was not in shame, rather mention of the word 'hang', for any reference to gallows or rope left him shuddering in the coldest of fears.

"Do you know General Davidson?" Parchman asked the middle-aged captain who headed the escort. The officer looked bored with army life, he had already told Parchman several times about his home, his family and his business as a trader of goods with England.

"I know a Major Davidson, sir, but there is no-one with that name of the rank of general."

"You do know him, Captain, for he has just been promoted." This was an important part of the plan to frustrate Phips and stop the tit-for-tat strikes across the border between New England and French Canada. The whole plan had originated as the germ of an idea from the unassuming Davidson, been cleverly altered by Simon and Cartwright. And now was being magnificently distorted by Parchman who had no time for Davidson's original peace-loving ideas. The intention was to embarrass all those involved in the war in America in order for Whitehall to take control of policy. The motive had moved far from the original peace-loving aims of Major Davidson, who believed commerce and industry would promote community and co-operation. Now the objective was to create maximum chaos and then to benefit from it in all possible ways.

But Parchman's refinement cared not for whether Whitehall grabbed the policy initiative. He simply defined success as failure; provided Phips and his rabble were unsuccessful, he would obtain his pardon and, most importantly, a new position in government. He cared nothing for foreign policy and empire, preferring the insidious and underhand manoeuvres of domestic matters. He would deal his blow on Phips and get back to London as quickly as he could to collect his pardon.

"I see, sir. General Davidson is close by." The bored and middle-aged captain stressed the rank, dubious as to its validity. "In fact, he is just three days march west of here. He is in an area of New England I know well, sir, having visited several times to buy and sell the goods I trade with England. Did I tell you, sir, that I trade mostly in…"

"Just get me there in two days."

"Sir, that is impossible. We have to cross the mountains…"

"Then, Captain, your first order from me is to make it possible. Am I understood?" He kicked his horse forward, as if demonstrating the need for speed, for urgency.

The middle-aged captain responded to the challenge set upon him. At first, he seemed to do nothing, still plodding his horses steadily northwest in the direction of distant Canada.

"This pace sickens me," Parchman complained after half an hour of the same gentle routine. Can't we quicken it a bit, man?"

"Sir, I am thinking out the possibilities. Bear with me a moment longer." Again, Parchman snorted and drove his horse forward, as if the escort was tied to his horse's tail and he could drag them on at a faster pace.

For time was all important to Parchman. He now knew that Phips planned an attack on Quebec. He was sailing there this very moment. He would move into position at the head of the army he landed and stood every chance of making a great success of it.

And it was Parchman's job to ensure he failed.

"How can I help, sir?" Davidson asked, stepping out of his tent to greet the government official from England.

"First, I have good news for you, Davidson. You are hereby promoted Major General."

"What did you say?"

"You are now Major General Davidson. What is more, I have orders concerning out next actions in this theatre of the war."

"Forgive me, sir." Davidson sat down on the camp chair, called for the orderly and asked for brandy. "You will have some, sir?" His promotion was so out of the blue that it seemed to be hanging in the deep-blue sky right above his heads.

"Not for me."

"Leave the bottle, Clarkson."

"Very well, sir." As the orderly left, Davidson turned to his strange visitor.

"How do I know this…promotion is genuine?"

"You have my word, Davidson." That clearly was not going to be enough. "And your brother sends his best wishes."

"Do you know my brother, the duke?"

"He asked me to pass on the following message." He cleared his throat, feeling slightly ridiculous at what he was about to recite.

Wiltshire House is very fine
Now I live there all the time
Wiltshire House is very fair
From Wiltshire House I will not stir.

"So you do know my brother!" Parchman did not answer for he had never met the tiresome duke, rather had learned the password rhyme from Cartwright, who had learned it from Simon. And Simon, in turn, had learned it from Major, now Major General, Davidson.

And the circle was complete but not in the way the major had intended when he had set it in motion. Whatever material made that circle had changed beyond belief on its journey twice across the Atlantic, once in each direction. It had started with a blend of integrity mixed with good intention and returned as pure deceit.

For Parchman had become involved. And he could wind any thread for his own evil purpose.

The beauty of Parchman's plan was the extra dimension. He chuckled to himself as he went over it again.

"What was that you said, sir?" Parchman was back in Boston, after four days in the hinterland.

"Nothing, Davidson, just a rumination, is all." He would have to be careful that he did nothing to arouse suspicion. "I'll draw up your orders directly but, in the meantime, be so kind as to commandeer a fast vessel in the King's name. She will need to take you and your new general staff to Quebec quickly. "

"Can I have an overview of my instructions, sir, so I might ponder them while the ship is made ready?"

Parchman was about to deny Davidson's request, the curt words already formed and ready to flow, when he reconsidered. It was important to keep this new general on his side, at least for the time being.

"On second thoughts, send an aide to commander the vessel, and come and dine with me at my lodgings. There is much I should tell you, Davidson."

Two questions crossed his mind as he issued this invitation. First was how little could he manage to divulge of his real plans without losing Davidson's fragile confidence, without confirming he meant war not peace? It was a tightrope between retaining the willing co-operation of this simpleton and maintaining the secrecy as to his actual intentions for the colonies.

Then the second question overtook the first. How would he bear sharing his food with another when he took no pleasure in eating and certainly no pleasure in company?

This was another example, he reflected, of the sacrifices Parchman made for the cause.

The only cause.

Chapter 31

Being in love three times in one year is remarkable but somehow Thomas managed it, although it was only years later that he would acknowledge it.

He had started 1690 in love with Bridget Browne, author of the heart-rending but simple eye-witness account of the Siege of Londonderry. He had escaped with her from Ulster in late '89 and married her in March, snow lying heavily on the ground, perhaps freezing all emotions for, as abrupt spring gave way to rich and indolent summer, the love did not seem to germinate. Another familiar plant grew in the garden. When Thomas took care, day and night, of Amelia Grimes, his love for Bridget shrivelled in the heat and shrunk to almost nothing. He was consumed with Amelia and sought nothing else.

And who could blame him? Amelia had suffered greatly since he had made the simple mistake of assuming she had lain gladly with his sister, Elizabeth. Thomas had run away from the horror of two naked female bodies, deaf to explanation, thinking only of hurting Amelia, who had offered him so much hope but apparently without any sincerity.

He had intended to go to the New World, thinking a complicated and confusing formula in which distance and difficulty of travel would compound the emotions of regret and sorrow engendered. But the formula was broken or not proven and the strain of the physics sent him instead into Ireland, at the southern tip of a hostile land, roused by the forces of James Stuart who had once been king. He had no choice but to travel the length of the country, south to north, in the company of his new friend, Tristan Browne, a lost young Irishman seeking his way to a home he had never known.

He met two other people who had made a great impression on him during that danger-spotted trip up the country. The first was Fr O'Toole, a sailor turned Catholic priest, who helped them escape twice.

But more importantly, the priest had set a kernel inside his young heart, a kernel of great beauty for his particular religion. And that kernel was still alive and growing. He had invited Fr O'Toole to his wedding during that frozen March and had sought the company of his Catholic friends and family, asking, but not asking, the same question of each:

What it was like to be a Catholic? To hear the sweet, lulling rhythms and chants of religion, to know the absolute security of what came next.

And so he learned that their God placed good works above faith. This troubled him severely for it was his own religion turned upside down. He warmed to this idea, for Thomas was a good man, despite his sins, and wished to do good in this world, perhaps to counter the damage he had done last year through his blind pride.

That being the damage to Amelia and then to Bridget, the second remarkable person his Irish travels had brought him into contact with.

Thomas had fallen out of love with Bridget through being consumed by Amelia's troubles. Some argue a man can love two women at once. Thomas was not such a man. His pride still reigned and governed him. Bridget had been the replacement for Amelia and now there could not be two.

Except there was to be another chapter to this story; the third falling in love of 1690. For as Amelia repaired herself, gaining new strength every day, attended by Thomas, cared for by Milly, who had taken her for her own, Amelia's strength began to impose itself once again.

"You cannot have me, Thomas," she had said one morning when Milly had gone to fetch warm water for Amelia to wash.

"I love you, Mealy."

"But you are committed to another and she is a wonderful person, Thomas. You are to make your marriage work." Issued more like an order than a request, yet it did not wash with Thomas.

"I should never have married her. I should have stayed single and waited for you."

It was at this point, or rather after many minutes of similar attempts at persuasion, that Amelia committed a sin.

She told a deliberate lie.

"But I do not love you, Thomas. I did once but no longer."

And Thomas, blind in pride and lost in confusion, believed the lie and, however painful, accepted it.

Life can be so sweet and so sour. It can send sunshine or rain. And into every life a little rain, at least, must fall.

But this was one of the moments when the rain dried up quite suddenly and the sunshine broke out; no rainbows for the rain was quite gone already.

"You know those cottages you are troubled about at Dew Drop?"

"Yes," replied Thomas, wondering what earthly relevance they had to their discussion.

"Take Bridge on a walk over there. Take a picnic with you."

Thomas had done as Amelia had instructed, fearing both loss and gain at the same time. Yet this was destined to be life at its sweetest, for Thomas, with a little help from Plain Jane and none at all from Big Jim, was re-awakened to the sharp angular beauty of Bridget, the wonder of this strong yet slightly awkward lady, the lostness yet the togetherness that made her. She became his bridge again and, like the first ever bridge he had built over the Stour, it remained strong and true down the generations.

And that is the story of Thomas, who fell in love three times in the year 1690.

The duke did not even recognise John Parsons when he arrived at Wiltshire House on Sunday afternoon.

"You want to stay the night and eat me out of house and home, no doubt?" he complained. Penelope had introduced them, although they had met before, then announced that she was retiring to rest and change after the journey.

"Might I have a maid to help me change, Your Grace?" she asked sweetly. He looked shocked, then reconsidered.

"Take my housekeeper. She will attend to your needs. Now, Mr Whatever-Your-Name-Is, are you intending to impose upon my hospitality for I am sorely pressed with financial concerns that make life here pretty threadbare."

"No, Your Grace. I shall depart the moment I have done my business and then return tomorrow for the ceremony in the church."

"I'm glad to hear it. I cannot stand the fuss of social indulgence. Every man is an island, I say, and must strike out for what he sees fit." The mixed metaphor was not lost on John, who had received a better education than the duke, despite his considerably lower standing.

"You desire to marry tomorrow morning, as I understand, Your Grace?"

"I do, no time to waste. I must bed her and get a son quickly. Don't look so surprised, man, this was as much her idea as mine."

"Of course, Your Grace. I do not offer judgement." He had, equally, not been at all surprised. Penelope had remembered the desperate plea made by Eliza Davenport, once Lady Merriman, to help her new maid, Milly, the previous year. She had gone over her plan in some detail with John Parsons, Milly's godfather.

She had acted on a whim when she had told the duke that she would arrange a best man for their hastily scheduled wedding. She had driven her trap over to Ashenham, a small village ten miles distant and on the edge of the Wiltshire holdings. She had stopped at the inn there, the Oak and Ash, wondering why the village had been named Ashenham, rather than Oakenham.

"Sir, I seek John Parsons, lately of Ashenham." She remembered the man well enough from the visit last year. Eliza had brought him to Great Little in a desperate attempt to raise the money to buy the estate of Ashenham from the duke. He had demanded £5,000, an outrageous price. They had not been able to put together £500 at that time, for both Great Little and Bagber were suffering from the duplicitous contracts set up by Parchman and Simon Taylor and administered by Grimes, their brutish henchman. And so, the great injustice to Milly's family was left unaddressed to Eliza's great dismay for she had rashly promised some resolution to the matter.

"He lives at Oakenham, Your Grace, two miles up the road."

"Oh, I did not realise there were two villages, Ashenham and Oakenham."

"They form one estate," came the sullen reply. They recognised her as the dowager-duchess and had no love for the Wiltshires. Her husband, the previous duke, had emptied the village following the perceived insult of not being recognised during an unplanned visit there. He had filled it again with new tenants. Perhaps they at least should have been grateful to their landlord? Except the new duke had doubled and doubled again the rents, avarice so often winning over wisdom.

"So, there is an oak to go with the ash?"

"There is, Your Grace. I am going that way if you will give me a lift in your trap." A young man drank his beer at the bar, slammed the pewter tankard down and turned to leave. He was heavy, strong and had a menacing air about him.

"Gladly, sir," said Penelope, wondering if she was biting off more than she could chew, wishing for the companionship of Sally.

But outside the sun shone and the man smiled, bowed and smiled again.

"I am John Parsons' son, Peter," he said, "I heard report from Milly and from my father that you wanted to help last year. I am glad to make your acquaintance, Your Grace."

"Why, Mr Parsons, were you so grave in there?" She allowed him to help her into the trap. "You made me quite frightened."

"I apologise, Your Grace. It's just that it doesn't do one much good around here to show any friendliness or co-operation with the Wiltshires."

"You must tell me more about it as we drive to see your father, sir." And Penelope was amazed to hear the update on the sad plight of both villages, even since last year. Over half the tenancies were vacant. The Oak and Ash Inn was hanging on by a thread, the landlord having borrowed from every source to keep the business open, "for people can't spend what they don't have, Your Grace."

Oakenham was as sad, or sadder, than the larger Ashenham. John Parsons and his extended family lived in a three room, single story cottage on the edge of the hamlet. But they met outside on the green which once had been framed by an inn, a shop and a quaint little church.

"I would not take you indoors, Your Grace. We can sit on your trap, if you are so inclined, and take a view of the church."

"It is boarded up." Penelope felt the obviousness of her words as soon as they had left her unthinking brain.

Yet her brain was working and working well for she had come up with a plan.

"You understand, Mr Parsons, that my interest is purely selfish. I wish to ingratiate my friend, Lady Roakes, with Mrs Davenport, Milly's employer, for purely personal reasons."

"I understand, Your Grace." He knew something of the personal reasons, for who in the area had not heard the tale of the Witch of Bagber and her disappearance and miraculous re-emergence at the time of the Monmouth rebellion? Who, now, could claim ignorance of the fact that Lady Roakes had a dark past but was now bent on good? Who, also, did not realise that there was some connection between these two? And that two great and neighbouring estates in Dorset had an enmity – no, nothing so hot as that, rather a coldness, for each other?

John Parsons could not believe the luck suddenly falling on his broken community when the dowager-duchess outlined her plan.

"I will play my part in it fully and absolutely, Your Grace," he said with a smile. "Might I make a couple of recommendations for improvement?"

Now the plan was in motion and Penelope and John Parsons had everything to play for. He had returned with her to Wiltshire House to discuss matters with the duke.

Except, strangely, Penelope was not in the room at all, apparently letting the plan go on in the absence of its architect.

Was that wise or reckless? But they were sticking to their script, for this was one of John Parsons' improvements, in fact two of them rolled into one.

"Knowing his bigoted nature, he is more likely to discuss business with his intended bride out of the room," he had said. "And might I suggest you use the opportunity to change after your journey into something quite…er…"

"There is no need to mention what you mean, sir. I comprehend entirely and have just the dress for the occasion."

"You mentioned business, sir. Pray tell me what it is so we can be done with such matters." Perhaps it would provide a windfall to the duke; it seemed the sun continued to shine at present.

"I wish, Your Grace, to buy the village of Ashenham from you."

"The price is £5,000," the duke quickly replied, remembering the negotiations that the Witch of Bagber had started last year. "Do I know you from somewhere?" He looked more closely at John; something linked him with the past but he could not place it.

"I have common enough looks, Your Grace. People do at times confuse me for someone else." It had happened so it was not a lie but it was right on the edge. "I was thinking of a smaller sum in recognition of the service I am doing you tomorrow."

"You extract a price for it, sir?" The duke's eyebrows shot up, half rage and half astonishment.

"It is customary to give the best man a gift, sir. And as, in respect of your request for minimum fuss, I will also be giving away the bride, I do think it is a reasonable request."

"That is for the Dowager-Duchess to negotiate, something for giving you away, I mean." But the duke was flustered by the logic and was finding argument difficult to marshal. So John went in for the kill.

"If you would prefer to find another at such short notice then I shall go and be about my own affairs." He deliberately left out 'Your Grace'; the matter was moving along well.

244

"No, I would not prefer so. It seems we must come to some arrangement. But I cannot dispose of property in entail that is not fair value. My gift is to consider the sale to you but not to take the price below the market." It was a brave effort, throwing John completely. They had not allowed for this level of cunning in the negotiations, thinking him too consumed with passion on the one hand and anger that his brother should succeed him on the other.

"Your Grace," they both turned to see Penelope enter the room. In fact, she had been in the doorway for a few moments, gauging how the discussion was going, deciding now to play her ace.

She was a picture of radiance. Her mauve dress with black underskirt flowed from her tiny waist. It was a waist pinched in by her stays and then tightened again and again. The housekeeper could attest to that with her exhausted limbs and ragged breathing from heaving on them. Over the top was the most exquisite but impracticable mauve netting from neck to ankle. It seemed to invite the duke to open the package and explore the delights within.

He had to have her, come what may.

The resulting price was entirely within John Parsons' capacity to pay.

"I can fund some of what you cannot afford," she had offered when sitting on the trap two days prior, looking onto the old church with the boarded-up windows. But he would have none of it.

"We get it for a price I can afford or we do not do it."

There was one little extra Penelope threw in at the last minute.

"Add Oakenham to the mix, Your Grace," she said, fluttering her eyelids and inviting him in.

He agreed readily enough for there was an unspoken part of the deal that passed between the eyes of the duke and his bride-to-be.

He would have her tonight, one day early. That was the price of the hamlet of Oakenham.

Chapter 32

At the beginning of September, Amelia heard something that warmed her heart.

"Bridge and I are going to Ireland to see her family."

"And so I can add something of Ireland to my new book," Bridget said.

"Tell me, what is your new book, Bridge? I have missed so much this year."

"It is called *A Female View and Perspective on the Wonders of Our Modern Nation,*" she replied, evidently proud of her work. "It is only half written and I estimate it will take another six months to complete, I would like to add something of your perspective to the mix when I get back."

"Fame at last!" Everyone smiled except Milly who saw things literally.

"Are you truly now famous, Miss Mealy? I did not know. Perhaps the matter with your..." Her voice petered out, lost in confusion. But everyone now accepted Milly's term of address for Amelia, along with her curious and direct remarks. It was as if she had joined the family.

"I'll explain later, Milly. But now we must say goodbye to those who hunger for travel."

"Goodbye Master Tom, I mean sir, and also Miss Bridge. I am so glad you are together again." She curtsied and left the room while others broke into smiles, charmed by Milly's mix of direct innocence and wisdom. Thomas looked at Amelia and noticed the blush; he wondered whether perhaps he had been deceived by Amelia's declaration of no feeling for him, for blushes so often follow the trail of love.

"It's only the improvement in Mealy that lets us go, sir," Bridget said when they were settled in the coach in Shaftesbury. They would change at Wincanton and arrive two days later in Bristol.

"Why so much luggage?" Thomas had asked when he had seen the pile Bridget was bringing with her. "Surely not all clothes?"

She had laughed and explained that two cases were full of books for her father. "He has such a longing for reading material. See, I have here several new treatises."

"Including '*Principia Mathematica Philosophiae Naturalis*' by Isaac Newton?" he had asked.

"Why yes, why do you ask, sir?"

"Because I have taken the time to read it. It was recommended to me by a wonderful lady who I am very much in love with."

"Then I am consumed with joy, sir, for my feelings are the mirror image of yours."

"They are one and the same, two ends to the same bridge, I would say."

Sally was anxious. Penelope had told Alice she would be gone a few days and that now stretched to ten as September broke its glories upon Dorset. The harvest was all in and most was gone to market fetching record prices.

"The estate is well on its way to mending, Lady Roakes," she had reported.

"You've done well, Sally. I think it is time for Tomkins finally to retire."

"He will enjoy that, Lady Roakes, he has his grandchildren nearby; he said as much to me just the other day."

"Then we will act upon it immediately, Sally. You have effectively been assistant-steward since the spring, still learning a little from Tomkins. Now you will come out from under that tutelage and shine in your own right."

"Thank you, Lady Roakes."

"And another thing, Sally, when we are alone or with Penelope, there is no need to stand on ceremony. Please call me Alice at such times. Furthermore, I wish you to be the steward all the time and would not have you part-time a maid."

"It pleases Penelope…Alice. I think it gives her some ownership, some connection with the past when we first fell…"

"I understand and I will raise it with Penelope whenever we see her next. This horse fair in Devizes is going on forever!"

Penelope waited alone in the bridal bed. It was not the first time she had waited for the duke for he had come the previous night as part of the deal for Oakenham. The marriage ceremony had been a miserable affair that morning and it had been hard to keep the duke's hands off her all day long.

She had insisted that John Parsons be invited to the bridal festivity. The housekeeper had prepared well within the inadequate allowance she was given. There was only one cook and one kitchen maid, both of whom complained about every task placed upon them until the housekeeper threatened to have them replaced and they sullenly fell into line.

For a while.

The rest of the establishment, Penelope learned that morning, consisted of the steward, who dared not contradict his master in anything, and a valet to the duke who doubled as a footman.

"Who will dress me?" she asked of her new husband.

"You'll need to bring your blackie," he replied. But that was not in her plan. She most certainly did not want Sally to know what she had been up to.

Not just yet.

"She does not work for me anymore." This was a slight stretching of the truth for she had two positions; as assistant-steward, she worked for Alice, the owner of Great Little and, hence, not for Penelope.

"Well, Mrs Barrington, the housekeeper, will have to do it, or else the kitchen maid. What's her name again?"

"I know a lass from Ashenham who would suit," John put in. But the duke would not consider hiring what he now called an 'outsider', "for Ashenham is no longer part of my estate so they can be damned, every one of them."

The deal they had come to the day before was an excellent one for John Parsons. The village of Ashenham and the smaller one of Oakenham had passed to John's ownership for a little under £400, such was the duke's desire to have a son by bedding Penelope in all her sensual finery.

"Wear the same dress tomorrow," the duke had instructed as she had, thankfully, stripped it off that evening.

"I had thought, Your Grace, to wear something a little less heavy, more delicate."

"I said I want you in that dress tomorrow." And Penelope had nodded her obedience and then suffered a second day in 'the Purgatory Dress' as she and Sally had named it.

But now, at least, it was off and her husband could not demand it be worn a third day. She lay back on the pillows, feeling the freedom from the tight stays that made the dress look right, reflecting that Mrs Barrington would also be pleased not to have to pull vigorously for a third morning. She did not complain, seeming to accept her lot, but Penelope rather liked the older woman who had put up with so much from her master since he had inherited the title two years earlier.

"Two hours at most and it will all be over," she said to herself but out loud.

"What was that dear?"

"Eh?"

"What did you say?"

"Oh just two hours or more of pleasure ahead."

"Just two hours? I think I can last longer than that!"

But, in actual fact, it was a lot less. He had felt a little strange during the evening, putting it down to anticipation, despite the taster the night before, also perhaps he had drunk a little too much brandy. There was an irritating throb in his temple. He climbed into the bed, feeling the effort a little too much.

"Damn that brandy," he said. "Damn, damn and damn again." Penelope had moved over to let him in, now rolled back, real concern shining in her eyes.

"Sir, what is wrong?" No answer, just a jerking of his slumped body accompanied by a breaking of wind and a spreading of urine across the sheet.

"Sir, go to the privy!" she called, scrambling off the bed, going around to his side. "Your Grace?"

An hour later the physician pronounced him the victim of a massive stroke.

"Your Grace," he explained to Penelope as if to a child, "the Duke has suffered an attack in his head. The blood has broken through the veins and flooded the brain."

"Will he live?"

"Not for long, I fear. But I must ask, Your Grace, why you were in his bedroom at night and dressed yourself for bed?"

"We were married this morning," she replied, then thought quickly and added, "we consummated the marriage just now. He rolled over and fell into a swoon from which he has not recovered."

"I see, Your Grace. I am very sorry for your loss."

The physician ran through some instructions for his care and said he would be back first thing in the morning and they were to send a messenger if the duke deteriorated. Penelope was glad that Mrs Barrington was listening to the physician because she could not.

Her world was turned this way and that. Had she not hoped for this to happen, deep down? Had she taken Alice's joke about him not living long and somehow made it reality? Had she forced the death of this odious old man?

"There, there, my dear," Mrs Barrington was soothing her, stroking her long dark hair and squeezing her shoulder blades.

And Penelope actually cried. She cried for a man who had put himself first all his life. She wept for a man who had not been able to think of others except as objects to use and abuse. The sadness was cruel and many-strained. She would never dream of shedding a tear for the man alive and well but was flooding tears now that he lay close to death in his bedroom next door.

It was cruel because she was without child. It was deceitful for they had never consummated their marriage as man and wife. And the irony was clear; the only time she had slept in his bed was the night before they were joined in matrimony.

The next duke in line arrived four days later. He came with a flare of followers as befitted his expected position, anticipation in every deep line of his face.

And he was, in Penelope's view, much worse than his older brother. Physically, there was no comparison. He was tall and lean with muscles that rippled when he walked. He looked ten years younger than his 58 years with not an ounce of fat hanging on him.

"You must be the Dowager-Duchess," he said with derision threaded through his voice. "What are you doing here? I hope not waiting for scraps from the high table."

"I am the Duchess, sir." She explained about the wedding and suffered his snorts of ridicule.

"Tell me immediately when the old man is dead," he said, mounting his horse and waving to his entourage like a cavalry commander giving the order to move out.

Mrs Barrington was an older lady but she lived on to a great age. When she finally left employment at Wiltshire House, she went to live with her granddaughter and always told the tale of the duke and the attack in his brain.

"And the most amazing thing of all," she would say, time and time again, "is how the young Duchess behaved. She went to the Duke's bedroom the moment his brother's party had disappeared down the drive."

"And what happened next?" her great-grandchildren would cry, although they had heard it many times before.

And old Nana Barrington would hug them on her lap and tell of how the great duchess fell to her knees in front of the duke and begged him to live as great big tears rolled down her face.

"And after a long while, children, she rose and, still gripping his hand, she spoke of her decision. He was to move in gentle stages from Wiltshire House to Great Little where she and Alice and Sally and all the staff would care for him day and night. Now isn't that a nice story of two people in love? They left the very next day and arrived at Great Little in Dorset a few days later. They took me with them for the journey and then bade me come back and look after Wiltshire House. And do you know what?"

The children would all cry, "what Nana?"

"Well, the Duchess came to me before I left Great Little and said for me to care for the house for his heir. And she patted her tummy as she said those words and I do think she knew even then."

The reality was, as always, a little different, less like a fairy tale. When Penelope watched the duke's brother trot down the drive of the house he expected to be his, she was, for the first time in her life, on the receiving end of arrogance. Prior to this, she had always dished it out. Her mind was in turmoil as she watched the last straggler of his entourage disappear around the bend at the end of the drive. She went to her husband, not with any certainty of mind but with utter confusion to offer him.

And she offered him her despair, much as someone would to God, only Penelope did not pray, had never prayed. Then her mind wandered a while, thinking of many things quite incidental to the central topic of what she was to do.

Get a grip, woman, seemed to sail through the air in the duke's voice. Yet had the physician not just said that the duke would not speak again?

Get a grip, woman, or I'll whip some sense into you. There was the voice again. She looked at the duke but there was no sign of communication. Could she be imagining it? Perhaps imagining what he might have said?

The truth was Penelope was so without religion that she did not imagine God might speak to her in this way. And in a language she could understand. Hers was a world where you could touch everything, whether it was valuable or not. Well, almost everything, for you could not touch the love she had for Sally or the fondness for Alice.

But she always wished she could, if just for a moment.

After a while, the trees and the birds and the wind and the rain, all joined in the words she had heard, creating a mighty coalition of a chorus, almost deafening her yet never seeming to tire of the question.

What will you do now? What will you do now? Get a grip, woman, get a grip.

The only decision she remembered making throughout this mass of confusion was to take her new husband to Great Little, to take him where there were two people she could count on to help her.

And so, the next morning, they set out on their slow, hesitant journey to Great Little. It took a week, journeying a little each day and resting often and long. They stopped in Salisbury for a day and found a man of medicine who knew something about blood clots in the head. He saw the duke, pronounced him seriously ill but not incapable of life and promised to come regularly to see him. They stopped a night also at the Homeless Pig, on the road outside Andover. There the new landlady said she had in residence a fine doctor who sold tinctures for every ailment. Penelope bought six bottles from Dr Mowbray for a guinea. A week later, Sally threw five and a half bottles of the sweet-smelling liquid away.

They arrived, tired and battered by the rough roads, in the middle of September. Sally saw them arrive first and rushed to the door, calling Alice to follow her.

"Pen, what is it? Are you alright?" There was an edge of panic in Sally's voice that Penelope quickly quelled.

"Yes, Sal, I'm fine, other than missing you. Pray get help for my husband…"

"Your husband?" But her eyes said, "you did it then, you actually did it?"

"Yes," she said, in answer to both questions.

Chapter 33

Eliza set out for Great Little the same day that John Parsons came to visit Bagber.

At first, she had thought something had happened to Milly's mother but the broad smile on his face belied any troubling news.

"Welcome, Mr Parsons, I trust you are well?"

"Very well and the bearer of excellent news, my lady." There was a lot of confusion about Eliza's title. Had she ever correctly been called Lady Merriman? Or did the title fall into abeyance when her father had been murdered in the grounds of this very house with no male heir to take his place? To manage the issue, she responded to all and every respectful reference including 'my lady', 'Your Ladyship', 'Lady Merriman' and plain 'Mrs Davenport'.

"Should not Milly hear it, then?" Milly was summoned and blushed when her servant-like curtsey to her godfather was met with a hug and a kiss.

"Uncle John!" she cried, bashfully.

"I have very good news to tell you, Milly."

He asked if Milly could sit and found a stool for her. "Now listen Milly, listen carefully." He told of the great trade between the dowager-duchess and the duke, the resulting purchase of Ashenham, "and Oakenham into the bargain". He went lightly over the terrible price that Penelope had to pay but Milly knew for she had seen the duke several times before she had left for London and service with Eliza.

"We've already started improvements, Milly, even 'though it has been less than two weeks since the purchase. I do not think I have stopped once in those two weeks, hence my belated visit to pass on the news to you both. We urgently seek a good builder to sort out the years of neglect and know that Lady Merriman…"

"Mrs Davenport you mean, Uncle John."

"Yes, you do well to correct me, Milly. We know that Mrs Davenport has a brother-in-law who has an excellent reputation as a builder."

"Oh, you mean Mr Tom! Yes, he is a fine man, sir."

"Thomas Davenport is indeed my brother-in-law. He is in Ireland at present, visiting the family of his wife, but he will be back soon and Mr Milligan, the old owner, is deputising in his absence."

"Thank you, my lady." He turned to Milly. "Don't you see, Milly, this means you can come home."

"I am home already, Uncle John. Bagber has become my home, not because the home in Ashenham with my family is any less important but because I am happy here, sir. Lady Merriman has made it her task to make it so." Confusion over titles again.

"Well, I never!" he replied, quite taken aback at the display of maturity that sat so oddly in her youthful body.

"Milly, you may go about your duties now. Your godfather and I will talk some more about the particulars then I will send him to find you. You may take the afternoon off to spend with him."

"Oh, thank you, miss, I mean my lady, Mrs Davenport."

"She gets lots of things wrong, Mr Parsons, yet has such a wise head on her shoulders. She really is quite remarkable."

Eliza did not take Mr Parsons with her that day; he was, after all, promised to Milly for the afternoon. She thought of taking her husband, Matthew, or perhaps Elizabeth, recently widowed and saddened at the loss of the man she had struggled to love. She finally went alone but not until she had explained to Elizabeth that she felt she had to go alone. Then she went to see Matthew in his study, explaining the same and asking permission to go.

"I rather think you must go, my dearest."

"Thank you, sir, you are very kind."

"Be gentle with everyone today, Eliza my dear, just as Jesus is gentle." His words sounded trite but Eliza knew her husband much better than that.

In the end, she changed her mind again, wasting another hour as new permission was sought of her husband and new preparations made. She would take their daughter to meet young Sir Beatrice, together with a nursery maid.

It was mid-afternoon on a heavily-clouded day that the carriage rolled out of Bagber Manor to cover the ten miles to Great Little.

Eliza started to point out to her baby daughter all the land that was theirs. They had started tentatively buying fields and woodland again that summer.

"Bagber Manor was never hit as badly as Great Little," she said to baby Eliza, who gurgled happily as the carriage made its way south and then east, headed for Sturminster Newton, which it would bypass, then on to Fiddleford, Okeford Fitzpaine and up Okeford Hill. "Now, we cross from our land to that of Great Little," she told her baby, who would listen with equal glee were her mother to read aloud a shopping list or a Sunday sermon.

The rain broke out at the top of Okeford Hill. It steadily increased as the carriage went slowly down the other side, towards Hedge End Farm. They were now firmly in Great Little territory. She wondered what it would be like to have a different sounding name to her own estate, such as Great Little. She remembered the Little family as a child; Sir Jacob had been a good friend of her father. She had done this same journey often enough but years ago; not so often in recent years. It pushed her mind onto less happy thoughts; the brutal murder of her kindly father, the snatching away from her of her first born, the pig farm in Yorkshire, her confused state when held there and, again, when subsequently chained to a sink in Bristol, trying to work out who on earth she was.

And then the question came to her with the answer as neat as a row of soldiers. She might be a Christian but she was not ready to forgive, not yet at any rate. Outside, as if applauding her decision, the rain struck with more force, while thunder added to the clapping around them. The coach slowed to a crawl.

They came eventually to Winterborne Stickland. The driver suggested seeing out the storm at the Crown Inn but Eliza wanted to get on.

"It's only three more miles," she shouted through the gloom and heavy downpour. "And there is an inn halfway should we not be able to make it. We go on, Stevens."

"Yes, my lady." The baby started wailing. The nursery maid, frightened by the violence of the storm, had to be persuaded into assisting. The coach was going so slowly now that they could change the wet baby on the bench seat, Eliza helping the fumbling fingers of the maid. Both baby and carer quietened a little with the activity but still whimpered against the cold and violent thrashing of the storm that was everywhere around them.

They made another mile, then came to the small inn, bolted shut against the storm. Eliza saw a figure at one window draw away when his presence was noted; presumably they would not want to be disturbed at a time like this, even by wealthy aristocrats prepared to pay well for their comfort.

But then the same figure, enveloped in a huge coat and hat, came out to talk to them. The driver stopped the horses and dismounted from his seat. Now Eliza could see the figure from the inn more clearly. She had supposed him to be the landlord but he was just a boy of twelve or so.

"You can't go on, my lady, come in to the dry."

Eliza thanked him for his generosity but waved a decline to the invitation, determined to make her destination that day.

"What is your name, boy?"

"Peter, my lady. Peter Taunton. Please come in, my lady. We have rum aplenty and bread and cheese. My mother can make some soup if I rouse her." It struck Eliza as odd that her mother should be sleeping at five o'clock in the afternoon with an inn to run. She looked again. The Spirited Duck was anything but spirited; it sat sadly on a rise above the road, worn by weather and neglect into a resigned state. It seemed to say 'I'll be an inn if I have to be but I would much prefer to be a hovel or a pigsty.'

"See, my lady, you are cold indeed." The boy seemed triumphant in his observation.

Eliza took a shilling and pressed it into the boy's skinny hand. "Bring glasses of rum for each of us, an extra one for Stevens, our driver. We'll go on. We've not far to go."

He came back with the rum within a few minutes.

"Do you know who I am, Peter" The strong liquid forced calm on them. Eliza suddenly felt they could go on forever, so long as kind and spirited boys presented a glass of rum every few miles.

"No, my lady."

"I am Lady Merriman." Why did she giver her maiden name? Was it vanity?

"The Witch of Bagber!" the boy replied, but with a twist to his mouth to say it was nothing to fear.

"I like you, Peter. Come and see me at Bagber Manor. I would know you better, young man."

Eliza's decision to go on was in agreement with Stevens who she consulted while the boy fetched the rum. Great Little, despite the tension, offered much greater hospitality than a tired country inn where the landlady slept at five in the afternoon. It was less than two miles to Winterbourne Whitchurch and Great Little lay before that. The boy had confirmed it was less than a mile to the turning.

But the storm seemed determined to stop them, sending great puddles of pooled and rushing water. The horses were skittish but Stevens knew his trade and, chief amongst the necessary skills was keeping the horses steady.

"It is us against the elements," Eliza said to the inside of the coach, rather liking the thought.

"And, my lady, I fear the elements are winning." The nursery maid spoke through fear; there was nothing exciting to her about a storm like this.

"Never, my dear." But did she speak too soon? Stevens pulled the exhausted horses to a stop and climbed down a third time. He was quite some time around the coach on foot before coming to the window to report.

"Our rear left wheel is very loose," he said. "It must have been that big rut back there."

"How far to go, Stevens?"

"The drive is just ahead on the next corner but I cannot see it in the early dark."

"And the drive is a quarter of a mile long?"

"More like half a mile, my lady."

"We go on, very slowly, mind you."

Sally saw them approach, or rather she first heard the neigh of terrified horses as they stumbled, the sound piercing the storm like a blade. She looked from the front portico up the long sweep of the drive that followed the ridge.

"It's a coach," she cried. "It seems to be in trouble. There are people outside in the storm." The staff at Great Little was back to full-complement , and fourteen able-bodied servants, wrapped quickly against the weather, made their way to the stricken coach, two hundred yards along the drive. Alice led with Sally hanging back slightly, sensing that Alice wished to be in charge, that she divined some importance in her actions that evening. A stable lad, despatched by Alice, harnessed a covered cart with a plough horse and came along minutes behind.

"Thank God for help," cried Stevens. "We got so close but not quite there." It was obvious that the wheel had come off; the coach listed dangerously and an anxious young face peeked out of the window. She was lodged against the seat back and window frame, both arms clutching a baby.

"How many in total?"

"Just the maid inside and Lady Merriman's baby. Lady Merriman came out to help." Alice looked and saw the woman she had held captive for five long years. She was soaked, holding on to the coach with grim determination to prevent it turning over completely. She smiled and received a nod in return.

Alice took command. She detailed three servants to help Stevens unharness the panicked horses. Eight more were asked to manhandle the broken coach to get it upright. Then they hauled it to the side of the drive while the rest made a human shelter with their coats so that when the stable lad drew the cart alongside, the nursery maid could hand the baby out to Alice and then be helped herself across the narrow gap and into the dry cart.

The same human shelter operated when the cart pulled up to the front portico, newly rebuilt after the fire two years earlier.

Meanwhile, Alice had sent two young girls back to the kitchen, charging them to boil water for baths.

"Then, I want brandy served to all who have helped today. Bring it to the Great Hall and make sure the fire is stoked up."

"Yes, Lady Roakes." But both their words and their ragged curtsies were lost to the storm.

"I came to thank you," Eliza said, when sufficiently warmed by the fire, a shawl of Alice's across her sodden dress.

"Never mind about that," Alice replied. "First we must get you into a hot bath and then into some dry clothes. Elsie, is the bath ready?"

"One more load of water, Lady Roakes. If Lady Merriman would like to make her way to the guest suite in two ticks, I'll fetch the last of the water by the back stairs and meet her there." Eliza was not so fatigued that she did not notice most people referring to her as Lady Merriman, the name she was born with. But, as she crossed the hall to the half-built staircase, she heard two young servants refer with a giggle to the Witch of Bagber. She smiled to herself, rather liking the mystery surrounding her.

Myth and legend have their purposes quite apart from storytelling on wet and windy autumn days. Eliza demonstrated this statement as she ascended the grand staircase, still waiting for its bannisters to be carved and fitted. She spoke to the Little family, painted on the wall that divided the staircase from the Great Hall, addressing them at their perpetual feast started all those years ago.

"Hello Littles, great and small, it is I, the Witch of Bagber, come to visit you once more."

Supper was served in the Great Hall. There were four present in a room that could hold a hundred easily.

And all were female. Lady Roakes put Eliza as far from her as she reasonably could, thinking it best not to assume any association. Penelope sat on one side and Sally on the other.

It was a first for both Sally and Eliza, as they realised when talking before they were called to the table.

"I have never eaten at this table before. I have served often enough but never actually sat at the table."

"I have never eaten as a guest of Lady Roakes, much like you, my dear. My past, too, was very different to what you might imagine on seeing me today." Eliza seemed about to go on and then thought better of it.

"Penelope is not too pleased that I am here," Sally replied, unaware of Eliza's pause, more concerned with her own situation, which had not been easy.

They had been delighted to see each other on Penelope's arrival back at Great Little three weeks earlier, Penelope spilling out everything she had done at Wiltshire House. It had seemed the perfect reunion after two weeks apart. But then they had retired to change for the evening and everything had come undone.

"Where's your uniform, Sal?"

"I don't wear it anymore, Pen. Alice does not like it now that I am officially the steward with sole responsibility for running the estate. Tomkins has retired fully while you've been away." But Penelope was concentrating on one small part of these two sentences from Sally, one word giving insight into enormous change.

"Alice, not Lady Roakes? I would never believe it!" And that was the start of a furious row that still burned to the touch. Penelope had said Sally had no right to change their finely balanced agreement.

"And you have no right to charge off, pretending to go to a horse fair and come back sold yourself!"

"It was your idea, Sally Black."

"It was but it was just an idea." She stressed the last three words, aware that it was unfair to do so; she had been all for it when it was just an idea. "You took hold of it and made it happen without telling me, or Alice for that matter."

Sally had since moderated her position, seeing how upset Penelope was. She had reverted to 'Lady Roakes', causing Alice to frown slightly on each hearing. But it kept a fragile truce between Penelope and Sally. They still shared the big bed but did not talk and did not cuddle against each other. Instead they turned, one left and one right, like a big exotic plant folding its leaves for night.

In public, they were excruciatingly polite to each other but, when back in private, a cold wall immediately descended between them; talk was impractical for it risked reigniting the argument.

"Am I right in understanding, Your Grace, that you have married the Duke of Wiltshire, having been married to the previous duke of the same title? He had a collapse on your wedding night and has not long to live? You have brought him to Great Little, over almost forty miles of varying roads, in order to care for him here?"

"Precisely, Lady Merriman." Penelope fell into the same trap as the servants; next she would be referring to the Witch of Bagber, such was the distraction caused by the rift with Sally.

"Can I see him?"

"Of course, Lady Merriman. He has some rooms at the back of the house on the first floor. You are aware that he understands what people say but cannot talk?"

"Yes, it is just his ears I need, your 'double-grace'." Said with a smile in recognition of the news that Penelope had twice married into the same aristocratic family. "I wish to tell him how delighted I am that he changed his mind and sold Ashenham to Mr Parsons and for such a reasonable sum as well!"

It was sometime later, close to midnight, that Eliza and Alice found themselves alone together in the library. Penelope and Sally had both retired and Alice had sent the servants to bed.

"There is a decanter of Burgundy in the library if you would care to sit with me for a while?" Alice's words were stilted and no eye contact was made.

"Gladly," Eliza replied but not meaning it. She welcomed a glass of wine but would preferred to have taken it up to her bed where she could remove the dress she had borrowed from Alice and put on the nightdress, also on loan. Then she would sit with her back propped against the piled-up pillows, sip her wine and try and make sense of her feelings.

A luxury she did not have. For here she was, instead, sitting in a high back chair, facing Alice in another that matched hers. The wings of their chairs came forward, seeming to funnel their concentration onto each other.

"I'm sorry..." began Alice, as every personal conversation with Eliza had begun and ended over the last few years.

"I know that, Lady Roakes, you don't need to keep saying it."

"I crave your forgiveness." This was exactly what Eliza had expected, prepared for since first understanding why John Parsons had come to her that morning.

And why she had felt obliged to go to Great Little in order to give her thanks to the one woman she could never forgive.

She had rehearsed it two-dozen times, running through the words in her head, varying slightly the reaction from Lady Roakes to test her own response, which she held to be firm under each scenario.

"I can't..." she started to speak, then stopped, noticing the dim light in the eyes that stared from one wing-framed chair to the other. "I can't..." she repeated, aware suddenly of the power she had over the pain of regret that faced her. She owned that power, why should she ever give it up?

But another voice spoke through the fog and mist that was her mind. It was the voice of her father, long ago; the gentlest and happiest of men. He seemed to reason with her, or rather to take her in hand and explain how things should be. But that same voice then had the tones of her beloved husband. Then she heard the words he had said that very day to her, "Be gentle with everyone today, Eliza my dear, just as Jesus is gentle."

"I can't..." she started once again to those dimmed and disappointed eyes across the way. "I can't hold it against you any longer." Where on earth had those words come from? They turned who she was on her head.

"What?" Clearly, Alice thought the same.

"I see that you have changed. I for…" Was she going to stumble right now? A journey half done is not done at all. A meal half cooked cannot be eaten safely. Why start if you do not intend to go on?

Eliza took a deep breath and then let the words come tumbling out.

"I forgive you, Alice Roakes, I forgive you wholeheartedly."

Chapter 34

Parchman had a duty to do. It involved putting up with the soaking spray and discomfort as the boat, manned by twelve rowers and a coxswain, made its slow way against the tide. It would be easier, he reflected, if they were there in winter and the River St. Charles were bound in ice; they would be able to walk across with a little care, simulating a walk on dry land.

Why was travel always worse at the ebb and flow of seasons, when the stillness of summer and winter were being pushed in or dragged out?

Why did poets go on about the beauty of travel and the beauty they found in the countryside? There was nothing of promise here, just grey rocks and water that got everywhere. Give him a city any day with its vibrant stench of human life, its winding, twisted streets perfectly suiting his furtive ways. Quebec up there looked miserable, a pathetic excuse for a town. Place him back in London and he would never ask for anything more. Once in London, he would never leave that glorious, stinking cesspit again.

But Parchman had a duty to do and that duty was wholly to himself. See this through, he told his uncomfortable body and his natural instinct to flee, and you shall have London and all its wicked ways.

They were four hundred yards from the Six Friends, Phips' squat flagship. In a moment, he would have to meet the odious Sir William Phips. Not on dry land but on board his flagship. Parchman had delayed travelling from Boston to Quebec as long as possible, sending Davidson with his small contingent of troops and urgent instructions to Phips to desist the attack on Quebec.

Only there were two sets of instructions carefully recorded in his temporary office in Boston. Two sets to cover the two ways this could work out.

He had seen the ship Davidson had commandeered anchored with Phips' fleet when he had arrived the previous evening in the White Lady. Davidson's ship had brought the major-general to Quebec and then evidently sat around like a spent musket that no-one knew how to reload. He hoped his ship, the White Lady, would not stay long at all; soon, it would be making fast passage back to England.

With Parchman aboard.

Just a few more days and he would know which way the wind was blowing.

And, therefore, which set of instructions would become a part of the official records.

He used every opportunity to go over the plan again; success depended on the most careful planning. First there was the original mission to consider. It had all started with Davidson. Detesting the tit-for-tat raids across the frontier between New England and New York on the one hand and New France, or Canada as it was known, on the other, he had decided to use his influence back home to force a change of policy. Davidson came from a large aristocratic family, giving him powerful connections in England. Being a younger son, he had chosen to settle in this ugly New World, but that did not mean he could not make use of his contacts from time to time, sending messengers back from New England.

There was that 'new' again, getting everywhere with its crude attempt to carve something from nothing that obsessed the human race so completely.

And so pointlessly, for everything man could ever want was already there in London.

Back to the point; wandering minds caused failure, it was essential to focus.

Davidson had sent that fool, Taylor, who Parchman knew well, back to England to rouse up his influence with a view to changing policy in that part of America that bordered Canada.

Wealth creation is what we are about that we may better serve his majesty with new coin rather than bullets which will only ever be returned with fresh bullets in our direction. We need peace on the frontier to create the wealth that eases the way for everyone.

That was the essence of Davidson's argument; Parchman had heard it often enough. And it had looked like holding sway, except for two things that had saved the day. Parchman knew that weak people craved peace while others, like him, profited enormously by the chaos and disruption of constant change.

And what better than war to create that change?

First of the two fortunate happenings; Taylor, the messenger, had become stuck in a mire of sentimental emotion, killing a perfectly capable operator in Grimes and, no doubt, losing his own life into the bargain.

At the end of a rope. Something that held such fear for Parchman. He disliked many things, some intensely, travel by sea being one of those. Yet the only thing he really feared was dangling at the end of a noose, his precious life draining as he slowly choked to death. He woke often, feeling an imaginary noose around his neck, clutching at the rope with scrabbling, urgent fingers, screaming into the silence with his panicked voice.

He brought his mind back to the plan once again. It kept wandering which concerned Parchman. He had always had such discipline, such control of his mind. Now, at the critical point of success, it seemed to wander like a pilgrim seeking the way to the shrine.

The second happening was that clever Cartwright had twisted the plan for his own ends. And this had given Parchman his own idea. Cartwright was not interested in peace. Further advancement came much more rapidly in times of war.

As did demotion, even disgrace, but that was the game that Cartwright was signed up to.

The clever new minister, trained by Parchman, had changed Davidson's simple plan from peace to aggression, thus creating naked opportunity by stripping away its pious clothing. Davidson, who everyone knew to be a capable officer of the militia, would be ordered by London to take control of the war and lead a decisive blow against the French; no more tit-for-tat but one focused invasion into the heart of New France.

The fact that the merchants of Boston would be paying for Davidson's expedition was a bonus that made Parchman smile. It was war as a neat commercial endeavour; neat because it was funded by those of business who took all the risks. But the glory would remain with the politicians.

The particular politicians who strove to make it happen.

The simple instruments of Cartwright's manipulation of the plan were the rapid promotion of Davidson and the supply of vital war supplies to make Davidson rather than Phips effective. These were the munitions that had sailed with Parchman on board the White Lady to Boston. They were now housed in that same ship anchored safely a short distance from the fleet. The master of the White Lady had thought it a clever extra cargo for Cartwright to arrange, making a useful contribution to the war effort.

And a sizeable packet of money for him.

If they ever received them, of course. And this is where Parchman's plan was a step above Cartwright's. Without the munitions, Phips' expedition could not succeed. Parchman controlled the armaments, hence he controlled the course of events.

In Cartwright's version of the plan, Davidson would take possession of the weaponry and supplies and work out a new attack, shattering the very heart of New France. Most importantly, it was to be directed from Whitehall when Boston had failed. Parchman had learned this, not from Cartwright, but from the loose-tongued master of the White Lady, who had been easily impressed with the closeness of Parchman to the centre of power.

Parchman had kept the weapons in the hold of the ship and could, therefore, play it either way. He would judge first whether Davidson was likely to succeed, giving him free rein if he looked promising or holding back on the supplies totally. It was entirely in Parchman's gift. If Cartwright had trusted Parchman enough to tell him of the cargo, he could have passed along the responsibility to discharge the lethal stores to Davidson. He would have had no choice but to obey. But he lacked faith in his messenger and this had left Parchman in complete control.

In control as always, he thought, allowing a chuckle of appreciation for how things had worked out.

Faith and power were connected in more ways than one, Parchman considered as he drew his coat tighter against the spray.

The boat bumped against the side of the ship, someone above called for the coxswain to be careful and the coxswain swore in response. Parchman stood, ready to clamber up the netting that hung over the ship, ready also for the next stage of the plan he had made his own.

Chapter 35

Anne Aspley was delighted to hear from Sally that Thomas was back in Dorset after the six weeks they had spent staying with Bridget's family in Ulster. She had waited for him patiently, honing her idea while he was away. She immediately wrote a letter, reminding Thomas of their acquaintance and asking if she might come and visit him to discuss an idea she had.

This morning a reply had arrived, in fact an invitation to stay overnight at the Davenport home in Sturminster Newton. At the bottom of the letter from Thomas were a few dozen words, mostly in capitals. Formed with elongated letters and sharp corners, they expressed a desire by Mrs Thomas Davenport to meet with Miss Aspley of whom she had heard interesting things. It mentioned the book she was writing covering a female perspective on the modern nation and expressed a strong desire to meet her in that regard with a view to including her in the book.

"To think, you will be immortalised in print!" joked Mr Jarvis when Anne showed him the letter.

Bridget and Anne became firm friends from their very first meeting. There was enough practicality about the intellectual Bridget to relate to the intellectualism hidden in the intensely practical Anne.

"We're like two halves of the same shell," Anne said, thinking that they were odd halves for she was rounded with what was left of her puppy fat while Bridget was taller and all angles and shapes in a strangely beautiful way.

Anne arrived when Thomas was still out at work so Bridget was alone.

"Don't apologise for coming early, Miss Aspley, it gives us time to get to know each other."

"That's kind of you, Mrs Davenport." It was the only time they addressed themselves formally. Within minutes of the introductions, they were on first name terms.

When Thomas entered the parlour, newly opened and prepared for Anne's visit, a few more 'Miss Aspleys' were employed, but it was not long before it became Anne and Thomas.

Anne was clearly excited to discuss her idea.

"Tell us your idea, if you will," Thomas said as he settled into an unfamiliar chair in a room they hardly ever used.

"It's nothing unusual," she replied, suddenly bashful. "Quite ordinary, in fact."

"I don't believe a lady of your business acumen would travel halfway up the county to tell us something ordinary."

"Well, it's just this. It's all about smoothing out your cashflows, Thomas, as a builder I mean."

Thomas listened intently to the detail. Bridget listened equally, but with two different perspectives. She was interested in anything that might help her husband with the biggest headache of his building business; how to ensure the payroll in the bad times as well as the good. She was also fascinated as a commentator on modern life, observing a brilliant young mind at work. She was framing the questions she would ask her the next day when Thomas was at work again.

"You would start a bank?" Thomas asked as Anne drew to a close.

"I would, sir, if you said you would be my first customer. I have a little excess capital as the insurance business has been excellent these first few months."

"Will it be enough?" Bridget asked, thinking a disaster might wipe out much of the insurance company capital.

"Far from it but Mr Fellows has agreed to back it."

They talked on over supper. Bridget was impressed with Anne's thoroughness and her capacity for detail. She laughed easily but one sensed that the business purpose was never far from centre-stage.

The letters flowed shortly after Anne left the next day in the afternoon. First was a personal note thanking them for the hospitality. She had enjoyed herself thoroughly, not least the fascinating discussion she had held with Bridget in the morning.

It was followed a few days later with a business-like but friendly letter informing them of progress towards setting up the bank. It included a letter from Mr Fellows' lawyers in Dorchester, along with a subscription agreement.

"What is this, Thomas?" Bridget asked.

"Did you not listen to that bit, Bridge?" he replied, teasing her gently. "Anne offered us a shareholding at the subscription price of £10 a share. I did not commit for I meant to talk to you about it first but, I confess, I became distracted by the amount of work going on at Great Little. You know they have started building at the main house again?"

They agreed later that day to take up four shares of £10 each. It was a considerable investment for them.

"But it will give us four thousandths of the new bank as ours," Bridget said happily. "Although, when you read the detail, it seems only half is payable now."

"Who are the other proposed shareholders?" Thomas asked.

"Mr Fellows has forty percent and I believe, yes, Anne has most of the rest."

"Where on earth did she get the money from? That must be quite a few thousand."

"I suspect that Mr Fellows has loaned it to Anne," Thomas said, after thinking a moment. And he was spot on with his suspicion. Mr Fellows, close to a hundred years old, thought it a perfect harnessing of his capital with Anne's energy and determination.

The third letter to arrive announced the setting up of Aspley Bank, limited by £10,000 of share capital, half paid-up and half pledged by the shareholders. The fourth letter arrived the following day and contained a loan agreement allowing Thomas' firm to draw on £250 of credit secured against his stock of building materials.

Bridget sat back at her writing desk in the study she shared with Thomas. She had her quill poised but not employed; rather it hung from her hand, the mind working through several ideas at once. She had notes from her conversation with Anne and referred to them frequently, reminding her of the words Anne had used, the points she had made.

Presently, she drew a clean piece of paper and started on it. It was to be a new chapter entitled

Into Every Life (A Little Rain Must Fall)

She resisted the temptation to underline the chapter title and instead moved down the page to write:

They say that misfortune becomes the manure on which good fortune can thrive. I say, with examples to make my point, that it depends on the gardener and the skill that gardener applies to the task of turning the plot around.

Take a lady I have recently met. In the space of a few short weeks, she lost the male half of her family. Her brother, the soldier, went first. But he died of some terrible wasting disease contracted in the New World, the circumstances being far from the blaze of glory one imagines a soldier's end to be. The father, a merchant, died shortly after hearing the news. The medical men will argue a weak constitution or a growth gnawing at his insides. But no- one will convince me otherwise than that it was a case of a broken heart. His only son, his one hope, was gone while his business matters looked dire, according to my source which is very close.

This left the female half, about which I will concentrate this chapter on. The mother was, understandably, distraught and unable to cater for herself, let alone her diminished family. Everything fell to the daughter.

This young lady could have survived. She had the goodwill of some of her creditors and could have eked out a living as a piano tutor or some such. Instead, she grasped all her problems, like clutching at nettles with bare hands, enduring the pain which only, in actual

fact, lasts an hour or two. She used her judgement and considerable force of personality to make a difference.

And most importantly, she knew her limitations and sought advice and assistance where she needed it. Her garden is now well on its way, I am happy to report.

Bridget paused at this moment, wondering whether to continue with her analysis of Anne Aspley or to bring in other people to back up her theories. There was, for instance, the strange story she had heard of Penelope becoming the Duchess of Wiltshire twice over. And then the circumstances she had experienced directly while visiting Great Little, concerning the duchess' relationship with Sally Black.

Now Sally Black was someone she could relate to. She, like Anne, had a practical bent that was perfectly suited to the world of business. Whereas, Penelope…"

"Bridge, where are you?" Thomas' voice echoed down the hall. "I have a grand commission for a new house along the Salisbury Road. The contract was signed this morning and toasted in claret!"

Bridget put down her quill and sighed, then collected herself and went to see her husband.

"Well done, sir, I know you worked hard on this contract and now you can look forward to another successful project."

"I have another idea to celebrate," Thomas said, leading his wife up the stairs, stopping to kiss her on each step, such was his exuberance.

"I am so happy for you, sir." And she meant every bit of it for his happiness made hers and her writing would be better for it.

Chapter 36

The bombardment was unannounced and unexpected. The White Lady, with its precious store of cannon and ammunition, was anchored away from the main ships, out of harm's way. It gave the sailors a long haul on the oars to reach Phips' flagship but, Parchman thought, that is what they are there for.

"What on earth are the buggers doing?" he asked the master of the White Lady, not expecting an answer, just voicing his incredulity. "I need to go to the flagship."

"Again, sir?" A question but said with considerable deference.

"Again and immediately."

Parchman's thoughts went back and forth, up and down, as he was being rowed the two miles through choppy waters. At first, he felt a growing elation. The idiot Phips had played right into his hands. Parchman was the senior and yet Phips had deliberately disobeyed him. Parchman had come down on the side of withdrawal at the last minute, while climbing the netting to reach the deck of Phips' flagship the previous day. But once made, he stuck to the decision, as if espousing a lifelong principle. He had issued a curt and loud command to withdraw, intending for it to be as embarrassing as possible. It had brewed into an incredible row, voices spilling out of Phips' cabin with stabs of fire like the cannon themselves.

"I thought, sir, you might be bringing the supplies we desperately need."

"What made you think that, Phips?" Convention dictated 'Sir William' but Parchman delighted in denying him his title. He did not believe in the vanity of aristocracy; even less so with jumped-up commoners.

Parchman had successfully avoided answering Phips' question regarding the armaments and ammunition. He was glad of this. Some people had a knack of identifying a lie, however cleverly disguised, so it was far better to avoid lies wherever possible. Besides, Phips made him uncomfortable, as if the man could see right through him.

"We have been asking for the extra supplies all summer and into autumn. Our success in this mission depends on them."

This is when the row had really flared. Phips could not accept that he was likely to lose this mini-war.

Normally, with an argument like this, Parchman would have settled it with one of the long, thin knives he always carried, perfect for finding the slits between the ribs.

And so satisfying to win the argument.

But these were not normal times. They called for extraordinary cunning. And now, as the sailors hauled on their oars to take Parchman back for the kill, Phips was playing right into his hands. He chuckled.

"Sir?"

"Keep quiet and steer the goddamned boat," he snarled.

But, as he got closer, he realised something else. The bombardment was being returned from high up in the city. And Phips' little ships were being hit continuously. He had a sudden fear; would the enemy see him as a high-level government official come to set up counsel with the general? Would they turn their guns on him, seeking to destroy him before he got to the Six Friends? Could they fire with such accuracy? Parchman knew nothing of war and vowed to remedy the gap in his knowledge.

If he made it through this day.

The awkward journey up the side netting was never easy but Parchman made it while retaining a little dignity, although losing his hat which an enterprising sailor caught in the boat below and handed back with a grin.

"Looks like your headgear went on a separate journey, sir." Parchman liked the cheek, gave the man a penny and asked him his name.

"Rose, sir, Alfred Rose."

"Bring that heavy-looking man with you and follow me."

There was no reception party. Everyone, Phips included, seemed preoccupied with the bombardment; clearly, they were receiving much worse than they were giving.

"Not very Christian, is it sir?"

"What do you mean?" Could Rose mean they were deliberately ignoring him? Parchman had considered and dismissed that idea; they were just very much absorbed with the pounding they were receiving. He did not know any of the names but ropes and blocks were flying all over the place, while the sails half-furled above were clearly holed so the ship looked like a beggar, ragged and disordered; only half dressed.

"I meant, sir, this ship is not giving more than its receiving, is all sir. Not very Christian that, sir." Rose was a sharp one, for sure. Whereas the heavy behind him walked blank-faced, avoiding eye contact. He was the muscle whereas Rose was the brain. Parchman would remember that.

They climbed the ladder to the quarterdeck. Just as Parchman's head reached deck level, a cannonball scoured its way along the wooden planks, missing Parchman but sending a huge splinter within inches of his face. That same cannonball took down two sailors standing at the wheel, turning their lower bodies into a mass of blood and gore. Parchman saw the bewildered expression on both faces as they were hurtled along like skittles to land in a heap by a closed hatch. He felt a surge of emotion, loving the element of surprise that took life so suddenly; yet preferred it when he dealt out that surprise.

"Good work will be done today, Rose." He hauled his still-fit body onto the quarterdeck and beckoned for Rose to follow him.

"I'm sure it will, sir, I'm sure it will."

"Can you write, Rose?"

"For sure, sir. I was a magistrate's clerk in another life, sir." It was perfect to be sent such beautiful coincidence at the very point of need.

"You know something of the law, then?"

"I do sir, quite a bit as it happens."

"Then listen to every word said and write it down as soon as you get a chance."

278

The second argument with Phips was short but equally tense. Not explosive in itself, more strained voices than shouted words. The excitement came from the bombardment.

"This is foolish, Phips, and directly in contradiction of my orders."

"I am the senior military commander and I judge…"

"You know nothing of military matters. Why is your land detachment sulking on the far bank of the river, for instance? Why not cross the river and attack the city?" Parchman had listened to Rose at the top of the gangway as he had sketched over the strategic position of the army under Sir John Walley, his wiry arm pointing out the key positions.

"You have more than the law at your disposal, Rose."

"Thank you, sir. I was a soldier once."

"You certainly have useful experiences and I am thankful for the advice."

Parchman had used this new-found information to get at Phips who, knowing little of war, stood blankly a moment until an aide whispered in his ear.

"They are pinned down, sir. Now please leave me to direct our efforts from my flagship. You are most welcome to use my cabin if you like."

"I will stay where I damn well please, Phips. Somebody has to sort this mess out."

"I must insist…" but he got no further for there was the sound of air being sucked in as another cannonball hit. It seared across the rear of the deck, destroying the handrail that ran across the back. It caused no loss of life, in fact no-one was hurt at all. It seemed a miracle, although Parchman rather hoped for a few more mangled bodies to make his point. He jerked his head to watch the ball fly away. It hit the sea with a dull thud twenty yards ahead.

But there was damage, perhaps far more serious. Phips's ensign had been flying from the stern of the ship, proud in the strong wind. It still seemed to stand although the structure all around was broken. It held for a moment and then dipped its head, as if recognising the solemnity of the occasion. Ten seconds passed as it slowly broke free of whatever still held it and fell in stately fashion into the sea below.

It took several minutes for the sequel of this act to get underway. Several minutes during which it seemed the bombardment lulled on both sides. There was cheering from the shore but it was distant, like the cries of a riot in another street altogether. There were discussions still to be had on the quarterdeck but they were postponed. Everyone stared at the flag as it bravely fought the sea, refusing to sink below the waves which now seemed so reasonable in their gentle efforts to submerge it.

"There's a boat coming out!" someone cried, tearing into the pause with cruel reality. Thus ended a moment that could have gone on forever.

"It's a canoe, sir," said one of his officers with a telescope. "What harm can a mere canoe cause us? Are we to tremble in our shoes?" He turned as he spoke, expecting laughter at his joke. But Rose got there first.

"It's coming for the flag, isn't it?" There was no 'idiot' at the end of his sentence, but he might as well have tagged the insult on.

"Muskets to the quarterdeck!" shouted an officer. "I want every one of those audacious buggers riddled with balls."

Scrambling boots spread out over the taffrail that was no longer, muskets at the ready, waiting for the canoe to come into range. And for the order to fire.

Around them, the battle rose up again, finding a pitch all of its own. Parchman ducked when balls came near, wondering again if they would focus their aim on him. He much preferred his way of operating; quiet streets and shady corners, springing out suddenly, the element of surprise paramount.

"Fire!" The order was given and twenty muskets shook their fury onto the canoe. Only one hit the hull of the craft, no damage evident.

"Reload!" They were much closer now, Parchman judged them to be fifty yards from where the ensign floated in the slightly rising tide, seventy yards at most from the stern of the Six Friends.

The second volley had a little more effect. One canoeist slumped down, not dead but Parchman could clearly see his right arm, a mess of bloodied flesh. Another ball snapped a paddle in two, although the enterprising canoeist simply dropped his half paddle and grabbed that of his wounded comrade.

The order was given to reload and fire at will.

"Take careful aim, boys!"

The canoe was just yards away from them now. One man leaned over and snatched the ensign from the water, giving the command to turn about as he perched dangerously over the side. They completed a neat about turn and made to leave, Phips' colours rammed into the bottom of the vessel, single musket shots chasing them away.

All too soon, they were beyond range.

A little afterwards, Parchman left in disgust. His contempt was beautifully orchestrated, his role played perfectly. Sir William watched the hunched shoulders and the clenched fists of the departing man from England and felt the early wind of the official fury to come his way. He would have to work hard to counter the failure of this campaign.

He was visibly and vocally defiant, ordering the gun crews to new speeds of reloading to punish the Canadians for their audacity.

And to revenge the indignity of having his flag taken, plucked from the sea beneath his very own quarterdeck.

Should he leave now? Try and get back to England before Parchman? But that would mean abandoning his post at a critical time. He had been foolish to think that it would be an easy conquest of Quebec. The French under their able governor, Frontenac, had outwitted, out-schemed and out-planned him at every stage. He thought of Major Savage, sent three days earlier to demand a French surrender. Frontenac had played games with him, blindfolding him to disguise their lack of strength, buying time until Sir William's scouts reported the militia reinforcements arriving from Montreal. That, undoubtedly, gave the French numerical superiority, evidenced in the fierce resistance to his landing party, pinned back on the wrong side of the St Charles River.

But the psychological games had gone further. Major Savage returned a terrified man. Frontenac, no doubt all planned, had pleaded in council for the major's life. They had wanted his immediate death as the ultimate insult in reply to the surrender demand.

Sir William should have seen that it was all a ruse. Instead, like many before him but neither explaining or excusing his stupidity, he had believed in what men around him had said. Perhaps they had all wanted to believe that the French defence would crumble. Perhaps some knew the truth but dare not speak out. Perhaps some even wanted failure.

Major Savage had not been murdered in Quebec. Instead he had returned with a cleverly worded answer to Sir William:

I have no reply to give your general other than from the mouths of my cannons and muskets.

He must have known his reinforcements were fast approaching Quebec, sealing the fate of this ridiculous campaign.

A thought came to Sir William. Could he blame Captain Schuyler and his pathetic attack on Montreal? If that had even half-succeeded, Frontenac would not have been able to call for reinforcements from the area and perhaps the Quebec invasion would have stood a chance.

In the end, whatever excuse he dreamed up, it was his campaign and he would have to answer for it. Not financially, for the £40,000 cost had come from the merchants of Boston. They knew the risks and could shout and cry all they liked when the invading army returned with its tail between its legs and no sign of any plunder as return on the investment.

No, the answering would have to be to the government in England, to men like Parchman who see duty performed as equating to success, no allowance for failure.

A man in public life is only as secure as his last success. Yet success is the foundation of failure as it brings the envious snapping around one's feet.

He needed to terminate this foolish attack with half an ounce of dignity and get to London as soon as possible. If he could just get something to call a victory... Or a treuce, maybe? He would send an emissary right away.

Two days later, while his thoughts were still on salvaging some dignity, he heard that the White Lady had slipped away, sailing into the ocean and, he was sure, with a course set for England. Another ship, a smaller one, had left at the same time.

The man who reported the White Lady's departure was an experienced seaman. It was clear he had something on his mind.

"What is it, Reynolds?"

"Sir William, when the White Lady came to its mooring the other day, it was low in the water."

"So?"

"Meaning it was laden with something."

"And now it is much lighter?" Sir William asked, thinking more provisions to charge to the expedition cost and a lighter ship to travel more quickly to England.

"No, Sir William, it was still low in the water. I thought this strange and enquired of the officer in charge of the moorings as to what had been unloaded from the White Lady."

"And there was nothing?" Sir William now knew the extent of Parchman's trickery. The long-promised munitions had sailed into the Quebec basin, moored for three days within two miles of his present position and now had sailed away again.

"That's right, Sir William, nothing unloaded, just a considerable amount of fresh food and water taken on board."

Epilogue

News of the disastrous expedition to Quebec reached London in early December, courtesy of the White Lady. It was as Parchman intended, why he had sailed from Quebec on 22nd October, the moment the truce was negotiated and the exchange of prisoners had started.

He promised a fat reward for speedy passage, not caring how that reward would be paid or who would meet the bill. Rather than dock in Bristol, he ordered the master of the White Lady to go around the southern coast and into the Thames directly. "That way you'll get your bonus the quicker," he said, thinking he could pass it on to Cartwright and it would probably get lost for years amongst the clerks and paperwork that made the administration of a great office of state.

Now he was in Cartwright's spacious rooms, shown in by a man who was bent double yet managed to avoid colliding with the furniture, no doubt through having some plan of the layout built into his head. He wondered what the old man would be like in an unfamiliar setting.

But that, like the captain's reward, was of no consequence now. He only had to report to Cartwright, glory in the success of the plan and then take up his new office.

And what an office awaited him! Not the actual rooms, although they were grand enough, but the activities he would be involved in. He had full responsibility for rooting out Catholic attempts to undermine authority throughout the realm. It was Heaven-sent and he relished the job ahead.

"We'll have to get you an assistant, sir." Cartwright said after listening with rising excitement to the report from Parchman. "For your new role, I mean." He had not expected Parchman to fail but the level of success was outstanding. Parchman had moved a step up in initiative, humbling the colonials completely. Cartwright could now impose control on the miserable New Englanders, reaping praise for the new and aggressive approach in pursuing the war against the French across the known world. And they still had a cargo load of munitions to do as they would with.

The only niggling concern was a thought at the back of his head; what had he brought back into power in exchange for this success? He shivered suddenly, feeling a chill on the back of his neck; what had he unleashed in his deal with Parchman? For some reason, he thought of Michael Bars, the chief jailer in charge of Taylor's execution. He had received confirmation of Taylor's death, heard second-hand the nobility of his address to the crowd, feeling something missing in his own life. How could one single world contain so much good and bad? How can one table host Parchman on the one hand and the likes of Michael Bars on the other? He felt a sudden envy for the good of this world, for the decent men like Bars and the Davenport brothers. But then he shook himself; they would never become ministers of state.

"Yes, what was I saying? That's it, we need to get you an assistant, sir."

"No need, Cartwright," Parchman replied with typical lack of respect for the man who had once been his assistant but now was a minister of state and a lord, "I have someone in mind and have already intimated as much to him." Alfie Rose was the perfect candidate for the job. He knew something of the law, of government and of soldiering as well. In fact, he seemed to know a little of everything.

They had parted in the Quebec basin, shaking hands on a deal that would benefit them both. Parchman had set sail in the White Lady heading straight to London, while Rose had been briefed to take a smaller vessel, the fastest available after Parchman's ship, to Boston. He carried a letter of authority from Parchman allowing him entry to Parchman's office in the town, an office Parchman expected never to visit again.

"Your sole purpose, Rose, is to take away the orders requiring Phips to attack Quebec, leaving those that require him to desist. I want the orders you extract brought to me in London."

"And what then, sir?" Rose had fished and had caught something of note immediately.

"Then we have a golden future together, Rose. You are exactly the type of assistant I have need of and we are going to be busy in the years ahead."

They say that good news travels faster than bad. No-one has done a survey or tried the theory out. But generally it is held to be true.

Oddly, in the case of the Battle of Quebec, resounding failure that it was, the news travelled rapidly. But this does not challenge the theory, rather it reinforces it in the strangest of ways. For what sounded like bad news was actually excellent for those that hoped for failure, Cartwright chief amongst them.

And he had the power to spread the word.

The news was all around Dorset within a few days of being announced in London.

"Being trounced by the French like that!" Henry exclaimed on hearing the details in the library at Great Little. It was exactly the response Cartwright hoped to get from the aristocracy and landed gentry throughout the land; from the people who made up both Houses of Parliament.

And from the people who, generally, had younger sons or brothers sent or gone to the Americas. For, Cartwright reasoned, the greater the perceived failure of the colonists, the greater his influence and control in the future.

It was on such clever moves that the minister of state's strategy depended.

As well as the pure luck of bumping into Parchman again.

Henry and Grace had become regular visitors to Great Little. Henry had taken an interest in the insurance business following the investment Grace had made. Aspley and Associates, Marine Insurers, started having its monthly board meetings at Great Little without any conscious decision to hold them there. Penelope claimed total ignorance of marine insurance yet asked several penetrating questions at each meeting in her languid, arrogant way. Sally was altogether different. She loved the detailed calculations that Anne Aspley took her through and rapidly became an expert at understanding risk upon the sea.

"It's a wonder you don't sometimes meet in Dorchester, Sally," Alice had said one evening before the next scheduled visit. "All those records that Anne has to bring with her each time!"

"We cannot, Lady Roakes." It was back to the formal in deference to Penelope's wishes. "For the Duchess will not leave her husband, even for half a day." Thus displaying the curious mixture of admiration and frustration that had wallpapered the relationship between duchess and maid-come-steward in recent weeks.

There were other reasons for the visits; Grace and Penelope had always got on reasonably well but the fact that Grace had listened and acted on impulse to aid Penelope caused a notch up in their friendship.

Penelope was the type to love her friends awkwardly and she did so, adding Grace and eventually Henry to the very short but growing list. And once on that list, one was never taken off.

A list that did not contain Sally, because Sally was essential and not a choice. They remained furious with each other, but that did nothing to stop the need.

Henry had another brace of reasons for wanting to go to Great Little. Before making the commitment, he had first been to see his birth mother, Eliza Davenport, to ask her if she minded him going to Great Little to advise Penelope on her horses, "For she has started to consult me by letter which I find flattering. But I know of your difficulties with regard to Great Little and will not go without your blessing, mother." Very few people knew that Henry's real mother was Eliza Davenport, or Lady Merriman as she had been at the time. Knowledge of his illegitimate status would deny him the earldom and, with no other male heirs, make the title defunct. His grandfather, the old earl, had gone to enormous lengths to keep his illegitimate status from the world, including burying his birth mother away, first on a pig farm and then in a laundry in Bristol in which Alice Roakes, then Alice Beatrice, had been her jailor.

"My dearest Henry," she had said, "I am quite reconciled with regards to Lady Roakes as is now or Mrs Beatrice as was then." She stopped a moment and Henry saw a shadow of pain on the pretty face of his mother. "What's more, my son, Penelope Wiltshire is the unlikely architect of those reconciling forces so I would not want to hurt that great lady in any way." She told her son of the negotiations to buy Ashenham from the duke and of the tremendous price the duchess and Mr Parsons had achieved. "I do not know how she did it but the cost was well below the market rate and she got the little village of Oakenham thrown in too!"

"I think I know how she did it, mother. She married the Duke."

"Yes, I know, but consider this. She looks after him with remarkable dedication now that he is so ill. She is quite the saint wrapped in a devil-may-care skin."

"There is more to it than that, mother." He told her of the latest news and Eliza clapped her hands with joy.

"She will make an excellent mother."

And strangely, Eliza's words rang true.

Sally had somehow known of Penelope's pregnancy first. And in a world turned stranger than storytelling, with showers of rain thrust into the deepening cold but sunny days of a Dorset winter, it proved to be the most peculiar thing of all.

"It will be a boy."

"I pray so, Sal, although I would prefer a girl myself." But what the duchess wanted mattered little in the bigger arrangement. A girl would not inherit a dukedom; that was a fact. Instead the stricken duke's brother would take the title and all the wealth and land that came with it.

"I, too, would prefer a daughter that we could dress in the prettiest of clothes but it cannot be, Pen. If we were allowed a choice, we would both have to make our marks for a boy."

Penelope looked oddly at Sally, as if examining a horse she had suddenly seen something in.

"What's up, Pen?"

"Nothing." That was a typical answer from Penelope when pressed on emotional matters. And she had to be pressed again before she would reveal what had prompted her look-again at Sally.

"It's just that you called me Pen." But bright Sally was not up to speed on this; even the brightest can be stupid at times. "I mean, Sal, it is the first time you've abbreviated my name since…"

"Snap!" said Sally, getting the drift. "It's the first time you've abbreviated mine too."

"Since the row, I mean. Now, Sal, let me dress you for soon I won't be able to bend to tighten you up with this great little lump about my body!"

The baby became the Great Little Lump or G.L.L. in their private shorthand. Alice soon worked it out and shared in their secret for a week before word got out to everyone. It could not long be a secret for Penelope suffered extraordinarily badly from morning sickness, combining it with intense irritation at everyone around her.

Except for Sally who now could do no wrong.

And the duke, who she cared for with a tenderness that surprised everyone, even Penelope herself. She ran the recently enlarged staff ragged with demands for soup of a certain temperature and consistency, herbs for a particular scent that she believed he craved although he gave little evidence of a preference, sheets changed at all hours of the day and night and a host of other requirements, some reasonable, most not.

But, throughout it all, she was there for her husband, the man she had detested and married for money but who now was central in her life for some inexplicable reason.

He was the father of the child she carried. But there was something more, much more, than inheritance and money. As the weeks passed, she would pat her growing tummy and place the duke's lifeless hand on it. In return, she received a half-smile from time to time. It spoke of conspiracy well entered into.

The odds were reduced from one in a hundred to evens. The child just had to be a boy and the duke and Penelope would both have achieved their goals.

"Does the duke know?" Bridget asked one evening. She and Thomas had been invited to stay at Great Little as the building project to both the main house and the estate was taking much of Thomas' time.

"Does the Duke know anything?" Alice replied, feeling suddenly she was host to a large extended family. She and Bridget were in the library while Thomas and Mr Milligan were touring the works. In the Great Hall there was a board meeting going on for Aspley and Associates, Sally having rushed there from the estate meeting Alice had concluded an hour earlier. Soon they would come together for supper. She thought of the Little Family, perpetually feasting halfway up the stairs, frozen into a painting that had been the only thing of worth to survive the fire.

So much had happened since the fire had raged through the house. She thought of her husband, Sir Beatrice, murdered days before the fire in what had been his study, now a part of the enlarged library. Then there was the birth of baby Sir Beatrice, the new joy of her life, although a constant reminder of the husband she had lost.

Would all this activity, sorrow and joy, despair and hope, hate and love, just become one scene in a painting, like the Littles of Great Little in their perpetual feast? Could an artist paint such emotion into the stillness of a painting? Does emotion not imply movement, for instance racing hearts and pounding stomachs, fists that clench and unclench?

"Alice?" Bridget was shaking her.

"Sorry, sorry." She could not focus immediately on who had wakened her from her trance. "Who..." but then she stopped for she had recognised her new friend, Bridget Davenport.

To think the Davenports would ever be counted amongst her friends.

Book One of the Dorset Chronicles
A New Lease on Freedom

1680s England is on the brink.

Thomas and Grace Davenport are the wilful youngest children from a strict puritanical Dorset family who are torn apart by the death of their mother.

The ambitious Duke of Monmouth, illegitimate son to the old King, Charles II, lands with a small force in Dorset, seeking to depose his staunch Catholic uncle, James II, for fear of him re-establishing a Catholic dynasty in a precarious Protestant country.

Thomas and Grace meet Henry, the heir to the corrupt Earl of Sherborne, who falls deeply in love with Grace but a Catholic nobleman is forbidden to marry a Puritan. Their budding relationship is ripped apart when Henry is forced to take up arms to join the fight against Monmouth.

Lady Merriman, a vivacious woman with a tragic secret that would threaten the foundations of the Earldom, becomes a surrogate mother to Thomas and Grace but goes missing in extraordinary circumstances and they become determined to track her down.

Against the background of civil war, brutal imprisonment, and fierce determination borne of love, they face an immense struggle in their quest to find their beloved friend and overcome intense personal battles to achieve stability and order in the most turbulent of times.

A must-read for those who love the history and drama of an emerging nation.

Book Two of the Dorset Chronicles It Takes a Rogue

It's 1688. England, a nation struggling with its identity, is staring at yet another momentous rebellion, this time led by William of Orange.

Henry, the new Earl of Sherborne, has a deep secret to keep. Recently married to Grace Davenport, he walks a tightrope between loyalty and rebellion.

Grace's elder brother Matthew Davenport, exiled in Holland after the disastrous Monmouth Rebellion of 1685, jumps at the opportunity to return to Dorset as a scout for the planned invasion. Their brother Thomas, free from the oversight of their strict Presbyterian father, has found his vocation in building. Desiring nothing more than a quiet life, he is dragged into a world of espionage in order to save his brother.

Penelope Withers, selfish & cold-hearted, sets her sights on marrying above her and enters into a marriage of convenience with the Duke of Wiltshire. She hungers for human warmth yet is ice-like with others. That is until she meets Lady Roakes, who is compassionate and kindly despite her own wicked past. Together they forge a friendship through tragedy that fundamentally changes their lives, both learning that a rogue need not stay a rogue forever.

Parchman, no first name, is motivated to terrible evil through hatred. Appointed the King's Keeper, the question is, will he stay loyal as others desert their king in droves?

Set in the very heart of Dorset amidst the threat of competing political and personal forces, these lives are dramatically intertwined through ambition, love and revenge.

Following on from the first in **The Dorset Chronicles** *(A New Lease on Freedom)*, *It Takes A Rogue* is a must-read for those looking for a thrilling tale of anguish, adventure and suspense set amidst the forging of modern England.

Book Three of the Dorset Chronicles A Simple Mistake

Anyone can make a mistake…
Believing himself spurned by the woman he loves, Thomas Davenport leaves Dorset, intent just to get away. He ends up in Ireland, at the height of the 1689 James Stuart invasion. He meets Tristan Browne, an Irishman born in Barbados, coming home to a land in uproar.

The Siege of Londonderry, like so much in the Seventeenth Century, puts countryman against countryman in a bitter war of attrition, starvation and resilience. Bridget Browne is caught up in it and writes a startling account, full of insight.

Unknown to Thomas, his brother Matthew is also in Ireland, wishing only to be on the pulpit in his native Dorset, but his sense of duty prevails.

Thrown together by fate, the four must flee Ireland when Matthew uncovers a corrupt scheme, the work of old adversary Parchman, who is also wreaking havoc back home in Dorset.

Can Great Little and Bagber Manor survive as we have come to know them, or will Parchman succeed and see his foes out on the streets, beggar bowl in hand?

As we move relentlessly towards the modern age, our heroes and villains have their own struggles, which build into the drama of an extraordinary nation in the making.

The Story Continues

The 1690s are upon us. Some things have settled down following the Battle of the Boyne. But much remains in turmoil and Parchman is, once again, let loose in government to wreak the havoc that makes him what he is.

Both Great Little and Bagber Manor are thriving after the terrible damage done to them, growing in confidence as they expand and take on new ideas. These landed estates are driven by the determination of Lady Merriman and Lady Roakes, the fierce joy of life that is Penelope Wiltshire and the quiet competence of Sally Black. Both Dorset and the nation as a whole are at the forefront of expansion, looking out to the world at large, developing new business models, new ways of life, making a new and vibrant society from the remnants of the past.

But the sun shines only partially on Britain. There are still many obstacles to grapple with and much to do in the forging of our modern nation. As always, personal ambition, hatred and revenge have the potential to wreck the lives of those who strive to make the most of their circumstances.

And that is before taking politics into account and all the viciousness that entails.

Book Five of the Dorset Chronicles does not have a name yet but it is coming very soon to follow our characters through the action, the history and the drama that made this remarkable period of our past.

I have a feeling that some of our main characters may be going north to the wild glens of Scotland.

But that is another story.

Printed in Great Britain
by Amazon

40221349R00179